D0558409

A CHRONICLE of the

Roman
Twilight

A CHRONICLE of the

Roman Twilight

A Novel

John Ranger

A CHRONICLE OF THE ROMAN TWILIGHT
A NOVEL

iUniverse books may be ordered through booksellers or by contacting:

iUniverse
1663 Liberty Drive
Bloomington, IN 47403
www.iuniverse.com
1-800-Authors (1-800-288-4677)

ISBN: 978-1-5320-4517-2 (sc)
ISBN: 978-1-5320-4518-9 (e)

Library of Congress Control Number: 2018905539

Print information available on the last page.

iUniverse rev. date: 05/16/2018

PREFACE

I ONCE READ THAT every great civilization eventually produces a generation that is no longer capable of either bearing the burdens or living up to the expectations of the past. Beyond doubt, the generation whose members were selected to bear that cross for Rome were the ones in charge of the Eastern and Western Roman Empires from AD 383 to 408. They were the ones who lost the future. The calamities that befell the empire during those years would eventually prove themselves impossible to surmount.

Up to the beginning of that period, the empire had seemed invincible. Its capacity to absorb tyranny, barbarian invasion, civil war, murderous plagues, and devastating economic collapse seemed infinite. Regardless of how appalling the effects of such disasters, the state always rebounded one way or another. The resilience was always there. At the beginning of 383, the Western Empire was strong and appeared secure while the Eastern Empire was still struggling to recover from the terrible losses it had suffered in its defeat at the Battle of Hadrianople five years earlier. To the extent that the East would recover, it would be largely due to an influx of soldiers from the West. But the Fates are capricious. A quarter century later, it was the *western* half of the empire that was struggling as never before: Britain had been abandoned; much of northern Gaul was ungoverned; a number of the fortresses on the Rhine River that had protected civilization for four and a half centuries had been destroyed; western Spain was a political no-man's-land, and the authority of the Roman government in much of eastern Iberia was little more than a vague rumor; stretches of land on the south bank of the Danube had been given up with little hope of ever being secured for the empire again; and north Africa was in revolt.

Every generation believes that its passing marks the end of an era. As the end of the first decade of the fifth century approached, people started to witness not just the conclusion of an era but the end of an epoch. Events were in motion that would shatter the western half of the Roman world.

The Battle of Hadrianople in 378 has long been considered the key event that led to the fall of Rome a century later in 476. More recent thinking on the issue suggests that this is not the case. The fictional memoir of this novel is dedicated to the proposition that it was the chronic political instability of the West that led to its disintegration.

At the end of his great history of Rome, from the reign of Emperor Nerva to the fateful reign of Emperor Valens, Ammianus Marcellinus advised subsequent historians, be they professional or amateur, to "cast what they have to say in the grand style." It is up to you to judge the degree to which I have succeeded.

John Ranger
Wappinger Falls, New York

CHAPTER 1

Childhood's End

Sorrento: October 25, 439

THE BOY WAS AWASH with sweat and almost breathless as he raced down the steps and onto the magnificent tiled veranda.

"Grandpa, have you heard the news?" he gasped.

"What news, Gratian?"

"Carthage has fallen to the Vandals."

The old man's expression didn't change. He and his oldest grandson had always been very close. As they looked at each other during a brief silence, the boy knew instinctively that his grandfather wished to be left alone. As the boy left to go inside, the old man looked off toward the northeast across the bay. A low mist obscured Naples, but Vesuvius loomed off to the right as majestic and menacing as ever. He arose from his table and walked slowly over to the railing. Looking down the cliff to the sea, he noticed two small fishing boats far beneath him. Their like had been passing by this point for a thousand years and more. He had known this day would come. Its arrival had been inevitable from the moment that Count Bonifacius had brought the Vandals over to Africa from Spain. But the realization of imminent evil never makes its final attainment any more acceptable. How could things have gone so badly? When he looked back over his life, it seemed that the empire had stumbled and groped from expectation to failure in an endless succession that he could never have foreseen when he was young. Perhaps his greatest mistake was simply in hoping itself. He felt as though his very soul cried

1

out from within him: "It was all for nothing. Every dream we dreamed, every ambition we cherished, every struggle we fought were all in vain. All our victories were mere preface to disaster."

He returned to the chair at his writing table and looked across to Vesuvius again. Had it all really happened? After all, even with young people, the passing of time tends to warp the perspective, with reality and the imagination often becoming intertwined. Britain seemed so remote now, both in time and distance. Far greater than the thirty-two years and 1,200 miles that now separated him from his birthplace there.

He had seriously questioned the value of recounting and reanalyzing the events of three decades ago both for himself and for others. For the most part, these profound and terrible disasters had become so many distant yesterdays. At least they would have been if the bad news didn't keep getting worse. His initial feeling was that he should be content to leave them that way. Even after the passing of so many years, they still evoked considerable discomfort. The intensity of the agony they brought on had subsided considerably, as the sufferings caused by all such calamities must. If they persisted, then we would be unable to survive. But the deep-rooted sense of loss remained, as indeed it should. That brought on the most troublesome aspect of the enterprise. However, he had finally given in to the urgings of his two sons. They were eager to know of his boyhood in Britain, what their grandparents were like and, above all, of his experiences with Stilicho, Alaric, Gainas, and that host of other men at the turn of the century who had been so instrumental in determining the future course of national events.

He had started the book once before, based on diaries and letters that he had kept right up until 410. At that point, the chaos of the times forced him to suspend his efforts. But after digging everything out of a trunk two years ago, he decided to continue with it. The more he reviewed the writings of those years, the more he came to feel that he could make a substantial contribution after all. For the truth as he saw it, pertaining to much of that period, differed considerably from the views of several writers. The Catholic Church historians, above all that damned fool Paul Orosius, were the most odious of the lot. The ridiculous manner in which they continually allowed their religious

2

convictions to distort what should have been an objective analysis was pathetic. They were not really historians but at best chroniclers, at worst mere propagandists. On the other hand, those of the pagan persuasion, showing their usual contempt for "the Vandal" had, for example, made statements about Stilicho's campaigns against Alaric in Greece that were downright libelous or should have been. It is often stated that historians write with the benefit of hindsight. But the old man wondered, *If hindsight is all that beneficial, then why do historians so continuously debate great past events, often on the basis of having observed the same evidence?* It was advisable to keep Tacitus in mind on these matters. He had once referred to a specific incident nearly four centuries earlier that could be applied to much of history in general. He remarked that it was "subject of every variety of misrepresentation, not only by those who then lived but likewise in succeeding times: so true is it that all transactions of preeminent importance are wrapped in doubt and obscurity; while some hold for certain facts the most precarious hearsays, others turn facts into falsehood; and both are exaggerated by posterity." It appeared to him that hindsight only broadened the scope of the debate rather than bringing about any universally accepted conclusions. And so he had started compiling and revising. After two years, he wondered if he would ever finish, but he managed to console himself with the notion that at least he was in the homestretch now. He smiled at the irony because he remembered another homestretch many years ago ...

I was born in December 364 on my father's ranch near Cirencester in southwestern Britain. I am certain that I could not have asked for a choicer location in which to enter this world. I am not one of those who automatically reflects upon his childhood as being the happiest and most care-free period of his existence, as many are prone to do. Childhoods are pervaded with problems that are every bit as severe to us as children as later problems are when we are adults. But what I do remember above all about this period is its almost universal tranquility. It stands in such sharp contrast to the life I have had since migrating to the continent. The area in which I lived is one of the most heavily Romanized districts on the island. And Britain itself, throughout my youth and for many decades previously, had been one of the empire's most prosperous regions. Admittedly, the island suffered from 367 to 369 from massive barbarian attacks. In particular, they struck near York and in the area known as the Saxon Shore.[1] But military attacks on the island were the exception and not the rule.

My father was descended from a Germanic mercenary who settled near London after retiring from the army during the reign of Septimius Severus. All my relatives on my father's side still live in London or its environs. My mother's ancestors had come to Britain from Caledonia during the mid-200s. Since my father also had a Celtic background, my parents were fluent in both Latin and Celtic. As a result, my brother, two sisters, and I were also bilingual. When we spoke to one another, we often inadvertently mixed the languages up. We would often speak one sentence in Latin and another in Celtic, much to the consternation of our more or less strictly Latin-speaking friends in Cirencester.

For a businessman enjoying commercial ties with both urban and rural communities in Britain, as my father did, bilingualism was essential. In the cities, while everyone spoke Latin and the upper class, on rare occasion, spoke Greek as well, a sizable percentage could also speak Celtic. In the countryside, the reverse was true but in greater degree. By the time I was born, the Celtic language had absorbed and corrupted hundreds of Latin words. This osmotic process had developed both as a result of the Celtic language's inadequacy in expressing new concepts and for the sake of convenience. In spite of Britain's having been a part of the Roman Empire for almost four centuries, the Latin language and culture are not as deeply rooted there as in Gaul and Spain. In the latter dioceses, the original Celtic language and culture has all but disappeared except for a few isolated areas. Their increased degree of Romanization is due to their having a larger percentage of their populations descended from Roman settlers, coupled with their having been a part of the empire for a longer period.

Materially, we led a very good life. As I mentioned, my father owned a large sheep ranch that contained a sizable quarry. Our sheep were the famous Cotswold lions, the largest in the empire, having been brought to Britain shortly after the conquest for the purpose of clothing the legions. By the time I was born, the herds had grown so large that most of their wool was exported to the mainland provinces. They were willing to pay quite handsomely for it. Most of my father's income was derived from the wool trade, although we also grew a moderate amount of grain that would also return well in a good year. Any adversities brought about by fluctuating grain or wool prices, however, were more than offset by compensation from the quarry. It provided the stone for many of the gray-walled buildings that now stand in this area. It is difficult to know how to compare conditions in Britain as recently as the 390s with the circumstances prevailing there today. I have it on reasonably certain authority that the area around Cirencester is relatively unmolested in spite of Irish attacks along the coast of Wales. But it must be kept in mind that current conditions have deteriorated from those that I am describing in the Britain of several decades ago.

It has been over forty years since I last saw my father's ranch. The last I heard, it was owned by my sister Maria Patricia and her husband. When I was a boy, the ranch was of considerable area. But like most all other men with sizable landholdings, my father reserved only the woods and pastures for himself and farmed only about a quarter of the arable land. The remainder was let out to farmers whose families had hereditary tenure. As in the continental provinces, British tenant farmers are allowed to pick deadwood from the forests and graze their animals there. Since money was in short supply then, as now, they paid for their farming, foraging, and pasturing privileges mainly by working for my father. The time they spent in such labors ranged from two to four days a week, depending on the season, and consisted largely of cultivating and harvesting the crops. In addition, they would also obtain supplies, repair fences, perform errands, and work in the quarry. The tenant farmer's monetary rent is very small and generally consists of only one-tenth of their annual crop produce. Their existence is rather primitive by middle-class standards. Legally, these farmers are free, but their "freedom" is of a much-circumscribed variety: they cannot leave the estate to which they are born, can choose a wife only from that same estate, and can never volunteer for the army. During times of military emergency, they can be conscripted but only on condition that they return to "their" farms as soon as the emergency has subsided. When the landowner sells his estate, the tenants go with it. Like runaway slaves, runaway tenants can be reclaimed and severely punished if the landowner feels so inclined. But in the real world, these laws are frequently bent and broken. My father owned no slaves, and neither did any of our neighbors, although certain richer families in the cities did. With foreign expansion brought to a close so long ago, the availability of slaves had long been in decline. This became more pronounced the farther north and west one went. Besides, even restricted free labor will out produce slave labor almost anytime.

Although the work was more difficult, as soon as I was old enough, I chose working in the quarry over being a shepherd. Herding sheep I found quite boring. To this day, I cannot comprehend how some men can perform this mind-numbing task for most of their lives. But in stone cutting, I obtained a much greater sense of accomplishment, and it must be admitted, the monetary return was superior. A great deal of caution had to be exercised because the stone found in the region is soft in places and can disintegrate quite unexpectedly while being worked. I took great pride in seeing the stone I had helped fashion being used to expand or repair certain of the stately mansions and public buildings in the district. During this period of my early teens, I considered becoming an architect. It was one of numerous dreams that would go unrealized.

One thing for which I have long been grateful (though I don't recall any such feeling at the time) is the school that I attended in Cirencester. It had been expanded considerably during the reign of Valentinian I (364 to 375). This emperor is best remembered for his excellent military capabilities that were tragically combined with a savage temper. But in addition, he had a profound respect for education. He built or reconstructed a number of schools throughout the western half of the empire, including the one I attended.

He became emperor nine months before my birth and died during my eleventh year. He started his reign mildly enough, as even the worst of sovereigns usually do, but as the years wore on, his temper ever more frequently got the better of him. He often condemned men to death for trivial offenses that had not previously been capital crimes. Never once did he commute a death sentence, as even the worst tyrants had done at least on occasion in times past. The fact that he terrified our foreign enemies was little consolation for those innocent Romans who suffered so unjustly as a result of false accusations during his reign. My earliest recollection of a political statement was hearing my father say, in connection with an egregious miscarriage of justice in Africa, "The trouble with our emperor is that he seems to have difficulty remembering which side of the Rhine or Danube he is campaigning on."

Fortunately, he was speaking to my mother after dinner one night, and the remark did not leave the house. Comments like that, made in the wrong company, had led many a man to the executioner in both the East and the West. Once he felt secure in his position as chief of state, the basest aspects of Valentinian's nature soon manifested themselves. One day when my father appeared grumpier than usual, I asked him what was wrong.

"You must not repeat this to anyone," he said. "When I was in town this morning, I was told of a most terrible event by a man that I know. Our emperor had ordered a new and very elaborate breastplate to be made by one of his most experienced craftsmen. The man completed his work and took the new breastplate to Valentinian. The emperor at first appeared to be very pleased by it but then took the piece and placed it on a scale. Because it weighed just slightly less than was called for in the original specification, Valentinian ordered the craftsman to be executed immediately by decapitation. See how lucky we are to be living in Britain? Remember when you are older that the farther away that you can live from the seat of imperial power, the better off you are. At least when the country is being run by a malevolent degenerate like Valentinian and that worthless brother of his in the East. There are numerous other outrages of this nature that our two emperors have committed. Living under these brutes, it's almost as though the empire has passed under barbarian control and we don't even know it. I admired Valentinian when he came to the throne. Talk about misjudgment. His apologists point out that in his free time he is a painter and sculptor. Sure. And Nero was a poet and musician."

I had never seen my father so bitter at the government. Nowadays, six decades later, as a result of the calamities that have befallen us, Valentinian I is seen in a far more positive light. He died of a stroke in 375 while arguing with a barbarian delegation on the Danube. He was idolized by the army but hated by civilians. Their taxes had been jacked up considerably late in his reign to pay for the massive rebuilding program to strengthen our fortresses on the Rhine and the Danube. But in all fairness to the emperor, he was not a fiscal illiterate. He knew how seriously excessive taxation could hurt the economy and reduce tax revenues in succeeding years. As a result, he held them constant until it was impossible to do so any longer. Valentinian's biggest failures were entirely of a personal nature. Criticism of his political appointments he interpreted as disloyalty to himself and thus the state. He saw himself as an absolute monarch, would never admit to having made a mistake and frequently allowed corrupt officials to remain in power regardless of how they abused their offices. Like Septimius Severus, Valentinian I strove to make the legal system as equitable as possible. He introduced a special appeals court to aid the poor and prevent the wealthy from abusing their social privileges. But like Septimius Severus, he considered himself to be far above the law that everyone else was subject to and acted accordingly. He was succeeded by his sons Gratian and Valentinian II.

Shortly after Valentinian I died, a number of terrifying natural events occurred. They foreshadowed many of the great evils that subsequently befell our greatest of empires. During a heavy thunderstorm, the imperial palace at Sirmium and its associated forum were struck by lightning and severely damaged in the resulting fire. For many generations, Sirmium had served as a headquarters for the emperors while they conducted operations across the northern Balkan Peninsula. At the same time, Crete and much of Greece were badly shaken by a series of earthquakes. In the following year, our entire defensive posture on the lower Danube was undermined by the admission of the Visigoths into the empire. This subsequently led to the most appalling devastation of Thrace and Greece, with which I would become only too familiar. But this came much later.

In 378, the terrible Battle of Hadrianople occurred in which the Eastern Roman Emperor Valens and twenty thousand men were slain in a single day by the Visigoths. Many historians consider it to have been the most salient defeat in our national history and the cause for the decline of the West. They are mistaken. It was the damnable civil wars subsequent to that tragedy that did us in. But Hadrianople, by itself, was bad enough. I was thirteen when this calamity happened. When I checked my atlas, I determined that Hadrianople lay over two thousand miles from Cirencester. What possible danger could the Visigoths pose to us from such a distance? Most people throughout the Western Empire were thinking in terms of how their taxes would be raised again to help pay for rebuilding our shattered eastern army. No one thought of a direct Visigothic impact on the West itself. Not then.

While my family could be considered upper middle class and I never suffered material want in any way, my feelings about my boyhood in Cirencester are at best ambivalent. Even with the passage of so much time, my feelings toward my father are still uncertain. He was the biggest man I ever knew, standing six feet four inches tall, weighing 275 pounds, and measuring an astonishing five feet around the chest. Not the sort of man whose admonitions one would take lightly. He was a very strict disciplinarian and ruled the household (and especially me) with an iron hand. He only thrashed me once, as I remember, for some trifling misdemeanor when I was about six. But the fact that I still remember it nearly seven decades later must testify to its severity. When I performed a task properly, nothing was generally said, because this sort of thing was expected. But whenever I fouled things up, criticism was leveled, often severely, without the slightest hesitation. While I grew up to respect and fear my father, I cannot say that I ever held any genuine affection for him. But perhaps the feeling was mutual.

The blackest episode between us arose on the occasion of my sixteenth birthday. A large celebration was held and many friends were invited to our home. My father and I started arguing over some minor matter and he simply erupted at me. He yelled that I had always been a disappointment to him and had never done anything to make him proud of me. He then proceeded to give quite a comprehensive catalog of my shortcomings, complete with unfavorable comparisons to virtually every other boy in the district, some of whom I barely knew. He had deliberately humiliated me before every friend I had, and I never forgave him for it. It was only when I broke down and started crying that my mother convinced him to leave me alone. One incident like that was one too many and I decided that as soon as possible I would leave home for good. No way would I live like that for the rest of my life. I suppose I had something like London in mind when the idea first occurred to me. After all, one hundred miles is a monumental distance to one whose previous travels have been limited. Unfortunately, the "opportunity" to leave came somewhat prematurely. But then the future always arrives before we are ready for it.

Seven children were born to my parents at their villa near Cirencester of which I was the second eldest. But three of my brothers died before reaching the age of five and these tragic losses, naturally, exacted a terrible toll from my parents. The death of my older brother, Valerius, two months before my twin sister, Valeria, and I were born particularly affected my father. My mother told me that he had dearly loved the boy and was inconsolable in his grief. I have often wondered if the death of Valerius governed his attitude toward me. With Valerius gone, I was the surrogate eldest son, and on one occasion after a dispute between us, I heard him tell my mother that he was certain Valerius would not have turned out the way I had. It seemed that all my failings were being measured against Valerius' imagined successes. In my darker moments, I felt that Valerius was fortunate in a sense; at least he didn't have to put up with the rubbish I did.

This discordant state of affairs was only aggravated by the relationship that prevailed between my father and my brother Gratian. He was eleven months my junior but very precocious. Gratian possessed a totally different personality than I had. He was a born comedian and as sly a fox as ever I knew. My father rarely got angry with him because he realized that doing so was a waste of time. Whenever he was scolded for misbehavior, Gratian, in rebuttal, could always be relied upon to come up with some subtle wisecrack. It was always of just the proper flavor to start whoever was reprimanding him laughing. Parents, churchmen, schoolteachers—the source of disapproving authority was irrelevant. Gratian could charm them all and cleverly talk his way out of any predicament. Any except the last. Another attribute that endeared Gratian to our father was his taking to certain of the manly pursuits to a greater degree than I did. While I generally enjoyed the salmon-fishing trips that the three of us would occasionally take to the Severn River, I never really enjoyed hunting, being instead more academically inclined. Gratian and our father, on the other hand, frequently hunted together using dogs and went after anything that moved. There was of course the ongoing problem of keeping the fox and wolf populations down and providing deer for our meat supply.

While my brother Gratian was handsome, highly amusing, and quite charming, he was also basically aimless. While I was poor at athletics, Gratian was very proficient. But he failed to develop this proficiency in any positive manner. At sporting meets sponsored by our city, Gratian was often too lazy to enter the various events, although he always performed well when he did. It was a similar story in school. We attended the full five years of elementary school, beginning when we were seven years old and completed the three years of secondary school at age fifteen. Or at least I did. Gratian progressed so well that the teachers allowed him to skip the second grade and to catch up with me in grade three. But apart from the initial years, he never exerted himself the way he should have. In fact, skipping the second grade was his crowning academic achievement.

My sister Valeria and I should have been quite close I suppose, being twins. But such was not the case. We were friendly enough, but that was as far as it went. The only one in my family for whom I felt genuine affection was my younger sister Maria Patricia, who was three years younger than Valeria and I. She was a very bright and attractive girl.

In the primary grades, the reading and writing of Latin and Greek were heavily stressed. Good writing was strictly enforced, and we spent countless hours at the wooden templates we all used to trace letters on our wax tablets. In addition, history, the use of the abacus, and arithmetic were taught. In the latter subject, I recall having a great deal of trouble with fractions, as did almost everyone else. In the three secondary grades, we had more history, geometry, gymnastics, poetry, rhetoric, philosophy, and music, and I fared better in those subjects for some reason.

Our home was typical of the large villas that are common in the countryside of southern Britain. Built about the year 210, it had been in my mother's family for three generations. Alterations had been performed on various parts of it during the intervening years. The original house had been of a rectangular design consisting of six rooms and a veranda. Eventually wings had been added to both ends to give it an overall length of about 120 feet. One distinguishing feature of the British villas that tends to make them larger than their Mediterranean counterparts is the inclusion of kilns for drying grain. These are necessitated by the wetter British climate. Our bathhouse was, of course, separate from the villa in order to lessen the risk of fire. Like most villas, ours was well situated with respect to a highway and its chief market a few miles away in Cirencester.

There had been a great deal of home construction in Britain during the late 200s and early 300s, both in the cities and the countryside. This was due largely to immigration to the island from the Rhineland frontier and northern Gaul. The terrible devastation to those regions wrought by barbarian invasions during the third century had instilled a deep-rooted and permanent fear in their citizens. Certain of those who could afford it decided to leave and move to more secure provinces such as those in southern Gaul, Spain, and Britain. By far, the greater number of those emigrating chose safer havens on the continent. But those moving to Britain made a relatively greater social and economic impact on the local economy, owing to our much smaller population. As a result, Britain had become more prosperous than most continental provinces by the late 300s.

Throughout the winter and the cooler months of the spring and autumn, my brother and I had the responsibility of stoking the furnace for the hypocaust. Around the Mediterranean, most urban Romans are familiar with this device from the manner in which the warm rooms of the public baths are heated. The warmer climate obviates the need for this type of extensive heating arrangement in most private homes there, and the larger continental mansions and villas have them located mainly under their living rooms. In Britain, again due to the climate, many villas have a hypocaust system covering virtually the entire ground floor. At a nearby villa under construction, I had the opportunity to see one being built. The floor of the hypocaust consisted of tiles two feet square laid in a concrete slab. Small square pillars, about eight inches to a side, were placed in the center of each floor tile to support the raised floor above. Flues ran up the exterior walls for added warmth and to allow the smoke to escape. It would take almost two days to warm up the floors at our villa once the hypocaust was started. After that, the furnace had to be stoked only two or three times a day with wood or some coal to maintain it.

My seventeenth year had started in about as inauspicious a manner possible. Things eventually cooled down, but the bitterness remained, and the event itself proved only a prelude to what was to come. To this day, I still have the most confounding emotions about the spring and summer of 381. It was at once the happiest and most beautiful summer I had known to that point and at the same time the most destructive and hate filled. In the autumn of the previous year, my father had purchased the entire estate that lay to the north of us. As a result, his already considerable land holdings were increased by almost one-third. The couple that owned it had grown too old to manage it anymore. Not having any children, they decided to sell and move to Bath. The winter of 380–381 had been rather severe, and I hadn't had a chance to acquaint myself with our new property. By March, all the snow was gone, so one day I rode over to get to know the terrain and introduce myself to at least some of our new tenant farmers. When I arrived at the home of a Frankish family, I saw a girl who was more beautiful than any I had ever known. Her name was Ardovanda, and I fell in love with her at first sight. I had no way of knowing that the incomparable elation I felt that spring and summer would be the source of a near-endless desolation. The feelings that I remember now stand as testament to the intensity that I felt at the time. We all have crushes that come and go, but this was different. I knew that she and I belonged together, and I wanted with all my heart to spend the rest of my life with her. I had never felt for anyone what I felt for Ardovanda, and in all honesty, I have never felt quite that way since. When we were together, I felt transported to another world.

I had not been particularly secretive about my relationship with her. Neither had I gone overboard in advertising it. I simply felt that what did or did not happen between us was our business. One day when my mother asked me where I was going, I made the mistake of telling her. I had always gotten along well with my mother to that point, and her reaction took me completely by surprise. She exploded at me in a manner quite reminiscent of the argument I had with my father on my birthday. I turned away and rode off as the most immediate solution to yet another family dispute. I was coming to realize that one never discussed anything of personal consequence in my family in a reasonable manner. As I expected, when I returned home, all hell broke loose. My father was on a business trip, but my mother obviously had been practicing her tirade for some time. She started off by denouncing me as a disgrace to the family for stooping to consort with a girl of such low station.

"What would the neighbors think?" As if I actually cared.

She said that my father would be furious when he found out who my girlfriend was, but that turned out to be untrue. When eventually told by my mother, his reaction was quite subdued. She railed on and on about how embarrassed the whole family would be and how difficult it would be for her to face friends and neighbors. When I naively remarked that she would like Ardovanda if she knew her, my mother shrieked back at me, "How can you be so stupid to think that I would ever want to know anyone like *that!*"

She then went on to describe Ardovanda, a girl she had never seen and never would, as conniving and deceitful, and she continued to denounce her in almost every way imaginable. The fact that Ardovanda's family were tenant farmers was bad enough. Their being Franks as well only added insult to my mother's notion of injury. At this point, I reminded her that her own ancestors were Caledonians and that where barbarism was concerned, the building of Hadrian's Wall was hardly an academic exercise. This brought forth another eruption from her to the effect that I was never to mention the Caledonians and the Franks in the same breath again. The upshot of this dismal encounter was that I was forbidden from seeing Ardovanda under any circumstances.

In the days that followed, the atmosphere around our home was the worst ever. I had kept my temper during our first confrontation, and after a period of about five days, I approached my mother in the vain hope that she might be more reasonable about the matter. The hopeless quarrelling started all over again. She constantly demanded that I promise never to see Ardovanda again, and with equal persistence, I refused to answer her. I stormed out of the house and rode off on horseback simply to be alone. After that second confrontation, I wrote my mother off as a prize bitch that would never listen to reason on the issue. But what could I do? One thing I did was keep seeing Ardovanda but in a secretive way and with far less frequency than I would have liked. I also determined to approach my father on the matter when he returned from his lengthy business trip. I felt I had nothing more to lose, and on the first opportunity when he and I were alone, I raised the issue once again. His reaction puzzled me. He never raised his voice and showed a surprising degree of understanding about the issue. His almost apologetic tone made me wonder if he was reflecting on some long-ago love of his own that had failed for some reason. He hardly looked at me once through the entire conversation. But he also made it clear that the matter was closed: my relationship with Ardovanda was over. The day after this discussion, I spent the entire time mending fences on the south side of our estate. When I returned to my bedroom, I found a new, small leather bag with my initials on it in the center of my desk. I opened it and discovered a number of gold coins. It was an extraordinary amount of money and obviously a peace offering from my father. He always thought in monetary terms and probably thought that this gift would be sufficient to make me forget that Ardovanda ever existed. I placed the coins back in the bag and let it sit in the middle of my desk for two months. I never thanked him for it, and I never mentioned Ardovanda's name again. I had reached a watershed with my parents. There was no future for me in Cirencester.

For the next few weeks, my father had Gratian and me working at a feverish pace along with certain tenant farmers doing various chores.

I never thought much about it at the time, but we were mending fences and repairing buildings only on the original part of the estate. At no time were we working on the newly acquired property to the north. I assumed we would get there after we had tended to our original property. Then one morning my parents asked me to come into the living room. They announced that they had arranged a marriage for me.

"She's a lovely girl, dear," my mother remarked.

The way she said "dear" reminded me of a cobra spitting venom. The girl they referred to was named Veronica. Her father owned a transport company, and on the surface, it probably appeared to our fathers to be an ideal matchup, given their complementary business interests. But as far back as I could remember, the fair Veronica's only interest in our family had been my brother Gratian. She generally regarded me with about as much affection as a piece of the furniture. My father, true to form, then went on at great length about the size of the dowry. He concluded by saying that late September or early October appeared to be the earliest time for the wedding. That was due to the heavy and conflicting business schedules that he and Veronica's father had until then. My mother then chimed in again about how beautiful Veronica was. For the last time in our lives, my mother and I agreed on something. Veronica was a knockout, but the two of us would be an appalling mismatch. Whenever our families had visited, she and I had almost never spoken to one another, although she had all the time in the world for my brother. I thought she and Gratian would have made a far better match. But what had precipitated this sudden marriage announcement was the Ardovanda affair. My parents had doubtless concluded that they best do something for my adolescent bodily appetites and quickly, lest I go off and embarrass the family again.

"Is that it?" I asked.

This bland reaction caught them both off guard.

"Uh, well, uh, I suppose it is," my father stammered. "Is that all you have to say?"

I told them it was and left the room.

I rode to the area where I was supposed to be working and then took off on a rather circuitous route to Ardovanda's home. As I came to the top of a hill that overlooked the place, I saw that the northern boundary of our expanded property had been partly changed since my last visit. A section of it had been moved south several hundred feet. The home of Ardovanda's family was now part of the farm to the north of us and was empty. I rode over to the farm of another tenant family. They told me that Ardovanda's family had moved out two weeks earlier, but their whereabouts was unknown. I went to the villa of the landowner, a man named Silanus, and asked him why the boundary had been realigned. He replied that my father had approached him with a view to swapping pieces of property of similar area and value.

"And what was the purpose behind that?" I asked.

"If you didn't know, you wouldn't be here," he replied.

"All I want you to do is fill me in on the details," I said. "I know they are gone, and I want to know where you sent them."

"Since your father instigated the transfer, why don't you ask him?" he replied.

"My father isn't home right now," I lied. "And besides, the Frankish family is your property. That's why I'm here asking you. I'll find out sooner or later, and I'd appreciate it if you would make it sooner."

He was a friendly man whom I had known for about ten years. He obviously felt himself in a difficult position. There was an awkward silence, and then he said, "All right. After all, there isn't much you can do about it. Your dad and I agreed that, as part of the property swap, I would move the family in question north to my other estate near York at his expense. I'll be bringing another family from my York estate down here to take their place. Your father and I have been friends for many years, and I owed him a favor. I'm sorry that it had to be at your cost, but you're young, and you'll get over it. Incidentally, your father gave a generous cash allowance to the family through me. I thought you might like to know that."

I thanked him and left.

I rode back the way I had come. Eventually, I stopped the horse and just sat there for the longest time, staring off into space. York was over a week's ride away. I had never felt so alone in my life. I was devastated and cursed both my parents in ways I would never have thought possible.

However, as I headed back to where I was working I started to put a plan together. The more I thought about it, the better I liked it. My home leaving, which I had first daydreamed about the previous December, mainly as an act of spite, had now become a necessity.

An annual celebration was held every August 1 to commemorate the troop landings of Claudius Caesar in 43 to start the Roman conquest of the island. Originally, these fairs had been sponsored by the nearest military garrisons. But as the conquest spread north and west, the cities evolved into civilian municipalities. They eventually took over responsibility for hosting these holidays. We Britons thought our circuses pretty exciting. However, in later years, I came to realize, after witnessing exhibitions in Rome and elsewhere, that the typical British circus was a rather tame affair. All the commonplace events were present. But the only exceptional features of the British circus were the bear acts. Britain and, to a lesser extent, Caledonia had become the chief supply sources for circus bears in the western provinces. North Africa, their original source hunting ground, had been almost emptied of them for generations. British circuses lacked exotic animals, however; they were too expensive to import.

The fair's biggest occasions were the horse races. They have always had a powerful appeal to the people of southern Britain, and I suppose they always will. It must be something in the blood. Anyone over the age of sixteen could enter whatever race he chose. The races were of varying length, and the prize money differed accordingly, as did the entry fee. The feature race was one and a half miles, and it held the greatest interest. I had no horse of my own to enter, but that was of no concern. I would enter my father's best horse, Cymbeline, a north-African breed. He would never give me permission for this, so I would simply do it on my own. Cymbeline was one of the finest horses in the area. While my father had frequently given me permission to ride him, I had been strictly forbidden to run him at any speed because of his advanced age. On occasion, when out of sight of our home, I would give him full rein, albeit not for a great distance. The surge of power when I let him go the first time frightened me. But the more I let him do this, the greater my conviction became that in any race this horse would be a certain winner.

My father had always taken the entire family to Cirencester for this holiday, although on two occasions we had attended the fair in Caerleon, about sixty miles to the west of us. For the August 1 fair of 381, however, I had known for quite a while that my father would be off to Alchester on a business trip. My mother had no interest in attending, and besides, she had to stay home with Valeria, who was sick. So, when the big day arrived, Gratian, Maria Patricia, and I went to Cirencester on horseback, my mount being Cymbeline. The last thing that I did before leaving home was pocket the pouch with the gold coins in it. The fair was centered on the five-thousand-seat stadium just outside the city. Since the crowds were always large, we arrived shortly after it opened. We quartered our horses at a stable just a short distance away. We met some friends of ours there, and Gratian and some of his pals eventually drifted off on their own. This was just as well for what I had in mind later on. Shortly after midday, I left the stadium to get some food for my sister and me at the concession stands. While doing so, I entered Cymbeline in the feature race. After we were through eating, I told her what I had done. I had never seen her look more surprised.

"You must be crazy," she almost yelled at me. "Father will string you up when he finds out, and besides, you've been in enough trouble lately."

Like Gratian, she was sometimes overly forward for her age but usually in an amusing way. This time, however, her tone was quite uncompromising. But it didn't matter. I was satisfied that Cymbeline could win, with or without her blessings.

The large field of entries contained some that were little more than plow horses. We lined up, the starting rope was raised, and we were off. By the one-mile mark, Cymbeline had seized the lead, and I never looked back. He was racing like the wind, leaving the rest of the field farther behind with each succeeding stride. As we thundered across the finish line, I thought of renaming him Pegasus. Then it happened. I was sent hurtling through the air and hit the ground hard, landing flat on my back on the inner trackside. I was badly dazed but not unconscious. The rest of the horses sprinted past as people came running over to help me. I was very groggy, and it took a while before I could maneuver without assistance from anyone. As soon as my head cleared, I realized that my father had been correct: Cymbeline was too old. His heart had given out on him and he had collapsed and died. I was looking in disbelief at Cymbeline when my siblings approached. For once, Gratian was at a loss for words. That spelled out above everything how he felt about the gravity of my predicament. But my sister started laying it on without hesitation.

"You've really had it this time, Marcus. Dad will kill you when he gets back home. I told you the idea was stupid, but you wouldn't listen to me, would you?"

As I thanked her for her reassurances, a local magistrate approached and presented me with my prize money. He also said that the race officials would dispose of Cymbeline.

When I finally regained my composure and the initial shock had passed, I realized that what I had been planning for this day would only have to be modified slightly. My brother clumsily excused himself, claiming that he had made prior commitments to the friends he had met earlier in the day. The truth was that he wanted to put as much distance between us as he could in case some of my misfortune was to rub off on him. Our father had taken me with him several times when purchasing horses and had taught me what to look for when examining them. I put this knowledge to good practice and used part of my prize money to purchase a horse that was for sale along with dozens of others. Since it was late in the afternoon, the prices had dropped, and I got a pretty good bargain. After having our supper at the fair, we bade farewell to our friends and headed for home. The journey was spent mostly in silence. The die was cast, the Rubicon crossed. When we were about a quarter mile from the ranch entrance, I stopped and told Maria Patricia of my plans.

"I won't be returning with you, Pat. I'm leaving home for good."

I said that with no small amount of dread. Thinking about leaving home was one thing, but actually hearing me say it out loud crystallized the idea and gave it a certain frightening irrevocability. My sister appeared stuck for something to say.

"Do you really mean that?" she finally asked.

"Yes, I do," I replied. "Things have gone tragically wrong for me ever since my last birthday, and they show no sign of improving. I've been planning this for a long time. My intention when we left this morning was to see you safely home and then leave. Cymbeline's death hasn't triggered anything; it only confirmed my original plan. The contempt in which our parents hold me is absolute, and they've earned my unyielding disgust in return. To our father, in particular, I will never be any more than an exasperating remembrance of his unachieved ambitions for me, whatever they were."

My sister just looked at me in silence.

"The last eight months have been the worst I have ever known. I have generally considered myself capable of making pretty sound judgments, but those two don't care about anything I think or feel. Incidentally, I know exactly where I'm going and what I'm going to do. But I can't tell you any more than that. I don't want you to be pressured into telling them anything that I don't want you to. Tell them that I'm sorrier than they will ever imagine that things have turned out so badly between us. But as far as I'm concerned, they have no one but themselves to blame. I want you to impress upon them that it was not the accidental death of Cymbeline that caused my home leaving. Above all, it was their reaction to my feelings about Ardovanda. I'll never forget what they said to me, and I'll never forgive them for what they did. Their next scheduled humiliation for me, as you know, is that they want to stick me with that witch Veronica for a wife. Well, I'm tired of the buggering that I've had from those two, and I'm not going to take it anymore. Furthermore, you can tell the old man that I'm glad his blasted horse is dead. The only thing I'm sorry about in that connection is that I didn't run the bloody thing into the ground sooner. Whatever belongs to me is yours. I don't want the others to have any of it."

With tears running down her cheeks, she hugged me tighter than she ever had before. She finally accepted that I was leaving home for good and that there was no way of knowing when or if we would ever see one another again.

"This is goodbye love," I said.

I then kissed her, slapped her horse, and sent him on his way. I followed her at a distance until she safely entered our main gate. Then I turned around and headed south back to Cirencester.

The city covers 240 acres and, like most cities, resembles the hub of a wheel with four highways leading out of it. By the late 300s it had become the second largest city in Britain, after London, with a population of ten thousand, including the suburban villages. Originally the site of a small Celtic village, Roman Cirencester had been established in the year 45 as an army fortress on the initial Roman frontier in Britain. As the conquest pushed westward into Wales, the city continued to develop as a purely civilian center. As the saying goes, trade follows the standards. Merchants who had originally established themselves in the city to cater to the army continued to prosper after the army moved on. They were instrumental in helping the erstwhile fort develop into a successful market town. During the late third and early fourth century, Cirencester received two augmentations to its population and economic well-being in quick succession. In addition to the influx of European immigrants, it became a provincial capital as a result of the decision by Diocletian and Maximian to divide the island into four provinces.

Continuing along Ermine Street West, I entered Cirencester through the Gloucester Gate and passed down four blocks until I came to the forum. As it was the supper period, business was rather slack. The magistrates, local officials, and businessmen had closed their offices in the basilica. There were, however, numerous traders still selling their goods in the marketplace, and the usual number of idlers had gathered. So I tied my horse to a hitching post and purchased some fruit along with some bread from a nearby bakery. I packed them in my saddlebags for the journey the following day. At this point, I had a sudden bit of good luck. A man named Silvianus, who lived in the city and had business dealings with my father, hailed me. Our families had known one another for many years and we became engaged in a lengthy conversation. Silvianus was about to leave on a business trip to Marlborough. He had borrowed a sum of money from my father several weeks earlier and now he was asking me to take his repayment home. Silvianus had placed me in a rather awkward position but I couldn't very well refuse. So I assured him that my father would receive the money as soon as I saw him upon his return from Alchester. Strictly speaking, I meant what I said. My money concerns were over for the time being. The street crowds were starting to get rather heavy so Silvianus and I bade one another farewell and I mounted up. Large crowds in Cirencester are common during the summer. The city has several large and luxurious hotels. They cater to tourists visiting Bath, about forty miles to the southwest on the Fosse Way. As I rode along, I studied the buildings with a special intensity that I never had before. The goldsmith's shop, the restaurants and hotels, the stores all receded behind me until I arrived at the wall. I turned around and paused to take one last look. Then I passed through the Silchester Gate that came to symbolize my childhood's end.

It had been an extremely hot day and the heat had continued into the evening. We had eaten well at the fair so I knew I wouldn't be hungry that first night on the road. I continued for about three hours, taking advantage of the long British twilight. This is a difficult thing to explain to people in the Mediterranean area where night falls quicker during the summer. Cirencester lies on the southern edge of the Cotswold Hills. The relatively low-lying and rather swampy area to the immediate south and west of the city contains the headwaters of the Thames. As a result, the highway is carried over it in several places by a system of trestles. I had to get over this portion of the road before I could camp overnight on some higher ground about ten miles to the southeast. It was getting dark as I got across that last trestle and made the drier ground I was aiming for. I had ridden my new horse a fair distance, and it was starting to tire. I didn't want to terminate his existence as I had done that of Cymbeline. Besides, in spite of spreading a thick blanket across the saddle, my backside was extremely sore. I couldn't have ridden any farther if I wanted to. So I pulled off the road, tethered the horse, and went to sleep. This was the first time I had ever slept in the open countryside alone. I was surprised when I awakened the following morning to find myself sopping and seemingly freezing as the result of a heavy dew. As soon as I was on the road, I recalled that during the night I had experienced the strangest dream.

Most dreams are of short duration and are quickly forgotten after we awaken if, indeed, they are remembered at all. This dream was different. It remains as clear to me now as the night it occurred almost sixty years ago. In it I became dimly aware of a bearded man I could not recognize, frozen in space against a background as bright as the sun. This image remained stationary for the longest time. And then slowly, almost imperceptibly, the background started to darken and became a deeper red. Blood red. With equal slowness, the bearded man started to move in my direction, ever so gradually quickening his pace, until he was running at top speed straight at me. As he approached, his features became more distinguishable. I experienced a very dull sense of recognition, though I still could not place him. Suddenly, the dull red background vanished, and the man was part of an enormous throng of people moving south. But my focus was on this bearded man. He passed through cities and valleys on his way to some undisclosed destination. I had never seen so many people before, numbering as they must have in the tens of thousands. I noticed tremendous mountains that were far higher than anything in Britain. But where was this and who was this individual upon whom my attention was so fixed? At that point, I woke up shivering in my dew-sodden blankets. While the dream remained in my mind for several days, I eventually forgot about it. But as a man barely across the threshold of middle age, this bizarre fantasy would transform itself into a most grotesque and terrifying reality.

When our father had humiliated me on the occasion of my previous birthday, I had immediately considered leaving home. But lacking the fortitude for such an undertaking at the time, I had discarded the idea. It was just as well since, unprepared, I would have bungled it. But I had interpreted that fracas as a warning of worse things to come and had started laying the groundwork for my eventual departure. For our eighth birthday, our parents had given Valeria and me a splendid atlas containing detailed maps of every province in the empire. I had never before realized that it was so large and diverse. In the years ahead, I spent countless hours studying every map in great detail. The major cities, the mountains, the highways, the rivers, I knew them all. But perhaps most important was the historical section in the back of the atlas showing the world as it had been in prior ages. That book truly served as my introduction to history and stimulated the great interest in the subject that I maintain to the present day. This plus my later studies both in school and the excellent library in Cirencester developed my fascination with the military. I had never really considered joining the army until after the fiasco of my sixteenth birthday, and this created a problem.

According to the laws of hereditary bondage, I was expected to follow in my father's footsteps as a farmer and sheep rancher. However, with the exception of certain occupations that the government deemed vital, these laws were neither strictly enforced nor conscientiously obeyed. This was especially true after the catastrophe at Hadrianople in 378. At that time, the requirement for soldiers in the east became so acute that almost anyone, regardless of background, who wanted to join up, was accepted. Few if any questions were asked. I had given little consideration to the details of how I would go about joining. I felt that would take care of itself when the time came. Recruiting for most infantry units is done on a local basis. The vast bulk of the cavalry (though not all of it) is comprised of Germanic mercenaries. Because I would probably be stationed somewhere in Britain if I joined up on the island, I was determined to get to the continent via the Gallic Strait[2] so as to join a front-line unit on the Rhine.

The distance between Cirencester and Silchester is forty-six miles. I had a very long ride ahead of me if I was going to reach Silchester in a single day. The first full day on the road was uneventful. I did, of course, maintain the usual tourist's interest that arises when passing through territory one has never before seen. I had traveled to Bath and southern Wales on several occasions with my parents, but I had never before been east of Cirencester. The day soon warmed up, and there was a good westerly breeze blowing, but that didn't mean anything. The most characteristic aspect of British weather is its variability. Our climate is different from that of the more southerly provinces on the Mediterranean. In Britain, precipitation falls the year round. Near the

Mediterranean, the summers are quite dry, while the greater percentage of annual rainfall comes during the winter. The cloudier British skies generally prevent the days from being too hot and the nights from cooling down too much. As a result, the daily temperature range in Britain is small, while in the Mediterranean provinces it can be rather large. As I proceeded to the southeast, I left the Cotswolds behind. At Wanborough, there was a small group of buildings that couldn't even be said to constitute a village, the sort of cluster that is common at every minor highway intersection. Southeast of Wanborough, the highway ascends the Marlborough Downs' escarpment. It does so at a rather steep angle without any zigzagging to reduce the gradient. But as I continued my progress, the journey became easier. I passed through a hilly, heavily wooded area. Then, as the afternoon wore on, the local relief started to diminish so that I could make better time. My next port of call would be Speen, approximately thirty-four miles southeast of Cirencester.

Speen is only a small village and started out as a station in the imperial postal service, having a herd of about forty horses available at all times. An average rider on a good mount can travel twenty-five to thirty miles a day. A courier in the postal service can cover as many as 250 miles a day in good weather in those areas where the stations lie only a few miles from one another. Or so it is claimed. This was the function of Speen, Alchester, and countless other postal stations like them throughout the empire until the time of Diocletian and Maximian. During their joint reigns, taxation in kind became universal. The authorities realized that an enormous number of collection points would have to be established in short order, and they would have to be fortified. The larger cities could absorb this new role with comparatively little effort, but the small towns and villages had to be expanded considerably. Thus, Speen and Alchester and countless other hamlets like them suddenly assumed a new importance. They acquired a few of the trappings of the larger urban centers, though they would generally remain villages at best.

It was evening as I reached the floodplain of the Kennet and Lambourn Rivers near Speen. I misjudged the length of time required to pass through the hills leading to this village and expected to arrive earlier. I had always thought of Speen as being a miniaturized version of Cirencester, but this was far from the case. All the buildings were of wood construction and were government owned. Apart from several administrative offices, there were granaries and warehouses for storing the produce and supplies obtained through tax collection. There were also stables and corrals for housing the animals used by the imperial postal service and the companies that transport government provisions. Overall, it was quite a disappointment. Just outside the village proper was a small cluster of buildings that might be thought of as a suburb. It consisted of several small private homes and a restaurant that was preparing to close down for the day. The only thing the woman who ran the place had to offer was ham and eggs, so I had a double order of each. It was a pleasant change from the bread and fruit that I had been eating thus far. The little restaurant raised its own pigs, chickens, and vegetables. But with no major market in Speen, travelers possessing more exotic tastes would have to bring whatever else they might want with them for the proprietor to prepare for a fee. The woman was quite talkative, and I was thankful for the conversation, what with my not having spoken to anyone since the previous evening. She remarked that it had been a good business day, primarily due to travelers returning home from the recent holiday. The traffic I had passed on the highway, however, was not excessive; an occasional lone rider or small caravan and that was about it. But the unfortunate news was that there was no inn available to the public at Speen. I had slept badly on the ground the previous night and I thought a regular bed might improve things. That was not to be. So, having finished my supper, I was soon back on the road.

Within a mile, I came to the Lambourn River. After tethering the horse, I laid out my bedroll and settled down for the night. I lay there for a while staring at the countless stars, trying to contemplate my future. I even permitted myself to consider, however briefly, that this entire adventure was some terrible error that I should best correct by returning home at once. But that was out of the question. My parents had made their decisions, and I had made mine. The home life I had known was a thing of the past. Whatever home I would have in the future would be one that I made myself. The course of action that I had decided upon was irreversible. While it was to be filled with more heartbreak and disappointment than I could have ever imagined in that summer of 381, I have never regretted having chosen it.

The next morning I awakened early before sunup but the light was good enough to travel by. I was immediately into a more heavily farmed region, and the population density gradually increased as the morning proceeded. So did the wagon traffic in both directions, which I took as a good sign. Lonely stretches of road are open invitations to highwaymen. While criminality of this sort was not severe in southern Britain (certainly not by continental standards), it was advisable not to journey long distances over empty roads alone if it could be avoided. About midmorning, after crossing the Kennet River, I passed the milestone indicating that I was only five miles from Silchester. It warmed up considerably after that and, while the highway traffic became quite heavy, I reached the city somewhat before noon. I was halfway to London.

Silchester is laid out like a disjointed octagon. It has an area of about one hundred acres that makes it a little less than half the size of Cirencester. Prior to the Roman conquest, Silchester had been the capital of the Atrebates tribe. Like Cirencester, it had developed into a full-fledged Roman town with most of the trimmings. But I had no time for the role of a tourist there. Just outside the wall, my horse had thrown a shoe, so I dropped him off at a blacksmith shop. I have always been surprised at the extent to which horses still go unshod. In addition to screening the hoof from injury, horseshoes improve the footing on all but the hardest surfaces. They will also enable a horse to travel a given distance faster and in greater comfort. Since several jobs were to be performed ahead of mine, it would be a while before the horse would be ready. This was satisfactory, as I had to make several purchases and needed a bath in the worst way.

I stopped first at a tailor shop, where I purchased a new tunic, and then went to the main bath. It has quite an impressive entrance that leads to a courtyard where people can work out if they want to. Beyond that is a rather spacious locker room. Because of the heat, the first thing I did was plunge into one of the small, cold pools that are located on either side of the locker room. They only measure about ten or fifteen feet to a side and are not swimming pools of the type that are generally found only at resorts such as Buxton or Bath. After that, I relaxed in the warm bath before visiting the steam room. I had picked a good time to attend the baths, as only about a dozen people were there apart from the attendants. The main crowd would be arriving later on.

While I was scraping myself down, I received my first intimation of what conditions were like in Gaul. They were not encouraging. A pair of businessmen had come in before I had and were preparing to leave. One, named Arturius, remarked that his son-in-law had returned a week earlier from a trip to Spain and Gaul. Spain, according to this man, was doing reasonably well, being neither conspicuously prosperous nor overly depressed. Southern Gaul was in good shape but northern Gaul was another story. He went on to state that vast tracts of once prosperous farmlands there had been abandoned and were overgrown with trees and weeds; once beautiful country villas were standing idle and overgrown, in many cases burned out; once large and prosperous cities had been reduced, in some cases, to only a fraction of their former size. I then asked if either one of them had visited Gaul recently.

"I was there about two years ago," Arturius replied.

"I'm interested," I explained, "because I'm on my way to London on family business. I thought that while I was so close I might take a brief trip from Dover to the continent if I could afford the transportation. I've never been there before."

"Well," he considered, "crossing the strait to Gaul is safe enough since we haven't had any trouble with Saxon pirates for quite a number of years now. But I would not recommend that you venture very far inland on your own. As you just heard me mention to my friend Licinius, conditions in northern Gaul are not good. There are numerous bandit gangs on the prowl composed of runaway slaves and tenant farmers as well as army deserters and all sorts of riffraff."

"Added to this instability," Licinius stated, "or perhaps one of its root causes is the damned barbarian settlements that the government has been creating all over that region. It's an indication of just how depopulated northern Gaul has become that so many Germanic prisoners of war have been settled on abandoned lands that were once productive under

Roman ownership. Most of these buggers still have one foot in Germany and won't be satisfied until they have dragged the rest of us down to that level as well."

"The policy of barbarian settlements within our frontiers carries risks," rejoined Arturius. "But not all of these settlers were prisoners of war. Many entered Gaul as normal immigrants. In any case, the empire has fewer people today than it did two hundred years ago. Gaul has suffered as large a population decline as anywhere. We need people. And you must remember that Gaul is the linchpin of the whole Western Empire; without it, Italy has no direct links with either Britain or Spain. Most of our Celtic ancestors became Latinized. I don't see why we should not expect to have similar successes with German settlers in Gaul and elsewhere in the long run."

"Then why hasn't this policy accomplished more positive results?" Licinius came back. "We've been pursuing it long enough. I would remind you of the unreliability of certain of the Visigothic settlers resident in Thrace prior to the onset of our current troubles in that region. There have been far too many instances of these people being all too ready to join up with any enemy barbarian raiding party that passes through their neighborhood. These people simply cannot be trusted."

"Come on, Licinius," Arturius replied. "That last remark of your little harangue is simply not true. The Franks have proven to be reliable settlers and even more reliable as 'Roman' soldiers. After being settled in Gaul, the Franks and others have no desire to see their new homes savaged in raids by their distant relatives that have remained east of the Rhine or north of the Danube. The Franks that Probus settled here in Britain, mostly up in the Midlands, have been successful."

"I can vouch for that," I interjected. "We have two families of Frankish tenants on our farm near Cirencester, and they are a hardworking lot that never give any trouble."

Licinius' response to that was bitter.

"What you've just said only substantiates the remark that Emperor Julian made: 'The German is either at your throat or at your feet.' Your touching example doesn't change anything, sonny. Visit northern Gaul, and you will see all the damage they have done. The only time the barbarians stop killing us is when they are too busy killing one another."

Licinius said that with the relish of a chess master who had just made the final move of the game. But Arturius was far from beaten.

"When it comes to killing one's own kind," he countered, "we Romans wrote the book on the subject eons ago. As for Julian, I respect your adoration of the man. But with religious toleration in rather low relief these days, I would caution against your trumpeting that admiration injudiciously. Personally, I think he did as much to combat barbarism in the West and to restore Gaul to prosperity as any emperor in this century except Valentinian I. But Julian was a daydreamer. He thought of himself as a young Trajan or a reincarnation of Alexander the Great. He, above all, should have realized the precarious state of the empire's human and financial resources, especially in Gaul. Instead he chased his Iranian fantasies across the Mesopotamian desert and with largely Gallic troops at that. In the very year that Julian launched his fatal campaign against Iran, the Garamantes tribe destroyed the city of Sabratha in Tripolitania. That was only eighteen years ago, and to this day it remains in ruins. And don't forget that just four years after that the Saxons and Picts launched the most devastating raids this island has endured since it became Roman territory. Not to needle you, old boy, but the Iranian campaign was vintage Julian all right. Whenever I think of him, I think of the old Greek philosopher, Thales I believe, who tripped and fell down a well one night while walking along looking at the stars."

The discussion then started going off on tangents. The businessmen excused themselves, and we bade one another farewell.

On my return to the locker room, I took a plunge in one of the cold pools again. The water in both of them was frigid indeed, indicating that it was drawn from very deep wells. After toweling down, I donned my new tunic and left. An excellent restaurant was close by, so I gorged myself there, realizing that it would be the only major meal I would have during the day. I picked up my horse from the blacksmith and departed Silchester through its London Gate. It was midafternoon and London was forty-four miles away. It was only after I arrived in London that I realized how important Silchester is to Britain's leading city. In spite of its distance, Silchester is, in effect, an advanced western suburb of London. It acts in this capacity by connecting the capital with the southern and southwestern sections of the island as well as southern Wales. There are other routes from London to these regions, but the road through Silchester is the main one. It carries by far the greatest volume of east-west commercial traffic across the island.

The highway traffic remained heavy, but I was able to keep a good pace. The first couple of miles, I was again traveling through rich farmland. This, however, came to a rather abrupt halt at the edge of a large oak forest. The first village I would come to would be Staines where I would be meeting the Thames again at the halfway point between London and Silchester. But that would be on the following day. In the meantime, I had several hours of riding to look forward to across fairly level land that would present no obstacles. The journey to London proved somewhat monotonous. Along most of its length, the highway passed through heavily forested land that was broken only on occasion by open areas. As the main highway across southern Britain, I expected its surrounding territory to be more built up. The sparse population in this region is further attested to by the few villas along the route, plus the fact that not a single major road branches from or intersects this highway throughout its entire length. The absence of privately owned land along any highway means that the government alone is responsible for its upkeep. In Britain, as in the continental provinces, the highways outside the towns must be maintained by any private landowner whose property they border on. The army frequently sends out inspection teams to ensure that they are kept up to government standards. My father would discharge his obligations to the highway bordering his ranch by contracting the work out to a construction company in Cirencester. This is the common practice.

With the approach of evening, the sky started to darken as a typical late-afternoon thunderstorm developed. I had ridden several miles without seeing any buildings at all and was fearful of getting drenched. Then I spied a structure some distance back through the trees. It soon started to drizzle so I had little choice but to investigate whatever shelter it might offer. The building was back about a quarter mile from the highway and located on a small hill. The road that led to it was badly overgrown and appeared to have been that way for years. It turned out to be an impressive villa, much larger than that of my parents and far more Mediterranean in its design. It had extensive two-story porticoes and a round temple pavilion at its main entrance. But what had happened to the place? I immediately thought of the conversation that I had earlier in the day in Silchester concerning past devastations in northern Gaul. This was my first indication that conditions in Britain might not be quite as unblemished as my heretofore restricted vantage point had suggested. The villa had been largely burned out. But was it an accident or had it been caused by Saxon raiders in years past? It was impossible to know. The villa was about forty-five miles from the sea. The Saxons tended to keep their raiding parties closer to the shore where they possessed greater mobility and could retain their element of surprise. A foray this far inland was unlikely, but I couldn't help but wonder. In the period 367–369, a number of villas in Somerset and Devon had been attacked and burned by Scottish raiders from Ireland. Fortunately, they had come no closer than fifty or sixty miles from our place.

I entered the villa and brought the horse with me, as the rain had started to come down heavily as soon as we reached the place. The western wing had been badly gutted by fire, and the roof had collapsed, but the eastern wing had escaped largely intact. So I camped there for the night. I spent the remaining daylight exploring the villa as well as I could. In the first instance, I wanted to make certain that no squatters were living in or near the place. Secondly, I had the naive belief that I might find something of value. Both searches proved negative. It was such a shame. The western wing was severely damaged, and the gardens, fountains, and reflecting pools were in a serious state of disrepair. But nowhere had damage been done to the extent that restoration could not have been made. And yet, apparently, no one had even tried. The heavy rain continued for hours. The noise of the storm, added to the sheer eeriness of the place, did nothing to pave the way for an easy night. I slept fitfully and awoke for the final time just before dawn. It felt good to get back on the road again.

With over thirty miles to go, I would not arrive in London until the following day, but I rode hard just the same. Well before midday, I arrived at Staines on the bank of the Thames. Staines is a small village, but its main claim to fame is that its bridge crossing the river is one of the first Roman bridges built on the island. I spent the remainder of the day both riding and walking the horse. Having ridden hard during the morning, I didn't want to overwork him. I continued walking until after sunset and then spent my final night on the road. In addition to wanting to spare the horse, I wanted to tire myself out so that I would sleep better than I had the night before. The next morning, I was awake before dawn in full knowledge that I would be in London by noon.

It turned out to be a beautiful day with a pleasant breeze afforded by southwesterly winds. The early-morning traffic started to pick up and was soon far heavier than anything I had experienced earlier in my journey. It was indicative that I was approaching the city that was the financial and political capital of the island. The suburbs of London are extensive. Like Silchester, the relative absence of villas in the surrounding countryside reflects the fact that most of London's encompassing farmland is cultivated by people living within the city itself. The city of London has purely Roman roots, unlike most other towns in southern Britain. It is located on the north bank of the Thames, just down from where a north-flowing section of the river makes an abrupt ninety-degree turn to the east. The river is deeper at the city itself than it is either immediately upstream or downstream. Opposite the city, on the south bank, is a large mostly unreclaimed marshland with very little settlement. London originated as a result of the early Roman decision to build what is now "London" Bridge across the river in the course of the conquest four centuries ago. The choice of this site was influenced by the need to cross the Thames as far downstream as possible. Once the conquest had swept far beyond London to the north and west, the importance of the then village as a river crossing diminished. London was then developed as the river port of St. Albans but soon outstripped its supposed parent by becoming the financial center for the island. It evolved rapidly, mainly because of its convenient access and capacity for defense. The wall that surrounds the city was added in the early 200s. It stands twenty feet high, ranges from six to eight feet thick, and is built of stone brought in from Kent. It contains twenty-one bastions. London is a largely self-sustaining city. It requires no aqueducts to tap distant lakes or rivers, as gravel deposits within the city contain an ample water supply. The large forest, which I had ridden through on the trip from Silchester, provides plentiful timber for fuel as well as the construction of buildings. In addition, its profusion of wildlife satisfies much of the meat supply for the area. All the grain the city requires is more or less provided locally. The Thames and surrounding waters provide a rich fishing harvest that includes salmon. The city is almost perfectly bisected into an eastern and western half by the small Walbrook River that is really just a creek. Four of its tributaries start to the north of the city and are channeled under the north wall by brick-lined culverts. Colchester was Britain's first capital, but London, even before assuming this function officially about the year 60, had already become Britain's largest city. From the beginning, it possessed a cosmopolitan population that was more commerce oriented than was that of the original capital.

The destruction that occurred in all the western provinces, except Britain, during the third century is well known. But, ironically, Britain was the first to fortify its towns with walls on a province-wide basis. The process was started about 196 when Clodius Albinus made his ill-fated bid from Britain to seize the throne. The island was fortunate that it did. The continental cities only constructed walls when the barbarian onslaughts left them little choice. By that time, the currency had become worthless. Thus, the costs of constructing the defenses of the British towns, having accrued when the currency was stable and the island was at peace, were easier to bear than on the continent a couple of generations later.

It was well before noon when I entered London through the more northerly of its western gates. The London basilica is the biggest on the island and stacks up well against the largest in Europe. In the nearby forum, there is an impressive statue of Emperor Hadrian. At the basilica, I checked the addresses of my relatives in the city directory. The first one I visited was my father's older brother, Lucius. He lived only a few houses away from where the Walbrook joins the Thames. He had recently retired after spending most of his life working for the largest freight-hauling company on the island. It was a private company, but since a high percentage of its business was performed under government contract, it was virtually a government agency.

My relatives were happy, not to mention surprised, to see me. There was, of course, the obvious problem of explaining why I had come. Having thought about this the previous day, I concluded that the best policy would be almost honesty. I stated that the reason I had left home, which I assured them would be only temporary, was that my father and I didn't get along very well. I went on to say that we had suffered a disagreement of rather marked intensity and that I decided to leave home for a while to allow things to cool down. To my surprise, my uncle, who had last seen me when I was two, laughed.

"It runs in the family I guess," he said. "Your father and I never got along with our father either. He was a miserable old bugger that liked to work his family like dogs. I cannot once remember ever having seen him smile, at least not with the boys. He got along well with the girls, but his sons were another matter. Fortunately for your dad and I, your grandfather died while we were still in our teens. That sounds like a hell of a thing to say, but it should give you as complete a statement as you need on what conditions were like between us. Just a few months before he died, I got into a fistfight with him, and I was afraid one of us would be killed before it was over."

At the time of my paternal grandfather's death in 344, the family was living on their small farm to the northwest of London on the road to St. Albans. When the owner of a large neighboring estate offered them a good price for the place they took it. My grandmother then moved the family to London. She sent my father and uncle to school for two years to enable them to become literate. My father remarked to me on several occasions that he and his brother felt very uncomfortable during those years because they were so much older than the other children in class. But, embarrassed or not, their limited education had proven to their advantage in subsequent years. After that, they had both joined the transportation company for which my uncle worked until his retirement. My father, as a result of his traveling about the island in the company's employ, came to know my mother's father at Cirencester. They became friends and business associates. Since two of my mother's brothers had died as infants and the third had died of pneumonia at age sixteen, my maternal grandfather was left without male relatives to whom his estate could be left. My father, never one to turn down a good business opportunity, resigned from the transportation company, married my mother, and took over the managerial duties on my maternal grandfather's ranch.

My uncle had remained in London and was a remarkable man in many ways. Shortly after starting work with the transportation company, he had learned the blacksmith trade. He and two of my cousins built a sizable shop of their own at his home and, after he retired, they developed it into a thriving business. I had never seen so many tools in one place. They manufactured tongs, chains, chisels and hammers, handcuffs for the constabulary, saw blades and wedges for splitting wood. In recent years, he had even started exporting to the continent. Later in the afternoon, my cousin Lucilius dropped by on his way home. He worked for the same company his father had. I was invited to his place to have supper and to stay for the remainder of my visit. He lived in a relatively new home with his wife and young children. I hadn't seen Lucilius in two years. He used to visit us occasionally in Cirencester when he was on the road, but the trips came to an end when he obtained an administrative job in London. That evening, he took me on a tour of the city.

London has a population of about twenty-five thousand and an area of 330 acres within its walls. Under Diocletian and Maximian, it had become the capital of the Diocese of Britain and thus the residence of its vicar, the supreme civilian political officer on the island. It is to the vicar that the governors (or to be more accurate, the "presidents" as they are now called) of each of Britain's five provinces report. I referred earlier to the four provinces into which Britain had been divided a century earlier. Shortly after I was born, a fifth was carved out of the most northerly province and named Valeria in honor of the reigning emperors, Valentinian I and Valens. Its capital, Carlisle, at the western end of Hadrian's Wall, is the most northerly provincial capital in the empire.

Lucilius took me first to the vicar's palace just a couple of blocks to the east of his father's home. Fronting on the Thames, it is a large, impressive structure surrounded by a high, thick wall with a typical Mediterranean-style design. The chief administrative building is built on an east-west axis and bisects the site. Running the entire length along the inside of the walls are colonnaded buildings that connect to the central vicar's palace, thus forming courtyards on both sides of the main building. Everything was closed of course since it was evening, so we could not go inside. A quarter century would pass before I would view the interior of the building under circumstances that I could not possibly imagine now. We also visited the forum and basilica that I had dropped into earlier. After that, we took a leisurely ride along the walls until we arrived at the fort at the northwest corner of the city. After that, we returned to my cousin's home where we talked and drank long into the night. After covering a host of topics, mainly family matters, Lucilius asked me when I was getting married. We had been going at the wine for some time now and were starting to loosen up.

"I was wondering when you were going to ask me about that," I replied. "Actually it's somewhat of a sore spot and part of the reason I'm here. My father arranged a marriage for me with an absolutely gorgeous girl named Veronica. Her father's transport company runs yours competition in the southwest. But as far back as I can remember, the fair Veronica's only interest in our family has been brother Gratian. She couldn't care less about me. Gratian's marriage has also been arranged to the only daughter of a landowner whose estate lays a couple of miles away from ours. Gratian is not exactly overjoyed with his marital arrangements either because he has feelings for Veronica just as she does for him. So he suggested to our father, without asking me, that we simply switch. Always the altruist, he wisecracked that at least one of us should be satisfied with his connubial provisions. But dear old dad paid no attention. He replied that to change the plans he had made would make him look like a fool—a typical response. I feel sorry for Gratian's prospective bride. I'll give their marriage about two weeks before he starts screwing around on her. No marriage he ever makes will last worth a damn."

"What a rascal that brother of yours is, eh?" Lucilius remarked. "You are so totally different. I remember the first time I met the two of you. Even then, though you were both quite small, I knew that Gratian was fated to be the black sheep of the family. Based on what you told me, he appears to be living down to my expectations."

We both had a good laugh, but the time had arrived for a more serious discussion. I told him about my interest in visiting the continent and asked his advice on how I should go about getting there. He replied by giving me a recitation on conditions in northern Gaul that was only marginally less depressing than I had heard in Silchester. After he had finished, he asked me if I wanted to reconsider. When my response was negative, he told me that he would see what he could do.

"We have ships leaving for Gaul all the time, though a large percentage of them call in at Dover or one or another of the coastal ports en route. I'll see if I can get you on a ship going straight to Boulogne. That way, you will save half a day or so getting there. We'll discuss it more in the morning."

That said, we called it a night.

I spent the following day visiting relatives in other parts of the city. They received me warmly in spite of their never before having met me. One of the most immediate impressions they made on me was the varied nature of their religious beliefs. My immediate family was Christian, though my father had converted just shortly before he and my mother were married. Most of my cousins were Christians also, but this was principally due to smart politics rather than any deep-rooted spiritual convictions. One of my older cousins, a retired army veteran, had long ago been admitted to the cult of Mithras. My uncle and aunts still worshipped the old pagan gods in spite of the increasingly repressive edicts that the government had promulgated in recent years on behalf of Christianity. My brother and sisters and I were raised as strict Catholics. However, when I was older, I was impressed with the credibility of Arianism compared to the more irrational aspects of Catholicism. I never broadcasted these views to any degree because of the political unwisdom of such an act, especially by a civil servant or soldier. Nonetheless, I have long had the nagging thought that the wrong branch of Christianity emerged triumphant from that conflict.

At this time, the population of the Eastern Empire was about 60 percent Christian. Within this Christian population, the majority were Catholic, although the Arian minority was strong. In the Western Empire, a solid majority of the population was still pagan, while its Christians were and are overwhelmingly Catholic. On August 3, 379, the emperors proclaimed a new law. It declared all non-Catholic branches of Christianity to be heretical and illegal. It was reaffirmed six months later with the appended threat of government harassment for noncompliance. Having crushed, at least on paper, all Christian enemies of Catholicism, it would now be the turn of the pagans. On January 10, 381, another law was issued that was a milestone in the history of the empire: Catholic Christianity would be our only legal religion. All three emperors, Gratian and Valentinian II in the West and Theodosius I in the East, were westerners. Just as western leadership had been recently enforcing its political will in the East, so too would it put in force there its religious inclinations. The pagans up to this point had been rather disinterested, or at the most amused, observers of the fratricidal "political" struggles going on among the Christians. Many pagans had respected Valentinian I for the policy of strict religious neutrality that he had maintained during his eleven-year reign. Because of this, they had reason to hope that, following his death in 375, his sons would carry on his policies. In this they were mistaken.

The conflict between Arian and Catholic Christians had been going on since the reign of Constantine I. Arius was a Libyan priest who had a large following in Alexandria. The main premise of Arius was quite logical: Jesus Christ was similar to but different from God and was subordinate to Him. They are not identical. The Catholic position is that Jesus Christ is the manifestation of God on earth. Whereas Arians believe that Jesus did not exist until He was born of Mary, the Catholic position is that Jesus Christ has always existed. Every manifestation of God mentioned in the Old Testament is in fact Jesus Christ. The Arians believe that God cannot be divided, and, therefore, God and Jesus Christ are different; Jesus is only semi-divine. The Catholics believe that Arianism is a step back from monotheism. Since Christians worship both God and Jesus, monotheism demands that God and Jesus be the same. The controversy has gone on for decades. In the East during the reigns of Constantius II (337–361) and Valens (364–378), Arianism was ascendant. The law of January 10, 381, put an end to that. Among the barbarian peoples beyond the frontiers, however, Arianism was the supreme version of Christianity and continues to be so. This would serve as yet one more point of conflict between us and them.

At the time of their accession in 375, Gratian was seventeen, and Valentinian II was four. The latter was, because of his age, of no consequence at the time and unfortunately never would be. Gratian was an extremely zealous Catholic. His suppression of Arianism in the West was politically astute; the Arians there were but a small minority, and their ruination had placed the Catholic Church solidly behind him. However, in the end, it would not be enough.

When I arrived back at Lucilius' home, everything was ready. He had made the necessary arrangements to obtain my passage to the continent aboard a ship that was leaving London for Dover the following morning. At Dover, it would take on additional cargo and then sail for Boulogne. He also handed me an official government passport authorizing me to make the passage. It stated who I was, where I was from, and the nature of my business. The latter was, of course, rather vague but made some general reference to my father's wool trade. The passport was required because of the serious problem of runaway tenants and slaves. If a person ever inquired about boarding a ship at a shipping office, then he had to produce the document authorizing such a journey. Without a passport, arrest was possible on suspicion of being an escapee.

The next morning, I accompanied my cousin to his office on the Thames River and was introduced to the captain and crew. I thanked Lucilius profoundly for the hospitality and friendship he and his family had extended to me. As a token of my appreciation, I told him that he or anyone else in the family could use my horse as they wished in my absence. The previous night, I had given the stableman enough money to quarter the horse for the five days that I "expected" to be away. I felt a wave of remorse for having deceived Lucilius in the way that I had, but he was my only means of getting to Gaul, and that was all there was to it. We stated our farewells, and I boarded the ship. Soon after setting sail, we passed under London Bridge.

Estimating shipping schedules is always a hazardous undertaking due to the unpredictability of the winds. The water-borne distance from London to Dover is approximately eighty miles. With a good westerly breeze at our backs that afternoon and evening, the trip would be completed by noon of the following day. A better-than-average time I was told. The first day proved uneventful. London was soon out of sight, and the population density started to drop considerably. Apart from ships passing upstream on their way to London or an occasional villa on higher ground to the south, few discernible signs of life appeared anywhere. By the time we entered the Thames estuary, shore activity of any kind had seemingly disappeared. The coastal area was almost pristine in appearance. This was, in part, due to lengthy sections of marshland somewhat like that lying to the south of London. The shoreline presented no notable relief until, as evening descended, we arrived at the Isle of Sheppey with its range of low-lying cliffs. Shortly after we passed the island, night fell. During the day, I had busied myself helping the deckhands when I was needed, but for the most part, I was preoccupied with the sheer excitement of my first sea voyage.

One of the most difficult aspects of both developing and defending Britain has been its small population. Including both civilians and military personnel, it comes to about 800,000 compared, for example, to 5,000,000 in both Spain and Italy and about 5,750,000 in Gaul. Because of this low level of settlement, Britain is the most underdeveloped of all the western dioceses. In addition, this population is unevenly distributed.

Perhaps 60 percent to 70 percent of the inhabitants live south of the line running northeast from the estuary of the Severn River to The Wash. Even within this most heavily populated area, vast tracts such as Cornwall and the heavily forested region between Silchester and London remain, in which there has been very little settlement. Those areas of Britain that are cultivated are generally zones containing light soils that can be easily cleared of their thin cover. The thickly forested regions have remained uncleared because the low rate of population expansion has not required it.

Shortly after we passed the Isle of Sheppey, I lay down on a pile of hides and fell asleep. By this time, the breeze had died down, and the ship was making slow progress. I awakened briefly when the ship reached the port of Reculver, at which point we turned south to pass between Britain and the Isle of Thanet.[3] After that, the night continued without incident. Shortly after dawn, we entered the strait and passed the port of Richborough. My first captivating view of the famous white cliffs of Dover is forever fixed in my mind. We soon saw the smoke rising from the larger of the two lighthouses there. It puts out smoke by day and fire by night to guide channel shipping. My cousin's suggestion that I sail rather than ride to Dover had proven its wisdom. The overland journey of seventy-two miles is shorter but would have taken three days.

It was around noon when we landed in Dover. Since the ship would be spending several hours taking on new cargo, I set about exploring the place. Its port facilities are second only to those of London, as befits the closest British port to the continent. The town is guarded by one of the larger forts of the Saxon Shore, which is located near the harbor. After looking it over, I took the road up to the lighthouses on the heights that rise to 375 feet above sea level. I was fortunate in being given a brief tour and history of the more easterly of the two lighthouses by a very kindly man of about my father's age. He had been involved in maintaining them for many years. The lighthouse he took me through stands about eighty feet high and was constructed about two hundred years earlier. He explained that the other one, the older of the two, was still well maintained because it had to be used when the bigger one was down for repairs. I spent considerable time wandering over the cliffs, absorbing the magnificence of the scene. Someone once wrote that traveling through regions one has never before visited can take on an almost spiritual dimension. Standing there on the cliffs of Dover, I understood full well what that meant. But at the same time, I was perplexed with that special anxiety and sense of loss that a person always feels in the full knowledge that he will be leaving his native land, perhaps forever. Intruding upon the profoundness of the moment was a small but distinct column of smoke on the southern horizon. It was rising from the great lighthouse at Boulogne, thirty miles to the south on the coast of Gaul, reminding me to head back to the harbor, as my ship would be embarking soon.

It is important when writing about any series of historical events to keep the chronology straight. At this point, I must digress from my strictly personal story and bring the reader up to date on political and military happenings that had occurred in recent years to the point where I left home in August 381. This will involve a relatively detailed account of the background of the Gothic nation and the events leading up to the catastrophic Battle of Hadrianople in August 378.

CHAPTER 2

Those Perfidious Goths

VALENS THE VACILLATOR. He had spent his entire life in the shadow of his older brother as a man of the second or third rank. Valentinian had always been in the first and had had an outstanding military career, while Valens' had been mediocre at best. Everyone knew that Valens would never have reached imperial status if his brother had not appointed him to it. The embarrassing truth had been out well before he had ascended the throne. Valentinian had been proclaimed emperor on February 26, 364, and shortly thereafter held a meeting with his top officers. At his proclamation, the soldiers had made it plain they wanted to be ruled by two joint emperors instead of one. With the sudden deaths of the previous emperors, Julian and Jovian, within eight months of one another, the empire had been fortunate to have avoided civil war. Neither ruler had named a successor. The army wanted no such danger to arise in the future and demanded that Valentinian appoint a co-emperor to reign with him. At the meeting, he asked the assembled officers to make their suggestions on an associate. An understandable silence fell over the group. Then Dagalaif, the chief of cavalry, courageously stated that if his first concern was to establish a dynasty, then Valens was the obvious choice. If his primary consideration, however, was for the empire, then he should look elsewhere. Valentinian was stunned by this response and took an entire month to make his final decision. The time delay was yet another vexation for Valens, who had already felt himself demeaned somewhat by his brother's having appointed him to *his* personal staff as a tribune upon his own proclamation in February. Valens, with a very limited understanding of Greek, would have felt more at home in the West. But with the greater military danger to the empire being in the West and his brother being by far the superior soldier, that was out of the question. While everyone was glad to see two emperors reigning, the citizens of the East soon felt shortchanged in the man who came to rule over them.

The brothers were from Cibalae, a town in the province of Pannonia Inferior about midway between the Sava and Drava Rivers, not far from the Danube. Valentinian was born in 321 and Valens in 328. Valens had been grateful when his brother gave him a free hand to rule his territories in the East as he saw fit. His citizenry, however, were soon far less appreciative and with good reason. Valentinian, although a Christian, followed a policy of strict neutrality in the West on all questions of a religious nature. Valens, on the other hand, pursued a policy of persecuting non-Arian Christians in order to create "unity" among Christians throughout his realm. A fool's errand if ever there was one. Militarily, Valens had not done badly, but he always performed short of expectation. Invariably, his campaigns were described as "successful but inconclusive." In spite of his brother's being dead for three years, Valens was by no means considered the "senior" emperor. That really smarted. Valens was fifty years old, and his teenaged nephew in the West was nineteen. But Gratian let it be known from the beginning of his reign that he considered himself to be the senior of the two emperors because his father had been such. Rather pretentious, but there it was. Perhaps the opportunity had now arisen that would change this.

Valens was of two minds as to what to do about the confrontation with the Visigoths. Should he go to war or negotiate a peaceful settlement? If it was to be the former, then should he wait for Gratian to arrive from the West with the reinforcements that he himself had requested or should he go it alone? Recent battles with the Visigoths had gone Rome's way. If he could defeat them singlehandedly, then his place in history would be assured. The embarrassing comparisons to his uppity young nephew would cease too. Valens had listened to the conflicting advice of his generals but was undecided. So on the extremely hot day of August 9, 378, the army lacked a firm battle plan and had rehearsed for none of the possible situations that might emerge. The emperor had been unable to assess with certainty the numerical strength of the Visigothic Army. (The most frequent estimate was ten thousand, but the actual number proved to be twice that.) So perhaps he should wait until the western reinforcements arrived to be on the safe side. But if he did that, then historians would probably say that credit for the victory belonged to Gratian. His uncle would come off looking second best once again. At the same time, going to war with the Visigoths under any circumstances would mean that his original decision in 376 of admitting them into the empire had been a colossal misjudgment. He would be seen as a loser regardless of what decision he made. At least he had that right.

All nations great and otherwise have origins that are wrapped in obscurity. The Gothic peoples are no different. While they are generally considered to be the greatest of the German nations, perhaps the word "Germanic" rather than "German" would be a more fitting word to describe them. They did not originate in Germany, although their language resembles that of other German peoples. They arose in southern Scandinavia, and from them the island of Gotland in the Baltic Sea derives its name. Due to population growth and a lack of arable land, a large percentage of them were forced to leave Scandinavia and Gotland. Under the leadership of King Berig, they migrated south across the Baltic Sea to the region around the mouth of the Vistula River. This considerable distance of 150 miles shows that the Goths were experienced seafarers centuries before they came into contact with Rome. The exact date of this emigration is not known, but it happened sometime during the first century BC. This first great collective sea voyage set the standard for their descendants when they launched their invasions across the Black Sea to strike the empire during the 250s.

Our great historian Tacitus recorded information about them. At the time of his writing, they were settled on the south shore of the Baltic Sea in a region that they called Gothiscandza. There is also a river called the Guthalus[4] that flows into the Bay of Danzig, giving further testimony to the fact that the Goths were once settled there. Tacitus noted that the Goths lived under kings who were apparently more powerful than those ruling over other German nations. Kings were the exception and not the rule among the Germans at that time. Their nations that did choose kings limited their power and appointed them only during wartime.

In Germany, the Goths came into contact with more nations than they had known in Scandinavia, including the Vandals, Burgundians, and Rugians. Struggles against these peoples saw the Goths emerge as the strongest nation in the area and the submergence of some of the lesser tribal groupings into the Gothic nation. Around the middle of the second century, they were forced to migrate to the southeast under King Filimer. Their numbers had been growing in Gothiscandza for two hundred years. While the land could sustain them, the sea could not. The Baltic Sea has a very constricted access to the Atlantic Ocean between Jutland and Scandinavia. As a consequence, its waters tend to be somewhat stagnant and unhealthy and support only a limited fish population. Their remigration carried them through the Pripet Marshes, and by the year 200, they had established themselves on the north shore of the Black Sea and the Sea of Azov. This overall distance is about the same as that from Paris to Naples. In 238, they had their first military clash with Rome. It marked the beginning of the great conflict between us that continues to this day. The Goths would eventually devastate Thrace, Greece, and western Anatolia before meeting with disaster.[5] After the terrible defeats they suffered at the hands of Gallienus (268), Claudius II (269), and Aurelian (271), they were fairly well behaved for almost one hundred years. Rome had only to conduct occasional campaigns against Gothic raiders during this period. It appeared that they had taken the lessons of the previous century to heart.

But during this period of relative tranquility, Gothic strength increased. Numerous other German and non-Germanic peoples either voluntarily joined them or were subjugated. By the time I was born, the

Gothic "nation" consisted of Alans, Heruls, Finns, Slavs, Rosomons, Huns, and Sarmatians as well as the descendants of the original Goths themselves. And certain Romans also. These Roman Goths consisted of certain traitorous army deserters as well as the descendants of innocent civilians who had been taken into captivity during the 250s and 260s. To sum up, the Gothic nation had been transformed into a multiethnic collection of peoples whose non-Gothic elements had joined under a variety of circumstances. This nation was led by Goths at the very top. But the lower-level groupings could be led by men of any of the above-mentioned nationalities. At the same time, the human traffic flow was not all one way. Shortly after their arrival on the coast of the Black Sea, Gothic volunteers started entering the Roman Army. They still are. After the crushing defeats that the Goths suffered during 268–271, they split into three distinct groups. The Dniester River became the boundary between the two major divisions. The Goths to the east became the Ostrogoths, while those residing to the west of it eventually became known as the Visigoths. The Gepids became a separate people and have tended to operate in an independent manner from the other two. The splitting up of the Gothic nation in 291 may have reflected a difference in public opinion among them with respect to the institution of the monarchy.

After Rome had abandoned Dacia, north of the lower Danube, as being no longer defensible in 271, various Germanic peoples moved in to fill the vacuum. The Visigoths moved into contact with us on the lower Danube. The Gepids shifted to the area lying to the north of them beyond the Transylvanian Alps. This territorial acquisition, however, led to conflict. They were soon struggling with their Carpian, Vandal, and Bastarnian neighbors over who should get what portion of the territory. As a result, the Bastarnians who had lived for centuries in an arc around the western shore of the Black Sea were driven from their homeland. In 279–280, Emperor Probus allowed them to settle in Thrace, where they have since been assimilated into the local population. This struggle went on for several decades.

The monarchical form of government that was a centuries-old institution among the Goths was retained within the Amal dynasty of the Ostrogoths only. It would take several generations for the Baltha dynasty to emerge among the Visigoths, and that occurred after they had entered the empire. At the time of their separation, the Visigoths were not as united as the Ostrogoths. The basic political unit among the Visigoths was the subtribe in which blood relationships were most important. A subtribe was headed by a chief that the Goths called a *reiks*. Sometimes several subtribes would band together under a semi-monarchical leader called a "judge" for the purpose of making war, but this was a temporary position. When the period of danger was over, the judge would step down. It is an odd coincidence that the ancient Israelites, prior to the establishment of the Kingdom of Israel, were also led by men who used that title.

During this period, another source of conflict arose both between and within the subtribes: the advent of Christianity. Many of the Roman civilians who had been enslaved by the Goths in the 250s and 260s were Christians. Their religious beliefs soon took root among their captors. The reiks reacted much as the earlier Roman emperors had. They viewed the new religion as a threat to the traditions and culture of their people. Not wanting to offend their ancient gods, they were determined to stamp it out. They feared the spread of Christianity among their people would pave the way for the development of pro-Roman sympathies as well. In 348, a Visigothic leader named Aoric carried out the first persecution of Gothic Christians. It forced their emigration by the thousands into the empire. Included among them was Ulfilas, bishop to the Goths, who was the grandson of Romans driven into slavery back in 257. They would remain steadfastly loyal to the empire in spite of the vicissitudes that would beset us all in subsequent generations. Aoric was eventually succeeded by his son Athanaric, who was appointed a judge and leader of all the Visigoths in 365. Due to a bitter dispute between Aoric and Constantine I, Athanaric was forced by his father to swear an oath never to set foot on Roman soil.

Athanaric led the Visigothic forces during Rome's drawn-out campaign against them in 367–369. Valens defeated the Visigoths in minor engagements fought well to the north of the mouth of the Danube. He failed, however, to vanquish Athanaric's army in a major battle that was the object of the entire exercise. One thing that Rome did in each of these three years was destroy large portions of the Visigothic grain crop. Within a decade, this achievement would come back to haunt us in a most savage manner. In 369, tired of the course the war was following, Valens determined upon a drastic expedient: he promised a financial reward to his soldiers for every barbarian head they brought in. Enemy skulls quickly started to pile up, and Athanaric started feeling the pressure. This take-no-prisoners attitude by Valens, the destruction of their farmlands, and large-scale flooding by the Danube in 368 forced Athanaric to come to terms. The emperor returned to Constantinople and, in the time-honored tradition, took the title "Gothicus"—prematurely, as subsequent events would demonstrate. Athanaric returned home and from 369 to 372 conducted a vicious persecution of Gothic Christians. The war had inflamed anti-Roman hatred among the majority of the Visigoths and whetted their appetite for such slaughter. It also split them. The Visigoths had established several major "judgeships" during the fourth century. They were drawn from the Baltha family, an indication of things to come during my own lifetime. The subtribal reiks, however, did not like to see anyone hold this office for too long. Their fear was that a prolonged judgeship could evolve into a monarchy limiting their own power. Fritigern, one of the reiks, played on this fear and also used the persecution of the Christians to his advantage. He contacted Valens and received imperial support for raising a revolt against Athanaric. In return, Fritigern agreed to become an Arian Christian. The implication was that if the subtribal reiks became a Christian, then the bulk of his followers would follow his example. For four years, an on-again off-again civil war raged between Athanaric and Fritigern, with Athanaric gaining a marginal victory.

In 376, the Huns suddenly appeared out of the east and destroyed the Kingdom of the Ostrogoths. A Visigothic army under Athanaric went to assist their Ostrogothic cousins but arrived too late. The bulk of the Ostrogothic nation at this time passed under the domination of the Huns. The tens of thousands that remained free fled to the west to join the Visigoths. The Visigoths themselves had suffered a decade of turmoil by this time. The Huns got behind Athanaric's army, and once again the Visigothic breadbasket was laid waste. Athanaric's people were facing famine, and soon panic broke out. At this point, Fritigern and Alaviv, the leaders of the opposition to Athanaric, suggested that the Visigoths apply to Emperor Valens for permission to enter the empire. This would be presumably on the same basis that other Germans had done in times past. The majority of the Visigothic subtribes agreed and deserted Athanaric.

Alaviv and Fritigern led a delegation to Antioch during the spring of 376 to visit Valens. They sought to settle in the Diocese of Thrace where they could live under imperial protection. They, in return, would provide troops to the Imperial Roman Army as well as provide a federate army of their own to defend the empire. Valens's court was in a quandary, and the problem was this: Letting the Visigoths in would provide the Eastern Roman Army with many thousands of recruits. This in turn would allow landowners to avoid providing conscripts. Instead, they would pay the imperial treasury a per capita monetary tax for the men they did not have to provide. So the army would get bigger, and the state would get richer. There was, however, the very serious question of whether the Visigoths could be trusted. If they could not then their entry would dramatically undermine the entire strategic basis of the line of "Diocletianic" fortresses running the length of the Rhine and the Danube. These fortifications had safeguarded the frontier for eighty years. The system was designed to slow down our enemies until the central field armies could arrive to defeat them. Now Constantinople was considering a plan of action that could jeopardize this entire concept. If the Visigoths rebelled for any reason after settling in Thrace, then what would the government's strategy be? The enemy (one of them at any rate) would be south of our defensive belt of frontier strongholds to begin with. Our field armies would have a far more difficult time containing the Visigoths, and the frontier garrisons would be of only limited value in the process. Was the risk worth the danger? As a result of their conquest of the Ostrogoths, the Huns now had a large number of these warriors fighting in their service. Our knowledge of the Huns was very sketchy then, but the one thing we knew was that they had been moving west for years. Romans first heard of them about the year

370, the same year they overran the lands of many of the Alan peoples to the north and east of the Black Sea. Those Alans that did not submit to the Huns fled west and joined the Goths.[6] When the Kingdom of the Ostrogoths collapsed in 376, Visigoth and Roman alike feared that this terrifying plague in human form would soon arrive at the Danube. They already had thousands of Alans and Ostrogoths in their employ. Did we want them to subjugate the Visigoths in the same way, or did we want the Visigoths to fight with us?

Valens was in the process of making the most fateful decision that a Roman emperor had ever made. He could have refused entry altogether. But if he allowed them to immigrate, then it would be absolutely essential that proper planning be done to ensure a responsible reception when they arrived. Hard intelligence about people living beyond our frontiers, even those whom we have known for generations, is frequently difficult to come by. Major decisions must often be based on what is largely guesswork, and the Huns appeared to be the greatest danger we had faced in a century. The emperor signed a compact with the Visigoths, granting them entry. The fates of the Gothic and Roman peoples were sealed.

THE ROAD TO HADRIANOPLE

The initial estimate was that one hundred thousand people would enter, but it was difficult to have confidence in such a number, given the fluid conditions on the frontier. Whenever barbarians of any number were admitted as immigrants, they surrendered their weapons to Roman authorities at the frontier crossing points. This condition was agreed to between the government and the Visigothic delegation that signed the compact at Antioch. But when large numbers of Germans had entered the empire at the invitation of the government before, it had been over an extended period of time. We had been admitting Franks, who now number several hundred thousand within the borders of Gaul, over a period stretching back a century. The admission of three hundred thousand Bastarnians was accomplished in 279 and 280 over a period of several months. And during the reign of Constantine I, three hundred thousand Sarmatians settled in the provinces bordering the Danube. But the entry of the Visigoths would occur over a period of only a few days. Planning, communications, and control would have to be of the highest order.

The decision to settle the Visigoths in Thrace was somewhat ironic given the manner in which their ancestors had trashed the place a century earlier. The basis for this decision was the high fertility of the soil and the protection that the belt of frontier fortresses provided. The Visigoths in turn would be adding thousands of soldiers to our forces in Thrace, thus adding to their own defense and that of the empire in general. It had been agreed to in the compact that the Visigoths would cross the Danube at the city of Silistra.[7] This would enable the Romans to count the Visigoths as they crossed and to collect their weapons as they did so. From the beginning, things went badly. The central government in Constantinople took only minimal responsibility for the crossing. It was incumbent upon local officials to manage almost the entire enterprise and they lacked the resources for such a massive undertaking. Valens himself should have been present to oversee their admission but he was not. He was still in Antioch dithering over the situation on the eastern frontier. The emperor should have authorized military and civilian officials of the highest caliber to draw up detailed plans for receiving the Visigoths. These plans should then have been disseminated to all levels of personnel involved and understood by everyone. None of this happened. In fact, the officials that Valens did send out were the ones that exhibited the most abominable behavior. In a sense, this was to be expected. Strong and responsible emperors are never afraid to appoint the most capable men available to the most important political and military postings. But Valens was a weak ruler. He was riven with self-doubts about his own capabilities and tended to promote men who were only of indifferent talent; men who would not pose a threat to him. Thanks to imperial ineptitude, neither shelter nor food was provided in anywhere near the quantities required. History had shown that receiving a large influx of foreigners was possible when done properly. But past immigrations had been handled by strong emperors and capable officials.

These ingredients were most conspicuous by their absence this time. The crossing at Silistra was an utter fiasco.

Most of the local officials did their best to ferry the Visigoths across the river in an orderly fashion but to no avail. Many factors, natural and man-made, fused themselves into a hideous alliance that would eventually plunge the empire headlong into disaster. To begin with, the Danube was in a state of flood along its lower reaches due to extremely heavy rains in previous weeks. They continued throughout the period of the crossing. This made the river much wider than normal, and the incessant rain only added to the general hardship and confusion. Fearing the Huns might attack them from the rear, the Visigoths were terrified. They had agreed to cross on ships provided by our Danube Fleet in a systematic way. Instead, they started making dugout canoes and building rafts to transport themselves. We soon lost control of who was coming across and where. Many tried to swim the river, but that was impossible under the circumstances. Hundreds drowned in the attempt. The government called in units of the nearest field army as well as garrison troops to regain control of the situation. But by denuding the frontier fortresses, even more barbarians, including Alans and Ostrogoths, started pouring in.

The total number of barbarians involved in the crossing was closer to two hundred thousand—or twice the original estimate. Even with the most conscientious planning, it would have been extremely difficult to receive such a huge number of immigrants in such a short period of time. Notwithstanding that, how could Valens and his government have been so negligent? Officials acted as though they were entirely ignorant of the danger. In fact, many of them deliberately aggravated the already appalling conditions. A worst-case situation soon developed.

Lupicinus was the general that Valens had placed in charge of the operation, with Magnus Maximus as his deputy. Lupicinus had a good service record. That made the frightful incompetence he displayed during the crossing and its aftermath all the more difficult to understand. Magnus Clemens Maximus also had a sound military background, but at Silistra, he also betrayed a streak of venality and unfitness that would equal that of his master. Lupicinus would pay for his dereliction of duty with his life; to the regret of us all, Magnus Maximus did not. At least not at the time. To the half-starved Visigoths arriving on the south bank of the Danube, these generals offered only small quantities of dog meat. The immigrants were stunned by the degraded nature of their reception. Nonetheless, they surrendered up the sons of many of their leading tribal elders as hostages to the Romans, as Fritigern and Alaviv had agreed. This standard practice had worked well in the past. It guaranteed good behavior by the Germans and educated their future leaders in the Roman way of life. The hostages were disbursed to various cities in Asia Minor. While top Roman officials behaved outrageously, many instances of kindness were shown by local Roman farmers and landowners, some of whom were of Gothic descent. They gave such food as they could spare to the refugees.

Fritigern and Alaviv immediately recognized the disastrous situation for what it was. They had to take charge themselves since no leadership of any kind was being displayed on the Roman side. Gathering their people together, they marched for several days to the city of Marcianopolis about seventy miles south of the Danube.[8] Lupicinus met the Visigothic leaders and invited them to a banquet inside the city. Ostensibly, it was to smooth the current difficulties over and allay the fears of the immigrants. It is not known what his real intentions were. Marcianopolis had been ringed with Roman Army units to keep the Visigothic hordes away from the city walls. At the same time, the mass of the Visigoths were demanding admission to the city to obtain supplies. Hostilities soon broke out between Roman and Visigothic soldiers. The Roman Army was heavily outnumbered, and a large number of Roman soldiers were killed and stripped of their weapons and armor. Upon hearing this, Lupicinus ordered the slaughter of the bodyguard that had accompanied Fritigern and Alaviv. The leaders on each side suspected that they had been marked for death by the other. Fritigern, however, quickly persuaded his host that, in order to prevent further bloodshed, he should be allowed to return to his people. This would enable him to restore order. Lupicinus agreed. Fritigern and Alaviv left with the realization that all-out war was looming. Historians will forever wonder just how the leadership of the Eastern Empire could have been so inept at such a vital turning point in our relations with such a potentially dangerous people. Valens and his government were hopelessly out of their depth. During the ensuing two years, everything the government did aggravated the overall situation. If it had been their intention to treat the Visigoths in such a despicable manner, then why had they invited them into the empire in the first place? All of them, top to bottom, left to right, back to front, conducted themselves like a bunch of utter ignoramuses. The empire, to this day, has not stopped paying for their criminal disservices.

Lupicinus gathered all the soldiers that he dared risk and went forth from Marcianopolis a distance of nine miles to meet the Visigothic Army. Again, heavily outnumbered, the Roman Army suffered serious casualties. Lupicinus fled back to his headquarters in the city and committed suicide after finally realizing the degree to which he had disgraced himself. At the same time, things started to unravel in the surrounding territories. After the fighting at Marcianopolis, certain Roman authorities began to suspect the loyalty of regular army units comprised almost entirely of Visigoths. Valens ordered one such unit, stationed outside Hadrianople, to a city near the Hellespont. He wanted to keep it away from the rapidly deteriorating situation to the north. The urban prefect of the city denied this unit provisions to which they were entitled and then attacked the Visigoths with a quickly organized militia. The Visigothic unit reacted by attacking the city. Failing in this endeavor, they retreated north and joined Fritigern. From here on, Fritigern's army spent its time sacking undefended estates throughout the immediate countryside. Government unpreparedness was quickly causing Thrace to deteriorate into the same turmoil it had suffered a century earlier. This time, however, the Visigoths would receive local volunteers to assist them. A number of Roman tenant farmers and miners from nearby gold mines joined the Visigoths and guided them to the richest estates. Travesty after travesty quickly ensued, with many men, women, and children being raped, slaughtered, or dragged into slavery. What goods the Visigoths could not carry off with them they torched.

While all this was going on, Valens remained in Antioch still trying to patch up a quarrel with Iran over Armenia. Finally recognizing the danger, he requested reinforcements from his nephew Gratian and returned to his capital. The population there had ideas of their own. When Valens entered Constantinople, large and intensely angry mobs had no qualms about displaying their feelings toward him. They drove him from the city and forced him to set up his headquarters on one of the imperial estates. Gratian sent units under Generals Frigeridus and Richomer, the latter being the commander of Gratian's household troops. In 377, the Eastern Roman Army, still heavily outnumbered, drove the Visigoths north of the Balkan Mountains. They also fought a large portion of the Visigothic Army to a standstill at the Battle of Ad Salices between the lower reaches of the Danube and the Black Sea. Smaller gangs of Visigothic marauders, however, continued to range over much of the rest of Thrace. To recover the situation, our soldiers started moving all available foodstuffs into the fortified towns and cities. In addition, the passes in the Balkans were garrisoned to prevent a breakout southward by Fritigern's forces. The Visigoths were not to be outdone. They invited Alans and Huns, who had also crossed the Danube, to join them in a breakout through the passes. The Roman forces were more heavily outnumbered than ever by now. Their commander made the fateful decision to withdraw them from the mountain passes rather than risk their annihilation. Since the western reinforcements had not yet arrived, the commander may have had little choice in the matter. The barbarians poured through, and Thrace was again subjected to the most terrible forms of devastation and degradation.

Shortly thereafter, western soldiers started to arrive under the command of Frigeridus. They quickly encountered a large collection of bandit gangs led by the Ostrogothic chieftain Farnobius. This mob of several thousand was almost exterminated, and its survivors were sent into slavery to work the estates around the northern Italian cities of Parma, Modena, and Reggio. The Roman Army appeared to be gaining the upper hand during 377 and the winter of 377–378. It was decided that Emperor Gratian would lead another large contingent to the East to act in conjunction with his uncle. When news of this western troop transfer seeped into the Black Forest of southwestern Germany, the Alemanns took advantage to launch a massive attack of forty thousand men. Counterattacking, the Roman Army scored a brilliant victory, with only five thousand of the enemy escaping slaughter or capture. Gratian, who had conducted himself with great bravery in this campaign, then resumed his eastward march. Prior to hearing of Gratian's victory, Valens had finally received some good news of his own. His general Sebastian had selected three hundred men from each of several legions and composed a special task force of approximately two thousand. He trained this unit relentlessly to attack small Visigothic units loaded down with loot and lacking mobility. Finally it was ready for bigger game. A large Visigothic band had been detected, laden with plunder, heading north in the vicinity of Hadrianople. It presented the choicest target to date. Sebastian kept his forces well concealed and struck the Visigoths completely by surprise. Enemy casualties numbered into the thousands. So much loot was recovered that imperial storehouses in Hadrianople were unable to hold it all. It had been a splendid victory and one in which Roman casualties were very light. What made the casualty ratio all the more impressive was that the Roman task force had been, once again, heavily outnumbered. But the lopsided nature of our victory was tempting to misinterpret. That is what Valens did. Every army loves to catch their opponents completely off guard. The battle that the Roman Army had won on the banks of the Hebrus (or Maritsa) River was not necessarily an indication of how the two armies would come off in a fair fight. Also, Sebastian's task force was a special elite unit consisting of the best soldiers across several legions. This, too, Valens overlooked.

Fritigern was badly shaken by this defeat. He quickly summoned his plundering regiments to meet him near the city of Cabyle some fifty miles north of Hadrianople. He was determined to suffer no more ambushes by Sebastian or anyone else. After Sebastian defeated the Visigoths, Valens received from Gratian the letter informing him of his own victory over the Alemanns. Gratian also informed his uncle that he was continuing eastward with all possible speed so they could destroy Fritigern's army once and for all. Poor Valens. His beleaguered army no sooner scores a major victory than he gets a letter from his hotshot nephew informing him of his own far more massive victory over a far larger enemy. Valens and his associates had bungled the entry of the

Visigoths in the first place and had been slow to contain them during the next two years. He felt that he would now appear paler than ever in comparison with his western colleague. That might have been the deciding factor for Valens. The lead elements of Gratian's army were already arriving at the base camp Valens had established outside of Hadrianople. At the same time, Valens held a meeting with his top generals. He wanted their opinion as to whether they should go forth to confront the Visigoths on their own or wait for Gratian to arrive with the rest of the western forces. Opinion was divided, but those in favor of going it alone won the day. With Gratian's western army less than a week away, Valens was persuaded by a majority of his generals that the battle was as good as won. They knew what the emperor wanted to hear, and he was gratified by what they said. Their confidence was bolstered by the fact that this was the first time since the entry of the Visigoths that the Eastern Roman Army would outnumber them in a full-scale confrontation. The Roman side numbered about twenty-five thousand men. Valens was satisfied; the time had come for him to claim his place in the sun.

✳ THE BATTLE OF HADRIANOPLE—AUGUST 9, 378

In the days prior to August 9, Fritigern sent a church envoy to Valens. The Visigoths offered to make peace with the Romans on the basis of the conditions that had originally been agreed to at Antioch. We know now that the purpose of the unwitting envoy was to buy time for Fritigern's allied cavalry to join him for the battle that both sides realized was inevitable. Given all the human and material destruction that the Visigoths had committed over the past two years, no Roman emperor and government could agree to the status quo ante. During the morning of August 9, the Roman Army marched north eight miles to where the Visigoths had established themselves. A hallmark of the Goths has always been the manner in which they use their wagons as a mobile fortress by drawing them into a defensive circle on or near the battlefield. The Romans with their legions in the center, flanked right and left by cavalry regiments, faced north toward a Visigothic army whose infantry was enclosed by its circle of wagons. There was a large contingent of Visigothic cavalry on Fritigern's left flank but nothing on the right. Fritigern again expressed the desire for a peaceful settlement, but it was just another stall. When King Ermanaric of the Ostrogoths was defeated by the Huns in 376, he had appointed a pair of Alans, Alatheus and Saphrax, as the guardians for his young son Videric. Once it became apparent that the former Kingdom of the Ostrogoths could neither be defended against nor recovered from the Huns, King Ermanaric committed suicide. Alatheus and Saphrax then assumed the leadership of that segment of the Ostrogoths that refused to submit to the Huns and joined the Visigoths. Their request to Valens that they also be permitted to settle within the imperial frontiers with the Visigoths was denied. The government realized that the empire would have its hands full dealing with the Visigoths alone. But with all the confusion attending the Visigothic entry, these Ostrogoths barged in too. Fritigern kept in contact with them, and they would now play a pivotal role in his confrontation with Valens. At least they would if they ever showed up.

On a sudden impulse, the cavalry of the Roman left flank launched a sudden charge on the wagon fortress. Precisely at this time (Valens's luck, one might say), a large Ostrogothic cavalry contingent under Alatheus and Saphrax appeared on the scene and drove into the side of our charging cavalry regiments. The Roman charge was blunted and then routed. After engaging in relatively little combat, the cavalry on our right, which was composed largely of Batavians, simply fled the field. Seeing the disintegration of both our cavalry wings, the Visigothic infantry came charging out of its wagon fortress. Our infantry was attacked straight on while their cavalry assaulted our relatively unprotected flanks and rear. A near endless rain of arrows poured into our surrounded infantry, who were prevented from staging an orderly retreat by the enemy cavalry. The Roman infantry units realized they were doomed but were determined to take as many Visigoths with them as they could. Many units fought bravely to the last man in a battle that raged for hours in spite of the fact that its outcome had been foretold early on. Valens was trapped with the doomed legionnaires. Soon after night fell, the emperor was critically wounded by an enemy arrow. Under cover of darkness, he was taken to a nearby fortified farmhouse by his few remaining imperial guardsmen. They were spotted. The Visigoths attacked the farmhouse but did not know that it was Valens who had taken refuge inside. Unable to break in, the enemy soldiers piled up straw around the house and set it on fire. Only one guard escaped, and he related this story once he was safely back among Roman soldiers. That which was utterly unthinkable had happened. The empire had suddenly been plunged into the worst crisis since the depths of the third century.

As the final act in connection with this catastrophe, the Visigothic hostages who had been taken at the Danube crossing in 376 were dealt with. There were several thousand of them distributed throughout the East where they had spent the past two years being given a Roman education. Under orders from Julius, marshal of infantry, they were all executed. What did their parents and leaders think would happen to them?

In 370, a charge of sorcery was brought against an eclectic group of little-known entertainers in Rome. Tragically, this group was soon connected by Valentinian's officials to members of the Roman Senate, their families, clients, and associates. Charges of adultery were soon made as well, and these in turn led to accusations of treason. None of the conspiratorial charges were ever proved, but a number of the lesser indictments were. Valentinian I always demanded the maximum penalty for any crime, regardless of the nature of the offense. As a result, numerous men and women were executed in Rome primarily because their moral conduct failed to measure up to the puritanical standards by which their chief of state lived, at least where sex was concerned. Before long, these judicial outrages would have an echo in the East, prompted by the question of the imperial succession.

In 368, Valentinian I had endured a severe illness. As a result, he proclaimed his then eight-year-old-son, Gratian, as full emperor in order to secure, as well as he could, the succession to the western throne. Valens and his wife, Albia Domnica, had two daughters and a son named Valentinian Galates. The boy was born in 366 but died at an early age. This left the question of the eastern succession open. From 371 to 373, a series of sordid treason trials were held in Antioch in which Valens proved himself every bit as brutal as his brother. Several men had been charged with resorting to sorcery to ascertain who would succeed Valens, who, since the death of his son, was absolutely paranoid on this issue. To be charged was sufficient proof of guilt for the emperor of the East and his cohorts. As a result, terrible miscarriages of justice occurred. Dozens of innocent men were executed, and their families impoverished by the confiscation of their estates and other assets. Valens perverted the judicial system to appease the almost insatiable greed of himself and his associates. Throughout the empire, people heard of wealthy citizens in the East setting their entire libraries on fire. They feared government agents breaking into their homes and finding some book containing references to magic and the occult. Possession of such information was considered sufficient to be condemned to death, and few that were so accused escaped the ultimate penalty.

I like to think that in his last panic-stricken moments, as Valens was in the hideous process of being burned to death while suffering from painful battle wounds, the curses without number that were screamed at him by his victims as they died at the hands of their merciless torturers all came back to haunt him. Apart from his immediate family, no one mourned his loss, catastrophic as the battle had been for the empire. Even his nephew Gratian, staggered as he was by the magnitude of the defeat, did not appear to be overly upset at his uncle's demise.

The Roman Army lost twenty thousand men at Hadrianople. In times past, we had lost far greater numbers. But what made the Battle of Hadrianople so critical were the political consequences that derived from it. More on this subject will be discussed in subsequent chapters.

The battle was not without cost to the Visigoths; they must have lost several thousand men, although I have never seen an estimate of what their casualties were. Roman prisoners, eager to gain favor with their captors, wasted no time in telling them of the vast treasure that resided inside Hadrianople. In addition to that portion of the imperial treasury that Valens had brought with him, there was the treasure that Sebastian had recently captured back from the Visigoths. The enemy spent several days attacking Hadrianople, but it proved impregnable. Tempting as the treasure was, the sight of hundreds of Visigothic dead strewn around the walls of the city was one to which Fritigern had no desire to add. Coupled with this was the fact that Emperor Gratian was marching eastward with his army. Fritigern had no intention of becoming involved in another major engagement so quickly after August 9. Such an encounter might destroy his exhausted forces.

Fritigern was neither a king nor a judge, and he could govern only with the consent of the governed. Such consensual attitudes only existed during periods of extreme danger. Once the Battle of Hadrianople was over, the Visigoths were not in a very consensual mood. Fritigern was starting to lose control, and he knew it. He advised his men against attacking Hadrianople, but they did it anyway. Now their imaginations were fired by stories from Roman captives who, for a share of the loot, volunteered to join the enemy. They recommended that the Visigoths now move about seventy-five miles southeast to the port city of Perinthus on the north shore of the Sea of Marmara. Estates of rich individuals both inside and outside the city were theirs for the taking. Numerous attacks were made on villas near Perinthus. A number of families that had not taken refuge within the walls of the city itself were murdered. But no attack was made on Perinthus itself. Its walls were too formidable. Realizing they were about forty-five miles from Constantinople, the Visigoths decided to give it a try. This now-largest city in the Roman Empire is overwhelming to anyone who sees it for the first time or any time for that matter. Its incalculable riches were far too tempting to pass up. So the Visigoths launched an attack on it, but it was a complete and costly waste of time. They suffered heavy casualties while doing little damage to the defenders. After this rebuff, the Visigothic army split up into a number of smaller units. They headed west to conduct raids in Thrace and Macedonia as little more than bandit gangs. Fritigern had led them to their greatest triumph since King Kniva had destroyed Decius and his army 127 years earlier. But now, just weeks later, Fritigern was becoming yesterday's man. He was coming to realize how Athanaric must have felt when the people abandoned him.

Decius and his army had been annihilated in 251, and it took almost two decades for Gallienus (in 268) and Claudius II (in 269) to avenge him by crushing the Goths. Valerian had suffered the humiliation and disgrace of capture, enslavement, and death at the hands of Sapor II in 261. It took almost four decades for him to be avenged by Galerius in his brilliant victory over the Iranians in 297. So now the question arose of by whom and when would Valens be avenged? The answer would be "No one, not ever."

THE IMMEDIATE AFTERMATH OF HADRIANOPLE

Emperor Gratian established his headquarters at Sirmium. He was nineteen years old but had the maturity to realize that he had to replace his late uncle with an effective leader. Since his young brother Valentinian II was only seven years old, dynastic considerations would have to be set aside. A frightening vacuum had developed in the Balkans. In the short run, no one knew how and when it would be filled. The Visigoths were on the verge of realizing what their ancestors had failed to achieve in the previous century: the establishment of a Gothic state within Roman territory in the Balkan Peninsula. The Visigothic "wedge" had cut off the West from the Asiatic provinces. The first order of business was containing and suppressing that intrusion. But how?

There was no mobile field army in Thrace anymore. While the garrison troops were holding up well in their fortresses, the military command structure that had formerly governed them was destroyed. Gratian wanted no one as co-emperor who had been connected in any way with the recent debacle. It would therefore be someone from the West, but he would have to be familiar with Illyria and Thrace. This narrowed the choice to the son of Theodosius, the late count of Africa, who also bore the same name. Theodosius the Younger was at the time thirty-two, retired from the army and living on his ancestral estate in Spain. At the age of twenty-eight, he had been Duke of Moesia and was quite familiar with the lands of the lower Danube. He had attended his father when the elder Theodosius was Duke of Britain. His father had been responsible for repelling barbarians from the island in the latter 360s. Theodosius thus had a very broad military background and had risen to the highest levels of the officer corps at a very young age. By 378, his uncle Eucherius was one of Gratian's top advisers, which did him no harm either. He received a summons to attend Gratian in Sirmium during the autumn. He was to become Marshal of Infantry of the East. Theodosius no sooner arrived at Sirmium than a large band of Sarmatians invaded across the Danube. Using the remnants of Valens's army along with a number of western units, Theodosius led them to victory over the Sarmatians, whom they drove back across the Danube. That was all Gratian needed to see; he proclaimed Theodosius as emperor of the Romans on January 19, 379.

To give Theodosius greater latitude in suppressing the Visigoths required a territorial transfer. The prefecture of Illyria was turned over to the Eastern Empire on a temporary basis. Several top men in Gratian's government were sent east along with a number of western legions and regiments. Gratian then returned home to deal with a new threat by the Alemanns on the upper Rhine. Theodosius established his headquarters at Thessalonica in eastern Macedonia for the following reasons: Its well-protected port facilities would guarantee the safe arrival of supplies from almost anywhere. Its central location placed him in close proximity to where the army would be required, while Constantinople was too far to the east for use as a command center. In addition, communications were too disrupted for a site further inland to be selected at this time.

Military hereditary obligations were now rigorously enforced throughout the East, and all provinces were hit with new conscription levies. The Balkan Peninsula is absolutely vital to the empire's security. All main east-west land communications run through it, and these had to be reestablished as quickly as possible. The central question was how.

Theodosius, cautious by nature, would only resort to major military engagements as a last resort. He avoided large-scale battles because he had to husband his reduced resources. If he lost them in a major battle, there was no way to determine what the future course of the empire would be. Even if he won, the army would still probably suffer so many casualties that it would be too weak to respond to the next crisis. As the terrible news from Hadrianople spread beyond the Rhine, Danube, and Euphrates, our dangers mounted. Theodosius determined early on that his military operations against the Visigoths would consist of small-scale struggles across a broad front. Nothing too great would be chanced in any single encounter.

The chaotic situation prevailing in the Balkans led to periodic surges of other barbarians across the lower Danube. Ostrogoths, Alans, Huns, and others, in addition to the Visigoths, were devastating the provinces in that area. The Diocletianic belt of frontier fortresses performed its function. They fought admirably, and the vast majority of them were able to withstand the enemy onslaughts because the barbarians lacked siege equipment. The problem was that Theodosius I required time to rebuild the shattered and demoralized field army that he had inherited. Fortunately, the Rhine had remained quiet following Gratian's sound defeat of the Alemanns in 378.

The year 380 was a bad one for Theodosius and the Balkans. He suffered a serious illness early in the year and some minor military losses after he recovered. His illness was so grave that by February it looked like he would not survive. The Catholic Church spared no effort in praying for his recovery, and he received the sacrament of baptism. When he recovered in the spring, Catholic Christianity realized that it had as staunch a supporter on the throne as it had ever possessed. Theodosius immediately took to the field with an army that he knew was not yet combat ready. He had little choice in the matter. During his recent illness, the processes of major government decision-making, military and civilian, had been paralyzed. Several garrison towns had recently surrendered to the Visigoths. They feared that no support from the central government would ever arrive to relieve them. Theodosius resorted to restricted military action to allay these apprehensions but suffered several marginal defeats. Once again, the emperor of the East had to send to the emperor of the West for military assistance.

The year 381 was much better. In January, the former Visigothic leader Athanaric, who had been all but forgotten after 376, took seriously ill and was suffering severe hardship in Transylvania. Theodosius saw this as an opportunity to show the entire Gothic nation what cooperation with Rome could bring. He gave Athanaric and his few thousand remaining followers permission to settle within the empire. The old Visigothic judge was welcomed to Constantinople with a great public celebration. Two weeks later, Athanaric died from his illness, and Theodosius gave him a state funeral. These events made a profound impression on Goths everywhere and started generating the desired results.

The emperor and his generals soon started conducting a large number of small-scale operations against the enemy once again. These were generally successful. During 381 and 382, Visigothic fortunes went rapidly downhill. They carried out a horrendous amount of destruction during the first year after Hadrianople. Then they had to relearn a lesson that had confronted their ancestors in the previous century. When a region was too severely pillaged, it was often impossible for it to come back into production the following year. As a result, from 379 onward, serious outbreaks of famine occurred. Coupled with this came several attacks of plague. As if these circumstances were not bad enough, their ranks were further thinned by desertions to the Roman side that had started soon after the disaster at Hadrianople. The most important man to switch sides at this time was a relative of Athanaric named Modares. He soon inflicted an impressive defeat on a small army of Visigothic marauders weighted down with plunder. This might sound surprising, but the more thoughtful among the Visigoths simply desired a permanent place to settle. They wanted to spare their families the threat of disease, starvation, and constant battle. Only a permanent peace with Rome could achieve this end.

The Visigoths who were slow political studies had to learn the hard way. In 381, Gratian and Theodosius conducted joint operations. They succeeded in driving those Visigoths who had not come over to the Roman side out of Illyria altogether. By 382, Fritigern and his army were bottled up in the valley of the lower Danube where they had first landed in 376. They had lost most of their captives and plunder and after six years of constant warfare were back at square one. By October, they were pretty much a spent force. One thing that helped to focus minds on both sides was an attack across the Danube during the winter of 381–382 by the Huns and the Carpodacians. This attack was driven back. It served, however, to remind both Romans and Visigoths that, while the immediate Hunnish threat had been overestimated in 376, the danger was still there. It was just building more slowly than had been originally anticipated. So in the autumn of 382, Theodosius reached an agreement with the Visigoths in which they were recognized as federate allies. At this same time, Fritigern simply disappeared. No official explanation has ever been given regarding his death. One rumor had it that he died of natural causes in Thrace, while another claimed that he had returned north of the Danube for some reason and was murdered there.

Under the conditions of the treaty, the Visigoths would settle in the Diocese of Thrace between the Balkan Mountains and the Danube River. They would provide regiments to our army of Thrace. These units would patrol the 140-mile length of the Danube from Oescus (where the Iskur River enters the Danube) downstream to Silistra, where all our recent unpleasantness began. Since 376, this section of the border had been a gaping wound. Barbarians had poured through whenever they felt the urge because there was nothing to stop them beyond the frontier. Now, for the first time in six years, the front-line garrisons had a mobile field army operating behind them—even if it was one that would, in part, keep them looking constantly over their shoulders. The Visigoths would govern themselves under their own, not Roman, laws and would provide recruits to the Roman Army as requested by the emperors. Here again, the new relationship between Romans and Visigoths would have novel aspects to it. Individual Visigoths could volunteer for the Imperial Roman Army, as they had been doing for a century and a half. If they became officers, then they could advance to the highest ranks if qualified. The Visigothic subtribes would be subject to conscription as the emperors saw fit. But such conscripts would serve under their own chieftains, wear their own uniforms, use their traditional tribal weapons, and be trained as Visigothic, not Roman, soldiers. These chieftains would be commissioned as officers in the Roman Army but were barred from the top military posts. They would receive an annual subsidy from the Roman government to sustain themselves and train their subtribal armies. Such "federate" soldiers did not receive Roman citizenship regardless of how long they served. It was this aspect of the agreement that formalized the beginning of the "barbarization" of the army. Barbarians in Rome's service had almost always been Romanized through assimilation. This would not happen to anywhere near the same degree among the federate allies. It fell short of the peace for which the Roman public had wished. Gratian and Theodosius, however, had concluded that it was the best that could be accomplished under the prevailing conditions. The recent victories in the Balkans had been achieved to a high degree by the western armies led by Bauto and Arbogast. But pressures were building on the Rhine, and these units could not remain in the Balkans forever.

In the four years since he became emperor of the East, Theodosius I had accomplished much. The cardinal principle that had guided him during this period was that a major defeat was to be avoided at almost any cost. Under the circumstances, this was probably the most responsible course of action to pursue. But with the benefit of a half century of hindsight, one might ask whether the refusal to risk defeat did not, in fact, guarantee it in the long run.

CHAPTER 3

A Gallic Intermission

SHORTLY AFTER I BOARDED ship, we set sail. I stood there almost transfixed by the gradually receding coastline. The white cliffs of Dover are a remarkable sight, but I had too little time to enjoy them. While watching them contract on the horizon, the full impact of what I was doing registered. Nothing had ever worked for me in Cirencester. Nothing ever would. I felt trapped inside a cocoon that would never open. No aspect of my life was my own, and I had no sense of belonging there. At the same time, I strongly believe that within the vast majority of civilized people is a strong attachment to the place where they were born. An almost magical bond exists that certainly goes far beyond my capacity to describe. Yet here I was in the process of breaking that connection. I was closing the formative chapter of my life and was certain that from that point on I would be concentrating all my efforts on the future. It was a naive notion. We often like to fool ourselves into believing that what is past is truly past. But the most unfortunate components of our lives never really fade far enough over the horizon for us to be completely liberated from them. The tragedies, the failures can always be disinterred at the appropriate moment of self-pity for yet one more exercise in self-flagellation. These contradictory emotions kept churning within me until finally the cliffs were lost in the haze. When I could distinguish my homeland no longer, I turned south to be reassured by the smoke rising from the lighthouse at our next port of call.

In London, I had dropped into the library and copied a map of northern Gaul. The trip from Dover to Boulogne, about thirty-six miles, generally takes several hours, so I had plenty of time to think about what to do once I arrived on the continent. My original intention was to start east from the coast to Cologne, a distance of about 260 miles. I figured I could cover it in a little over two weeks. At this time, second thoughts began to occur over the issue of joining the army. Was that really what I wanted to do? The stories I heard in recent days over security in northern Gaul raised concerns on just how dangerous such a trek might be. Having departed Britain, I decided to see what the civilian sector might offer; after all, there was no need to rush these things. For the remainder of the voyage, I busied myself helping the crew whenever required. By the time we arrived in Boulogne, it was starting to get dark. After presenting my passport at the harbor master's office, I headed into town.

Boulogne has the most important Saxon Shore fortress on the continent. Like most of these settlements, it resides on a high hill overlooking its harbor and extends well beyond its walls down to the shoreline. Its most eye-catching aspect is its lighthouse that lies just to the north of the town. It stands fourteen stories high, and like its counterparts at Dover, it keeps burning 365 days a year. From this area, Julius Caesar launched his two "visits" to Britain in 55 and 54 BC. Almost a century later, from the by then thriving seaport, his great-great-grandnephew, Claudius I, undertook the Roman conquest of the island. In addition to its importance for trade and national security, it is also a substantial fishing port, thanks to both the large volumes and considerable varieties of species that are found in these coastal waters.

In general, the forts of the Saxon Shore network extend along both the British and Gallic shores of the German and British oceans.[9] The network was constructed from 260 to 300. Some individual sites had been fortified before then, but during this period, they were all brought up to a common standard. Their tactical function is to act as a system of naval bases for the British Fleet to counteract assaults by pirates, to provide strongholds from which both cavalry and infantry can respond to invasions in their vicinity, and to block penetration by barbarians of river systems that would carry them into the interior of Gaul or Britain. They provide a similar defensive role to the Rhineland fortresses by frequently being positioned at the mouths of rivers that serve only too often as avenues of attack.

After leaving the docks, I headed up the hill toward the forum. I was curious to see what job openings might be available, and like all cities and towns, there would be job listings posted there. I didn't expect much, but one that caught my eye was an advertisement for teamsters by a transportation company. It appeared to be the newest ad on the board in comparison to the others that were rather weather-beaten. After obtaining directions, I went there half-expecting the place to be closed at this late hour. It was just outside the northeast wall of the town, and I was surprised to find men still working. Assuming that he was in charge, I approached the oldest man I saw.

"Pardon me, but I noticed your ad in the forum for teamsters, and I wondered if you still had any openings?"

He seemed like a grandfatherly type, probably in his late fifties with balding white hair. He looked me over rather suspiciously. He probably eliminated the possibility of my being a runaway slave or tenant to begin with and recognized my accent as British. Motioning for me to come off to one side out of earshot of the other men, he introduced himself as Victor.

"Tell me about yourself," he said. "Where you're from, how old you are, what your job experience is, what your family situation is. Also, are you a Christian?"

"Isn't everybody these days?" I replied. "By the way, is that a prerequisite for the job?"

"No." He grinned. "But if it was, I assume you wouldn't mind going back to the church in the center of the town and submitting to an instant conversion would you?"

"Whatever it takes." I smiled.

I gave him a condensed briefing of what had prompted my leave-taking from Britain. I described my familiarity with driving wagons with heavy loads and pointed out that, from the standpoint of hereditary bondage, my younger brother would gladly and greedily take my place when it came to running our father's ranch when the time came.

"What will you do if I don't hire you?" he asked.

"If I can't find anything else around here," I replied, "then I'll head east and join the army at Cologne."

Victor paused for a few moments to consider what I had told him.

"I'm short three people for the next eastbound wagon train. If I don't get them, then we'll have to redistribute the load from a couple of these wagons to the ones that we have drivers for. The highway inspectors won't like it, but they'll accept the fact after the proper amount of cash lubricant is applied. By the way, if you haven't already guessed, you're hired."

At this news, I was elated. He went on to explain that the company transported goods back and forth between Britain and the Rhineland and throughout northern and eastern Gaul. Both military goods and civilian wares were handled. He also held out the possibility of my being involved in trips south from the Rhineland to the warmer Mediterranean climes. The pay was better than that of a private soldier, and I silently congratulated myself on rethinking my plans during the voyage. Being wishy-washy can prove advantageous sometimes. I went to the town baths, had a late supper at a restaurant, and then returned to the transport company. In addition to a large barn for the animals, they had a garage for storing and repairing the wagons and a bunkhouse for the teamsters.

We were up just before dawn the next morning when Victor announced a change of plans. I was teamed up with a Frank named Marcomus who was to lead a small caravan of just three wagons. We were going south eighty miles to Amiens on the south bank of the Somme River. Marcomus was a likable enough chap in his midfifties. An army veteran with extensive experience, he had become a soldier when Constans was emperor of the West. Fighting on the losing side at the civil war Battle of Mursa, he served in the Mesopotamian campaign of Julian before finishing out his service in Africa. We had deliveries to make to several large villas near Amiens. After that, instead of returning to Boulogne, we would take the highway running northeast from Amiens to Arras to rejoin the main wagon train. Transportation companies dislike running wagons empty for any distance. The loads would be redistributed in part from the main caravan to the three empty wagons once we reunited with them. The hope was that the entire convoy would then cover the remaining distance to Cologne in less time.

First, we had to get the paperwork done regarding my being hired. I had arrived too late the previous evening to do it then. By signing on as a teamster, I was assuming an unalterable, hereditary obligation. It would theoretically fix me as a carter for the rest of my life, as well as my oldest son whenever he was born. But as we all know, these "obligations" are being broken all the time. I assumed this responsibility with a very cavalier attitude. At the tender age of sixteen, I had no intention of spending the rest of my life staring at a pair of ox butts during every waking hour. Having escaped (not really, too strong a word) from Britain, my immediate concern was to secure steady employment with a guaranteed income. Hereditary obligation or not, I felt I would probably have no trouble breaking it when the time came. Victor put my home as Cologne. He explained that by doing that, I would be able to work the north-south caravans between southern Gaul and the Rhineland as well as the routes across the north. I asked him if the provincial authorities ever checked into the validity of such work authorization papers once they were filed. He assured me they did not.

"The government assesses financial penalties against the late delivery of goods when we are transporting items for the army or when we are delivering the annual taxes in kind," he said. "They don't care who conveys the goods as long as they arrive on time. This is especially the situation with respect to the army. There have been rare cases of transport chiefs being executed when deliveries were late during wartime. So we always try to give ourselves plenty of leeway to allow for bad weather, wagon breakdowns, and so on. This run we're starting today won't be too difficult. Within several weeks, we'll have to start delivering the year's harvest to the various towns. To the greatest degree possible, grain deliveries are made by sea because of the cost advantage. Even the fortresses on the lower Rhine, like Utrecht and Nijmegen, are supplied from Britain rather than the interior of Gaul when the crops near those towns are insufficient to meet the local requirements."

"What exactly is your position here?" I asked.

"I'm the assistant superintendent in charge of our northern convoys. We always have several wagon trains on the go at any given time, and it's my responsibility to see that everything goes well. I'll take charge of our eastbound train while Marcomus is in charge of the group going south. When we reunite at Arras, Marcomus will take over as the convoy master while I keep tabs on the others."

The signing-on process completed, we were on our way.

Like all major freight companies, ours provided both regular and express service. With regular service, the wagons are drawn by oxen. Express service utilized teams of eight horses in summer or ten during the winter months, with an additional charge being applied for the faster service. Much of northern and north-central Gaul is rather flat. While its soils provide rich farmland, certain sections are still heavily forested. For generations, its economy has been based on the agricultural output of large villas. But during the third century, much of it was ruined by plague and invasion, and it suffered a sharp population decline. During my time there, the results of this havoc were still much in evidence. I soon saw many large estates that had been abandoned then and subsequently reclaimed by nature over the ensuing decades. Some of them were deserted due to the general panic at that time by owners who simply wanted to put as much distance as they could between themselves and the frontier. If they had enough money, they could afford to abandon even a large villa and build or purchase one elsewhere. When the government failed to get Roman owners for these vacant lands, it settled Franks on them to bring them back into production. But even with large-scale barbarian settlements, there are still numerous abandoned farms, some of which have fallen into total ruin. With some working villas, the owner's national origin is readily apparent; if the homes of the tenant farmers have a Germanic rather than the more standard Gallic structure, then the villa owner is probably a Frankish chieftain.

After five days, we finally reached Amiens, and it too turned out to be an educational experience. What I had studied in school about the two great plagues and the impact of the barbarian invasions suddenly came to life. In the first two centuries of its existence, Amiens had developed into a thriving city that eventually extended its area to approximately

450 acres by the time of Marcus Aurelius. Its population then was at least ten thousand. When I visited the town in 381, its area had been reduced by 90 percent from what it had been two hundred years earlier. But the reduction had taken place in the course of a much shorter period because the town walls had been built during the latter 200s. The forum and the amphitheater that were originally in the north-central part of the city are now incorporated into its south wall. Outside the walls, I walked along some of the ancient blocks of the original city whose vestiges were still quite prominent. Some buildings, about a block south of the amphitheater, were still used. But virtually everything else had been torn down to ground level to provide building materials for the town fortifications. Block after block of ruination was kept in view only by the animals that grazed there and kept the grass down. Acres of abandoned foundation stones educed a tragic nostalgia for what must have been. More than anything else, they now symbolize the devastated ambitions of a superior age.

What I witnessed at Amiens I would see again and again in a majority of the places I visited in Gaul: shrunken towns with diminishing prospects. Autun had contracted from almost five hundred acres to just twenty-seven; Bordeaux was reduced from 309 to seventy-seven acres, and Paris had shriveled from 131 acres to a mere twenty-two. The only cities that avoided this description were the fortress towns of the Rhineland. After Constantine I died in 337, the construction of new public buildings declined throughout the empire and especially in the West. As the army expanded, an ever-increasing percentage of tax revenues were funneled into military expenditures. And as the government became more closely allied with the Christian Church, an entire new area presented itself for the empire to spend even more of its scarce resources on. By the time I arrived on the continent, the only new buildings the government was constructing were churches, and many of these were simply pagan temples that had been remodeled. I do not mean to imply by the foregoing that no one lives outside the walls of the cities I have mentioned. In many places, they do. What the area comparisons do provide, however, is a profound sense of how drastically our civilization has shrunk socially and economically over the past two and a half centuries. This is particularly true for the cities that are located well back from the frontier. And block after block of razed buildings certainly testify to a devastating demographic collapse, regardless of how precisely its degree can be determined.

A peculiar aspect of Gaul is that in spite of its having always had a larger population than all of Roman Africa (excluding Egypt), it has never had proportionate political influence. It has produced a much smaller number of both senators and equestrians per unit of population than Africa. Roman Africa was colonized about a century before Julius Caesar's conquest of Gaul, and the former never suffered the type of major invasions and other political and economic disruptions that Gaul did. But after allowing for this, it is still a mystery why Gaul has not achieved more political authority.

After delivering our goods to the villas near Amiens, we headed north to Arras, where we linked up with the main caravan and headed east. Because of heavy rains and a couple of wagon breakdowns, it was slower going than we had hoped. The further east we went, the greater was the degree of Frankish settlement. Their legal status, however, is that of any other Roman municipality. East of Tongres, we crossed the Meuse, and after skirting the northern Ardennes, we arrived at Cologne. Unfortunately, I did not get much of a chance to see the city at that time. We were immediately transferred to a convoy that was heading back west the following day.

By the time I had returned to Boulogne, Victor had hired several more teamsters and decided to hold a one-day introductory class to educate us on company policies. We were about an hour into the program when he suddenly said, "Marcus. Thanks to your recent trip to the Rhine, you are the most experienced among the new hires. Tell us if you noticed anything special about the highways you traveled on."

My mind was a complete blank and then I remembered something that I had noticed first while traveling across Britain and later in northern Gaul as well.

"One thing that I thought was rather strange was the number of times that the highways turned on hilltops," I replied.

"Anyone have any ideas?" Victor asked.

Silence.

"Such high points enable army surveying parties to sight in several miles of road at a time in a straight line," he went on. "This activity is frequently carried out at night, using lanterns for enhanced accuracy. Or at least it used to be. Nowadays, where highway work is concerned, we are more involved with maintaining what we already have rather than constructing anything that is entirely new. There are other things that you will notice about our roads, as well as laws that you will be subject to in the course of your travels. Widely admired though they are, the knowledge that many people have of them is superficial. The primary function of the system is and always has been to facilitate the all-weather transportation of the army, especially the infantry. This role it executes to perfection. And on these highways, the army always has the right of way. You will often find that your wagon train will have to pull off the road to allow troop concentrations to pass. But by their very nature, our highways have two serious drawbacks. They are very costly to maintain, and they do not serve commercial transport proficiently, other than in bad weather. You have probably already discovered in those areas where the surface consists almost entirely of paving stones a shod horse is in danger of slipping because the metal shoes cannot get enough traction. Whenever the surface consists of packed gravel, there is generally no problem. Nonetheless, even unshod draught animals have problems. The constant traffic wears the stone surfaces until, in some cases, they are almost like glass. The wagons themselves tend to slide around more as well, and the steeper the gradient, the more severe the problems. Whenever it rains, of course, things are all the worse. As a result, any wagon traveling on a highway has to carry a lighter load than its structure is capable of supporting. By law, and you must be very careful about this, a four-wheeled horse-drawn wagon is restricted to a maximum load of one thousand pounds. Similar ox-drawn wagons are limited to fifteen hundred pounds. But there is another reason for limiting wagon loads. The pivoted front axle is a recent invention that has revolutionized the simple process of turning a corner. But since the older wagons still have rigid front axles they can turn only with difficulty. It appears so obvious now that it seems incredible that no one thought to invent it centuries ago. In any case, the heavier the load, the worse the problem. Another reason for load restraints is the need for a daily minimum mileage to be maintained by all vehicles carrying goods under government contract, and these rates govern the entire empire. If you stay in this business long enough, you will learn of the enormous difference between the costs of land and sea transportation. A wagon load of wheat might have its basic cost increased by as much as 75 percent while being transported one hundred miles across country over a period of two weeks. This increase covers the driver's wages, freight charges, and highway tolls. But for a cost increase of only 35 percent, this same volume of wheat can be shipped from any one of the major Syrian port cities of Tyre, Sidon, or Tripoli the entire 2,500-mile length of the Mediterranean and beyond to Lisbon on the Atlantic coast. This is why almost all cities with access to the sea prefer to have their goods transported by ship, regardless of distance."

I spent the next six months of my life transporting goods between the Rhineland and the west coast of Gaul, as well as making more numerous local deliveries. From the Rhineland, we carried pottery and glassware, wine, bronze ware, and brass goods westward to towns and country villas and sometimes to Boulogne to be transshipped to Britain. In the reverse direction, we occasionally brought tin from Cornwall to the metal processing region southwest of Cologne and Bonn. There it was alloyed with locally mined copper to produce bronze ware. For generations, Britain and Spain provided tin for this industry. But when Spanish supplies started running out during the third century, Cornwall took over as the sole supplier. Most British tin, however, was transported by ship to the Rhineland because of the lower costs. Not all the goods we carried from the coast were destined for the fortresses on the Rhine. A steady volume of British woolen textiles and lead were destined for delivery to various places in Belgium and other parts of northern Gaul. In general, Gaul is by far the most industrialized region of the Western Empire. The pottery factories of Trier and the Rhineland and the glassworks of Cologne supply all the western provinces. The Gauls drove their Italian competitors in these lines of enterprise out of business ages ago and industry of any kind in Spain and Britain has never amounted to much in comparison. Even in Italy, wealth is based to a very large degree on land rather than commerce.

Most of the deliveries that we made were of a local nature. We took a number of trips to Tournai to collect stone from the quarries there for deliveries to towns and villas in that area, and we also hauled a lot of lumber. From sawmills, we made deliveries to the army at locations along the Rhine for maintaining the fleet as well as to private lumber dealers. We delivered barrels to the various wine producers up and down the Moselle Valley; from the imperial woolen mills at Trier we distributed new army uniforms throughout the Rhineland. In addition to uniforms, we also delivered weapons manufactured at Trier to the fortresses on the Rhine. The armament deliveries were always made under heavy army escort. The most disagreeable undertakings that we made for the army were the deliveries of lime from the great kilns near Bonn to the many area fortresses for repairing or extending fortifications. These kilns are large both in size and number and are capable of generating twenty-five thousand tons of product per year. Like the armament factory at Trier, this lime factory served all the fortresses of the lower Rhine.

Victor was not exactly a slave driver but none of his teamsters were allowed much time to themselves. Constantine I had decreed early in the century that Sunday would be a universal day of rest. However, since the vast majority of the population lives on farms and farmers are exempt from this rule, it has never meant much to most people. We always ran on pretty tight schedules. Between equipment breakdowns, bad weather, frequent last-minute schedule changes, we usually worked seven days a week from sunrise to sundown. I was on the road practically all the time. Like me, Victor was a Roman, but most of the teamsters were Franks. Because I was well educated, I soon found myself handling most of the paperwork since most of the Franks were at best semiliterate. This enabled me to meet some of the higher-ups in the company and placed me in position to gain promotion quicker than I might have otherwise.

Victor took an instant liking to me. He was a widower who lived with one of his two married daughters in a large home just outside Cologne. His other daughter and her family lived at Remagen about twenty-five miles up the Rhine. He also had had a son in the army who had been killed in action during a campaign undertaken by Valentinian I along the Neckar Valley in Germany. Victor was understandably bitter at this loss and had a general hatred for all Alemanns. While in Cologne, I never extended my social contacts much beyond Victor's family and that got me to wondering. When I departed Britain, I was leaving behind an impending marriage to Veronica that I knew would be a thoroughgoing calamity. But if one's marriage was not arranged by one's parents, then how did you go about getting married? I had never given it any thought before and it was a little late in the day to be concerned about it now. But I concluded that time alone more or less takes care of things in that regard.

Once the harvest is in, every transport company in the empire is involved in delivering grain supplies. For us, it meant carting wheat and barley from Britain and northern Gaul to granaries located in every walled town in Belgium and the Rhineland that could not be reached more economically by water. We also hauled large quantities of fruit and vegetables. When I joined the company, Victor told me that it suffered a rather high turnover in personnel and it did not take long to see why. We were working all the time and while the pay for a teamster was pretty good, the work never stopped.

I soon realized why the government is always issuing ever-more drastic laws to assure that people in jobs deemed vital to the national well-being stay put. It is because the laws are ineffective, at least in the frontier areas. In the more settled parts of the interior, the government can bully people into submission with greater ease when problems arise on this issue but along the frontier it is a different situation. The Franks were hard workers but when they got tired of being teamsters, they simply quit and usually went back to their settlements. While the Franks are settled all across northern Gaul, they are most heavily concentrated in Batavia and Toxandria. Batavia is the most northerly region in Gaul, lying in the difficult terrain between the northernmost branch of the Rhine, on which Utrecht resides, and the Meuse River. Toxandria lies south of the Meuse. Many Franks that worked for us lived in these territories. Since the majority of them had been born there, they were Roman citizens like the rest of us regardless of what their first language was. However, the government was reluctant to enforce the laws of hereditary bondage on these people, fearing that a minor irritant might quickly expand into a major crisis. So they were allowed pretty much to come and go as they pleased.

One good thing at this time was that the frontier was quiet. The reverse side of this coin, of course, was that the frontier never stayed quiet for very long. Emperor Gratian had headquartered himself at Trier during 377–378 for the purpose of conducting operations against the Alemanns east of the Rhine and south of the Main. The emperor's forces inflicted severe defeats on the Alemanns and that, coupled with several bad winters, had forced the West Germans to behave themselves for a period. Trier had become the second largest city in the Western Empire during the fourth century. Constantine I had used it as his capital early in his reign and embellished it accordingly. Constantine II, Constans, Valentinian I, and Gratian had used it in a similar fashion, but in 378, Gratian left Trier and moved to the upper Danube to confront a growing menace there from invading Alans. It was shortly after this that the Battle of Hadrianople occurred. Several years later, growing pressures on the upper Danube caused Gratian to return there and to move his headquarters finally to Milan in 382. He never returned to Trier.

The winter of 381–382 was quite severe in our region and it took a toll on all of us. The larger caravans would generally have a military escort provided by garrison troops from one town to the next. This was to protect against local bandit gangs or marauding bands of barbarians that came across the Rhine surreptitiously. In November 381, one such eastbound wagon train was caught in a terrible snow and sleet storm just east of Tongres. When two wagons skidded off the road, soldiers and teamsters alike struggled to get them back on with great difficulty. Marcomus was the oldest man in the group. With plenty of help, he didn't have to overexert himself to the extent that he did, but Marcomus was the sort of man that always led by example. This time it proved fatal when he suffered a massive heart attack. He died instantly. In the worst possible weather, we still had over sixty miles to go. It took us a week to cover the remaining distance to Cologne. Since I had been working most closely with Marcomus since joining the company, I was given the responsibility of conveying his body to his family down the Rhine at Nijmegen. The family had already been notified by our company headquarters. The farther north down the Rhine valley that I traveled, the greater the Frankish presence became. By the time I reached Nijmegen, it was almost like I had entered Germany. If it were not for the well-maintained highways and the stone-walled fortress towns, then it would be impossible from an ethnic and cultural standpoint to know which side of the river I was on. The number of villas had thinned out by the time I reached my destination, and the ones that I did see were all occupied by Franks. Marcomus' widow lived on a small farm just outside the town. She was a very gracious woman and seemed to take her husband's death better than I did. They had had two children, a daughter who had died as an infant and a son who was serving in a legion on the Danube. There were, however, plenty of other relatives around. The funeral was held according to local pagan rites the following day, and shortly after, I started back to Cologne. The family was genuinely grateful for my bringing him home to his final resting place, and they treated me very well for the short time that I was there.

The population of Gaul has declined by about 25 percent over the past two centuries. It would be considerably lower were it not for its Frankish settlements. Their numbers, however uncertain, have been very large. Northernmost Gaul is the most Germanized part of the empire. As I returned from my first visit there, I could readily understand why many people referred to this area as "Francia." The Frankish colonization of northern Gaul has, on the whole, been a good thing. They have risen to the highest ranks of the army and the civil service and their loyalty has almost never been in doubt. Neither have they ever hesitated to defend Roman (now also their) territory against barbarian invasions, including those by German Franks. One thing in our favor has been the relative lack of sophistication of the Franks from a political standpoint. There is no "king of the Franks." The highest title to which a Frank can aspire within his own society is that of a tribal chief. Rome deals with these tribal chiefs in Gaul just as we did with Celtic chieftains in centuries past. Our relationship with the Roman Franks stands in total contrast to our disastrous relationship with smaller numbers of Goths in Thrace that arrived, for the most part, not over generations but in the matter of a few days.

After the Roman conquest, Gaul developed a north-south cultural division that essentially reflects the climatic differences between the two halves of the region. Southeastern Gaul is largely an extension of Italy in terms of climate and culture. Like Italy, this region is pretty dry in the summer and frost-free almost every month with year-round sunshine. The winters are mild, and that is when most of the annual precipitation falls. It is more heavily urbanized than the north because initially most of the Roman immigrants to Gaul settled there; most of the large landowners still live in the towns. The largest cities in Gaul without a direct military function are still concentrated in the south. As you move further west and away from the Mediterranean, the climate gradually transforms into that of northern Gaul and Britain. While buildings in Aquitania still have the distinctive architectural style of their counterparts in Italy, their roofs have a steeper pitch to accommodate the heavier rainfall. Southern Gaul is less of a unit than is the north because the south is split in two by the Massif Central, an elevated thirty-five-thousand-square-mile region. Due to this large land block, the southwest and southeast quadrants of Gaul have always found it easier to communicate with the north than with each other. Northern Gaul has more in common with Britain than with its own south. The most important northern cities (excluding those on the Rhine) were originally Celtic tribal capitals that were rebuilt and expanded after the Roman conquest, just as were their later counterparts in Britain. The villa-based economy is more pronounced also, just as in Britain. There is year-round precipitation, and the summers are markedly cooler than they are in the south. The growing season in northern Gaul and Britain is longer than anywhere else in the empire or in the barbarian regions of central Europe. These factors all contribute to making Gaul one of our richest regions.

It was while returning from Nijmegen to Cologne that it really came through to me just how lonely and rudderless my life had become. I decided to ask Victor for at least a temporary change of scenery. I had been traversing northern Gaul for three months and had concluded that three months of northern Gaul went a long way. I would push for working on the north-south routes so that I could at least see the Alps and the Mediterranean. I wouldn't mind further assignments in the north, but as a steady diet, the place was starting to get to me. Victor proved to be understanding on the issue and promised to come up with something. Finally, in February 382, he told me that I had been assigned to a wagon train that would be starting from Trier and going all the way to Arles. What more could I ask for? When Victor told me this, he leaned back in his chair with a big grin on his face.

"So you want to visit the sensuous south, do you? Not before time I suppose. The fellows that you will be working with are a completely different crew from what you've been associating with so far. They're a wild bunch and after one trip in their tender, loving care, I can guarantee that you will return a new man."

"That means we're going to get you laid, kid," a voice boomed out from behind me. "I'm Julianus."

He was a big, good-looking, good-natured Gaul and, as I soon discovered, a notorious drinker and womanizer. In other words, the sort of chap that us rather quiet and socially awkward types wish that we were like.

"Julianus here is as good a teamster as we've got, and if you don't believe me, just ask him," Victor joked.

I subsequently discovered that the only reason Julianus had a job with the company at all was that an uncle of his was a part owner.

"Why is the wagon train going all the way to Arles?" I asked. "Wouldn't it be cheaper to transfer the goods to barges at Lyon or some other river port and ship them downriver from there?"

"It depends on the time of year, the strength of the mistral, and the spring runoff coming down from the mountains," was the reply from Julianus. "You've never experienced either the Rhone River or the mistral. Once you have, you'll understand. Whenever we have to go all the way to the coast on these southbound junkets, we usually try to offload at Arles because it's easier than Marseille. There are several disadvantages to shipping out of the latter. In spite of having a first-rate natural harbor, wagon traffic has a difficult time with the steep grade on the only road north out of the place. Besides, it's a little off the beaten path as far as major highway traffic is concerned. The main east-west highway across the south lies about eighteen miles to the north. That alone adds an extra two days to the round-trip. It depends on what our local agents can schedule with the harbor master's offices at the two ports."

The sources of the Rhone and the Rhine rivers are less than fifty miles apart in the Alps just north of Italy. The Rhone has a length of 505 miles. Due to the heavy runoff it and its tributaries receive from the Alps, its current is very strong. This heavy outflow coupled with a relatively steep gradient and the effect of the mistral, a strong, cool, dry wind that comes from the north, makes it difficult to navigate for almost its entire length. This wind is at its strongest and occurs most frequently during the winter and the spring, so traffic on the Rhone and Saone Rivers can have a very restricted season. It does not get under way until well into the summer when the previous winter had heavy snowfalls and frequently has to be terminated early in the winter when the mistral starts to pick up.

The next day, we took the highway southeast from Cologne and picked up more wagons as we moved along the Rhine through Bonn, Remagen, Andernach, and Koblenz. From Koblenz, at the confluence of the Moselle and the Rhine, we headed up the Moselle Valley to Trier. This lowest reach of the valley contains hillsides covered with the vineyards from which the famous Moselle wines are produced. It's a very rich area with expensive villas lining both banks of the river. Even without having to pick up the wagons in the other towns, we would still have taken this more roundabout route to get to Trier. There is a highway that runs southwest from Cologne directly to Trier, but it goes through the Ardennes. This forested tableland can be very dangerous in the winter. It gets cold at the higher elevations and can be hit with sudden severe snowfalls. During the time that I worked as a teamster, several instances occurred of isolated wagons being trapped on the Cologne-Trier highway during such storms. In one case, several people froze to death. For that reason, we only took it during the warmer months. I disliked traveling through the Ardennes Forest at any time. Tucked away, for the most part, in eastern Belgium, this area is one of the most sparsely populated regions within the Western Empire. It will probably never be much good for anything. The Ardennes plateau forms a watershed between the tributaries that flow northwest into the Meuse River and those that flow southeast into the Moselle. Because of the incessant rainfall, much of the land is waterlogged. That which is not has had the natural soil nutrients leached out of it to the point where it cannot be farmed. Its constant dreariness, caused by the almost never-ending precipitation and fog, always filled us with foreboding. Fortunately, the barbarians must have felt the same way. About the only people we ever saw in the region were in wagon trains or army columns.

South of Trier, we started to leave the wine country and entered a district where the land is more given over to cattle and grain farming. The Moselle region is subject to severe weather during the winter and the valley has an annual snow cover that lasts for about thirty days. Fortunately, there was little snow on the ground, and it offered no obstacle to us. Continuing up the Moselle, we passed through Metz to Toul, where we crossed the river for the last time and then left it. From

Toul, we climbed through low-lying and heavily forested mountains to the town of Langres from which we entered the valley of the Saone River. Passing through Dijon and Tournus, we continued down the Saone valley to Lyon. This is where the Saone empties into the Rhone River flowing down from Lake Geneva and the Alps. The remaining third of the journey took us down the Rhone River valley to Arles and the Mediterranean.

Upon entering the Saone valley, we entered southern Gaul. On the lower slopes of the hillsides are some of the finest wine-growing areas anywhere. Large agricultural estates, dominated by fine villas, also produce various grain crops. While there has been some German settlement permitted in the area, it has been on an individual basis as tenant farmers rather than a clan basis. The Saone valley, twenty miles and more in width and over 150 miles long, runs in a southerly direction through east-central Gaul. It is definitely more Latin than Germanic. This, of course, is what one would expect from a region that has formed part of the Roman heartland in Gaul for four centuries. During one of my journeys to Marseille, the caravan had to digress from the usual route to pick up goods in a small town. It was on a less-traveled highway, and I had never been there before. What caught my attention as we approached the place was what appeared to be a village on a hilltop a good distance from the road we were on. What puzzled me was that it seemed quite substantial, and yet it was missing on the map I had of this region. It was my first view of a fortified villa or, if you will, a private castle.

Around the middle of the third century, certain members of the senatorial class in the West made a drastic reappraisal of their position in society. These landed aristocrats had traditionally provided the manpower pool for the top political and military offices throughout the empire. But as that century passed its halfway point, a growing number of them simply withdrew from public service. They were fed up with having their estates plundered by government, usurpers and barbarians alike. If current conditions prevailed much longer, then they would be driven into bankruptcy. Such men realized that the day when the Roman Senate played a major role in imperial politics was coming to an end anyway. Having been banned from the army, seeing their political influence restricted, and being sick and tired of their ever-increasing rates of taxation, they started to vacate the cities. They "retired" to fortified villas that were constructed in locations that would not be overly accessible to either government soldiers or marauding barbarians. On readily defendable hilltops, their new villas came to resemble small fortress towns.

In such strongholds, they would be far more difficult targets for avaricious tax collectors, and their families and assets would be much safer. As the trend continued throughout the fourth century, these landed aristocrats would start to evolve new spheres of influence. The decline of the cities and the evolution of fortified country estates were much more pronounced in the West than in the provinces of the eastern Mediterranean. The plagues and barbarian invasions had injured the West in terms of both degree and extent more severely than was the case in the East. This in spite of the intensity of the destruction in provinces bordering the Aegean and Black seas. With the exception of Thrace, parts of Illyria, and the west coast of Anatolia, urban life held together better in the East. Except for the areas just mentioned, there was no withdrawal by the rich from the cities to the country in the East because there was no need for it. As a result, the central government in Constantinople could keep greater control over its populace than could its counterpart in Rome or Milan.

This private estate had grown into a small village in all but name and had fortified itself with a wall that would be a credit to a military detachment. It had grown slowly over several generations in both legal and extralegal ways. The locals I spoke to were quite open about it. Estates such as this had long ago started accepting runaway slaves and army deserters as certain landowners started building their own private armies. These "estate militias" had been started in the third century to protect senatorial properties from any kind of attack. But they quickly assumed a collateral offensive function. When barbarian armies were returning home loaded with plunder, they started to find the tables turned against them. Now they were the targets of these private Roman militias, and the landowners suddenly found themselves growing richer as the successes of their militias mounted. The government constantly demanded that such confiscated goods be returned to their rightful owners. In cases where the raids had been local, some efforts would be made in this direction. Where the invaders had ranged over a large area, it was impossible to make such restitution. The rich simply had to content themselves with getting richer. These senatorial manors were constructed by men who were and are survivalists. They and their forebears had suffered disaster after disaster. They concluded that if they could not maintain themselves as a political class nationally, then they would do everything they could to survive as a social and economic class locally. That became their collective objective above all else.

These private castles inevitably have their own water supply secure within their own walls, and the lords of the manors are very selective on whom they admit to their estates on a permanent basis. Pantomime artists and singers of song need not apply. To obtain security within these citadels requires skills that the landlord can use. Carpenters, stonemasons, butchers, men with plenty of hunting experience. Leather workers are in demand for the manufacture and repair of shoes, reins, bridles, saddles, wagon covers, and so on. Armorers are required for the upkeep of military equipment. Insofar as these manorial "armies" are concerned, there is usually no trouble outfitting them initially, as the deserters usually bring their uniforms and weapons with them. During the last quarter of the fourth century, as certain of these estates acquired the unofficial status of a town, they started to assume legal duties. As authority in the West deteriorated early in the fifth century, more and more of these senatorial proprietors assumed judicial obligations, though without being formally invested with them by the state. It was only natural that local legal authority would default to such men not only because of their social position but also because they generally had trained and sometimes practiced as lawyers. Many of these estates would eventually have their own prisons. These fortified villas have also contributed to the ongoing deterioration of the nearby towns. In extreme situations where a town has had the singular misfortune to be located near several such villas, it has been abandoned altogether. The blacksmith shops, clothing stores, lumberyards, brick kilns, the whole host of goods and services that towns have traditionally provided to their urban and surrounding rural populations have been siphoned off into such private castles throughout Gaul, Spain, Italy, and Illyria. The economic multiplier effects that large urban centers always generate have been much reduced since the time of the Antonines as the cities and towns themselves have been reduced. We are much the poorer for it.

All urban centers strive toward self-sufficiency to the greatest degree possible because of the high costs of overland transportation. But we learned long ago that when you trade, you grow richer by concentrating your efforts on those items that you can produce most efficiently while trading for items that you cannot. Striving for self-sufficiency in everything only creates a lower standard of living. But in the far from ideal circumstances that have faced us from the middle of the third century, this could not be helped. The chronic instability that shipwrecked much of the West and the Balkans during the third century and the increasingly oppressive taxation that afflicted all provinces during the fourth drastically reduced trade. Two centuries ago, a large number of shipping companies like the one I worked for existed, but now there are relatively few.

While traveling through Gaul, I noticed something else that has yet to happen in Britain: the establishment of monasteries. The first of these in Gaul was set up by Bishop Martin of Tours about 360. They have since spread like a plague throughout the region. I confess to a thorough contempt for people that join these institutions to escape the responsibilities and dangers the rest of us have to face on their behalf. During the reign of Diocletian and Maximian, the government found itself in a paradoxical situation: it was slaughtering thousands of innocent Roman citizens because they were Christians, while simultaneously settling tens of thousands of barbarian soldiers and their families on Roman soil because of our never-ending population shortage. Here we are a century and more later with the self-contradictions continuing. In the face of economic decline and the increased barbarization of the army, we permit thousands of men to join the Catholic Church every year. It has reached the point where in excess of one hundred thousand men (and several thousand women besides) have joined the ranks of the Bride of the Lamb in various monastic orders. This in addition to the thousands of priests. And all the while, the government taxes the hell out of the productive population to support these useless drones. These are men that could be in the army, the civil service, or employed productively by industry or agriculture.

Starting with Constantine I, the government, already strapped for cash, exempted all church lands from taxation. It then piled the taxes that the church should have been paying onto everybody else. Great Constantine's successors, with the exception of Julian, have only worsened the situation by granting more exemptions. The Catholic Church, which survived three centuries on its own, sometimes enduring the most savage persecutions, suddenly found itself inundated by government generosity. Now the church is convinced that without such munificence, it could continue only with the greatest difficulty. The government pays all bishops large salaries, builds new churches all over the place, and provides empire-wide free travel to the clergy whenever they desire. In return, the Catholic Church provides nothing toward the well-being of the empire. Economically, the monasteries act in the same way the fortified villas of the senatorial aristocracy do. They stress self-sufficiency and detachment from the surrounding world. In so doing, they further undermine the viability of the nearby towns. Their tax exemptions are only encouraging their proliferation. Wealthy men, who two centuries ago would have been building libraries, theatres, and triumphal arches in their hometowns, now make bequests to churches and monasteries instead in order to buy their way into heaven.

I was too young to understand what I was actually witnessing as I viewed my first fortified estate. With the passing of many years, I realize it was the ever-so-gradual transference of authority from government to private hands. With so many towns dying in the West, powerful landowning senators were allowed to collect taxes for the government with sweetheart arrangements for themselves. This was followed by the unofficial recognition by government that in cases where the towns could not dispense justice, the landed senators in the vicinity could do it instead. However, the greatest shock of all regarding the privatization of what had been strictly government responsibilities arose not in the West but in the East. The treaty with the Visigoths in 382 would make their independent army partly responsible for imperial defense on a vital stretch of the lower Danube. The twisted course of events during the ensuing thirty years would make this decision of greater import in the West than in the East. Government in the West was gradually starting to evanesce.

At Lyon, we entered the Rhone Valley. Lyon itself, in spite of its past tribulations, remains the chief trading center for Gaul and thus its most cosmopolitan city. Whatever past glory it may have lost, it still abounds with traders from every corner of the empire and occasionally as far away as Iran. When wind and river flow permitted, we could transfer our goods to ships there. In this region, such delicate crops as mulberries, grapes, cherries, and peaches are grown on the southern slopes of many hillsides. There are numerous grain and vegetable farms as well and no trace of German settlement of any kind.

A geographical appreciation of Gaul helps to bring its history alive. The combination of the Rhineland and the Saone-Rhone Valleys may be thought of as constituting the "spinal column" of Roman civilization in Gaul. Everything else that we have accomplished there is secondary to what has been achieved in these districts. The river networks have provided excellent land for constructing highways and developing a rich agriculture. In the south, it connects to the Mediterranean plains and thus to Italy. The Rhineland has provided the military foundation for the protection of civilization in Western Europe. In combination with the Saone-Rhone Valley, it has furnished the economic underpinnings as well.

As our convoy pushed ever closer to the coast, the force of the mistral at our backs diminished, and the humidity and temperature started to increase; the "sensuous south" indeed. A region that rarely sees frost and where the natives proved to be extremely friendly. We reached Arles and discovered that because of scheduling problems we had been rerouted to Marseille. This was a frequent issue when shipping from Arles. Schedules constantly had to be corrected to allow for the frequent silting of the river there. After another three days on the road, we arrived at our destination, and I finally set eyes on the Mediterranean. The others had all seen it before, but for me it was a milestone. The first thing I did was take a long walk along the shoreline in the all too short period we had there. After we unloaded the wagons and visited the baths, one of our members suggested a visit to the Golden House. The others all laughed and readily agreed.

"After thirty-two days on the road," Julianus said, "we've all earned an evening at the Golden House, and I'm certain that none of our number will enjoy the establishment's infinite charms quite so much as our new friend, Marcus, here."

The others all started laughing again. After that, it was quite clear as to what type of establishment we were heading for.

Marseille is the oldest city in Gaul. Greek colonists from the Asia Minor city of Phocaea founded it in 600 BC. This was when their colonies were spreading everywhere. In general, it was through Marseille over the following centuries that many people throughout Gaul were introduced to and attracted by the most positive aspects of Mediterranean civilization. This made it difficult for the Gauls to present a united front against the Roman invasion when it eventually came.

The Golden House was as fashionable a brothel as one could imagine. It was located in a large villa on the outskirts overlooking the city. We entered the villa through its large main gate and started climbing up a flight of stairs to an open-air bar and restaurant the next floor up. I'll always remember looking up into a sea of the most beautiful faces I had ever seen smiling down the stairwell at us. The thought quickly passed through my mind that I had died and gone to heaven. Since we arrived early in the evening, we had our pick of the offerings. I immediately sighted a girl who reminded me incredibly of Ardovanda. I was dumbstruck. Her hair was darker, her eyes were a different color, and she was a little older, but they could have passed for sisters.

Her name was Maria like half the rest of the women in our civilization. Julianus noticed my infatuation. He went over and spoke to her, and she sauntered over to our table. She stood there smiling down at me for a few moments and then suddenly yanked down the top of her dress, dangled both boobs in my face, and said "Nice, eh?" No argument there; time to put the dream aside and enjoy reality. A big cheer went up from my confreres when Maria and I retired to her room.

"Where are you from?" she asked.

"Britain."

"I'll bet you left a lot of broken hearts behind." She smiled, putting her arms around my neck.

"Only my own," was my self-pitying reply.

"Well then, you've certainly come to the right repair shop." She laughed.

One thing about getting laid for the first time in an institution like the Golden House is that it certainly sets high standards. Maria was absolutely gorgeous, but like all good things, it came to an end too soon. When my time was up, I returned to the main bar, by which time my associates were either off coupling away themselves or getting drunk. So I had some wine and sat down on a chair by the railing, where I was provided with an excellent view of the city and the Mediterranean. Out of the corner of my eye, I saw Maria playing up to client number two for the evening: a short, fat old fart that looked like he had more money than I'd have in ten lifetimes. The place was filling up by this time, so I had more wine and started to feel the effects of it. Just like I'd never had sex before, neither had I ever really been drunk. But the Golden House was just the place for having both experiences for the first time. Oddly enough, I suddenly thought of my parents and my home back in Cirencester. It had been almost seven months since I had left Britain, but it was beginning to feel more like a decade. My straight-laced parents had smashed up the innocent relationship that I had with the only girl I had ever loved and tried to harness me to a vixen. Now here I was, less than a year later, getting laid and loaded in one of the swankiest whore houses in the empire. The transposition was somewhat disquieting. I was less than pleased with this picture, but it would have to do until something better came along.

That was how I spent the next several months of the year 382, traveling up and down the main north-south highways between Cologne and the southern ports. Every journey was not a round-trip. Sometimes coming up from the coast I would be transferred to a convoy going south if it was a large train and short of workers. I was getting to know the various routes by heart, and, of course, there was always a visit to the Golden House whenever we arrived in Marseille. I was also introduced to a similar house of harlotry when we delivered to Arles. On my second visit to Marseille, I looked forward to spending another evening with Maria, only she wasn't there. A girl named Aemelia informed me that Maria had gone off to Italy with a rich landowner and was living somewhere between Rome and Naples. Probably that sweaty little fat guy whom I saw her with on my first visitation. So Aemelia became the instant object of my affections this time around. Usually girls don't stay in places like the Golden House very long. They move around frequently from place to place and it doesn't pay to get hung up on one of them for any length of time. Still it would have been nice if that one particular fantasy in the flesh had lasted just a little longer.

The year 382 had been most pleasant. For that reason alone, I should have known that the circumstances in which I found myself would be of short duration. On a return trip from the Mediterranean, early in May, I was sitting in a bar in Strasbourg, when news suddenly swept the place that the government would soon be issuing new conscription notices. This rumor had made the rounds several times in recent months. The military situation in which the West found itself was increasing its chances of becoming a reality. Several times since the Battle of Hadrianople, western army units had been sent to the East when the fledgling army of Theodosius I suffered a defeat or new invaders crossed the lower Danube. Four years had passed since Hadrianople. While the

Eastern Army was steadily improving, it had not recovered to the point where Gratian's units that had been helping to contain the Visigoths could be sent back to the West. The drain on western resources was such that our own security was starting to be placed in jeopardy. Several weeks later, we were hauling loads of oysters encased in barrels of brine from Arles for delivery to towns in eastern Gaul. Along the way, we were informed that the conscription orders had been posted. There was constant talk of what their impact would be on us, but we wouldn't know for certain until we were informed by our superiors. We reached the Rhine near Augst, our last delivery point for the oysters, and headed downstream to Cologne. Upon arrival, we all heaved a general sigh of relief when informed that, as an essential business, we had avoided the draft.

In June, I was posted to Trier and joined the company headquarters mainly because of my good education. When the company was short of drivers, I might be called upon to make local trips, but the long-haul journeys were over for the time being. I was made responsible for establishing an order tracking system and improving their inventory system that was somewhat of a mess. It was a pleasant change from what I had been doing for the past year and I welcomed the opportunity. I also got an apartment of my own and started to feed my historical curiosity to a greater degree than ever. Whenever I had any spare time during my travels, I frequented the libraries in the towns that we passed through. Some were pretty small and didn't have much to offer, but there was always something of a historical nature to read. Trier was different. Its library was the largest I had ever seen to that point, and to start off, I earnestly dug into the *History of Carthage* by Claudius Caesar. Most people have forgotten that he was a historian before he became emperor and was an excellent writer.

I frequently noticed a very attractive blonde-haired woman at the library. She was always elaborately dressed and made up and had an aristocratic bearing to her. In her mid-thirties I assumed. Other than the librarian, I never saw her speak to anyone. It was uncommon to see a woman in a library, especially that often. So she obviously had an education superior to most. I was quite surprised one afternoon when she approached me at the table where I was sitting.

"Pardon me, but the librarian told me that you have our only copy of old Claudius's *History of Carthage—Volume II.* I was wondering how long you would need it. I'm a teacher, and I require it for a class I'll be holding starting next Monday," she said.

She was quite striking, and I was rather tongue-tied by her approach and sudden request. I finally managed to blurt out, "Well, uh, tonight I'm going to run some army supplies up the Rhine and planned on leaving here shortly anyway. So I guess you can have it now."

She thanked me and left.

Several weeks passed before I saw her again at the main market. She was in the company of a servant woman, but both of them were pretty loaded down with groceries. I offered to help carry their purchases home, and we started to get to know one another. Her name was Margareta Silanus, and she was a tutor to the children of government officials and high-ranking officers in the city. Now that Trier was no longer an imperial capital, many government personnel, both civilian and military, had left for Milan. As a result, her business had taken a downturn. In addition, she held evening seminars in history and current affairs for adults that would be starting up early in September. She asked me if I was interested and I replied in the affirmative. The seminars would cover the whole broad sweep of civilization from its dawning in pharaonic Egypt and the city-states of Mesopotamia and the Indus River Valley down to the present day. We were to study economic development, the evolution of literacy, and current events. I learned through a couple of others in the class that Margareta had been a widow for many years. Her only son had died as an infant.

Several weeks later when I arrived at work one morning, Victor asked me to come into his office. While his official residence was in Cologne, he also had an office in Trier where he spent much of his time when he wasn't on the road. It was all over very quickly: new conscription notices had been published throughout the Western Empire. We had all heard that the earlier call-up had failed to take in nearly enough men. There would be a second one including people that were employed in vocations that were generally protected from such acts. I was not surprised.

"I'm sorry that it's come to this, but I've had to give you up to the draft," Victor said. "The numbers everywhere are far larger than anyone feared. The manpower level of the Army of the Rhine has fallen so low that it is questionable whether it could withstand a full-scale barbarian assault. I hope that things get settled in the East quickly and that your service proves to be only temporary. The company is losing thirty men all told. It's staggering."

I replied, "When and where do I report?"

"Tomorrow at noon at the army headquarters here in the city. I'm sorry to see you leave, Marcus. You've done some fine work for us, and we'll miss you. In this day and age, with so many Germans flooding into the army, this might seem quite antiquated, but I've prepared a letter of introduction for you. It used to be a tradition that a young man entering the army would present such a letter to his commanding officer once he was assigned to a unit. In earlier times, such letters were required along with the appropriate legal documentation to determine the status of the inductee. Such information was used to determine whether the individual would be assigned to a legion, to the auxiliaries, or the fleet. To what extent it is still done among Romans joining the standards I don't know. But it will certainly work to your advantage. In it I've mentioned that you are well educated, that you know how to take shorthand, that you are good when it comes to handling horses and oxen, that you have experience in wagon repair, and so on. I apologize for the short notice. It is usual to inform a man at least a week ahead of time so that he can get the required legal documentation together, and the rest of the people that we gave up were so instructed. But you were the last one to go on the last list that we provided to the authorities, and you do live locally. Either later this afternoon or tomorrow morning, you must drop by the basilica and get your proof-of-residence document. I would suggest today because there will probably be quite a crowd of men showing up there tomorrow for the same reason, and you don't want to leave it too late. So Godspeed, and I hope that we will see you back here soon."

He was rather choked up, so I simply thanked him for everything he had done for me over the past year and left. I spent some time handing over my responsibilities to a fellow that I had been working with. After picking up my final pay, I left. It was a strange feeling. I went to Margareta's home and told her that I had been drafted and would, therefore, be unable to attend her seminars anymore. It was a shame because, while the class had been going for only three weeks, I had found the sessions quite informative. I explained how much I had enjoyed them and wished her good luck. She gave me a truly haunting look, then came to me with her arms outstretched and hugged me and kissed me.

"It doesn't matter that you are a Christian and I am a pagan. I will pray for your safe return every day, and if you get a chance, either during your training or your period of service, to drop by my place, then by all means do so. I'd like that."

I was most pleasantly surprised.

"Every day, I will pray for your safety and well-being also, and I promise that I will come and see you at the first opportunity," I replied.

I then took her in my arms and hugged her, and we made our final farewells. As I walked back to my apartment, my head was spinning. There was something very special in her tone of voice and whole attitude that I had never experienced before. She was a generation older than I, but that was of no consequence. That was no mere peck-on-the-cheek sendoff that she had given me. I had the distinct impression that if others had not been present at her home, then perhaps ... Well, that was my fantasy for the day anyway. I spent much of the afternoon at the basilica getting the required documentation.

CHAPTER 4

A Call to Arms

THE NEXT MORNING, I appeared at army headquarters. Several hundred other young men were present for the same reason, and I could envision this scene being repeated in every city throughout Western Europe at this same time. Generally, when one joins the army as a volunteer, it is for twenty-five years. The first twenty years are called "standard service," during which one serves as a regular soldier. The last five are referred to as "veteran service," in which the soldier is exempt from certain of the more onerous duties while living in above-standard accommodations. In other words, after completing his twentieth year, the regular soldier is sort of superannuated into the role of an elder statesman of his unit. Among the more permanent benefits that derive from this latter status are that the soldier and his family are exempt from the poll tax and certain public responsibilities. For conscripts, the situation is different. Being drafted to respond to a specific set of circumstances, the draftee is usually released back to his previous occupation once the emergency had passed. However, if there is a serious shortage of skilled and seasoned warriors, then draftees could wind up as regular soldiers. After Hadrianople, they usually did.

At noon sharp, a centurion called us to order and gave a brief speech welcoming us into the service. We were then broken up into different groups to undergo a medical examination. In recent years, these exams had become increasingly perfunctory as the need for warm bodies increased. Certain landlords, corporations, and towns had become notorious for unloading their least productive tenants, employees, and citizens into the draft. As the army's desperation level went up, recruiting standards went down. About the only thing the medical inspectors were interested in was ensuring that we were at least five feet six inches in height, could see, and had all our fingers. In addition, any identifying scars or birthmarks were noted for the record. Once this was complete, a tribune ordered us to be drawn up in ranks for the purpose of swearing our initial oaths of allegiance to the three emperors. When an individual soldier volunteers for the army, he repeats the entire oath himself. When a large group of men are being inducted at the same time, one of them is chosen to read the oath. After that, each of the others repeats the phrase "the same for me." This process is repeated every New Year's Day by all soldiers for the remainder of their military careers. The tribune asked which of us were literate, and I was one of only a few who raised their hand. Probably because I was in the front rank, he ordered me to come up on the dais and to stand beside him.

"Read in as loud a voice as you can muster this copy of the oath so that everyone in the assembly can hear you," he ordered.

"Yes, sir," I replied. "I swear in the name of God, our Lord Jesus Christ, and the Holy Ghost and in the names of our beloved Emperors Gratian, Valentinian II, and Theodosius, who, next to God, should be honored and admired by all of humanity, to discharge my duty carefully, diligently, and without question in whatever their majesties may order me to do. I will never desert and if need be will lay down my life in the defense of the Roman Empire."

Rank by rank, each new recruit in turn replied, "The same for me." After the swearing-in ceremony, each of us was branded on his upper arm to be permanently identified as a soldier. In the far happier times of the Caesars or the Antonines, the mere suggestion of such a procedure would have been considered an outrage. But after the chaos of the third century, all soldiers were branded (as are men in all key occupations now) in order to be identified more easily as deserters. After this, we were paid our joining-up bonus and shipped off to our respective units.

The legion I was posted to was Legion XXII Primigenia in Mainz on the left bank of the Rhine where the Main River joins it. This legion was named after the ancient goddess of fortune, Fortuna Primigenia. It was created by Claudius I in 41 to replace a legion from the Army of the Rhine that was being sent west to participate in the invasion of Britain. Even though Christianity has officially replaced the ancient religions, the legions continue with their original names. I viewed my assignment to this legion as a good omen. Legion XXII Primigenia has a lengthy and illustrious history. Depending on the fluctuating fortunes of the times, it had occasionally been relocated to Nijmegen and Xanten downstream. Sometimes an individual regiment[10] would be shipped out for special duty elsewhere, but for most of its three-and-a-half-century history, the legion had been stationed at Mainz. Its officer corps was as solid as that of any frontier unit, and its training facilities were as good as could be found anywhere.

The ten weeks of basic training that followed my induction were the most exhausting of my life. The only thing I could be grateful for was that in the days of the Caesars and the Antonines, basic training lasted four months. We started every morning at 6:00 and continued until 8:00 in the evening. One ancient writer said of the Roman Army: "Their drills are bloodless battles and their battles are bloody drills." I would soon discover the truth of that maxim. From time immemorial, the first thing every soldier has learned is how to march. To civilians, parade square drills appear to have only a ceremonial purpose, but in reality, nothing could be further from the truth. They instill discipline, and proper discipline is vital to any soldier in wartime. On the march, it prevents stragglers from being picked off by the enemy and keeps the unit on constant alert. It sets ranks tight in close-order combat, preventing enemy breakthroughs and limiting casualties while spacing individual soldiers so that they avoid getting in one another's way. In addition to learning the various drills via voice order, we were trained to respond to trumpet commands. These are important during combat when voice commands become inaudible over the battlefield noise. By the time our basic training was over, we could march twenty miles in five hours during good weather with our backpacks on. Marching drills were carried out for an hour each morning and afternoon. Calisthenics and physical training in general were heavily emphasized during basic training, and after, we joined our regular regiments. Once basic training was over, regular track and field meets were held between the different centuries within our regiment, provided we were at peace. The top men in each activity from the two regiments would be pitted against one another in an overall legion championship. Dashes, relay races, the long jump, the high jump, and, during warm weather, swimming contests comprised these games. The long jump and the relay race were my best competitions. In addition to the physical training, they fostered a team spirit among everyone. This program of fundamental conditioning for all soldiers went back five hundred years to the close of the second century BC when the training methods of the gladiatorial schools were adapted to the army.

After several weeks, we were introduced to weapons drill. The shields and swords we used for training purposes were twice as heavy as the regular weapons used in combat. After we had been instructed in their proper use, we spent many hours at what are called "the stakes." Generally, the recruit had to pound a long, thick stake into the ground, at least six feet of which stood above the surface, for use as a dummy during sword drill exercises. Our legion was more fortunate than most in this regard. Having resided for so long at the same location, it had substantial training facilities. Instead of mere stakes, we had actual wooden dummies in human form to practice against. Our instructors trained us in how and where to strike to achieve the deadliest effect, how to assault the head, the sides, or the legs, how to advance, and how to withdraw. Defense was emphasized as much as offense. When a sufficient degree of proficiency had been achieved with the training weapons, we started training with regular arms. Then, toward the close of basic training, we started drilling against our fellow recruits for an added degree of realism. Once we were capable with the sword and shield, we started training with the javelin and the bow and arrow. These training weapons were also twice the weight of those that were used in regular service. The need for the soldiers of the frontier legions to be capable archers increased during the fourth century as these most ancient of our army units became more defensive in nature. Our training with the bow was just as intensive as it had been with the sword. We were instructed on how to use it both from a standing or kneeling position on the ground and from horseback. With the bow, we had to be capable of hitting a target the size of a man at a distance of six hundred feet. Finally we were trained in the use of lead-weighted darts that can be used against either men or horses from close range. We carried five of these in a small rack attached to the inside of our shields. Darts, however, are expensive to make, so their manufacture is concentrated in those armament plants that are located in areas of greatest danger, such as the Rhineland, Italy, and the Balkans. Their distribution is restricted to soldiers serving in those theaters. What we hated above everything in basic training was when our instructors would have us cram our backpacks with about forty pounds of rocks and then order us to run up and down the steepest hills they could find. It was fortunate that winter settled shortly after this practice began. The snow made the hill climbing treacherous, and so these exercises were soon abandoned for the season to avoid undue injuries.

Since we had been conscripted so late in the year, we had to conduct some of our training indoors during inclement weather. Most, if not all, legionary fortresses have large training halls for both their infantry and cavalry units. But during both basic training and after we had been assigned to our regiments, the more sadistic of our drill sergeants seemed to take great pleasure in putting us through our parade square exercises outside, especially when it was raining or snowing.

Once our basic training was over, a brief graduation parade was held. Then we were assigned to our centuries within the two regiments that comprised our legion and transferred to our barracks. After we had settled into our new quarters, our centurion, who was named Julius Aranius, came by to introduce himself and to get to know us on a more individual basis. In his latter twenties, he did not appear to be that much older than the recruits themselves. At this time, I presented him with the letter of introduction that Victor had written for me. He called the new recruits around him and said, "It has been a hectic and tiring ten weeks. You are being given the next two days off, more or less, so you can be properly documented by legion headquarters. Starting first thing tomorrow morning, you will be interviewed by members of the adjutant's staff first in order to create your legion personnel records. The second order of business is that all new recruits, upon joining their regular regiments, are required to write a will or have one written for them."

The centurion paused for effect, and the room fell deadly silent. It was at this moment that the full significance of our having joined the army was driven home to us as with a sledgehammer. He then went on, "Once you have completed these two documentation procedures, your time over the next two days is your own. Get to know the city of Mainz and, under all circumstances, be on your best behavior. Any law breaking by any of you will be punished with the utmost severity. Insofar as your writing your wills is concerned, we realize that most of you are not literate. Those of you who fall into this category will be dictating your wills to a scribe."

Later that day, he came over to see me.

"I've read the letter of recommendation that your former supervisor wrote for you. It's impressive and rather unusual. It used to be that soldiers were required to have such a letter to introduce themselves to their commanding officer. However, in recent years, the tradition has largely fallen by the wayside as a result of so many barbarian volunteers joining up. We get the odd one, but they are rare. Nowadays most such letters are used when entering the civil service rather than the army."

"A sign of the times," I replied, trying to sound closer to his age than my own.

"Unfortunately it is. You seem to have had an excellent education, and as a result of it, I think you can be a big help to us. Most recruits are neither literate nor numerate. You are both, and in addition, I see that you can take shorthand. That's certainly a rarity in an army recruit these days. I'm going to pass this information up the line to our tribune because it's a certainty that he'll be interested. In the meantime, I'd like you to help the illiterate recruits by writing their wills for them. Over the next few days, I've assigned you to the adjutant's staff to help his people with this requirement. His scribes are, for the most part, on veteran service. At times like this, when a wave of new recruits comes in, they get swamped with the paperwork. In addition to writing the wills, you will also be completing the individual personnel records that must be put together for each new man. You can report to them immediately."

I thanked him and went to the adjutant's office. I was handed an outline of what a last testament should look like, and then I wrote my will, in which I left all my worldly possessions (whatever they might be at the time) to my sister Maria Patricia. This was handed in to the adjutant. For several days, I spent all my time generating men's wills, having their marks properly witnessed, and writing up their personnel records for the legion headquarters. The wills were usually short, and the completion of personnel records consisted for the most part of filling in the blanks in standard forms that the staff had already drawn up. I was kept on for an extra couple of weeks due to the workload. By the time we were finished, it was New Year's Day, 383.

Another recruit who had been ordered to act as a scribe at this time was a young man named Gregorian, a year older than I. He was the only son of a centurion from Lusitania who was serving in another legion. Well educated and a native of Bonn, he was required to join the army as a hereditary obligation. I envied him in several respects. He was tall, muscular, and quite handsome and was engaged to a girl who was the daughter of another officer serving in his father's legion. They were to be married the following summer. He was a very gung-ho type and had been looking forward to joining the army for as far back as he could remember. He struck us all as the type best described as a "born leader" and appeared to have a good future ahead of him. The two of us also started chumming around with three other draftees of roughly our own age: Marcellinus and Stephanus, Celts like myself, and a Roman-born Frank named Chlogius who came from Xanten. We would remain the best of friends.

During basic training, we had been introduced to battle tactics. After assignment to our individual centuries, our capabilities in these skills were tuned to a higher degree through constant instruction and practice. As soon as we had acquired a sufficient level of proficiency, we started regular patrol duty along our bank of the Rhine. At Mainz, the Rhine changes its direction where the Main River empties into it from a northerly to a westerly flow. Our legion sent out patrols that would meet up with detachments from the fort at Bingen, about twenty miles to the west, and from the fortress town of Worms approximately thirty miles to the south. Sometimes these patrols were conducted as route marches, but more often than, not we performed as mounted infantry. For the most part, they proved uneventful. Nonetheless, because the Germans are renowned for striking when they are least expected, such patrols had to be conducted. The winter is usually the quiet season for the military in Europe. Frozen rivers, however, have often provided avenues of invasion that were just too inviting to pass up. The deadliest attack ever inflicted on the West would occur at exactly this time of year, but that lay well off in the future. For the time being, the frontier was peaceful.

Through late January and February, the patrol work was rather routine. On occasion, we would apprehend two or three generations of several families that had come across the frontier together, but that was about it. We would take them into custody, and they would be shipped off to work as tenant farmers on estates further back from the frontier. It was all rather amicable. That was all they were looking for anyway, simply a safer and better life than the one they had lived in Germany. During the better weather, they were picked up on the frontier highways constantly. We often thought how easy life would be if all Germans wishing to emigrate into the empire chose to enter in this fashion. But as soldiers, we were looking for more than this. Above all, we wanted to be "blooded," though not too seriously of course. We wanted combat with the barbarians so that we could consider ourselves as veterans. We were tired of being derided as virgins by the real veterans and were beginning to wonder if we would ever participate in a genuine battle. We needn't have worried. Our opportunity would come in early March.

While patrolling well south of Mainz with another century from our regiment, we came across a large force of about 350 Alemanns. They were engaging a couple of our centuries on duty north of Worms, the ones we were scheduled to meet up with before returning to Mainz. It had been a close contest, but when the Alemanns, minus any cavalry support, saw our centuries coming up behind them, they were in a quandary. To break out of the impending trap, their leaders called an immediate retreat. Since a cavalry squadron from our Worms garrison kept penning in their flanks, the only direction the Germans could head was straight north toward us. (Incidentally, we had been warned repeatedly during basic training that in addition to attacking the enemy, another function of allied cavalry is to cut down, if need be, any deserters *from our own ranks*.) The Alemanns' only hope was to break through our units before we had a chance to get into battle formation. To affect this, they cleverly formed a column on the run in order to apply maximum pressure at some point through our newly arrived troops. Fortunately, the distance for them to realize this was too great. Our battle line was ready before they were upon us.

A battle line can be anywhere from four to sixteen ranks deep, depending on both our manpower resources and the strength and organization of the enemy. Our centurions quickly formed us into six ranks to face the onslaught. As it charged us, the German column started to break down. While such a formation was best for rupturing our lines, it presented all too compact a target for our attacking cavalry and archers. The column started taking heavy casualties, and its advance slowed. The soldiers from the Worms garrison had been ordered to halt their pursuit until the Alemanns had struck our front lines. Separating themselves from the Germans enabled our sixth rank to lay down volleys of arrows as the enemy approached.

I was positioned in the front rank. Normally, as the enemy closed, our front two ranks would have hurled their darts at them. But because they were charging as a column instead of a line, that was ruled out. Our centurions ordered the front two ranks to kneel down behind our shields and to ram the end of our spears securely into the ground. With their business ends slanted out, we prepared to accept the full brunt of the enemy attack. All the while, we were yelling out our battle cry. One powerfully built German with long hair flowing down past his shoulders was charging directly at me with a spear whose length could have skewered three of us. He was quite tall, and in his desire to escape his southern pursuers and break through our lines, he had outrun his comrades by a considerable distance. He was wearing a complete set of Roman body armor, obviously taken from one of our dead soldiers in some past battle, but no helmet. The man in behind me yelled, "Look out, Marcus! He's coming right at you!" Then another yelled something similar. When he was almost on top of me, his mouth suddenly dropped wide open, his eyes winced shut, and he dropped to his knees. He appeared momentarily frozen, and in an instant, I broke formation. I heard our sergeant major yell, "Get back in formation, Cedranus." At this moment, however, my main concern was the German in front of me and not the sergeant major five lines to the rear. I leapt forward, plunged my spear into his throat, and then resumed my position in the line as he fell over with a look of the most terrified disbelief. A cheer went up from our lines, and then our battle cry resumed. It was only when he hit the ground that I saw the arrow protruding from the back of his right leg. He had taken the wound some time before. Only when he had reached our lines could he no longer stand the pain.

As the Alemanns started throwing their spears at us, our centurions ordered our fourth and fifth ranks to hurl their spears at them. Several German spears entered the ground close by, and I heard several "thuds" as some struck Roman shields. Our spears and arrows took a frightful toll because many Germans had previously dropped their shields to gain speed in their escape. We braced for and received the full force of the German charge, but it was uneven, and we had only minor difficulty withstanding it. At the moment of contact between opposing front lines, all combat becomes localized. Units will almost automatically break down into ad hoc subunits to destroy their nearest opponents without regard to what is happening elsewhere on the battlefield. We were ordered to advance into the Alemanns, and when this happened, our southern forces resumed their attack into what was now the German rear. At this point, the battle turned into a massacre. The enemy was already tired and hurting from their initial battle and their command structure soon broke down completely under this attack from opposite directions. Our arrival had given second wind to the Roman units already engaged and outnumbered while demoralizing the Germans. The Alemanns fought well but were soon defeated. At the end, about seventy-five surrendered and were shipped off for interrogation prior to being sold into slavery. That would also be the fate of the lightly wounded. A few escaped. The rest were either dead or dying from their wounds. We finished off their seriously wounded as they lay on the battlefield since it was pointless to prolong their agony. We also collected all weapons, both Roman and

Alemann, from the battlefield and stripped the dead of their armor. The captured weapons and armor would be analyzed by our officers back at the base camps both to determine how to improve our own weaponry when possible and to establish where these men may have fought previously. Of course, some of the captured weaponry was simply pilfered.

The price of victory had not been cheap. It never is, but then the price of defeat is always far greater. The medics had arrived, and we were directed to carry our wounded and our dead into their field hospital. There is a medical section attached to each regiment, and a squad of these medics always accompanied our patrols. It may seem odd that our dead were taken there, but this is standard practice to facilitate the full accounting of all casualties that the officers must carry out after every engagement. All soldiers killed in action must be identified by their commanding officers prior to being placed aboard the mortuary wagons for the trip back to their home base for burial. As their bodies were being loaded for transport back to Mainz, I was astounded to see that one of those slain was my friend Gregorian. He had died from a ghastly head wound while positioned in the second rank, kneeling behind his shield as we had been ordered. A German spear crashed through along the line where two of the half-inch-thick boards of which it was manufactured were joined. The spear had penetrated deeply into his forehead just below the helmet and above his right eye. He had been killed instantly without ever having struck a blow himself. The frightful image of that promising future precluded is still as firmly ingrained in my memory as if it had happened yesterday. To this day, I still think of Gregorian and the others, forever young.

Some of us wept openly with no sense of embarrassment over the tragic loss of our comrades. We wept with a sense of pride, love, and admiration for those among us who had made the ultimate sacrifice. It is an emotion that overcomes raw recruits and veterans alike and has nothing to do with the number of times the Fates force us to endure it. Before that first day of battle, we had been friends. Forever after, we would feel as brothers in a manner that is deeper than a blood relationship. Men who have never fought for their country cannot understand the experience. Three were recruits slain on their very first day of combat without ever entering what should have been the prime of their lives. When a person to whom we are close dies, I think we all feel our own lives, our sense of worth diminished in some indefinable way. We all felt an appalling emptiness, and I knew that Gregorian's parents would be forever heartbroken: their only child lost, the grandchildren they would never have. I had met his father and mother briefly when they had come by to visit him at the barracks in Mainz about two weeks earlier. I cannot say that I actually knew them, but I prayed for them daily for years afterward. It would be many years before I would have the opportunity to visit his resting place at the cemetery in Bonn. His gravestone was inscribed in the ancient Roman tradition: "The Last of His Line."

Our centurion addressed us: "Our century entered the battle with sixty-eight men and emerged with sixty-three. You know the comrades that we lost: two were veterans, and three were seeing combat for the first time. Our loss of five men, in addition to being grievous to us as individuals, constitutes 7 percent of our entire complement. In addition, eleven of us have suffered wounds, some serious but none life-threatening. This brings our total casualty rate for this day to 24 percent. As a unit so top-heavy with recruits, you performed quite well. But if we continue to take casualties like this, then we will soon cease to exist. One thing that I know you have learned this day is that all victories have their price, even relatively minor victories like ours. We've got a lot to review and work on, and we'll be doing that as soon as we get back to base. During the battle and while we were killing off their wounded, you should have noticed one thing: we were fighting a unit of battle-hardened veterans today. I didn't notice anyone that appeared to be a teenager among them. That's another reason to congratulate yourselves. I'm damned proud of the way you performed, and so should you be. As is typical in combat, the enemy outnumbered us, but because of our superior training and discipline, we won. In battle, we will usually be outnumbered by our enemies, but do not let this chronic adversity in numerical strength concern you. We outnumbered the Visigoths at Hadrianople, but a fat lot of good it did us. That's another reason to take pride in what you have accomplished this day. Unquestionably, you are now veterans."

At this point, we sent up a big cheer.

"But just remember," our centurion continued. "You're only as good as your last battle. What I'm going to say now is for the benefit of the recruits. The battle that we fought this afternoon will never be recorded in any history book. It is, however, typical of the sort of engagement that will comprise the vast majority of the clashes in which you will participate throughout your military careers. Major battles are generally few and far between. Some soldiers pass their entire career without ever seeing one. Now get all your gear together, as we'll be heading back in one hour."

I had no idea at the time that the wills I had prepared at the end of the previous year would start to be executed so soon. We had cheered when we were called "veterans," but to a man we felt that there was precious little to celebrate. The other century from Mainz and the soldiers from Worms had suffered more severely than we had. A lot of us new recruits simply felt hollowed out, but we all had to accept the losses and continue on. Having stripped the German dead of anything worthwhile, we heaped their bodies into circular pens and set them on fire. As we stood watching the flames and smoke twisting tortuously into the sky, our centurion spoke to us again.

"While you are watching the enemy corpses being incinerated, remind yourselves that, as soldiers, what you are really witnessing is the cost of being second best on the battlefield. Death or slavery is the price of defeat and is a price that this unit will never endure."

Along with the other recruits, I had passed a personal watershed this day. We had started the march as boys, regardless of what our age was, but we had finished it as men. Messengers had been sent to both Mainz and Worms to fetch cavalry and mounted infantry to come and accompany us back to our respective barracks. There was a danger that more Germans might be lurking in the vicinity, and we did not want to be caught off guard in our weakened condition. The trip back to base was uneventful. The reinforcements brought a supply convoy to replenish us with everything we required: weapons, water, medical supplies, food, and so on.

My first night back in Mainz, I wrote down the details of my first campaign. I would continue to be an inveterate diarist for the remainder of my military career. When finished, I wrote a letter to Margareta and enclosed the description of the day's battle. In the letter, I asked her to put my battle characterizations together in safe keeping for me as a chronicle that I could retrieve at a later date. In the years that followed, she kept the diaries and the accompanying letters together, and I eventually used them as the basis for this book. I hated paying the high costs that private couriers charge for delivering mail, but as long as the distance was not too great, I could afford it. When I was in the Balkans, I would simply hang on to my diaries until I could get to a point that was closer to Trier.

Our first full day back at Mainz, we went through the recent battle over and over again with our centurion and senior noncommissioned officers. This was to ensure that the mistakes we had made would not be repeated at any point down the line. Both individual and collective shortcomings were pointed out. I was criticized for breaking formation to achieve my first kill. I took the judgment positively, as was intended, but with the memory of Gregorian all too fresh in my mind, I was in no doubt as to what I would do if I had to do it over again. In addition to our regular training, my background as a teamster led to my spending time repairing wagons for the upcoming campaigning season. This new responsibility had just begun when we were suddenly given new orders. Our regiment was heading east.

There had been no rumors of any kind prior to this directive landing on us. The signs, however, had all been there. We were just too inobservant to see them. Within our legion, a preponderance of the new recruits had been placed in my regiment, and some veterans had been transferred to the other regiment to make room for them. This by itself was suspicious, but no one had drawn the proper conclusion. As mentioned earlier, on October 3, 382, a peace settlement had been drawn up between Rome and the Visigoths. In spite of this treaty, the East would still require troops from the West for an unspecified period of time as insurance that the Visigoths would stick to the letter of the agreement. From now on, western troops would be rotated to the East instead of being transferred there. Our experienced troops that had been serving under Theodosius would return to the Rhineland and be replaced by new ones. These in turn would revert to the West once the government felt that the crisis in the East was finally over. Two days later, we were on our way.

The manpower shortages in the East had been brought about by more than the loss of the twenty thousand men at Hadrianople. Shattered armies not only encounter difficulties attracting new recruits but also have problems keeping their remaining soldiers in the ranks. The Eastern Army was riven with desertions, and draftees seemed to be disappearing as fast as new levies could be raised. When units of the Western Army started being shipped to the East, the desertion rate went up in the West as well. The age of volunteers and draftees usually ranges from nineteen to twenty-five. But it was soon lowered to eighteen and then to the year in which one turned eighteen. That's how I fell into the selection process. The sons of veterans who have not yet seen service are always subject to call-up to the age of thirty-five.

The preparations had been going on for some time, and our legion was by no means the only one involved. Among the troops being relocated to the East were those belonging to both frontier garrison legions such as my own and independent cavalry regiments. Military terminology had become rather confusing during the fourth century. A regiment consists of six centuries of eighty men each, plus specialized troops such as cooks and blacksmiths. Prior to the reigns of Diocletian and Constantine I (284 to 337), there were ten regiments in a legion. Building on the earlier model of Gallienus, these emperors developed a system of independent cavalry regiments stretching from Gaul to Syria. Many of the troops for these new commands were initially drawn from the frontier legions that became more and more static in nature. The number of frontier legions was increased dramatically, but their size was reduced from ten to two regiments, that is, from about 5,500 to 1,200 men. The mobile field armies also contain legions that act as mounted infantry. But by far the most common unit in the field armies is the independent cavalry formation known as the "Palatine" regiment. There are dozens of these Palatine regiments, especially in the West. While the frontier legions are quartered in their garrisons, the mobile field army regiments generally have no such permanent home bases. Their units are constantly shifted according to the manner in which the danger of the moment veers from one location to the next. As a result, many soldiers of these mobile units wind up being quartered along with their families in the homes of private citizens. Any citizen can be forced by law to surrender up to one-third of their home for this purpose if need be. Many ugly incidents have been recorded over the decades since this unfortunate practice came into being.

We traveled south from Mainz through Speyer, through Strasbourg to the "great bend" in the Rhine where it swings from an east-west to a north-south direction after flowing past Augst. Downstream, the Rhine is open to commercial navigation. Upstream, it is too difficult for this. For our mutual protection, we traveled in the company of regiments from two other frontier legions as well as a Palatine regiment. We were especially glad for the company of the cavalry because it provided outriders for the entire column that were constantly on the lookout for Germans. Included in the column were not only the soldiers but also the wives, children, and concubines of the veterans. The column totaled about four thousand. As we marched south toward the great bend, we were continually haunted by the highly elevated slopes of the Black Forest on the German side of the river. At least once a week, we would stop at a major center to rest up and bathe, repair any of our kit that need repairing, and have any medical or dental problems looked into. Constant stopovers were required, especially since we were traveling with so many women and children. Fortunately, the weather was good for this time of the year. It was cold, but we did not encounter any blizzards. At the great bend of the Rhine, we entered the Jura Mountains. This mountain range starts in eastern Gaul and extends to the northeast where it continues across the Rhine into Swabia in the southwestern corner of Germany. Because of the severity of its winters, this section of the range is nicknamed the "Raw Alps." The name is pretentious, however, as their average elevation is fairly low.

Augst dates back to the time of Julius Caesar. It was one of the original Rhine garrison towns that was constructed to protect the then recently conquered territories in Gaul. Well situated on a plateau overlooking the south bank of the river, Augst is a very pleasant city. It has a theater that holds eight thousand people as well as a large amphitheater and two baths and generally appears more Mediterranean than do the other more northerly Gallic towns. There is, of course, a stone-walled fortress on the banks of the Rhine, but most of the town lying outside the walls is still occupied and in good shape, unlike most other Gallic towns with which I'm familiar. After we left Augst, we spent the next three weeks marching east. Several days later, we entered Rhaetia and passed to the south of Lake Constance in the Alpine foothills.

At the extreme southeast corner of Lake Constance, we stopped over in the town of Bregenz. It lies at the foot of Pfander Mountain, a short distance to the east of where the southernmost stretch of the Rhine flows into the lake. The town was quite prosperous then, although it had been reduced in size from what it had been in earlier times. Located at the intersection of major east-west and north-south highways, it is important as a commercial center. It has a small army garrison and, more importantly, is the headquarters for the naval squadron that patrols the lake. The surrounding area is heavily forested, although there are small wheat and dairy farms along with modest cattle ranches to support the local population. Hides obtained from the ranches support numerous leather craft shops in the few surrounding towns. Upon leaving Bregenz, we turned northeast and continued our march toward Kempten, where a detachment of Legion III Italica is stationed. We were about ten miles out of Bregenz when a group of outriders came galloping toward us from up the highway. After speaking briefly with our centurion, they continued on their way, and Julius Aranius lined us up in proper formation along the roadside.

"Those officers just informed me that Emperor Gratian will soon be passing this way. As you've been trained, I will salute him first, and you will all in unison immediately repeat my salute."

The emperor had been inspecting fortifications on the upper Danube. He had come up from Verona through the Brenner Pass that is open the year round. It was a brief tour of inspection prior to the opening of the campaign against the Alemanns scheduled for June. The emperor would soon be returning to Milan. We suddenly heard what sounded like thunder coming up ahead of us. We heard it before we saw it, but we knew instinctively that it was the emperor and his three-hundred-man Alan bodyguard. They suddenly appeared over a hill traveling at top speed. Our centurion saluted and yelled, "Hail, Augustus!" at which point our entire century saluted and repeated, "Hail, Augustus!" The emperor returned our salute, and his entire Imperial Guard was soon past us. I had seen the emperor! My eyes remained fixed on Gratian until I lost sight of him when the column started to round a bend to the left in the road. The vast majority of people, even most soldiers, go through their entire lives without ever seeing their monarch. I would see several and be a friend of one, but there would be tragedies of a direct or indirect nature associated with them all. None of us would ever see Gratian again. We resumed our progress to the northeast.

The upper Danube valley and the northern Alpine foothills are scenic but heavily forested and sparsely populated. In fact, there was an eerie emptiness to northern Rhaetia. Most land in this area is ill suited to agriculture. However, around some of the towns, small numbers of Alemanns had been permitted to settle and establish farms. Many of them were retired army veterans, and their sons were now serving in various legions and regiments along the Danube. At the valley of the Inn River, we passed from Rhaetia into Noricum. There we came across small farms and saw occasional areas where trees were being harvested. To the south of us in the Alps and their associated foothills, iron, coal, and salt were mined and shipped by river or road to the Danube for further processing and distribution. One noticeable contrast to Gaul and Britain was the absence of large villas. We followed the Inn toward the Danube. As we pushed on to the northeast, we left the Bavarian Alps to our right farther behind.

We passed only a few western units heading back to the Rhine. Most had been scheduled to take other routes, either to the north or south, so as not to over task the supply depots along any given highway. Occasionally we met regiments traveling west or north in preparation for Gratian's impending campaign against the Alemanns. Some would eventually be part of the army that he would take into Gaul to combat Magnus Maximus. They would all betray him. We finally reached the Danube near Passau.[11] The great river's flow increases considerably here due to the influx it receives from the Inn River carrying runoff from the northern Alps. In fact, at their point of juncture, the tributary actually has a greater flow of water than has the Danube. Because of all the rivers feeding north from the Alps, we had crossed over many bridges between Augst and Passau. Their construction was a remarkable tribute to the engineers who had built them in centuries past. About fifty miles downstream, we came to the city of Lauriacum.[12] Legion II Italica, founded by Marcus Aurelius, is still stationed there. Above this point, the Danube River does not completely freeze over due to its turbulence. What I remembered as we camped there overnight was that Lauriacum was to be the southern anchor point of the new frontier that Augustus Caesar wanted to establish near the end of his reign almost four centuries earlier. That campaign culminated with our catastrophic defeat involving the loss of three legions at the Battle of the Teutoburg Forest in the year 9. The objective was to advance our boundary of the Rhine and the upper Danube northeast to the line of the Elbe and Vltava Rivers. The southernmost point of the Vltava in Bohemia is about thirty miles from Lauriacum. If only … We proceeded along the Danube to Vienna. We were constantly on our guard against German attacks, but the weather stayed cold, and the numerous ice flows on the Danube made any attempt to cross the river hazardous.

Vienna is a large city with a population of almost twenty thousand. It is centered in an alluvial plain that provides excellent agricultural land. Its commercial importance originated in its location near the ancient amber route that connects the Baltic Sea and the Adriatic. It comes as a surprise to many people to learn that Vienna, in spite of its position on the frontier, is one of the oldest cities in the empire. One thing that was becoming clear was that almost every substantial city is located in close proximity to either the sea or a river. Trade and defense have dictated this. The home base of Legion X Gemina, Vienna has many of the amenities that the smaller cities along the Danube do not possess to the same degree. However, other units in the process of being transferred had been scheduled into Vienna before we arrived. So we were shunted thirty-some miles downriver to Carnuntum, the home base for Legion XIV Gemina. We had averaged twenty miles a day during actual travel days. The elapsed time to cover the 650 miles from Mainz to Carnuntum had come to a little over seven weeks. Once there, we were allowed to rest and recuperate for a few days. In spite of the beautiful scenery, we were all tired of marching and needed a lengthy layover. Carnuntum had an illustrious history, but we were shocked to see the dilapidated state into which it had deteriorated. It had been destroyed during the barbarian invasions of the latter third century and then rebuilt as a stone-walled fortress town that still had a sizable civilian population outside the walls. What contributed to its current ramshackle condition was its subjection to several attacks by barbarians since Hadrianople. Much of the town lying outside the walls had been seriously damaged. Carnuntum has a rather peculiar layout to it. It is scattered for a distance of two and a half miles along the river. The legionary fortress is located at its eastern end, while the civilian town is in the west. With so many cities in Gaul and the Balkans having contracted during the third century, it was odd to see a town on the very edge of the frontier still so spread out. The military and civilian sections of the town each had their own amphitheater, the civilian edition having been built over two centuries earlier by a town councilor who had originally come from Antioch, Syria. By the time it reached Carnuntum, the Danube had stretched out to over one thousand feet in width.

While at Carnuntum, I first heard the name of a young man who was destined for great fame and great tragedy. His father was a Vandal army officer, but his mother was a Roman. I was surprised to find that a man of such common origins was engaged to be married to Serena, the niece and adopted daughter of Theodosius I. This was quite out of the ordinary. Then again, he was no ordinary man; his name was Stilicho.

Our original orders had been to proceed to Carnuntum with the understanding that once we arrived, we would be informed as to our final destination. With nothing better to do on one of our days off, I visited the two local cemeteries with my friend Stephanus. One was in the civilian sector, while the other was closer to the legion fortress, although civilians were buried there also. Some of the stones went back three centuries, but what was most disturbing was the number of fresh monuments, attesting to the savagery of recent Germanic attacks on the town. On our third day there, our centurion called us together.

"Gentlemen, at sunup tomorrow, we will be leaving for Belgrade that is just inside the Diocese of Dacia. Once we arrive there, we will be detached from Legion XXII Primigenia and reassigned to Legion IV Flavia Firma. At the same time, we will pass under the supreme authority of His Majesty Theodosius. Belgrade is approximately 370 miles from here, so we've come almost two-thirds of the total distance. We will be patrolling the Danube just as we were doing previously on the Rhine. I'm told that this region has been stabilized for some time, but we'll find out more about that after we arrive. That's sunup tomorrow. You will be ready."

It was true that the frontier of the lower Danube had quietened considerably during the past eight months. But we would learn the hard way that "stability" is a word that can be interpreted in a rather elastic fashion. While recent pressure had been mounting on the upper Danube, we had experienced no problems thus far. The only real gripe was sore feet and the cold. East of Carnuntum, the degree of danger would increase considerably. From there all the way to the mouth of the Danube, there had been serious hostilities over the past five years. We witnessed numerous burned-out homesteads, and most of the towns had undergone sieges of varying severity. Our caravan was strengthened by the addition of two other regiments that afforded us all greater protection. Fortunately, we encountered no hostilities during our march through Pannonia. In fact, the weather proved to be the greatest obstacle. Heavy rains slowed us considerably, but during the third week in May, we entered Belgrade, our new home base.

Several centuries were given an official welcoming ceremony at the legionary fortress inducting us into Legion IV Flavia Firma. A banquet was laid on with the finest food and the best wine. After returning to our new quarters, Julius Aranius called us together and gave us a brief address.

"We've been given the next three days off to relax, rest up, and get our gear in shape. I'll be conducting a full-dress inspection on Friday at sunup. All your equipment will be battle ready by that time. If you have difficulties getting anything repaired or replaced, then come and see me. You know where my office is. Whenever I leave the base, I'll give the sergeant major the name of the centurion who is covering for me. Try and get familiarized with the city and the local surroundings. I'm certain that our newfound confreres will be only too glad to acquaint you with the restaurants, bordellos, and so on. Now, on a much more serious note, I was informed a short while ago that a revolt has broken out in Britain against the government of our beloved Emperors Gratian and Valentinian II. It is led by Magnus Maximus, count of Britain, and started at least two weeks ago. That's all I can tell you at the moment. I'll be sure to inform you as new information becomes available. Or you can inform me should you find out anything before I do."

We all laughed at our centurion's last remark, but it was an uneasy laughter. The rest of the evening was consumed in trying to guess how the revolt would affect us. The consensus was that it would be snuffed out as had every other western revolt across time, save that of Constantine the Great. But then what did we know.

For Emperor Gratian, 383 had been a very sad year, with far greater tragedy to come. He had followed his father's example by the tireless energy that he expended in securing the West. He had become emperor when he was only sixteen but had learned well what his father taught him. The understandable fears of the populace over such a young man taking over from such a ruthless but capable soldier were soon put aside when Gratian simply took up where his father had left off as far as military affairs were concerned. He had proven himself to be far more capable as a field commander than the sons of Constantine the Great had. Gratian had married Constantia, the only child, born posthumously, of Emperor Constantius II. Early in 383, she had given birth to a son, the only great-grandson of Constantine the Great. Soon after, both the empress and the baby died. It was only too powerful an omen of what lay ahead. Gratian was brokenhearted at his losses, as was the whole country, but soon after this, he had taken his second wife, Laeta. Just when things seemed to be getting back to normal for the imperial family, everything suddenly went wrong for them and the empire. At the time of the Danube crossing by the Visigoths in 376, Magnus Clemens Maximus had acquired an unsavory reputation as a result of his extortionate behavior toward the Visigothic refugees. However, he was a smart enough general. Once in revolt, he quickly crossed to the continent. Emperor Gratian, who was about to launch his expedition against the Alemanns on the Danube, quickly cancelled these plans and rushed westward to combat the usurper. Gratian and his army arrived at Paris during the latter part of July. For five days, the two armies confronted one another with only minor skirmishes taking place. Then suddenly a portion of the emperor's Moorish cavalry deserted to the usurper. Shortly after that, the rest of his army deserted him as well. The emperor fled south with his three-hundred-man Alan bodyguard in an attempt to reach Italy, but bad news always travels quicker than the fastest horse. Gratian's entourage found the gates of every city they approached closed to them. Finally, the governor of the province whose capitol is Lyon admitted them. Pretending loyalty, this governor had already been bribed by agents of Maximus into going over to the usurper's side. He delayed the emperor at Lyon just long enough for Andragathius, the usurper's marshal of cavalry, to catch up with him. After supper on August 25, the governor betrayed Gratian to his enemies, and he was murdered. It had been thirty-three years since an emperor had been assassinated (Constans in 350). A quarter century of relative tranquility and growing prosperity that had been brought to Gaul by Julian, Valentinian I, and Gratian now stood in the balance.

Gratian had been an excellent emperor, the only one that ever achieved the office as a teenager that could be described in that manner. He was well liked and was provided with an exceptional education conducted by the Christian poet Ausonius, who had strong connections with pagan senators in Rome. An eloquent speaker, Gratian was above all a fine soldier. In all our history, no imperial succession from a father to a natural son transpired with greater ease or with more positive results.

Gratian's administration had overseen the executions of a number of his late father's officials who had been responsible for the reign of terror in Rome. Under the guidance of Ausonius, relations between emperor and Senate were vastly improved. For decades, senators who aspired to political office had been limited to holding governorships and vicariates in the prefecture of the Italies alone, including Africa. Under Gratian, similar offices were opened up to them throughout the prefecture of the Gauls as well, although the emperor still appointed his own people from the civil service in many cases. The young emperor had fought the barbarians tirelessly almost from the day he came to the throne. He was a devoted husband and was looking forward to fatherhood until the various tragedies of 383 started to unfold. Had he lived, he might have ranked with the best of our chiefs of state. He certainly tried to emulate their finest qualities to the best of his ability. He is criticized by some historians as liking to clown around a little too much with his cronies. But to describe such a trivial habit as a "fault" in an emperor is truly to grasp at straws. On a more serious level, he ignored the policy of religious toleration that his father had followed during his eleven-year reign and, as a devout Catholic, started persecuting all forms of heresy. He also offended the pagans by removing the Altar of Victory from the Senate house in Rome and stopping funding by the central government of all pagan religious practices. But none of these "shortcomings," either real or imagined, played any significant role in his subsequent overthrow.

Apart from unbridled personal ambition, there was one strategic reason for Magnus Maximus to revolt. He felt that Trier, in northeastern Gaul and just a short distance from the Rhine frontier, was the best place to situate the main headquarters for defending Western Europe from German invasions. Many people throughout the prefecture of the Gauls shared this sentiment. For almost a quarter century, an emperor or vice emperor had resided somewhere in Gaul, and during these imperial residences Julian, Valentinian I, and Gratian had provided a staunch defense of all Western Europe. Milan, where Gratian had relocated his capital, was thought by many to be too remote from the main German invasion routes to provide a sufficiently swift response to aggression across the Rhine. The reasoning that had previously placed the emperor of the West in Trier was that for the past quarter century, the main threat to western security had been on the Rhine. The upper Danube had been relatively quiet. The strategy was that if the Germans broke through on the upper Danube, thus threatening Italy, then eastern units could assist the local forces if need be until reinforcements arrived from Gaul. This was a continuation of the policy of Valentinian I. However, the catastrophe at Hadrianople had completely undermined that concept. This fact was not lost on the Alemanns, who started to refocus their attacks from the upper Rhine to the more weakly held upper Danube.

A body of opinion evolved in the British, Spanish, and Gallic provinces to the effect that with the Balkans in chaos, the East would never be able to assist the West, and especially Gaul, in case of a future invasion anywhere. Very few people had faith that the peace treaty would be upheld. The Visigoths were firmly ensconced on Roman soil in the Balkans. Constantinople would thus be reluctant to commit a sizable portion of its mobile forces to the West for however short a period, due to the increased danger of a Visigothic revolt to their rear. Western resources had been already stretched thin on the Rhine to provide more strength to the upper Danube. Gratian's moving his headquarters from Trier to Milan only confirmed the worst fears of the far west.

In 380, while sending more regiments to his eastern colleague, Gratian had first to deal with an invasion by Ostrogoths and Alans into Pannonia on the central Danube. He scored a marginal victory over these intruders led by none other than Alatheus and Saphrax. This was not a case of tens of thousands of Germans trying to migrate into the empire as had been the case with the Visigoths. These barbarians were essentially soldiers of fortune and either had no immediate families or, if they did, had not brought them along. After their surrender, however, Gratian permitted them to join units of the Roman Army and bring down their families from north of the Danube, which they did. The number of soldiers they contributed came to about fifteen hundred men.

Yet they had played a crucial role at Hadrianople out of all proportion to their numerical strength. It was a wise move all around, though not universally regarded as such. In the service of Rome, these barbarians had no inclination to realign themselves with the Visigothic mobs to the east that now appeared to be losers anyway, Hadrianople notwithstanding. It was from this defeated army that Gratian selected his three-hundred-man Alan bodyguard. This settlement outraged public opinion. Gratian felt, however, that by settling these Ostrogoths and Alans as Roman allies, he would be preventing them from rejoining Fritigern, thus causing more grief to Theodosius, who was already in difficulty enough. It was a responsible course of action. But an immediate consequence of this agreement was a lowering of public support for Gratian.

The most important strategic decision that any emperor can make is to dedicate himself to solving the most pressing danger engaging the empire at any given time, regardless of its geographical location. As the Rhine was quiet, Gratian did not have to be there. His proper place from 378 onward was on the Danube, and those who think otherwise are wrong. With the benefit of hindsight, it might have been wise to send young Valentinian II to Trier when Gratian left for Milan. Though just a little boy, the mere fact of a legitimate imperial presence in the prefecture of the Gauls may have been enough to dampen any treasonous ambitions in that area. A certain benefit for his young half brother would have been to get him out of the oppressive clutches of Bishop Ambrose. As for Gratian himself, he was being worn out traveling back and forth constantly between Trier and the Balkans. Every time Theodosius's army got into trouble, Gratian had to rush eastward to assist him.

One thing that distanced Gratian from the army was the recent acquisition of his Alan bodyguard. The Alans are a non-German Caucasian people that originally lived an entirely nomadic existence to the north of the Caucasus Mountains and the Black Sea. In spite of their racial differences, they have far more in common with the Mongoloid Huns than they do with Caucasian Europeans. The Alans were unpopular with both the Germans and the native Romans in our army. Many of these Romans and Germans were veterans of many years. The sudden popularity of these nomadic strangers with the emperor only served to create a gap between him and the regular troops. Gratian soon started to appear before the army dressed as an Alan warrior wearing fur robes and carrying Alan, not Roman, arms. He also consorted ever more with his Alan bodyguards on the hunting indulgences that he had for too long been carrying to excess. There was also another reason for public indifference to his assassination. The settlement with the Visigoths had been signed in the previous year. While Theodosius I had been the chief Roman negotiator, his western colleague had agreed with its terms. A strong majority of public opinion, East and West, were astonished and bewildered by this arrangement. The public expected another Battle of Naissus like Claudius II conducted back in 269, but this ambition was not to be realized for reasons I have already explained. To sum up, Emperor Gratian had unwittingly made himself an ever-ripening target at the time that Magnus Maximus revolted. But to put things on a baser level, Maximus might have revolted for the simple reason that he thought he could get away with it. After all, he was a fellow Spaniard who had served with Theodosius and his late father. There was also a story that the usurper and Theodosius were distant cousins. He had been an enthusiastic supporter of Theodosius when the latter was elevated to the throne. Because of this, he might have felt slighted when he was subsequently reassigned to Britain, but given the way in which he had botched things in 376, how did he think he should be treated? Britain was about as far away from Hadrianople as one could get and still be on Roman territory.

On another item, the usurper had totally misjudged Theodosius. Maximus may have felt that by killing Gratian he would gain favor with the emperor of the East. When Valentinian I died on November 17, 375, Theodosius's father had been arrested in North Africa, taken to Carthage, and summarily executed. The circumstances surrounding this outrageous miscarriage of justice have never been satisfactorily explained. It appears that certain advisers of Gratian suspected that the count of Africa might be entertaining imperial ambitions of his own. The popular belief that no such conspiracy existed is substantiated by the fact that no one else was ever arrested in this connection. In any event, the young emperor had no knowledge of this incident until after the execution had been carried out. Theodosius understood this and bore Gratian no ill will. They had discussed it at great length among themselves when they met after the Battle of Hadrianople, and the issue was closed as far as both men were concerned. It didn't take Maximus long to realize how completely he had miscalculated on this as on other issues.

To many, the assassination of Emperor Gratian remains a mystery. It need not be. Possessing the most rectitudinous character is no protection for an emperor against the rapacious greed of the basest elements that are always prepared to risk everything for the throne. Magnus Maximus was just such a base element. A number of men had started revolts against the established authority from the West, and every one, except Constantine I, had failed. This dismal record of defeat notwithstanding, here was one more fool willing to risk not only his own life but also that of thousands of others as well as the integrity of the state for his own self-gratification. And at a time when the empire could least afford it. Civil war is the costliest form of warfare because it pits Roman army against Roman army. Regardless of who wins, Rome always loses, and Magnus Maximus felt that he could use this to his advantage. What made this revolt all the more irresponsible was that it occurred a mere five years after the Battle of Hadrianople. What probably emboldened the usurper's confidence was that Theodosius I had his hands full. He was rebuilding the eastern mobile field armies while simultaneously trying to ensure that the Visigoths abided by the recently signed peace treaty. Magnus Maximus was convinced that the advantage lay with him and not the East. An additional factor working for the usurper was the recent deposing of old King Ardashir II of Iran. Theodosius would not want to take any precipitous action against the West until he had ascertained what the attitude of the new Iranian monarch, Sapor III, would be toward Rome.

The assassination of Gratian could not have happened at a worse time. He and Theodosius had worked extremely well together and had recovered, in large measure, the situation that Valens had lost in 378. The Battle of Hadrianople is regarded by historians as the most decisive in our history from the standpoint of the manner in which the West was subsequently dismembered. However, it would never have achieved the historical gravity that it has were it not for the terrible civil wars into which we were plunged as a direct result of Magnus Maximus' usurpation. People of a future age will be puzzled as to how the Battle of Hadrianople, which occurred deep in the Eastern Roman Empire, could have led to the disintegration of the empire in the West over one thousand miles away, as so many contemporary writers maintain. It is the main theme of this writing that it did not. The consequences of that terrible battle had been contained by 382. They would have remained that way had not the West snatched defeat from the jaws of victory in 383 by going into revolt. It is my intention to show that by doing so, the West precipitated its own destruction in a way that was impossible to foresee at the time. In 383, the West was much stronger than the East. Five years later, the success of the policies of Gratian and Theodosius in integrating the Visigoths and certain others into the Roman framework would become all too evident. So too in the final civil war of the reign of Theodosius I in 394. But I will also show that this last civil war, perhaps more than anything else, destroyed the alliance between the Romans and the Visigoths and led to the disintegration of the West that appears irreparable.

The more shallow-minded Gauls and Brits hailed the victory of Magnus Maximus, claiming that now they had "their own" emperor who would put western interests first and foremost. Many in Britain supported his revolt, at least in the beginning. However, his removal of thousands of soldiers from Albion to Gaul gave even his most fervent adherents there cause for second thoughts. The political division of the empire in the late summer of 383 was this: The usurper held the prefecture of the Gauls; Valentinian II nominally controlled the prefecture of the Italies and Greece, but he was only twelve years old; Theodosius I held the prefectures of Illyria and the East. This situation would hold for several years. But everyone knew from the beginning that it could not last indefinitely. Theodosius owed his elevation to Gratian, and he would never falter in his loyalty to the House of Valentinian I. He would eventually be united to it by marriage. It was only a matter of time before East and West came to open conflict.

Immediately upon securing power, Magnus Maximus sent embassies to both Valentinian II at Milan and Theodosius I at Constantinople. In both he displayed a marked political ineptitude. An offer of peace to Valentinian II was conditional upon the twelve-year-old boy residing at Trier under the "protection" of his brother's murderer. Could Maximus actually have been mindless enough to think that the young emperor and his mother, Justina, would agree to this? Everyone was dumbfounded when news of this ludicrous offer became public. The court at Milan, however, made the offer the basis for a series of embassies between Milan and Trier, several of which were headed by Bishop Ambrose. This enabled Valentinian II's Frankish general, Bauto, to occupy the Alpine passes between Gaul and Italy that would help to delay an invasion by Maximus for another four years. The offer to Theodosius was just as brazen. The murder of Gratian was attributed to the overzealousness of Andragathius, and no apology was proffered. Maximus presented Theodosius with a simple choice: peace including joint operations against all enemies of Rome or civil war between themselves. Theodosius appeared to accept the status quo; Magnus Maximus assumed that he had achieved recognition.

The death of Emperor Gratian marked the end of that long line of Illyrian emperors that had done so much to preserve the empire during the past century and more. With one exception, we have not seen their kind again, and the empire has been much the worse for their absence. Gratian was the last legitimate emperor in the West to truly exercise executive authority, and the magnitude of his deplorable loss would be manifested all too quickly.

Since mid-March, we had come just over one thousand, miles but as westerners, we felt serious anxiety about the revolt. After all, the West was our homeland, whereas the East was terra incognita. Subsequent events, however, would prove our transfer to have been, for most of us, our great good fortune. During the months of June, July, and August, our regiment assumed patrol duties along the Danube, and we were trained in highway construction and the maintenance of our fortress. While occupied by our new responsibilities during a very hot summer, our thoughts were constantly on the West and what was happening there. We received maddeningly little news of any kind. Then, at the beginning of September, we were informed of the murder of Gratian. We instantly realized that we would remain in the East and that when civil war broke out, we would be fighting our former comrades. It also should have been evident to everyone in the West that the many thousands of western soldiers serving "temporarily" in the East would not be returning.

When traveling anywhere in the empire, one can see by the roadsides the small temples dedicated to those little minor goddesses that our ancestors called the Fates, now abandoned and mostly in ruin. There are times, when considering the capricious path that history has taken recently, that I think we were overhasty in discontinuing the worship of those little rascals. They do not appear to be taking their unemployment lightly.

CHAPTER
5

The Caldron
(383–387)

I WAS THIRTEEN WHEN the Battle of Hadrianople occurred. From then on, whenever conditions in the eastern Balkans were discussed, that blood-drenched peninsula was usually referred to as "the caldron" and with good reason. In the areas the Visigoths infested after 376, the wreckage in the countryside was terrible. Estates and farm sites that had been built up from the ruination of the previous century had been destroyed all over again. But the cities, with few exceptions, held out. By 380, the Gothic threat had been contained, and with the peace treaty of 382, the caldron had cooled down considerably. By that time, Alavivus, Athanaric, and Fritigern were dead, and no leader had emerged to replace them. As a result, the peace treaty was signed repeatedly with small individual bands of Visigoths since by 382 there was no cohesion among their different groups. Some of these bands, usually composed of single men without families, would continue to operate as bandit gangs for some years to come. But the worst appeared to be over. This was the general situation when our regiment arrived in Belgrade.

Belgrade and Sirmium, just to the west, are the two main cities in the Central Danubian Plain. This region contains the valleys of three right-bank tributaries of the Danube: the Morava, Drava, and Sava Rivers. In combination, they constitute the central Danube's breadbasket. These riverine plains are subject to severe flooding, but as a result, they contain rich alluvial soils. Great quantities of wheat, oats, and barley are grown and large cattle herds are raised for both beef and dairy products. The rivers also provide a rich fish harvest. The region, however, is lacking in minerals and coal. These must be shipped in from either farther up the Danube or from the southeast. This area east to the mouth of the Danube has the most varied climate in the empire. The summers are as hot as in the more southerly provinces, but the winters are colder than anywhere else. In view of the latter, I was surprised to find vineyards resident here along with orchards. This territory had suffered barbarian inroads during the aftermath of Hadrianople but with nowhere near the severity of the provinces further east. The rolling hill country to the south of Belgrade rises in places to an elevation of about three hundred feet above the river level. It is thick with small farms along with a number of large estates. Belgrade itself is strategically located at the junction of the Danube and the Sava Rivers on a promontory that is surrounded by the rivers on three sides. The city has always been important as a center of trade. After 376, its significance was greatly enhanced because the security of the highways leading from the downriver ports was completely undermined by the Visigoths. Belgrade, along with three other ports lying within the next fifty miles downstream, became the most easterly riverine assembly points for caravans transporting goods south into Greece and Asia. Wagon trains from all four ports would eventually funnel south up the Morava Valley to Naissus, the birthplace of Constantine the Great.[13] While the Visigoths were rampaging, the caravans would head southwest from Naissus to Skopje, from where they would follow the Axios River down to Thessalonica on the Aegean Sea. Since the signing of the peace treaty, the trade caravans could once again travel southeast from Naissus through Sofia, the Succi Pass, Philippopolis, and Hadrianople to Constantinople.

I suddenly awoke with a resounding jolt, briefly wondering if an earthquake, which I had never experienced before, had struck the building. I was sound asleep when my friend Stephanus had raised the end of my bed up and suddenly dropped it.

"Rise and shine." He laughed. "Come on. Let's see what this place has to offer in the way of nightlife."

Sitting up and pretending to be somewhat alert, I remarked, "At the banquet, a couple of our new fellow legionaries mentioned a place called the Waterfront Inn. Did you hear anything about it?"

"Yes, I did," Stephanus replied. "It's several blocks outside the wall near the Danube. I got pretty good directions on how to get there. If we get lost, we can ask somebody. I was told that the natives are quite amicable. We know what that means, so let's go."

After picking up Chlogius and Marcellinus, we headed out. After passing through a gate leading down to the Danube, we found ourselves in the sort of waterfront area common to any sea or river port: warehouses everywhere, open-air markets selling well into the evening, sailcloth manufacturer's shops, flour mills, and so on. Finally we came to the Waterfront Inn, an old converted warehouse at the river's edge. We entered and quickly grabbed the first available table. After ordering a round of wine, we started looking over the girls hanging around the bar. There were only a few of them.

"Well, chaps," Marcellinus asked at length, "have we all made our selections for the evening or is a lengthier period of contemplation required?"

"I'm going to need another round of the grape first," Chlogius suggested. "After all, you can't fly on one wing."

"I might need considerably more than that," I confessed. "I don't know about you guys, but the offerings that have appeared thus far strike me as a pretty rum lot. That one down on the far end is the best looking, but they all look as hard as nails."

"Listen to our expert here," Stephanus gibed. "Do I detect yet another harangue on how wonderful the girls of Marseille and Arles are?"

"Spare us please." Chlogius laughed. "I think the trouble with our friend Marcus is that he is too well bred. If he had been born lower down on the social ladder, he'd be a down-and-dirty type like the rest of us. I mean hell, the bugger can even read and write."

A lot of good-natured kidding like that went on for a while. Eventually, the girls started dropping around our table to give us a better opportunity for inspection. My three comrades eventually paired up and headed off into the rooms at the back or upstairs. I didn't though. I was tired and disinterested at the moment, so I spent the rest of the evening concentrating on the wine and conversing with some of the other soldiers who had wandered in. I was starting to learn what comes to the knowledge of every young soldier sooner or later: the army, any army, is an excellent training ground for young drunks. That night, however, I didn't mind getting plastered because we had the following day to sleep off the hangover.

"Hey, soldier," I heard from out of the haze. "You still awake?" It was Chlogius.

"Where are the others?" he asked.

"Still humping I would think," I replied. "They haven't come back yet. Do fill me in on all the lurid details of your evening's romp."

"No, no," was the reply. "I doubt that your delicate constitution could withstand the full particulars of my evening's sexcapades. Sometimes I'm so manly I just can't stand myself. However, since your carnal yearnings tend, so you would have us believe, to the more exotic, I might have some good news for you. My lady of the evening, Martina by name, informed me that a Syrian merchant was here last week and spoke to the manager of the establishment. She's the portly trollop that welcomed us when we arrived. The upshot of their negotiations was that the Syrian will be providing this establishment with an influx of wenches from the Kingdom of Axum in Africa. They are supposed to arrive during the next month or so."

"That could be interesting," I replied. "I never saw a Negro before I started visiting the Mediterranean ports, and I only saw a handful there. I'm certain there are none in Britain. Have you ever seen any?"

"No," he replied, "but these people are not pure Negroes. They are a frontier race with an admixture of Caucasian and Negroid blood. An uncle of mine served with the army years ago, and for part of his enlistment, he was in a garrison on the Nile right on the southern frontier of Egypt and Nubia. Axum, or Ethiopia, is the next country beyond

Nubia. He said the women who served the soldiers there were absolutely gorgeous. In fact, a friend of his married one of them and brought her back to Belgium with him when he retired. It's an incredible world we live in, isn't it? To think of a Frankish-born Roman soldier serving on the southern frontier of the one-time land of the pharaohs, marrying a woman from Axum, having three children, and moving the whole family back to northern Gaul upon retiring. We should all be so lucky."

At this point, Stephanus and Marcellinus returned and immediately started in on Chlogius.

"Boy, you didn't last long, did you?" said Marcellinus. "I'll bet you were back in a fraction of the time that it took us. Right, Marcus?"

"The only reason you clowns were in the back for so long is that it took you all this time just to get it up," Chlogius responded.

"I trust your natives were friendly," said Stephanus. "Mine decidedly was not. But that's the luck of the draw I suppose. I would have been better off staying with friend Marcus here and getting smashed."

The others had a few more rounds of wine, and we headed back to the barracks. The next day, we were all badly hung over. Each of us, on more than one occasion, swore never again to raise the cup on high. At least until the next time. There were several establishments of a similar nature that we would frequent from time to time, but their wine was just as expensive, and their women were even tougher. Welcome to Belgrade.

Our patrol duties along the Danube resembled those along the Rhine. In addition, we became heavily involved in another military activity that was a centuries-old tradition at this time of the year: highway maintenance. Within the confines of areas that enjoy a Mediterranean climate, this is not that great a problem; the difficulties that arise are generally those of normal wear caused by traffic. But in areas that have a more continental climate and in the more mountainous regions, the alternate freezing and thawing during the winter wreaks additional havoc on the road network. At this time, the roads in the Balkans were the worst in the empire. The incessant warfare had prevented almost any maintenance from being done on them during the summers. As a result, after six years of neglect, the entire network was starting to fall into ruin. With the return of peace, an enormous amount of work had to be performed on all bridges and highways. Much of our time over the next several years would be consumed by this backbreaking activity. While landowners are generally responsible for the upkeep of highways that border their property, so many estates had been destroyed that the army was obliged to do most of the repair work. With other units, we worked on the highway that parallels the right bank of the Danube both up and downriver from Belgrade. In addition, we worked on the roadway that joined Belgrade with Sirmium almost forty miles to the west. Sirmium periodically served a similar purpose on the central Danube to what Trier performed near the Rhine—a central military headquarters for conducting defensive and offensive operations in the region.

One day, while on a rest break upstream from Belgrade, I noticed a convoy coming down the river, accompanied by a large naval contingent from the Pannonian Fleet. Later in the day, our centurion called us together for an announcement.

"There will be a change in your duties starting tomorrow," he said. A big roar of approval went up from our assembly. "Yeah, I know. It will break your hearts to be torn away from these illuminating endeavors. However, I think we could all do with a change of scenery regardless of its brevity. We will be returning to base tomorrow to get our gear in shape. Three days from now, we will be escorting an overland convoy to Naissus along with some other units. It's approximately 170 miles from Belgrade. We'll follow the Danube east to Viminacium and then turn south up the Morava River Valley to Naissus. There we will turn over our escort duties to a unit coming up from Sofia. For those more downcast members of our company who do not appear happy at the prospect of a 340-mile round-trip, we will be traveling as mounted infantry."

Cheers all around.

"Why did they pick us?" a decurion asked.

"I specifically asked for this responsibility when I heard it was available. Now that the Balkans are peaceful again, it will be a good opportunity for our century to become acquainted with the surrounding region. After all, we should know it as well as the Visigoths do."

At the appointed time, our century was on the docks in Belgrade. The convoy that had passed us on the river had come a long way. It included coal supplies for fortress towns on the Danube and civilian trade goods. The wagons were loaded and ready to go. During our first "pee parade," I struck up a conversation with the civilian in charge of the convoy. His name was Josephus, and he came from the town of Rhodiapolis in the province of Lycia in southwest Asia Minor.

"How far has your journey taken you?" I asked.

"Traveling in the wilds of Germany, we measure the distance in terms of time rather than miles," Josephus replied. "The amber trade is quite lucrative, but a lot of work and negotiating is involved."

"How deep into Germany do you go to obtain it?" I asked.

"It comes from the sands along the south shore of the Baltic Sea," he replied. "That area contains the largest amber reserves in the known world. I only made the trip to the Baltic once though, and that was a good many years ago. On this trip, as with all the others I take, we only went as far north as the town of Calisia."

I remembered Calisia[14] from studying the amber routes during my last year of schooling. Located about 270 miles north of the Danube, Calisia is more than halfway to the Baltic Sea.

"How does the quality of the amber routes in Germany compare to our own road system?" I asked.

"There is no comparison," was his swift reply. "Within the empire, the old amber routes have been absorbed into the Roman highway network and have lost their original identity. But in Germany, they are best described as passable tracks. In swampy areas or on the approaches to riverbanks, where the rivers are shallow enough to ford, a log surface has been laid down to handle wagon traffic. In mountainous areas, the tracks have been improved also, but that's the extent of it. There are several such amber routes coming down from northern Germany to the empire. They are the most ancient roads in Europe. It is believed that the Etruscans played a major role in laying out the western trails, while the Greeks had a similar responsibility for the more easterly routes. I've heard that the building of these lines started about 1900 BC. It's remarkable to think of them predating the founding of Rome by over a thousand years."

"Are any of the rivers there navigable or do you travel overland all the way?" I asked.

"I don't know about the other routes," Josephus replied. "The only one that I've ever traveled is the one that goes north from Carnuntum to the Baltic Sea, and the only time that we're ever on the rivers is when we're fording them. They really aren't navigable, and even if they were, there would be the problem of constructing proper docking and loading facilities. The locals lack such capabilities."

"Speaking of the locals," I said, "what about your safety? I would think that taking caravans through Germany would be extremely dangerous at the best of times."

"The potential for danger is always there, especially when the Germans are feuding among themselves," Josephus explained. "What makes the whole enterprise work is that everyone makes money from the caravans. We pay the local Germans to keep the route clear, to maintain those parts of it that are log covered, and to provide local security."

"Sounds like the sort of trip I might like to take some time, once anyway," I thought out loud.

"Perhaps you will," he replied. "All Roman caravans traveling into Germany or Iran carry former soldiers in their retinue to act as intelligence agents. These are men who have either retired or whose service time was reduced for some reason."

"What is Calisia like?"

"Calisia comes as a very welcome surprise to visitors. It is partly a Roman town. It serves as an entrepot for Germans coming down from the Baltic with their amber, furs, and other goods and Romans coming up from the south with their merchandise. There are baths, hotels, restaurants, and numerous warehouses that might appear somewhat rustic to those of us down here, but you have to remember that I'm talking about a town that is far beyond the northern boundary of the empire. Of course, after seven weeks or so on the road, such as it is, almost any permanent rest stop looks good."

"What are the people like that live there permanently?"

"Some Romans are more or less permanent residents there, but most of the people are, as you would expect in the heart of Germany, Germans.

These, however, are peoples with whom most Romans have little familiarity. They are mostly Lugians and Helisians with a smattering of Rugians from the Baltic coast. They are relatively prosperous, as most middlemen are. It's a shame more Germans are not like them. We would have a far more peaceful and prosperous world if they were."

"You mentioned that you made it to the Baltic Sea once," I reminded him.

"Yes, but I wouldn't recommend it. Rugium, the capital of the Rugians, is at the mouth of the Vistula River where it empties into the Baltic Sea. It is 180 miles beyond Calisia and is a rather bleak, woebegone place, not at all in the same class as Calisia. Besides, north of Calisia, the quality of the road deteriorates badly. It is difficult enough getting wagons from Carnuntum to Calisia, but north of there, one is pretty much reduced to using pack trains. It's simply not worth the effort. By the way, did they ever teach you anything in school about Marcus Aurelius's Marcomannic War?"

"It was mentioned in passing, but we never went into it in detail," I replied.

Josephus went on, "On my journeys up to Calisia, I have often thought of how convenient it would have been if that war had been continued to a successful conclusion. If so, then the first 120 miles of the route north from Carnuntum would be paved all the way to the Moravian Gate."

At that moment, our centurion gave the order to mount up and hit the road again. I thanked Josephus for a most interesting discussion. It was his mention of the Marcomannic War that had ended two centuries earlier that first piqued my curiosity on the subject. To this point, my familiarity with the central Danube was limited to a forty-mile radius of Belgrade. All that was about to change. Continuing eastward along the Danube, our caravan grew in size first at Aureus Mons, then again at Margum and Viminacium. It would make a very tempting target for any bandit gang, but with such a large contingent of mounted infantry, our officers felt that sufficient security had been provided. It was also hoped that the convoy would prove to be so alluring that some bandit gangs would attack it. By drawing them out in this way, we would be spared the effort of having to beat the bushes looking for them. Let them come to us when we were expecting them.

As we headed south from Viminacium, up the valley of the Morava River, the countryside looked healthy. Crops on both the large estates and the small peasant farms were coming along well. Numerous vineyards abound here along with apple and peach orchards. Some coal mines exist in the region, and on our way south, we passed a convoy under escort heading north, carrying lead, copper, and zinc from several local mines. The area that we were now entering had long formed the main land bridge between Western Europe and Asia Minor. The region that runs southeast from Belgrade to Thessalonica on the Aegean Sea is defined by the valleys of the Morava River in the north and the Axios River in the south. The strategic importance of this region to the empire cannot be overstated. Should control of it be lost to an enemy, the empire would be split in two and unable to transport troops across the Balkans in an east-west direction.

Late in the morning of our sixth day south from the Danube, smoke was seen rising in the distance to our left over a hill. Our century was leading the convoy at this time, so we were ordered to investigate. As we approached the crest of the hill, we halted, and our centurion selected his decurions, Chlogius, and me to accompany him. Chlogius and I looked at one another. We were puzzled as to why we were being chosen to accompany the others since we were simply private soldiers. We dismounted and finished climbing the hill. As we approached the crest, Julius Aranius led us off to the side of the road where we could observe the fire while crouching under the cover of trees and brush. We heard screaming as we climbed the hill, but even though it was far off, it was tortured enough to tell us someone was being put through hell. We could see a large villa ablaze with a number of men running about carrying things from the house. Well off to the left in one of the farm fields, we saw a man on horseback cut down another man who had been trying to escape to a wooded area.

"Huns," Julius Aranius hissed. That word sent a chill through us all. "Do a quick count of how many you see."

"Twelve," I said while another claimed fourteen, another eleven, and so on.

"Allowing for some more inside the villa, let's say twenty all told," our centurion concluded. "I don't see anyone else moving around anywhere. Do the rest of you?" We didn't.

Our centurion and the decurions were reading the land for the best way to approach the villa. Our hill continued to the right of the highway down to the Morava River, a distance of about a quarter mile. Our centurion led us back to the rest of the column, and a plan of attack was quickly prepared. Two riders were also dispatched back to the convoy to inform the others of what we had discovered and to request assistance. There was not time to take everyone up to the hilltop in small groups to fully inform them as to the lay of the land. If we were to save any lives down there, time was of the essence. On a patch of clear dirt beside the road, our centurion drew up a map of exactly what we would be doing. Each decade (eight-man unit) knew what was expected of it. We went over the plan twice and then mounted up. We pulled off the highway and headed west toward the Morava until we almost reached the river. Rounding the end of the hill, we passed through a forest heading south until we felt we were in line with the road leading off the highway to the villa. At that point, we turned east and headed through several hundred yards of forest. As the trees started to thin out, we could see that we were a little north of where we wanted to be. At full gallop, we thundered across the highway, through a small peach orchard, and then centered ourselves on the quarter mile of road to the burning villa. There was a small decorative wall that surrounded the place and stood about three or four feet in height. Our horses would jump it without difficulty.

We were divided up with four decades on either side of the approach road to pass over the wall two decades at a time as planned. The danger of trying to pass the entire century through the main gate, even if that were possible, was that we would present too concentrated a target at the point of entry. When we were about halfway there, a Hun suddenly appeared at the gate. He ran off yelling to warn his comrades, but in no time, we were pouring over the wall. Each decade had a specific task assigned to it. From the hilltop, it had been noted that the Huns had quartered their horses in the northeast corner of the villa grounds. The task of our decade was to slaughter those horses so the Huns would have no chance to escape. Once over the wall, we wheeled to our left before the Huns could organize a defense. I felt a thud and heard an instant ringing sound as an arrow glanced off my helmet. We killed the two Huns that were guarding the corral and then set to slaughtering the horses. Distasteful as this was, we all recognized its necessity if the Huns were to be prevented from committing any more atrocities like they had at this place.

I have always hated melees of this nature. All soldiers do. Anything can come at you at any time from any direction. Now most set piece assaults degenerate into such struggles also. It's just that in the latter case at least a degree of control exists during the initial stage of the battle that is simply not there in the type of attack that we were involved in. What made the job of our decade doubly dangerous was that we knew that as the Huns tried to escape, they would head directly for their horses and therefore us. In the open country surrounding the villa, it was impossible for them to escape on foot. As a result, our centurion had one decade protect our backs while we were killing the horses with our spears. Suddenly our decurion, a Roman-born Frank named Chlodomirus, ordered us to forget the horses. Half a dozen Huns made a life-or-death attempt to get to them, but the decade supporting us felled them all with arrows. Our decade advanced to finish them off with our swords. The entire battle had been quite short. Our century had suffered seven men wounded. The one among them that did not require medical attention was my friend Marcellinus. At full gallop, his horse suddenly balked at the idea of jumping the wall. His rider, however, sailed onward. Marcellinus was knocked unconscious by his impact with the wall and the ground and did not come to until the fight was over. He was kidded for days over how, while the rest of us were risking life and limb for the greater honor and glory of Rome, he had dozed through the whole affair. Once the battle was over, I picked up the bow and a knife from one of the two Huns that we had first killed. Their bows are much prized by all soldiers, regardless of nationality, and when you are presented with the opportunity to obtain one, you seize it.

Twenty-three Huns had been in the raiding party, and fourteen of them were killed in our assault. We captured the remainder, but they would soon regret that they had not died with the rest. Unfortunately, we had arrived too late to save the estate owner and his family from being slaughtered. The Huns' victims were all lying before the villa. The husband had been decapitated, and from the manner in which his wife's legs were splayed apart, it was obvious that she had been repeatedly raped before dying from multiple stab wounds. Their two young sons, aged about ten and twelve, had also been cut to pieces. The only good news was that two younger children, a girl of about three and a boy of five or six, were found hiding (or perhaps where they had been hidden) in an implement shed. It was now time to deal with the Hunnish captives.

All the prisoners had been bound, and our centurion, after inspecting the implement sheds, came upon an ax with a very large blade. He immediately sharpened it on a nearby grindstone. We selected the biggest and meanest-looking Hun of the lot, whom we assumed to be their leader. He was bound hand and foot and forced to kneel in front of our centurion. He was then tied to adjacent trees in such a way that he could move neither forward nor backward nor from side to side. Our centurion stood in back of him, not off to one side as an executioner normally would to behead a criminal. Most of us were puzzled at this but only for a moment. After our entire century had gathered round to observe, Julius Aranius raised the ax overhead and drove it down perfectly into the crown of the doomed man's skull. His head was cleaved in two as the ax penetrated well below the shoulder line and the two halves of the skull, shattered, flopped over. Many of us were almost stupefied at this horrifying sight, but we passed it off as entirely justified. After the execution, our centurion ordered two of his decades to scour the surrounding woods to bring back any other family members, slaves, or tenants that might still be hiding from the Huns. The problem of what to do with the remaining prisoners, some of whom were badly wounded, was handled expeditiously. The Huns were parceled out one to a decade to be hanged from a giant oak tree that stood along the south side of the road leading from the villa to the highway. I have always had an intense dislike for hanging as a method of execution. However, having seen the savagery that these Huns had visited on their victims, the method of extermination seemed grimly appropriate. One by one they were all strung up. Strangulation is as excruciating a manner of being slain as one can imagine, with the exception of being burned to death. But to a man we felt no sympathy for any of them. After all, how many other innocents had they slaughtered in getting this far? Shortly before the execution of the first Hun, another century from the caravan came to assist us and was disappointed to see that we had been able to handle the situation with such dispatch.

The two units then combined to bury the family and their servants who had been murdered. A couple of servants were found seeking safety in the woods and were brought back to the villa. While we were executing the Huns, the fire in the villa had mysteriously burned itself out. We took the young children with us to hand over to the authorities in Naissus, who would try and place them with relatives. Thus concluded my second combat experience. It also marked my introduction to the Hunnish people. Negative as my comments have been about the Huns to this point, I do not mean them to stand as a condemnation of their race as a whole. In the years ahead, I would meet a number of Huns who volunteered for service in the Roman Army and in that capacity would serve as loyally and capably as any of us. I was only eighteen, but during 383, I matured at a far quicker pace than ever I would had I remained in Britain. My boyhood had receded into the background at an astonishing speed.

The rest of our journey was uneventful. We handed over our responsibilities for convoy duty to units that had just arrived in Naissus from Sofia and returned to our home bases on the Danube. As we passed the villa where we had wiped out the Huns, we halted. Julius Aranius rode over to the insect-covered corpse of the Hun whose skull he had split and placed a sign before the body that he had made up in Naissus. It read simply "An Enemy of Rome." After he returned to our column I approached him.

"Sir, Chlogius and I were curious as to why you selected us to accompany you and the decurions to scout out the villa prior to our engagement."

He replied, "I've been impressed with the way the two of you handle yourselves. You've been with the unit less than a year, but if you keep progressing in the way you have to this point, then I think you will find yourselves promoted to decurion in the not-too-distant future. The scouting exercise was just a little on-the-job training. You can tell Chlogius what I've said, but don't say anything to anyone else. Just keep up the good work."

The summer of 383 was very hot, but apart from our single engagement with the Huns, things remained quiet militarily. While we did not have any more "bloody drills," we certainly did have plenty of "bloodless battles" to consume our days, in addition to our periods on patrols and highway maintenance. In another sphere, the Syrian merchant finally delivered on his promise of Axumite prostitutes. (Is there anything that Syrian merchants do not sell?) When our group showed up at the Waterfront Inn the night after they arrived, we were very impressed. There were a dozen of them, and they were all absolutely beautiful. All in their late teens, they had been trained to speak a little conversational Latin. They had been shipped north up the Red Sea from the Axumite port of Adulis[15] on a slave ship to the Egyptian port of Myos Hormos, from which they had eventually made their way north. Suddenly Belgrade was not such a dull posting after all.

My companions had become rather boisterous after a few drinks. That night, however, I was not in a drinking mood. In no way was my sexual appetite going to be dulled when there were treasures as these available. The girl who caught my eye first was named Makila. She smiled and approached our table from the bar. When I got up to go with her to her room, my friends were quite surprised.

"Chaps, a historical moment in our association has indeed arrived," Stephanus wisecracked. "I think that our friend Marcus here has at long last found Miss Right."

"Not before time," Chlogius continued. "You know, old fellow, we were starting to harbor the nastiest thoughts as to just what your libidinous interests really were."

"Or if you had any at all," Marcellinus chimed in. "Go get her, tiger."

"Yeah, and be quick about it," Stephanus added. "We'll all probably want a crack at her before the night is out."

I enjoyed their entertainment at my expense as much as they did. Makila was pure ecstasy, and our time together that first night was all too short. There would be many other such nights, however. I took one of the other girls only when Makila was not available, as happened sometimes. But it was Makila to whom I was attracted above all. With the addition of the Axumite girls, the inn's reputation was greatly enhanced, and it started drawing better crowds than it ever had. On occasion, a rich, widowed or divorced landowner would rent a girl and take her off to his estate for a romp of several days. In the highly uncertain times that the Balkans had endured in recent years, a number of the aristocrats had found it to their financial advantage to simply rent a prostitute for a few days rather than buying her as a slave.

It was there that I enjoyed my most pleasurable evenings during July and August 383, but it was also there in early September that our world was suddenly turned upside down. I had just finished another delightful interlude and was returning to our table. My comrades were either still getting laid or in the pissoir. A decurion seated at another table called out to me.

"Marcus, have you heard the news?" Lucius asked.

With some hesitation, I asked, "What news?"

"We only have two emperors. Gratian was murdered at Lyon on August 25," was the startling reply.

"You know this for a fact?" I asked.

"I was told by our centurion just as I was heading over here," he said. "Our entire legion will be assembled first thing tomorrow morning, at which time the prefect will officially inform us all as to exactly what happened."

"Jesus Christ," I replied. "Just when things in the East are finally brought under control, the West has to erupt. What happens now?"

"I don't know," Lucius replied. "I don't think anybody does. But the smart money says there is no way in which Theodosius will accept this. He owes his throne to Gratian, and he won't abandon our late emperor's family now."

At that point, Marcellinus arrived, and I informed him of what the decurion had told me.

"I guess that gibes with the latest imperial utterances posted in the forum today," he replied. "Theodosius has issued a decree that no one can own any property that cannot be subjected to a tax. That's certain to make everyone in the Eastern Empire happy. Just think: tax assessors can barge into your home at any time and place a value on your wife's dresses or the books in your library or anything else they take a notion to."

"At that rate," I said, "the government will soon be taxing people down to their underwear, which, of course, shouldn't be a problem for anyone in this place. However, since you and I are in possession of neither wives, books, nor homes at the present time, it won't bother us. But it certainly will be trouble for all civilians. I think you are right. Theodosius knows that from now on he won't be able to get any more troops from the West, regardless of what goes wrong here in the East. He's going to stock his treasury so that he'll have plenty to pay his army, however much he has to enlarge it, when we march West, as march we will."

The following morning, our entire legion of almost one thousand men was gathered and addressed by our commander, the prefect. He gave us the details on Gratian's betrayal and murder as I related them in the previous chapter. At the time of the Battle of Hadrianople, the prefecture of the East and the Diocese of Thrace had constituted the Eastern Empire. The remaining three prefectures formed Gratian's and Valentinian II's Western Empire. When the Visigoths spilled out of Thrace into the Illyrian Dioceses of Dacia and Macedonia, most of the prefecture of Illyria was transferred to the Eastern Empire to facilitate Theodosius's campaign to contain the enemy. This transfer was to be strictly temporary. As the Illyrian dioceses were purged of the enemy, they were returned to the Western Empire. By July 383, these transfers were complete. At our assembly, the prefect informed us that Theodosius was reannexing Illyria, minus Greece, once again as a defensive move against the usurper. The government of Valentinian II, with most of the Western Army in Gaul, agreed with this. The prefect ended his address by ordering us all confined to barracks until noon. At that point, our centurions would inform their individual units of changes in their responsibilities.

The centurions (century commanders) and the tribunes (regiment commanders) met with the prefect (legion commander) for much of the morning. At noon, our centurion gathered our unit together to inform us of what had been discussed.

"All right, the situation is this. Our current responsibilities of border patrol and convoy escort will continue. In addition, we are going to be trained as river marines. Other units stationed here permanently have been trained in these capabilities, and we are going to be brought up to the same level of proficiency. The purpose of this training is to enable us to provide escort duty for convoys providing supplies to besieged river fortresses should the need arise. Secondly, in this capacity, we will also provide protection to ships transporting trade goods to these same ports to ward off activity by bandit gangs. Our marine training will commence at the beginning of next week. These new responsibilities had been planned before the murder of our beloved Gratian. Events of the last five years have shown that individual units, be they in frontier garrisons, the mobile field armies, or simply reservists, must be more flexible, and by that I mean capable of filling in for one another in case of disaster. The world is changing, and we no longer have the luxury to be specialists in only specific military arts. We must, at least to some degree, be familiar with them all. On the subject of bandit gangs, our land patrols are to be expanded. In addition to our border control responsibilities, we will be conducting mounted infantry expeditions against bandit groups whenever called upon to do so. Just as we will be escorting river convoys, we will also be providing protection for their overland counterparts. Instead of being an exception to the rule, as our mission to Naissus appeared to be earlier this summer, overland convoy protection is going to become one of our ongoing responsibilities. As you can see, our unit mission has been drastically expanded, but keep in mind that we will not be trying to do all these things at once. We will be sharing these duties on a rotating basis with other units stationed nearby."

In the weeks ahead, we were trained intensively as marines. We practiced boarding "enemy" ships, firing volleys of arrows accurately from a pitching deck, making riverine landings, and so on. During this period, we were also given a series of undertakings that we found rather demoralizing: along with other units, we razed to the ground a number of small, fortified watchtowers along the south bank of the Danube as far east as the Iron Gate. A number of them had been destroyed or damaged during the aftermath of Hadrianople by barbarian assaults. These structures had provided advance warning of barbarian incursions to units stationed in nearby major fortresses and had provided a vital function as long as the level of engagement was low. However, a number of their isolated units had been wiped out by massive assaults even though the attacking Visigoths lacked what we would consider to be proper siege equipment. The decision was made by Theodosius to abandon both the damaged and surviving watchtowers and to raze them all to the ground. The men formerly stationed in these places were reassigned to units in the major fortresses to satisfy the manpower shortages in the garrison legions. I was too young at the time to fully appreciate the strategic consequence that was prefigured by abandoning these small outposts. In times past, we had retreated from overly ambitious frontiers without suffering any adverse effects. The Antonine Wall in Caledonia had been abandoned in favor of the much superior Hadrian's Wall to the south. We had withdrawn from our original province of Dacia, north of the Danube, when barbarian pressures rendered it indefensible. However, the act of forsaking these outposts on the frontier that had been established at the time of Julius and Augustus Caesar was of far greater import than the value of any one of them might indicate. This frontier went back to the very period when the imperial system of government was established. If minor outposts were to be abandoned on the Danube, might not the Rhine suffer a similar process? And if we could justify (or at least rationalize) relinquishing them, might we not soon be departing from, or at least reducing the size of, major fortresses on what we had for centuries considered our natural frontier? This, as we know, would eventually come to pass, all in the name of a more economical use of resources.

As September passed into October, one thing became quite clear. Even if considerations pertaining to the Visigoths and the Iranians had not precluded it, it was too late in the year for Theodosius to consider a counteroffensive to destroy the usurper. We were told by our centurion that such a campaign could occur no sooner than 385, if then.

A significant point that is often overlooked in discussing the aftermath of Hadrianople is that the Roman Fleet never lost its control of the Danube. Security on the river itself is a responsibility shared by the Pannonian Fleet, centered at Taurunum, and the Moesian Fleet, whose headquarters is at Noviodunum[16] near the end of the Danube. At the point where the Sava River flowing east and coming up from the south empties into the Danube, it forms the boundary between Pannonia on the west and Moesia to the east. At the confluence, Taurunum is on the west bank, while Belgrade is on the east. While Belgrade is much larger than Taurunum, the latter headquarters the Pannonian Fleet though it uses the facilities of both ports. The boundary line separating the zones of responsibility of the two fleets varies periodically, depending on the military demands of the time. After the Battle of Hadrianople, the two fleets were responsible for supplying all the fortress towns from Belgrade to the mouth of the Danube (a distance of about seven hundred miles). The respective hinterlands of these cities were too insecure to supply even basic foodstuffs. The Moesian Fleet would bring supplies that had frequently originated in Greece and Asia Minor upstream from the mouth of the river. When I arrived in Belgrade, the Pannonian Fleet was operating as far downstream as the Iron Gate. Previously, it had been functioning farther east by using the canal system that Emperor Trajan had built around this gorge over 250 years earlier. The Iron Gate is the last and most dangerous of a series of gorges that separate the Transylvanian Alps to the north and the Balkan range to the south. It is roughly two miles long and over five hundred feet wide, with soaring cliffs to either side. The earlier gorges are navigable, but the Iron Gate itself is almost impossible. Apart from occasional adventurous souls who chance it in small boats, all military and commercial traffic uses Trajan's canal to bypass its rapids.

As the autumn wore on, we spent more time on our expanded responsibilities. On November 11, the first day of winter, we were busy razing a watchtower downstream from Viminacium. On my nineteenth birthday in December, our century was scouting as mounted infantry for reported bandits in the Morava Valley. We did not find them. Thus, 383 passed into 384. To celebrate, I spent the evening of New Year's Eve with Makila, and then on New Year's Day itself, after taking our annual oaths to our emperors, Theodosius and Valentinian II, I wrote a letter to my sister Maria Patricia and sent her some gifts. In the two years and five months since I had left home, I had made no attempt to communicate with my family. Such contact was long overdue. I also gathered together the diary that I had been keeping of my experiences thus far and mailed both packages off to Cirencester and Trier respectively, by a reputable local courier. In spite of the impending civil war, normal communications had been kept open between the prefecture of the Gauls and the rest of the empire. Neither side wanted to needlessly aggravate the situation.

Whenever I had any spare time, I often rode out for trips in the countryside. There is really only one highway out of Belgrade, and that is the one that continues eastward along the right bank of the Danube. There is no highway to the south, and to head west you must first cross the Sava River to Taurunum where the highway forks. One road heads to the northwest up the Danube. The other develops into a network that heads up the Sava valley and connects with the head of the Adriatic Sea. Since Sirmium served as an occasional imperial headquarters it had a well-stocked public library and I visited it occasionally during my posting at Belgrade. For the most part, however, I tried to avoid the highways that I was employed to patrol and repair and to enjoy the back roads instead. I met a few girls, but none of them ever showed much interest. Soldiers are often regarded as a necessary evil in areas where they are stationed but I was never that much of a socializer anyway. Where women were concerned I stuck to the ones at the Waterfront Inn. My life had settled into somewhat of a pattern, and to this point, I was not especially disappointed with the way in which things had turned out.

During 384 and 385, a large number of Visigothic volunteers joined our Legion IV Flavia Firma to bring it to full strength. At the time of our arrival, the legion consisted of about a thousand men, but during our first two and a half years there, we lost about 150 of our original complement. Only a few had been killed in action while conducting escort or patrol duties. The rest had been lost to us due to retirements, discharges due to wounds or construction injuries, a few desertions, and so on. At full strength, we would number 1,200. The influx of such Visigothic volunteers was going on throughout many of the legions and cavalry regiments along the central and eastern Danube, and it struck a sour note among many of our veterans. Early on, there were instances of outright hostility between Roman soldiers (regardless of their nationality) and the new recruits, but they gradually dissipated over time. Working together and fighting against common enemies would aid the integration process considerably.

Starting in 385, regular Palatine cavalry regiments on the lower and central Danube started receiving Hun recruits. That came as a surprise to all of us. The implication was that at least some of the Huns were displeased with the conditions they found north of the Danube. They preferred to cast their lot with Romans who were complete strangers to them racially, linguistically, and in every other way, rather than stay with their own kind and continue to suffer hardship. Generally these Huns were not assigned to the garrison legions. However, since our century was being used to an increasing degree as a mounted infantry unit, our legionary prefect requested that some of the Huns be posted to Belgrade to instruct us in their methods of mounted warfare, especially in using the bow. After all, they had proven very effective against the Goths. These Huns, who were a rather affable group, were soon training us in the manner in which they fired their arrows either to the right or left while galloping at top speed during attack or retreat. An odd thing about them was that, in spite of their having inspired the utmost dread in native European populations for the past decade and a half, we felt no great degree of animosity toward them as a people. Apart from the crimes of small groups of criminals that are common to all nationalities, the Hunnish nation had not committed much in the way of aggressive acts against Rome to this point. In that respect, we got along better with the Huns than we did with the Visigoths.

After a long day of repairing roads in the summer of 385, our intrepid group agreed to meet at one of the smaller bars after a visit to the baths. As the evening wore on, it was obvious that something was bothering Chlogius. He was very quiet, which was unlike him, and he seemed distracted by something or other.

"What is it that has you preoccupied this evening?" I asked.

"Is it that obvious?" Chlogius replied.

"Yes. In fact, it has been for a couple of days now."

There was an awkward silence as Chlogius considered how to respond.

"It's the Visigoths. I'm just uncomfortable with them."

"Why?" Marcellinus asked. "Most of them seem all right to me."

"They seem that way to me too," Chlogius replied. "On an individual basis, I really haven't had trouble with any of them. What bothers me is the fashion in which the government is treating them collectively. This business of letting thousands of them join regular Roman Army units in areas where Visigoths have settled is, to my way of thinking, a mistake and potentially a dangerous one."

"Why do you say that?" asked Stephanus. "Things have worked out well with your people. Hundreds of thousands of Franks live in northern Gaul and serve loyally in local units. What's the problem?"

Chlogius paused again for a few moments before answering. "The problem is the manner in which these Visigoths, who until recently were our deadliest enemies, are being accepted into local Roman Army units as though they were native born. I'm a third-generation Roman. Both my grandfathers, when they emigrated into the empire from Germany and joined the army, were posted to units on the farthest frontiers. Initially, one served on the lower Danube, and the other in Syria. Removing them far from their homeland Romanized them in the quickest possible time.

Both men were eventually transferred to legions on the Rhine where they completed their service. Their sons, since they were Roman born, were Roman citizens and treated like anyone else. But as immigrants, my grandfathers paid their dues to obtain Roman citizenship by serving wherever Rome wanted them. I don't see these Visigoths doing that."

"Visigoths have served in the past and are probably serving now on the eastern frontier against the Iranians," I reminded him.

"The key words in what you just said were 'in the past,'" Chlogius replied, "meaning pre-Hadrianople. By serving locally, the Romanization process will take longer with these new people if, in fact, it takes place at all. When I get back to visit my relatives and friends in northern Gaul, I'll speak German to those whose Latin is poor or who don't know it yet or just because I feel like it. But so what? We think of ourselves as Romans. Marcus, you've mentioned that in Britain you frequently spoke one of the Celtic languages among your friends and at home, but did that make you any less of a Roman? Of course not. Through conquest or immigration, our ancestors were assimilated into the Roman culture and political system. By allowing well in excess of a hundred thousand Visigoths to settle in Thrace and their sons to serve in Roman Army units there, the government is undermining the Romanization process that other immigrants like the Franks and Bastarnians have undergone in the past. Take me for example. My Frankish name is Chlogio, but I always insist on using its Latin version of Chlogius. It's the same with our decurion Chlodomir. We always address him as Chlodomirus, and neither of us would take kindly to being addressed by the Frankish version of our names. Perhaps I'm expecting too much too soon, but I'm looking forward to the day when our Visigothic friends start Latinizing their names."

"Interesting points," Stephanus said. "Perhaps Theodosius and Gratian had originally intended to send at least some of the new Visigothic recruits to serve in the West prior to the revolt there. We'll probably never know now. Every large Germanic settlement within the empire has the element of a crapshoot in it, but they've worked out pretty well. The big test will come when we move against Magnus Maximus. How do we think the Visigoths will behave in Thrace while the bulk of the Eastern Army is off fighting in the West? Will they conduct themselves as they are supposed to or will they start rampaging again?"

"The peace treaty is only three years old," Marcellinus said. "I don't think the Visigoths are in any shape to go on the warpath anytime soon. From what I understand in conversations I've had with some of our new Gothic confreres, in their broken Latin, their folks back home are still busy getting used to their new surroundings. I agree with what Chlogius said on the issue of Romanization. Every barbarian that has ever been allowed to settle on Roman territory has had to live under Roman law just as everyone else in the empire does. Until now, that has also included settlements of pre-Hadrianople Visigoths. But this business of letting these latest Visigothic arrivals live under their own laws is total nonsense. What will happen when a native Roman and a Visigoth have a dispute of any kind? Whose laws will prevail? Having granted this legal concession to the Visigoths who were formerly under Fritigern and, therefore, our worst enemies, what's to stop previous groups of Visigoths that settled peacefully in the empire twenty or thirty years earlier from demanding the same concession? Why shouldn't all barbarian settlements within the empire, then make similar demands?

"Another thing that has thoroughly pissed off all citizens everywhere is the exemption from paying taxes that was granted to Fritigern's mobs. Are all other barbarian groups in the empire going to demand this exemption also? Without their paying taxes, how are the highways and bridges in their areas going to be maintained?"

"The assholes will probably solve that problem by ripping up the highways in order to use their paving stones to construct houses," Chlogius wisecracked.

"Seriously though," Marcellinus continued, "I'm afraid that the peace treaty with the Visigoths is one for which we might wind up paying a terrible price down the road. By agreeing to it, Gratian and Theodosius planted a seed that could cause a terrible unraveling process to start eventually. The only thing that has kept the Visigoths in a state of reasonable behavior so far is that they have the Hunnish problem north of the Danube to worry about."

"Speaking of the Huns there," I said, "whatever happened to them? Ten years ago, they were the greatest danger that civilized humanity had ever faced. Yet the only ones that we've ever seen in combat were the ones that we slaughtered back at that villa on the way to Naissus two years back. As we know, they are even volunteering for service in *our* army now. History is filled with ironies. Wouldn't it be the damnedest thing if the pure hell that Thrace and the surrounding dioceses underwent for six years was prompted by a danger that didn't even exist in the first place? We let the Visigoths in because they are in a panic over the Huns, who are supposedly at their heels. Then the Visigoths spend the next six years trashing their new homeland and weakening both themselves and the empire while paying almost no attention to the Hunnish menace at all. I trust I am not alone in my ignorance of the matter, but I readily admit to being rather confused."

"Aren't we all," said Chlogius in a resigned tone. "Stephanus, you graciously mentioned, a few moments back, what model immigrants my Frankish ancestors and their co-nationals turned out to be. However, another problem exists in connection with settling German immigrants in frontier areas. The geographical proximity of Franks living on both the Roman and German sides of the lower Rhine has created problems in the past that might serve as a forewarning with respect to the Goths. As recently as thirty years ago when Julian was in charge of Gaul, Franks on the German side of the Rhine felt they had a right to move to the Roman side in Batavia and Toxandria simply because other Franks lived there. They felt no obligation to be bound to any treaty of obedience under Roman law. They regarded these regions as Frankish and not Roman. Julian had to take military action to impress upon them the errors of their ways. We have allowed over one hundred thousand Visigoths to settle in Thrace, but what is to stop them from allowing other Gothic tribes, trans-Danube, from moving in as well? How are we going to monitor such activity, or are we?"

Our perplexity over the Gothic influx would only deepen in the years ahead but not immediately. In those first years after the peace treaty was signed, most of the Visigoths were model immigrants. To be certain, there were problems with bandit gangs among them but nothing that appeared overly dangerous. Most of them were as tired of fighting as we were. The big question in the minds of most of us, however, was how long would it take them to get their second wind? And when they got it, would the empire be faced with yet another round of conflict or would they choose to live peacefully as other barbarian immigrants had? The main reason why Rome had not had major problems with the Huns to this point was that they were having trouble solidifying their hold on their newly subjugated peoples north of the Danube. They were gradually succeeding, though, in their traditionally brutal fashion. This was not lost on the Visigoths.

The economy of Thrace was gradually getting back on its feet. Small Visigothic settlements and farmsteads started dotting the landscape in the northern part, and the great estates started returning to life. There had been as yet no emergence of the Visigothic "national army" that had been permitted under the Treaty of 382, and many of us tended to disregard that provision as the years went by. We had, however, forgotten the old adage about politics abhorring a vacuum. No national leader had emerged among the Visigoths since the deaths of Athanaric and Fritigern. It was naive to think that situation would last forever.

In 384, young Valentinian's general, Bauto, conducted a successful military expedition against Germanic tribes on the upper Danube. It was essentially a scaled-down version of the campaign that Gratian was in the process of conducting at the time of Maximus' revolt. Thwarted by Valentinian II's army, these Germans next attacked Gaul. It suited Maximus to see this as a plot to undermine his authority there, and relations between Gaul and Italy almost came to the boiling point. As a result, a meeting took place between Theodosius I and Valentinian II in September 384 at Aquileia, resulting in a closer working relationship between their two governments. It was a busy year for diplomacy in the East as well. Stilicho, a surprisingly young general at age twenty-four, headed an embassy to Ctesiphon in response to an Iranian mission to Constantinople. Heretofore, such a responsibility had been unheard of for a man with such an ethnic background. It was obvious that Theodosius was deeply impressed by Stilicho and had great plans in store for him. It had taken the new Iranian government of Sapor III the better part of a year to consolidate its control over the country. Stilicho's mission marked the beginning of a series of negotiations to resolve outstanding issues between Rome and Iran regarding our common frontier. It would include the partitioning of Armenia. Another three years of arduous diplomatic activity would be required to obtain a successful outcome. Later in 384, when Stilicho returned from Ctesiphon, he married Serena. She was the surviving daughter of Theodosius's late brother Honorius and had been adopted by her uncle shortly after her father's death. This marriage left no doubt in anyone's mind as to who the emperor's second-in-command would be, at least from a diplomatic standpoint, from now on.

Theodosius was in a bind. Since the emperor could not wait forever to attack Maximus, time was on the side of Iran; the longer they drew out the discussions, the more concessions they were certain they could exact from us. The seemingly endless bargaining to "finalize" the partition of Armenia did delay the opening of the campaign against Magnus Maximus, but this was not entirely to Rome's disadvantage. It provided time for the peace treaty with the Visigoths to mature without major disruption.

This raises an important point with respect to establishing security along the eastern frontier as opposed to the situation along the Rhine and Danube. The Persian Empire of Iran and our Eastern Empire share a common frontier of approximately eight hundred miles or more. When political agreements are signed between Constantinople and Ctesiphon, the agreement holds for our entire common frontier. Along the Rhine and Danube, there has never been a single group that controlled anywhere near that length of frontier. Wars with Iran are always very costly to both sides, but given that theirs is a unified civilized nation with an area somewhat comparable to our Eastern Empire, there is generally a much better chance that political disputes between the two can be resolved by diplomacy. This in turn would be less demanding of manpower and financial resources from a military standpoint. This was never the case on the Rhine and the Danube where military operations were almost always the only way to respond to the security problems posed by the Germans.

In 385, Theodosius arranged for one of his own chief civil servants to be appointed praetorian prefect of the Italies. This was Flavius Neoterius, who earlier served with distinction as praetorian prefect of the East when the struggle against the Visigoths was at its peak. In addition, that same year, Theodosius had the Mauritanian chieftain Gildo, an associate of his late father, appointed to his father's old office as count of Africa. Thus, Theodosius established a de facto protectorate over young Valentinian's territories in Italy and Africa. This last appointment would serve the emperor well but not his successors.

Desultory negotiations went on between Trier and Milan over the sordid affair of having Gratian's body transferred to Italy for proper burial by his family. The assassin refused to surrender it. For the first three years of his usurpation, Maximus tried to get official recognition of his regime from both Constantinople and Milan but especially Milan. Getting nowhere, Maximus then tried to outflank Milan and get the Catholic Church on his side. In correspondence with Pope Siricius, the usurper pointed out that while he himself persecuted Arian heretics who denied the divinity of Christ, the young Valentinian II tolerated them. The church, however, refused to recognize Gratian's murderer as a legitimate emperor. Like the negotiations with Iran, this endless bickering had also served to buy Italy and the Eastern Empire the time to gain additional strength.

In the summer of 385, I was promoted to decurion. The individual legions train their own decurions, and I had completed the relevant coursework during the previous winter. Our centurion, Julius Aranius, had been promoted to tribune and had taken over as our regimental commander. A man of Frankish ancestry named Fredemondus had been promoted to centurion and named as his replacement. There had been much shuffling of personnel among the numerous units stationed along the Danube during the previous two years. Men with families tended to be assigned to the frontier legions. Single men, on the other hand, were most frequently assigned to units in the mobile field army. While part of a frontier legion, I found myself acting more and more in a mounted infantry roll. This arrangement suited me and other younger men. It got us away from routine garrison responsibilities and into the field.

Escorting civilian and sometimes military convoys and hunting down bandit gangs provided a better chance for promotion. The latter activity, in addition, provided the opportunity for confiscating the plunder found on any bandits we apprehended. The rules attending such discovery were, and still are, conveniently vague: Any non-Roman thug captured anywhere wearing any part of a Roman Army uniform was executed on the spot. The assumption was that there was only one way in which he could have obtained it. Any Roman discovered to be operating as a member of a bandit gang could also be summarily executed for murder (assumed) and treason (known with absolute certainty if operating in the company of Visigoths). Any loot taken from bandits captured on the property where their crimes were committed was to be returned to the surviving victims if there were any. There have always been unfortunate stories of Roman soldiers acting as badly as the bandits themselves in such instances. If no victims survived, then all valuables were to be turned over to the office of the quaestor (i.e., chief financial officer) of the province. He would then return a certain percentage to the military unit involved as a reward. This percentage would vary from region to region, and I believe it still does. The loot taken from any bandit gangs captured in the open was pretty much fair game, although this was certainly not government policy. It too was supposed to be turned over to the quaestor. Unless something was a rare work of art or in some other way readily identifiable as to who its owner might be, it rarely found its way to the quaestor's office. As for cash, well, the reader can draw their own conclusion.

Most bandit gangs operating in Thrace, Dacia, and Macedonia consisted of relatively small numbers of men. If their numbers grew too large, then they would be more easily detected by nearby army patrols. Remaining small meant that they would be more difficult to spot, but on the other hand, they would almost certainly be wiped out if they were apprehended. Their plight had reached the point where they were in a quandary as to what to do. Fearing the latter more than the former, a number of smaller gangs banded together in the valley of the Morava River during the late summer of 385. Many large estate owners in the regions infested with the bandit gangs had retreated to the nearby cities where they also had residences. They were now operating their estates as absentee landlords. Some, however, transformed their villas into regular fortresses the way that some larger estate owners in Gaul had done. With the unfortified estates already picked clean and the fortified villas and the cities impregnable, the bandit gangs had to seek new opportunities. This resulted in civilian convoys traveling the region becoming ever more tempting targets.

A little over two years after we attacked the Huns at the villa, we were again escorting a large civilian convoy down the Morava River Valley. This time we were on the highway going down the west rather than the east side of the river. Since we had had our own way whenever confronted by hostile forces, we were perhaps not as attentive as we should have been. Our outriders had detected nothing when suddenly we were ambushed by a large gang of rebel Visigoths. They charged from the forest to our right against our part of the convoy, and a furious struggle ensued. We were taken completely by surprise, and our casualties quickly started to mount. It was the worst battle that most of us had ever been in. Though we were into the autumn, it was a very hot day, and the sweat had been pouring off us before the battle had started. Initially I saw similar attacks taking place up and down the length of our right flank, but in the rising dust and chaos, I soon had no idea of what was happening elsewhere. This is the course that most battles follow. Our centurion and century sergeant major were among the first to go down with serious wounds, while three of our ten decurions were killed in action and two others were wounded. From somewhere in the confusion, I was struck across the helmet by a sword, and my head suddenly felt a ringing sound as though it were being used as the clapper in a church bell. The blow caused me to lose my orientation. With perspiration running into my eyes, I was momentarily blinded, and as I blinked with as much intensity as I could to ease the stinging, I received a sword slash across the face. The man who did it was quickly killed by another man in my decade, but, ironically, the wound helped to bring me back to my senses. The screams and groans and curses of the dying, wounded, and struggling seemed to be coming from every direction. Fortunately, there were sufficient numbers of us so that we managed to drive the Visigoths off before they did any damage to the convoy itself. The battle was only a marginal victory for us. Of the seventy-six men in our century alone, eleven were killed and twenty-three were wounded. We had withstood the brunt of the attack. Another century also acting as mounted infantry came to our assistance and took casualties as well. We never did determine how large a force had attacked us, but by the time they were driven off, they had left twenty-three dead on the battlefield and another twenty-eight seriously wounded. Our casualties were so severe that there was no room for generosity after the action was over. Those of us who had survived soon saw to it that the enemy wounded joined their dead.

My facial wound was not that serious. It had bled profusely at first, and as a result, my uniform was covered in blood. I looked a lot worse off than I was, and I had to keep explaining to the medics that men hurting more than I should be tended to first. I was finally told to shut up and lay down while a doctor sewed me up. The stitching was very painful, but I was grateful that they were using linen and not woolen sutures because the latter can shrink considerably, thus adding to the pain and disfigurement. Later I discovered that another soldier, more seriously wounded than I was but with a similar cheek wound, was unconscious when his face was stitched. When he awakened, he was horrified to discover that the doctor who operated on him had accidently sewn his tongue to his cheek. Thus, the stitching had to be cut out and redone all over again. When I heard that, the pain in my own cheek lessened considerably. One should not think unkindly of the quality of care we received from our medical staff. Nowhere on earth do doctors work under more formidable conditions than those who work in wartime or quasi-wartime circumstances. They always did the best they could for us in environments that no civilian doctor can imagine. I had always been clean-shaven, but as a result of that wound, I grew just enough of a beard to cover it and allow it time to heal. A number of my friends had grown beards, but I had always been loath to do so. Now I had no choice. Eventually I came to like it and decided to let it stay.

With so many of our senior personnel killed or wounded, I was ordered by the commander of another century to take our dead and most seriously wounded back to Aureus Mons on the Danube. Those whose wounds were minor stayed with the convoy. After loading all our casualties aboard wagons, we left immediately. I had with me my own decade plus four others that had also suffered heavy losses. We had backtracked north a considerable distance when an incident occurred about which I still have mixed emotions. We spotted a small convoy of six unescorted wagons heading toward us. It had probably left Aureus Mons the day after we had. Since it was small and unescorted, I concluded that it was probably carrying bulk goods of no great value for a relatively short distance. The problem was that it was strewn all over the road. The wagon master was not exercising proper discipline, and I rode up ahead to tell him to get his wagons over to the side so that we could pass by him.

"Sir, pull your wagons over to the side. I have wagons filled with dead and badly wounded soldiers that I have to get to Aureus Mons immediately."

I was astonished that the man who appeared to be in his early fifties simply ignored me.

Thinking him deaf, I repeated what I said to him in a louder voice. He looked over at me and snarled, "I don't have to take orders from some young son of a bitch like you. You goddamned soldiers think the whole bloody world owes you a living. Well, I owe you nothing. So go screw yourself."

"Sir," I repeated, "for the last time, get your wagons over to the side of the road. I have wounded men that I must get to a hospital."

At this, he raised his whip and threatened to use it on me. I immediately backed off and raced back to my ambulance convoy to the south. I was so enraged I went ballistic. I picked half a dozen soldiers from the five tattered decades under my temporary command. After informing them of the situation and what I was going to do about it, we galloped back to the civilian convoy that was still clogging up the highway and went straight for their miserable excuse for a leader. He laid his whip on one of my soldiers, but we quickly seized him. Since none of his fellow teamsters raised any protest at this, I assumed that he might be as popular with them as he was with me. I ordered the man tied to a stout oak tree and had his shirt torn from him. I then laid into him with his own whip. The more I flogged him, the more I wanted to flog him. He was a tough old bastard. For the first twenty lashes, he never uttered a sound, although he continually twisted in agony. Soon after, he started groaning but never really cried out in the way that I thought and hoped he would. Eventually he went unconscious, and his contortions stopped, but I just kept flailing away at him. By the time I was finished, blood had been splashing everywhere. My fellow soldiers were astounded at what I had done and I did not know whether the man was dead or alive. Neither did I care. I ordered one soldier to get a bucket from one of the wagons and fill it with water from the roadside ditch. After tossing it and several other buckets full on the man, he started moaning and said something that was unintelligible. I didn't give a damn what he was trying to say as I grabbed him by his beard.

"You've held out pretty well, you old cocksucker," I sneered at him. "I flogged you 110 times: seventy-six for each man in my century when we entered combat early this morning; eleven more for the men who died trying to keep this highway safe even for ungrateful buggers like you; and then I gave you an additional twenty-three visits from the lash for the gravely wounded men in my century who might yet join the dead in part because of your ingratitude. Let this be a warning to you, Fuzzy. The next time that you see a Roman Army column on the road, show some respect and move to one side. And if you think there is the slightest chance that I might be numbered among the ranks of that column, you'd better head for the tall grass because if I ever see you again, anywhere, I'll have your balls for bookends. By the way, now you know what a son of a bitch really is, don't you."

I dropped his head and walked back to my horse without ever looking back at the man. By the time I had mounted up, all the wagons were off to one side of the highway and our own convoy had caught up to us.

We got the wounded back to Aureus Mons as quickly as we could, but for three of them it was too late. After we arrived back in Belgrade, our battered unit was a given several days off to rest and recuperate. Of the twenty seriously wounded who survived, several were crippled badly enough to receive discharges. In one of the bars one night, we sat around thinking about the past week's events. We were disgusted by the manner in which we had blundered into the ambush. In particular,

I had a strangely ambivalent feeling about my own behavior with the irresponsible wagon master that I had almost flogged to death. Ever since the incident occurred, I had been wondering about what past experience in his life might have triggered his hateful attitude toward the army. What concerned me even more was the nature of my own reaction to him. I had never behaved so violently toward anyone except in a combat situation. Had a dark side of my character, of which I had no prior knowledge, suddenly revealed itself? It was deeply disturbing, and I was uncertain as to how I should handle it.

"You know the latest line making the rounds through the entire legion, don't you, chaps?" Marcellinus asked rhetorically. "It's whatever you do, do not ever get our friend Marcus pissed off at you. Flogger Cedranus here might just wind up becoming a legionary legend."

"You didn't witness the near-execution though; I did," Stephanus added. "It was more than just a flogging. I think the byname might more appropriately be Shredder Cedranus based on my firsthand observations."

They were having great fun at my expense, but I was less than amused.

"That actually places him in pretty good company based on what I've heard about Theodosius," Chlogius suggested. He had been wounded in the arm by a sword thrust and was in the process of recovering. "The emperor apparently has quite a violent temper, but as quickly as he explodes, he usually cools back down again before any real harm is done."

Five years, literally, down the road, there would be the most terrible exception to that general rule imaginable.

It was decided that our unit would be taken off patrol and escort duties until our wounded had recovered and new recruits (meaning Visigoths) had been obtained to fill in the holes in our century's roster. We were first employed tearing down ruined or abandoned watchtowers on the Danube as we had done earlier. When we razed these structures, we loaded every stone, brick, and board onto the ships that had transported us to the site. The rubble was then delivered to various points on the Danube where it could be reused in maintaining roads or rebuilding the fortresses. We were kept busy that way until it got too late in the year and the Danube shipping season came to an end.

We trained hard, as we always did during the winter months, to be fit for any action in which we might have to engage. Near the end of 385, we were surprised when we received orders to report to Skopje in southwestern Moesia just north of the border with Macedonia. In an earlier age, this city had been a legionary base. At Skopje, we were more than twice as far from Belgrade than we had ever been. We had been sent to this region in the upper reaches of the Axios River Valley because a large bandit gang had been operating there for several months. Normally a unit such as ours would not be operating at such a great distance from its official home base for what are essentially police duties. However, the top military authorities wanted us there for two reasons: If it was the gang that we had tangled with the previous autumn, then it was hoped that we might be able to identify it as such. The fact that we had a score to settle with these outlaws would be an additional motivating factor in our hunt for them. Thus 385 passed into 386.

The other units with which we were cooperating in the search were also mounted infantry units. It would be self-defeating to use cavalry for a campaign like this because speed was of the essence. Whenever information was received that the bandits had been spotted, the military forces pursuing them had to be able to get to the scene as soon as possible. Mounted infantry can travel quicker than cavalry, and the enemy was not expected to be heavily armored. Only some of the men we fought in our previous battle wore any armor, while the rest wore little or nothing in the way of extra body protection. Pickings had been slim lately and were getting slimmer. We had been on the hunt for almost four weeks and had neither heard nor seen anything of the enemy. The terrain in the region of the upper Axios River is mountainous. Combining the two, we were beginning to despair of ever coming to grips with the men that had almost defeated us the previous year.

Then one afternoon we got lucky. There had been a light dusting of snow the night before but not nearly enough to hamper us. We were off the main highway patrolling a back road that led toward the mountains when we saw some civilians running down the road toward us. However, when they saw us, they panicked and started running every which way off the road to get away from us. We were patrolling with two other centuries, and we immediately divided and started chasing down these people to determine what the problem was. We eventually rounded everybody up and determined that they were tenant farmers working on an estate that had suddenly been attacked by a large gang of outlaws. They were terrorized and appeared very suspicious of us, even though they now realized that we were on their side. We took five of them with us to show us where the estate was and to fill us in on any particulars that we should know about the place. We continued for almost a mile along the road past well-tended fields. Finally we rounded a hill and saw a fortified villa under siege. The attack had taken place so quickly that these tenant farmers had been unable to reach the safety of the villa. By the time we arrived, the Visigoths were furiously hurling themselves against the main gate with a small battering ram. They lacked any other siege equipment and had already paid a heavy price to the archers on the walls.

The wall surrounding the villa more than made up for what the site lacked in elevation. Like the villa where we had attacked the Huns, this one was situated about a quarter mile off the highway. Its entry road met our road at a right angle. The property had a heavy line of mature trees lining both the highway and the approach road that acted as a shield for us. In the confusion of the battle at the villa, the Visigoths failed to see us approaching until we were all lined up ready to attack them. All thoughts of breaking into the villa were dropped. The Visigoths were doomed, and they knew it. With their backs literally against the villa's front wall, they formed a battle line to defend themselves against us. We poured volley after volley of arrows into them while at the same time they were taking fire from the private archers on the wall. Possessing far more ammunition and manpower than the Visigoths did, we were able to cut them down at an almost leisurely pace. At the end, there were only about a dozen of them left when they threw up their arms in surrender. Looking over the captives and the bodies of the dead and wounded, we failed to identify any of them positively from our battle of the previous year. Neither could we exclude the possibility of their having been there.

The villa's owner came out and thanked us for the assistance we had rendered, but he did not invite us in. That was something no owner of one of these fortified estates would ever do. We went around dispatching the wounded and left it up to the private army of the villa owner to burn their corpses. Since we had done most of the killing, we stripped the dead of everything of value, which incensed the archers lining the wall. However, there was nothing they could do about it.

We took the prisoners to Skopje, where they were tortured by government interrogators that had been sent up from Thessalonica about 120 miles to the south. Some of them did confess to having been in battle with us the previous autumn and admitted to numerous other crimes as well. Of course, after the inquisitors had worked on them for only a short time, the cutthroats would have gladly confessed to anything. They were then all shipped off to Thessalonica where they would be thrown to wild animals in the arena. The Christian Church had done its best to eliminate this type of capital punishment. While its frequency of occurrence had declined in recent decades, even the most pious of emperors reserved to themselves the right to use it in extreme circumstances. The terror to which bandits had subjected the Morava-Axios valley regions in recent years was sufficient to justify its use in this case. We were sorry that we could not attend. Before we left Skopje, our centurion, Fredemondus, gathered us together for a brief address.

"Tomorrow morning, we will be leaving Skopje and returning to Belgrade via Naissus," he began. "You men can all take great pride in what you have achieved through our policing campaigns in recent years. You have discharged your responsibilities in the most exemplary manner possible, and I'm proud to be the commanding officer of every one of you. It is the conclusion of our top commanders that, with our elimination of the last major criminal gang in this area, our mopping up operations are at an end. Local units should be able to handle such activity from now on. Mission accomplished."

Our return to base provided us with very little rest. Once there, we returned to the more standard garrison duties while new recruits continued to join our ranks. By the beginning of April, five men in my decade were Visigoths. Almost one-third of our entire legion was composed of them by this time. The most important thing, once they joined, was teaching them to speak Latin. Many of those whose families had migrated into the empire prior to 376 could already speak it or at least had a working knowledge of it since some of them had been born south of the Danube. Near the end of April, while out for a night's carousing with my usual group, two of the new Visigothic volunteers in my decade entered. I invited them to join us and introduced Sigismund and Hilderic to the others.

"Where are you fellows from?" asked Chlogius rather coldly.

"We both come from near Oescus," Hilderic, the more talkative of the two, replied. "If you've never been there, it's far to the east of here, roughly halfway between Belgrade and the Black Sea."

"How did you wind up here?" asked Marcellinus. "I thought you fellows were mostly being recruited for the legions and the Palatine regiments in Thrace."

"That's been true until recently," Sigismund replied. "When the two of us showed up at the headquarters of Legion V Macedonica, which is stationed at Oescus, we were told that their quotas were full. So here we are. More and more Visigoths that join up are finding themselves in units based farther to the west all the time."

"I've heard that the garrison in Milan is largely composed of both Visigoths and Ostrogoths," I said, "but I always felt that that was done more for political purposes than anything else. You know, showing the newly found unity between the Gothic and Roman peoples, showing how much trust we have in you, putting Hadrianople behind us and all that."

"Before you guys start dumping all over us as 'the enemy,' Siggi and I want you to know that we are native-born Romans," Hilderic was quick to point out. "Our parents migrated into the empire when they were only children, with our grandparents in the reign of Constantius II. Fritigern and his mobs did us no favors at all at Hadrianople, and none of us joined him afterward."

"How much time did you spend in basic training?" asked Stephanus.

"Ten weeks," Sigismund replied, "same as everyone else. Have any of you heard anything about the possibility of another invasion on the lower Danube?"

We veterans looked at one another questioningly.

"An invasion by whom?" I asked. "The Huns?"

"No," Hilderic replied. "There were rumors back in Oescus, just before we left, of a large number of people on the move, mostly Ostrogoths, but nobody seemed to know exactly where they were heading. Last year, a large group of them forced their way across the lower Danube in the Dobruja and briefly captured the small town of Halmyris before being chased out. Whether this is going to be the target again no one seems to know. There was also nothing definite as to whether it included entire families or just soldiers or what the exact number was. It was all quite vague, but that was three months ago. We haven't heard anything since then. I asked some recruits that we went through basic training with, including Visigoths, if they knew anything about it, but they said they did not."

The Battle of the Danube

Early one morning, about a week later, our century was taken off regular garrison duties and told that we would be moving into the field. Our centurion, Fredemondus, would give us no further details. We were given the rest of the day off, confined to barracks, and told to have our equipment ready for inspection by four o'clock in the afternoon. At that time, we would receive further orders. That night, we were on the Belgrade docks awaiting the arrival of transport ships from the Pannonian Fleet stationed at Taurunum next door. Even after we boarded and were underway, we were not informed as to what our final destination was. One thing we noticed was that we were traveling in the company of two other centuries from our legion. We instinctively sensed a major operation of some sort, but the only thing we knew for certain was that we were heading downstream. We traveled only at night, putting in at convenient ports during the daylight hours. We passed through the towns of Aureus Mons, Margum, Viminacium, and a couple of other smaller places until we reached the region of the Iron Gate. The approach to the Iron Gate was not too difficult at this time of the year because the Danube was still filled with the spring runoff from its numerous tributaries. We passed through Trajan's Canal to bypass its rapids and then reentered the Danube. It was all very mystifying.

During the winter, early in 386, another crisis had taken shape in the form of a Germanic alliance under the leadership of an Ostrogothic chieftain named Odotheus. He led his polyglot hoard, consisting of many thousands of people, to the left bank of the lower Danube in the Dobruja region. There he was confronted by a Roman army under the command of the experienced General Promotus. Odotheus demanded entry into the empire under similar conditions to those agreed to by Fritigern's Visigoths in 382. Theodosius, now possessing greater confidence in his rebuilt army, rejected this petition and prepared for war. One nation of potential troublemakers inside the empire was enough. Promotus evolved a brilliant strategy. He had a group of his Visigothic soldiers, in whom he had complete trust, approach Odotheus under the guise of being willing to betray the Roman Army for a very large sum of money. Odotheus balked at paying such a huge amount, but Promotus had instructed his "traitors" to insist on the entire amount or nothing. This they did during determined bargaining, and their stubbornness paid off. Odotheus became convinced that their treachery was sincere and made a large down payment to them with the rest to be paid after the battle was over. Prearranged signals were agreed to, and a night crossing of the Danube was planned further upstream where it was believed Roman Army units were less concentrated and in any case would be asleep.

Odotheus had not played his cards well. His army was sizable enough, but he had misjudged the weather. In the northwestern Balkans, the Mediterranean climate prevails. However, as one continues to the east, in the Danube valley, the climate becomes increasingly continental. The winters along the lower Danube are the coldest in the empire, and they last longer than anywhere else. As a result, the river usually thaws upstream much earlier than it does in its lower reaches. The still-frozen

Danube in eastern Thrace could not handle the enormous spring runoff from central and western Europe. Severe flooding was the result. So Odotheus and his invasion force and their families were stalled just as much by the weather as they were by the ongoing negotiations. Spring was almost over before the river was back within its banks. This gave Promotus plenty of time to fine-tune his strategy. All officers are taught that in making riverine and lacustrine landings, it is vitally important to choose a place that offers a broad front and few if any obstacles. The broader the front, the more soldiers can be landed on the bank or beach at once, the quicker a foothold can be secured, and the more difficult it is for the enemy to concentrate their forces. On a narrow front, an invader is limited as to the number of troops that can be landed at one time, the landing craft tend to pile up, making it more difficult for successive waves of troops to land, and the easier it is for a defender to mount a successful counterattack. For the "invasion," Promotus chose a long length of the east bank that offered a gentle slope and few impediments to securing a quick foothold. Odotheus bought it.

After exiting Trajan's canal, our officers still told us nothing of where we were headed. Once past the Iron Gate, the Danube passes through broad plains that extend on either side of the river. Its velocity slows drastically. As a result, sedimentation is a problem along the river through most of its remaining length to the Black Sea. River pilots must use extreme caution in many places. We stayed over for one day at the fortress town of Ratiaria.[17] Shortly after leaving it, we crossed over into the Diocese of Thrace and what had once been the heart of the caldron. The Danube, which forms the northern boundary of the diocese, soon presents a startling contrast between its two shores. To the south, the banks become quite steep, towering in height from four hundred to six hundred feet above the river level. These high bluffs have long facilitated Roman fortification and domination along the lower Danube. To the north is an area of marshes and lakes that parallels the river and serves as a buffer between the Danube and the northern plains. Between the Danube and the Balkan Mountains to the south lies the Moesian Plateau, the new Visigothic homeland. This flat, windswept plain is best suited to cattle and sheep grazing, although there are some wheat farms. The plateau is dissected by several meandering rivers that have cut deep valleys in winding their way from the Balkan Mountains north to the Danube. The valleys are more clement than the plateau but are sparsely populated. Only when this plateau approaches the Black Sea does the climate moderate and permit the growing of fruit crops.

The further into Thrace we sailed, the greater our sense of unease. After we passed the fortress town of Novae[18] it was obvious that Hilderic and Sigismund had been right. Perhaps the Dobruja was our destination. We continued ever eastward past Transmarisca and Silistra where the fateful Visigothic crossing had taken place ten years earlier. Soon we turned north and knew at that point we were in the Dobruja. Belgrade sits on the boundary between the Moesian Fleet (downstream) and the Pannonian Fleet (upstream). Since we had left Belgrade, we had covered 75 percent of the river that is patrolled by the Moesian Fleet, yet we had hardly seen any of its ships. Where was it and where on earth were we going? Then suddenly we stopped, and each centurion informed his troops of their mission. Many thousands of soldiers, marines, and sailors were involved. The army had quietly brought up a large number of legions and Palatine regiments from both the mobile field army and some of the more southerly garrisons and positioned them just east of the river. The Moesian Fleet had been doing from the east what the Pannonian Fleet had been doing from the west: bringing troops and supplies from a number of different provinces to determine the fate of the Ostrogothic hoard decisively and with a maximum loss of Germanic blood. After night fell, the trierarch in command of our ship positioned us in the first of the three ranks into which the ships of both fleets had been arranged. The rank of "trierarch" comes from the time when all the mainline ships in the navy were triremes. These ships were propelled by three rows of sailors but went out of use during the reign of Constantine I. They were replaced by the faster single-decked vessels like the one we were on. Everything was ready.

The Ostrogoths and their allies attacked on what was a moonless night but were stunned by what was waiting for them. Promotus had gathered an enormous number of ships and had arranged our three ranks for a distance of almost three miles. Odotheus had expected a rather easy victory, and that was achieved—except this time the Goths and their allies were on the losing side. After waiting in the dark for what seemed like an eternity, the word was whispered to us that the enemy was on its way. By this time, we were into the small hours of the morning. We then heard the noise of their enormous flotilla of rafts approaching. The sky then suddenly lit up as our land-based soldiers sent a barrage of incendiary arrows high into the pitch-black sky. The entire river seemed to be illuminated, and the thousands of soldiers and marines aboard ship and land sent volley after volley of arrows into the stunned Ostrogoths. Unknown to us, hundreds of catapults had been brought up behind us. They started hurling missiles into the river, and while only a small number of their stones scored direct hits, their misses certainly added to the confusion on the Ostrogothic side. The battle quickly turned into a massacre, with the Germans losing several thousand dead, while Roman casualties were quite small.

Because of our base of origin, we were placed on the southern flank of the defenders. Some Ostrogoths did break through the center of our line well to the north of us where they had concentrated proportionately more of their forces. But those that actually landed on the right bank were quickly cut down by our land-based forces. No enemy Germans in our sector got to within one hundred feet of us. The land-based archers with their incendiary arrows kept the river very well lit. As a result, we could level our fire accurately at the enemy. We so outnumbered the Ostrogoths attacking us in our sector that many of them were only able to fire their arrows blindly; the hail of Roman arrows and stones upon them was so continuous. Just as dawn was starting to break, Fredemondus ordered us to cease fire. By this time, the carnage we had caused was visible without any artificial light. Looking off to the right, we could see the sluggish river carrying a large number of corpses. Many of the Ostrogothic dead that night drowned while trying to swim laden with whatever armor they were wearing back to the western bank. It was a hopeless notion.

"Sir," I yelled, "why the cease-fire order? There are still a large number of Ostrogoths alive on the river."

Fredemondus turned and faced us. It was a safe thing to do; no enemy arrows had been fired in our direction in over an hour.

"Gentlemen, the cease-fire order has come directly from the emperor. The trierarchs are about to set course into the central part of the river. Our ships were not arranged in their three ranks by the vicissitudes of fortune. The first rank was selected to act as an invasion force once the Ostrogoths had been defeated. Our forces will be supplemented by some land-based units that will be transported across by ships located downstream. The second and third ranks of ships will now start scanning the river for survivors. We are to take as many captives as possible. Anyone resisting is to be killed. After all this, I don't think we'll find too many diehards over there. Based on our intelligence estimates, the bulk of their army has perished either in battle or through drowning. While the major portion of the battle is over and it's time to make the slave markets happy, we must constantly be on our guard."

"Sir," I asked, "did you say that the emperor is here?"

"Yes. He arrived yesterday at the headquarters of our supreme commander. I would think that he will be reviewing us all when the campaign is over, but that is just speculation on my part."

The entire first rank of ships sailed across the Danube. Having just butchered the invading army, we landed in a "cold" landing zone with no hostile forces anywhere. Nonetheless, we wasted no time getting ashore. Fortunately, it was also devoid of marshland, unlike much of the left bank of the lower Danube. Most men we encountered were middle aged or elderly and offered little resistance once they realized their army was history. We captured several thousand civilians who had accompanied the invaders and were awaiting a signal to cross from the far bank that never came. Those Ostrogoths who survived and were fit were allowed to settle with their families in Phrygia in western Asia Minor and join the army. Those unfit for military service were sold into slavery.

It had taken several hours to obliterate the Ostrogothic army. It took the better part of two days to round up all the prisoners on the west bank along with their wagons, animals, and other goods and ship them across the Danube. This had been the greatest victory of Theodosius's reign. In terms of casualty ratios, it compared favorably with Julian's great victory at Strasbourg in 357. After dispensing the prisoners, we were informed by Fredemondus that the emperor would inspect all participating units the following morning. Not having slept in two days, we then got a good night's rest under the stars.

The next day, the inspection took place. With the possible exception of Julian, Theodosius I was the most informal emperor to reign during the fourth century. He was a soldier's soldier and was determined that every man in the army would see him that way. Strung out for miles along the highway, it was impossible for the emperor to address us all at once. So our units were grouped into clusters to economize the monarch's time. Being on the southern flank, we were the ones that Theodosius spoke to last. He was thirty-nine, a rather good-looking man and dressed more flamboyantly than we had expected. After Theodosius had ridden along the highway to the center of our group and turned his mount to face us, we saluted him. The emperor returned our salute and commenced his address:

"Soldiers of Rome. I cannot congratulate you enough for the bold and courageous manner by which you delivered this calamitous defeat to our enemies. God only knows it's about time we had an easy one, eh?" We all laughed. "The victory that you have achieved is the most decisive that Rome has accomplished since I became your emperor. I appreciate that many of you endured long and arduous travels to arrive here but that you, nonetheless, were able to hurl yourselves into the conflict to defend the honor and glory of our sacred land.

"We are estimating five thousand enemy either killed in action or drowned and ten thousand men, women, and children taken prisoner either on the western shore or from the river itself. Let the unconstrained greed and thoughtlessness of our recent enemies, whose corpses now lie burned in heaps everywhere or on the bottom of the Danube, thanks to your brilliance and bravery, stand as a warning to all enemies of Rome on all frontiers. By your dedication and determination, you have embellished the honor and tradition of Roman arms that extend over one thousand years. You were chosen carefully for this undertaking. We knew, based on the records that you have amassed in a variety of undertakings that the enemy's destruction was assured once he encountered your arms. You men have risked your lives in numerous operations to defend and secure the motherland in the past, and we had the utmost confidence that you could be relied upon to add glory to the might of Roman arms once again. There have been few times in all of Roman history in which the ratio of enemy losses to our own has been so enormous. Distressing as our losses are, these men can be buried with distinction and our everlasting gratitude. Your exploits in our just cause will not go unrewarded. May God grant you a swift and safe journey back to your homes."

The emperor and our units exchanged salutes, and we soon boarded our ships for the return trip up the Danube. Once back in Belgrade, we returned to routine duties that filled up most of the summer. My evenings I spent with Makila whenever possible. In August, I was called into the centurion's office.

"Marcus," he said, "I am reassigning you. As you know, Lucianus is retiring next month. With his departure, the office of century signifer is open, and I want you to take it."

"I'm grateful for the offer, sir," I replied, "but I prefer to continue operating in the field."

Fredemondus smiled. "I'm not leaving it up to you to accept or reject. I'm ordering you to take it. You've been with this century for three years now, and you've proven yourself in the field. You will have opportunities to prove yourself there again. After all, the situation with Magnus Maximus is not going to go on indefinitely. When Theodosius eventually confronts him, every able-bodied man in the army will be needed. My need, this century's need, for a new signifer is immediate. I feel that with your education, you are probably as well qualified as anyone for the position. The responsibilities of a signifer require a man both literate and numerate. That's you. Starting tomorrow, you will be acting as Lucianus' understudy so that when he retires you will be able to fill in for him right away. I have a replacement for you, as decurion of your decade that I will be announcing shortly. Apart from the century's immediate need, I believe you will find serving as a signifer beneficial to you insofar as future promotion is concerned. You have a far better education than most, you get along well with everyone, you command your men well, and you are respected by them. Whenever you are offered a position that is foreign to your experience, take it. It will serve to broaden your familiarity with military organization and responsibilities. If I didn't think that both you and the outfit would benefit, I would never have recommended you for the posting."

Sensing that he was right, I accepted and thanked him.

As signifer, I was the standard bearer for our century and responsible for our portion of the regiment's savings bank. In times past, each legion had maintained its own bank. However, on more than one occasion back in the old days when a legion contained 5,500 men, the savings banks contained so much money that legionary commanders were able to use them as a financial basis for furthering their almost always fatal political ambitions. Nowadays, legions only number 1,200 men, and savings banks are maintained at the level of the regiment, not the legion. In addition to maintaining our portion of the regimental bank, I was also our unit paymaster and in charge of keeping all century personnel records. In the days of the Caesar, Flavian, and Antonine dynasties, personnel records were maintained by men with the title of librarian. However, as the level of literacy declined in the third century and the manpower crisis set in, the position of librarian was gradually folded into that of signifer. Office postings always seem somehow less manly to a combat soldier than a field position. This is especially true when we are young. However, my centurion was right. Taking the position was a good career move because it familiarized me with the record-keeping responsibilities of a century. In addition, it served to introduce me to the staffs of the other centuries in our regiment as well as those at the regimental and legionary level.

In September, Fredemondus again called me into his office one morning. Eventually about twenty of us jammed into a room that had never been designed to hold so many.

"Gentlemen, good news," he said. "The emperor is holding a triumph in Constantinople on October 12 in honor of the Battle of the Danube. He wants representatives from all units that participated to attend. It's up to the discretion of the centurions and tribunes of those units to determine who goes. Now you all know why you are here. Get your affairs in order because you will be leaving tomorrow. As you all probably know by now, Theodosius, his piety notwithstanding, has a reputation as quite the party animal. So by all means enjoy yourselves but do try not to humiliate your beloved legion too much by excessive behavior, eh?"

We were all stunned: Constantinople! None of us had ever dreamed that we would one day get to the eastern capital. The next day, we left Belgrade and traveled familiar ground to Naissus. We had never been east of that city before, but that would all change now. From Naissus, we traveled up the Nisava River valley toward Sofia. The city of Sofia is located in a basin amidst elevated and jagged mountains. The region is well drained by four rivers that flow to the northwest (the Nisava), the north (the Oescus), the south (the Strymon), and the east. It is well located from the standpoint of being militarily defendable. In fact, Constantine the Great had considered it as the site for his "New Rome" before initially selecting ancient Troy and then finally settling on Byzantium.

Just east of Sofia, we entered the Diocese of Thrace, more particularly that section of it that lies south of the Balkan Mountains and north of the Rhodope Mountains and the Aegean Sea. This region constitutes the true heartland of Thrace and consists of a series of well-watered river basins containing rich farm land. In spite of the terrible vicissitudes to which Thrace had been subjected, its population had remained consistently at about one million.[19] The Balkan Mountains run about 330 miles west to east and effectively split the Diocese of Thrace into a northern third (the Moesian Plateau) and a southern two-thirds. This mountain chain reaches a maximum elevation of 7,800 feet and acts as a climate barrier between the continental climate of the Moesian Plateau (the new Visigothic homeland) and the Mediterranean climate to the south. The mountain range itself is sparsely populated, although some mining and quarrying activities are carried out there. Sofia had held out well during the Visigothic invasion, but once we moved east of the city, we started to see just how savage that onslaught had been. Not far out of Sofia, we saw our first devastated estate and rode into it to get a firsthand look. It was or at least had been a typical Mediterranean-style villa and had evidently been quite prosperous at one time. There were several graves in the front of it, and all its fields were overrun with weeds. We could detect no activity of any kind on the property apart from a few untended animals off in the distance. An eerie stillness and silence pervaded the place. Attempting to reopen it would be an expensive proposition. Every building had been burned to the point where nothing, except the villa, could be rebuilt. We returned to the highway and pressed on, climbing upward to the east.

After we passed through the Succi Pass, we descended into the area where the Mediterranean climate prevails and the culture changes from Latin to Greek. Fruit crops of almost every description abound here: apples, pears, plums, cherries, peaches, grapes, and a number of others. We saw a couple of fortified estates that appeared to be recovering from the war, but they were the exception and not the rule. The further east we progressed, the worse the destruction. Estate after estate had been attacked, and their ruination was such that they could not make any sort of recovery in the foreseeable future. In some cases, the owner and his entire family had been murdered. Even in those cases where the estate had survived, it shrank anyway because so many of its tenant farmers had been conscripted into the army or had simply run off. As more Visigoths entered the Roman Army, many of these tenant farmer conscripts had been released back to their former estates. It would, however, take years for these farms to get back to their original level of prosperity if, indeed, they ever did.

We were now into the Maritza River valley, and as we approached the city of Philippopolis, the situation started to improve. The unfortified estates near any city had suffered less than those located a greater distance away. Visigothic gangs tended to avoid operating too close to urban centers because of the danger of being attacked themselves by regular army units from their garrisons. Aristocratic landowners, whose estates were near a walled city or town, often established residences in those towns. It was a cheaper alternative to fortifying their country estates. This was the opposite of what I had witnessed in much of Gaul. Continuing east from Philippopolis, the degree of destruction increased as we distanced ourselves from the city. There were instances where, for mile after mile, every single building had been destroyed. The croplands, orchards, and vineyards had all gone to ruin. When the situation started to improve again, when we saw villas being repaired and herds, flocks, crops, and orchards being tended, we realized we were approaching Hadrianople. Throughout the length of our journey east of Naissus, we had passed army units hard at work repairing the roads and bridges. We also started seeing more small collections of soldiers on the highway. Like us, they were veterans of the Battle of the Danube and were traveling east to Constantinople for the triumph. We journeyed north from Hadrianople the several miles to the site of that terrible battle. It hardly looked like any action had taken place there at all. Theodosius had seen to it that the dead were buried as soon as the army had secured the area, and all visible evidence of the catastrophe was eliminated.

It is 132 miles from Hadrianople to Constantinople, and the population density started to increase at a rather impressive rate as we neared the capital. This area had suffered initially from the Visigoths when they launched their futile attack on the capital in 378 but had quickly recovered. The port town of Perinthus, centrally located on the north shore of the Sea of Marmara, marked the midway point of this last leg of our journey. We felt that with so many soldiers arriving in the capital, there would be enormous pressure on the services of even so large a metropolis as the city of Constantine. We had made good time, so we spent two days in Perinthus just relaxing and enjoying ourselves. After all, we expected to get little rest in the great capital. One thing I certainly indulged at Perinthus was my predilection for seafood that is in notably short supply, to say the least, at stations on the central Danube. The capital was only three days away.

No complete legions or even regiments were present. Subunits from each infantry and cavalry regiment that had participated in the battle were invited for the triumphal parade along with similar representations from the naval squadrons. In addition, Theodosius wanted his triumph to pay tribute to the tireless efforts that had been performed by the rest of his army in suppressing the Visigoths since 378. Hence, the presence of units that had not taken part in the Danube campaign. What we found awaiting us on the western outskirts of Constantinople was the biggest tent city any of us had ever seen. Preassigned accommodations had been set up to house us all. Units were rehearsed in the order in which they were to march, and early on the morning of October 12, we were all lined up outside the southernmost gate in the Wall of Constantine. Much has changed in Constantinople since I first visited it in the autumn of 386. At that time, the wall that protected the city was the Wall of Constantine. As the city rapidly expanded to the west, it became necessary to extend its fortifications in that direction. As a result, in 413, the urban prefect of the city, Anthemius, commenced the construction of a new wall to encompass the suburbs. Known as the Wall of Theodosius II, it lies the better part of a mile to the west of the original. It has a length of four and a half miles and stretches from the Sea of Marmara on the south to the Golden Horn on the north. The wall stands thirty feet high and is sixteen feet thick with ninety-two watchtowers standing sixty feet in height. In the year in which I completed this work, 439, the construction of sea walls began. Along the Golden Horn, the sea wall will also stand thirty feet high and contain 110 watchtowers. The wall that stretches along the shore of the Sea of Marmara will stand twenty feet high and will include 188 watchtowers when complete.

The units that participated in the Danube campaign were aligned according to their geographical disposition during the battle. Since we were on the left flank, we were located at the very end. That, however, did not diminish our enthusiasm. The parade had been divided up into sections of several hundred soldiers, and each section had been provided with its own marching band. On the proper command, we set off to the beat of trumpets, drums, and a number of other instruments I had never seen before. Once we passed through the gate, we were met by an enormous and still boisterously cheering throng. They knew that the army, at enormous cost, had delivered them and the Eastern Empire from great danger, and the capital's populace was not reluctant in showing its appreciation. There were large banners welcoming us to the city, and flower petals rained down from every direction. In fact the road was quite slippery with them. Shortly after entering the city, we marched through what is now called the Forum of Arcadius.

Continuing along High Street, we passed through the Ox Market and over the Lycus River, the main watercourse through the city. As High Street approaches the Aqueduct of Valens from the southwest, it makes almost a ninety-degree turn to the right and runs more or less parallel to the aqueduct as it heads off to the southeast toward the Forum of Theodosius. One thing that struck us all as we marched along High Street was the incredible number of bronze and marble statues that lined both sides of this broad, beautiful, tree-lined avenue. Many of them went back to before the time of Christ. I knew that when Constantine established (or rather reestablished) this city, he had ordered the ransacking of pagan temples throughout Greece, Asia Minor, and elsewhere to obtain works of sculpture to adorn it. Nonetheless, until now, I had little idea of the extent to which this legalized thievery had been inflicted. It was ironic to see this most Christian of cities decorated with seemingly endless lines of pagan statues. This applied not only to High Street, the main thoroughfare, but also to all major streets, avenues, and forums. But the more I saw of these magnificent sculptures, the more disheartened I became as I realized just how severe the artistic destitution of other provinces had become in the process. I came to look at Constantinople as being to the other eastern cities as an elite army unit is to the rest: so many cities had suffered aesthetic impoverishment to enrich this newly reborn jewel on the Bosporus.

The last great square that we entered was the Forum of Constantine, containing its enormous statue of him. I believe it is the largest statue of any emperor ever constructed. That was where the parade disbanded. The city's chief officials participated in the parade, as did the highest-ranking members of the Catholic Church. At one square, the Senate cheered us; at another city officials; at another, the lesser church officials; and so on. People lined the street, the rooftops, the balconies, and every window on the upper stories seemed to have a dozen faces struggling to get a look at us. It was a wonderful event that every participant would treasure for the rest of his life. As each section entered the Forum of Constantine, the parade would halt, and the section would turn, salute the emperor, and be dismissed to enter the Hippodrome. Theodosius and his family reviewed the parade from a platform that had been specially constructed for the occasion. He and Empress Aelia Flavia Flaccilla had been married for ten years by that time. They had had four children, but only two had survived. Their oldest son, Gratianus, had died when very young, and their only daughter, Pulcheria, had died in 385. Their two surviving sons, Arcadius, aged nine, and Honorius, who had turned three the previous month, were with them. To our everlasting regret, these two specimens of human deadwood were destined to be the next emperors of the East and West respectively. Sadly, the young empress died before the year was out.

After dismissal, we filed into the Hippodrome that was close by for further events and entertainments. The Hippodrome in Constantinople has the same U shape to it as the Circus Maximus in Rome. As its Roman counterpart, this stadium has chariot racing for its prime sport, although it does cater to other activities. Construction on it had started in 203 during the reign of Septimius Severus. Subsequent emperors had added further embellishments, the most notable of which had occurred during Constantine the Great's tenure. The latest adornment, of which I am aware, was an Egyptian obelisk added by Theodosius I. After all the parading troops had entered and tens of thousands of civilian spectators had taken their seats, the emperor made a brief address. He thanked the attending troops and the units they represented and paid tribute to those who had sacrificed their lives on Rome's behalf. He introduced a number of civilian and military officials, but the first man he introduced received by far the loudest ovation: Promotus, the architect of our victory. After official ceremonies were over, we were entertained by chariot races and numerous circus acts. We newcomers were overwhelmed by the size of the Hippodrome. Of course, at that time we had not seen the Circus Maximus in Rome.

After several hours, a group of us left the stadium, as it was getting into the latter part of the afternoon. We had not eaten since early morning. We walked across the Forum of Augustus lying just to the east of the Hippodrome and then visited the Church of St. Sophia, a most impressive building. After an excellent roast beef supper at a restaurant near the church, we headed back west along High Street to the Forum of Theodosius. We walked about a mile to the forum and then headed north on the street containing the best-known brothels in the city. The problem was that by the time we arrived, unimaginably long lines had formed coming out the doors of each of them. To save time, we each chose a different sink of iniquity in which to indulge ourselves but it was hopeless, just as I knew it would be. The lines hardly seemed to be moving at all, so I gave up and headed off on my own simply to walk around the city. Several streetwalkers propositioned me, but the idea of doing it standing up against a wall in some seedy back alley has always been just a little too down-market for my tastes. Besides, the long lines were just the excuse that I was looking for to avoid these places without losing face with my comrades. Increasingly over the last couple of years, my love interests were concentrated entirely in Belgrade.

Just as on High Street, the most beautiful statues lined every main avenue that I came to. Like High Street, great sadness attended all this decoration. Had this city been rebuilt during the age of the Caesars or the Flavians or the Antonines or even the first Severans, everything would have been fresh. The statues would have been new even if they were copies of great artworks elsewhere. That, however, was during the period of what historians call the High Empire or Principate. Even the Arch of Constantine in Rome contains artwork taken from the Column of Trajan. Another sign of the times: why create when you can steal? I had passed the main parade ground in the northeast part of the city when I realized I was lost. A large prison nearby told me more than I wished to know about the type of neighborhood I was in. I wanted to get back to High Street, which was some blocks to the south, but several streets that I tried to get there turned out to be dead ends. In any case, the streets were very badly lit in comparison to the main arteries. Their only lighting came from nearby apartment windows. The blacker the streets became, the more apprehensive I was. There weren't very many people on the streets in this area, and eventually things reached the point where there was no one at all. I then drew my Hunnish knife to be ready for any eventuality. Finally, I came to a street that appeared to go all the way to High Street, but it was just as dark as the rest. I decided to give is a try.

I was approaching the entrance to an alleyway when I heard a slight noise that appeared to come from it. I had just started to move out to walk down the center of the street when someone lunged at me. Quickly stepping to my left, I just barely avoided his knife as it shot past my neck. At the same moment, I plunged my own lengthy blade into his stomach to the extent that it protruded slightly from his back. He let out the most agonizing groan and then went limp, crashing to the ground. My next reaction was to look around quickly to see if he had any accomplices. Not seeing any, I extracted my knife and dragged him off into the alley. As I dropped him up against a wall, I heard a clinking noise that sounded promising. I knelt down and felt his throat for a pulse, and at that moment, he groaned again. I then gave him a deep, twisting knife thrust to the heart.

Upon frisking him, I discovered a pouch containing a large number of coins. He had apparently had a busy evening before coming up against me. I carefully wiped my knife on the dead man's clothing and reentered the street. Fortunately, it led to High Street, so I was on my way. At one point where the lighting was good and no one was close by, I took a look at the purse I had just appropriated. I was surprised to see that the coins were all gold and silver. I walked the several miles back to our tent city and was fast asleep before any of the rest of my comrades returned from the night's revelries.

The next morning, I arose early, but this time I rode into the city. In spite of having killed a man the night before, I slept well. Like the old saying goes, "a heavy purse makes a light heart." Having walked about ten miles the previous day, I had no intention of repeating the entire effort all over again. At the Ox Forum, I turned southeast and followed the Lycus River to its estuary at the Sea of Marmara. Turning east, I followed the shoreline to the Port of Julian that lies due south of the Forum of Theodosius. I continued to ride east past beautiful mansions overlooking the sea until I came to the palace grounds whose western boundary is the east side of the Hippodrome. Being unable to go any farther, I stabled the horse and visited a nearby bath. After having breakfast, I walked to the extreme northeast part of the city to the Gothic Column. This magnificent monument in the Corinthian style commemorates the triumph over the Goths of Claudius II Gothicus. I spent much of the day simply walking around the city, connecting in my own small way with so many facets of our remarkable country's history. Unlike Rome, Constantinople, the "New Rome," is a very Christian city where churches outnumber pagan temples by a large margin. Until recently, it had also been an Arian city, but Theodosius changed that. From the day he first entered the capital in 380, the emperor worked tirelessly to drive the Arian priests and bishops from their churches and replace them with Catholics. Many of the Arian prelates had to be forcibly removed, quite literally at sword point. Their Catholic successors were frequently installed in the same fashion.

I walked west along the north shore of the city and passed by its main port facilities. I had never seen so many ships of all sizes, both naval and civilian. London had been the largest seaport that I had ever visited, but to see the docks of Constantinople was to be simply astounded. At the same time, Constantinople has about ten times the population of London. Trading ships carried every imaginable type of goods: glass, timber, and silk from Phoenicia (with the last-named item having been shipped from China); linen, wheat, papyrus, rubies, emeralds, incense, spices, and perfumes from Egypt; marble, wine, and woolen goods from western Asia Minor; lead from Isauria; silver from Cilicia (under strict military escort); bronze ware and more marble from Italy; Negro slaves shipped in from Carthage and Leptis Magna to where they had been transported from equatorial Africa across the Sahara Desert. There were goods from Spain and Gaul and ships from almost every province that has a coastline. Eventually I found myself at the north end of the street where the brothels had been jammed to capacity the night before. Time to head south, so I did toward the limestone Aqueduct of Valens. (At least "His Ineptitude" had been able to do something right for the city.) After supper at one of the restaurants on High Street, I got my horse and headed back to the tent city. The next day, we started back to Belgrade taking the same route by which we came, except this time we skipped the side trip to Perinthus.

Back at the home base, we resumed our standard garrison duties. As century signifer, most of my work was office work, but I was called out on patrol duty occasionally. On the trip back from Constantinople, I had given a lot of thought to my feelings for Makila. We had developed an affection for one another over the past year. The feelings that I had for her were the strongest that I had felt for any girl since my innocent affair with Ardovanda. I readily admit to having been captivated by her from the first moment I saw her. There are those exceedingly rare women in the world that have just the right combination of white and black blood in them that renders them beautiful beyond comparison. Certainly to me at any rate. As mentioned previously, several girls racially akin to her worked in the place. None of the others, however, possessed her personality. There was a charm and openheartedness to Makila, in a profession that nurtures neither, that I had not enjoyed before. Finally, on my twenty-second birthday in December 386, during the course of a blinding snowstorm, I asked her to marry me, and she accepted. I had never had a greater sense of fulfillment than I did at that moment.

We would need a considerable sum in order to purchase her freedom. Makila and I had each, in our own way, saved up a reasonable amount of money, and I was on good terms with "Big Julia," the proprietress of the establishment (the one that Chlogius always referred to as the "fat trollop"). I approached her one night and asked how much it would cost to spring Makila from the place. She showed no surprise at my question and stated a sizable amount based on her having to get someone in to replace Makila and all the expenses that would entail (both real and imaginary). I haggled her down a little. The main point was that we agreed to a final amount. On a normal soldier's pay, it would have been difficult to obtain. However, thanks to the confiscated plunder I had acquired in various ways over the years, I could easily afford it. We agreed that I would purchase Makila on the following February 1. I could have done it sooner, but I did not want to raise any suspicions as to where and how I might have acquired such sudden wealth.

On January 1, 387, we swore our annual oaths of allegiance to Theodosius, Arcadius, and Valentinian II. What was important here was that Theodosius had sent out some deliberately confusing signals. By allowing portraits of Magnus Maximus to be posted in Egypt, the emperor had implied recognition. At the same time, he never formally made public such recognition and never conducted negotiations with representatives of the usurper that finalized the matter. When the name of Magnus Maximus was again conspicuous by its absence from our annual oath of fidelity, our suspicions were confirmed.

In February, Makila and I purchased her freedom, and we were married. As a married soldier, I could live off the base, and we obtained an apartment close to the business district in Belgrade. I was twenty-two, and she was twenty. It was the most beautiful period of our lives. Since much of my time was spent on staff work, we were able to spend a lot of time together. I was not involved in maintaining roads anymore and only on occasion was I called out on mounted infantry patrols. On numerous evenings during the spring and summer, we would eat out in the better restaurants and perhaps attend the theatre afterward. On my days off, we would frequently go for a picnic in the countryside. In October, she became pregnant. This was truly life as it was meant to be.

In the spring, a special tax was levied throughout the Eastern Empire on landowning town and city counselors. It was to help pay for the army expansion required for the impending campaign in the West. People have complained about their tax burdens since the first tax was invented. But in Antioch, Syria, the reaction was extreme to the point of being all out of proportion. We first heard about it one morning while on border patrol ten miles east of Belgrade. Fredemondus was informed first by the commander of a century from Aureus Mons patrolling west in our direction. Our centurion imparted to us what he had been told and was immediately hit with questions.

"Is it a full-scale revolt?" asked Hilderic.

"No, nothing like that," replied our centurion. "One revolt at a time is plenty. It appears that a curial committee, understandably pissed off over this latest tax to be laid on them, went to present a petition to the provincial governor in Antioch, requesting a substantial reduction in the tax. This they had every right to do. Unfortunately, at the same time, a large mob started storming through the city, apparently on behalf of these aforementioned landowners. After wrecking several public buildings, they eventually attacked the governor's palace but were driven off. Failing in that exercise, the mob then destroyed bronze statues of the emperor and his family located at certain public buildings and forums, as they are in all cities. As you know, such misbehavior constitutes an act of treason. The original mob broke up into several gangs of degenerates that started attacking homes and innocent people and commercial establishments indiscriminately. They got completely out of control. Mobs always will when authority does not clamp down on them. Once the small local military garrison was called upon by the governor to intervene, the mobs were quickly broken up and dissolved."

"Has anyone been executed?" someone asked.

"Yes. The count of the East soon arrived on the scene, and certain leaders of the riots were arrested, tried, and executed. A number of other men were imprisoned for participating in the riots, but the emperor soon granted them clemency and ordered them released. Rich landowners whose estates had been confiscated also had their property returned."

"What is it about Antioch?" asked Hilderic. "I've often heard how difficult the city is to govern in spite of its being one of the richest in the empire."

"Maybe that's its problem," Fredemondus replied. "It's too damned rich for its own good. As a result, a lot of people who live there think they're entitled to special considerations that do not apply to the rest of us. For some reason, its population has always been more riot prone than populations elsewhere. It is primarily a Greek city remember and our Hellenic brethren have often tended to be more disputatious than the rest of us. Or so we've been led to believe. An older cousin of mine served there for several years and he loved the place. Antioch and Alexandria have a lot in common. They were both founded and populated by Greeks. The temperament of both cities is similar but I can't speak from firsthand experience. I've never visited either place. Both have a reputation for instability and luxurious living and probably always will."

Our centurion was an insightful man, but being ambitious, he usually played his cards very carefully where discussions of a political nature were concerned. He was only twenty-nine but already had eleven years of military experience behind him. A couple of weeks later, back at the garrison, several of us were talking to him one afternoon. We were all anxious about what would happen next in the West, but our conversation always seemed to come back to events in the East.

"Now that the troubles in Syria appear to have subsided, do you think Theodosius will now move against Magnus Maximus?" I asked.

Fredemondus paused before answering. "I'm not certain that the unrest in Antioch or elsewhere in the East is necessarily over," he finally replied. "The government has, for far too long, been sowing the winds of religious discord throughout Syria and Phoenicia and elsewhere. Now it is reaping the whirlwind of political conflict, and it could easily spread. For years, the government of the Eastern Empire has been legitimizing mob action in the name of furthering Catholic Christianity at the expense of other religious denominations. Such actions have never been sanctioned by previous emperors. But once you, in effect, authorize mob violence in one area of public life, how do you stop it from becoming an accepted means of political action in other fields?"

"You can't," I ventured. "I think Theodosius's appointing his friend and fellow Spaniard, Maternus Cynegius, as praetorian prefect of the East has been a disaster from a political standpoint. His promotion has led directly to the destruction of the Temple of Edessa in Osrhoene, the Temple of Zeus at Apamea in Syria, and the ruination of a number of other great artistic and architectural works. While we've been putting our lives on the line here in the Balkans to defend and rebuild the empire, the government in these other provinces has been employing mobs and sometimes even soldiers to attack these great buildings as though they were enemy citadels. Can this be anything other than madness?"

"The law of unintended consequences strikes again," Marcellinus said. Slightly built with sandy brown hair, he had a rather soft voice to match. "I'm a pagan. So I don't care what disagreements Christians have among themselves. It's just that I see this religion that Constantine the Great honestly thought would make a substantial contribution to national unity fragmenting and dividing us in a way that religion has never done before."

"As you know, I'm a pagan also," Fredemondus said. "Past persecutions of Christians notwithstanding, the pagan religions have almost always been tolerant of one another. Government persecutions of Christians prior to the reign of Constantine I had little to do with the actual philosophy of Christianity. But they had everything to do with the Christian attitude of total intolerance toward the religious beliefs of all non-Christians. That, in turn, led to the refusal of Christians to perform public acts of obeisance to the ancient gods of Rome under any circumstances, even in times of dire national emergency. Nowadays, even the 'triumph' of Christianity is insufficient to satisfy their leaders. It's not good enough simply to be a Christian. One must be the 'right' kind of Christian. The notion of a 'right' or 'wrong' kind of any religion strikes all pagans as ridiculous. To this point, with the exception of such desecrations as Marcus just mentioned, the government has been focusing its prosecutorial energies on Christian heresies. But if Christians cannot be spared government-sponsored criminality by their fellow Christians, then what hope is there for the rest of us?"

In the autumn of 387, Magnus Maximus felt sufficiently confident to move against Valentinian II. Most importantly, for the first time in his misbegotten "reign," he acted like neither the thug nor the fool he had played in the past. Ironically, the government of young Valentinian would provide the artifice that the usurper would utilize to break through the Alpine passes. Valentinian II entrusted a special embassy to his top official, Domninus, whom he sent to negotiate a treaty that appeared to grant a certain degree of recognition to the usurper. Magnus Maximus received the delegation graciously and offered to send army units from Gaul to assist Valentinian's generals in a campaign against barbarians threatening Pannonia. This offer was declined, as similar past offers had been. However, Domninus agreed to take back with him a small token force as a show of unity between the young emperor and the usurper on the issue of repelling barbarians. This small force would ostensibly act as an addition to Domninus' bodyguard on the return trip.

Magnus Maximus had an entirely nefarious purpose for it. From his standpoint, their primary function was to prevent anyone in Domninus' loyal bodyguard from noticing that several miles in the rear, they were being followed by the bulk of the usurper's army. The plan worked to perfection. The units in Valentinian's army defending the pass failed to realize that the rebel army was, in fact, a rebel army until it was too late. Having been duped, they were left with no choice but to join the usurper. Maximus' army broke out of the Cottian Alps and entered the Po Valley heading straight for Aquileia. The units in Valentinian's army that were guarding the other Alpine passes, upon realizing that they had failed in their purpose, went over to the usurper. So did a number of other army units in northern Italy. Valentinian II, his mother, Justina, and his sisters boarded a ship and escaped down the Adriatic to the Macedonian port of Thessalonica. Here the western imperial family was met by Theodosius and a delegation from the Senate at Constantinople.

For the recently widowed Theodosius, who was only forty, it was love at first sight once he spied Galla, the oldest of Justina's daughters. They announced their betrothal, and plans were soon being laid for the reconquest of the West. Theodosius almost always ensured that only men of the highest caliber occupied the most important political and military positions. There had been certain egregious exceptions to this general rule in the past, and there would be in the future. But for the time being, Theodosius was at his best in this regard. The top commanders were Promotus as master of cavalry, Timasius as master of infantry, and Stilicho as count of domestics (i.e., imperial bodyguard). In the political sphere, the emperor realized that peace and tranquility were vitally important in those portions of his realm that would be farthest removed from his reach. Fortuitously, order in the Orient was facilitated by the death at this time of Maternus Cynegius. In his place, Theodosius appointed Tatianus and made Tatianus' son, Proculus, the urban prefect of Constantinople. Both men were pagans with excellent reputations. Religious ferment was a luxury that the empire simply could no longer afford. At least not for now.

Reunion (387–388)

CHAPTER 6

IN BELGRADE, OUR LEGION centurions called their troops together once they had been informed by our prefect that a state of war existed between East and West.

"So the inevitable has finally happened," I said to Fredemondus later.

"Yes, but it's all rather curious," he replied. "I explained to the century what we were told by the prefect. Namely, that Magnus Maximus employed a clever stratagem to get through the one Alpine pass and into the Po Valley. But I wonder if there isn't more to it than that. In 383, Gratian's army deserted him, in part because of bribes the usurper offered certain Moorish units and others that had previously served under him in Europe and Africa. The sudden assault through the Cottian Alps seems almost too perfect. It leads one, at least this one, to wonder if the real method this time wasn't the same as the one used four years earlier. The quickest way to get from Gaul to the head of the Adriatic is to take the one and only highway that runs through the Cottian Alps. It runs from just south of Valence in the Rhone Valley through the Mt. Genève Pass and on to Turin near the head of the Po Valley. It's an easy trip from there to Aquileia if there are no intervening armies in the way. And that raises the question of just what the Milan garrison, among others, was doing at this time. There are a lot of awkward questions that demand answers. I think Theodosius might have served his political cause to the better by paying more attention to Italy instead of spending so much time trying to ram Catholicism down the throats of his unwilling subjects farther east."

"What is it about Spain that seems to breed such ferocity on the matter of Catholic Christianity?" I asked. "It's almost unique among the western dioceses in this regard. No such feelings exist in Britain, where most of the population is still pagan, or Gaul either, from what I saw when I lived there. Theodosius has appointed a disproportionately large number of Spaniards to political offices in the East, and they all appear to be as unbending as he is on the matter of religion. One cannot simply be a Christian; one must be a Catholic Christian."

"Maybe it's the water. Or the grapes," Fredemondus replied. "By the way, just before he invaded Italy, Magnus Maximus ordered the execution of Merobaudes."

"On what grounds?" I asked.

"No one here in the East seems to know yet," Fredemondus answered. "Merobaudes was instrumental in proclaiming Valentinian II as emperor in 375. He was one of the most capable generals in the Western Army, and he and Gratian, as I understand it, were always on good terms. And yet when it came to making the most important decision in his life, Merobaudes betrayed his emperor. Was he planning on turning again, and was that the reason for his execution? We'll have to crush Magnus Maximus to find that out, I suppose."

Throughout the autumn and early winter of 387, the army was working twelve hours a day training, getting the highways and bridges ready, allocating supplies, and so on. The invasion of Italy by Magnus Maximus had actually come as a relief. Everything we did now was focused on the impending campaign, and the intensity of all our endeavors was magnified several fold. Like all staff members, I was swamped with paperwork by the flood of new recruits coming in as soon as the harvest was over. Road and bridge repair was concentrated in the Sava River Valley. In October, because of my background as a teamster, I was assigned to a task force of officers and veteran noncommissioned officers whose responsibility was to inspect and test out new wagons that had been manufactured for the quartermaster corps. Armories all over the Eastern Empire were manufacturing swords, javelins, shields, bows, arrows, and armor for both men and horses and every other manner of armament that would be required for the forthcoming campaign. On a number of occasions, our century escorted overland convoys in bringing up equipment from southern armories to units on the Danube.

As soon as the ice was off the Sava River in 388, ships from the Pannonian Fleet along with civilian ships and barges were used to carry stores upstream to the various resupply points. River transportation is cheap, but in the case of the Sava also quite time-consuming. By highway from Belgrade to Sisak is 231 miles, while the river distance is about 130 miles longer. Our century was involved in these transportation activities for a while, but one day in the spring after returning to Belgrade, we were called together by Fredemondus for a special visit by our regiment's tribune, Julius Aranius.

"Any of you still remember me?" he asked jokingly. "It's been a long time since we've had a chance to get together like this. For those of you who might be wondering, you are still considered part of Legion IV Flavia Firma." We all laughed at this. "Over much of the past four years or so, you've been assigned to special duty so often that you've almost become an independent century. Both under my command and that of Fredemondus, you've all done yourselves proud, and you can rest assured that it's well appreciated at legion headquarters. But we no sooner get you back to operating as a regular century than you find yourselves being drawn off for special duty again. That's why I asked Fredemondus to gather you together for this meeting. You are going on another special assignment. The next two days are yours to spend with your families or whomever you please for those of you who are still single. Your centurion will inform you of your mission at the proper time. You will be departing Belgrade at eight o'clock this coming Friday morning. Good luck."

Makila and I spent every moment of the next two days together. This would be the first time that we had had a prolonged separation since we were married. Her pregnancy was starting to show, and I was concerned for her since I had no idea how long I would be away. Fortunately, Makila had remained on friendly terms with Julia, who assured me that she and

Makila's girl friends would take good care of her. Two days later, we were on the march as regular infantry. This was a definite downer, and our direction was east instead of west.

"If we are off to fight the enemy in the west, then why are we going east?" one of the Visigothic recruits hollered.

"Who gives a shit," Marcellinus answered. "If the war is to the west and we're marching east, that suits me fine. A guy could get killed going in the other direction."

We were all puzzled, but Fredemondus would throw no light on the matter. At Margum, we turned south and headed up the Morava. At Naissus, we headed west and then south to Skopje, where we had helped eliminate that bandit gang two years earlier. Entering the Axios River Valley, we followed it all the way to Thessalonica. Our 320-mile march took us almost a month. As soon as we arrived at the Aegean seaport, we were met by a tribune who drew Fredemondus off to one side. We could not overhear what they were saying, but it was apparent from the hand gestures and occasionally raised voices that all was not going well. Tempers eventually cooled down, and a lengthy discussion ensued. After saluting one another, Fredemondus returned and explained the situation.

"Gentlemen," he said, "There is some good news and some bad news. The attack on the West is to be a two-pronged assault. The one in the north is under the supreme command of His Majesty Theodosius. That one we know all about, after having spent the past several months busting our collective asses on its behalf. The assault in the south, under the supreme command of His Majesty Valentinian II, has been prepared for in a similarly assiduous manner. Our original orders were to march from Belgrade to Thessalonica, where we would board ships. For security reasons, I'm still not at liberty to inform you of our final destination. What I can tell you is that the ships that were to provide our transportation and that of a number of other units have been called away to provide troops to Egypt."

"Why?" asked Chlogius. "Has a revolt broken out there too?"

"Not to my knowledge," our centurion replied. "It is widely known, however, that Magnus Maximus has political support in Egypt. I would think that the supply of additional troops to that diocese is to forestall any attempt by the usurper to translate that support, isolated though it may be, into a military uprising. The upshot, as far as we are concerned, is that we will have to continue our journey on foot. Personally, that suits me fine. The idea of sailing around the Peloponnese Peninsula at any time is not my idea of a joyride. Its surrounding waters can be very rough. Some of you might have noticed me expressing my, shall we say, disappointment over the fact that a messenger was not sent up north to inform us sooner so that we could have taken a shorter route to our eventual destination. But these things happen. We do have three days off here to rest up and get our gear and ourselves in shape for the next leg of our march."

We eventually arrived at a large tent city and stayed there for the next four nights. I visited the dock area of Thessalonica on my own and was astounded by the number of warships and civilian transports that were present. It was obvious that the upcoming campaign was going to be larger than the Danube expedition in 386.

Before the start of his drive to the West, Theodosius utilized the predictive talents of a peculiar monk named John. This monk, who was quite old, had spent almost fifty years living in seclusion at a monastery in the small town of Lycopolis in southern Egypt. No one had seen him since he entered his cell, and outsiders could only conduct interviews with him through intermediaries from the monastery. Even they could not come in contact with him directly. (Given that John had gone half a century without a bath, I don't know why anyone would want to.) In any case, he was supposed to possess an unblemished record for predicting the future, so the emperor sent an embassy to Lycopolis to sound him out on the prospects of military success. Big surprise, old John predicted Theodosius would emerge triumphant! I wonder what the emperor expected the old man to forecast. Monks, like courtiers, are certainly not averse to telling their monarchs exactly what they want to hear. After all, what did John have to lose by predicting victory? If Theodosius defeated

Maximus, then the emperor's gratitude would take the form of imperial largesse for the monastery. If the East was defeated, then the imperial head (minus its owner) would go on a provincial tour, and that would be the end of it. John would have had to be a total idiot to predict defeat. As soon as the embassy reported back to the emperor, he ordered the operation to get underway.

At Thessalonica, we saw the imperial family: Valentinian II, his mother, Justina, and his younger sisters. The emperor of the West was now seventeen years of age, a handsome young man who was quiet and rather shy. The moment I saw him, I was reminded of the one and only time I had seen his older half brother five years earlier. I uttered a silent prayer that the reign of this emperor would be a happier one than that of Gratian. It went unanswered.

Our army was to march west from Thessalonica along the Via Egnatia to its western terminus at Durres on the Adriatic coast. The distance is about 220 miles. The Via Egnatia had been constructed almost six centuries earlier during the Macedonian wars that ended with Rome annexing Macedonia as its first eastern province. At first, the journey was easy as we crossed the coastal flood plain formed by the deltas of several rivers, the most important of which is the Axios. These are the largest plains in Macedonia and the most effectively cultivated. They form the heartland of what was the ancient kingdom. On the second day, we entered Pella, the ancient capital, where Alexander the Great was born. After Rome annexed Macedonia, Pella declined into a rather nondescript provincial town. Its importance is heavily overshadowed by that of Thessalonica, about twenty-five miles to the east. In spite of that, it is still a pretty and well-kept municipality. Fortunately, Macedonia and Greece have the same Mediterranean climate as Italy and southeastern Gaul, so, given that it was by now summer, we were not hampered by bad weather.

West of Pella, we reached the end of the floodplain and started climbing to Edessa. This ancient city is said to predate the civilization of Greece itself and is located on a high rise of land overlooking the Loudhias River Valley. Edessa would be our last taste of civilization for a while. West of that city, the terrain becomes rougher, consisting of alternating mountain ranges and valleys that are sparsely populated. This is the least developed part of Macedonia. Nomad sheepherding is the main activity, and agriculture is restricted. After swinging around the southern end of Lake Bigorritus, we headed northwest to the city of Bitola, several days distant. Bitola lies at the western margin of the plain that carries its name. Another quiet, provincial backwater, it centers a small agricultural area that focuses on cereal crops and livestock. We remained there for two days. Bitola marks roughly the halfway point between Thessalonica and Durres. West of Bitola, the terrain becomes considerably more difficult, with steeper mountains and plunging valleys alternating in rapid succession. About thirty miles west of Bitola, we came to the city of Ohrid on the northeast shore of the lake of the same name. If the region had a greater population density, it could be a great resort area. Lake Ohrid is quite large and is ringed with several good beaches. While there, we were able to sink our teeth into the lake's plentiful fish harvest. Overall, the city is fairly prosperous. The Via Egnatia played a vital role in Rome's conquest of Macedonia and Greece back in republican times. However, once Augustus Caesar pushed the frontier to the Danube, the highway's strategic importance declined. In spite of this, it has remained vital as the shortest link between Rome and Constantinople. It has always carried heavy diplomatic traffic between East and West over the centuries, and as a result, its cities have excellent public facilities. The Gothic catastrophe that befell Thrace gave fresh life to the Via Egnatia and its cities. When it came to providing troops and supplies to Theodosius to contain the Visigoths, the more northerly Balkan routes had initially been too insecure. The Via Egnatia was pressed into service, and its cities had been enlarged with supply depots and their attendant personnel. Someone always benefits from someone else's disaster.

Much as we hated to leave Ohrid, we did have a schedule to meet. The last ninety miles from Ohrid to Durres made up the loneliest stretch of the journey. After two more mountain passages, we entered the Genusus River Valley, and from there it was all downhill. Just as I had when I first marched from Mainz to Belgrade, I marveled at the incredible work those ancient engineers had performed in putting this highway through this empty land over five hundred years earlier. In the valleys where the drainage was poor, the roads had been constructed in a special way. Vertical posts were driven into the ground along the edges of the roads, and logs were laid between them in the direction of the highway. On top of the horizontal logs went successive layers of clay, pebbles, and gravel, cambered in order to provide drainage to either side. It had been a long, hard march. Numerous other units beside those in our force were participating in the invasion of Italy. Regiments from farther up the Danube were descending on Durres and other ports on the coast of the southern Adriatic. We couldn't all arrive and board ship at the same time. Those we were to use had sailed from Constantinople and the Aegean ports, and it was of paramount importance that all units be precisely on schedule. We had just arrived at Durres and caught our first sight of the Adriatic Sea when Fredemondus called the century together.

"There is going to be a delay of several days," our centurion announced. "The day after we left Thessalonica, a plot was discovered in a couple of our legions and cavalry regiments up in the Sava River Valley. Certain Visigothic troops had accepted bribes from the usurper to desert to the West shortly before the first engagement took place. Fortunately, the plot was discovered in plenty of time, and the would-be deserters were put to flight. After being surrounded in a swampy region in Macedonia to the north of Thessalonica, the traitors were wiped out almost to the last man. However, this effort caused a delay in launching the northern wing of our offensive, which has set back our own schedule by about two weeks. We slowed our march across Macedonia to soak up most of this time so that we would avoid placing too much strain on the resources in Durres after we arrived. We must keep the northern and southern campaigns in sync with one another."

So we had a few days to relax prior to the uncertain struggle that loomed ahead of us. Lounging in one of the baths, Marcellinus asked me, "What do you think of this campaign of ours?"

Not catching the direction of his question, I replied, "It suits me fine. Personally, I'm just as happy that we are avoiding what will be the main battle at the head of the Adriatic. A better shot at longevity and all that."

"No, that's not what I'm getting at," he replied. "What do you think the *real* purpose of our expeditionary force is? To draw strength from up north to make it easier for Theodosius to defeat the usurper's main army?"

"On the surface, yes. But perhaps you have been thinking what I have in recent weeks. With several thousand men in our company and more joining us, we should certainly be able to give a good account of ourselves if Magnus Maximus discovers our flanking move on him."

"Discover it—hell, he probably knew where we were going before we did," was Stephanus' cynical interruption. "Come to think of it, we still don't really know where we're heading once we land in Italy, do we?"

"Maybe," I went on. "But getting back to the original point, Theodosius has already granted the title of Augustus to his older son, Arcadius. Do we think that he will do any less for his number-two son? Not likely. Theodosius, at age forty-one, is still a relatively young man, and long may he live. But he has already had one critical illness that almost took him from us several years back. Barring any unforeseen developments, when he passes from the scene, he will be leaving the empire to three successors: Valentinian II, Arcadius, and Honorius."

"Quite so," Marcellinus said. "Now suppose our invasion force is subjected to a serious attack either while crossing the Adriatic or after we've landed. Should Valentinian be killed in the onslaught or be executed following capture, the succession would be secure for Theodosius's sons alone. After all, we don't see them accompanying either army, do we?"

"Are you suggesting that the purpose of our enterprise is to get our young emperor killed?" asked Stephanus.

"Not for a moment," Marcellinus replied. "Theodosius is a decent and deeply religious man, and I'm certain that he is far above such lurid behavior. But if the Fates were to turn against us, then the eventual transference of power, when it comes, would be simplified. History plainly shows that an imperial succession involving more than two people is inherently unstable. Witness the mess after Diocletian abdicated or the civil war between the sons of Constantine the Great. If misfortune should befall young Valentinian, then Theodosius will have a clear conscience. He could simply pass it off as God's will. But I honestly think that we are being too cynical. Valentinian II is emperor of the West, and this is a campaign to recover *his* throne. There is no way in which he could avoid participating in this conflict, even if just as a spectator."

There was quite a bit of noise in the baths, as there always is, but we kept our voices low throughout so as not to be overheard. Another group of men entered the pool in our area, so we changed the subject, and nothing more was said on the matter. Prior to my first seeing him at Thessalonica, I had never given Valentinian II much thought. After all, Gratian and Theodosius were emperors in the full executive sense of the word, while young Valentinian was just a figurehead. He was now seventeen, but what was of concern about him was that his older half brother had been conducting armies in the field at that age. Valentinian I had done a superb job of training Gratian, while he was still a boy, for his future responsibilities. I believe that Gratian would have done the same thing for his brother had he lived. No one, however, had taken Valentinian II under his tutelage for the awesome political and military responsibilities that were truly his. His mother certainly couldn't do it, and the biggest male influence in his life to this point had been Bishop Ambrose of Milan. Enough said on that score, at least for the time being.

Only after we arrived in Rome did we receive more detail on the Visigothic rebels that had triggered the delay to the onset of our campaign. The area of marsh and forest in Macedonia into which they had been chased covers several hundred square miles. Our expeditionary force had passed through the southern reaches of that area just a few days before the rebels arrived. Far from being wiped out, as we had been told, a sufficient number of them had survived to cause severe difficulties for the inhabitants of the region for years to come.

Our transports arrived, and we quickly transited from Durres to Brindisi across the southern end of the Adriatic. Once ashore speed was of the essence, so I had no chance to explore this city where our greatest poet, Virgil, died in 19 BC. Its close proximity to the southern part of the Balkan Peninsula establishes its significance in maintaining communication with the East. It's a pleasant town with a fair-sized harbor that is always busy. Since no major river flows through Brindisi, there is no problem with the harbor silting up. We immediately started marching toward Rome. As we headed out of the city, we marched past the two columns that mark the southern terminus of our first and most famous highway, the Via Appia. When we left Thessalonica, we were told only that we would be marching along the Via Egnatia to Durres. We were not told where we would land in Italy in order to keep word of it from leaking out to Magnus Maximus. There were rumors that we were headed for Rome, but most of us younger soldiers thought that was too good to be true. Nonetheless, here we were on the oldest highway in the empire, and its ultimate destination is the Eternal City.

Between our leaving Belgrade and arriving in Brindisi, two months had passed. I worried constantly about Makila. I trusted Julia to take care of her as she had promised, but I still felt guilty about not being there when the baby arrived. It was due in late July, but I had no way of knowing what had actually happened and would not until I returned to Belgrade. All I could do was pray for the best.

It is one thing to prepare a line of march for an army when it is traveling through one's own territory, as was the case while we advanced from Belgrade to Durres. It is an altogether different situation when that army must advance through hostile or potentially hostile country. Such was our situation once we landed in Brindisi. After we disembarked, the navarch (squadron commander) informed us that marines had already landed at Taranto, on the other side of the heel, to secure it for us. Remarkably, all the ports in southern Italy were undefended. The next objective for the navy was to seek out any enemy fleet in the area and destroy it. From Brindisi, we marched to Taranto. The fleet could have taken us directly there from Durres by sailing around the heel of the peninsula. However, its primary objective was to land us in Italy at the earliest possible moment. The danger was that Magnus Maximus might have sent his fleet at Ravenna down the Adriatic to prevent a landing in southern Italy, whether he had any direct intelligence on it or not. Numerous ships in our fleet were packed with marines for just such an eventuality. The longer the sea journey to land us in Italy, the higher the probability could be that our fleet would be intercepted by the enemy with us still on board, and it was essential that this be avoided. We had never had to live off the land before. It's not the sort of activity that endears an army on the march to the locals. Southern Italy had not seen an "enemy" army on the prowl in centuries. If only things could have remained that way.

By taking the Via Appia, we stayed away from the east coast, thus avoiding contact with enemy forces until the last possible moment. Our objective was to seize Rome and then continue our march into the north of Italy to attack the army of Magnus Maximus from the rear. If the usurper discovered us marching up the Via Trajana on the east coast, then he would land an army to stop us without hesitation. By keeping to the inland routes, we made it more difficult for him to know where we were. Fortunately, things went well for us. We met with no resistance anywhere. The civilian populations of both Brindisi and Taranto welcomed us warmly, but then they would have done the same for the usurper's army if it had arrived first. This was understood.

We have all heard the expression that "south of Naples is Africa." The substance of this remark lies in the fact that economically and climatically, southern Italy has more in common with North Africa than it does with the northern part of the country. Several of our major historians, such as Strabo, have assigned the impoverishment of the region to the plundering by the Carthaginian Army under Hannibal between 218 and 203 BC. The enforced absence of local farmers conscripted to serve in our army at that time caused the long-term abandonment of the land that conjoined with Hannibal's depredations to worsen matters. The countryside never recovered from this devastation and the later introduction of large-scale sheep ranching only denuded the land further. This theory is open to question. Six centuries have passed since the visitation by Hannibal's army and, in all fairness, one cannot go on forever blaming these long-ago foreigners for the permanent impoverishment of the area. In the third century, the eastern Balkan Peninsula and Asia Minor suffered terribly at the hands of barbarian invaders, and yet their economies recovered to a reasonable degree within several generations. The climate of southern, and in particular southeastern, Italy alone raises the question of just how prosperous this region would be in the best of times.

The Apulian lowlands lie between the Adriatic Sea and the Apennine Mountains and extend from the tip of the heel roughly halfway up the east coast of the Italian boot. These lowlands, which vary in width from roughly twenty to thirty-five miles, receive the lowest rainfall and suffer the worst droughts of any part of Italy. There are numerous large estates in the area, but the dryness of the climate limits what they can produce. As a result, grazing is widespread because of the difficulty of raising cereal crops except in areas where the local water supply is sufficient. Even when grain crops can be grown, their yields are low due to the soil quality. The upside of the meteorological conditions is that the region produces the strongest wines in the land. They are exported to other parts of the peninsula to fortify their weaker varieties. At both Brindisi and Taranto, there are large salt companies. Cities on the lower Adriatic and Ionian Seas are ideally situated for this industry. The true Mediterranean climate here promotes long, hot summers with very little, if any, precipitation. The low rainfall causes the salt content of the surrounding waters to be much higher than that of the Atlantic Ocean or the more northerly reaches of the Mediterranean and upper Adriatic. The high temperatures enhance the evaporation process that is carried out in large basins. These are fabricated in such a way as to catch seawater between the levels of high and low tide. In all likelihood, this region, the most sparsely populated part of Italy, is forever destined to be economically and politically of little consequence.

Pressing north, we soon left Taranto and its gulf behind. One thing I noticed as we marched through the countryside was the absence of dairy herds. In the north, in the Po River Valley and the Alpine regions, dairy cattle are plentiful because the heavier rainfall there promotes the growth of grass, as it does over all the northerly reaches of the empire. However, while the south is not cattle country, there are ample herds of sheep and goats. We passed by sheep ranches along with orange and olive orchards as we continued ever northward to Rome. One local custom we witnessed was the shepherding of goat herds into the villages early in the morning to be milked for waiting customers.

Far removed as we were from the scene of the main campaign, we were not completely in the dark as to what was going on there. At Taranto, we had received some good news. Magnus Maximus had left a sizable army back in Gaul to protect both the Rhine frontier and the throne in Trier on which he had placed his young son, Victor. Two of his generals, Nannienus and Quintinus, were soon involved in repelling a Frankish invasion that occurred near Cologne. Quintinus pursued one of the invading armies across the Rhine but suffered a defeat with heavy casualties. With Gaul open to the danger of another invasion, the usurper could hope for little in the way of reinforcements from that quarter.

The more southerly reaches of the Apennines have the lowest elevation of the entire chain. Nonetheless, erosion has cut ravines and valleys through much of the region, making east-west communications awkward. We passed through Benevento and continued on to Capua and the Mediterranean coast. Marching northwestward through Campania, we were within a week's march of Rome when we were approached by a small, mounted detachment sent down from Aquileia. It brought great news. Before we were officially informed, rumors started sweeping through the ranks that victories had been won at Sisak and Poetovio and that Emona had fallen without a fight.[20] Valentinian II and his commanders debriefed the officers on the details of Theodosius's campaign. Word was then passed down the line to the centurions who informed their rank and file of what had happened. Fredemondus addressed our century:

"Magnus Maximus, as we know, had established his headquarters at Aquileia. He subsequently was in the process of building his most easterly defensive position at Sisak on the Sava River about 165 miles to the east when Theodosius attacked. The emperor used cavalry units with large numbers of Huns and Alans. Our victory was complete. The army then moved to combat the usurper's main force coming down from the north at Poetovio. The rebel army was decisively defeated in this second battle after a long struggle. Casualty figures are unavailable for either battle, but for the second engagement in particular, the number of dead and wounded was serious on both sides. After Poetovio, the usurper's army started to disintegrate. Some units went over to Theodosius, and the remainder retreated westward. The city of Emona surrendered to our army without a fight, leaving the road open to Aquileia. At this point, a group of rebel officers, recognizing that their cause was hopeless, arrested Magnus Maximus and surrendered him to Theodosius. The usurper was decapitated on August 28. The empire is once more united."

At this, we all gave a long, loud cheer. Similar shouts could be heard from the other centuries as their centurions passed along the same information.

"Now we are going to be formed into larger contingents," Fredemondus continued, "for an address by His Majesty Valentinian II, who will provide us with additional information."

We formed up in a field belonging to a large estate. We were rather surprised at the fact that the young emperor was going to speak to us. So far as we knew, he had never given a public address to any audience, let alone thousands of soldiers. He rode out in front of the assembled army, and we exchanged salutes.

"Soldiers of Rome," Valentinian began, "I know that you must be both elated and disappointed at the announcement that you have just heard. Elated because we have won, disappointed because you no doubt feel that we played no direct role in the victory. My colleague Theodosius and I want you all to know that, in the latter instance, nothing could be further from the truth. During interrogation sessions with soldiers that deserted to our army after the Battle of Poetovio, it was discovered that they already knew that our army had landed in Italy and was in the process of conducting a pincer movement on them from the south. This prompted the usurper to move against us in the north several weeks ahead of his original schedule and before his entire battle order had arrived in position. In addition, our presence here proved to be a determining factor in the decision to arrest the usurper and hand him over to my colleague for execution when our northern army reached the outskirts of Aquileia.

"As you know, our late, beloved Gratian was first betrayed in Gaul by a regiment of Moorish cavalry. These men subsequently formed the bodyguard of the usurper. They too have all been captured and executed en masse." At this, a deafening roar went up from our assembly that lasted for several minutes. The emperor raised his right arm, and the cheering finally died down.

"We have been in continual communication with the fleet since leaving Taranto. This morning, prior to the arrival of the contingent from my colleague, we conferred with a group of naval and marine officers that escorted us across the Adriatic. Four days ago, our navy landed at Ostia and Portus Augusti, and several regiments of marines immediately marched on Rome. The city came over to our side without resistance."

At this, another great cheer went up from the assembly.

"Our preapprehensions about Magnus Maximus suspecting a flanking movement by our army were confirmed. The usurper had sent his field marshal, Andragathius, with a fleet of dromon warships to intercept our invasion force before we could land in Italy. The murderer of my brother was no doubt on his way to complete the task that he had started five years ago. He spent several fruitless days scouring the

211

southern Adriatic and northern Ionian Seas for us, but, as we know, he came up empty-handed. According to a statement made by a member of his fleet, Andragathius was on the verge of landing at Brindisi when he was approached by a vessel from the north informing him of his master's defeat and subsequent execution. Knowing the fate that would eventually befall him, Andragathius hurled himself overboard, preferring to commit himself to the deep rather than the executioner's blade." At this, another huge cheer went up from our ranks. Valentinian continued, "Andragathius' fleet wandered around in the Ionian Sea for several days and was eventually defeated by our supporting fleet off the coast of Sicily. I know we're all devout Christians here, but Nemesis, that ancient goddess of retributory justice, has never looked lovelier, has she?" At this, another great cheer went up that the emperor let go on for some time. He then concluded his address.

"During the course of the past three months, some of us have marched and sailed as much as a thousand miles on this campaign. The empire owes a debt of gratitude to you all that it will pay in the traditional way of a special donative." More cheering. "We have been informed," Valentinian continued, "that a senatorial delegation is on its way from Rome to welcome us and offer congratulations on the success of our campaign. I believe that we all would have had a greater sense of appreciation for the gesture if they had met us on the docks at Brindisi, but magnanimity being one of the cardinal aspects of our nature, we shall welcome them in a spirit of friendship and cooperation." We all laughed at this, as did the young emperor. We exchanged salutes, and he rode off.

"What did you think of his speech?" Marcellinus asked me.

"I liked it. He showed a maturity beyond his years that rumors had not encouraged us to expect. I'm impressed by what I heard and I hope he gets a fair chance. He might turn out to be a chip off the old block after all."

"All this good news in one day is almost too much to handle," Stephanus remarked.

Our sense of vindication, however, would be only too short-lived.

We continued our northwestward march through Latium, the true Roman heartland that is now the most northerly part of the expanded province of Campania. Our concerns over rations were suddenly over, as the Senate ensured that our supply requirements were amply provided for. We arrived at Rome within a week, where we found that a large tent city had been constructed for us, much like the one that we had experienced at Constantinople two years earlier. Valentinian II and his advisers had persuaded the Senate to contribute rather substantially to his donative for the troops. They did with little hesitation. The reason for their generosity had much to do with the fact that many senators had been on friendly terms with the usurper during his brief residence in Italy. The Senate had sent a delegation, led by the highly respected Symmachus, to Milan early in the year for the celebration of the consulship of Magnus Maximus. Under the circumstances, the Senate was in a difficult position, and Theodosius and Valentinian II understood this. For it not to send a high-ranking group of representatives for the occasion would have been almost unthinkable. But what transformed this discomforting event into an act of political stupidity was the delivery of a panegyric on behalf of the usurper by Symmachus. Fortunately for him and the rest of the Senate, Theodosius and Valentinian II were in a forgiving mood. The meetings between Valentinian and his entourage and the Senate were all quite amicable.

We had been given five days to relax at Rome before heading back to our home bases. The single chaps headed off to indulge in the usual forms of fun and frolic when in the big city. Fredemondus and I, being happily married, stuck pretty much together and spent most of our time as tourists. On the first day, we entered the Appian Gate and soon passed through the Arch of Drusus that carries the Severan aqueduct over the Appian Way to feed the Baths of Caracalla. These are the largest public baths in the Roman Empire and are enclosed within an area measuring 750 by 380 feet. In addition, the grounds of the baths contain exercise courts and outdoor swimming pools that are quite extensive. The area of the entire complex—baths, grounds, and associated facilities—measures over one million square feet! Not only is the scale of the architecture overwhelming, but also the magnificence of the artwork on the walls inside is of such a nature that it is highly questionable whether it could be duplicated today.

Roman summers are long and early September can be just as hot as July and August. That was certainly the case when we were there in the summer of 388. We spent a good deal of time in the frigidarium (cold pool), which is enormous. It contains almost 380,000 gallons of water and must be refreshed several times a day. To our amazement, this refreshment process is completed in a rather short period of time. Overhead was the largest flat ceiling ever constructed anywhere. We would conscientiously look up at it from time to time, wondering if the whole thing might not come crashing down upon us at any moment. The tepedarium (warm pool) is just as impressive but in a different way. It has a large arched roof that is supported by eight granite columns that measure about six feet in diameter. The architects cleverly used pumice stone for the roof instead of more standard, heavier materials in order to lighten the load on the columns. Everywhere you look, you see the most beautiful statuary in marble and bronze. Enormous mosaics, bas-reliefs, cameos, and imperial busts are everywhere. The Baths of Caracalla are truly one of the great architectural and artistic masterpieces of the empire.

After refreshing there for quite a while, we continued on up the Via Appia and, after passing the Appian aqueduct, we came to the Circus Maximus located between the Palatine Hill to the north and the Aventine. This place has to be seen to be believed. We thought the Hippodrome in Constantinople was huge, but the Circus Maximus is definitely the more impressive structure. Of course, with a seating capacity of 285,000, it should be. Measuring approximately two thousand feet by six hundred feet, it is the largest hippodrome-styled (i.e., U-shaped) stadium in the empire. We spent the better part of the afternoon enjoying the chariot races before heading several blocks north to Trajan's Forum. We had supper there at one of the many outdoor restaurants.

"I guess I should be happy that our Eastern Army won," said Fredemondus. "After all, it certainly beats the alternative. But there are aspects to our victory that I find disquieting."

"What are they?" I asked.

"It's been ten years since the catastrophe at Hadrianople. At that time, the mobile field army stationed in Thrace was shattered, and if it wasn't for the West sending troops, such as us, continually eastward, then the Balkan area might have collapsed completely. Yet now the army of the East has recovered to the point where it can defeat that of the West."

"As a pair of westerners, about the only bright spot in what you just said," I replied, "is that quite a number of those eastern units came from the West. But that must be cold comfort to the Western Army itself right now. Also, the civilian population there cannot have had their morale boosted by their army's defeats in both the civil war and the Rhineland."

"True," Fredemondus responded. "I hadn't thought of that. Another thing that disturbs me about our recent victory is that so many of our Roman cavalry units appear to have a disproportionately large percentage of recent barbarian recruits in them. Even if they are led by Roman officers, I'm uncomfortable with the thought of barbarian troops defeating a more truly Roman army under any circumstances."

"I know what you mean," I replied. "What sort of a message does it send both to our own population and that of the barbarians recently settled on both banks of the Danube?"

"It was awfully decent of you to omit the Rhine in your last remark." Fredemondus smiled. "But the defeat on the Rhine bothers me just as much as this civil war has. Defeats of Roman armies are rarely stand-alone events. They inevitably serve as the go-ahead sign for further incursions. I just think that the manner in which we achieved victory in this civil war, by relying so heavily on barbarians, does not bode well for the future."

"Let's just hope that this recent civil war turns out to have been our last," I said. "The time has long passed when they could be described as anything but suicidal luxuries."

"I heard an interesting rumor pertaining to an impending reorganization of the Eastern Army," Fredemondus said, changing the subject. "Apparently, Theodosius has plans to drastically alter the organization of the mobile field units. There might be as many as four or five separate armies."

"Five mobile field armies?" I asked incredulously. "How the hell will we ever be able to afford them or obtain their manpower? As last year's riots in Antioch indicated, we can barely afford the military we've got now. One such army would be the one stationed on the eastern frontier. But obtaining as many as four others would not be easy."

"Based on its original configuration," Fredemondus considered, "the Eastern Empire does not need that many field armies. If the rumor is correct, then I don't think Illyria will be returned to the West. What I've heard is that there will be a separate mobile field army for each of Thrace and Illyria. Where the others will be is anybody's guess."

"Annexing Illyria to the East permanently would make for a better geographical balance," I reasoned. "But territorial 'loss' of any kind always causes hard feelings of one sort or another. If Theodosius does hang onto Illyria, then it will be interesting to see how it plays against political feelings here in the West."

Looking back after the passage of several decades, our concerns for the future were only too well founded if ill-defined. At the time, what else could they be? The warmth of the afterglow of our civil war victory of 388 faded slowly at first and then plummeted as conditions deteriorated in both Gaul and Thrace. Any cynic could have predicted the latter and many of us did. But the former would take us completely by surprise.

The following four days, I spent, sometimes by myself, sometimes in the company of others, touring this magnificent capital to end all capitals. The eastern seat of government might be in Constantinople and its western counterpart in Milan (later moved to Ravenna in 402), but the spiritual capital of this remarkable empire of ours will always be Rome. Where else could it be? On the second day, I traveled to the northwest corner of the city and visited the Mausoleum of Augustus by the Campus Martius. After crossing the Aelian Bridge, I toured Hadrian's Tomb and saw the Circus of Hadrian at Vatican Field. I was surprised to find that this latter part of the city lies outside the protective wall built by Aurelian and Probus. One of the buildings I wanted to visit most of all was the Pantheon. This masterpiece was originally built in 27 BC, the year that the imperial form of government was established. Emperor Hadrian completely rebuilt it a century and a half later, and Septimius Severus and Caracalla made some minor alterations early in the third century. Its dome, 142 feet in diameter, is the largest ever constructed.

The enormous circular interior of the building is illuminated only by a twenty-seven-foot skylight at the center of the dome. After visiting the Pantheon, I relaxed in the Baths of Agrippa, the oldest that I have ever visited. Just across the street from the Pantheon, they were constructed in 19 BC and receive their water from the Aqueduct of Virgo. On the third day, a group of us went to watch the gladiatorial exhibitions at the Coliseum. This is the largest of all the amphitheaters in the empire. By "amphitheater," I mean those circular or elliptical arenas designed specifically for showing gladiatorial combat and wild beast fights. It has a seating capacity of fifty thousand. On August 23, 217, the Coliseum was hit by several lightning strikes that resulted in a serious fire. The damage was so severe that it was closed until repairs were completed in 223 under Alexander Severus.

The top story had been most severely damaged. Although we had good seats at a lower level, I could see, even from where we were sitting, that the repair work to the upper story looked peculiar. During a break in the show, I went up to the upper level to inspect the repair work and was quite surprised at what I saw. The restoration work was quite shoddy and I was reminded of what some of the protective walls of the shrunken cities of Gaul look like. The workmen of the time had used damaged pieces from the Coliseum along with materials from nearby older buildings that were in the process of being demolished. They were cemented together in a way that would have disgusted the original builders.

The growing influence of Christianity had tried to suppress gladiatorial exhibitions but to little effect. (Christian leadership throughout the empire will not be satisfied until it has ruined everybody's fun.) Constantine I in 325, Constantius II in 357, and later Honorius in 397 would all in their time issue laws to abolish these games. However, when faced with public outrage over the matter, these emperors decided to satisfy themselves with the proclamations alone and never mind the enforcement. Nonetheless, one unfortunate incident in 404 led the spineless and stupid Honorius to put an end to gladiatorial combat once and for all. Only wild-beast fights and boxing and wrestling matches have been permitted in such arenas ever since.

Late in the afternoon, I broke from the others and went off to the northeast to visit the Arch of Gallienus on the Via Labicana. I have always admired this much-abused man who tried so hard and paid such terrible personal sacrifices to hold the empire together. My respect for him has only grown as conditions in my own lifetime have deteriorated apparently beyond recall.

With the intense heat, we understandably spent a lot of time in the various baths around the city, including those of Constantine, Diocletian, and Trajan. There are 956 baths in Rome! I have sometimes wondered how many forests were chopped down over the centuries to keep them heated. Most of the wood for this purpose now comes from Africa. I also took in a couple of theatrical presentations and visited some of the more famous gardens. The last place I visited, however, was to my way of thinking the most symbolically important though perhaps the least impressive from the standpoint of appearances—the House of Romulus where the incredible story of our commonwealth began. Our visit to the city was a marvelous experience, but as all good things must, it soon came to an end. It was just as well. I was anxious to get back to Belgrade and see Makila and the baby.

With our Roman holiday over, the various units took leave of the Eternal City and headed back to their home bases. A good many would be traveling by ship, and so they marched to either of the twin ports of Ostia or Portus Augusti at the mouth of the Tiber and departed from there. For units from the central Danube, such as our own, the quickest way to return to base was overland. After a campaign that had taken months and in which we had not fired a single shot, we were going home.

CHAPTER

7

A Future Foreclosed
(388–392)

EARLY THE NEXT MORNING, after breakfast, Fredemondus called our century together for what turned out to be a very special meeting:

"Gentlemen, we have had a change of plans. We are not returning to Belgrade immediately. His Majesty Valentinian II and his family will be traveling to Milan. They will meet with His Majesty Theodosius to discuss political affairs in the aftermath of our victory. As you know, there are seven Palatine Guard cavalry regiments in the Eastern Empire that constitute the Imperial Guard under the command of Stilicho. When His Majesty Valentinian II left Italy last year, part of only one of his Palatine Guard regiments made the trip with him. For our just-completed campaign, this regiment was brought up to strength by borrowing several squadrons from Stilicho's regiments. These squadrons have been ordered returned. His Majesty Valentinian has requested that several units originally stationed in the West be assigned to him as replacements to act as his bodyguard on the trip north. We are one of the units so selected. This is a profound honor, and you've earned it."

"Do we know what the status is of the other western Palatine Guard regiments?" someone asked.

"Not at the present time," our centurion replied. "If those regiments, in fact, fought for the usurper, they will be disbanded. Their soldiers will be distributed to other less prestigious cavalry or infantry regiments as punishment. His Majesty Valentinian and his advisers are still conferring with senators and other officials, so our departure has been postponed until tomorrow. You won't be too disappointed, I trust, to learn that for the journey from Rome to Milan, we will all be mounted." Cheers all around. "I am ordering each of you to be on your best behavior at all times," our centurion continued. "Good conduct is demanded under all circumstances. At this particular time, however, your deportment must be of the highest order in every way. Remember we are in the imperial presence. Screw-ups by anybody will not be taken lightly either by me or the officers in charge of this force."

After this briefing, I approached Fredemondus. "If the western Palatine Guard regiments are disbanded, then might our century be incorporated into one of the new regiments that will be raised to replace them?"

"I honestly don't know," Fredemondus replied, "but I suspect that might be the case."

"It's an exciting prospect," I went on. "Their pay scales are substantially higher than the regular regiments and they have other privileges as well."

Fredemondus paused for a moment before replying. "This is strictly between you and me," he said. "I asked the tribune who requested our century the same question. He replied that if I was making an informal request for such a posting, it would be taken into consideration if such a restructuring of the Western Imperial Guard becomes necessary. As I said, don't mention a word of this to anyone. I don't want to raise any false hopes. I don't think the fact that we are an infantry century would make any difference as to whether or not we are chosen for a Palatine Guard regiment. We could be retrained as a cavalry unit. My knowledge about the Palatine Guard is not exactly firsthand. I believe that only the First Palatine Guard Regiment acts as the actual bodyguard. The remaining ones take part in a lot of nonmilitary missions to the point where they constitute a sort of mobile civil service to some extent."

"Okay," I said, "thanks for the information."

"One more thing," Fredemondus said, "and this too you must keep in strict confidence. I'm uncertain how our new assignment will affect this, but my intention, as soon as we returned to Belgrade, was to recommend you for officer candidate school. Every year, centurions make such recommendations to their regimental tribunes, who in turn review the submissions before passing them up the chain to the legion prefects. Just because I make the recommendation does not mean that it will be accepted. However, given that Julius Aranius is our regimental commander, I think there is a good chance that you will be admitted. The school lasts for ten weeks and would be held in Sofia. It's the closest one to Belgrade. It all depends on what happens once we reach Milan."

It was remarkable news all around. The idea of becoming an Imperial Guard member and attending officer candidate school was almost too much to take in at one time. My excitement, however, was immediately tempered when I suddenly remembered my father's warning of years ago, reflecting on how lucky we were to be far removed from the seat of imperial power. It had been a wise caution. But of course I ignored it.

Valentinian II had not held an official triumph in Rome, but it had been the next best thing. The Senate had, on rather short notice, laid on a splendid round of celebratory activities that were hardly disinterested in their primary objective. The senators had amends to make given the friendship many of them had with the usurper's regime. As a result, they had laid it on lavishly: the finest drivers were available for the chariot races; the best gladiatorial combats in years were quickly arranged at the Coliseum and other arenas, along with boxing and wrestling matches; gymnastic exhibitions, wild animal displays, and theatrical presentations were held all over the city. The Senate had done well, and our appetites were pretty well sated by the time we left.

Valentinian II and his family were now traveling in two elaborate carriages, provided courtesy of the Senate. His ad hoc bodyguard, consisting of both cavalry and mounted infantry, was composed of about three hundred men. As we passed through the city, there were large, cheering throngs lining the streets everywhere. It seemed as though half the population had turned out. Their rousing sendoff was certainly a morale booster. Marching past those ancient forums, I could not help but reflect, for what seemed like the thousandth time since my arrival, that this was where it all began. How could this single city have acquired the greatest empire in history? Rome: creating new institutions in response to new circumstances while maintaining others a thousand years old. Everywhere one looked, the scene could only be described as magnificent. The churches, temples, amphitheaters, stadiums, theaters, statues, and public buildings brilliantly reflect the splendor of this grandest of realms. Even though the style might have originated many centuries in the past in Greece, the artistry we saw in every direction was original. Constantinople, on the other hand, proudly displays artworks that have been stolen from practically every province in the empire that had anything worth making off with. The more I saw of Rome, the more my opinion of the capital of the East declined. Class versus swank. Even though imperial expansion had come to an end centuries earlier, Rome gives the impression of a city looking forever outward. Constantinople, on the other hand, represents not grandeur and innovation but fear and stagnation. We continued north, passing in succession under the arches of Diocletian, Claudius, and Marcus Aurelius until we departed the city by the Flaminian Gate.

Several miles north of Rome, the Via Flaminia crosses the Tiber River, at which point we passed from Latium into Etruria (Tuscany). Immediately after this, the highway divides in two. We took the left branch, known as the Via Clodia, which continues in a northwesterly direction through Etruria. Given that we were all mounted, our journey up to Milan would proceed at a much faster pace than had the trek from Brindisi to Rome. Etruria is bounded on the north by the Apennines and on the east and south by the Tiber River. The region's topography can best be described as confused, consisting as it does of hills and valleys, restricted plains, and areas that are inadequately drained. It receives considerably more rainfall than southern Italy and as a result is one of the more prosperous agricultural areas on the peninsula. The wines produced in Etruria are perhaps the best in Italy because of the area's fertile soils, abundant sunshine, and the experience of vintners extending back over many generations. It is also well known for its olives, and grain farms are widespread, along with the raising of numerous livestock.

In spite of the more favorable agricultural conditions, many districts in Etruria are sparsely populated because of the danger from nearby swamps and lakes of malarial infection.

We continued up the Via Clodia and around Lake Bracciano. We passed through the city of Saturnia and on to the point where the Via Clodia ends by joining the Via Aurelia that runs along the entire coast of Etruria. One of the most pleasant places we stayed was at the small naval base of Pisa. One thing about traveling in the imperial presence is that one eats extremely well. Messengers had informed each city that we visited well in advance of our arrival. As a result, they put on lavish feasts at every stop along the line. The distance from Rome to Milan is about 340 miles, and there are a lot of cities along the route. You get the idea. After a particularly sumptuous meal at Pisa, our centurion, Fredemondus, called us together.

"I don't know about the rest of you guys, but if I eat much more on this trip, I'm going to wind up weighing more than my horse," he joked. We laughed, but for most of us, the laughter was a little painful since we were all stuffed as well. "Lord, these Italians know how to eat, don't they?" he went on. "On a more serious note, I was just informed that immediately after the execution of Magnus Maximus, His Majesty Theodosius sent Arbogast to Trier, where he executed Victor, the usurper's son, who had been elevated to the title of Caesar just before his father invaded Italy. Arbogast has been commissioned to get those defenses of Gaul that were damaged during recent Germanic invasions back into working order. His Majesty Theodosius is currently in Milan awaiting our arrival among other things. That's all I have in the way of news for the moment."

"What do you think about the appointment of Arbogast?" someone asked.

"I think he is a first-rate choice," Fredemondus replied. "As a Frank, he is quite familiar with the area. In 380, Emperor Gratian sent his top general, Bauto, with Arbogast as his deputy to assist in the recovery of the Balkans after Hadrianople. These two generals were largely responsible for the success that we enjoyed in eventually bottling the Visigoths up in northern Thrace. I don't think a better selection could have been made for the task of strengthening the Rhine."

It sounded good to the army at the time as it did to people everywhere. We had no way of knowing that the first few bricks had just been laid in a whole new road to Hell.

From Pisa, we traveled along the coast to Luna before turning north onto another highway. This road took us through a pass in the Apennines and then followed the Parma River to the city of the same name. In the process, we left the province of Etruria in the Diocese of the City of Rome and entered the province of Aemilia in the Diocese of Italy. The province takes its name from the famous highway. The Apennines are much more impressive in this area than they are in the south and reach elevations of several thousand feet in places. At Parma, we linked up with the Via Aemilia. This highway runs in a southeast to northwest direction from Rimini on the west coast of the Adriatic across northern Italy to Piacenza. Aemilia, being on the north side of the Apennines, is a very rich province, as are most districts in the Po Valley. Its climate, while technically classified as Mediterranean, has certain of the more continental aspects to it. While its summers are as hot as in the rest of Italy, its winters are colder, and the palm tree does not grow there. Generally, the farther up the valley one travels, the more severe the winter. The more equitable northern climate is not just due to its higher latitude. The prevailing winds in the Po Valley are from the east, whereas those in the more southerly two-thirds of the peninsula blow up from Africa. In the north, rain generally falls throughout the year, and there is more of it. From the Via Aemilia north to the Po, a broad, rich plain exists that contains some of the richest farmland in Italy. The drainage basin of the Po is half as large as Roman Britain. For the first time since we landed at Brindisi, we started to see large beef and dairy herds. At Parma, we turned to the northwest again. We started to leave the Apennines behind, and after crossing the Po at Piacenza, we arrived at Milan. There followed a heartwarming reunion between both branches of the extended imperial family. Late in 387, the recently widowed Theodosius, at age forty, had married Galla, the teenaged sister of Valentinian II. The new empress of the East was pregnant when Theodosius left for the West. She would give birth to a daughter who would reign as empress in her own right: Galla Placidia.

We all knew Theodosius would have to remain in the West for a while to get affairs in order for his young brother-in-law. In addition, the West had every right to expect that the highly experienced Theodosius would provide the education in statecraft and the guidance in its practice that Valentinian II needed. The young emperor was four when his father died and twelve when his half brother had been assassinated. The most influential man in his life to date had been Bishop Ambrose. While the bishop had performed diplomatic duty on behalf of Milan in the aftermath of Gratian's assassination, his chief interest was furthering the interests of the Catholic Church. The bishop's intellect was renowned throughout the empire, but his was a one-dimensional mentality. Theodosius would provide the much-needed secular extensions to Valentinian's understanding of the world. At least that was the popular hope. What would soon manifest itself was that Theodosius's scheme for the future management of the West had more than one name attached to it.

The rumor was true. Shortly after arriving in Milan, Theodosius substantially reorganized the Eastern Roman Army. Its mobile field armies were drastically increased from two to five. Three of them were "territorial" in that they were responsible for maintaining the security of a specific region. One each was assigned to Thrace, Illyria, and the East (meaning the frontier with the Persian Empire of Iran). The remaining two were "imperial" field armies that could be assigned anywhere the emperor felt circumstances warranted. A master of soldiers (or field marshal) would head each of these armies. This was great news for the East. However, the downside for the West was that a number of its best cavalry regiments were transferred to the East to meet these new manpower requirements. Theodosius did not want to become more dependent on the Visigoths than he was already.

What concerned me personally about this transfer was that an inordinate number of the best soldiers in Britain were shipped to Thrace and Illyria. It was standard procedure to transfer rebellious units to different areas once their revolt had been suppressed. But in Britain, their numbers were not replaced. The British defenses were being stripped to bolster those on the continent. It was not the last time that such a troop removal would hit the island.

Shortly after our arrival in Milan, Fredemondus called us together for another brief announcement:

"Gentlemen, it is my honor and privilege to announce that our century has been chosen as a component of a new Imperial Guard regiment that …" A great cheer went up from all of us that drowned out the rest of the sentence. "The old western guard regiments are being disbanded because of their disloyalty during the recent crisis," he went on. "Those of us with families back in Belgrade will be permitted to return there soon to fetch them here, where we will be stationed for the foreseeable future."

A huge banquet was held shortly after we arrived in Milan to commemorate the reestablishment of Valentinian II as emperor of the West. Bishop Ambrose attended, as did members of a senatorial delegation from Rome. Also present were numerous important civil servants and army officers. However, it was not just restricted to big shots. Those of us comprising the new Western Imperial Guard were also invited even if we were segregated off in a far corner of the hall for the main dinner. In Constantinople, I had seen Theodosius only at a distance, but at this dinner in Milan, things were much less formal. The emperor loved to show himself off as a man of the people. The idea of affecting a pose of oriental aloofness that so many of his predecessors had assumed was totally foreign to him. He never feared for his personal safety and was always willing to plunge into a crowd to get to know people better. In this manner, he refused to distinguish between civilians and the military, much to the constant concern of members of his bodyguard.

After the dinner, he came over to where a group of us were standing and struck up conversations with everyone that he could. He wanted to know where we were from, how long we had been in the army, where we had served, what our fathers did, and so on. For the most part, his conversations were limited to the top officers who tried to hog all his time. Nonetheless, the emperor would frequently break away and talk to some of us in the ranks as well. I was flabbergasted when he approached me.

"And where are you from, young fellow?"

"Cirencestor in Britain, sir," I replied. "My name is Marcus Cedranus."

He smiled at this. "I remember Britain fondly. I served there on my father's staff when I was only about your age, and I liked it very much. It's a pleasant country, and I've always envied its relatively peaceful history. It's unfortunate that the whole empire could not be more like Britain and Africa in that respect."

"Your father's name will always be revered in Britain for what he accomplished on our behalf," I said.

"Thank you," Theodosius replied and then glanced off for a moment with an unfocussed look in his eyes. "Is there any special question that you would like to ask me?"

I was surprised at this. Looking back now, it might have been due to the wine's influence, but I decided to ask anyway. "My lord, almost from the beginning of the usurpation of Magnus Maximus there was the rumor that you and he were related in some way. Is that true?" I saw some of the officers in our group, Fredemondus among them, wince when they heard what I said. But it did not appear to bother Theodosius.

"Yes," he replied, "he and I were distant cousins. That's why I have arranged to have his daughters adopted by joint relatives of ours."

At that point, one of the officers asked him a question on a different matter, and my audience was over. Perhaps it was felt that I had best be stopped before I asked the emperor any other questions of such a personal nature. What crossed my mind then was the old Sicilian saying that "the more things change, the more they remain the same." At the dawn of the imperial system, the great civil war fought between Augustus (then still known as Octavius) Caesar and Mark Anthony was also an enormous family quarrel. Those two men were distant cousins as well. Mark Anthony's maternal grandfather, Lucius Caesar, was an uncle of Julius Caesar. Thus, Mark Anthony's mother and Julius Caesar were first cousins. And here we were over four centuries later having just completed another civil war between relatives. Our officers might have feared that I was going to ask the emperor about his execution of young Victor, the son of Magnus Maximus. There was no fear of that. Every educated man learns early in life of the admonition to Augustus that "it is unwise to have too many Caesars."

227

None of us had had a chance to gain any appreciation of Milan when we had to leave for Belgrade. We traveled southeast to Cremona where we linked up with the Via Postumia. It would carry us eastward through Verona and Concordia to Aquileia at the head of the Adriatic. The Po River Valley is the best watered area in Italy, and, having been a recent visitor to Apulia, the contrasts between the two districts are considerable. There are numerous rivers in the area around Milan, and all of them flow into the Po. North-central Italy also has many lakes, and for a short time, my wife and I would discover just how beautiful this area really is. Districts near the central Po Valley receive about twenty-four inches of rainfall per year, and about three times that amount falls in the mountainous areas to the north. Given its more "continental" climate, I was surprised to see olive orchards this far north. There are numerous irrigation and land reclamation projects in the region, and many of them date back centuries. The clearing of forests and the draining of swampland have led to the establishment of large wheat farms and cattle ranches as well as the raising of other types of livestock. These projects have increased land productivity greatly. Not only are grain farms larger than those in the south, but their yields are much higher. Fruit orchards and vineyards are also in abundance.

Continuing eastward, we started to get farther away from the Po and entered the province of Venetia and Istria. At Aquileia, we took a day off from our journey to tour this vitally important seaport where so much recent history had taken place. To the east of this city, we entered the Julian Alps and started to climb. These mountains form an important part of the watershed between the drainage basins of the Black and Adriatic Seas. We next arrived at the strategic city of Emona. Its importance lies in its location near the eastern entrance to the pass containing the main highway through this range. This pass provides the most direct access between Italy and Pannonia. Emona served as a milestone of a sort because there we entered the valley of the Sava River. Continuing to the southeast down this valley, we arrived at Sisak. The towns downriver from there were the ones we had started provisioning a year earlier for the northern wing of the campaign. We continued along the highway on the right bank of the Sava until it crossed the river at Marsonia.[21] Several days later, we caught sight of Taurunum, the headquarters of the Pannonian Fleet on the other side of which lay Belgrade. The whole journey from Milan to Belgrade had covered almost six hundred miles.

It was early evening when we entered the city. With great trepidation, I approached our apartment after stabling my horse. I could hear women's voices, but I couldn't tell who they were. I knocked on the door, and after a few moments, Makila answered. With her long black tresses tumbling halfway down her back and around her shoulders, she never looked more beautiful. She simply smiled and said, "Welcome home, Daddy." We wrapped our arms around one another and enjoyed one of those long, wet kisses that you would like to see last for about a week. For an instant, I thought I might have cracked one of her ribs when she gave out a short yell. Fortunately, everything was fine.

"What do we have?" I asked.

"You are the proud father of twin daughters," she said, taking me off to a corner of our living room.

"Twins?" I gasped.

"Twins. Each one has ten fingers and ten toes, and everything else appears to be normal as well."

Two of Makila's friends were there as well and had been coming over for several hours every day to help her look after the babies. Julia had been true to her word and had proven an indispensable help in that regard. The two friends soon left, knowing that Makila and I had a lot of catching up to do. Before I had left on the campaign, we had chosen two boys' and two girls' names that we both agreed on, though we never for a moment expected to become the parents of twins.

"Meet your little girls, Pops—Demetria Makila and Justina Teresa, just as we agreed."

I sat there for what must have seemed like an eternity to Makila. Holding each one in turn and then just staring back and forth from the one to the other as they lay in their bassinets, I just couldn't take my eyes off them. Makila had already eaten, but I hadn't, so after I made a hurried trip to the market, she cooked supper for me. During and after the meal, I spent a lot of time describing our campaign, such as it was.

"And you guys never even saw the enemy during the entire war?" she asked disbelievingly.

"That's right, hon, not even once. Believe me, it would be great if all wars could be fought like the one that our century just went through."

I described as much of the Macedonian and Italian countrysides as best I could and went all out to characterize Rome. After that, it was time to start making up for all those months that we spent apart. The next day, we started out like the previous evening had finished. I've always been a morning man where sex is concerned. Finally, Makila had to feed the babies, and I fell asleep again. When she climbed back into bed, I awakened and decided that it was time to tell her.

"I was going to tell you this last night, dearest," I said, wrapping my arms around her, "but we had more important things to do if you will recall."

"I have a vague recollection," she said with more than just a trace of concern in her voice. "Tell me what?" Her Latin had become pretty good in a rather short period of time, and her thick Axumite accent made her even sexier.

"We're moving."

"Where to?" she asked. "I like it here."

"Fredemondus told me while we were in Rome that he was going to recommend me for officer candidate school."

"Terrific," she responded. "Where?"

"Well, that's where things get complicated. It's a ten week course. If we were staying in Belgrade I would have to go to Sofia for it. But while we were in Milan it was announced that our century was being detached from Second Regiment, Legion IV Flavia Firma and being reassigned to a new regiment of the Western Imperial Guard that will be established shortly. We're moving to Milan, gorgeous. It's a whole new world."

"Where is Milan?" she asked. "I've heard of it."

"In northern Italy, and it's the capital of the Western Empire. In terms of population, it's the second largest city in the West after Rome. I would estimate it will take us about forty-five days to get there. That is, provided the weather holds and we don't get caught in any early snowstorms."

Three days later, our convoy started west.

We had heard for years of how Bishop Ambrose dominated the court of Valentinian II, but we had written that off to the youth and inexperience of the western emperor. The notion of a priest, even a bishop, dictating to an adult emperor was absurd. Now that Theodosius was also resident at Milan, we were confident that such clerical contemptuousness would be brought to an end. Bishop Ambrose was by far the most dominant figure in the Catholic Church. This was not surprising given that his aristocratic background, upper-class education, and brilliant intellect permitted him to debate circles around anyone. What would astonish us all was the manner in which he would soon convince Theodosius that the emperor's secular responsibilities as chief of state were of secondary importance to his duties as a Roman Catholic, as defined by the bishop of Milan. His colossal arrogance and total contempt for all opinions that were contrary to his own meant that people either admired Ambrose or detested him. There was no middle ground. The most reasoned arguments for religious toleration, whether they originated with the Roman Senate, his fellow churchmen, or elsewhere, were always met with unyielding hostility. Whenever young Valentinian tried to accommodate the diversity of religious opinions within his realm, the bullying Ambrose was always there to threaten excommunication and eternal damnation if he did so. Ambrose's main purpose in life was to eliminate the pagan religions along with all non-Catholic branches of Christianity. In pursuing these objectives, he had no concern over how socially disruptive his methods were. To Ambrose, the ends always justified his means. At a time when the need for religious toleration was paramount, Ambrose tended to consider anyone who was not a Catholic as Lucifer's henchman. With an ever-increasing number of Visigothic volunteers, who were Arian Christians, joining the Roman Army, how did Ambrose think they would react to a proscription on their religious practices? He probably couldn't care less. He may quite properly be thought of as God's own sonofabitch. In any case, he certainly acted like it.

Ambrose was born in 339 at Trier into a Christian senatorial family. His father held the office of praetorian prefect of the Gauls during the reign of Constantine II, but he died shortly after Ambrose was born. Raised in Rome by his widowed mother, he pursued the standard political career of men of his class and in 370 became governor of the Italian province of Aemelia-Liguria, whose capital was Milan. He was quite popular in this capacity. In 374, the office of bishop of Milan fell vacant, and contesting factions were unable to agree on a successor. In a totally unforeseen development, Ambrose was proclaimed bishop as a compromise nominee, and he accepted. Shortly after the elevation of Ambrose, Valentinian I died. The late emperor had followed a policy of strict toleration with regard to all matters of a religious nature. It is interesting to think of how subsequent church-state conflicts would have evolved if the elder Valentinian had been granted a longer life. With Gratian, who for the latter part of his reign had moved his court to Milan, there was no problem between bishop and emperor since Gratian was a zealous Catholic. But with Valentinian II, the situation was different because his mother, Justina, attempted to pursue her late husband's religious policy. In 386, the dowager empress, acting as her son's regent, undertook to obtain a church for the Arian minority in the city. That minority included a sizable number of Gothic soldiers who had recently enrolled in the city's garrison. Ambrose adamantly refused any concession to these heretics.

The bishop was a demagogue in the fullest sense of the word. In this confrontation, he never hesitated to fuel public opinion against the imperial family. He did this through religious prejudice and also by fanning ethnic bigotry within a section of the Roman populace toward the Gothic soldiers defending them. Ultimately, the empress had to withdraw her request after Catholic mobs, stirred up by Ambrose, threatened to riot. Shortly after we had left Milan in the autumn of 388, an incident occurred that we did not learn about until we reached Belgrade. At the frontier town of Callinicum[22] on the Euphrates a mob of Christians set fire to a Jewish synagogue and the small church belonging to a sect of Christian heretics. First of all, Theodosius ordered the bishop in charge of Callinicum to pay for reconstructing the destroyed synagogue. Ambrose countered by commanding Theodosius to withdraw the order and threatened him with devastation by the Almighty if he did not. Theodosius, as was his nature, reconsidered his original directive on the matter and demanded that the entire community of Callinicum be financially responsible for the reconstruction. Ambrose, seeing that he had the emperor on the run, decided to increase the stakes by refusing to hold communion until Theodosius had rescinded the rebuilding order altogether. In addition, Ambrose forced Theodosius to drop all plans to bring the people who had destroyed the synagogue to justice. Theodosius, fearing that Ambrose would send mobs into the streets of Milan and make the city ungovernable, capitulated just as Empress Justina had done in 386. In effect, Ambrose was saying that in the eyes of the church, an act that would be considered a crime in any other circumstance was "legal" (or at least acceptable) if the person committing it was a Christian acting to further the interests of Catholicism at the direct expense of its enemies, whomever they may be. By implication, Ambrose was demanding that heretic Christians, pagans, and now the Jews have the protection of the law withdrawn from them where attacks on their person and property by rampaging Catholic Christian mobs were concerned.

Theodosius should have foreseen that his policy against pagan temples and the churches of heretic Christians would permeate into other areas. The decision at Callinicum now rendered Jewish synagogues unsafe from self-righteous Catholic rabble. In addition, there had already been an instance near Antioch where a Catholic gang used the "discovery" of the bones of some previously unheard-of martyrs on some valuable farmland as the pretext for seizing the property to enrich themselves. No temple destruction was involved. Before they met, Theodosius, with limited objectives in Constantinople, and Ambrose, with all-or-nothing determination in Milan, were independently pursuing similar policies. It was only when their plans of action collided in an undistinguished town on the farthest reaches of our eastern frontier did the two men come into open conflict with one another. The entire empire was stunned when this imperial reversal was announced. Our convoy only discovered the outcome when it arrived in Aquileia. The first duty of any chief of state is to maintain the external and internal security of the realm. Emperor and bishop, however, were exercising personal policies outside the law that were causing internal disorder in some quarters to match the external chaos that had been reigning quite recently on the frontiers. Each man saw his consequences-be-damned attitude as a manifestation of God's will, and this state of affairs would only worsen.

A biannual pattern was emerging that we should have recognized earlier. In 384, Ambrose led the charge against the restoration of pagan privileges that had been requested by his distant cousin, the famous pagan senator Quintus Aurelius Symmachus. These prerogatives had been withdrawn earlier by Gratian. In 386, Ambrose stood down the dowager empress over the issue of the Arian church in Milan, and now in 388 Theodosius had felt compelled to submit to Ambrose's demands over the issue of the Jewish synagogue. The victory of Ambrose over Theodosius had been just as complete as his earlier "triumphs" over Valentinian II. The bishop had won his greatest victory in personal terms yet, but a far greater one lay just two years ahead.

Our convoy continued westward. With women, children, and household goods in tow, our rate of progress was understandably slow. Our biggest concern was the weather. We pushed as hard as we could because we wanted to make it through the Julian Alps before the bad weather started. Makila and I were both concerned for the welfare of our daughters. Their health was good, but, still being in the first year of their young lives, we worried constantly over them. Fortunately, our luck held. Storms held off while we made it through the mountains and into Venetia. After leaving Aquileia, the weather soured, and we spent my twenty-fourth birthday riding through a driving rainstorm. On December 15, we entered Milan during a light snowfall, the first of the season. Instead of living in a private apartment as we did in Belgrade, we were assigned to married quarters specially reserved for the Imperial Guard on the outskirts of the city. This large barracks had been empty since the original regiments in the old bodyguard were disbanded. As a result, we had the pick of the best apartments. Several days after we arrived, Fredemondus informed me that I had been accepted for officer candidate school along with Chlogius. It was great news, and at least I would know someone there.

As Christmas approached, I could not help but be appreciative for the good fortune that had befallen me during the course of the past year. My beautiful wife had presented me with two fine children; I had not suffered so much as a scratch in combat; I had visited Rome, been advanced to the Imperial Guard and been accepted into officer candidate school. Life was good. It was very good. As an act of gratitude, I made a large (for me) financial contribution to a Catholic orphanage in the city. It was the least I could do. In the brief time between our arrival and the start of the New Year, we tried to become more familiar with our new home. However, the season limited these efforts and more detailed explorations would have to await the spring.

Milan is a very ancient city that was founded by Gallic peoples about 600 BC. It is located in the center of a rich agricultural area between the Ticino and Adda Rivers, two northerly tributaries of the Po. At a sufficient distance from all these rivers, Milan escapes the floods that periodically inundate other cities lying within the Po basin. It is also the capital of the Diocese of Italy. It serves as the hub of a highway network that links the city in an east-west direction up and down the Po River Valley as well as north to Lake Constance on the frontier and south into the heart of Italy. Its origins, location, and surroundings are slightly reminiscent of Vienna. Over a century earlier, when the frontiers collapsed, Milan had taken over from Rome as the chief administrative center of the land. Once established as the capital of the Western Empire, Milan gained predominance over Rome that it has never lost. Prompted by barbarian invasions, this political move reflected the economic ascendancy of the north of Italy over the rest of the country. The cultural heartland might be the central portion of the peninsula, but when it comes to commerce and politics, the north reigns supreme.

On January 1, 389, all troops from the Imperial Guard and the garrison formed up on the main parade square to swear our annual oaths of allegiance to Theodosius, Valentinian II, and Arcadius. Soon after that, the ten-week officer cadet school began. At lunch that first day, the main topic of conversation was Theodosius's recent capitulation to the bishop. Chlogius wasted no time in ragging me about it.

"Well, Marcus," he started. "Good Christian that you are, you must be delighted with the latest humiliation of an emperor by the incomparable Bishop Ambrose."

"I'm no more satisfied with it than you are," I replied.

"I remember on our march up from Rome," Chlogius continued, "how we all agreed on what a fine example Theodosius would set for the youthful Valentinian. He would certainly show his immature colleague how to handle strong-willed advisers—above all, uppity priests—wouldn't he?"

"We seem to have misjudged the 'savior of the East' somewhat, have we not?" I said. "I think I'm going to have to attend some of Ambrose's services if for no other reason than to gain a better understanding of the man. He must have something going for him."

"Above all, what he appears to have is the biggest ego in the empire," Chlogius complained. "Can you imagine any of the great emperors of the past permitting themselves to be kicked around by a priest? Why is Theodosius doing this? I thought you might know since you're on such intimate terms with the man."

We both laughed at this reference to my brief conversation with him.

"I think Theodosius was simply overwhelmed by the powerful intellect of Ambrose," I offered.

"I've heard that from a couple of others as well," Chlogius replied, "but I don't buy it. Intellect and wisdom are not the same thing. In 384, when he rejected the request from his cousin Symmachus to restore the Alter of Victory to the Senate in Rome, Ambrose heaped contempt on the notion that the ancient gods had granted our ancestors dominion over our enemies. The strength of the army all by itself had guaranteed that. But now, just four years later, Ambrose is claiming that the strength of his army had nothing to do with the victory that Theodosius gained over the usurper. It was God's will alone that brought that about. Then the good bishop went on to threaten Theodosius with God's infuriation in the form of no more military victories if he ordered the Jewish synagogue to be rebuilt in Callinicum at public expense. What happened to the strength-of-the-army argument over the past four years? The least Ambrose could do is be just a little more consistent in his contentions."

"No argument from me," I agreed. "The smartest thing Theodosius could do is ban the bishop to some obscure island where he could ponder the consequences of his intemperance over the next several years or the rest of his life for that matter."

"Unfortunately," Chlogius reminded me, "as Empress Justina discovered in 386, Ambrose does have a large and volatile following in the city. Any attempt to do as you say would undoubtedly lead to riots. They could make life rather awkward for the imperial family."

"Then let the army make life difficult for the mob," I replied. "Let the populace make a choice: do they want the capital of the Western Empire resident here or do they want Bishop Ambrose? There are several other cities in northern Italy that would make just as good a capital as Milan. Or for that matter, move it back to Trier. Let Theodosius pick another bishop for the city. He's forced priests onto their congregations literally at sword point in the East. There's no reason why he couldn't do the same thing here as well."

"Yes, but the clerics forced out in the East were Arians being replaced by Catholics. Theodosius is as Catholic as the pope. He won't do it," was Chlogius' final word on the matter. He was right.

"Theodosius, as a politician, knows that in purely political matters, compromise is necessary," I tried to sum up. "But Ambrose is that type of thoroughly abrasive individual that sees concession as synonymous with surrender. The big question is whether or not Theodosius has learned anything from this humiliating experience. Ambrose, throughout his tenure as bishop, has been able to hold a whip hand over Valentinian II. As a result of his first contest with Theodosius, it appears that the bishop will be able to hold the same degree of mastery over him as well. Ambrose, perhaps more than any other bishop, tries to intrude religion into every dimension of political life. Given that, I'm afraid Theodosius will be in for a difficult time here if he does not find the backbone to stand up to him." He never would.

The officer training course was quite intensive, and it was the middle of March before we had completed it. For Chlogius and me, the situation was rather confusing. The infantry centuries in our new regiment were in the process of being retrained as cavalry units. Infantry regiments are headed by a tribune and divided into six eighty-man centuries headed by centurions. Each century is divided into ten decades headed by decurions. Cavalry regiments are also headed by a tribune but are divided into sixteen thirty-man squadrons, each commanded by a decurion. A decurion is thus an officer in the cavalry but a noncommissioned officer in the infantry. Having completed officer cadet training did not mean that promotion to officer rank was anywhere on the horizon. It simply meant that you would be considered for such promotion when one became available, as they frequently did. However, unless the officer cadet was quite exceptional in his qualification, the promotion often took years. So that we didn't become rusty in what we had learned, there were periodic refresher courses that we all had to take. The need for a large reservoir of officer cadets, I would come to realize, was necessitated by the fear of civil war as much as foreign invasion.

The period from the end of 388 until the spring of 392 would be the happiest of my life. The days of road maintenance and fortress construction were behind once I was admitted to the Imperial Guard. The military training, however, was much more heavily emphasized. This was especially true for my regiment since we all had to be retrained as cavalrymen. We spent a great deal of time jumping ditches and walls and learning to use our swords and spears from the saddle. The most dangerous part of the training was learning to swim with our horses while fully suited up in armor. Every year, men were lost during such training exercises. Sometimes we were drawn off for nonmilitary activity, as in the spring of 389, when we had to assist flood victims from the Adda and Ticino Rivers. An unseasonably warm and early spring had quickened the Alpine runoff. We found ourselves evacuating villagers and their belongings as well as we could, but in spite of our best efforts, we were unable to prevent a number from drowning. Flooding is a recurring problem during the spring in northern Italy. Flood evacuation is something in which all local army units are called upon to assist.

Makila and I, in addition to being deeply in love with one another, came to love this area of Italy as well. Our only regret was that we would spend too little time there. In April 389, we made the twenty-five-mile trip up to the resort town of Como on the southwestern branch of the lake with the same name. The town has a very pretty setting adjoined by two-thousand-foot mountains. A large number of wealthy families have their villas around its shore. Some are so close to the lake that their owners can catch fish out their windows or from their verandas. Como's most famous son, or at least its most grateful, was Pliny the Younger. He organized the construction of a private school in the town so that local families would not have to send their sons off to Milan for an education. In addition to richly endowing the school from a number of lucrative farms that he owned, he enlisted the help of his friend, the great historian Tacitus, to provide a faculty for it. He also had constructed public baths and a library that he also endowed. Over three centuries later, these institutions are still there. It was while on this brief vacation that Makila became pregnant again. She could not have conceived in a prettier place. Life was good and getting better.

After arresting and executing Victor, the son of Magnus Maximus, in September 388, Arbogast's next priority was the reorganization and reconstruction of the Rhine defenses. First, he added to the field army that he had brought with him those mobile units under the command of the usurper's generals, Syrus and Carietto. Arbogast demanded of the enemy, German Franks, that they surrender all the plunder that they had stolen, plus the leaders that had started the recent war. In doing this, the field marshal overplayed his hand. With the recent defeat that the army of Quintinus had suffered firmly in mind, Arbogast was reluctant to go into immediate combat with the enemy when his demands were refused. After hesitating, he decided to write Valentinian II, requesting how to respond to this awkward situation. The reply from the young emperor's advisers recommended a peace treaty with the German Franks rather than going to war with them. This was duly negotiated. As a result, more Franks were allowed to enter Gaul in the traditional manner by which previous Franks had settled there. As a guaranty of good behavior, these new arrivals also gave hostages. These resettlement activities continued throughout 389. Gaul was in the process of being repacified and relations between the field marshal and his young chief of state appeared proper. There was, as yet, no suggestion of any problems.

In late April 389, the emperors jointly announced that Valentinian II would be taking up permanent residence in Trier. We were all ordered to our quarters to start packing. Unfortunately, I had a lot of paperwork to complete that day, so I arrived back at our apartment later than usual.

"Rough day at the office, hon?" Makila asked after a long and delicious embrace.

"No, not really. I'm late because I had to process the paperwork for a number of Ostrogothic recruits we're taking on. There are a lot of them settled hereabouts as tenant farmers on various estates. I just never realized there were so many."

Makila was feeding the children, and since there is never a good time for imparting what might be taken as bad news, I informed her that we were being reassigned to the Rhineland.

"It would have been nice if you had given me a little more warning than just three days," she said, sounding none too pleased.

"It was the best that I could do. I think you will like Trier. It's a pretty town, somewhat smaller than Milan, with a climate that is not all that different. I wish that we could have spent more time here, but in the army, transfers can come on rather short notice, as you are starting to find out."

I took her in my arms and held her tightly.

"I'm not surprised at this," I went on. "Almost everyone in the Western Empire, outside of Italy, has come to feel abandoned by their rulers. It's been almost half a century since a reigning emperor visited Britain. I can't remember when one last toured Africa or Spain. I would expect Theodosius to visit the more westerly provinces himself once he gets the situation here in Italy settled down and back to normal. We're heading north, sweet stuff. Our tour of duty here is at an end."

Because of the suddenness of our departure, Bishop Ambrose held a special service to baptize recently born children of Imperial Guard soldiers. Makila had been attending classes herself at the cathedral in preparation for entering the Christian faith. Her baptism was rushed forward to this service as well so that all three of my "girls" were baptized at the same time. We spent the next two days getting our belongings packed onto wagons. Before leaving, I sent a letter to Margareta in Trier. Makila had been rather suspicious of this woman to the far north and I was not entirely certain that I had allayed those fears. Before leaving Milan, a scouting party had ridden ahead to investigate conditions in the pass through which we would be traversing the continental divide. They reported back that it was clear. Most of us were apprehensive because of the season. Nonetheless, we were all excited at the prospect of traveling directly through the heart of the Alps.

Passing through the town of Bergamo, we continued up the east shore of Lake Como. At the northern end of this lake, the mountains rise in some cases to eight thousand feet. From here we traveled up the steep valley of the Liro River to the Splugen Pass that lies at an altitude of a little over 6,900 feet. This pass marks a division between the Lepontine Alps to the west and the Rhaetian Alps to the east. North of it are the great watersheds of the Rhine and the Danube. To the south lies that of the Po. The highway through this pass is almost always closed during the winter and has long had a reputation for being subject to avalanches during the spring. Fortunately, our transit through it encountered no problems. The scenery during the trip was overwhelming with the towering slate grays and snowcaps of the mountains and the plunging valleys almost every shade of green. Once we were safely through the pass, we entered the valley that contains the headwaters of the Rhine. It is a rather narrow mountain river at this point, giving no hint of its future greatness. Its banks are quite steep and heavily forested, with just an occasional bald patch in places, indicative of a probable landslide. We would pass through the towns of Curia, Magia, and Clunia.[23] Not far from Curia, the Rhine plunges into a narrow, menacing gorge known as the Via Mala. The noise is incredible, and above the gorge, there is always a fine water spray in permanent suspension. The riverbanks are vertical at the gorge and very close. We suffered a temporary delay at Curia when we were hit by a late-spring snowstorm. Fortunately, the temperature climbed quickly thereafter, and we were on our way as soon as the highway was passable. Midway between Curia and Bregenz, the plain of the Rhine broadens out somewhat, and small farms start to appear. It had been six long years since I first passed through Bregenz on the shore of Lake Constance. While those years had been extremely productive, exciting, and rewarding, it was gratifying to see this beautiful region once more.

At Bregenz, we found that Theodosius was going to hold an official triumph in Rome on June 13. This announcement had been made only a few days after we left Milan and its timing had a most invidious aspect to it. Everyone recognized that Theodosius was the senior emperor regardless of the fact that Valentinian had held office four years longer than his eastern partner. It was, nonetheless, extremely poor protocol for Theodosius to be upstaging his colleague in his own territory. To make matters worse, Theodosius had sent to Constantinople for his younger son, Honorius, to accompany him. However unintentional, this was a deliberate slight to Valentinian II. None of us in his company liked the idea.

"What's bothering you?" Makila asked me later that day.

"I feel uneasy about this coming triumph," I replied, "and I'm also beginning to question Theodosius's capacity for making responsible judgments. The announcement of the triumph has to be demoralizing for Valentinian."

"Why?" she asked. "Valentinian was certainly given a pleasant reception at Rome back in September of last year according to what you told me. Why should he be displeased with the Senate's extending its hospitality to Theodosius as well? After all, it was Theodosius that won Valentinian his throne back."

"Valentinian was given precisely that, a 'pleasant reception,'" I replied. "That is not the same thing. The coming triumph should be a joint affair with both eastern and western emperors attending. It should be symbolic of the reunification of East and West. There is no question that Theodosius has to visit Rome to patch up relations with the Senate. His nature appears to be such that he will probably do an excellent job of it. But, to me, the most disturbing aspect of the celebration is not just that Valentinian will not be there but that Honorius will be."

Makila did not see it that way. "I think you are reading too much into it. Theodosius misses little Honorius, who is only four years old. Look at how much you missed our little girls during the same period of time. It's only natural for the emperor to want to see his son."

"I hope you are right." I smiled at her. "But whenever a reigning emperor presents his son to the Senate, either in Rome or Constantinople, it is for one reason only: he is showing them their future sovereign. Without question, Theodosius will bestow the title of Augustus on his younger son just as he already has with Arcadius. It's not proper. The West is Valentinian's patrimony. If Theodosius wants both his sons to be emperors, it should be as co-emperors in the East. It's in the 'New Rome' that Honorius should be presented to the Senate, not the old one. The fact that Honorius is going to Rome speaks plainly that Theodosius intends for the West to be divided between Valentinian and Honorius. Valentinian has spent his entire life as emperor in shadows cast by others. First his brother, then Ambrose, then a usurper, and then Theodosius. Now he finds himself being upstaged by a kid that isn't even five years old yet."

Tragically, the problem of Valentinian II and Honorius sharing the West would be only of academic interest.

Leaving Bregenz, we traveled along the south of Lake Constance among hills cloaked in vines and a variety of fruit trees. We followed the Rhine westward to the small town of Basel. In addition to being a small fortress, it also serves as the uppermost port for the heavy traffic that travels the river between there and the North Sea. By this time, the river had broadened out to almost nine hundred feet. After Basel, we turned north through the "elbow" that the Rhine follows in passing between the Black Forest to the north in Germany and the Jura Mountains to the southwest. We were now into the plains of the upper Rhine that are about ten miles in width and stretch as far west as the Vosges Mountains. Wine country. We continued through all the fortress towns that some of us had passed through in the opposite direction in 383. We followed the Rhine as far as Mainz before turning west to Trier. The distance from Milan to Trier is over five hundred miles, and every city we passed through celebrated the return to legitimate government. As with our procession through Italy in 388, everyone wanted to proclaim their loyalty to Valentinian II. Boy, were they ever glad to be rid of that tyrannical maniac, Magnus Maximus! We all got a kick out of these often-strained protestations of attachment. (I include the imperial family itself in this.) Not wanting to offend anyone, of course, we all soaked up as much of this hospitality as our systems would allow.

Because of all the partying en route, it was mid-June before we arrived at Trier, the birthplace and new capital of our young emperor. Valentinian II had just turned eighteen, and Trier had been the seat of power of the man who had overthrown and murdered his brother six years earlier. Trier had a lot to live down and certainly did its best. Arbogast, accompanied by a large delegation from the city council, welcomed the imperial family outside the city and escorted them to their palace. The Imperial Guards were shown to their quarters, which were every bit as nice as what we had in Milan. Spacious as they were, there were not enough of them to house us all. Housing allocations were made on the basis of seniority. Those who could not be accommodated at the barracks had to be billeted in private homes.

A huge banquet was given that first night back in Trier. Every available grandmother and single teenage girl in the city appeared to have been rounded up to provide babysitting services for those of us who required them. No time to get acquainted with one's surrounding for those among us who were new to the place. Arbogast had seen to it that the city spared no expense in welcoming Valentinian II back home. All the top civilian officials of the prefecture along with the vicars of its dioceses attended. In addition, many top military officers were present along with leading members of the local aristocracy. Regarding the Imperial Guards, all officers and officer cadets were invited, which was how Makila and I got to attend. Roast beef, roast lamb, ham and pork, honeyed chicken, almost every food combination imaginable was available. No matter how glutted one's tastes might be, no end of additional culinary enchantments was available as added temptations. The emperor gave a brief but engaging speech that was both understanding of his audience's anxieties and forward-looking in its outlook. Valentinian II appeared to have a natural aptitude for public speaking, which he had first exhibited to his troops south of Rome the previous year. He also appeared to be gifted, or well trained, in the arts of diplomacy. During the many speeches that he had given at the various banquets, his theme was always one of reconciliation and building for the future. Everywhere, he made it known that the sort of reprisals that emperors of earlier times had indulged in when revolts were put down were a thing of the past as far as he was concerned. Arbogast thanked the emperor and introduced the next speaker, Constantianus, praetorian prefect of the Gauls. He had been appointed to his current post in 388 by Theodosius and Valentinian II and had previously served Theodosius as the vicar of the Diocese of Pontus in northern Anatolia.

Once the speeches were over, it was time for the guests to mingle. While our group of officers and their wives tended to stay together, I excused myself, telling Makila that I wanted to see if anyone that I happened to know from my previous stay in Trier was present. There was, of course, only one person that I knew from the "old days" who could have been. After wandering through the crowd for quite some time, I spied Margareta sitting at a table containing a large number of men who were certainly important in their own eyes.

Approaching her from the side, I asked, "Remember me?"

"Marcus!" she exclaimed. "I hardly recognize you with that beard." She got up, and we kissed and hugged one another.

"It's good to see you again after all this time," I said.

"All right, all right, who is this guy?" asked an elderly gentleman with a big grin as he stood up to the right of her.

"Rufius, this is Marcus, the young soldier that has sent me those interesting diaries and letters of his. Marcus, this is my husband, Rufius Cornelius Anicius. Marcus, we have so much to catch up on. Rufius and I were married almost two months ago."

"My belated congratulations to you both," I said. "You're a fortunate man, Rufius."

"Don't I know it," he laughed.

"Excuse us," Margareta said to the group at her table. "I have to con young Marcus here into attending my history and government seminars now that he is once again resident among us."

She led me away from the table and outside onto a large patio where it was much cooler. She informed me that she had saved the letters and diaries I had sent her and had found great value in them. This in spite of the substantial interruption in our correspondence in recent years. I was then asked to attend a series of seminars that she would be starting at the beginning of September. She wanted me to come as an occasional guest speaker, and I agreed. Now that the seat of the western government was once more located in Trier, she felt that there would be more of a demand for her courses.

"Were you surprised to see that I'm married?" she asked.

"What always bewildered me in that regard was that you had not remarried many years ago. You've been very special to me and I wish you both the very best. How did you meet?"

"His country estate borders mine," she answered. "His first wife died over a year ago, and our coming together was sort of natural, I suppose. It's rather trite to observe that I'm not getting any younger." Then she added, laughingly, "Besides, you were already married. Come on and introduce me to your wife. I assume that you brought her."

I felt the full rush of confused feelings I had experienced when I knew her six years earlier. I did not know how old she was then, apart from recognizing that she was almost a generation ahead of me. The age difference was of no consequence. She was a remarkably beautiful woman, and I was still mesmerized by her. I took her back inside and introduced her to Makila. In the months ahead, our families would become good friends, and we would frequently visit back and forth. After a brief conversation, I escorted Margareta back to her table.

"Marcus, I am stunned," she said as we crossed the great banquet hall. "Makila is absolutely ravishing and such a remarkable racial combination. By the time you leave tonight, you will be the most envied man in Trier."

We agreed to get together once Makila and I had settled down and well before Margareta's new seminars were due to start. It was only at that point that any mention of politics was made. She reflected that everyone throughout the prefecture was satisfied with the excellent job Arbogast had done to get the frontiers in order. This was in accord with what we had been hearing back in Milan. The empire had weathered the recent civil war in better shape than anyone had dared to expect when hostilities began. Throughout the West, the frontiers were quiet, with the usual minor exceptions, and the economy was improving. All the indicators were pointing up. Three years later, we would be staring into the abyss.

Rufius Cornelius Anicius was a member of one the richest families in the empire. He had estates in the Moselle Valley and Aquitania. His brothers and cousins also had estates in Gaul and Italy as well as Spain and Africa. Land ownership in the West is of a different order than that of the eastern provinces. Western senatorial families have existed for centuries, with many of them going back to republican times as do their patrimonies. Most eastern senatorial families have relatively recent origins. They were created during the latter part of the reign of Constantine I to populate his new Senate at Constantinople. As a result, their estates are much smaller than those of their western confreres, and their political influence is more restricted. So are their opportunities for avoiding tax payments.

The following afternoon, all officers and officer cadets of the Imperial Guard were called to a special meeting ordered by Arbogast. He welcomed us to our new responsibilities and wasted no time in making his cardinal points.

"Gentlemen, as officers in the service of Rome, your personal integrity must be beyond reproach at all times. We have all heard stories, at one time or another, about corruption in both the civilian and military branches of government. It would be silly to deny that such practices exist in some quarters. It would be equally foolish for any of you to think that such conduct will be tolerated by me at any time, under any circumstances. Our late Emperor Valentinian I was known as 'Maximum Val' to many of us who had the honor to serve him because he enforced the maximum punishment for every crime and never once commuted the sentence of anyone for anything. So it is with me. Any officer found guilty of padding the enrollment of his unit or units so as to skim off the pay allotted to such nonexistent soldiers will be executed. Any officer found guilty of accepting bribes to promote either subordinate officers or men in the ranks will be executed. Any superior, be he an officer or a noncommissioned officer, who accepts a bribe to excuse a soldier under his command from any duty, will be executed. The empire requires soldiers who can perform any task assigned to them, and above all, it requires soldiers who are there.

"Imperial Guard regiments constitute the finest units in the army. Unless there is a need for you to act as the personal bodyguard of the emperor, I intend to use you as regular cavalry as requirements dictate. After all, we wouldn't want any of you to get rusty now, would we? The Imperial Guard regiments in the East have gained the reputation lately for being a bunch of overpaid 'pretty boys' whose main purpose in life is to adorn parade squares in fancy uniforms and to act as a branch of the civil service. Rest assured that will not be your purpose here except on special occasions."

Arbogast went on to explain that while the frontiers were secure, he was planning a minor campaign in which we would be involved in the weeks ahead. In the meantime, it would be endless drilling and field exercises as usual. He told us that each month several squadrons from our regiment would be assigned to the emperor. These would turn out to be easy assignments unless Valentinian was traveling somewhere. After Arbogast's address, we were dismissed and given the next two days off to get settled into our new quarters.

I had just returned home when there was a knock on the door. I was surprised to see Margareta's husband, Rufius.

"Hope I'm not interrupting anything," he said in his usual jovial way.

"Even if you were, you would be welcome anyway," I said. "Come on in."

"I'll only stay a few moments," Rufius continued. "I figured that you would be home by now because I heard at the banquet last night that you new arrivals would be given a couple of days off to get settled. We stayed overnight at Margareta's home here in the city, and we got to wondering if the two of you and your children would like to live at Margareta's villa just a few miles up the Moselle. It's not large as villas go, but you would have much more room there than you have here. The place has been empty since Margareta and I were married. She used to have a couple of elderly slaves to help look after it, but they both died during the years that you were away. We maintain it minimally with slaves from my place now. The rent will be small. The only condition that we will impose is that you will be responsible for maintaining the place with help from the slaves from my villa. We want the place lived in; otherwise, it will suffer from the atrophy of disuse. My children have their own places, and we would like to have someone that we know living there for obvious reasons. So, what do you think?"

Makila and I looked at one another with disbelieving grins. We expressed our heartfelt thanks to Rufius and his wife for their generosity and agreed to meet them in one hour to ride out to their country estates that were on the highway heading south to Metz. I rented a wagon from an agency a few blocks away, and we drove along the Moselle to the estate. Margareta ushered us in the main door of her villa, and Makila said, "We'll take it." There was no need to look any further, although we did go on a complete tour. By aristocratic standards, the villa might have been small, but by the standards of a common soldier, it was beyond my wildest dreams. The largest villa that I have ever seen in my travels throughout the empire is in the Moselle valley. It has a floor area of over a hundred thousand square feet and contains over one hundred rooms. We immediately returned to Trier and had our belongings shipped out to the villa the next morning. We couldn't believe our good fortune, and neither could my comrades. The villa was larger than any place we had ever envisioned ourselves living in and had a most pleasing view of the Moselle. Its design was in the true Mediterranean style. It was the interior, not the exterior that reflected the real beauty of the place. The rooms faced primarily onto the inner courtyard and by design were not overly well lit. This was mainly to avoid the summer's heat, as in the more southerly climes. Three sides of the courtyard were surrounded by a colonnade that was covered by an extension of the villa's roof. The center of the courtyard had a small pool that could be drained, as required, by a sluiceway that led down to the Moselle. When the weather was hot, we would eventually let the children splash around in it to cool off. Smaller villas, such as this, are used generally as summer retreats and not lived in all year-round. In the winter, the owners return to the city, with only occasional visits to keep an eye on things. There are large working villas or manor houses as they are also called throughout the Moselle Valley that are farms in the true sense. Rufius' large estate next door to us was one such place. It too was built in the Mediterranean style, unlike the "villas" in Britain that, I suppose, might be thought of as having a more Celtic design to them. Our villa also had a large library that I put to good use whenever I was not in the field. Margareta had moved some of her books into Rufius' villa but had left most of them behind since Rufius had quite a well-stocked library of his own. Makila remarked jokingly (I think) that my continual reading at every opportunity would lead to the ruination of our marriage. Bookworm that I am, no way would I ever permit that to happen.

Theodosius's triumph in Rome was quite successful. He was a born politician, and this trait certainly came to the fore when he met with senators and their families. He let everyone know that he took no personal offense at their association with the usurper. In the next couple of years, Theodosius and Valentinian II would appoint many of them to the highest offices in Italy and Africa. There would be no question of course, in the minds of the appointees, as to the name of their real patron. The famous Gallic pagan poet and orator Pacatus delivered a panegyric to the emperor in which he praised Theodosius's passion for clemency while denouncing the late, unlamented usurper's persecution of Priscillianistic heretics. Understandable issues to be raised at the time but there was no need to fear an imperial purge. Theodosius realized that he and his young colleague needed the cooperation of the aristocracy to administer the Western Empire, the religious or recent political persuasions of its members notwithstanding. The emperor of the East met with senators both at the Senate itself and in their homes. He impressed upon all that he wished to work with them for the betterment of the state. The commoners got to see him attend theatrical performances as well as various circus games. I subsequently found out that Pacatus, in his panegyric, had referred to the fact that Theodosius and Magnus Maximus were related. The previous year, when I had asked the emperor about it during my first meeting with him, my friends had chided me for having made a "career-limiting move." The subject was supposedly taboo. When I heard that Pacatus had mentioned it also, I felt much better. In the following year when Pacatus was appointed proconsul of Africa, I felt better still.

Everyone who toils in close proximity to the throne, regardless of capacity, has an interest in whose political star is in the ascendant at any moment. There could be no question that, among the members of the eastern government, the man who was enjoying the most meteoric rise, apart from Stilicho, was Rufinus. He had been appointed master of offices in 388 and left in charge of the Eastern Empire when Theodosius marched west. It is difficult to know what recommended this man to Theodosius. He was born in Aquitania, about seventy-five miles southeast of Bordeaux, the son of a shoemaker. Entering the civil service in his youth, he had no military background. He was a good administrator and had risen to prominence on merit. Given Theodosius's preference for advancing westerners in his government, along with Rufinus' fanatical Catholicism and you have a combination that might explain his climb up the political ladder. It would also prove to be a formula for disaster. Rufinus had brought Honorius to Milan and had accompanied the emperor and his son to Rome. This Gaul was not to be taken lightly.

Since the campaign that Arbogast was planning did not materialize before August, I spent time with Margareta, over several weeks, preparing some of her seminar topics. Usually one never criticized a living emperor or his policies unless one was absolutely certain of one's company. As a result, though Margareta and I were good friends, I still felt a need to be circumspect in what I said, all the more so as I was a member of the Imperial Guard. Government secret agents were everywhere then (and still are throughout the East), and a neighbor, close friend, or even a relative might turn into an informer if they thought the government would reward them with the property of the accused. When Valentinian I and Valens were alive, this was an absolute rule, and it continued into the joint reign of Gratian and Theodosius I, although both men were of a more liberal frame of mind. After Magnus Maximus completed his revolt, however, public discussion of Gratian's and Theodosius's policies with respect to the Goths was encouraged throughout the regions that Maximus controlled. The decisions made in 381 and 382 had aroused a great deal of public indignation in the East and West among both Christians and pagans.

The emperor and his army that we had lost at Hadrianople would go largely unavenged. Those surviving Goths who had slaughtered them would be rewarded for their efforts by being settled on Roman land after suffering only a string of minor defeats, although their cumulative losses had been considerable. Magnus Maximus took full advantage of the public disgust with those responsible for these decisions to enhance his own standing. As a result, he was quite willing to let the public enflame its feelings on the issue to the greatest degree possible. Freedom of speech had been encouraged as never before and this newfound habit would prove difficult to break even after the usurper had been decapitated.

At the beginning of August, our Imperial Guard regiment, in association with a couple of cavalry regiments from the Army of Gaul, conducted a sweep all the way down the Rhine from Koblenz to Utrecht. There had been rumors of a possible invasion by German Franks somewhere along this part of the frontier, but nothing came of it. Perhaps knowledge of our presence had been a sufficient deterrent. Arbogast had been conducting such patrols along the Rhine for months by the time we arrived. In addition to keeping German Franks out, apart from peaceful immigrants, Arbogast also wanted to cement the links between the Roman Franks of northern Gaul and the rest of the diocese. The garrisons of Utrecht, Nijmegen, Xanten, and a couple of other towns further downstream, on or close to the North Sea, were Frankish to a man. This area, while conquered, had never been colonized by Rome apart from the forts on the Rhine. By the time we returned to Trier at month's end, we had covered in excess of four hundred miles. I had been concerned about Makila living at the villa alone with the children for the entire month. So I arranged with Margareta and Rufius to check in on her to see that all her marketing needs and so on were taken care of. By the time I returned, Makila knew the local markets better than I ever had when I lived there before. She and Margareta had also become friends, which I was glad to see.

On the return patrol, I broke away for a couple of hours to visit the grave of my friend Gregorian. I dropped by the office of the graves' registrar at the garrison headquarters in Bonn to determine its location. Six long years had passed. I knelt beside where he lay and found myself crying openly once again as though his tragic death had happened only yesterday. I would visit the grave whenever I passed through the city and swore on that first occasion that I would continue such visits for the rest of my life. I made that vow with the best of intentions. Now resettled in the West, with a future that appeared secure, I felt that I would remain there permanently. We all learn the hard way, however, that sometimes promises cannot be kept. Far sooner than I would have thought, the day came when I would visit Bonn for the last time. While there, I learned that Empress Justina had died. This courageous woman had represented her son's interests to the best of her abilities throughout his reign, including the most trying circumstances. Always a strong spokeswoman for Arian Christianity, she was a conciliator in an age of ever-deepening intolerance. She would leave behind a line of imperial descendants through her daughter Galla, who was empress of the East. Everyone who knew her admired her, and she would be sorely missed, above all by her son, who now found himself more alone than ever.

Margareta's seminars started up early in September on a night when a severe rainstorm limited attendance. As a result, only seven men made it to her house: myself, a merchant, and five civil servants, including a young Frank named Gaiso, who was destined for a great career. Margareta got the discussion going.

"I'd like to start off this seminar in current affairs by introducing you all to Marcus Cedranus. I've known Marcus for seven years, the last six of which he has spent in the Eastern Army. He is a member of the First Western Palatine Guard Regiment and was transferred when the decision was made to reestablish the capital of the West in Trier. I've asked him to attend a number of our meetings because of the insights he has gained during his time in Thrace and Illyria."

I was immediately taken back by the intense hostility that was felt toward the settlement agreed to with the Visigoths. Many westerners felt that similar conditions would be demanded by other groups of German "immigrants," present and future, leading to a loss of Roman authority in our own lands. Western opinion appeared to be well informed on goings-on in the East. Those present accepted the dangers inherent in an all-out campaign to defeat the Visigoths. However, given the casualties the Visigoths had suffered after Hadrianople, they were at a loss to understand why the government had given in to so many enemy demands. There were also questions on the true nature of the Hunnish danger that were similar to discussions that my friends and I had engaged in.

Gaiso summed up the feelings of many when he said, "Unlike other German settlers in the empire who have blended in pretty well, the Gothic peoples seem to have an especially nationalistic and, from a Roman standpoint, unstable element about them. Other Germans migrating here have eventually become Romans. The Visigoths want to remain German."

"If our peace treaty with the Visigoths goes on the rocks," Margareta asked, "then what will the outcome of such a failure be?"

At this point, the merchant, Antonius, spoke up. "We will probably go bankrupt fighting them. Theodosius has raised taxes throughout the East, almost to the breaking point to rebuild and expand our army there, largely at the expense of our Western Army. Even the people of Thrace, who have suffered so terribly, have had their taxes raised. One wise guy remarked that the government is now busy seizing from the citizenry what barbarian 'charitability' left behind." We all laughed at this, but it had the ring of gallows humor. Antonius continued, "One other item I would like to mention, because I think it bears directly on the central issue, is that of demoralization. Not only have the people of Thrace had their homeland devastated, but as a result of the agreement, their taxes are going to pay the Visigothic federate soldiers that are now supposedly our allies. These are the very men who robbed, raped, and in many cases murdered or temporarily enslaved their families and friends. The populations of Thrace and Macedonia feel completely betrayed by their government." There was a long, discomforting silence at this point.

"So where do we come out on the question of the Visigoths?" Margareta asked. "Have we imbibed an elixir or have we swallowed a poison?"

I felt we had talked enough about the East for one evening. "If no one minds, I would like to switch our focus to the West to ask what prompted all you traitors to go over to Magnus Maximus in 383." This caught everyone off guard, and for the first few moments, the only response was the shuffling of feet accompanied by a few sheepish grins.

Finally, Margareta replied, "I know Marcus better than the rest of you, and I know he was only kidding with his 'traitor' wisecrack. There was no widespread dissatisfaction with Gratian prior to Magnus Maximus raising his revolt in Britain. When Gratian's army dissolved on him, the rest of us had very little choice but to go along."

"Magnus Maximus had an obvious appeal to Gratian's Moorish cavalry," Gaiso suggested. "They had served under him in Africa and respected him simply because he was older and more experienced than Gratian. A lot of well-placed bribes didn't do any harm either."

"His 'maturity' and 'experience' didn't count for much at the time of the crossing of the Visigoths at Silistra," I reminded them.

"You must keep in mind," said the merchant, "that the usurper played to the hilt the fact that he and Theodosius were distant cousins. Add to that the fact that Theodosius did not take action against him for four years, coupled with the vague hints that Theodosius tossed out from time to time that he might even extend recognition to the new western regime, and you can understand why no serious counter-revolt broke out among any army units."

"What about Merobaudes?" I asked. "Here was a man who had served Rome faithfully for over twenty years, was responsible for raising Valentinian II to the throne, and yet still betrayed Gratian to the usurper in 383. What caused Magnus Maximus to execute him?"

"We don't know much more than you do on that one," Gaiso replied. "At the time of his execution, it was announced that he had been planning a revolt against the usurper and the plot had been uncovered. Pretty standard stuff. If he was planning a revolt to avoid civil war with Theodosius, then it's difficult to know how he intended to explain to both Theodosius and Valentinian II his earlier treason in 383. His execution is a mystery to us all."

The discussion continued later than it would have normally because no one wanted to get soaked in the downpour. At last the rain stopped, and we all bade Margareta good night, as she would be staying in the city. As we left, Gaiso approached me.

"I noticed you writing rather feverishly on occasion during our discussion this evening, but I couldn't decipher what you were putting down," he said.

"We discussed some important items this evening and I just wanted to keep them in mind for possible future use. If ever I decide to become a historian then it's always beneficial to be able to have an accurate picture of what people were thinking at a given time instead of trying to go from a faulty memory. I was writing in shorthand. Why, were you thinking that I might be a government spy?" I half-kidded him.

"Well, one can't be too certain these days," he replied. "Where did you learn to write shorthand?"

I explained how I had taken a special course in it when I was still in my teens. When he expressed great interest in it, I agreed to teach it to him, and in that way, Gaiso and I started what became a lifelong friendship. The regular government course on the subject for civil servants would not be starting for several months. This way I would help to give him a head start. He was some years younger than I, and after a while, we started hitting the local bars together once the night seminars were over. He would ride out to our villa several evenings a week, and within a couple of months, he had become quite a proficient shorthand writer.

In December 389, on my birthday, Makila gave birth to our third daughter, Serena Aemelia. The year 389 had been a good year all around, both for me and my family and for the empire. There had been no military problems or civil disturbances of great importance, and prosperity was returning everywhere. We all looked forward to the New Year as being a continuation of the old. That was not to be.

Theodosius was at heart a kindly man, and his consideration for others was manifested on many occasions during his reign. But the emperor was also possessed by an immature streak that was reflected in his quick temper. He had had it since childhood and never outgrew it. There were frequent instances of his anger getting the better of him when some new problem arose. He would frequently issue an order for some precipitous action that he immediately regretted and felt compelled to countermand. The frequent revoking of such severe orders only served to display the more humane side of him and to enhance his popularity throughout his realm. Unfortunately, there would be an incident for which the revocation of an outrageous order would come too late. This failure would be catastrophic.

Early in 390, Valentinian II requested the commander of his Imperial Guard to provide him with a personal military training program. I thought it was an incredible oversight that the young emperor had not started training as a soldier long before now. Theodosius as much as any man knew that to be an emperor, it was absolutely necessary to be a soldier. And yet Theodosius had done nothing to prepare his young colleague with the military qualifications that every emperor needs to be a responsible and fully capable chief of state. At least the emperor of the East was consistent in this: he had never given his older son, Arcadius, any military training either. (At the time, Honorius was too young.) In due time, we would all learn the impossibility of training the sons of Theodosius to be competent in anything. Much, much more on that later.

The commander sent the order down the chain, and a group of us were chosen to be the emperor's trainers: riding, archery, swordsmanship, the works. That was how I got to know Valentinian II. He was a good-looking young man, athletically built, and nineteen at the time. I was one of his trainers in archery and infantry tactics. He turned out to be a pretty good shot and an excellent horseman. As a gift, I presented him with the Hunnish bow that I possessed, courtesy of the first member of that race I had killed. I impressed upon the emperor that the Huns probably manufactured the finest bows of anyone. Not that our own were bad. It was simply that the Hunnish variety was superior. Valentinian was genuinely grateful and to maximize his capabilities with it, I brought in the lone Hun in our squadron, a man named Denzic. He trained the emperor in the way the Huns ride and fire the bow while riding at full speed. The senior officers in the guard provided instruction across the host of other military responsibilities. For the first time in his life, I believe the emperor felt he was on the verge of becoming his father's son instead of merely his namesake. He had the right idea, but the Fates were aligned against him.

In the early summer of 390, the most disgraceful and appalling event took place in the otherwise distinguished reign of Theodosius. The city garrison of Thessalonica in Macedonia consisted largely of Visigothic troops commanded by a Romanized Visigoth named Butheric, who was highly respected by Theodosius. It performed constabulary as well as military duties in the city and its surrounding territory. In this former capacity, Butheric had ordered the arrest and imprisonment of a highly popular charioteer on a charge of homosexual rape. Coming as it did on the eve of special celebratory games, the most rabid fans of this charioteer were incensed that he would not be allowed to participate. A large mob formed at Butheric's headquarters demanding that the charioteer be released and when Butheric refused, the mob went on a rampage. During the ensuing carnage, Butheric and several of his officers were murdered and their bodies mutilated and dragged through the streets of the city. When news of this outrage reached Theodosius in Milan, he flew into a fury that would have the direst consequences. He appointed a new commander for the garrison and ordered him, at the nearest opportunity, to seal off the hippodrome and massacre the audience. This was in a sense typical of Theodosius, though on an unheard-of scale. Three years earlier, after the disruptions in Antioch, a board of inquiry had determined who was guilty of the crimes committed by the mobs. Theodosius had issued serious reprisals against the guilty but, on reflection, realized that he had gone too far and called them off. So too with the egregious orders that he had sent to Thessalonica. However, the big difference this time was that the emperor had bypassed the legal process altogether. There was no inquiry held to determine who the killers and the leaders of the mob actually were. The revocation arrived too late, as did the emperor's realization of the oriental proverb that "the reputation of a thousand years can be determined by the conduct of a single hour."

Once the order had been received in Thessalonica, the Visigothic garrison, under its new commander, went about putting it into practice. At the next day's chariot races, the garrison sealed off the hippodrome and poured troops into the stands. They simply slaughtered everyone that they came up against—men, women, and children, young and old. In the worst instances, young children were decapitated by slashing swords, and even pregnant women were butchered without pity. People trying to escape found all the exits blocked by soldiers who slew anyone trying to get away from the murderous insanity being conducted inside. As more people fled down the stairways to escape, they ran into the piles of the dead and dying plugging the exits. These people would die much slower deaths. While desperately trying to squirm and claw their way over the casualties in front of them, they were being crushed and trampled by the sea of humanity that kept flooding up behind them. All outlets were soon clogged with dead bodies, making escape impossible. In a last-ditch attempt at salvation, dozens of people hurled themselves from the top of the hippodrome to the ground below. A few of them survived, but the vast majority either were killed on impact or slain by onrushing soldiers as they lay terribly injured on the ground. Inside the arena, the seats and aisles and stairways were drenched in blood and severed limbs and portions thereof. The number of people attending the races that day is unknown, but by the time the massacre was over, seven thousand were dead. The only reason it came to an end when it did was that the soldiers were exhausted and could continue no further. It was the most outrageous act committed by any emperor against his own people since the abominable reign of Caracalla. The Greeks and Macedonians had suffered terribly in the third century and recently at the hands of the Goths. Now here they were being butchered by their age-old enemies again, but this time it was on the orders of the most Christian emperor that Rome had ever had, the man they had previously regarded as their savior.

The empire was staggered when news of the bloodbath got out. Nowhere was this more evident than in Milan, but precautions were also taken in Trier and Constantinople. The garrison and Imperial Guard in all three cities were put on alert against the possibility of civil disturbances against the government. The dangers of public disorder were far greater in Milan and Constantinople, but Trier took precautions just in case. The atmosphere was extremely tense and troops were on patrol constantly to maintain control, with various units spelling one another off. Fortunately, nothing happened, and after several days, all military units were ordered to return to their normal duties. It was business as usual during the daytime, but at night, the streets emptied quickly and stayed that way. In Milan especially, it appeared that the population was suddenly terrified of what this most pious of emperors might do and was cowed accordingly. The first day that the massacre became publicly known was the most difficult because we all expected the worst. It was well after midnight when I got home, but the welcome I received was less than warm.

"Where the hell have you been?" Makila said, not yelling but speaking quite firmly and somewhat louder than I would normally appreciate at that hour of the night. "I've been worried sick about you with all these rumors flying around. Margareta returned from the city today and told me what she had heard."

"I'm sorry, but there was no way that I could get word through to you that I would be late getting home tonight." I took her in my arms and tried to calm her down. "We'll be working in twelve-hour shifts for as long as the emergency exists. I'll be going in at noon each day and getting home at midnight." I recited everything that we had been told.

"How could Theodosius have done such a terrible thing?" she asked, repeating the question being asked by millions throughout the empire.

"That is what we have all been asking ourselves. For the past decade, Theodosius has been trying to incorporate the Visigothic peoples into the Roman nation. And now, after almost eight years of admittedly blemished success, the entire process has been undermined in the most hideous way imaginable. All the ancient wounds have been reopened. I don't believe anything will happen here. Valentinian is popular, and the public knows that he didn't have any role in this catastrophe. But we have to be on guard just in case."

"What will happen next?" she asked.

"God Himself might have difficulty answering that one," was all I could say.

The bishop knew his emperor only too well. Ambrose saw plainly that there was no need for him to play the role of the ranting seditionist as he had done to such effect in the past. Never before had the Roman Empire had a Christian monarch that feared so greatly for the salvation of his soul. After Thessalonica, he had occasion to. The bishop communicated with Theodosius in a lengthy letter that was both compassionate and understanding in its inclination. Ambrose indirectly excommunicated him by refusing to hold communion if he was present. The bishop ordered him to do public penance in a prescribed fashion. Those in attendance at the Milan cathedral would see over a period of several months the incredible sight of the emperor of the East dressed like a commoner, showing no hint of imperial rank. At each service, Theodosius would appear at the doorway and be met by Ambrose, who would remind him that since he was guilty of the crime of murder, as was Israel's King David, he must expiate his terrible sins in the manner that King David had. At every appearance, the emperor would publicly confess his sins and cry out for God's forgiveness. He would cast himself to the floor and denounce his crimes in a manner that could perhaps be best described as verbal self-flagellation. Theodosius was genuinely terrified of having his soul condemned to hell as no other emperor had ever been. The tears were real, the anguish profound. He would then leave the cathedral, and the regular service would go on. The public supported the bishop overwhelmingly during this crisis. In the disaster's aftermath, Ambrose stood as the embodiment of decency and responsibility. He was critical but with compassion. It is doubtful whether any man has ever had the opportunity to personify the public sense of right and wrong as Ambrose did at this time and he played the role to perfection.

In December 390, Theodosius was readmitted to the fellowship of the church. Harmonizing of relations between emperor and bishop during this period had been facilitated by Rufinus. Before a packed congregation, wearing his full imperial robes of state, the emperor was given communion by Ambrose. His period of penitence was over. At least officially. In the deepest sense, it could never end. At a higher level, the entire empire had been traumatized by the catastrophe at Thessalonica. The shockwaves created by it, like those of an enormous earthquake, are with us to this day. It soon became obvious to everyone that in matters of religion, the Catholic Church would dictate policy to the government. There would be no more conflict between the two. Nonetheless, there would be conflict.

Our duties as Imperial Guard members had taken on a routine in 389 that continued throughout 390. We had originally hoped that Theodosius would go on a western tour during the year, but it never materialized. Whether he ever considered one is unknown. Even if he had, such plans would have been overridden by events at Thessalonica that effectively froze him in Milan for the rest of the year. Throughout 390, we escorted Valentinian II on a number of tours of his Gallic domain. For me, it was a reiteration of sorts. The emperor paid visits to most of the fortresses on the lower Rhine where the Franks displayed a genuine affection for him. They had respected his father and, like his other subjects, wanted to make up for the tacit support they had provided his brother's murderer. Later in the year, Valentinian toured the Rhone Valley, and I found myself getting reacquainted with the cities of southern Gaul. I was on my best behavior at all times, but that didn't stop me from pointing out to my companions the local pleasure palaces that the typical young male might find of interest. Valentinian developed a particular affection for Vienne for some reason, and he mentioned on more than one occasion how much he liked the place. There would be a tragic irony to this attachment.

With the exception of Thessalonica, the year 390 was as uneventful as the previous year. The frontier remained quiet, and the economy continued to strengthen. I remained close with my original group of friends from Gaul as well as my decurion, Fredemondus, but a change had come over us since we had been posted to the First Western Palatine Guard Regiment. While on the frontier, in either garrison legion, we had never hesitated to hold some rather freewheeling political discussions whenever the inclination struck us. Once we were assigned to the Imperial Guard, however, there was almost a palpable reluctance to be quite so open with one another. All guard regiments are more "political" as regards the ambitions of their officers. As for the men in the ranks such as myself (officer cadet or not), there was always the danger that an injudicious remark could lead, once again, to a posting on the borderlands. Nonetheless, I approached Fredemondus in November 390 to discuss a number of things that had been bothering me of late.

"Is Theodosius planning to stay in Italy forever? He's been there for over two years now, and I'm bothered by the manner in which he is ignoring Britain, Gaul, Spain, and Africa entirely. Valentinian is doing his best, but he is too inexperienced to instill the confidence that a visit from Theodosius could."

"Some officers have expressed similar reservations," he replied. "Many of us expected a sweeping tour of all the westernmost dioceses by now. As we know, however, Theodosius has far more important things to do, such as groveling before Bishop Ambrose month after month to save that bloody soul of his. I just hope that by his ignoring our dioceses he does not wind up precipitating all over again the very situation that drew us here in the first place."

In February 391 came the edict outlawing all pagan religions and closing their temples throughout the empire. Ambrose had Theodosius just where he wanted him. This edict, while long expected, still came as a shock because of its incredibly intrusive nature. Individuals were forbidden to pray to their pagan gods, and government support for what had to this time been "state religions" was halted. Chlogius cornered me soon after the edict had been posted. The year 390 had proven a very good one for him. He had been married in the spring and during the summer had been promoted to decurion and assigned to command one of the other squadrons in our regiment.

"Marcus, old man," he assailed me. "What are your considerations on the latest commandments from Theodosius and Ambrose? Not quite composed on tablets of stone, from what I hear, but equally substantive nonetheless."

"I have never, until now," I replied, "heard of a civilization in which the purpose of the state was to serve religion in a completely subordinate role."

"Of course you have. Oh, it was hardly a civilization on a grand scale, but it was a nation state nonetheless. I'm referring, of course, to the ancient Kingdom of Israel. That is the way Theodosius now views the Roman Empire: Israel writ large."

"A fat lot of good being 'God's chosen people' has done the Jews," I said.

"And a fat lot of good it will probably do us as well," Chlogius went on, "with all the public discord this decree will trigger. It says that only Catholic Christians can worship either in public or in the supposed privacy of their own homes. All other forms of worship are forbidden at all times."

"Theodosius is nothing more than a puppet for that damned Ambrose," I exploded. "This edict, though aimed at pagans, in fact is directed at all non-Catholics. It will prove to be one more needless impediment to any kind of full cooperation between Rome and the Visigoths. His religious policies are operating at complete cross-purposes to his political objectives in the East. The antagonisms this edict will raise will also undermine all the fine diplomacy that Theodosius performed in Rome two years ago. It makes you wonder if he hasn't forgotten why he went there in the first place."

"The question," Chlogius suggested, "is whether the edict will be enforced now that it has been proclaimed. The Visigoths, since they live in the East, come under Theodosius's jurisdiction. If he tries to impose the edict on them then, I'm certain they will erupt. At the same time, the West is less Christian than the East and has more pagan administrators. Are these men now going to assume responsibility for Christianizing their fellow pagans? They detest Ambrose. The best that we can hope for is that the edict will prove to be unenforceable."

"This might also be the first major test that *our* emperor faces," I said. "By nature and upbringing, Valentinian is of a more pragmatic sprit, his recent belabored conversion to Catholicism notwithstanding. All his life, his mother encouraged him to treat religion as his father did, and our best hope, here in the West, is that he will."

The edict hit the empire like an earthquake. The large block of western senators and aristocrats that still adhered to the pagan religions felt betrayal and outrage. Toleration, what little there was of it, was at an end. Then two months later, with equal suddenness, Theodosius announced that he was returning to Constantinople. This was another aspect of Theodosius's character: long periods of lassitude followed by a period of considerable activity. It later came out that what had prompted the emperor's return to the East was a dispute between his wife, Galla, and his son Arcadius. I have never been able to determine just what the nature of their disagreement was.

In July, Makila and I invited Chlogius and his wife to our villa for dinner. Chlogius had just returned from his first long-range patrol down the Rhine as commander of his new squadron. On the way, he visited his family in Xanten. While our wives were busy with preparations in the kitchen, Chlogius and I withdrew to the courtyard to enjoy some of the local vintage.

"I haven't had much opportunity to speak to you since you returned," I said, "but I gather your tour of duty was a success."

Chlogius paused before replying, "On the surface."

"What happened?"

"Nothing that I can put my finger on," he replied. "From a military point of view, things went well. We picked up a few stragglers, but that was about it. Have you heard any rumors regarding Arbogast?"

"Nothing outrageous," I answered. "There is a story making the rounds that the field marshal was rather grumpy during recent meetings of the Sacred Consistory. Now that we've made Valentinian somewhat more knowledgeable in military matters than he was, he's been asking questions and demanding answers of a more detailed nature than Arbogast has been generally used to giving. That's about all though. Why?"

"When I was in Xanten," Chlogius continued, "I discovered a couple of things as a result of a visit I had with an old boyhood friend of mine. My friend's family is distantly related to Arbogast. He told me something odd. His younger brother, who is nineteen, was a member of the local garrison and a recent recruit. In spite of his inexperience, Arbogast reached down and assigned him to his personal staff here in Trier last February."

"Nepotism in the service of Rome?" I replied sarcastically. "Gee, that's a first."

"I know, I know," Chlogius responded impatiently, "but just hear me out on this. Two weeks later, according to my friend, another distant cousin of theirs, who is twenty and in the Army of Gaul, was also transferred to Arbogast's staff. The field marshal swore both men to complete secrecy and probably feels that the security of their mission, whatever it may be, is additionally enhanced by the fact that these couriers are blood relatives of his. To this point in their new careers, these men have made two round-trips to Rome. The men to whom they have conducted documents on Arbogast's behalf are Nichomacus Flavianus, praetorian prefect of the Italies, and Caeonius Rufius Albinus, urban prefect of Rome. My friend in Xanten has had a problem with alcohol ever since he was a teenager and this information was divulged during a night of barhopping. Upon hearing that I was a decurion, he might have been trying to knock me down a peg or two by letting me know that members of his family were doing quite well also, thank you very much. It appears that Arbogast's young relatives may not take the notion of secrecy as seriously as those of us of slightly more mature years do. Nonetheless, I believe that the information is genuine."

"The problem," I wondered out loud, "is what do we do with it? The timing of the arrival of your friend's relatives on Arbogast's staff and the objects of his communications in Rome certainly appear ominous. After all, why would the commander of the Army of Gaul need to communicate with civilian leaders in Italy? But Arbogast has been nothing if not completely loyal to the families of Valentinian I and Theodosius. You often hear him described as 'a Roman of republican virtues,' particularly by pagan aristocrats. I don't think it would be an overstatement to describe him as the most widely respected man in public service."

"I agree," Chlogius replied, "but do you think that these insane edicts proscribing paganism in all its aspects might be causing that loyalty to crumble?"

"If a serious attempt is made to enforce them here in the West, it could trigger a reaction. You mentioned a second matter."

"Oh yes," Chlogius said. "My friend Chlothar, who is a blacksmith, mentioned that one of the leaders of the Frankish invasion into Belgium back in 388 was a man named Arbitio who subsequently took part in the defeat of Quintinus later that same year. This Arbitio is also a cousin of both Arbogast and my friend Chlothar, and I gather is in his midthirties. Chlothar, who has never met Arbogast, told me that when Arbogast was a teenager, he killed a member of Arbitio's family. The circumstances of this crime have been hushed up ever since, but as a result of this killing, our esteemed future field marshal was expelled from his village and joined our army. There has understandably been bad blood between Arbogast's and Arbitio's families ever since. With Arbogast now supreme in the West, I've been wondering if any future invasions of Gaul by German Franks might not be touched off, in part, by this feud within his own family."

"An interesting possibility," I replied, feeling that the subject had pretty well played itself out. "Have you heard about what happened in Alexandria?"

"No," Chlogius answered. "Remember—I just got back from the field, where one is not particularly well informed on world events unless they are of a military nature."

"Last month, Theodosius issued yet another edict against paganism that applied to Egypt," I explained. "Apparently the pagan Alexandrians had continued the worship of their sun god, Sarapis, to guarantee the annual Nile flood. This in spite of the edict of last February. Not illogically, I suppose they felt that even Theodosius would be unwilling to risk a flood failure. All the more so since his capital is so dependent on wheat imports from Egypt. Add one more diocese to the list of those that have learned the intensity of His Majesty's devotion the hard way."

"Think about it though," Chlogius interrupted. "If the floods come next year, then their arrival will be taken as proof positive that the old gods do not exist and never have or that Christ has defeated them. If the floods do not come and widespread famine results then it will mean that God is punishing us for having taken so long to put an end to pagan worship. Another win-win situation for you Christians, old boy. I'm surprised that your spirits aren't more exalted."

This time it was my turn to be serious. "It gets worse," I continued. "A riot broke out between Christians and pagans, as they have long been prone to do. Christians were soon laying siege to the Sarapeum, the main temple to the sun god. It will probably go down as one of the classical 'last stands' of the ancient religions. When it was over, the emperor himself gave the order that all pagan statues inside the temple should be destroyed. Patriarch Theophilus, reading between the lines as even an illiterate could, then ordered the destruction of the entire Sarapeum."

"What?" Chlogius gasped. "I've often heard it described as one the great architectural masterpieces of the world."

"Past tense if you please," I continued. "It makes you wonder what it is that Theodosius has against the Greeks. First he slaughters seven thousand of them last year in Thessalonica. Now he orders the slaughtering of their religion. Alexandria is, after all, a largely Greek city. Carrying on with my news update, the civilians themselves proved unequal to the task of tearing down this beautiful work of art. So the army was called in to complete the demolition. Monks now occupy the site to prevent your coreligionists from sneaking in to retake the ruins and continue with their beastly and degrading rituals." It was my turn to smile.

"No wonder so many of those eastern soldiers aren't worth shit," Chlogius considered. "The only activity that many them have engaged in for the last ten years has been the smashing up of these ancient temples. The next time that you are talking to your good buddy, the emperor of the East, you might ask him if he is planning to introduce a program of study on the pulverization of temples into future officer cadet courses. I'm beginning to feel that you and I were shortchanged by the absence of such class work from the curriculum when we attended back in Milan."

"Now that you have finished interrupting me for the umpteenth time, am I permitted to continue?" I asked.

"You mean there's more?" He winced.

"Indeed there is. Here, let me refill your glass. An educated man like yourself will need additional fortification for the rest of what I have to tell you. The entire world has probably heard of the great Library of Alexandria."

"Oh, Jesus Christ," Chlogius moaned, this time smashing his head on the table we were sitting at. "Not that too?" The wine was starting to live up to its reputation.

"You are a quick study, aren't you?" I kidded him. "Unfortunately, the Library of Alexandria had, or did have, the tragic misfortune to be attached to the late, lamented Sarapeum. The good news is that the library is still standing."

"Hooray!" Chlogius shouted.

"The bad news," I continued, "is that there isn't much left to read there based on preliminary reports. Their destructive lust unsated by the mere wrecking of the Sarapeum, the momentum of the patriarch's mob carried over into the library. Fortunately, they were too worn out by this time to physically destroy the building. They did, however, devastate many of the contents. I read somewhere that the great library contained over one million volumes as either scrolls or books. A good many of them, no estimate available yet, were either burned or torn to shreds by the patriarch's devotees. Works of the devil, you know."

We sat there for a while just looking down to the Moselle and across to the villas on the other side.

"The Great Library," Chlogius said finally.

"The Great Library," I echoed. "It has been with us for seven hundred years, and during that time, the greatest mathematicians, astronomers, doctors, geographers, and writers have worked there. Yet here we are, in this beautiful setting, talking about a mob of Christian ignoramuses, many of Greek descent, who were probably oblivious to the fact that the building they were sacking was the very place where the Bible was first translated into Greek."

"They probably couldn't have cared less even if they did know," Chlogius replied.

"The Ptolemaic dynasty," I said, "collected books from all over the world, from Axum and Nubia, from Iran, India, Greece, and the Levant. No center of scholarship anywhere can compare. It was there that Euclid wrote and compiled his 'Elements of Geometry.' And Eratosthenes calculated the earth's circumference to be twenty-five thousand miles. Hipparchus, in part, invented trigonometry and compiled his great star catalogue there. He calculated the distance from the earth to the moon to be almost a quarter of a million miles, while resident in Alexandria, and also determined the length of the year. And on and on."

The two of us sat there for what seemed like the longest silence.

"By the way," I said, "at almost the same time that our army units in Egypt were trashing the Sarapeum, the tenth and eleventh squadrons of our regiment were suffering ten men dead in an attack by the Alemanns to the south of Mainz. The attack was beaten off."

More silence.

"You know," Chlogius finally said, "if this policy of deliberate government insanity continues unchecked, then some day we are going to hear that Theodosius has even gone so far as to abolish the Olympic Games."

We both had a good laugh over that ridiculous notion. Then Makila called us in for dinner.

Early in October, a trio of dispatch riders arrived at Valentinian's palace. Official documents always traveled back and forth between the two emperors, but this time something unusual happened. Shortly after the riders arrived, the presence of Arbogast and several top army officers was requested, and they stayed overnight. The following day, Valentinian called the officers and officer cadets of his Imperial Guards together and addressed us on the parade square near our barracks.

"Gentlemen, yesterday we received disturbing news from our colleague in the East. It appears that the Treaty of 382 between Rome and the Visigothic peoples has been deliberately broken for the first time. Early in September, the finally constituted Visigothic Federate Army struck south out of Moesia and through western Thrace to the marshlands of northeastern Macedonia near the city of Thessalonica. Based on information obtained from captured enemy soldiers, this army is composed mainly of warriors of that race settled in Moesia as a result of the Treaty of 382. In addition, however, a few of its elements come from families which have been living there for generations and had remained loyal to us during all the troubles that derived from the Battle of Hadrianople. Most disturbing of all in this latter respect is that the very leader of this rebel army appears to be a Roman-born Visigoth of the Baltha family. This is the leading family of the Visigoths and has provided most of their important leaders over the past century. In addition, this Visigothic Federate Army has been strengthened by the addition of hundreds of Huns and Alans, as well as certain Visigothic deserters from our own Army of Thrace.

"You will recall that in 388 a band of Visigothic rebels from the northern wing of our army deserted and fled to the southeast into the vast marshland that lies northwest of the city of Thessalonica. At the time, we were informed that this band had been all but wiped out. The bogus nature of that allegation was soon proven by the manner in which bandit gangs formed by these deserters have continued to plague the region to this day. Now, to make matters worse, these bandit gangs have joined up with the new invading army to form an even more serious threat. While returning to Constantinople, Theodosius and his entourage were attacked in those marshes. Our Generals Timasius and Promotus managed to route these rebels. However, heavy casualties were sustained by both sides, and Theodosius himself was, for a while, in grave personal danger. Promotus has been commissioned to wipe out this army once and for all. The reason for this address is to inform you that we are once again facing an enemy Visigothic army under unified leadership. We will provide you with more information as it becomes available. Based on what we have been told by captured enemy soldiers, the would-be 'Fritigern' of this new rebel army was not previously known to us. His name is Alaric."

The emperor then dismissed us.

Alaric would evolve into something, the nature of which, Fritigern probably never imagined. Alaric would succeed where Kniva had failed.

What exactly the measure of that success would be and how it could possibly be worth the price in any meaningful sense will forever be a matter for debate. All that lay in the future. None of us had ever heard of Alaric, but he would change the course of history as had no Goth before him.

While everyone had questioned the propriety of the Treaty of 382, we were nonetheless stunned and disappointed when the emperor broke the news of its violation to us. It consumed our private discussions for days afterward. Yet what I remember most about this time is how we could focus on what would soon prove itself to be a mounting disaster over a thousand miles away while at the same time being oblivious to one that was building right in front of us. The next seminar that I attended at Margareta's home, I was immediately assailed by Gaiso in his good-natured way.

"Let me make certain that I've got things straight, Marcus," he began. "The good Visigoths are the ones whose families had been settled in Moesia for a couple of generations prior to 376; those splendid folks who have remained steadfast and true in their loyalty to Rome through thick and thin; the very people that we want our more recent arrivals to emulate. The bad Visigoths, on the other hand, are those ruinous rascals that have arrived since 376 and caused so much devastation in Thrace and the surrounding areas. Now we are hearing that a leader has emerged from among the good Visigoths who has made common cause with the bad Visigoths to the point where he has made himself their leader and recently tried to kill our Emperor Theodosius."

"By Jove, I think you've got it," I interrupted.

"My only point of confusion," Gaiso continued, "is what did you say the difference was between the good and the bad Visigoths?" Everyone was laughing by this time.

"Go ahead, lay it on," I replied, taking the "insults" as they were intended. "As those of you who were here at the time will doubtless recall, I expressed the idea that as long as no man emerged as the leader of all the Visigoths, and as long as the empire remained at peace, we might have enough time to Romanize the Visigoths as we have Romanized other large groups of immigrants in the past."

"Yeah, well that leader has now emerged, and it appears that time has run out," Antonius the merchant remarked somewhat sarcastically.

"I'm new here," a young civil servant named Licinius said, "but can someone explain how the term 'federate' came to be applied to the Visigoths?"

Margareta answered. "When the Roman state was first expanding beyond the confines of Italy during the third and second centuries BC, we commonly allied ourselves with certain cities that were amenable to the strengthening of Roman influence in their regions. Such cities were granted 'federate status.' When the regions in which these cities were located were eventually taken over by Rome, these cities would be granted the status of an independent city-state. Rome granted each new province that it annexed or conquered a written constitution. That document detailed that previously federate cities would be 'independent' in the sense that the provincial governor would not have authority over them."

"The use of the term 'federate' to describe the relationship between Rome and the Visigoths is a perverse usage of this ancient term," I suggested. "Far from rewarding a trusted ally for furthering Rome's interests, we are now rewarding a constant enemy who has done nothing but undermine Rome's security with land and money."

"It was a logical next step on the downward slide that Valens started in 376," Gaiso added. "The catastrophe of Hadrianople had to be legitimized because the government is incapable of summoning the resources to avenge it."

"One thing," Margareta said, "that enabled Rome to settle Franks on Roman territory under conditions favorable to Rome was the fact that Rome has never suffered a major unavenged defeat at the hands of the Franks the way we did with the Visigoths."

"And when Frankish soldiers fight for Rome, they do so as soldiers in Roman army units," Gaiso continued. "The Visigothic federates, as distinct from Visigothic volunteers in the Roman Army, are to fight as allies (supposedly) of Rome but in their own units under their own leaders using their own weapons. I believe this Alaric has confirmed our worst suspicions on how seriously the Visigoths take their treaty obligations."

"I don't think it is overstating the case to say that politically and militarily the Visigothic settlement in Thrace has completely undermined the Diocletianic policy of creating a more defensible frontier," I added. "Our current policy is based entirely on the belief, or should I say slender hope, that all the Visigothic foxes that have been let into the Roman chicken coop will miraculously become herbivorous."

Before switching to other matters, Margareta summed up the hopes of us all: "Let's all hope and pray regardless of what our individual religions may be that Promotus is able to crush this new upstart so we can get back to living in the manner that civilized people are supposed to live."

At the time of Valentinian's address, and for some time thereafter, no one fully appreciated what was foreshadowed by this latest Visigothic treachery. Alaric's first campaign would fizzle out in the following year, and the situation would revert to the status quo ante. We once again half-convinced ourselves that the process of Romanizing the Visigoths could succeed in time. What we refused to recognize, to our universal peril, was that the entire house of cards that had been created by the Treaty of 382 was starting to collapse. Visigothic memories of how their numbers had been decimated after Hadrianople had taken a mere nine years to dim out. The skeptic's worst fears were about to be confirmed and who among us did not lay claim to that designation after the event?

As I mentioned earlier, the First Western Palatine Guard Regiment provided, on a rotating monthly basis, several squadrons of troops to act as the emperor's bodyguard. Our squadron and others accompanied him to Reims and Metz in October to deal with political matters in those towns. In the West at least, October was to be a quiet month. At the beginning of November, we were called out to attend to a minor invasion of Alemanns that occurred in the area of Speyer and Worms. This was close to where I had gained my first experience in combat almost ten years earlier. This time around, the situation was less bloody. The local defenders had handled themselves well, as they almost always did. When we arrived on the scene, most of the invaders, who were not mounted, simply surrendered, except for a few diehards. They died hard. Near month's end, we headed back to Trier. It was snowing lightly the day we arrived at the capital. Instead of dropping by the barracks as the rest did, I passed through the town and up the Moselle to "our" villa. As a result, I had no way of knowing. Entering the courtyard, I discovered Makila having a small snowball fight with the children. Demetria and Justina were almost three and a half, while Serena would turn two on the day that I turned twenty-seven. As soon as they saw me, all the "artillery" turned in my direction, and I threw up my hands in as abject a form of surrender as I could muster. After we had all hugged and kissed one another, Makila shocked me.

"Isn't it awful?" she said.

"Awful?" I replied somewhat bewildered. "Actually, I think it's all rather pretty as long as it doesn't get too deep and it's all melted by tomorrow noon. Those are my favorite kinds of snowfalls."

There was an awkward pause.

"I'm not talking about the snow," she continued. "I'm referring to the East. Haven't you heard?"

"Heard what?" I replied. "I've been in the field for almost a month, and when we returned to Trier, I came straight here to see you and the kids without stopping by the barracks. What happened?"

"Promotus is dead," she said. "Margareta and Rufius told me earlier today. He was killed in an ambush while fighting the army of this new Gothic leader, Alaric. I know that you admired him so much."

I was stunned, and all I could do was look at her with an expression of total disbelief.

"Go on inside and start getting supper ready," I suggested. "I'm going to check next door with Rufius to see what other details he might have on it."

The villa of Rufius and Margareta Anicius was only several hundred feet away from ours. One advantage of having friends in the western senatorial aristocracy is that they have an intelligence and communication network that is uniquely their own. The emperors might have restricted their political opportunities and eliminated them from the military altogether over recent generations, but the elite will always be the elite. When they became targets of unscrupulous emperors, they withdrew from the cities to the countryside. When their country estates became targets of the barbarians, they started turning them into fortresses. While the government has trouble filling manpower requirements for the national army, the aristocrats are able to find recruits to man their own private militias. Before any government law is posted, the aristocracy knows all about it down to the last detail. Certain aristocrats have suffered horribly in periods of turmoil just like the common folk, but as a class, they will always find a way to outlast the worst conditions.

The Anician family, as I've mentioned earlier, is one of the most powerful and influential in the Western Empire. It became dominant in financial circles before Constantine the Great came to power. Nonetheless, it was its close association with that emperor during his long period in office that propelled the family to the position of prominence it enjoys today. Rufius Anicius was in failing health by the time I met him, but in his earlier days, he had served in the Senate. In his friendly, unpretentious way, Rufius had referred to himself as a member of the "cadet branch of the dynasty." Nonetheless, as a retired senator, he was a most respected man. Of his children, one son lived on a family estate in Aquitania, another in Italy. One of his daughters lived in Trier with her family, while his other one lived with her family on another estate downstream from Trier. Margareta had implied that there was some ill feeling within the family over the father marrying a woman so much younger than he was. That's often the way. Rufius was an honorary member of the Western Sacred Consistory at Trier. In practice, he did not attend the regular sessions but was occasionally called in when special conditions demanded. When I arrived at their villa, a slave answered the door and led me in. Rufius bade me welcome and ushered me into his spacious library.

"You don't know how well I've been sleeping for the past month knowing that you were off patrolling the frontier on my behalf," he kidded me.

"With the lovely Margareta to keep you company, it's a wonder you get any sleep at all," I teased him back.

Another slave poured us some wine.

"Your continued good health," I toasted him.

"And yours," he replied, "along with our continued success with good-looking women."

We both laughed.

"Rufius," I said, "I just arrived home, and Makila informed me that Promotus is dead. I had not heard anything about it. What do you know?"

"I found out myself when I was in the city earlier today," he replied. "You've been away for almost a month, so I don't know what you may have heard regarding recent goings-on in the Eastern Sacred Consistory. Several weeks ago, at one of its meetings to which the general had been invited for consultation, an argument broke out between Rufinus and Promotus. Rufinus, always quick to anger, rudely insulted Promotus, and the general replied by slapping Rufinus hard across the face. For some reason, the emperor was not attending at the time. Rufinus immediately went to Theodosius and showed him the damage that Promotus had wrought upon him. The emperor, forgetting all about the ensuing consequences the last time he lost control of himself, immediately flew off the handle. In a thoughtless outburst he told the consistory that everyone had better get used to taking orders from Rufinus as master of offices because if they didn't, they might soon find him ruling over them as emperor. The thought of Theodosius sharing the imperial power with Rufinus or anyone else other than his two sons and Valentinian II is ridiculous. But it was just what Rufinus wanted to hear, whether he believed it or not. Shortly thereafter, the general returned to Thrace to continue his suppression of the Visigothic Federate Army under this young upstart Alaric, whoever he is. Promotus was ambushed and slain. I don't know how much faith one can place in them, but rumors are circulating to the effect that the two events are not disconnected. And to think that the purpose of the Visigothic Federate Army was to act as just another Roman field army to defend the Roman frontier in Thrace!"

"While I was stationed in Milan, my understanding was that Rufinus was one of Theodosius's most trusted confidants," I replied. "It's easy to understand why military men rise to positions of great importance. It's more difficult to ascertain why this is so in the case of high-ranking civil servants."

"Rufinus is a mystery to me too," Rufius replied. "Being an imperial guardsman, what do you hear about relations between our emperor and Arbogast?"

I sensed that Rufius knew more than he was letting on.

"After Valentinian's October address to us," I answered, "I heard that Arbogast was displeased with the frank nature of its content. Arbogast seems to have felt that it was mildly demeaning of Theodosius. As a member of his audience, I didn't find it that way at all. Valentinian has been reigning for sixteen years, but others have exercised the real power in his name for that entire period. As a result, I don't think that enough of his ministers take him seriously. For the first time in his life, he is independent, or at least he is supposed to be. But because of his previous dependence on others, I think he is having a difficult time making his authority felt. The emperor tends to be quite detailed in his addresses to us. I think that is a reflection of his being kept in the dark about what was going on around him for so long. He doesn't want to treat his subordinates that way because he doesn't like being dealt with in that manner himself."

"I agree," Rufius said. "Certain of the more strong-willed members of his Sacred Consistory do ignore him. I don't believe there is anything deliberately contemptuous in this. It is just that old habits are hard to break." Rufius looked down at the floor, deciding the extent to which he could confide his personal observations to me.

Finally he said, "At several sessions I attended, Arbogast and the emperor were both present. Whenever there was a difference of opinion between the two on any issue, Arbogast would not hesitate to contradict Valentinian, regardless of who was there."

"There have been numerous cases where the emperor has given an order only to have it vetoed by the field marshal. When I escorted the emperor to Reims and Metz," I continued, "he received notification of military appointments that Arbogast had made. Valentinian had requested Arbogast to inform him beforehand about any military promotions, transfers, assignments, et cetera that fell under Arbogast's aegis. This emperor has every right to do. But Arbogast seems to have objected to this 'interference' in what he felt was his own prerogative."

"Arbogast has been the supreme military authority here in Gaul for three years now," Rufius said. "This influence has overlapped into the civilian sphere and not without public support. Most civilian appointments throughout the prefecture were made by Theodosius on direct recommendations by Arbogast prior to Valentinian's arrival. As a result, Arbogast has strong civilian as well as military backing."

"That's true," I replied, "but Arbogast's immediate chief of state is Valentinian II. The emperor has the right to be informed by his subordinates on any matter for which they are responsible, in any manner that he sees fit. It seems to me that Arbogast and other members of the Western Sacred Consistory have lost sight of that. Valentinian has been in communication with both Ambrose and Theodosius lately. The rumor is that the letters detail Valentinian's complaints about his advisers simply ignoring him."

For the first time, there was a long pause in our conversation. I had the feeling that I might have said too much. It occurred to me that Arbogast and Rufius were both pagans and that the connection between them might be stronger than I had realized. But to what purpose? Maybe I was just being paranoid.

"How well do you know Arbogast?" I asked.

"We've met formally several times during Sacred Consistory meetings since Valentinian arrived. Before that, we met informally at several state occasions, but I really don't know him that well."

"As you know, Valentinian converted to Catholicism after Theodosius arrived in Milan," I went on. "I think he was simply tired of the badgering he was getting on the issue from Theodosius and Ambrose. More importantly, he has made no effort to enforce the edict on intolerance proclaimed earlier this year within his own domain. That point notwithstanding, I've heard that the edict has forced a wedge of sorts between Arbogast and Theodosius. Arbogast has long seen himself as Theodosius's man but the edict might be causing the cement in their relationship to crumble. Have you heard anything about it?"

"Nothing definite," he replied.

Rufius and I had another round of wine and spoke of many things for a while. Just before I left we agreed to keep one another informed on what we heard and that we did. It was still snowing when I left, though it had started to let up. Between our two villas, I could see several other estates across the Moselle lit up in the darkening twilight. It was a very pretty sight, the sort of view that lets you think, at least for a moment, that perhaps everything is right with the world after all. With the exception of the terrible loss of Promotus, I could stand there looking out at this small but very rich part of the empire and honestly feel that it was. But illusions cannot last forever.

Christmas and New Year's passed all too quickly. On New Year's Day, all soldiers gathered on the main parade square in Trier and once again swore our oaths of allegiance to Valentinian II, Theodosius, and Arcadius. We were starting to hear rumors of increasing restlessness on the part of various tribes on the other side of the Rhine. Another thing that started to strike certain of us was the manner in which our emperor became more withdrawn. Throughout the first two years of his residence in Trier, Valentinian had been quite outgoing. He enjoyed appearing in public and touring Gaul. There was talk of his visiting Spain and Britain, but nothing came of it. During the early part of 392, rumors continued to surface about the relationship between Arbogast and Valentinian deteriorating. Arbogast made numerous military and political appointments throughout the prefecture of the Gauls while Theodosius continued to do the same in the prefecture of the Italies. Appointments and decisions were made in Valentinian's name, in many cases, without his ever being consulted. Yet these two prefectures constituted the Western Empire, Valentinian's domain. As the year progressed, Valentinian felt more and more isolated.

I have always been at a loss to explain the way that Arbogast completely bungled his association with young Valentinian. Arbogast had served the families of Valentinian I and Theodosius with as much diligence and devotion as any man. He owed his career to Valentinian I whom he served throughout his reign. When Gratian assumed the throne, he made Arbogast a count and sent him to Illyria to assist Theodosius. In 383, after Gratian had been assassinated, Arbogast had been promoted to field marshal in Italy to defend the realm of Valentinian II. In that capacity, his relationship with the imperial family had been good. It was only after Valentinian II had assumed a supposedly independent role in the West that the relationship between the two began to decline. Arbogast should have been able to put Valentinian to good political use throughout the prefecture. The emperor had positive attributes that I have already discussed, and Arbogast was well acquainted with them. But such a role never materialized. Perhaps Valentinian wanted to be involved in military decisions for which Arbogast felt he was simply not qualified. At the same time, it was the field marshal's responsibility to see that his emperor was qualified regardless of whether Theodosius had given him specific orders on the matter. Arbogast simply could not bear to relinquish any of the authority that Theodosius had granted him. Instead of training the young emperor, Arbogast ignored him, and the civilian administrators, taking their lead from the field marshal, treated him the same way. For Valentinian, it was beginning to appear that his life was turning into an endless humiliation.

At the beginning of February, Fredemondus announced that I was being promoted to decurion. I was taking over a decade whose commander had been forced into early retirement due to injuries. The promotion would be effective immediately. It was the proudest moment in my army career to date and definitely time to celebrate. Makila and I had the biggest party that we ever held at our villa. I was a decurion at age twenty-seven with a beautiful wife, three wonderful children, and living in a villa. The horizon looked endless.

In April, an incursion of Alemanns came across the Rhine north of Strasbourg where we were patrolling with several other units. Our intelligence had been good, and we were able to apprehend the invaders before they penetrated very far inland. It was not a major invasion. However, they numbered about eight hundred, and the battle was the most difficult that I had participated in since returning to the West. Fighting broke out when one of the field army regiments ahead of us was ambushed by the main body of the Alemanns. Riders from the besieged regiment immediately rode back to summon us to assist them along with four centuries of mounted infantry. Such regimental couriers have a very dangerous responsibility. Whenever the Germans set an ambush, they almost always have men ready to chase after such riders to kill them before they can make contact with other army units. This is why several riders are always sent together. Depending on where a unit under attack is with respect to associated units, such groups of riders might be sent off in more than one direction. Three riders had been sent back to call us up, and one had been killed in the process.

Our units were under strength, as usual, so that we were outnumbered by the enemy by a wider margin than our unit designations would indicate. We arrived at the scene and joined the battle as soon as we could. The field army regiment, heavily outnumbered, had been taking the worst of it. As we approached the Germans, some of their infantry broke away from their main engagement and launched several volleys of arrows at us. Some found their mark in men or horses. Our mounted infantry centuries dismounted and attacked the Alemann infantry directly. Our cavalry decades aided in this while being ready to fend off any enemy cavalry attacks.

I have always felt more comfortable as an infantryman than as a horse soldier. The cavalry is fine from a transportation viewpoint. However, when battle is joined, it is often very difficult for commanders to maintain control of their men. This is why the basic cavalry unit, the decade, is smaller than the corresponding infantry unit, the century.

This complication holds for both corps of the service. But having served in both, I feel there is a greater danger for cavalry officers to lose their ability to govern events. Cavalry actions occur more quickly and are spread out over a much larger area.

The Alemann infantry, launching barrages of arrows at us, had only a small cavalry detachment to assist them, and it was busy elsewhere. Two of our centuries laid down an effective counter-barrage, after which we charged off into the Alemann soldiers and broke them up into smaller groups. We had gained the upper hand at the outset but that didn't make the fighting easy. The clangor of metal on metal as sword struck sword or helmet and the clatter of swords striking shields was coming from every direction. Immediately the screams and groans of the dying and wounded filled the air. Spring had barely begun, and yet the perspiration started pouring off our faces almost immediately. It would be a long afternoon. Ever since Hadrianople, the myth has taken root as fact that, during that battle, cavalry gained a permanent supremacy over infantry. During the battle, Gothic cavalry had first defeated Roman cavalry. They then assisted their infantry to defeat our infantry. If it had been a pure case of Gothic cavalry charging Roman infantry, then the battle's outcome would have been different. Early in our infantry training, we had been taught how to defend ourselves against a cavalry charge. This was not training that had suddenly evolved since that dreadful day in 378. It has been stock training for every Roman infantryman for centuries. What is vital on any battlefield is for infantry and cavalry to work in combination with one another. On this April day, fourteen years after Hadrianople, the Alemann infantry segment that we faced could not be protected by their cavalry. The reason was that they didn't have enough cavalry to go around and they couldn't be everywhere at once. These Alemanns also did not appear conversant with how to defend themselves against our onrushing cavalry. They saw us coming from a long way off but did not form up into a defensive square formation to defend against us.

Having broken the enemy up into small groups, our greater mobility gradually swayed the battle in our favor. Dust rose like a fog all around us, and we soon lost track of what was happening elsewhere. Finally, the enemy's losses hit the level where it became impossible for them to defend themselves any longer. Some surrendered and our infantry rounded them up. Those who didn't were cut to pieces. Once we had wrapped up activities in our sector, my squadron was ordered to assist our units that were besieged by the enemy cavalry. This was a different type of fighting altogether: horse soldier versus horse soldier. Our infantry had protected themselves well against the Alemanns. When our cavalry arrived to relieve them, the tide was turned. The attackers were now the defenders. Encompassed, with no way out, they fought almost to the last man. Shortly after engaging the Alemann cavalry, I took a sword slash across the lower part of my left leg. Almost at the end of the battle, I suddenly took an arrow through my left arm. I had no idea of what direction it had come from. I fought as well as I could for as long as I could, but I was losing too much blood from both wounds and getting weak. I ordered my deputy to take over command of our squadron while I withdrew to the field hospital that our medics had set up near the edge of the battle site.

I was in worse shape than I thought. The arrow had passed through my left arm. To remove it, the medics snipped off the head and then withdrew it back out the entry wound. The pain of extraction was excruciating and exceeded the pain of its entry. I had lost more blood than I realized from my leg wound. The medics applied thirty-five stitches to close it up. I thanked God that my injuries were not worse, but many of my comrades were not so fortunate. My squadron had suffered more casualties in both dead and wounded than any other squadron in our regiment. Both categories were loaded on wagons. The most seriously wounded were sent to hospitals in Worms and Mainz since these cities were closest to the battle site. The rest of us headed home to Trier.

Shortly after, Valentinian visited the wounded in the hospitals and returned to Trier in preparation for touring the cities down in the Rhone Valley. I spent the next three weeks at home recuperating, expecting everything to return to normal since my injuries did not appear to be that severe. It was not to be. To this day, I cannot lift or extend my left arm as far as the right, and I am still slightly lame in my wounded leg. The surroundings were certainly pleasant though. Late April in the Moselle is a beautiful time of the year, and I quite enjoyed the period there with Makila and the children. They were growing so quickly. I never doubted that they would be tall and beautiful like their mother. Demetria and Justina were almost four, while Serena was now two and a half. I could not have dreamed of a more enjoyable convalescence.

We visited back and forth with Rufius and Margareta more than usual during that time. At one of our visits, Rufius informed me that relations between Arbogast and Valentinian were getting worse. While the emperor appeared to have authority regarding lower-level political appointments, the highest civilian authorities continued to defer to Arbogast when making major selections such as those of provincial presidents. In Italy, Theodosius had made all the appointments even if they had been in the names of himself and Valentinian. Our emperor was coming to realize that Arbogast, not himself, was the de facto ruler of the West, that Theodosius had ordained it, and that virtually everyone accepted it. It could not go on forever.

After three weeks at home, I returned to my regiment, though I was still not 100 percent. The emperor's itinerary had been set. It had been almost two years since he had visited the lower Rhone Valley, so the tour would begin at Lyon and continue south from there. It went south all right. Five squadrons of Imperial Guards were selected as his escort, and mine was one of them. Valentinian would be accompanied by a number of his senior civilian officials. I kissed Makila and the children goodbye, telling them that I expected to be home in about a month.

The journey started well. From Trier, we traveled the route that I knew by heart to Lyon, the site of the first gala reception. Valentinian made a fine speech to the audience, met with all the local officials, and made a good impression all around. We then traveled on to Vienne, about twenty miles to the south. To our surprise, Arbogast was there dealing with a group of authorities from Italy. Valentinian had not been informed of such a meeting beforehand, and it created a most awkward situation. Arbogast was dealing with the Italians in the same large building that Valentinian used as a palace when he resided in the city. What led to the subsequent, devastating crisis was the topic of the meeting. The prefecture of the Italies has a lengthy frontier on the Danube that runs all the way from Lake Constance in the west to Belgrade in the east. Due to the ongoing need to ship troops to the Balkans, during the 380s, this part of the frontier had become dangerously under strength. Early in 392, barbarian peoples started threatening it. As a result, a delegation headed by none other than Bishop Ambrose visited Trier during the winter to discuss the transfer of troops from Gaul to help contain this pending invasion. At that time, Valentinian had expressed interest in leading such an expedition himself. Arbogast, however, had expressed his strong disapproval of the emperor's involvement. Nonetheless, reinforcements were sent. Now, a couple of months later, here was this second delegation discussing the same situation with Arbogast while the field marshal kept his emperor completely in the dark.

Valentinian had planned on spending several days at Vienne to rest up from the fast-paced nature of the journey thus far. Hearing of his arrival, the Italian delegation dropped around to bid farewell to the emperor as they prepared to leave the city. It was the proper thing to do, but it only made matters worse. Once again, Valentinian's nominal subordinates were acting as though he did not exist. The emperor was outraged at this latest insult. After briefly withdrawing to his quarters, he reemerged and summoned Arbogast to his presence. Valentinian II, tired of being ignored and humiliated by his chief general, had decided to act decisively. Arbogast entered, saluted, and approached Valentinian. The emperor gave him a scornful look and handed him a written decree relieving him of his command. Arbogast read the order, looked at the emperor, and smiled.

"I did not receive my current command from you and you lack both the authority and the ability to remove me from it."

At this, he contemptuously ripped the decree to pieces, threw it to the floor, and walked from the room. Everyone there stood speechless. Never had we ever heard of a Roman emperor being treated in such a disdainful manner. Mortified, Valentinian II left the room by another exit. Like all the other soldiers, I had the deepest respect for Arbogast as a commanding general. But as an officer of the crown, his conduct had been disgraceful. The gap between emperor and field marshal had now become a chasm.

The emperor ate alone in his quarters that evening. As officer of the watch, I was posted in a small office across the hall. Two guards were posted outside his door. The emperor's room was located on the second floor of the large, essentially square palace. It was off a long hallway that was sealed off at either end by doorways. There were no stairways leading from the first floor to the second in this section of the building. There were several offices off this main hallway. In addition to the guards posted outside Valentinian's room, I had two guards posted at the doors at each end of the hallway. The emperor's quarters and the offices along the inner wall of the palace faced out onto a large courtyard. After he finished his dinner, the emperor called for servants to take the dishes away, which they did. He then went for a short walk in the courtyard during the evening's fading light. I asked him if he wanted any company on his evening stroll, but he said no. When he returned, he motioned for me to come into his quarters for a moment. I closed the door behind me.

"Marcus, it's been a long day. I'm going to sleep in tomorrow morning. If I'm not up by eight o'clock, then knock on the door and get me."

"Yes, sir," I replied. Then I added with some hesitation, "I just want you to know, sir, that I think Arbogast's behavior this afternoon was absolutely detestable."

The emperor paused for a moment and then replied, "Yes, it was, wasn't it?" He was looking past me into the distance, but I could just see the tears starting to well up in his eyes.

"You can go now, Marcus."

"If you need me for anything, sir, I'll be right across the hall."

"There will be nothing more tonight. You will see me in the morning. Good night, Marcus, and thank you."

"Good night, sir," I said.

Those words have haunted me for the rest of my life. Not "I'll see you in the morning" but rather "You will see me in the morning." I've never been accused of being overly quick on the pickup. I thought at the time that it was an odd way of putting it but then the emperor was operating under a terrible strain. The rest of the night, I spent time checking the guards on a somewhat random basis. One never wants guards to be goofing off because they know their commanding officer keeps overly regular schedules. Earlier in the day, I had checked every other room in the section where the emperor's quarters were, and I checked them again, periodically, during the night. I had my old friend Marcellinus on watch with me. He was in another squadron now, but that didn't matter. Periodically I would check the courtyard where I had also posted several guards. Nothing unusual happened during our watch, so we thought.

By the time dawn came along, we were all pretty tired and looking forward to a good day's rest. Finally, at 8:00 a.m. on May 15, 392, I went to arouse the emperor, as he had instructed. I knocked on the door. No answer. After knocking several times, I asked the two guards posted at his door if they had heard anything inside.

"No, sir," one of them answered. "It's been quiet ever since you left his room last night."

"Your Majesty," I yelled, this time pounding on the door; again, no answer.

We stood there awkwardly looking at one another. At this moment, the new guard showed up with their decurion, a Gaul named Lucian. I explained the situation quickly and doubled the guard at the emperor's door and at both doors at the end of the hall. I took Lucian, and we raced passed the guards at one end of the hall and down the staircase to a utility room that I had checked out the previous day. Grabbing a long ladder, we ran out into the courtyard. Again I ordered the old guard to stay put, along with the new, until either Lucian or I released them from duty. We placed the ladder against the wall, and I climbed up to the window that the emperor had left open, as he always did, to catch the cool night air. I looked in.

"Jesus Christ!" I shouted.

"What's the matter?" Lucian hollered up to me.

"Get up here fast," I yelled down to him. "I need your help." While he was coming up, I climbed inside and moved a table under where Valentinian was hanging.

"Good God!" Lucian exploded as he ran over to help me cut the emperor down.

I sliced the rope with my Hun knife, and Valentinian's body fell into my arms. Lucian and I laid him on his bed and I cut the rope from around his neck. Lucian felt for a pulse, but we both knew as soon as we had seen him that we were much too late. His body was cold. I have often remarked that he was such a good-looking young man. But the most profound memory that I have of Valentinian II is that of him hanging from that rafter, his eyes bulging, his mouth twisted.

"He's been dead for hours," Lucian said. "You heard nothing at all?"

"No and neither did the men outside," I replied. "Order the guards down in the courtyard to put the ladder away. I'll go and tell Arbogast."

"I really envy you that chore," he said.

"I'll bet," I replied. "But it happened on my watch. Let's leave the double guard that we've posted until Arbogast gets here. Let no one in the room until we get back."

Lucian agreed.

I raced diagonally across the courtyard in the general direction of where I had been told Arbogast could be found. An official told me that the field marshal was still at breakfast with certain military and civilian officials in the dining hall. Two guards were posted at the door.

"Urgent orders for Arbogast," I said in as imperious a tone as I could muster.

The guards stepped aside and admitted me. Arbogast was conducting a business breakfast, as was frequently his custom. It was obvious that he was taking none too kindly to my intrusion. I had seen the man at a distance but had never met him in person.

"Lord Arbogast," I said, "I need a word with you in private, sir. It's an emergency."

"Who are you?" he replied coldly.

"Marcus Cedranus, sir," I answered, "First Western Palatine Guards Regiment. I need to talk to you in private."

"Does this involve the emperor?" he asked.

"Yes, it does."

"If that's the case, then there is nothing that you cannot say in front of these gentlemen," Arbogast said, almost chuckling as he looked around the table. As if on cue, the bureaucrats all started smiling as well. I had tried to keep the matter private as long as possible, but the field marshal had asked for it.

"The emperor is dead," I told the assembly.

"What?" Arbogast yelled as his associates gasped in disbelief.

"Come with me right away, sir," I said.

"Wait a minute." Then turning to a tribune that served as his adjutant, he ordered, "Quintus, get word to the garrison commander that the city is to be sealed off immediately, with no one being allowed in or out until further notice. All the gates are to be closed at once. Also, tell the Imperial Guard commander to post every soldier he has around this palace, sealing it off in the same way. The only members of the guard that are exempt from this duty are the ones that were in immediate attendance on the emperor last night. We'll want to question them."

Arbogast and I rushed out of the dining hall, across the courtyard, and up to the emperor's room. On the way, I explained how I had discovered Valentinian earlier and how the guards insisted that they had heard or seen nothing suspicious during the night. The field marshal ran in and stared at Valentinian, incredulous at what he was witnessing. I am firmly convinced that Arbogast's horror at what he, himself, had precipitated, however unintentionally, was genuine. It would take over two years for the series of events that had been initiated on that terrible night to play themselves out. As a result, the world would never be the same again.

After his initial shock was over, Arbogast quizzed me and other guardsmen repeatedly about what happened the previous night. The confusion surrounding Valentinian's death consumed the entire morning. Everywhere you looked, there were groups of men engaged in speculation as to what had triggered the young monarch's suicide. Rumors were soon spreading that it was really a case of murder. Subsequently, it became politically correct for certain historians to adopt this line to justify later developments. However, as the one who came as close to being a witness to the actual event as anyone, the emperor's death was a suicide beyond doubt. The idea that he was murdered is a convenient fiction. After interviewing everyone several times, Arbogast and his staff met in a large conference room down the hall from the emperor's quarters for about a half hour. When they emerged, Arbogast called all of us that had been on guard duty the previous night into the conference room.

"First and foremost, His Majesty Theodosius must be informed," he began. "Marcus, I want you to select two decurions, in whom you have complete confidence. They will accompany you to Constantinople, where you will deliver this letter to Theodosius. If he is not at the capital, then find out where he is and take it there. You must deliver it in person. After all, since you were officer of the watch last night, it's only fitting that you transmit the news." He then gave me what I can only describe as a slightly serpentine smile.

"If you have one of your secretaries write up a copy of this letter, sir, I could drop it off to Bishop Ambrose since Milan is on our way to Constantinople," I said. "I'm certain that you will want to inform him sooner or later. That way, we can kill two birds with one stone."

"No. I'll take care of that later," Arbogast replied. "It is imperative that Theodosius be informed as soon as possible. In the meantime, pick your two men and get your horses ready. I want to see the three of you here in one hour."

I saluted and left.

First, I dropped back into the emperor's room, and approaching the bed, I saluted him for what would be the last time. As I was leaving, I saw the Hun bow that I had presented to him lying on a large table against the far wall. I picked it up and left the room. Next, I saw Stephanus and asked him to inform Makila of what had happened to Valentinian and of the mission that Arbogast had charged me with. I then sought out my old friends Fredemondus and Chlogius and asked them to accompany me to Constantinople. We went to the stable and got our horses ready.

When I returned to the conference room at the palace, all was ready. I brought my two fellow decurions with me.

"We are ready to leave, sir," I said, addressing Arbogast. I then introduced him to Chlogius and Fredemondus.

Arbogast observed the three of us at length. "Very well, here is the sealed letter for the emperor. In addition, here are your passes to use the Imperial Post horses. I expect you to be in Constantinople in ten days. Any questions?"

"None, sir," I replied, and we left the room.

Arbogast then dispatched riders north to Trier. Their mission was to inform the late emperor's two young sisters, Grata and Justa, of the tragic news as well as members of the Western Sacred Consistory that had not accompanied the emperor on his last, fatal journey. All military commanders were notified, and the public was then informed. It was well into the afternoon by the time we got on the road. The distance from Vienne to Constantinople is over 1,400 miles. We would have to average 150 miles per day to meet Arbogast's schedule. I have often heard that a rider using the horses of the Imperial Post could travel 250 miles per day. I have long suspected, however, that this estimate was based on travel over relatively flat ground in perfect weather. We would have to traverse the Alps twice, and that could prove quite time-consuming.

I was dead tired from having been up by now for a day and a half. But the excitement of the terrible tragedy with which we were associated was enough to propel us ever further through the mountains. From Vienne, we headed southeast to Gratianopolis[24] on the Isere River. It was ironic that the first city we passed through would be this one. Shortly after returning to Trier in 389, Valentinian II had renamed the old city of Cularo to Gratianopolis in honor of his dead brother. The highway then swung to the south to pass through the valley of the Durance River that divides the Cottian Alps to the north from the Maritime Alps on the south. We then headed northeast and went through Briancon and the Mt. Genevre Pass. The route we were taking was the same one that the invading army of Magnus Maximus had taken five years earlier when he invaded Italy. His personal road to destruction had ultimately taken him to Aquileia. By an ironic twist of fate, the terrible tragedy of May 15, 392, would also reach its climax not all that distant from the same city.

The stations of the Imperial Post are generally positioned anywhere from ten to twenty miles apart, depending on terrain. In the mountains, they tended to be somewhat closer together than on flatter ground. We tried to be on the road for fifteen hours a day and sometimes eighteen, but this was not always possible. Accommodations are available at the post stations for riders that must stay the night. Going through the mountains, we were slowed somewhat by several heavy rainstorms, and as a result, it took us three days to get from Vienne to Turin. As we descended from the Alps, I happened to look back. It was a most remarkable sight. The sun had started to set and had just gone behind a large mountain. It had already darkened to the point where the bulk of the mountain appeared to be nothing more than a greenish-black mass. But on its left-hand side, the sun's rays, reflecting off the summit, seemed to have turned the sky and the air itself into the color of gold. It was one of the most beautiful sights that I have ever seen, but in a moment, it was gone.

By the time we reached Turin, we were in the upper reaches of the Po River Valley. It took only a little more than a day to travel across the whole of northern Italy, roughly the same distance that we traveled through the Alps. At Aquileia, the nonstop traveling started to catch up with us. We took time off to visit the baths at the garrison and get all the road dirt washed out of our clothing. The garrison commander there could not do enough for us. Upon hearing that we were heading for Constantinople, he invited us to dine with him that evening. He was hoping to pick up some piece of vital information that might drop during the course of our conversations. Using three decurions from the Imperial Guard as couriers was sufficient to raise his expectations in that regard. We dined sumptuously but were very careful in what we said. We heard nothing about Valentinian's suicide while there and we were gratified to know that word of it had not miraculously preceded us. But what he told us was most disturbing. The garrison commander, getting nothing of substance from the three of us, suddenly asked if we had heard the latest news from the East.

"What news are you referring to?" Chlogius asked. "Prior to being sent on this mission, we were campaigning on the Rhine for weeks. Marcus here still hasn't fully recovered from his wounds."

"I noticed you limping," the commander said to me. "If you would like, I can have one of our doctors check your injuries out for you."

I thanked him for his offer and asked him to arrange to have a garrison doctor check me out the following morning. Then I asked him what the news was from the East that he had referred to.

"The details are still murky," he replied, "but while you are in the eastern capital, make certain that you don't run afoul of Rufinus, the new praetorian prefect of the East."

"Praetorian prefect?" Fredemondus asked. "How did that come about?"

"In the worst possible way," the commander responded, "by way of a purge. Tatianus has been removed from office and banished to his home province of Lycia in Anatolia. His son Proculus, the urban prefect of Constantinople, has been executed by decapitation."

"What!" all three of us said at once.

"What the hell has happened?" Fredemondus almost yelled at him.

They were men of impeccable character who were universally respected in East and West by pagan and Christian alike. The fact that they had been deposed in a purge and that Proculus had been executed struck us all like a thunderbolt. The garrison commander was careful not to overstate his own feelings about what had happened. The reasons why Theodosius permitted the downfall of these two men has never been explained. It was nothing more than a blatant power grab on the part of Rufinus and Theodosius turned a blind eye when it happened. Rufinus, as master of offices, conspired to bring trumped-up charges of malfeasance in office against both men. He controlled the outcome of their trials through a combination of bribes to and threats against the men he had chosen to sit with him on the judicial panel. Theodosius, when told about the order to execute Proculus, tried to stop it, but he was too late. Incredibly, he did absolutely nothing to punish Rufinus for this deliberate breaking of the law. After the massacre at Thessalonica, Theodosius had issued a new law stating that anyone given a capital sentence anywhere in the empire would have it stayed automatically for thirty days for it to be reviewed by the proper authorities. Rufinus was fully aware of the law and ignored it. What made this disregard of the law all the more outrageous was that, as one of the four praetorian prefects, he was one of the empire's chief legal officers. The entire empire was disgusted with Theodosius's ineptitude on the matter. The execution of Proculus and the banishing of Tatianus only served to make the rumors of Rufinus' connection with the ambush of Promotus all the more credible. After the murder of Promotus, Rufinus was designated consul for 392. After the fall of Tatianus, Rufinus was appointed to Tatianus' office of praetorian prefect of the East. The common attitude became "what would one expect from the butcher of Thessalonica."

Rufinus would have fit well into the administrations of the worst of our emperors. He was avaricious and murderously ambitious as were the worst of their appointees. Theodosius, nonetheless, allowed him to increase his influence in areas that were not really in his realm of responsibility and ignored the outright reign of terror that he was exercising. Rufinus' terrible character failings were of no consequence to the emperor. Numerous members of the Eastern Sacred Consistory warned Theodosius continually about the increasing tyranny of Rufinus, but the emperor did nothing about it.

At the end of the evening, we thanked the garrison commander for his hospitality and for the information from the eastern capital. After having the dressings on my wounds replaced, we were back on the road the next morning, feeling very uneasy about what we were heading into. We passed through the Julian Alps in two days and into the Sava River Valley. The longest distance that we would cover in a single day was the 235 miles from Sisak to Belgrade. From there, the journey was an old one: Naissus, Sofia, Philippopolis, Hadrianople, and Constantinople. During this latter part of the journey, the only place we were slowed down was in the area around Hadrianople where the highway was thick with military traffic. Since the death of Promotus, Stilicho had taken over as the commander of the Army of Thrace. This army, consisting of twenty-one legions of roughly a thousand men each and seven cavalry regiments of five hundred men each, had been charged with containing the Visigothic Federate Army of Alaric that was still actively conducting itself in opposition to us. The containment seemed to be working, and an officer that I spoke to told me that Stilicho was off in the capital giving a status report to the emperor. Not wanting to raise any suspicions along the way, I had inquired as to the emperor's whereabouts only at Aquileia and Belgrade. In both cases, I was told that he was at the capital. This last conversation confirmed it. We arrived in Constantinople just eleven days after leaving Vienne.

As we approached the city walls, nearing the end of the Via Egnatia, we passed through the magnificent marble Arch of Theodosius I. It is now known as the Golden Gate, although it was not a gate then; it was a stand-alone monument. When we celebrated his triumph here in 386, we had heard that a triumphal arch was planned outside the city walls somewhere along the Via Egnatia. Exactly where had not been specified at the time. It was completed in 390. Since then it has been incorporated into the new Wall of Theodosius II. It was the middle of the afternoon as we traveled along High Street, following the same route that we had during the triumphal parade six years earlier. Good Lord, had six years passed already? We continued to the Imperial Palace grounds in the southeast corner of the city. On our last journey here, we had to content ourselves with looking at the place from the outside. What is referred to as the "Imperial Palace" is actually a collection of separate buildings. We presented ourselves at the main gate, and after informing the guards that I had an urgent message from Arbogast for the emperor, a courier rode off. I say "rode off" because the Daphne Palace, the main building in the complex, is almost a half mile from the main gate. After waiting what I thought was an overly long period of time, the courier finally returned with an official from the praetorian prefect's office. I repeated to him what I had told the courier, and the official, who introduced himself as Athemion, ushered us into the palace grounds.

The road wound through what must be the most carefully nurtured gardens in the empire. The only parts of the palace grounds not devoted to horticulture were the buildings and the roads. Otherwise, plants and flowering trees roll off in every direction from the urban walls to the sea wall. The Daphne Palace itself fronts to the southeast facing the junction of the Bosporus, to the east, and the Sea of Marmara (or the Propontis) to the south. The Imperial Port is also located there just to the right of the palace. It is small and is strictly for use by members of the imperial family and government officials. When we arrived, grooms were waiting and took our horses to the stable while the three of us were ushered into the palace by Athemion. The stateliness and luxuriousness of the building was overwhelming. Athemion took us down several long hallways until we arrived at the office of Rufinus.

"Please be seated," Athemion said. "I will tell Rufinus that you are here."

During our ride from the main gate to the palace, I had asked Athemion who the new master of offices was since Rufinus had been promoted. He said that Eutropius now held that position. The position of master of offices had become the highest office to which one could aspire in the civil service, apart from becoming one of the four praetorian prefects. The man who occupied this office controlled all secretarial offices across all ministries as well as the Imperial Post. At least Theodosius did not let Rufinus occupy both offices at the same time. Perhaps more ominously, Theodosius had placed the Imperial Guard under Rufinus' control since Stilicho had taken over the Army of Thrace in place of Promotus. This in spite of Rufinus' lack of a military background. Athemion returned and said, "The praetorian prefect will see you now."

We were ushered into Rufinus' presence and there followed a disconcerting silence as he continued to peruse a stack of documents on his desk without bothering to look up. This is such a tiresome exercise on the part of bureaucrats everywhere to impress newcomers as to how important they are. Finally, he leaned back and said, "What is this urgent business that you have with His Majesty?"

"I have a document in my possession that Arbogast has instructed me to deliver to the emperor personally," I replied.

"I can handle that," Rufinus responded, as I had assumed he would.

"I'm certain that you can, sir," I answered, "but Arbogast ordered me to hand the document to His Majesty in person and see the seal being broken. This is a matter of the utmost importance and involves the emperor of the West."

Rufinus paused at this point to consider what his next move would be.

"Perhaps you could conduct us to His Majesty, sir, and I could inform you both at the same time," I suggested.

After another pause, Rufinus replied, "Sounds good. Come with me."

We went with him down another long, elaborate hallway, and along the way, I caught a glimpse of the throne room. But it was only a glimpse. Wherever we were going to meet Theodosius, it would not be there. We went, instead, to an office next door with armed guards outside.

"Wait here," Rufinus said.

After a couple of minutes, he returned and told us that the emperor would see us now.

"Hail Augustus," we saluted upon entering what turned out to be a combination conference room and private office.

Theodosius saluted us back and then said to me, "Where have I met you before? You look familiar."

"Milan, my lord, in 388, following your victory in the civil war," I replied.

"*Our* victory, my boy, *our* victory," Theodosius said. "I remember now. You were the chap who had the temerity to ask me if I was related to that scoundrel Magnus Maximus." He was smiling when he said it so I didn't feel that I was about to join the erstwhile usurper anytime soon.

"Also," the emperor continued, "Rufinus, you should see the absolutely gorgeous wife that this man possesses. An East African girl, most fetching."

I smiled and nodded at this. Since Makila had not been with me when I spoke to the emperor at the banquet, he had apparently spotted her at some other occasion and made inquiries. Maybe I hadn't given enough credence to those rumors about him being somewhat of a letch. Or perhaps he just had a roving eye like all men do. Still, it would have been over three years ago, and he still remembered.

"What's the information that you have for me?" he asked.

"Nothing good, Your Majesty," I answered, handing him the document. "Your western colleague, Valentinian II, is dead."

"What?" the emperor erupted. "Dear God, no! No! No!"

"When and how did it happen?" Rufinus asked.

I related the tragic story once again. When I finished, there was an understandably long silence.

Finally Theodosius said, "Thank you, Marcus. You and your comrades must be very tired after your long journey. Rufinus, see to their quartering, feeding, and any other needs. When you've done that, send a courier to get Stilicho and then return here. We have a lot of work to do. I want the three of you back here at 7:00 this evening. Also, the three of you are to make no mention of this catastrophe to anyone."

"We understand, Your Majesty," I said.

"Sir, you and the praetorian prefect are the first ones we have mentioned this to since we left Vienne," Chlogius added.

"Good," Theodosius replied. "Okay. You're dismissed."

I then saw him break the seal that Arbogast had placed on his document. We saluted and left.

Rufinus put Athemion in charge of our needs. We were shown our sleeping quarters in a small but comfortable building used to house members of the Imperial Post. Then we hit the Imperial Guard baths, after which we dined at their mess hall. We met a couple of men that we had "campaigned" with on our swing through Macedonia and Italy in 388. We tried to pump information from them relating to the recent purge, but they were unable to add anything to what we had heard back in Aquileia. It would be a long evening. When we were ushered back into Theodosius's office, eight men were sitting at the big conference table. Rufinus was sitting to the left of Theodosius, while Stilicho was on the emperor's right. I had seen Stilicho before but only at a distance: the first time was in 386 at Constantinople and then, of course, at Milan in 388/389. Two generals and three other cabinet ministers from the Eastern Sacred Consistory were present. I was repeatedly grilled by various members of the group as to the details of Valentinian's suicide. After a while, the questions started to get repetitious and for a period of time I almost felt like I was on trial. Occasionally a question would be directed at one of my comrades, but as the officer of the watch on that fateful night, I was naturally the one to whom most inquiries were directed. We would sometimes be asked to leave the room while the big shots conferred and then were brought back in for another round of grilling.

About nine o'clock, when we were sitting alone in the hallway, Stilicho came out. He was the youngest of the emperor's advisers, being thirty-two at the time. My first thought was that he was being sent out to obtain information that the emperor and his advisers felt they had not yet obtained from us. If they felt that we were intimidated in their presence, then they were correct, although we had answered all their questions to the best of our abilities. Stilicho invited us down to a lounge located off the throne room, where a steward had prepared some wine for us. This youngest of the empire's field marshals asked us about our boyhoods, our military backgrounds, and our personal relationships with Valentinian, limited as they were. In return, I asked him about his campaign against Alaric. He told us that he hoped to conclude the campaign over the next several weeks. When he asked me about Valentinian's personal relationship with Arbogast, I did not hesitate to describe all the brutal details that I have related previously in this narrative. This matter had not been raised previously. I have sometimes wondered if my overly detailed answer might have played some role in subsequent events. Then he surprised us.

"As soldiers who serve in the West and as natives of that part of the empire," he said, "what do you think should be done to rectify the situation there?"

The three of us had discussed this question among ourselves a lot during our long journey. As a result, I was not stuck for an answer.

"The West needs an emperor of its own, sir," I replied. "Arcadius is only fourteen and too young for the job. In a sense, His Majesty is in a similar position to that of Emperor Gratian in 378. Gratian knew that the East required an emperor of its own to guide its affairs and recover from the disaster of Hadrianople. He recognized that since his only brother, Valentinian II, was only seven years old, he was completely inadequate for the job, so he reached outside his family and selected Theodosius. I think that His Majesty has several options: he can transfer Arcadius to Trier, he could choose one of his more mature distant cousins from Spain as emperor of the West, or he could choose someone else altogether to reign there."

"Whomever he selects," Chlogius interjected, "I believe that His Majesty should come to Trier for the investiture of Valentinian's successor. It has been obvious to many of us in the West that Theodosius's dynastic intentions have been to leave the East to Arcadius and divide the

West between Valentinian II and Honorius. Perhaps he should consider having his two sons rule jointly in the East and appoint someone more capable to manage the West. Whatever happens, the emperor must not leave a political vacuum there."

"The prefecture of the Gauls," Fredemondus continued, "has a population of about eleven million across all its dioceses combined. That's 30 percent of the population of the empire, and a good many of them felt humiliated by the fact that the emperor never bothered to visit them once during the almost three years that he was resident in Milan. I'm not referring to a small group of disgruntled soreheads. I'm talking about members of the aristocracy that I've spoken to, soldiers, friends that I have known for years, Christians and pagans alike."

"We believe," Chlogius added, "that the emperor should now visit the West, and by the West we do not mean Italy. I think he should visit all the dioceses of our prefecture, if possible, and let the people there know that he is concerned about their welfare. We are all certain that he is, but it is imperative that he display his concern graphically and unequivocally."

"In addition," I added, sticking my neck out, "it might be wise to transfer Arbogast back to Illyria. There is no question in anyone's mind, as far as I know, about the man's loyalty to Theodosius. But we've just had an all too brutal display of how he reacts to an emperor who is young and inexperienced or is not willing to give him a free hand to conduct both military and political affairs as he sees fit. His Majesty has several field marshals that could take his place and might be more, shall we say, diplomatically adroit."

"Sir, I have a question on another matter," Chlogius ventured rather nervously. "What caused the downfall of Tatianus and Proculus?"

"I'm not at liberty to discuss that," Stilicho replied but not coldly. "I was in the field when it happened."

At that point, we all fell silent.

"The three of you men," Stilicho finally said, "have certainly given us forthright and comprehensive answers to all the questions that we've put to you and we all appreciate what you've said. I'll convey your information to the consistory. We won't need you anymore tonight. The cabinet has its work cut out for a while. The three of you can relax and rest up tomorrow. Your time is your own. But I want you to return here the day after tomorrow at nine o'clock in the morning."

The next day, we just took it easy. We toured a couple of areas of the capital that we had not seen in our previous visit and just slacked off. Since the Hippodrome is right beside the palace grounds, we dropped in to watch the chariot races for a time before returning for dinner. One prominent new addition to the spine that runs down the center of the track caught our attention as soon as we entered. It is the large obelisk dedicated to Theodosius that was erected by Proculus when he was urban prefect in 390.

The following morning, we returned to the Daphne Palace, and Athemion escorted us to Rufinus' office. The praetorian prefect appeared quite friendly. If we did not have the knowledge we did about the execution of Proculus and the brutal fashion in which he had handled Tatianus, then it would have been easy to dismiss the stories we had heard about his ruthlessness. But then that is part of the secret of success of all tyrants, is it not? We were ushered into Theodosius's office once again. We exchanged salutes, and the emperor then handed me a document for Arbogast.

"I'm sorry that you lads could not stay longer to be more entertained by this beautiful capital of ours," Theodosius said to us. "But under the tragic circumstances, that is simply not possible. I am ordering you to return immediately to Trier with this information for the field marshal. I am also ordering him to use the three of you exclusively as couriers between Trier and Constantinople until the question of the succession in the West has been settled. I fully appreciate your determination to ensure confidentiality in conveying the devastating news of young Valentinian to us. However, in the future, all communications that you three convey to us are to be communicated directly to Rufinus. As I am certain you are aware, Rufinus enjoys my total confidence. I'm telling you this in person, and I have so instructed Arbogast in this document so that there is no misunderstanding on the issue. Safe journey home."

We left the palace as quickly as we could, each of us steaming on the inside but having the presence of mind to maintain our composure until we were outside the building.

"That was the last bloody thing that we wanted to hear," Fredemondus muttered through clenched teeth. "Rufinus will be the sieve for every communication that Arbogast sends to this city. There will be no way of knowing what information that is sent actually gets through to the emperor."

"The same goes for communications in the opposite direction," I replied. "There is a power struggle going on here, and we have no way of knowing what its ramifications will be."

Rufinus was playing a murderous game and it had only begun.

The three of us started west later that morning over the same route that we had originally taken. Near Lake Como, we turned north and followed the route that we had taken when we had escorted Valentinian II to Trier three years earlier. On our fourteenth day out of Constantinople, we arrived in Trier. It was the middle of June. It had been one hell of a ride in both directions, and we all bore saddle sores as reminders. We delivered the emperor's document to Arbogast and then underwent a grilling by the field marshal and his staff that was similar to the one that we had received in the eastern capital. Everyone was interested in the emperor's reaction to his colleague's death but what they were really interested in was Theodosius's reaction to Arbogast. That Valentinian II had complained to Theodosius about Arbogast's high-handed manner was common knowledge, but we had nothing to report in that area. I mentioned the lengthy conversation that we had had with Stilicho, omitting of course the part where I had told him what a son of a whore I thought Arbogast was. Fredemondus brought up what the emperor had told us about communicating with him only through Rufinus and expressed our misgivings about it. At length, the debriefing session was over.

Arbogast then said, "By the way, your Imperial Guard regiment has been attached to the Army of Gaul. As per the emperor's instructions, I'm making you three my official couriers to him. As a result, I'm relieving you of the commands of your squadrons until further notice. Go home and rest up for the next three days. After that, report to my office at ten o'clock every morning to see if I have any immediate need for you."

At the beginning of July, we had to make another dash to the eastern capital and back. It consumed most of the month and accomplished nothing. We had an audience with Rufinus, but that was it. We did not see the emperor, and Stilicho was back campaigning with his field army. Politically, nothing had changed, and the silence on that front satisfied some but disturbed others. My comrades and I were among the disturbed. At least the frontiers continued to be peaceful.

Upon our return to Trier, Makila and I had a dinner party to which my fellow decurions, Chlogius and Fredemondus, and their wives were invited. While the wives were busy inside, my fellow decurions and I set up shop, as usual, in the courtyard of our villa. We had been given five days off upon our second return, and I had spent all my time at home.

"Well, what do you think of the latest news from the East?" Chlogius began.

"What news are you referring to?" I replied. "You city lads always find out what's happening in the world before us members of the landed gentry do; anything of consequence?"

"You will both recall," Chlogius went on, "that Stilicho told us that he had contained the rebel Visigoths and was planning on wrapping things up soon."

"That's right," I answered. "And during our second visit, we assumed that he was out doing just that based on what we were told."

"Well, he wrapped things up all right," Chlogius continued. "After cornering this bastard Alaric and his glorified bandit gang somewhere along the lower Maritsa River, not far from Hadrianople, Stilicho defeated him and then let him go."

"What?" Fredemondus replied disbelievingly. "Why?"

"Direct orders from Theodosius," Chlogius continued. "The original plan was to wipe this Alaric and his army out completely once they were defeated, just like we did the Ostrogoths on the Danube back in 386. But for some reason, Theodosius, who was apparently in close proximity to the battle site, changed his mind and ordered Stilicho to let Alaric go. Beyond that, the fog of battle or rather diplomacy gets rather thick. It appears that negotiations of some sort took place directly or indirectly between Theodosius, Stilicho, and Alaric, and as a result, Alaric and his merry band of our Visigothic 'allies' are making their way back to Moesia, north of the Balkan Mountains."

"Never more to misbehave," Fredemondus added sarcastically. "Think of the propaganda value of having Stilicho administer a really decisive defeat to the Visigoths not all that far from Hadrianople. Why would Theodosius throw the opportunity away?"

"What we were hearing this afternoon," Chlogius went on, "once the information was made public, was that there is some question in the emperor's mind as to just how trustworthy the Visigothic soldiers in our army might be once they had to face their own brothers and cousins in the Visigothic Federate Army. This Alaric is apparently banking that they would rather switch than fight, and our emperor must share the same fears."

"Our Visigothic volunteers fought well on the Danube against the Ostrogoths in 386," I said.

"You have always said though," Fredemondus reminded me, "that the ultimate test of Visigothic loyalty would come when a strong, new leader emerged among them."

"There might be another reason," I suggested. "Theodosius may not have made up his mind as to what to do in the West. Perhaps he questions the validity of the official version of Valentinian's suicide. In addition to the letters that our late emperor had sent to his eastern colleague, he had also sent similar letters to his sister, Empress Galla. She is just as fully aware of Valentinian's problems with Arbogast as is her husband. Theodosius could be very well feeling pressure from that quarter. We don't know how relations now stand between Theodosius and Arbogast. If Theodosius does not buy what we know to be the fact of Valentinian's suicide, then he might be contemplating another war against the West. If that's the case, then it might explain why he decided to let Alaric and his army off the hook. He might have need for them in the near future."

"That would be crazy," Fredemondus said, and we all agreed.

"What you mentioned to Stilicho was perfectly sound," Chlogius said to me. "Theodosius should nominate a new western emperor."

"He already has." Fredemondus practically spat the words out. "And he is a nine-year-old boy."

"You're right," I agreed. "That is the ultimate intention. I find the silence on the issue almost deafening. What the hell can he be thinking about?"

As things would turn out, others were thinking more quickly than Theodosius.

When I returned from my first mission to Constantinople, I had dropped around to see Rufius and Margareta. Rufius, however, was quite ill, so I didn't stay. By the time I returned from my second mission near the end of July, his health had recovered considerably, so Makila and I invited them over for dinner one evening. Sitting in the courtyard, he seemed much more open on political matters than he had before. He was interested in my opinion on the confusing situation in the eastern capital. When I gave him my impressions of Rufinus, he was forthcoming on two matters.

"I received a letter from a cousin in Rome the other day," he said. "The overthrow of Tatianus and the execution of Proculus have certainly sent a chill through the governing circles in Italy. Most of them are pagan, and they are starting to wonder if what happened in Constantinople is a forerunner of what is going to happen next in Rome. Many members of the senatorial order there are starting to call into question just how permanent the arrangement is that they thought they had agreed to with Theodosius. His edict closing all pagan temples was the first blow and his inexplicable acceptance of Rufinus' murder of Proculus and overthrow of Tatianus, on charges that we all know were patently absurd, are making many think that instead of a friend, they now have a sworn enemy in Theodosius."

I then mentioned to Rufius the suspicion that I had as to why Stilicho had been ordered to let Alaric and his army go. I also remarked on my feeling that if war did break out between East and West again, that it might be the empress, rather than the emperor, who was behind it.

"That's a possibility I should have thought of," Rufius responded. "We all know that Arbogast botched his relationship with young Valentinian. But the way in which Theodosius is now mishandling his connection with Arbogast almost makes me feel sorry for the field marshal. While you were away on your second trip, I attended several meetings of the Western Sacred Consistory. It still officially exists in spite of our no longer having an emperor of the West. Arbogast stated that my neighbor, meaning you, had mentioned to Stilicho the need to quickly name a new emperor here. He expressed his complete agreement with that and commended you for saying what you did. I think he has a good opinion of you, Marcus."

I took comfort in that and expressed my gratitude.

"If Theodosius fails to appoint a new emperor quickly," Rufius continued, "then the legal process in Gaul, Britain, and Spain is going to grind to a halt soon."

"Why is that?"

"Laws must be created in the name of the sovereign," Rufius explained. "The prefectures of Illyria and the East constitute Theodosius's Eastern Empire but Theodosius has no writ in our prefecture. We need an emperor of our own for legal as well as military purposes."

"Can't Theodosius simply declare that, since the death of Valentinian II, he, himself, now reigns over the whole empire?" I asked.

"He could, but ten weeks have gone by and he hasn't done a damned thing," Rufius said, the tone of exasperation in his voice rising.

"Can't Arbogast simply issue laws in Theodosius's name as though such a declaration had been made by the emperor?" I asked.

Rufius smiled in his avuncular way. "You're not a lawyer, young fellow. It's not that simple."

It was the early afternoon of my fifth day home when Stephanus came galloping out to our villa.

"Hey, soldier," I hailed him, "what brings you all the way out here apart from the chance to enjoy some great wine, a beautiful view, and a splendid afternoon?"

"You're right," he replied. "That's exactly why I'm here. To enjoy them all for what will be the last time. We're being shipped back east in three days."

"*What?*" I asked in disbelief. "What's happened?"

"Orders from Arbogast," was the reply. "He received orders from Theodosius via a courier that arrived yesterday. Our Imperial Guard regiment is being sent east in three days. The rumble is that we are to act as a personal bodyguard for Arcadius. If that's the case, then I hope we will enjoy more success with him than we did with our previous employer."

"Arcadius is just a kid," I replied, "and a most unpromising one based on what I heard from a couple of friends back on the Bosporus."

"A lot of our comrades," Stephanus said, "are pissed off with the whole idea and are putting in requests for transfer to the mobile field army directly. I know Marcellinus is thinking about it."

Not wanting the day to be restricted to bad news, we sat down in the courtyard and enjoyed the view along with more than just a little wine. After an hour, Stephanus left, and I went in and broke the news to Makila. She took it badly, but I reminded her of how reluctant she had been to move to Trier in the first place and yet how well everything had turned out. I then rode into Trier to get clarification. After I returned home, I explained to Makila the decision that I had made.

"Arbogast is allowing Imperial Guard veterans with at least five years' experience, who were born anywhere in our prefecture, to transfer to the Army of Gaul if they so desire."

"Since you're British, you qualify," she said hopefully.

"I know. I love this place as much as you do, and I would like nothing better than for us to spend the rest of our lives here. But sooner or later, Rufius and Margareta are going to want to sell the place, and it is impossible for us to afford it on a soldier's pay. Besides, I'm afraid for the West. Ten weeks have gone by, and Theodosius has done nothing to appoint a new emperor here. The Western Army is a good one. But I sense an increasing danger of another civil war. If such a war does break out, then the forces on the Rhine would be reduced to such a degree that the frontier, only sixty miles away, might not be tenable. We cannot take that risk with our family."

Stating my position in those terms, she understood. I had even considered shipping her and the children off to live with my family in Britain and asking for a transfer there but decided against it. Apart from a few letters to my sister Maria Patricia, I had had no contact with my family in eleven years. Too much time had passed and the family bonds, such as they were, had dissolved long ago. When I told her that we would be passing through Belgrade, she perked up somewhat. After all, it had been almost four years since she had seen her friends there. We spent the next couple of days getting ready. I had been writing a lengthy letter to my sister for some weeks now and finally sent it off to her. We bade farewell to Margareta and Rufius and others we had met. Chlogius and Fredemondus, along with Marcellinus, had transferred to the field army (i.e. the Army of Gaul) and were both surprised and disappointed that Stephanus and I had not. We threw one last emotional farewell party at our villa and then our stay in Trier was over. Chlogius, Fredemondus, and their wives had become quite close friends over the years, and leaving them behind was difficult. We would never see them again.

At the beginning of August, our convoy of over a thousand men, women, and children started out on the same route that some of us had taken for the first time nine years earlier. During that period, the West had suffered the loss of two legitimate emperors and one usurper. Yet it was fairly prosperous and the frontier was secure. As we headed up the Rhine, I had the constantly nagging doubt as to whether I had made the right choice. In spite of what subsequently happened, I still think my decision was correct.

On August 25, we camped on the outskirts of Bregenz on Lake Constance. Two days earlier, we had crossed the boundary between the prefectures of the Gauls and the Italies. We pitched a large tent city there to rest up for a while after having traveled over three hundred miles since leaving Trier. We stayed for three days, during which we relaxed, visited the baths, made repairs to equipment, and requisitioned any supplies that we needed. The second day there, I took Makila and the children into town to visit the market and do whatever other shopping had to be done. The forum was jammed with people, and the place was in an uproar. I parked the wagon and headed off toward the crowd to see what the excitement was about. I soon saw my friend Stephanus emerge and head in my direction, away from the large bulletin board that was the center of attention.

"Stephanus," I hollered. "What's happening?"

"The West has a new emperor."

"And who might that be?" I asked, not quite believing what I had just heard.

"Eugenius Augustus," he answered with a big smile.

I stared at him with an obviously pained expression.

"What you're telling me without saying a word," he continued, "is that you have no idea who this clown is."

"Does the announcement provide any sort of curriculum vitae or are we just supposed to guess?" I asked.

"He's the former chief secretary to Valentinian II," Stephanus replied.

"*That* Eugenius?" I erupted. "Short, bald, overweight, and with no qualifications for the office whatever?"

"The same. You seem less than thrilled by it all. At least this should cause Theodosius to haul his head out of his ass and start paying attention to what is happening here."

"Let's not forget," I reminded him, "how Theodosius focused his attention the last time that a usurper arose in these parts."

Stephanus had to hurry off, so I gradually made my way to the bulletin board to read the pronouncement myself. It had Arbogast's imprimatur all over it. The proclamation had taken place on August 22 in Lyon. I returned to Makila and the children; we did the shopping and then returned to the camp. Everyone's worst fears were on the verge of coming true. Another civil war was now inevitable. Conversation for the next several days revolved around nothing else. It was an act of the most monumental stupidity because there was absolutely no way that Theodosius could see this but as an act of treason. I had met Eugenius on several occasions over the past three years. He was a likable and well-educated man but not a senator. He had come up through the civil service ranks and had for quite some time been a friend of Richomer,

Arbogast's uncle, who was one of Theodosius's top generals in the East. It was the connection with Richomer that had both introduced Eugenius to Arbogast and facilitated his entry into the government of Valentinian II. The story soon circulated that Eugenius had tried to resist his elevation to imperial stature, but as in most things, what Arbogast wanted Arbogast got.

The field marshal did not claim the throne himself for two reasons: He felt that his Frankish origins would aggravate Roman public opinion against him if he did. We have long been accustomed to Frankish generals holding the highest military positions from one end of the empire to the other. But to reach for the top prize itself would be just too much. Also, such an act would precipitate the very civil war that he wanted to avoid. With Eugenius totally dependent on Arbogast, the field marshal would have an entirely compliant political partner to complement his own military capabilities. This had never been possible with Valentinian II, whose claim to the western throne had been a birthright. The irresolution that Arbogast displayed following the death of Valentinian II has always convinced me that he was not directly involved in our young emperor's passing. Too many historians skip over the fact that three months passed before he raised the rather fatuous Eugenius to the purple. This delay alone hardly speaks of a carefully laid out plot.

We continued our journey eastward, and by the end of September, we arrived at Carnuntum. The week leading up to our arrival there had been unpleasant. In spite of the time of year, the temperature had been quite hot, and we had experienced no rain for several weeks. During the latter half of almost every afternoon, it had clouded up, and although there had been plenty of thunder and lightning, no rain had fallen. Seniority enabled me to get us registered in an old hotel down on the waterfront. I felt it would be a healthier place for Makila and the children, especially with all the heat. We had a nice view of the Danube, looking across to the lands of one of our most permanent enemies, the ancient Quadic peoples. The fortress of Legion XIV Gemina was close by, as was the forum, the governor's palace, and every variety of commercial establishments. With two amphitheaters, I thought we could pass part of the time taking the children to watch the various circus acts that had been scheduled while we were there. The only thing marring the scene was the presence of several coal barges unloading close by. But we could do nothing about that. This was the time of the year for getting the last round of shipments in from the west before the winter set in.

Just before our arrival, a minor Quadic invasion had occurred about twenty miles down the Danube. Our regiment, reduced in strength by the recent transfers, was asked to assist the local cavalry unit, comprised largely of Ostrogoths, in suppressing it. Local settlers, some of whose farmsteads had been destroyed in the raid, had pointed out the direction in which the barbarians had continued. Anticipating that they were heading south to round the southern end of Lake Ferto and attack the town of Sopron, we headed straight south. Sopron is located about forty miles south of Carnuntum in the foothills of the eastern Alps. Lying as it does astride the ancient amber route that comes down from the Baltic Sea through Calisia, it has a rich mercantile heritage. When we were about ten miles south of Carnuntum, we heard a loud explosive noise in behind us. Powerful as it was, it seemed to be a long way off. There were dark clouds on the northern horizon, but the noise sounded too sharp to be thunder. We put the incident out of our minds for the time being, as we had more immediate matters to occupy us.

Racing to Sopron, we saw no sign of the invaders. After camping there overnight, we sent out tracking parties early the following morning and had no trouble finding what we were looking for. They were a mixed group of infantry and cavalry and came to no more than one hundred men. We outnumbered them and put a plan together in which our Ostrogothic allies would circle around behind the enemy and then force them onto our regiment. The battle went our way, and the barbarians soon surrendered. As we rounded them up, one of them suddenly lunged at me with a knife that he had managed to conceal, stabbing me through my left arm from the back. I had only caught a glimpse of him at the last moment. Fortunately, one of our men killed him before he was able to get a second thrust at me. The wound was quite large, and as a result of this new injury, my use of this arm would be even more restricted. Overall, our casualties were relatively light. Our two regiments of cavalry had defeated the invaders within an hour once we had found them. Their critically wounded we finished off while our wounded, including myself, were tended by our field hospital. Those of the enemy that we captured would be sold as slaves.

I was lying on the ground to rest for a while after having my arm stitched up. I had lost a lot of blood and was feeling rather lightheaded. Stephanus came over to see how I was doing. He mentioned that someone had come out from Sopron to inform our tribune that a fire had broken out in Carnuntum. It appeared serious, but there was no word, as yet, of casualties. At the time, we made no connection to the explosion that we had heard the previous day. It was midafternoon before all the wounded had been tended to and all the men had been fed. We were all tired from a long day, but with so many prisoners, it would have been awkward to camp out overnight once more. Besides, we wanted to get our most seriously wounded back to the better hospitals at Carnuntum and Vienna. So, we headed back to the Danube, knowing full well that it would probably be almost two days before we arrived. As it darkened, we noticed a concentrated glow on the northern horizon. Something was wrong. Terrifyingly wrong. Later that night, we started meeting refugees coming south with the terrible story of what had happened. The situation was unclear, but it was claimed that during the morning of the previous day, a lightning strike had hit a large coal pile along the Danube where the coal barges were offloading. That may have been what caused the loud explosive noise we had heard. In any case the cause was never precisely determined. Strong northerly winds had spread the flames to the buildings on the waterfront. Everyone in the local legion was fighting to contain the fire, as were as many civilians as could be pressed into service. At that point, a number of us who had housed our families along the waterfront obtained permission from our tribune to return to Carnuntum immediately.

When we had covered about three-quarters of the distance, we arrived at the village of Parndorf. I bade the others to continue on while I rested up at the village for a while. By that time, the pain in my left arm had increased considerably, and the wound had opened up and was bleeding heavily. I was unable to continue any further. Fortunately, a medic who was traveling with us patched the wound as best he could.

The inferno's glow on the horizon was much larger now, and I was horror stricken by the fear of what I would find when I reached the Danube. We all were. Although it was the small hours of the morning, much of the village was still up because of the refugee influx. I spoke to several of them, and they repeated the earlier report that I had heard about the fire engulfing the waterfront. I searched among the refugees but saw no sign of my wife and children. When I described my family to them, none of the evacuees could remember having seen them. But they cautioned me that most people leaving Carnuntum had headed for Vienna, since it is much larger than Parndorf. With that slim hope in mind, I could not stay in Parndorf any longer. As I approached Carnuntum from the southwest, the conflagration appeared to cover the whole horizon. Under the influence of strong northerly winds, the air had been thick with smoke for miles. The scene was unbelievable. It was my first intimation of what hell must really be like. There must have over a thousand people hauling water up from the river to put out the fire. As I reached the forum, I realized that under the exertions of the previous night, my bandages had come undone, and I was bleeding again. I entered the legionary fortress off to the east and went to their hospital to have my wound restitched. Everyone had been working for almost two days without letup. After enduring the agony of having my wound cleansed and patched up again, I passed out from exhaustion and loss of blood. Dawn was already breaking over the eastern horizon.

I was suddenly awakened by a very loud clap of thunder and the faint sound of cheering. The firefighters were finally getting some help from nature in the form of an afternoon downpour that lasted for almost an hour. Feeling better, I left the hospital and headed for the waterfront. Soldiers had cordoned off the area and were letting no one through to prevent looting. The most soul-destroying sight of my life was that of the hotel, where I had last seen my family, burned to the ground. I could only hope and pray that they had gotten out in time. The firefighters were now going through the ruins trying to find the dead. Regiments stationed in Vienna had immediately been sent east to help contain the blaze and police the prisoners that were being brought up from the south. The strong winds, however, spread the flames so rapidly that little could be done to save lives in the vicinity where the fire had started. Once the fire was put out, our convoy proceeded eastward. Those of us who had loved ones missing stayed behind until our family situations were resolved. Those of us who could, helped the firefighters go through the ruins. With my arm in a sling, I did what I could, but for the most part, I could only stand and watch. Because so many people were staying there at the time, the hotel ruins were the first to be searched. There were several hotels along the waterfront, and they were all in close proximity. The slowness of the search only added to the heartfelt grief.

The army was stretched to the maximum, but the soldiers performed admirably. On the third day following my return to the city, the streets had been sufficiently cleared to allow survivors to pass through to the waterfront area. Adding to the confusion at the hotel where we had stayed was the fact that the second floor had collapsed down onto the first. It took two days to remove all the bodies. Everyone had been burned beyond recognition, and the stench coming from every direction was terrible. They were laid out in the street in a grid pattern that marked where they had been found in the building. Survivors attempting to make identification started vomiting, and men, who had not cried since they were children, were now to be seen crying everywhere. I immediately walked to the northern end of the grid since our room had overseen the river. It is impossible for anyone to prepare themselves in any meaningful way for what we had to go through. For me, it turned out to be terribly straightforward. I came across a cluster of four, one adult and three children. We had given our daughters identical lockets for Christmas in 391, and here I was kneeling before four bodies burned beyond recognition but with the identifying lockets still intact on the three small bodies. Serena, the youngest at two and a half, was fused to the body of her mother, who had clutched her to the very end. My four-year-olds, Demetria and Justina, were huddled with them. Although a half century has passed since then, I still think of them every day. We never escape the devastation of personal tragedy. We learn to live with it and the intensity of the agony lessens as time passes. But we never accept such disasters as being within a rational framework for the universe.

Several hundred people had died in the fire, and it took numerous mass funerals over the next two weeks to get everyone buried. My family was interred in the large cemetery lying about a half mile east of the municipal amphitheater. The attending priests did their best, and as usual, we heard the customary witless blather about the "will of God." I had never been one to see the hand of the Almighty as particularly visible in any aspect of human conduct or that of nature; even less so now. I felt completely consumed by self-doubt. If I had stayed behind in Trier, they would be alive. If I had shipped them off to live with my family in Britain, they would be alive. If we had had the luck to stay in Vienna instead of Carnuntum, they would be alive. If I had put them up in the tent city instead of trying for "superior" accommodations, they would be alive. With the best of intentions, I had put the four people that I loved beyond belief through absolute hell; I had inadvertently destroyed my family, and I have never forgiven myself for it.

I made arrangements to have a suitable headstone raised for them and then made preparations to leave. In a sense, I felt my life was over, certainly the most meaningful part. A year that had looked so promising at the beginning had turned into the most terrible year I had ever endured. So many futures foreclosed. But it was not the last time in which a year would start off propitiously only to end in total disaster.

The End of an Epoch (392–395)

CHAPTER

8

I SPENT THE NIGHT after my family's funeral at the barracks of Legion XIV Gemina, crowded as it was. Those of us who were wounded would rejoin our units when we were healthy enough to travel. Our casualties in the battle had come to about ten dead and thirty-five wounded, with the split in casualties being roughly equal between ourselves and the Ostrogothic regiment. I left the following day. Traveling alone did not bother me; in fact, I preferred it that way under the circumstances. I did not want to talk to anyone even if they were in a similar predicament to what I was. I headed southwest from the legionary fortress along the highway that leads to Sopron. About a mile down the road, I turned off to my right to visit the cemetery one more time. We had come here together; why could we not be leaving together? The old expression, "you can't change yesterday," came to mind, but that was certainly of no comfort. And the man who coined the saying "time heals all wounds" apparently never suffered much of anything. When I had identified their bodies, I had removed the three lockets that my daughters had been wearing. It was no easy thing to do because the intense heat of the fire had burned the locket chains into their flesh in places. I had given a larger version of these lockets to Makila for her last birthday, and she had liked it so much that we decided to get smaller versions for our daughters at Christmas. Every time I went off to campaign or on a mission somewhere, Makila would place her locket around my neck for good luck. That's why I was wearing it on the day of the fire and not her. I have worn it every day of my life since then and I always carry the small lockets of my daughters with me as well. I stayed for several hours at the cemetery. I didn't want to leave them, but as morning passed into the early afternoon, I finally had to face up to the fact that they had already left me. I headed south toward Sopron and beyond.

Our original orders had been to march to Belgrade, where we were to receive our final instructions. I was in no hurry to get there anymore and took a rather leisurely trip to link again with the Danube via Lake Balaton. This shallow, rather rectangular lake, while measuring about ten miles in width and fifty miles in length, has an average depth of only twelve feet. The lake provides a beneficial climate for fruit orchards on the north shore, but the south shore is rather swampy. Since the population density is sparse in this area, there are no towns for long stretches. As a result, I camped out for several nights. Sleeping under the stars by myself, I was reminded of when I had left home eleven years earlier. The same feelings of loneliness and frustration and rejection welled up in me again as they had then. Overwhelmed with these emotions when young, most of us have the understanding that our youth alone should present us with better opportunities in the future. I was only twenty-seven and in years was still young. But in terms of the bitterest of experiences that I had been forced to endure, I felt like I had aged a generation during the course of the past week.

It was almost the end of October before I arrived in Belgrade. I informed Julia and Makila's other friends of what had happened. Actually, few of her friends were there anymore, most having moved on to presumably happier conditions. At the office of the prefect of Legion IV Flavia Firma, I was told that my regiment had been ordered on to Constantinople. There had been some question as to whether we would be called upon to assist the Army of Thrace to keep Alaric and his Visigothic Federate Army in check. However, the latter had behaved themselves lately. The commander was most sympathetic to my situation and brought me up to date on political developments since Eugenius' elevation. On the diplomatic front, Eugenius (read Arbogast) had sent two delegations to the eastern capital in the forlorn hope that Theodosius would recognize the new western regime's legitimacy. One delegation included a number of academics, while the other consisted partly of clergymen. In both cases, Theodosius's response was unclear and highly reminiscent of the manner in which he had handled emissaries from Magnus Maximus several years earlier. All the indicators were heading downhill.

I had my wound redressed by the garrison medical team and then headed off to the city of Constantine. It was now the beginning of November. On the way, I stopped off at a health spa southwest of Sofia for a couple of days. While there, I learned that Theodosius had issued his severest attack yet against paganism. In this edict, issued on November 8, all pagan practices of all kind were to stop not only in public but also in private. The extent to which the government was now trying to obliterate all vestiges of paganism, short of holding a pogrom, bordered on madness. Among the restrictions: the will of any pagan could be negated by the courts to the extent that no portion of an estate could be inherited by pagan relatives or friends of the dearly departed; no government official could attend pagan festivals under any condition. This was particularly hostile to Italy. Theodosius, in his role of secular statesman, had willingly participated in pagan celebrations throughout his reign, especially in Italy; but no more. No one was permitted to take time off from work on a day on which a pagan festival was formerly celebrated. The terrible shadow of Thessalonica would hang over almost every piece of legislation that Theodosius inaugurated between February 391 and the end of his reign. The most tragic aspect of all these decrees is that none of them were necessary. The pagan religions had been declining for at least a century and would have continued to do. These government edicts hastened their demise but failed to generate an end result that would not have evolved in a far more socially acceptable manner without them. Not only pagans but also many Christians were disgusted by the intrusive and pervasive nature of these new laws. What was accomplished by these actions was the total alienation of the West and the "pagan reaction" that was most pronounced in Italy.

The greatest responsibility of any emperor is to maintain the security, tranquility, and prosperity of the empire. After Thessalonica,

Theodosius gave little thought to any of these things. His only concern was to get his soul into heaven and he could not care less about the social turmoil his legal resolutions caused in getting him there. He could do anything he wanted in this regard. Ambrose had assured him of that and that was all that mattered. Intolerance was the order of the day and God's will. Theodosius, to whom the empire owed everything during the decade of the 380s, was in the process of undermining his past accomplishments in the 390s. The price of getting our emperor into paradise would be far greater than the thousands of innocent souls that his hot temper and big mouth had sent to their doom on the north shore of the Aegean Sea that terrible day in 390. Half a century later, we are still paying the price for his single-mindedness and we will never stop paying.

I continued my journey with stopovers in Philippopolis and Hadrianople and finally reached Constantinople on December 1. Upon reporting for duty at the Imperial Guard headquarters, I was informed that my regiment had been broken up and distributed to the seven associated eastern regiments to bring them up to strength. To the greatest degree possible, the squadrons had been kept intact to preserve unit cohesion. However, a couple had been broken up piecemeal and distributed as needed to the general discontent of those involved. My unit had remained intact and was now the Fifth Squadron of the Fourth Palatine Guard Regiment. A number of the officers in our regiment had a small party for me. It was a good way to get introduced into the new outfit and to see old friends that I had not seen for quite a while. Everything was so different now. I took great pride in the fact that once I had become a decurion a number of comrades from my original squadron had transferred over to my new command. They had stayed with me during our western tour of duty and those who had elected to come east were still with me. Nonetheless, the number of close friends was much smaller now. Only Stephanus was still with me from our original group. The Visigoths, Hilderic and Sigismund, were also in my squadron, but the remainder were relatively new recruits. All my men were either Gauls, Franks, or Goths, mostly Goths.

Upon my arrival, I had learned that the emperor had held a big party for the newly arrived officers. As a measure of the man's essential humanity and as a reflection of the complexity of his nature, Theodosius had a special dinner for those of us arriving late from Carnuntum once we had all completed the trip. We had all suffered wounds, the loss of loved ones in the fire, or both. This was held in the Daphne Palace and was for all men so affected regardless of rank. The emperor visited with each of us prior to the dinner and to me he was especially solicitous.

"Marcus," Theodosius said to me, grasping both my hands in his and leading me off to one side. "I am so sorry to hear of the terrible tragedy that has befallen your family. You have lost more than any other man here and I have had prayers offered on your behalf and that of your fellow soldiers throughout the capital."

"I appreciate that, sir," I replied.

"It's the very least I could do," the emperor continued. "I'm hardly a stranger to the terrible agony that you have suffered and will have to live with for the rest of your life. My oldest son, Gratianus, died while quite young, and his twin sister, Pulcheria, died when she was only eight. Their mother died in childbirth, as did the baby, leaving me with Serena and my two boys."

"I like to believe," I added, trying to sound convinced, "that they are happy in the afterlife, waiting to greet us when our time comes."

"That's exactly the way that I feel, Marcus," Theodosius replied. "Faith is paramount above all. It's difficult for any of us to accept the tragedies that befall us, but we must all learn to live with them. At the time of my last bereavement, a priest remarked to me, 'Life is what happens while we are making other plans.' Sad but true. God will bring you through this terrible time in your life as He has brought me through mine. Believe it."

At this moment, Rufinus arrived to draw the emperor off on some political matter. I thanked him for his condolences as he left.

The rest of the month was somewhat of a blur. Both my birthday and the Christmas/New Year holiday season were the loneliest that I had ever spent. I simply wanted to get them out of the way so that I could get started on whatever our responsibilities would be in the New Year.

To pass the time, I wrote letters to both Margareta and my sister Maria Patricia, to inform them of the tragedy. At the time, I had no idea that it would be almost two years before I would be able to mail them. By then, there would be so much more to write about.

In the winter of 392–393, Arbogast conducted a large-scale operation against the German Franks in the valley of the Lippe River that flows into the lower Rhine opposite Xanten. Facing civil war with Theodosius, Arbogast wanted to avoid any military disasters occurring far to his rear along the lines in which Quintinus had been defeated during the last conflict. The expedition was a success, and in the spring, peace treaties were concluded with the Frankish chieftains in the area. As a result, thousands of new German Frankish troops joined the Western Army for our next round of civil war. This would prove to be the last campaign that the Roman Army ever conducted east of the Rhine.

On January 1, 393, we swore our annual oaths to Theodosius and Arcadius. Before the month was out, Theodosius had his younger son, Honorius, proclaimed emperor as well. The plans for the succession were now complete. However much the emperor wanted his younger son to rule the Western Empire, eight months had passed, and Theodosius had done absolutely nothing to secure it. Not garrisoning Italy left it wide open for an invasion from Gaul. It had the smallest military establishment of the four prefectures. In April 393, Arbogast and Eugenius overran Italy and hardly had to fire an arrow in the process. It irks me the way in which so many historians describe the government of Valentinian II as "ineffective" during the period 383–387 in spite of the fact that it managed to keep the previous usurper out of Italy for four years. Theodosius had to know what would happen after 392, given what had occurred in 387, and yet he frittered away his strategic opportunity. Every historian who has written about Theodosius has commented on his swings of mood and interest. It was the man's most perplexing aspect. In addition, he seemed to be incapable of concentrating on more than one or two major items at a time. He will always be remembered as a masterful military strategist and a first-rate army administrator. But none of his redoubtable military dexterity seemed to carry over onto the civilian side of government. With the exception of his increasingly oppressive edicts to further the advance of Catholicism, it's difficult to determine exactly what government business the emperor was tending to when he was not campaigning with the army. He was content to leave the civilian side of government entirely to the civilians that he had appointed to the various ministries. The most powerful emperors of the fourth century involved themselves with almost every facet of government but not Theodosius. Eleven months elapsed between the death of Valentinian II and the invasion of Italy by Eugenius and Arbogast. When one tries to determine exactly what Theodosius was doing during that time that prevented him from focusing his considerable potential energy on Italy, the answer is not very much. The emperor was devoted to his family and spent as much time with them as he could arrange. However, when one considers how his two worthless sons turned out, one cannot help but feel that his time might have been put to better advantage.

The emergence of Eugenius and his army into Italy set the stage for a backlash against Theodosius's edicts of intolerance to a degree that no one had foreseen. Eugenius reappointed Nichomacus Flavianus as praetorian prefect of the Italies, and Flavianus quickly resurrected every pagan religious practice and festival imaginable. This included some observances that had been abandoned for generations. The pagan reaction placed Eugenius, who was a Christian, in a predicament that only worsened as the year progressed. He knew that a revitalization of the ancient religions in the West would only impair whatever slender hope he had of reaching an accommodation with the East. Yet he was powerless to do anything about it. It probably didn't matter anyway. A second civil war had been ordained for my generation from the day that Valentinian II died. It would not be the last.

During the first four months of 393, our regiment drilled continuously but was not called out to campaign anywhere. Other than a few minor border raids from across the Danube, the frontier was quiet. Alaric and his Visigothic Federate Army continued to behave themselves after their marginal defeat by Stilicho the previous year. In late April, our regimental tribune, Lucius Verennius, invited me to his office. He was a Syrian who had spent most of his career in the Balkans once his basic training in his home province was over.

"Marcus, reviewing your record several months ago when you first joined us, I noticed that you had an extensive background as a teamster. Would you be interested in putting that experience to military use?"

"In what capacity?"

"It's the worst kept secret in the empire," he replied, "that another civil war is looming on the horizon. Whenever a large-scale campaign of any kind is planned, the quartermaster corps undergoes a considerable expansion to get all the supplies collected and distributed along the various lines of march. In part, these newly added people are drawn from personnel in existing units that have the requisite backgrounds. Others are conscripted from transportation companies for the duration of the war and then released when the campaign has been completed. The army always searches its records for people with backgrounds in the fields of both land and sea transportation for such undertakings. Your record shows that you worked for a transportation company prior to joining the army and then did a fair amount of work getting provisions in place along the Sava River Valley for the last civil war."

"Before you go on," I interrupted, "is this some kind of a demotion?"

During the few months that I had been in the regiment, I had not come to know my tribune all that well. There had been a number of social functions that all officers are expected to attend, but since the loss of my family, I had become somewhat reclusive and had hardly attended any of them.

"No, not at all," he explained. "Look at it as a chance to broaden your experience. Such a transfer would be temporary. Once all the supplies are in place, you would probably be transferred back to our regiment."

It was beginning to sound like the lecture that I had heard several years earlier from Fredemondus.

"You have been in the army for ten years now," my tribune continued. "How many people that you knew when you joined are still with us?"

"A select few."

"Exactly. You have an excellent record, your men like you and respect you, and you should have a promising future in the army. Never turn aside an opportunity to broaden your background. You never know when it will come in handy. Our various life experiences expand us as individuals in ways that we can never fully articulate. So too will a stretch in the quartermaster corps. Those of us in the infantry and cavalry corps tend to look askance at those who serve in noncombat roles. But the experience will place you in good stead when considerations for promotion come up down the line. I want you to consider making such a transfer. Come back and see me by noon tomorrow with your answer."

I considered what my tribune had said, and on the following day, I told him that I would take it. He was right about such experience looking good on my record. In addition, I needed a change in my life in the worst way. Why pass up this opportunity to get it? We talked of many other things. Eventually I mentioned that we had heard the story making the rounds that Arbogast had signed up a large contingent of Franks serving under a general of their own named Arbitio. I then related the story that Chlogius had told me about the distant relative of Arbogast's of the same name and wondered out loud if it might be the same person. So did my commander, who promised to send my information up the line.

The following day, I was called into Stilicho's office in the Daphne Palace. He had several Frankish officers with him. I repeated the story that Chlogius had told me to the best of my recollection about the blood feud between the families of Arbogast and the man named Arbitio. Stilicho, who always seemed to know a lot about everyone that counted or might eventually count for something, was obviously interested in whether the two Arbitios were in fact one and the same man. They thanked me for what I had told them, and I was dismissed.

The quartermaster corps had records from the civil war of 388 that contained just about all the logistical data we would require for the impending crusade. Upon joining that corps, I was made part of an ad hoc task force of officers. Our responsibilities were many. First, we had to determine our basic supply requirements. Standard figures are available for what each soldier requires for food and water, clothing, weapons, medical needs, and so on. Similar standards are available for determining the fodder requirements for horses and oxen. In strictest confidence, we were told that the only line of advance would be through the Sava River Valley to Emona.[25] We mapped out the lines of march for troops drawn from both the mobile field armies and the garrison troops that would be participating. The majority of these troops came from Illyria and Thrace, but there were also contingents from Anatolia and Syria. For someone dealing with such calculations for the first time, the numbers we worked up were staggering. In addition to the local crops, grain supplies would be flowing into the Balkan Peninsula from all over the Eastern Empire, including Anatolia, the Levant, and Egypt. Our having determined what our food requirements were, it was up to the praetorian prefects of Illyria and the East to arrange their procurement.

Secondly, we had to assess our land, sea, and riverine transport requirements. From the Central Records Office of the Eastern Army in Constantinople, we determined how many wagons were available province by province from each depot. This transport would be supplied in the main from Illyria, Thrace, and western Anatolia. What we had to do was confirm that this transportation was still available at each depot, and this involved a lot of traveling. In some out-of-the-way outposts, wagons had been sold off by corrupt officers. They were confident they would never be found out primarily due to the relative isolation of their locations. If that was their only offense, then they were flogged to within an inch of their lives and cashiered. In the most flagrant derelictions of duty, some officers, in addition to selling off some of their unit's transport, had padded their rosters so as to keep drawing the pay of men no longer in their employ. These men were summarily executed. Most transportation, however, would be expropriated for the length of the war from private sources. We spent much time comparing army records with current tax rolls to determine exactly what was available from the private sector, including transport companies and private estates. We did not take the Visigothic Federate Army into account in any of our transportation considerations. Under the Treaty of 382, they were to provide their own transportation. Where supplies were concerned, we were to provision them only when they were outside their "homeland" in Moesia between the Balkan Mountains and the Danube. In part, the annual tax payment that Rome made to the Visigoths was to enable them to provide their own transportation anywhere and supplies within Moesia.

Thirdly, we had to assess the condition of storage facilities along the various lines of march and all ancillary supply lines. We would be using the warehouses that were for collecting the annual taxes in kind. We spent months determining their state of repair. Where such was required, we submitted work orders directly to the offices of the two praetorian prefects.

All this work was exhausting, but it was just what I needed to keep me from dwelling too much on the loss of my wife and children. Not that I haven't grieved for them profoundly every day since that terrible tragedy occurred. But to focus overmuch on one's grief can have a corrosive effect on one's soul and I had obviously been fated to live the rest of my life without them. I had best get on with it.

While traveling through Philippopolis, I witnessed three curials (i.e., town councilors) being flogged in public for failing to raise the amount of taxation demanded of them by their provincial president's office. About a decade earlier, Theodosius had issued a new law that no whips with lead weights attached could be used to flog curials anywhere when they turned up short in their taxation quotas. Somehow I doubted that the three curials involved were overly grateful for that particular piece of legislative enlightenment. It was a ghastly sight. Yet emperors continue to wonder why it is so difficult to find men to fill such positions. I had heard of this sort of thing, but this was the first time I had come face-to-face with it. The government need for money always expands before a military campaign, and for this one, increases were implemented on every tax in existence. One reason Theodosius used for abolishing the state support of pagan religious rites was that these funds could more appropriately be spent on the military. He conveniently ignored the fact that the orders of magnitude more money the government squandered on the construction of Catholic churches and tax exemptions for the church was a far greater drain on military resources. If the church was paying its fair share of taxation then many of the outrages such as the one I witnessed that day in Philippopolis could be avoided.

By the end of 393, most of the work of our special task force had been completed. The laborious work of actually getting all the supplies to their destinations was handled by the regular units just as my century had done during the previous war. We were ordered back to our original legions and regiments. Although Chlogius and I had joked about the possibility back in Trier, Theodosius did indeed order the abolition of the Olympic Games that year because of their association with ancient pagan rituals. When I returned to Constantinople in January 394, I was assigned to the regimental staff where I was appointed assistant adjutant. A new decurion had been selected for my old squadron immediately after I had left on my special assignment. If I was going to return to a combat role, I would have to wait for an opening. A number of new recruits had joined the regiment since I had gone on special assignment. I was busy for some time supervising the creation and updating of personnel records across all our squadrons. Rather mind-numbing after awhile but work that must be done nonetheless.

By early 394, Theodosius had decided to stop vegetating and get busy. His plan of campaign would be similar to the one of 388. There would, however, be several major differences. There would be no southern campaign. In 388, with southern Italy undefended, a two-pronged attack promised to be most effective. That would not be the case this time. Arbogast, immediately upon taking Italy, had raised troops from there and quickly built up large garrisons for Bari, Brindisi, and Taranto. With these ports denied to us, landings in the south would be difficult. The eastern shore of Italy lacks large harbors apart from the three just listed. The remaining ports are too small to sustain a major invasion force. In addition, Arbogast built up the fleet headquartered at Aquileia, distributed its ships among all the ports on the east coast of Italy, and had them on constant patrol to guard against a southern strategy on our part. In that, he succeeded.

At the same time, there was a downside to Arbogast's strategy. By concentrating all his forces to the west of the Julian Alps at the head of the Adriatic, he had surrendered the most easterly provinces of the Western Empire to Theodosius. This meant that the eastern boundary of Eugenius' realm had been withdrawn three hundred miles to the west. Theodosius could now use Pannonia and Dalmatia as he saw fit. Pannonia yielded the Sava River and its valley to provision and transport the bulk of our troops to the eastern Alpine foothills. Dalmatia would provide us with the room to work in a left-flanking maneuver if we chose.

Another major difference between this and the previous civil war was that the Visigothic Federate Army would be taking to the field under its young commander, Alaric. Conventional wisdom had it that, in effect, it would act as a sixth eastern field army and operate in conjunction with the forces drawn from the five regular field armies. As it turned out, conventional wisdom and Alaric didn't have it quite right. His Majesty had other ideas. The emperor, as he had done in the previous civil war, chose his generals well. Initially, Timasius was chosen to command the infantry and Richomer, Arbogast's uncle, was chosen to head the cavalry units. Unfortunately, Richomer, who had been in ill health for some time, died during the summer and a restructuring of the command was required. Timasius was made the overall commander while Stilicho was selected as the second in command. Directly under them, the Eastern Army was divided into three corps led by the Visigothic general Gainas, the Alan general Saul, and the Armenian general Bacurius. All foreign born but Roman in the fullest sense of the word nonetheless.

Throughout the first half of 394, supplies were being transported to our depots along the Sava River. Fortunately, the winter had been mild, and spring arrived a little earlier than usual. There would thus be no delays to the start of the expedition. We knew the campaign was close when Theodosius once again sent a mission off to see John of Lycopolis down in Egypt for another prediction. The mission was headed by Eutropius, the master of offices. Once again, the hermit auspicated triumph for the East but this time he went into more detail. John foretold that Theodosius's victory would be attended by enormous slaughter on both sides and that the emperor himself would not long outlive the event.

This latter prophecy was concealed from the public until after it had come to pass. Understandably shaken by this prediction, the emperor, nonetheless, seemed galvanized almost as never before by the upcoming campaign. He seemed to sense that his ultimate destiny was about to be fulfilled and he rewarded the hermit on the Nile accordingly. To counter the first of John's predictions that almost immediately became public knowledge, a pagan oracle soon forecast the ending of what some esoterics call a "Great Year." This is a "year of years," a period of 365 years, at the end of which humanity enters a new age. The year in which Jesus Christ was crucified is not known exactly but is estimated to have been between 29 and 31. By conveniently choosing the year 29, the oracle had predicted the end of the "Great Year" of Christianity in 394. After that, paganism would once again reign triumphant. Christians immediately pounced on this and reversed the interpretation.

The whole crusade was billed by the leadership of the East and the pagan element within the Italian aristocracy as the ultimate, winner-take-all showdown between Christianity and Rome's traditional religions. But that was an oversimplification. Christianity had the power to eventually crush the pagan religions, but the reverse was not the case. Rome's ancestral religions and over a thousand years of traditions that were associated with them were simply fighting to survive.

The one part of the Western Empire that refused to recognize Eugenius was the Diocese of Africa. To ensure the continued loyalty of Count Gildo to the East, Theodosius promoted him to the rank of field marshal early in 394. Against the recommendations of several of his closest advisers, the emperor shrewdly permitted grain shipments to continue from Africa to Italy. Theodosius felt that cutting off food supplies to Rome would hardly endear him and his family to the populace. Besides, it would accomplish nothing from a strategic standpoint. If anything, the emperor felt that such generosity on his part to the Italians, in the face of such provocation, might even undermine the support there for the usurper.

In 386, prior to the onset of the previous civil war, the first wife of Theodosius, Aelia Flaccilla, had died. Now, incredibly, just before the outbreak of our second such war in six years, Galla, his second wife, died in May during childbirth, as did the baby. Many interpreted the tragic loss of the empress as an omen indicating success for the Eastern Army. But, in addition, I was impressed by how the loss of Empress Galla and her child compared with the last year of Emperor Gratian. This grievous presignification would prove correct on both counts.

Arbogast had set up his headquarters in Milan but had established his frontline positions to the northeast of Aquileia. He also had advanced positions further along the Adriatic coast to block any thrust through Trieste by the Eastern Army. Traveling westward from Emona to Aquileia, the highway emerges from a low pass in the Julian Alps onto a broad plain in the valley of the Frigidus River. This is several miles upstream from where the Frigidus empties into the north-south flowing Isonzo River. This river, in turn, empties into the Adriatic just east of Aquileia. On the northern bank of the Frigidus, Arbogast had created a very large and heavily fortified position that was almost a mile square. It could not be avoided by any army emerging along the highway from the narrow pass to the northeast. The hilltops marking the approach to this position were all heavily defended by the Western Army. Arbogast had not mistimed his initial deployments the way that Magnus Maximus had. John of Lycopolis had been correct: the attempt by the Eastern Army to force its way through the valley of the Frigidus would indeed be a bloodbath. The general disposition of Arbogast's forces had been known well in advance. No major fighting had taken place in the Frigidus/

Isonzo region in the previous war. But in numerous discussions among us officers, it soon became apparent that a large number had serious misgivings about having to attack the Western Army in such awkward terrain.

At the beginning of April 394, I was transferred from the office of assistant adjutant to that of regimental quartermaster. As such, I was responsible for seeing that each man in the regiment was properly supplied throughout the line of march, although we had not yet been informed as to when our westward march would begin. Should, at any depot, supplies be inadequate for any reason, it was up to me to determine the nearest alternate station from which we could obtain provisions. There would be no major supply problems on the westward journey, but on the return trip, things would be different. At the end of April, a meeting was held of all Imperial Guard officers to inform us of the plan of campaign. Similar meetings were being held all over the Balkan Peninsula at this time as all units involved in the expedition were simultaneously informed of their missions. Stilicho and Rufinus were joint chairmen of our gathering, but after making the welcoming and introductory remarks, Rufinus yielded the floor to Stilicho. We had heard much of an intense rivalry between these two men but had never detected any suggestion of it in public. A year later, there would be no aspect of it that was *not* public.

An elaborate sandbox model had been constructed that was quite accurate in depicting the difficult topography of the region. It showed Arbogast's forces aligned along the Frigidus River and occupying all the high ground along the approach road from the east. In addition, it showed his defensive positions along the Adriatic coast to the northwest of Trieste. The topographical advantages lay entirely with the West; our strategy was simply to keep feeding units piecemeal into a meat grinder until we eventually overran our opponents. Not an attractive prospect at all. Unit markers on the "map" were represented at the legion level for the infantry and the regimental level for the cavalry. The Imperial Guard regiments were roughly in the center of the line of march attending the emperor. Our primary responsibility was to protect Theodosius and his staff from enemy assault, but we could also be used as shock troops to exploit any weakness that suddenly developed in the enemy lines. Stilicho explained the strategy at a high level and our regimental responsibilities in detail. When he had finished his initial presentation a deep silence fell over the room. We glanced around with looks that wondered which ones among us would still be here when it was all over.

"Any questions?" Stilicho asked.

"I have, sir," I replied. "Has any consideration been given to conducting a flanking move through Dalmatia in addition to the central thrust? We've heard rumors as to how the campaign was going to be conducted for several weeks now and one thing that has made some of us uncomfortable is the fact that no plan exists for a flanking attack. Specifically, what I'm thinking of is an attack from Sisak to the southwest through the mountains to Senia on the Adriatic coast. From there we would advance to the northwest through Tarsatica and across the Istria Peninsula to Trieste. We would have to combat Arbogast's covering forces there, but once we were through them, we could launch an attack up the Isonzo River against the rear of the Western Army. The total distance for such a maneuver would be around 250 miles. But if I'm part of the main attack force on the Frigidus River, I'd feel a little more secure if the men I was driving against were themselves being attacked from some other direction."

A number of other officers supported me in this and the topic was soon taken up for discussion by the Imperial General Staff. Nonetheless, at a second meeting of the Imperial Guard officers a week later, Stilicho announced that the decision had been made to stick with the single thrust strategy and not pursue the possibility of any flanking movement through Dalmatia. The General Staff had concluded that it would be too difficult at this stage of the campaign to put a sufficiently large and effective force together and supply it as I and others had suggested.

"What role will the Visigothic Federate Army be playing in all this?" Julius Aranius, commanding one of the other Palatine Guard regiments, asked. "You show them in the vanguard, there in the sandbox. But unlike the regular Roman units, I can't tell how large their contribution will be."

"Right now, we're not certain," Stilicho replied. "Alaric claims he has recruited twenty thousand men but until we actually see them in the line of march, we can't be certain. Our own estimate places them at closer to fifteen thousand."

This was the figure that our planning task force had used.

"So this punk will probably be commanding as many troops as Gainas, Saul, or Bacurius?" my tribune Lucius Verennius said having been wounded in the struggle against Alaric in 391.

"Alaric will be operating under the direct command of Gainas," Stilicho replied. "Regardless of how many men his army consists of, he won't be commanding all of them. His Majesty will redistribute certain of the men that Alaric brings with him as he sees fit. I'm not at liberty to discuss exactly how these allocations will be made. There are bound to be some rough edges in this exercise; after all, it's the first time that we've worked together with the Visigothic Federate Army under the Treaty of 382."

Theodosius allowed himself only the briefest period of mourning for his wife and child before ordering his Eastern Army to start its march to the west. Arcadius was left in Constantinople, under the stewardship of Rufinus, with authority granted by his father to promulgate laws in his own name. It was the emperor's intention to bring his younger son to Milan or Rome to mature through his teen years since, after all, this would eventually be his domain.

Alaric assumed that his command would equate to those of Gainas, Saul, and Bacurius. Instead, as Stilicho had informed us, Theodosius put him under the command of Gainas. This was quite proper given Alaric's lack of experience as a field commander, with the exception of his rebellion against us in 391. Ridiculous as it might seem, it was precisely this act of treason that the supercilious Alaric thought qualified him for a command that was the equivalent of three of Rome's most capable generals. However, he would certainly not be lacking in experience once the upcoming battle was over. Stilicho saw to that by placing Alaric's forces in the spearhead of the East Roman attack.

The transfer of the emperor and his armies to the West took four months. Nothing of an untoward nature happened to us during that long summer. The first phase of the line of march would be almost the entire length of the Sava River Valley from Belgrade to Emona, where we arrived in August. This route was the same one I had taken late in 388 when I traveled from Belgrade to Milan with Makila and the children. Unlike the war in 388, the current enemy would make no attempt to combat us east of the Julian Alps and for good reason: he had a slaughterhouse in mind for us where the terrain was entirely to his advantage. Once past the crest of this mountain range, battle could be joined at any time. The strategy behind this single push through the Julian Alps was most unimaginative. However, given the excessive imperial loitering during the course of the past year, any alternative had been pretty well precluded.

Emona was our last supply depot. We spent several days there loading our wagons. From this point on, we would have to forage and commandeer our supplies when our current stocks ran out. Travel in the mountainous borderlands between Dalmatia, Pannonia, and Italy has always been difficult. It is not only the toughness of the terrain that causes this but also the density of the forests of chestnut and oak trees along with a variety of conifers that cover the slopes. There are few roads through this area. As a result, our baggage train was strung out for many miles along the highway. Much of the region is only thinly populated. As we slowly made our way through this southern fringe of the Julian Alps, it was difficult to grasp just what an enormous undertaking it truly was. Even among the officers, our range of view was limited by our individual responsibilities and the big picture was, in large degree, a blur. Almost half the entire Roman Army was coming into combat with itself. Each side was contributing about one hundred thousand soldiers. Our one hundred thousand included the Visigoths of Alaric's federate army. The size of the forces involved dwarfed those that participated at Hadrianople by almost five to one. Like that watershed conflict, this one had also been avoidable. Again, like Hadrianople, after what would become known as the Battle of the Frigidus River, the world would never be the same again.

As we pushed deeper into no-man's-land, our scouts determined where Arbogast had placed his most easterly outposts. When we approached, they withdrew to the west. We continued to follow them until the lead elements of our army were within a few miles of the Frigidus River. The westerners wished in no way to impede our progress toward the punishment they planned to inflict upon us. Eventually, one of Theodosius's scouting parties was ambushed. The battle could be joined at any time. The emperor chose a high hill from which he could observe far down the valley to the great earthwork defense that the Western Army had constructed. Pickets were posted on the high hills to our right and left to detect any attempt by the western forces to outflank us. No such attempt was made, at least not early on. We would have to go to them.

It took several days for Theodosius to get all his forces into position, but by the afternoon of September 5, we were ready. One problem the emperor had was with Alaric. He was outraged when Theodosius redistributed many of the units of the Visigothic Federate Army among the three corps commanders under Timasius and Stilicho. Theodosius reminded him that the Treaty of 382 said nothing about the Visigothic federates being subject only to Visigothic leaders during periods of common danger. Alaric accepted this interpretation but he wasn't happy about it. He was left with fewer than ten thousand men under his direct command.

Gainas' corps, including Alaric's reduced federate force, was placed at the head of our army. Approaching the Western Army from our starting line was somewhat like passing through a funnel from the small end. The narrowness of the valley prevented us from deploying in battle formation before engaging the enemy. As a result, we would have to approach the Western Army in column formation until the defile from which we were emerging became broad enough for us to change into our regular battle line dispositions. All the time, we would be under a withering fire of arrows and missiles from ten thousand men in the surrounding hills. And once we got past them, there were ninety thousand men in Arbogast's main army arrayed before their mile-square fortification. The stage was set.

The first contingent, consisting of Visigothic federates, marched quickly down the valley in a modified "turtle" formation. Their shields formed as solid a shell as they could under the circumstances. Initially, this protected them. But as large rocks started crashing through, gaping holes developed, and the endless rain of arrows started to find many targets. We had not known that Arbogast had situated catapults along each side of the valley; a significant intelligence failure. Alaric's men did as well as they could under the terrible conditions. Unfortunately, the first units sent down the valley were almost wiped out before they could get into battle line formation. This was repeated over and over again, with the results always being the same. The federates who survived the gauntlet were attacked by soldiers arrayed in front the palisade and wiped out there instead. We had lost a thousand soldiers, killed or wounded, before realizing that we would have to attack the defenders on the surrounding hills. Otherwise, our attack on the army before the palisade would never materialize.

Alaric's men were pulled back and ordered to attack up the hills on one side while soldiers from the Eastern Roman Army charged up the other. Once the defenders on the hills had something else to worry about, we resumed our march down the valley. The rain of devastation was still horrendous, but now more of our soldiers were surviving the trip through the "valley of death." Several well-executed attacks were made by Visigothic federates against Arbogast's main force but they were all repulsed. The attacking forces were just too small. The slaughter was developing into something the likes of which most of us had never seen. East Roman regiments were brought up and tried their luck but with the same results. If this carnage continued, then it would destroy the flower of the Eastern Roman Army. That was not all that would be destroyed that day.

Then someone came up with an apparently bright idea. We brought dozens of our transport wagons up to the start line. East Roman and Visigothic soldiers placed their shields in the wagons and then crouched under them. By slowly moving them down the valley, they approached the plain below. At first, all went well as the Western Roman Army was taken by surprise and did not immediately know how to respond. The hailstorm of arrows continued as before but now they no longer had much effect. The catapults on the hills rained rocks down as they had been doing before but without doing much damage. Their original ammunition stores had consisted of relatively small rocks since their targets were men and horses. The introduction of the wagons meant that the enemy would have to use larger stones if the catapults were to be anything but a nuisance. It would take a while to upgrade their arsenal in this way. As a result, we were able to get a number of wagons down the hill with men safely under them while our opponents decided what to do next. Even though the process was succeeding, it was frightfully slow. The number of men that we had put into position in front of the main western force was just a fraction of what was required. Then the late-afternoon sky suddenly lit up with hundreds of incendiary arrows flying down from the surrounding hills. Several of the wagons caught fire, and when the men underneath could no longer hang onto them, they went careening down the hill. Added to that, the catapults went back into action. The artillerymen could not come up with large stones but they did start firing sawed-up tree trunks instead. The combination of tree trunks and fire arrows was far more devastating than the original barrage. Some of the wagons smashed into one another, plugging up the road. The men who had been using them for protection were now prey, once again, to the western archers. Except now they were more exposed because their shields had continued down the highway ahead of them in the burning wagons. The whole afternoon had degenerated into a nightmare.

Early in the evening, Theodosius ordered a halt to all further attacks down the valley until the surrounding hillsides had been cleared of the enemy. The emperor then ordered the men who had reached the bottom of the valley to return to the start line. At this point, these men were attacked by the westerners and almost wiped out. Getting the survivors back proved almost as dangerous as sending them down the valley in the first place. As darkness fell, it became apparent that we had accomplished none of our first-day objectives in spite of the several thousand dead we had sacrificed. The fighting continued through most of the night to the regret of us all. Fighting in broad daylight is bad enough, but in the blackness of night, it is orders of magnitude more difficult. As the struggle progressed, it became apparent that Arbogast had made one serious misjudgment in positioning his troops. He should have placed more of them on the hills on either side of the valley. There were simply not enough of them to withstand the onslaught of ever-increasing numbers of East Roman and Visigothic soldiers that attacked them through the night. Theodosius was very concerned at the rate at which our casualties continued to mount. At one point, he was heard to remark, "If tomorrow turns out to be like today, I'll need the Imperial Guard to protect me from my own soldiers far more than from Arbogast's lot."

Arbogast's miscalculation soon became discernible to him as well. His problem was that he could not easily add to their strength from his position at the stockade. He then decided upon a clever stratagem. He selected a force of several thousand German Frankish warriors and had them launch a flanking attack against the right side of Theodosius's army. Moving these men a goodly distance downstream from his camp so that they would not be observed by the eastern forces, Arbogast had them strike straight north through the densely wooded hills. They were to make a right turn, once they had scaled the heights, and strike hard at their eastern adversaries. The man that Arbogast chose to lead them was Arbitio. The field marshal saw the Franks off and watched them until they vanished into the darkness. It was the last he would ever see of them.

The terrible slaughter continued throughout the night, but during that time, the Western Army took the worst of it. Its soldiers, fighting in relative isolation on the hilltops, were outnumbered and overwhelmed. Their morale, however, was incredible. In many cases, they fought to the last man rather than surrender. At times, Theodosius was almost given over completely to despair, and who could blame him, given the slaughter that had happened during the afternoon? His total casualties had been horrific on that first day: ten thousand East Roman and Visigothic dead and perhaps twice that many wounded. The emperor spent much of the night in prayer. So did many of his soldiers.

By dawn of the next morning, the valley hillsides had been cleared of western soldiers. In addition, during the night, Arbitio had made contact with the right flank of our army, but rather than fight, Arbitio and his five thousand men surrendered and joined the eastern cause. The emperor was rejuvenated when Stilicho informed him that this had happened. We were overjoyed to hear it too but puzzled given the way that things had gone for us during the previous afternoon. The details of Arbitio's transfer of loyalty would not become known until after the battle was over. Later on the morning of September 6, my tribune ordered me to take command of my old squadron. Theodosius, shortly thereafter, ordered almost his entire force to march down the valley. This we did in complete security from the previous day's dangers. If we had been most impressed with Arbogast's fortification from the distance, and we had been, then we were astonished by it up close. It was a remarkable work of military engineering in the grand old Roman tradition, the sort that one simply doesn't see anymore. It's fair to say that even Julius Caesar would have been amazed by it. Should the battle go against the western forces, they would withdraw into this stronghold, and we would have a terrible time breaking into the place. My regiment had not taken part in the previous day's fighting other than to help in getting many of the wagons to the start line in that ill-fated experiment. Things would be different this time.

The previous afternoon, the westerners had understandably come to the conclusion that they had almost won the campaign, and they almost had. The sight of those thousands of (mostly Visigothic) dead before them, while their own casualties had been kept small, had to make them question how long Theodosius could sustain such losses. This overconfidence caused Eugenius to break out the celebratory wine somewhat ahead of schedule. As a result, a good many of his soldiers were rather hung over at sunup the following morning. Once the battle began, however, their fighting ability did not appear to be impaired. The battle went back and forth during the midmorning hours with neither side able to gain an advantage. Our Imperial Guard regiments were kept in reserve ready to exploit any opening in the western defenses, but none occurred. We were beginning to wonder if we were ever going to see any direct action in spite of the thousands of dead all around us. And then it happened.

There is a phenomenon in this part of Italy called the "bora."[26] It is an extremely powerful wind that races down out of the northeast and across the Adriatic regions of Italy and Dalmatia. It is most common for this wind to occur during the winter when cold air crossing the mountains plunges down the valleys so quickly that it does not have time to warm up. Suddenly, on what had started as a warm late-summer day, such a wind struck us without warning. It came roaring down the valley to our rear and forced us forward onto the enemy. At the same time, Arbogast's army was facing into this terrible wind and could not withstand it. The shields of both armies acted like sails. The westerners were blown backward into one another in confusion, with dust blowing into their faces as though they were caught in a Sahara sandstorm. We easterners were blown along in a similar manner, but at least we could see where we were going and maintain better order. With a wall of dust blowing from our rear and blinding our enemies, the battle turned in our favor. Western archers suddenly found their arrows being blown back onto themselves and could not launch anymore. As a result, the Imperial Guard regiments along with other cavalry regiments started exploiting holes that suddenly developed in the western lines. As the wind blew cold and hard upon Arbogast's army, it finally broke. Individual soldiers and then entire units surrendered to us while others simply fled the field. They had no choice since it was impossible for them to fight. With mass surrenders occurring all along the line, the main entrance to the massive fortress was left open to us. By this time, the wind had died down, but it had lasted long enough to enable us to win the day.

We stormed into the fortress whose main gate had been left open in all the confusion. Several thousand rear echelon soldiers were located along with the usurper. Shortly before the final surrender of the palisade, I received yet another wound to my left arm as the result of an accidental sword thrust from one of my own men, the Visigoth Sigismund. It happened during a fight in close combat while we were attacking Eugenius' headquarters. The men in the usurper's bodyguard had not fully appreciated the extent to which their army had disintegrated outside the stockade and the fighting within the compound was heavily contested. My wound was not serious, but poor Siggi would spend much of his remaining active military career apologizing to me for it. Another Imperial Guard regiment captured the terrified Eugenius. Taken to Theodosius, he was summarily executed by decapitation. There was no alternative, but many of us felt sorry for the man. He had been hopelessly out of his element from the very beginning and had only accepted the position reluctantly. He had deserved a better fate. But then, during the past two days, so had tens of thousands of others.

Arbogast escaped into the hills to the northwest of the battleground where, upon realizing the hopelessness of his situation, he committed suicide a few days later. Two bloodstained swords were found at the scene indicating that he had been assisted in taking his own life. I like to think that during his final moments, he finally realized how young Valentinian had felt two years earlier. If there was ever a case of pride going before a fall then this was it. Nichomacus Flavianus, praetorian prefect of the Italies, also committed suicide. Arbogast was not the only general to die as a result of the battle. Bacurius, one of the East's three corps commanders, had also been killed in action.

The field hospitals from both sides were quickly blended into one organization treating the wounded indiscriminately, regardless of which side they had fought on. The wound to my left arm was quickly patched up and did not seem all that serious at the time. It was, nonetheless, the most repeatedly injured part of my body. Minor injuries can have an accumulative impact that is just as severe as that of a single more serious wound. As the wounded were being tended, we started cremating the thousands of dead. We were kept busy for days stripping their bodies of all weapons, equipment, and personal belongings and piling them into large cribs for cremation. The burning of the corpses went on for days up and down the length of the valley, on the hillsides and before the fortress. We had dodged a spear in the war of 388 when our casualties, as civil wars go, were relatively light. But not this time. The Visigothic

Federate Army of twenty thousand men (Alaric's count had been correct) had suffered five thousand dead on the first day alone and as many wounded. Half of these eventually died from their injuries. Coupled with their losses on the second day, Alaric's dead alone totaled close to ten thousand. It fostered yet one more bitter legacy that has forever poisoned relations between Goths and Romans.

As soldiers from both sides cremated and buried the dead and tended the wounded, an outsider from civilian life would have been stunned at the extent to which we cooperated with one another. Just a few days before, we had been slaughtering ourselves at an incredible rate. Yet most of us were getting along well enough now that the battle was behind us. The reason was that it had been a civil war. There were men from the East serving in the Western Army and soldiers from the West, such as Stephanus and myself, enrolled in the army of Theodosius. There were cousins and brothers serving on opposite sides of the conflict. After burying the dead and getting the wounded moved into our huge field hospital, many of us started visiting different units from East and West to determine who the survivors were. I am not trying to gloss over the hostilities that still existed. On a purely man-to-man basis, they diminished rather quickly. At the highest level, however, the antagonisms were more difficult to subdue. Stilicho was now made supreme commander of the Western Army. As the recent second in command of the Eastern Army, he had been responsible for inflicting tens of thousands of casualties on these same westerners. It would be tough for him to win their acceptance. He would have to earn it.

Arbogast had the same problem when he took control of the Western Army in 388. By strengthening the army along the Rhine, rebuilding fortresses in the region and conducting successful operations against our enemies on both sides of the river, he had soon won the loyalty and respect of the recently defeated westerners. His successor would face drastically different strategic problems. Stilicho was responsible militarily not only for the prefecture of the Gauls but also for the prefecture of the Italies. That meant he was answerable for the defense of Western Europe from Britain and the mouth of the Rhine to Belgrade. In addition, he was also accountable for the protection of all of Africa except Egypt. His obligations covered a much broader area than did those of Arbogast. What placed an even heavier burden on him was that, as Theodosius's son-in-law, he would come to see himself as responsible for the entire empire, not just its western half.

There have been claims made by certain historians, pertaining to the battle, that are in error. Some have stated that an eclipse of the sun occurred on the second day along with the arrival of the "bora." Mention has also been made of an eclipse with no reference to the bora at all. As one who experienced it at full force, I can testify to the arrival of the bora and its devastating effect on the Western Army. As to the eclipse, there was none. The new moon did not occur until several days after the battle was over. Some writers may have made such a claim simply to add an element of religious mystery to their recitation of the campaign.

On the second day after the battle, a courier from the emperor's staff sought me out, telling me that Theodosius and Stilicho wanted to see me immediately. Upon arriving at the emperor's headquarters, which he had moved from up in the valley to within the palisade enclosure, I was admitted to an audience with him, Stilicho, and a man whom I had never seen before.

"Marcus," the emperor began, "I hope your wound isn't too serious."

"The arm won't be of much use to me for a while, my lord, but after that I've been told that it should be all right."

"Good," Theodosius went on. "There is someone here I would like you to meet. Marcus Cedranus, this is Arbitio."

We smiled and nodded to one another.

"From that tiny acorn that you planted with us several months ago in Constantinople," Stilicho said, "we were able to harvest an oak forest consisting of Arbitio and his five thousand Frankish warriors who came over to us on the second day of the battle. Your suspicions were correct. I cannot go into detail but the men whom you met with me that day did the rest."

"We are very greatly in your debt, Marcus," the emperor said to me. "Once we are resettled in Milan, in several weeks' time, you will be amply rewarded, and I assure you that you will not be disappointed."

"Thank you, Your Majesty."

"It is amazing what has evolved here," Stilicho remarked, "from a casual conversation over wine in a villa overlooking the Moselle River. You must show it to me sometime, Marcus."

At that point, I was dismissed.

On the third day after the surrender, I was supervising a detail that was cleaning litter off the battlefield and determining what could still be used and what had to be destroyed. Stephanus approached me and said, "I think you should come with me. I just found Marcellinus. He's been seriously wounded in the side, and the doctors are not certain that he will recover."

Stephanus led me across the broad plain where the final conflict had taken place to the huge field hospital located inside the stockade. We both wondered if it may have been one of the largest such ever constructed. There were men lying on cots or on the ground for as far as the eye could see. Tents were being set up to protect them from the elements. Stephanus led me to the bed where Marcellinus was lying.

"God I'm glad that both you guys survived," Marcellinus said as I grasped both his hands in mine. "Our numbers keep getting smaller all the time. I'm so sorry to hear of your loss of your wife and children. Stephanus told me when he saw me earlier this morning."

We all had tears in our eyes.

"Unfortunately," Marcellinus went on, breathing heavily, "The bad news doesn't stop there. I don't know if you've already heard or not but our friend Chlogius was killed early last year during Arbogast's campaign in Germany."

"No, I hadn't heard," I replied, looking over at Stephanus. It was news to him also and the two of us just sat there stunned and shaking our heads.

"His squadron was caught in an ambush four days after we crossed the Rhine," Marcellinus continued. "He was a damned fine officer and was the only man killed in the attack. On the second day of our battle here, our old friend Fredemondus was killed. He was my decurion, and he went down just after the bora struck and just before I was wounded. This is all such insanity, just bloody, suicidal insanity!"

He winced in pain. The three of us remained silent for a while.

"That's exactly what it is," Stephanus said. "Marcus, I remember your telling us one time that 'civil war is a luxury that we can no longer afford.' Yet look at the capital that we've expended here in the course of just two days. I don't know what you've heard, but I'm hearing that the total number of dead has already topped thirty thousand on both sides combined, and they're not through counting. How the hell can we suffer a loss like this without the defenses of the empire deteriorating as a result?"

"I've heard a similar estimate," I said.

"I wonder," Stephanus said, "what historians will call this conflict. Arbogast's War perhaps? He was an excellent general, but if he wasn't such an arrogant bastard, over thirty legions' worth of men would be alive today and manning the frontiers or patrolling the interior."

"How about the War of Valentinian's Revenge?" I suggested. "In death, our late emperor has had a far more marked influence on affairs of state than he ever had in life. At the same time, I suppose we must also give credit to the late Empress Galla for exacting her own revenge from the grave."

Stephanus and I stayed with Marcellinus for a while longer but it was obvious that he was tired and in considerable pain. He did not look well at all. When we returned the following day, we were told that gangrene had set into his wounds. He died two days later. Stephanus and I took his body to Aquileia and buried it in a civilian cemetery with a proper gravestone. Thus, he joined that countless army of men down through the centuries that have died as strangers in a strange land, so far from home. A good soldier and a staunch friend, he had never married.

I regretted we had not been able to do the same for Fredemondus. However, when one is surrounded by thousands of dead bodies it is impossible to give them the individual care that one would wish. The danger of the spread of disease is too great and there had been suffering enough. Marcellinus had been correct. This war had been nothing but an act of "bloody, suicidal insanity." That it was bloody and insane surely no one would gainsay. The measure to which it had been suicidal would stretch far beyond the conflict itself.

The bora that blew down out of the Julian Alps that September 6 has been known ever since as the "Divine Wind" and with good reason. It was obvious to all, not just on the battlefield but throughout the empire, that the God of the Christians had delivered the Eastern Army to victory that day. To pagans everywhere, the implication was obvious. There would be no resurgence on the part of their religions. The tide was going out on them and the only time they had left was of the borrowed variety. However, there was no sudden surge in conversions to Christianity. Instead, it has been a gradual process over the course of two generations.

Writing this with the benefit of almost a half century of hindsight, it is easy to say that the triumph of Christianity had been foreordained. But even if the West had won, paganism would probably have enjoyed a prolonged afternoon at best. There could have been no more of a new dawn for the ancient religions of Rome in 394 than three decades earlier during the reign of Julian the apostate. Christianity had been in the ascendant for well over a century. If that ever-broadening dominion could withstand the great persecutions of the past and emerge stronger after each, then there is no way in which a single military defeat would have changed its progression.

During October and November, I was assigned to a task force that was responsible for analyzing the state of readiness of all the units that had participated in the recent conflict. I'll have more to say on that in the next chapter where its consequences were more relevant. As soon as conditions at the battlefield had been settled, the emperor started making plans for his return to Milan. Due to my task force assignment, however, I would be two months late joining him there. For the last time, the empire was under the control of a single emperor. Theodosius's entry into Italy was remindful of the end of the previous war six years earlier. He was generous in triumph once again even to those who had led the pagan reaction. He knew he had an enormous problem ahead of him in replacing the tens of thousands of soldiers who had fallen at the Frigidus River. But first he had to make new political appointments. The emperor, with his retinue and Imperial Guards, marched to Milan with the intention of eventually visiting Rome. This latter visit would never take place.

Once again, the Imperial Guard regiments were set up either in barracks or in private homes in Milan for the most part. Because my arrival had been delayed due to my task force assignment, all available apartments in the barracks had been taken up. It must have been a desire to indulge in some form of psychological self-flagellation that propelled me to visit the barracks where I had lived with my family six years earlier. Walking down one of the hallways, I heard the crying of a small child and was instantly reminded of that infinitely happier time. It was a mistake and I realized instantly that my being assigned to that task force might have been providential. The memories were just too painful to return to that barracks block and I wasn't about to impose myself on some private family. So I took a suite in an apartment building. I could afford it on the extra pay I received as an officer in a Palatine Guard regiment. Not far from the barracks but still far enough, it afforded me the sort of independence I had become accustomed to in my living accommodations in recent years. I frequented the library whenever time permitted and absorbed as much history as I could manage. The military training was routine but as rigorous as ever. While I could handle it, I was disappointed by the manner in which the movement of my left arm remained restricted. One of the first things I did upon moving into my new living quarters was to complete the letters to Margareta and Maria

Patricia that I had started two years earlier. I had been adding to them occasionally during this lengthy period and by now they bulked quite large. As a result, the courier service charged me quite a bit to deliver them (especially the one to my sister), but I certainly could not complain. After all, whom else did I have to correspond with?

At the end of November, I was called into Stilicho's office at the palace. Only Stilicho and the emperor were present.

"Welcome, Marcus," Theodosius said. "I will make this short and sweet." The emperor then presented me with a considerable sum of money. "It is only on extremely rare occasions that monetary rewards are made to soldiers for actions on the battlefield. Your information that led to Arbitio's changing sides constitutes such a circumstance. This award is symbolic of my personal gratitude, the gratitude of the Imperial General Staff, and for that matter the entire empire for what you helped to accomplish. Please accept this presentation with my heartfelt appreciation."

I thanked the emperor for this most generous gift and then Theodosius excused himself, leaving me alone with Stilicho.

"Marcus," Stilicho began, "we have reviewed your record and have been favorably impressed by it. You have gained a wide breadth of experience throughout the length of our European frontier. Your men respect you and your commanding officers have always filed complimentary reports on you. Would you be interested in taking on special assignments from time to time under my direct command?"

Here was another obvious occasion presenting itself to put myself on a fast track to my next promotion. With only the slightest hesitation, I replied, "Yes, sir, I would. What kind of assignments would they be?"

Stilicho looked off to one side and then turned back to me.

"Like no others that you have ever been involved with. His Majesty and I have put together a select group of officers known as the Special Service Squadron. All members report directly to me while on assignment. These are temporary postings. All members serve on an as-needed basis and must be available as required. The rest of the time, you are assigned to your regular units where you perform your normal duties. Certain orders that you will be called upon to execute you will find distasteful. You will discharge them anyway because to fail to do so will be interpreted as an act of treason. Should you decide to join the Special Service Squadron, you will have no choice but to carry out any order that you are given. You will not have the option of requesting that someone else be given the assignment instead. You will discuss your special assignments with no one except those with whom you will be acting. Having heard everything that I have said, do you still wish to join the Special Service Squadron?"

"Yes, sir, I do," I replied.

"Then welcome aboard. From this day forward, you are a member of the group. There will be no special assignments anytime soon but you must keep yourself in constant readiness for when they do arise. By the way, none of your special service assignments will ever appear on your personnel records. Officially, the Special Service Squadron does not exist. Are you sure that you don't have any questions?"

"How many of us are there?" I answered.

"I'm not at liberty to disclose that."

At that point, I was dismissed. I left the palace stunned. It was not enough for me to immediately contemplate retirement (even if it had been possible), but I had received a considerable amount of money. I immediately thought of my friend Chlogius, without whom none of this would have been possible. Had he still been alive, I would have split it with him fifty-fifty. As it was, I determined to seek out his widow at the first opportunity and share it with her.

The winter had set in and so did all the memories of the family life that I had once had. How could the time have gone by so quickly? Over two years had passed since that terrible day in Carnuntum. In early December, the emperor took ill, and from the beginning, rumors spread that it was serious. Word went to Constantinople to send Honorius to Milan at once. That only served to raise everyone's apprehensions. Ever since his first severe illness fifteen years earlier, the emperor's health had never been all that robust. A sense of unease soon emanated from Milan to every corner of the empire. However, we tried to make the best of things during the holiday season. I had met a couple in my apartment block with whom I had become quite friendly. They had me over for

Christmas dinner and there were several parties in the block that we attended between Christmas and New Year's. It buoyed everyone's spirits and we all started feeling relieved when we heard that the emperor's health was improving.

On New Year's Day, soldiers throughout the realm renewed their oaths of allegiance to Theodosius, Arcadius, and Honorius. In spite of what we had heard about the emperor starting to recuperate, his absence from our annual swearing-in ceremony started the rumor mill going all over again. During the first half of January 395, the central government became increasingly paralyzed as questions of the emperor's health multiplied. On January 17, after Honorius arrived, celebratory games were held, and both father and son presided. After a couple of hours, the strain proved to be too much and the emperor had to withdraw. Throughout the day, the skies had been a leaden gray, but walking home, I suddenly witnessed a blazing sunset low on the horizon that cast the strangest glow. Early in the evening, Theodosius died, six days after his forty-eighth birthday.

Whenever Rome had needed a man on horseback to deliver her from her most desperate tribulations that man had always materialized. Theodosius had filled that role after Hadrianople. But his passing marked not just the termination of an era. It would define the end of an epoch. With only one short-lived exception, no such emperor on horseback has emerged during the ensuing half century, the most politically destructive period in our history.

At the time of his death, I could not help but contrast my personal recollections of the man with the historical renderings of other great, or at least important, Christian emperors. The word "affable" frequently comes to mind in describing Theodosius. That is just about the last word one would use to describe any of his Christian predecessors, especially a stiff like Constantius II. (Back in 361, when told by a witness that Constantius II had died, one of his ministers had asked, "How could you tell?") Theodosius was warm, considerate, and as family oriented as any emperor. He had a genuine concern for the citizens of the empire, although that did not always come across well. Exceedingly few and historically blessed are those rulers, like Hadrian, who can project their own reign and good fortune through successors two generations into the future. No such fortuity would attend the reigns of Theodosius's children and grandchildren. Just as Constantine I fostered the notion that he was of the line of Claudius II Gothicus, so too would Theodosius put forth the claim that he was descended from the family of Trajan; his column in Constantinople closely resembles those of Trajan and Marcus Aurelius at Rome. He encouraged friends and relatives from Spain to join him in the East, and many of them occupied important political offices in support of his government. Certain of his relatives married into important eastern families to further his dynastic ambitions. In any event, he would be the last ruler of a truly united empire.

He had been raised as a soldier from his earliest years and was as competent a field commander as any man of his generation. At the same time, he never really seemed to like the role of "supreme warlord." By nature, he was a conciliator rather than a fighter, and he would usually never resort to warfare unless he had no other choice. Now that the bulk of the Visigothic nation was ensconced within Roman territory, he wanted to make their absorption into the Roman state as successful as possible. He had inherited an enormous mess and did as much as any man could to set things right. Perhaps it had been impossible from the beginning.

Honorius, at age eleven, was now emperor of the West, but the real power, of course, resided with Stilicho. When the death of Theodosius was announced, I remembered a story I had heard some time earlier. Serena had accompanied Theodosius to Rome at the time when he had ordered a halt to the spending of public money on pagan rites. As a result of this edict, all priests and priestesses of the pagan religions were eventually expelled from their temples. While this process was going on, Serena visited the Temple of Magna Mater. There she took a necklace from around the throat of the goddess Rhea, daughter of Uranus, god of the heavens, and Gaea, goddess of the earth, and placed it about her own. The last of the Vestal Virgins saw the emperor's adopted daughter adorn herself in this way and pronounced a curse on Serena, her husband and all her children for the commission of such a sacrilegious act. I never gave this story another thought. Not for thirteen years.

CHAPTER

9

A Pandemic Reborn
(395–396)

EVERY EMPEROR FROM CONSTANTINE I on had left his successors a diminished legacy. Theodosius was no different. The dangers we faced were not immediately obvious but beneath the facade there were deepening cracks in the political concrete. Stilicho would do his best to hold everything together. However, without mature and universally respected executive authority enthroned in Milan and Constantinople, this would be increasingly difficult. When Diocletian abdicated in 305, he passed on the empire to highly experienced soldiers East and West. They inherited the finest and largest military establishment it had ever had, along with its most equitable system of taxation. When Constantine I died in 337, his three young, inexperienced sons inherited an army that numbered 450,000 but whose frontier legions had been reduced to only 1,200 men each. Emphasis was now placed on its mobile regiments. The system of taxation now had to support the expanding empire-wide Christian Church in addition to the army and the thirty-thousand-man government bureaucracy. When Constantius II died in 361, his cousin Julian took over an army that just eight years earlier had suffered 54,000 dead in what was probably the costliest civil war in imperial history. Julian himself wasted the lives of thousands more in his poorly coordinated Iranian campaign in Mesopotamia. These numbers could not be made up easily. Valentinian I maintained the caliber of the army in the West. But his ignoring of Dagalaif's warning, by appointing his brother Valens as his eastern colleague, led to the disaster at Hadrianople in 378. The army that Theodosius I inherited was a shattered and demoralized ruin. The Eastern Roman Army could only be rebuilt in the short run by troop transfers from the West. Thus, both East and West were weakened by Valens's tragic misjudgment and not just the East alone.

The casualty figures for the Battle of the Frigidus have never been published. A reasonable approximation would place the total number of men killed at close to the number lost four decades earlier in the civil war between Constantius II and Magnentius. Added to the fact of a universally weakened Roman Army was the presence of a totally unpredictable state within a state in the form of the federate Visigoths under the command of their future king, Alaric. Faced by serious dangers without and uncertainties within, Theodosius I had settled the state upon his two frightfully incapable sons. As children, they were embarrassingly immature, and as adults, they would be nothing more than overgrown children.

Writing as I am now in the latter 430s, I have suffered the signal misfortune to live under two generations of the descendants of Theodosius I, and I pray to God that there will not be a third. This family has been an unholy blight of unfitness upon the land if ever there was one. The ancient saying that "the sons of great men remind us that great men should not leave sons behind" has once again been proven in the most capricious fashion. The same expression apparently holds for their grandsons.

Immediately after Theodosius died, Stilicho conducted a meeting of the Western Sacred Consistory and made a surprise announcement. Shortly before he died, Theodosius had an audience with Stilicho alone in which the emperor made him the guardian and regent for both his young successors, Arcadius (age seventeen) in the East and Honorius (age eleven) in the West. Since Stilicho was a member of his own family, the emperor had complete confidence in him. Stilicho acknowledged that Theodosius's original intent had been to have him act as guardian for Honorius while Rufinus fulfilled a similar role for Arcadius. But the appalling casualties of the recent civil war and Theodosius's growing suspicions about the extent to which Alaric and his army could be trusted changed all that. There had to be a strong military authority for the entire empire. His son-in-law was the only man capable of exercising such responsibility for the dynasty as a whole. There was no question of Stilicho's supremacy in the West. Shortly after the Battle of the Frigidus, he had been appointed marshal of infantry for the Western Empire. But when the emperor became ill toward year's end, he feared his affliction may be fatal. He recognized that his sons were totally incapable of exercising their obligations as responsible chiefs of state in their own right. Arcadius was as dull witted as they come, and Honorius, it was coming to appear, was borderline mentally retarded.

It was common knowledge that Theodosius had made the arrangement with Stilicho for Honorius. The revelation about Arcadius surprised everyone. Suspicions naturally arose that Stilicho had fabricated the latter "regency" since he had been the only one present at the time and there was nothing in writing. Ambrose, though he was not present, supported Stilicho completely. In spite of the bishop's support, Rufinus refused to accept Stilicho's assertion. The long-simmering dispute between the two was soon out in the open. Rufinus saw himself alone as being the eastern government. The notion of his blithely accepting this "new arrangement" strained the imagination. That also went for many others in the East.

On the surface, Stilicho's position made sense. Ever since the death of Jovian in 364, there had been a firm principle that two emperors should share executive authority in partnership with one another; the job was simply too complex for one man. As a member of the imperial family, Stilicho felt that the regency could best cement that collaboration if it was handled by himself. But there was an inherent inconsistency in his policy: how could one regent handle affairs of state that generations of experience had concluded required two emperors? The circumstances that Stilicho had inherited were unique in our history. They would eventually prove themselves incapable of resolution to anyone's satisfaction.

Rufinus had long been jealous of the power Stilicho was accumulating. As long as Theodosius was alive, he could do nothing about it. But now that there was no supreme authority at the top, he could start formulating plans to ensure his own supremacy over Arcadius. Rufinus recognized that his lack of military experience would prove a definite drawback in his attempt to ward off Stilicho's designs. Nonetheless, just the instrument that this shoemaker's son from Gaul thought he required would soon come to hand. With the passing of Theodosius, Rufinus was now the dominant personality in the East, though not without rivals. He was everything that his new emperor was not and could never aspire to. Rufinus was tall, handsome, quite an eloquent speaker, and quick witted. His new "boss," who was stunted in both mind and body, was made to order for him. Whenever Arcadius exercised his own judgment, without consulting his advisers, his actions were generally foolish or impulsive and the results unpredictable. The emperor's intellectual defects and his insipid character made it inevitable that he would be dominated by others throughout his adult life. Rufinus felt, of course, that no one was better suited to perform this mastership than himself. He had been brazenly unprincipled even under Theodosius, but he shared one overriding belief with his previous master: that the calamities stemming from the Battle of Hadrianople had been brought about by God's anger with government laxity in stamping out all forms of Christian heresy. Rufinus' extreme zealotry, on behalf of Catholicism, had induced Theodosius to look the other way even where his worst outrages were concerned. Now that the "old man" was gone, we would learn just how venal and downright criminal Rufinus could be. Rumors, later in the year, that he was trying to make himself emperor were unfounded. Similar accusations would, in time, be leveled against Stilicho as well and with a corresponding lack of substance. Rufinus was determined to remain the power behind the eastern throne but his ambitions would not extend beyond that. It was, however, the degree to which he was willing to pursue that end that would truly outrage public opinion to the point of utter disbelief.

At the end of January 395, Stilicho ordered Alaric and his Visigothic Federate Army to return to Lower Moesia. With the exception of the Imperial Guard regiments and the mobile field army units that had been retained in northern Italy, Alaric's army was one of the last of the eastern forces to be returned to their home bases. As a result, many warehouses that had supplied them along their westward trek were now empty. With little choice in the matter and no need for prompting, Alaric's men had to forage and expropriate supplies for themselves. In some places where provisions were critically short or nonexistent, the Visigothic Army attacked estates and undefended towns to satisfy their needs. Many that lived along their return route suffered almost as badly as if they had been victims of a full-scale barbarian invasion.

Between September 394 and the end of January 395, Alaric's army had been ensconced in the northeast corner of Italy. The ever-confident Alaric had performed brilliantly during the Battle of the Frigidus and, on that basis, soon placed on Theodosius the demand that he be given a top command in the Roman Army. Theodosius reminded him that if he wanted a command in the Roman Army, he should have joined it in the first place. Besides, Alaric was only twenty-four at the time. It had been made quite clear in the Treaty of 382 that Visigothic soldiers had a choice: they could join the Roman Army and be treated like everybody else or they could join the Visigothic Federate Army, in which case they were essentially on their own. The officers in this federate army would be treated as Roman officers during periods of common danger, but their ranks were not transferable into the imperial service. Alaric knew this all along but had decided to give it a shot anyway and see what happened. He then argued that the Treaty of 382 was meant to apply to dangers that were common to both Romans and Visigoths. On this he was on more solid ground. Alaric's position was that he and his army had gone far beyond what the treaty called for. They had served Theodosius's cause in a civil war that was really none of their business and had suffered terribly in the process. Special services demanded special rewards, according to Alaric, but Theodosius would have none of it. The emperor did, however, grant Alaric the title of "count" but no more. For any other twenty-four-year-old military commander, such an honor would have been satisfaction enough. But not for a future king.

To accede to Alaric's exaction would undermine the entire treaty. Indeed, if Theodosius had caved in to Alaric, there would be no incentive for any ambitious Visigoth to join the Eastern Roman Army. Such a precedent would mean that any Visigothic federate general could make similar demands on Rome, under threat of revolt, whenever the mood struck him. Where, then, would the borderline be drawn between the Roman and Visigothic armies? And what would stop other barbarian generals from making similar demands on Rome in the future? The possibility for confusion was endless.

The death of Theodosius was to transform the relationship between Romans and Visigoths by making the whole argument moot. Romans think of treaties as being between peoples, regardless of who their rulers are. The Goths, on the other hand, regard treaties as existing between rulers, not peoples. As far as Alaric and his followers were concerned, the Treaty of 382 was null and void the moment Theodosius died. Alaric immediately saw the opportunity to play both halves of the empire against one another. As he was leading his army back across the Balkan Peninsula to Moesia, he claimed to everyone within earshot that Theodosius had promised him a command in the Roman Army after the civil war was over and had reneged. No such promise had ever been made, but that didn't matter. Alaric simply used this accusation in order to justify his "outrage" at having been denied his "just rewards."

At the time of Theodosius's illness, there was another problem that had a direct bearing on the Goths. While the Visigothic Federate Army and the Roman Army of Thrace were on the Frigidus, the Huns finally consolidated their strength north of the Danube. They immediately struck south into Moesia. There was nothing to stop them once they had bypassed our frontier defenses. These raids continued into the winter and marked the first large-scale Hunnish invasions of the empire. The devastation they caused among both Roman and Visigothic inhabitants of the diocese was dreadful. By early 395, many of us wondered if the Hunnish danger that had caused us so much grief with the Goths over the past two decades was at long last going to materialize against Rome directly. These invasions into the Visigothic homeland fueled Alaric's anger all the more. He soon started contemplating the need for a safer territory for his people. But where? It would take almost a quarter century to answer that question. The point for now is that this became the primary concern of Alaric and his closest advisers. It was the main reason, or rationale, behind the tragedy known as the "Gothic Uprising" that occurred within a few months.

Theodosius lay in state in Milan. Ambrose delivered the funeral oration at the end of February, forty days after the emperor's death. The forty-day waiting period was all part of Ambrose's ambition to place himself in line with biblical traditions. There had been forty days and forty nights of rain during Noah's flood, forty years of wandering for Moses and the Israelites in Sinai, and forty days for Christ in the wilderness. The number would have an increasing role to play in the history of the Visigoths as well. After the funeral, preparations were made to escort the late emperor's body on a tour of the Illyrian provinces that would end in the eastern capital. There it would be entombed in the mausoleum that had been built by Constantius II. Unfortunately, the Gothic Uprising would delay its arrival until November. For the immediate future, more demanding issues called for attention. During the six weeks between the emperor's death and Ambrose's funeral oration, Stilicho finished making the political appointments for the Western Empire that Theodosius had started.

After the Battle of the Frigidus, Stilicho's main responsibility had been to assess the state of the units that participated in the conflict. I was one of the officers chosen to assist in this, particularly as the western legions and regiments were concerned. We had to consider the overall condition of each unit, and it was no small task since two hundred thousand Roman soldiers had participated. Alaric's army was not part of this analysis. The units were reviewed in the order in which they were to be returned to their home bases. The date of their release would depend on their total travel distance: the longer the distance, the sooner their release. The garrison units, East and West, were dispersed as soon as they could be supplied for their return journeys. It was essential that the frontiers not remain stripped of manpower for any length of time for obvious reasons. Next to go were regiments from the Army of the East. They had the longest distance to travel and there were not very many of them. For their return trip they were led by Timasius. The infantry legions and cavalry regiments of the mobile field armies of Gaul, Thrace, and Illyria along with the two imperial field armies were another question. They were the most important units in the army, and their casualties had been very high. The task force status reports on them reflected their shrunken state, especially that of the Army of Illyria. Just when our assessments had been submitted to our higher-ups, the emperor took ill and the whole process was frozen in place.

Several days after the emperor died, Stephanus and I went out for a night of barhopping. I had taken him with me as an assistant on the task force. When we were first stationed in Milan, I had encouraged him to take classes the army offered to soldiers wanting to become literate. He had done well. As a fellow son of the West and a veteran of twelve years like myself, I felt he could be of value when it came to interviewing the men in the ranks. Before hitting the bars, we went out for dinner and started discussing the new political world that we suddenly found ourselves in. The conversation eventually got around to our task force findings.

"What's your impression of the overall status of the army?" I asked.

"I'm not at all comfortable with what we found out," was the response.

"Neither am I," I replied.

"It's ironic, isn't it?" he went on. "You and I enrolled in the army over a dozen years ago. The main concern then was to rebuild the shattered Eastern Army. Where would you say we are today?"

"I'd like to be optimistic and claim that we are back at square one. Unfortunately, we've actually regressed far beyond that because now both the eastern and western armies have been badly smashed up."

"Is this what we've been fighting for all these years?"

"Not deliberately," I replied, "but ever since last September, I've been wondering about what I've accomplished over the past decade or so. When I was a teamster, I could look back at the end of the day and know exactly what I had delivered to whom. Now, like you, I can look back over twelve years and not know what I've delivered to anybody."

"What do you think will happen next?" Stephanus asked.

"Whenever the field armies have suffered heavy losses in the past, the best soldiers in the garrison legions have been transferred into them to replace their depleted numbers. That will no doubt happen this time as well," I replied.

"The westerners are getting pissed off with their being retained here," Stephanus said, altering the subject just slightly. "They don't understand why they haven't been released back to Gaul the same way the garrison units were. I could never come up with a good answer for them. Do you have one?"

"I think it's Stilicho's idea. They are his men now, and before sending them back, he wants to get better acquainted with them. He'd been having a lot of meetings with their officers down to the decurion and centurion level before Theodosius's condition worsened. Secondly, I think Stilicho sensed that Theodosius might not make it from mid-December on. Not knowing what Alaric's army will do, he wants as many resources at hand as possible for any eventuality. We all know they have a personal rather than a national attachment to treaties."

"Stilicho is an unknown quantity to the Gauls and Franks," Stephanus said. "They don't know how good he is and it bothers them."

"He's beaten them twice," I replied. "That should be good enough for them."

"Yes, but Stilicho is a Vandal and westerners are not familiar with them." If only things could have stayed that way.

"They'll come to respect him in time," I said, "just as you and I have. Actually, he faces problems from both camps."

"Why do you say that?"

"You and I interviewed only western units," I replied. "But in conversations I've had with other officers, it appears that some of the newer Visigothic recruits in our Eastern Army are buying into the notion that their cousins in Alaric's army were deliberately sacrificed against Arbogast. So there appears to be a question of reliability among elements of the eastern field armies. Will westerners follow a leader with whom they are familiar only as an enemy? Will Visigoths in the Eastern Army desert to Alaric? Our best hope is that we will not have to fight any wars anytime soon."

"Based on what we've heard about the Huns lately," Stephanus responded, "that hope might already be dead. If they try and hold the territory that they have invaded in Thrace, then we could be at war with them in a matter of months."

"The Huns are nomads. I can't see them trying to settle in a civilized region like Thrace. Our biggest problem is going to continue to be the Visigoths," was my not overly convincing response.

"What is it about the goddamned Visigoths that makes them feel so special?" Stephanus asked in a highly agitated manner.

"Every Roman in the empire shares your frustrations on that one," I replied. "I've heard some Goths boast that they are more 'Roman' than any other Germanic nation, and perhaps it's that feeling of superiority over their fellow Germans that has fueled most of our problems with them. Too large a percentage of them simply do not want to be assimilated."

"More Roman my butt," Stephanus replied, more riled than ever. "If any Germanic people deserve that title, it's the Franks. Frankish soldiers can be found serving on the Rhine, the Danube, the Euphrates, and even as far away as Egypt. Franks have held the highest military offices in the empire from marshal of Gaul to the dukes of Palestine, Phoenicia, and a host of other places. They occupy civil service positions to a much higher degree than any Visigoths do. We gave Alaric and his lot a homeland on the lower Danube and no sooner do the Huns show up on the north bank than the Visigoths want to bug out on us. You don't see the Roman Franks on the lower Rhine hightailing it off into the interior every time their German relatives drive across that frontier. As reliable allies, the Visigoths are useless."

"Up to this point, I'm in complete agreement with you," was my response.

"Another thing that irks me," Stephanus continued, "is the never-ending excuse that we are given for tolerating Visigothic insubordination: we need their soldiers. I think we would all admit that we do need them in the East, just as we require Frankish volunteers in the West. But what we need is recruits for the Roman Army, not the Visigothic Federate Army. This whole idea of a permanent foreign army operating on Roman soil in conjunction, supposedly, with ours has all the potential for a disaster."

"Again, I agree," I said. "We should know by now that the empire is regarded by Alaric and his followers as nothing more than an enormous target of opportunity. He will never be one of us. From a political standpoint, the one characteristic of Alaric that exceeds even his greed and vanity is his failure to recognize the long-range interests of his people as individuals. The Visigoths cannot expect to survive as a separate people within the empire. One way or another, they will be assimilated."

"The only question," Stephanus concluded, "is how long and bloody the road to that result will be." There was a lengthy silence, and then he continued. "On a completely different subject, old boy, have you met anyone new in the past two years and more?" It was a most delicate subject, and he knew it.

"I was introduced to a woman about six years younger than I am at one of the Christmas parties that I attended in my apartment block," I replied after some hesitation. "She's a sharp-looking girl who was dumped about a year ago by her husband who is living somewhere down around Naples. She has a cute-looking three-year-old daughter. We went out a couple of times but nothing really clicked. I don't imagine that we'll being seeing one another anymore."

"Too bad," he replied. "I was hoping that by now you might have met someone to fill the void. If you'd care to, I could always fix you up with one of the tarts that I hang out with."

We both laughed. Stephanus had always gone after streetwalkers and never seemed serious about settling down with anyone.

"Most generous of you, my loyal comrade. But as far as I'm concerned, I'm not really looking for anyone, and no one is looking for me. I'm content to let things stay that way for now." Stephanus understood and didn't press the issue any further.

By the end of January, Stilicho had created a new field army of his own: the Army of Italy. It consisted of units from the armies of Gaul, Illyria, and Thrace and consisted almost entirely of native-born westerners. He needed an army under his immediate command regardless of how depleted the other field armies were. There were a number of heated discussions with the commanders of these other armies, who argued against further reductions in their legions and regiments, but they knew that Stilicho had to prevail on the issue.

Shortly after arriving back in Moesia at the end of March, Alaric replenished his army in terms of numbers and initial supplies. As the result of a conference with his tribal chieftains, most, though not all, of the Visigothic families living there decided to seek a safer homeland elsewhere. These included the Visigoths who had settled there in the period 376–382 as well as a few who had arrived three decades earlier. The mounting danger posed by the Huns, they felt, was too great a risk. The fact that virtually all the Huns had returned north of the Danube said to many of us that the Visigoths were overreacting in the same fashion they had two decades earlier. Life on the frontier will always be dangerous but the way to handle these threats is with determination and foresight. Not by running away from them.

Thousands of Visigoths living in Moesia decided to remain there at peace with Rome. This confirmed in the minds of most of us that either the threat was not as serious as Alaric and his followers were claiming or that Alaric's real ambitions simply lay elsewhere. He was nothing more than a gangster at this stage of his life and saw the depletion of the eastern mobile field armies coupled with the fact that they were still stationed in northern Italy as a golden opportunity. His army and its attendants headed south. Their immediate destination was Constantinople. His purpose was not to capture the city. That was impossible. What he failed to achieve with Theodosius he now hoped to accomplish with Arcadius: field marshal rank for himself in the Eastern Army and a new treaty. His manner of achieving these objectives constituted nothing less than barbarism of the worst sort. His army and its associated horde cut a swath of devastation and bloodshed from the lower Danube to the capital. They attacked farmsteads and undefended villages to feed and supply themselves that the marauding Huns had not previously destroyed. Leave it to Rufinus to see this as an opportunity to further his own political ambitions.

Word arrived in Milan late in April that Alaric was marching on the eastern capital. In early February, after Alaric had left for the East, Stilicho had started making plans for a similar march by his own forces should the need arise. The available task force members who had planned the westward march of the Eastern Army in 394 were assembled and reassigned to the quartermaster corps once again. At the initial meeting of our task force, Stilicho addressed us.

"I regret very much," the generalissimo began, "that I have had to gather you all together so soon after our last campaign. But the news from the East is not encouraging. Based on intelligence reports that we have received over the past few months, it appears that a large percentage of the Visigothic peoples are preparing to leave their homeland in Lower Moesia. This has been prompted by the destruction caused by the Hunnish invasions of Thrace and the newly established proximity of the Huns on the north bank of the Danube. There have been numerous communications since he departed for the east between our friend Alaric and the tribal chieftains back in Lower Moesia. There can be no doubt that if the Visigoths do decide to move, then Alaric will be their leader. Our intelligence confirms that thousands of Visigoths have already abandoned their farms and are currently grouped in large encampments. They will soon be on the march. The only question is when and in what direction. I would think that their first objective would be to move south of the Balkan Mountains in central Thrace. This would afford somewhat more protection than the Danube offers.

"As regards the Huns, it appears that those remaining in Thrace are continuing to withdraw north of the Danube. So the main focus of our attention will continue to be the Visigoths. Your assignment this time is to provide for our supplies as far east as Thessalonica. What happens beyond there will be determined by subsequent developments. Copies of your analyses for the previous campaign were transported from Constantinople to Milan by Theodosius's headquarters staff and are available to you. As a result, you will by no means be starting your work at the beginning. Nonetheless, because the time constraints for this operation are far more severe than they were for last year's expedition, you will probably find yourselves working night and day to perform the analyses required. There will be one major difference this time: our entire force will not be advancing along the line of the Sava, Danube, Morava, and Axios River valleys to get to Thessalonica. Between our advance in 394 and the return marches this year by both our own forces and Alaric's, the Sava River valley is exhausted. It will still be able to sustain a reduced number of us but under no circumstances our entire expedition. Should a march to the East become necessary, our forces will be split in two. The northern wing, which will consist of the majority of our army, will follow the old Sava River valley route. The smaller southern wing will follow the route down the east coast of the Adriatic to the port of Durres. From there it will follow the Via Egnatia to Thessalonica where our entire force will link up again. The Adriatic route presents special problems because of its topography and climate. Because of that, a special group of you have been selected to do the analysis there. The Pannonian Plain in the north is a rich agricultural region. To the south in Dalmatia, however, the land is far more mountainous, and grazing takes priority over agriculture in many areas. The farms that do exist there tend to be smaller than in the north, and the grain yields are lower. That's the main reason why the southern wing of our advance will be smaller than its northern counterpart."

Stilicho's introductory speech wound up shortly, followed by a question-and-answer period, and then individuals were assigned to teams. I was placed on the team working on the logistics for the southern prong. It was obvious that we had a lot of work to do. Based as we were in northern Italy, we could draw on the resources of the Po River Valley to begin with. Dalmatia, however, would be a problem. In terms of area, it is the largest province in the Diocese of Italy and one of the largest in the empire. But its size is misleading. Dalmatia is effectively divided into two distinct climatic zones of vastly different areas by the Dinaric Alps. They run parallel to the Adriatic coast for the entire length of the province and beyond. Between this mountain range and the sea, the Mediterranean climate prevails. The width of this coastal region ranges from only fifteen to twenty-five miles and is the most heavily inhabited area of Dalmatia. To the north, a more continental climate prevails. Therein lay our main challenge: the vast majority of our supplies would have to be drawn from this narrow coastal strip. The volume of stores that we could obtain would govern the size of the force that was sent along this route.

Topographically, the Dinaric Alps constitute one of the most rugged regions of the empire, and the further south they go, the rougher they get. Rising in places to eight thousand feet, these mountains present a pronounced obstruction between the coastal and interior regions of Dalmatia. Few roads penetrate inward from the coast, primarily because of the forest density. The distance from Aquileia that lies just to the northwest of Dalmatia in Venetia to Durres, in the Diocese of Macedonia is 475 miles. Throughout this distance, only five highways lead inland from coastal settlements, including the Via Egnatia at Durres. It was in Dalmatia that I first became acquainted with what is called karst topography. The region along the eastern Adriatic coast contains limestone that is exposed at the surface. Groundwater can dissolve this type of rock, creating rather bizarre landforms. When limestone is exposed in dry climates, this type of topography does not evolve. But the humidity of the Dalmatian coast is ideal for these configurations to develop. The heavy rainfall enables the solution of the limestone to advance rather quickly, especially in rock that is fractured. Areas that are underlain by limestone can have large underground caverns created by this process. If the roof of such a cavern collapses, then a surface depression called a sinkhole results. Many sinkholes exist in Dalmatia, a typical one being perhaps a couple of hundred feet in diameter and anywhere from two to five stories deep. Sometime karst ponds or lakes form in these sinkholes when the bottom of the hole becomes clogged with silt washed in from the surface by rainfall. In some places, a chain of sinkholes will occur that have been caused by an underground river or creek. In the best watered ones, entire wheat farms exist, while in a number of the isolated sinkholes, gardens have been established. In some cases, vines are grown on their rough walls.

The Dalmatian coast is a beautiful place and has much in common with the rivieras of Gaul and Italy. Very few rivers flow into the eastern Adriatic, and of the six hundred islands that lie off its coast, only about 10 percent are inhabited. There are many large and rich estates in this region that belong to members of the aristocracy. Their agricultural wealth, like that of other Mediterranean regions, is based on such crops as grapes, olives, vegetables, and figs. The cities, however, are all generally smaller than those in Italy and do not have extensively developed hinterlands. Fishing is an important economic activity in much of this region. The heavier annual rainfall that the coast of the eastern Adriatic receives in comparison with the foot of Italy makes the waters off the coast of the former less saline than those of the latter. This makes the extraction of salt from the sea off Dalmatia more difficult. As a result, olive oil is used to preserve fish about one-third of the time.

When our task force members reached the coastal town of Butua, near Lake Scutari, we crossed the border into the Diocese of Dacia. Thus far we had been in the province of Dalmatia in the Diocese of Pannonia that, at the time, belonged to the prefecture of Illyria in the Eastern Empire. At that point, we were only about seventy miles from Durres. About 60 percent of the entire line of march of the southern wing of our advance from Aquileia to Thessalonica lay within the province of Dalmatia. The officials there were ultimately responsible to the praetorian prefect of Illyria, but because of the close proximity of Stilicho's military forces, they cooperated with us completely. Once we crossed that boundary, however, which authority would be recognized: Milan or Constantinople? The prefecture of Illyria had bounced back and forth between West and East several times since 379. It consists of the three dioceses of Pannonia, Dacia, and Macedonia along with the proconsulate of Greece. It had been attached to the Eastern Empire when Theodosius died and on that basis could be considered as part of Arcadius' realm. We were, therefore, not certain what our reception would be when we showed up on behalf of Honorius. As things turned out, there were no problems. Since southwestern Dacia and western Macedonia had no military garrisons, the civilian officials in charge of these areas proved most helpful. Their attitude was, of course, prompted by the fact that we had the nearest army.

In April, when word came that Alaric was marching on Constantinople, we were ready to move ourselves. Our main force departed Aquileia heading northeast to Emona and the Sava River Valley. Our smaller arm, traveling along the Adriatic, reached Durres in thirty-seven days. At that point, we were situated to reach Thessalonica by the end of May. After staying over for two days, at Durres we turned eastward up the Via Egnatia. Following the Shkumbi River, we soon left the coastal plains behind and headed into the mountains. As I retraced the route that we had taken in the opposite direction in 388, I could not help but feel that certain of the more fertile, intermountain valleys of Greece, Epirus, and Macedonia might make a good homeland for the Visigoths. Admittedly, such a resettling would negate our main reason for inviting them in the first place (i.e., frontier defense). But if it served to pacify them, then we could refocus our efforts to where their soldiers belonged on the Rhine and the Danube. We often forget that the population of ancient Greece and Macedonia combined at the time of Alexander the Great was three million. Now, after the passage of seven centuries, it is only half that, thanks to the Greek Diaspora that erupted with Alexander and spread all around the eastern end of the Mediterranean and deep into Iran. Greece and Macedonia can certainly support a larger population than they do today.

Many of the more mountainous regions there are not well suited to agriculture and a more pastoral way of life persists. But in the areas around Lake Ohrid and Lake Prespa, several valleys contain excellent farmland, and numerous other districts like that throughout the region are quite under populated. While such valleys are fertile, they tend to exist in isolation from one another, and transportation difficulties foster subsistence rather than market agriculture.

While we were on the march to Thessalonica, the situation at Constantinople was developing in a very awkward manner. When Alaric arrived at the eastern capital, he was met by Rufinus, who was all decked out in the garb of a Gothic warrior. Such sucking up to Alaric and his nation on the march certainly gained Rufinus no admirers anywhere in the East. This was especially true among those whose estates had recently been ruined and whose villages had been sacked and burned to the ground. It had also not gone unnoticed that Rufinus' estates in Thrace had escaped attack by the Visigoths in spite of their lying directly along Alaric's line of advance. Rufinus was in a bind. He had neither military authority nor experience and of the five mobile field armies of the Eastern Empire, only the one guarding the eastern border with Iran was in good shape. The other four were exhausted, under the command of Stilicho, and nowhere close. Rufinus saw his chance to gain an army of his own in the army of Alaric. Exactly what transpired is not known. No documentation has been found detailing what they discussed.

We were less than a week's march from Thessalonica when we received new orders at Edessa from Stilicho. Alaric's Visigothic horde marching west from Constantinople had entered the prefecture of Illyria, bypassed the heavily fortified Thessalonica, and struck south along the coast of the Aegean Sea. We were ordered to leave the Via Egnatia and force march southeast to the valley of the Haliacmon River. There we picked up the highway that circles around Mount Olympus and followed it south and then southeast to the town of Larisa in the valley of the Pinios River. The locals were in a state of panic and were very glad to witness our arrival. The Visigoths were reported to the east of Mount Olympus, only a few days from Larisa. We immediately marched northeast down the Pinios River Valley and into the Vale of Tempe that the river flows through before emptying into the Aegean Sea. The Vale of Tempe is as narrow as ninety feet, while to the south the soaring cliffs, in some places, reach a height of over 1,600 feet. Legend has it that Poseidon carved it out with his trident. Our vanguard that day contained regiments composed of Gauls and Franks from the Army of Gaul. Just as our lead elements were emerging from the Vale, they ran into the forward units of Alaric's army. Being heavily outnumbered, Alaric's men suffered a severe defeat before retreating back up the coast. With part of Stilicho's forces also somewhere to the north, the Visigoths withdrew to the northwest and set up camp on the slopes of Mount Olympus. This position they heavily fortified by surrounding it with a deep ditch and double palisade. We were not looking forward to attacking this redoubtable stronghold because our casualties could be terrible. For the moment, our orders were to form a blockade between the Aegean Sea and the mountain and prevent Alaric's passage to the south, which we did. If we couldn't stop him, then we were at least to punish him and his followers as much as possible.

As we passed out of the Vale of Tempe and filed past the bodies of the dozens of Visigoths who had perished there, I stopped to inspect the shields of several of their dead warriors. I noticed a small, peculiar marking on several of them that reminded me of a symbol that some third-century historians had recorded on Gothic shields of that period. Upon asking a Visigothic soldier in our regiment what it was called, he replied that it was known as a "swastika." I would learn in later years that it had originated many centuries in the past either in India or Mesopotamia as a good luck charm. How the Gothic people ever came in contact with it will probably always remain a mystery. Without fear of contradiction, it can readily be claimed that the swastika never brought any luck to any Roman.

The Visigoths were virtually surrounded, and they remained that way for the next four months. Much criticism has been leveled at Stilicho for his not having launched an all-out assault on Alaric's positions. However, most historians are not soldiers, and Stilicho's situation was quite similar to that of Theodosius after he assumed the throne. Just as the Roman Army had lost twenty thousand men at Hadrianople in 378, it had lost at least twice as many on the Frigidus in 394. Just as Theodosius had been forced to utilize his reduced manpower resources with great caution during the early 380s, so too did Stilicho during the middle 390s. Stilicho had many things to consider:

+ Less than a year after the last civil war in which the field army units had suffered horrendous casualties, the last thing he wanted was to involve the Roman Army in yet another bloodbath. It would take years to build these field armies back up to full strength as it was.

+ There was considerable animosity between certain eastern and western units and it was questionable as to how well they would cooperate with one another in actual combat. There had been all-out brawls between easterners and westerners during both the marches to Mount Olympus and during the period we were all stationed there.

+ The loyalty of the newest Visigothic recruits in the eastern units was not completely assured.

+ During our encampment in Thessaly, there had been a more or less constant bombardment of requests from Constantinople for the soldiers from the armies of Thrace and Illyria to return to their home bases. The eastern soldiers themselves were not shy about making similar demands themselves since they had not seen their families in over a year. The men from Thrace were fearful of the conditions of their homes and families as a result of the attacks of both the Huns and Alaric's Visigoths. For their part, the western soldiers were angered over having to serve in Greece instead of defending their own home territories over a thousand miles to the northwest on the Rhine.

+ For its part, Alaric's army was in no position to fight either, all his bluff and bluster to the contrary notwithstanding. His forces had suffered ten thousand dead at the Frigidus, so he claimed, and he had no desire to gamble everything on a battle that he might very well lose.

It was difficult to keep our regiments in top fighting shape while being stationary at Mount Olympus during the summer of 395. I drilled my men relentlessly during this period to keep them battle ready for any eventuality but it was not easy. The Visigoths probed our lines on numerous occasions, launching attacks by both day and night. But we held them in check, and these contests never amounted to more than localized skirmishes.

During that long summer, we received most unsettling news. The Huns had struck us again but not in a region where we expected. With the Roman Army in closer proximity to Thrace, the Huns had decided once again to hit us where we were weak. Or at least where they thought we were weak. Passing eastward along the north coast of the Black Sea and the Sea of Azov, tens of thousands of them struck southeast through the Caucasus. They then split up and simultaneously invaded both our Eastern Empire and Iran. The group that crossed the Euphrates caused widespread devastation in several of our easternmost provinces before being confronted and virtually destroyed by our Army of the East. We were overwhelmed when we heard about our victory there.

Suddenly, in early October, our situation changed. Stilicho received orders, signed by Arcadius, to release the eastern mobile field armies to their commanders and return them to their home bases. He was also ordered to evacuate the prefecture of Illyria and return the Army of Gaul to the West. There was no question that Rufinus had written up the order and simply had his thick-witted master sign it. Stilicho could have disregarded the order but I don't believe it ever crossed his mind to do so. Such a step would have constituted an act of treason against Arcadius and that was something that he had no intention of doing. Stilicho's ambition in the East was to be Arcadius' regent and going into revolt against him was hardly the way to accomplish that end. As relations would continue to worsen between East and West and as the strategic circumstances in the West would begin to deteriorate early in the next century, Stilicho would forsake this ambition entirely by 402 at the latest, if not before.

The Roman Army had been well supplied throughout the four-month standoff. The plains of Thessaly, on which we were located, are one of the finest farming districts in Greece, thanks to its rich soils and its rather flat terrain. We had all the wheat and barley we could ask for. At the same time, the Visigoths, confined to the lower reaches of Mount Olympus, had been reduced to rather desperate circumstances. They must have been getting pretty close to the bottom of the barrel, especially with winter looming on the horizon, when Rufinus saved Alaric's neck. Stilicho had intended to keep Alaric surrounded throughout the winter and, if possible, starve him into submission. The new directive from Arcadius (read Rufinus) put an end to that idea. Rufinus no doubt thought that his ordering Stilicho back to Italy was a master stroke. It turned out to be something quite different.

Stilicho ordered a number of officers and noncommissioned officers from the Imperial Guard regiments to his headquarters. I was one of the officers so summoned. He selected six men to deliver two documents to Constantinople. One was addressed to the emperor and contained Stilicho's acceptance of Arcadius' orders. He told these soldiers that Rufinus would probably not allow them to see the emperor in person but that they could give the document to Rufinus since he was the one for whom it was really intended. The other document was to be delivered to the eunuch master of offices, Eutropius. The messengers were then sent on their way. That just left me and two decurions that I had seen around, but whom I did not know, with Stilicho. A courier was ordered to fetch the Visigothic general Gainas to our meeting. It had been announced earlier that Gainas would be commanding the combined mobile field army group on its march to the eastern capital to be officially returned to Emperor Arcadius. After that, these armies would return to their home bases. The determinedly loyal Gainas soon arrived, and he, Stilicho, myself, and the two other officers would have a most private and confidential meeting. Something was in the air and I was puzzled why I and the two other decurions would be present at a meeting between two of the highest-positioned field marshals in the land. The answer was not long in coming.

Stilicho introduced us all to one another and then started speaking to us in a low but distinct voice so that what we said would not be overheard.

"Gentlemen, you three, along with Gainas, are members of the Special Service Squadron. You are about to undertake your first mission, but there is something that must be done first."

Gainas brought over a Bible from another table. Stilicho swore each of us to permanent secrecy pertaining to everything that we discussed that evening and all subsequent actions.

"Now," Stilicho continued, "as to why we are all here. You three will be operating under the direct command of Gainas until your mission is complete. At that point, you will return to your home units. Your commanding officers know nothing about your mission. The only thing that they were told was that I needed you. They need know nothing more than that."

Stilicho then went on to define our responsibilities for this operation. We three decurions gave one another a look of disbelief and Stilicho paused momentarily to let the realization sink in.

"Only six people know of this assignment at the present time," Stilicho went on. "The sixth man is in Constantinople."

"If you can call him that," Gainas wisecracked.

"You will be joined by certain others along the way," Stilicho continued, disregarding Gainas' remark. "Gainas knows who they are and when they will be attached to your group. We will have no other meetings on this matter. Gainas will fill you in on the details as required."

As suddenly as the meeting had started, it was over, and we three decurions were dismissed.

Stilicho sat back and tried to relax, but he simply felt worn out.

"To what degree do you trust Eutropius?" Gainas asked.

"I've known him for almost ten years now."

"That's the same length of time that you've known Rufinus," Gainas said. "We all know how much you trust him."

"Yes." Stilicho smiled. "But my relationship with Eutropius has always been of a more positive nature than the one with Rufinus. Eutropius doesn't get along with him any better than I do. I've been in correspondence with Eutropius for some time on this matter. If I didn't have complete confidence in him, I wouldn't be sending you and the others on this mission. He can be trusted."

"Let's hope so," Gainas replied. "After all, it's our necks that the axes will be aiming for if your confidence is misplaced."

"As master of offices," Stilicho went on, "he is the number-two civil servant behind Rufinus in the government hierarchy here, and like every number two anywhere, he would like to be number one. Rufinus suspects that I want to re-annex the prefecture of Illyria to the Western Empire the way it was prior to the Battle of Hadrianople. To offset this possibility, Rufinus promised to have Arcadius grant Alaric his wish on one condition: the Visigothic Federate Army must enter the prefecture of Illyria and prove it capable of holding it for the East."

"So Alaric is to become the new marshal of Illyria?" Gainas asked.

"It appears so."

"That should make the current holder of that office happy," Gainas continued. "Getting back to our mission, it's been common knowledge for years that you and Rufinus don't have any love for one another, but the notion of you and Eutropius as a political duet seems odder yet. Beyond our immediate undertaking, how much confidence do you have in him as a political partner?"

"Not much," the generalissimo admitted. "But give Eutropius credit. He took a lot of the wind out of Rufinus' sails on his own this year. My elder daughter, Maria, is going to marry Honorius. When their engagement was announced, Rufinus saw how he could similarly cement his connection to the eastern branch of Theodosius's family: he would marry his daughter to Arcadius. Unknown to Rufinus, Eutropius had plans of his own in this regard, with which I was quite familiar. He quietly arranged to have Eudoxia, Bauto's daughter, marry Arcadius, as they did on April 27. You and I know that Rufinus arranged the assassination of Promotus. So there was a certain degree of poetic justice in this choice because Eudoxia was living in Constantinople as a member of the household of one of the sons of Promotus. Rufinus was furious when the announcement of Arcadius' wedding was made. It took him completely by surprise and Rufinus does not like surprises."

"Wait until he sees the one that we've got in store for him." Gainas laughed.

"And Eutropius," Stilicho said, "will be your delivery boy."

In a state of uncertainty and yet relief, the field armies packed up their supplies in preparation for returning to their home bases. As we marched with the eastern units, Gainas held a number of meetings with the other two decurions and me to complete the details of our responsibilities. In addition, a number of new men were added to our group at various points along the way. Only a few were Visigoths. The Roman Army departed for the north, leaving Alaric and his horde to complete their original "mission". With probable disaster ahead, Alaric had, for the second time in four years, been saved by a directive from Constantinople. We marched along the coast of the Aegean Sea. The eastern field armies were to be transferred to Emperor Arcadius in an official ceremony just outside the southernmost gate in the Wall of Constantine. The distance from Mount Olympus to Constantinople is almost four hundred miles. The trip took us over five weeks to complete. By that time, Stilicho's main army had reached the Danube on its return to Italy while the smaller southern force was midway between Durres and Salona on the Adriatic coast.

While the stalemate at Mount Olympus was going on, the body of Theodosius was slowly making its way back to the eastern capital. The leisurely pace of the cortege was quite deliberate. The government wanted to allow as many people as possible to pay their last respects to their late emperor and thousands upon thousands did so. Once the Roman siege of the Visigoths had been lifted, Stilicho released soldiers to head north and act as an additional escort under the command of Gainas. Theodosius was entombed in the Church of the Apostles on November 8, 395. The bulk of Gainas' forces arrived on November 28. Upon approaching the city, Gainas rode ahead with a small retinue to the Daphne Palace to inform Emperor Arcadius that his returning soldiers had arrived. The turnover ceremony would take place at the Hebdomon palace about a mile or so to the southwest of the capital. Arcadius was quite enthusiastic about the impending ceremony because it would afford him one of his rare opportunities to appear like a chip off the old block. Rufinus had been unaware of these plans until they were well underway. Once again, the praetorian prefect of the East had been outwitted by the master of offices.

Stilicho and Eutropius knew that Rufinus, not wanting anyone to forget who had engineered this transfer in the first place, would accompany the emperor. Gainas had positioned us, in the guise of his personal bodyguard, in such a way that we surrounded Arcadius and Rufinus without arousing any suspicions. No sooner had the emperor, with Rufinus by his side, delivered a brief reception speech than Gainas gave a prearranged signal to those of us with more than a troop transfer ritual on our minds. We had known beforehand that the Hunnish bodyguard, in whose company Rufinus always traveled, was small. Quickly drawing our swords, the late arrivals to our group proceeded to slay all the Huns while we three decurions cut Rufinus himself quite literally to pieces. Gainas had to move swiftly to assure the terrified emperor that Rufinus was the only real target of the assassins. It was obvious to the large crowd of horrified civilian onlookers that the killers were enjoying their work. Well we should have. We had all been chosen in a most meticulous fashion. Most were veterans of the Army of Thrace and had served under Promotus, whose death Rufinus had masterminded.

The three of us went at Rufinus from different directions, and in the terror of his last moments on earth, it never occurred to him to draw the sword that he always wore for show. Not that it would have done him any good. Our biggest problem was to avoid one another's thrusts and blows in such a confined space. Each of us officers stabbed Rufinus several times, the other two in either side while I went at him from the front. But Rufinus was remarkably strong. Even with having sustained all these wounds, he did not sink to his knees until I stabbed him so hard in the stomach that my sword protruded from his back. At that point, the three of us stepped away. I said to the other soldiers in our group, "He's all yours."

"You didn't leave us much," one of our Visigothic veterans laughed, fresh from slaughtering the Huns.

"Be creative," I told him, and that they were.

One soldier sliced off Rufinus' left hand while another lopped off his right. Having suffered such hideous wounds and finally seen both hands severed, he could only stare straight ahead, his eyes bulging, in terrified disbelief at what the Fates had ordained for this most fervent of Christians. After being run through with swords innumerable times, Rufinus was finally decapitated.

"Good job chaps," Gainas said.

In the time-honored custom, he had Rufinus' head impaled on a stake and paraded around the city. One of the soldiers picked up Rufinus' severed right hand and, in a savage send-up using the severed hand as a begging bowl, approached the stunned crowd, pretending that even in death the venal Rufinus was still capable of shaking down innocent people. Gainas then gave instructions to the various commanders to take their troops back to their home bases. He took the three of us decurions with him to inform Eutropius what had happened. For the most part, we rode in silence, but finally one of the other decurions asked Gainas what he thought would happen next, now that Rufinus had been removed from office.

"Assassinating Rufinus was the only practical course of action left to us given the virtual treason that he committed recently with Alaric, but his 'enforced absence' from the Daphne Palace will not necessarily cause any advantage to accrue to Stilicho. Rufinus' foremost opponents here in the East have spent goodly portions of their lives and money acquiring personal political satrapies. Killing Rufinus might simply bring to power another Rufinus."

Eutropius showed no surprise when informed of his rival's demise. And that came as no surprise to us. He had conspired with Stilicho on the day's events from the beginning. In fact, Eutropius had been instrumental in persuading Rufinus to accompany Arcadius in the first place, not that much urging was required. Eutropius then had Rufinus' wife and daughter banished to Jerusalem. We stayed in Constantinople for two days to rest up and partake of the pleasures of that wonderful city. Then we headed west for Milan taking the Via Egnatia end to end before traveling north along the Adriatic. Thus the year 395 drew to a close.

On January 1, 396, all soldiers swore their annual oaths to Honorius and Arcadius. It seemed so strange, almost unnatural, not to be swearing that oath to Theodosius. Soon after arriving back in Milan, rumors started making the rounds about Stilicho. Questions were being raised by the Senate in Rome and by certain civilian officials in Milan as to why he had failed to attack Alaric's army at the earliest opportunity. Some were so outrageous as to suggest that Stilicho and Alaric were operating in collusion with one another since this was the second time that Stilicho had had Alaric in his grasp and "let him go." The virulence of the slanders that were raised only grew once the malevolence of Alaric's subsequent crimes in Greece became common knowledge. Thus, though he was generalissimo of the West, Stilicho was off to an uneasy start with the ruling political circles there. Such suspicions would remain for the duration of his supremacy.

Stilicho had risen to the position of count of domestics (i.e., chief of the Imperial Guard), marshal of Thrace, and now generalissimo of the West in rapid succession. But perhaps the saddest aspect to his career was that he would always be considered a foreigner by many aristocratic Romans. This in spite of the fact that his father, a Vandal, was a naturalized Roman citizen and his mother was born a Roman. We all know that it is the nationality of the mother that determines one's own nationality, but for too many, that was of no consequence. Although Theodosius had married him to his adopted daughter, Serena, and recognized their children as his grandchildren, that was still not good enough for the Italian blue bloods. They would always be suspicious and untrusting of him and men like him regardless of how destructive this distrust was of their own best interests. Nonetheless, Stilicho will always be remembered as the most outstanding example of how a man considered to be a foreigner or at least an "outsider" could be introduced into the Roman political scene and advance through a composite of resolve, perseverance, and capability to accomplish things that were by now far beyond the abilities the native aristocracy.

Once Rome's field armies had departed Mount Olympus, the Visigothic horde moved south. Now there was very little in the way of a military establishment to hinder Alaric, regardless of what he chose to do. Rome's field armies were either at, or on their way to, northern Italy, northern Illyria, Thrace, or Constantinople. There were some strongly walled cities in Macedonia and Greece with respectable garrisons. However, as events would soon prove, there were far too many that lacked fortifications in spite of the hideous legacy of the third century and far more recent reminders in the fourth. The Visigoths would feast on these.

Accurate numerical estimates of the people comprising the Visigothic nation under the command of Alaric are hard to come by. In addition to Visigoths settled on Roman territory, there were some trans-Danubian Goths who had escaped the Huns and had joined him quite recently. A fair estimate of the total number of men, women, and children who were situated at Mount Olympus with Alaric would be about eighty-five thousand. Feeding a multitude of that size on the march would have been a most difficult operation under the best of circumstances. With power vacuums where executive authority should have reigned and the increasing degree of infighting between East and West, conditions were far from propitious.

They soon passed through the Vale of Tempe unhindered and ascended to the Plain of Larisa like a plague of human locusts. There they replenished their badly diminished food supplies by expropriating everything in sight from the helpless local population. Continuing across Thessaly, the Visigoths then transited the Pass of Thermopylae. Critics have been quick to point out that the garrison at the pass should have been able to stop the Visigoths from getting through. But comparison to the valiant resistance put up by the Greeks under King Leonidas of Sparta to the Iranians in 480 BC serves no purpose. The general in charge of the defense of Greece south of Thermopylae was Gerontius. He was a capable commander who had first made a name for himself a decade earlier when, as garrison commander of the Black Sea port of Constantiana, he had courageously put down a rebellion by local Visigoths, although his own troops were outnumbered. The garrison commander at Thermopylae had previously received orders through Gerontius from Rufinus to permit safe passage to Alaric's army and their families. To refuse to do so would have been interpreted as an act of treason as, even at that late date, the East was still trying to treat the Visigoths as allies. Once through the pass, the Visigoths were a little over a hundred miles from Athens. Thanks to our well-maintained highways, it could be said that Rome had quite literally paved the way for the erratic wave of destruction that these barbarians would carry out in the land of the ancient Hellenes.

Shortly after exiting the Pass of Thermopylae, Alaric was informed of the assassination of Rufinus. The arrangements that he had made with the praetorian prefect were now of no consequence. Four months of being penned up at the foot of Mount Olympus had given Alaric plenty of time to think. Just as he felt Theodosius and Stilicho had betrayed him and his followers at the Frigidus, he started wondering why Rufinus did not appear to be doing anything to free him up so that he could settle his people somewhere in Illyria. Was this just another attempt on Rome's part to try to debilitate him and his followers? The shock of Rufinus' death made him think that perhaps he had been too cynical in his attitude toward his late Roman patron. The antagonism between Stilicho and Rufinus had obviously been greater than he had realized and there was an obvious lesson there for him as well. In dealing with Stilicho, he would have to exercise the utmost caution.

They struck south into the Department of Boeotia and sacked every undefended town that they came to. This should not be interpreted as meaning that the towns so assaulted were all destroyed. In most cases, they were not. But they were plundered of all foodstuffs and monetary wealth. Given that the frontiers had been so heavily fortified generations earlier, many cities in southern Greece felt that they were sufficiently secure from the reach of the barbarians. Only a minority had been fortified with stone walls. Such a city was Thebes and there Alaric met with his first rebuff. However, realizing that Athens was only thirty-five miles distant, Alaric led his forces across Attica and invested Piraeus, the port of Athens. Proper arrangements having been made, Alaric and a small delegation were permitted to enter the city, partake of the baths, and dine with the city fathers. Athens, itself, was able to buy its way out of trouble by handing Alaric a considerable sum of money.

Leaving enormously richer than when he arrived, Alaric struck west for the city of Eleusis that lay fourteen miles distant. He had bypassed it on his approach to Athens. Eleusis had been for over a thousand years one of the foremost religious centers of Greece. On the highway between the two, the Visigoths met one of Greece's better-known men of letters. They decapitated him on the spot and slaughtered everyone accompanying him. It was only a preview of what awaited the next stop on Alaric's itinerary. His attack on that city was as savage as any in his entire Greek adventure. Alaric, in his own perverse way, consistently saw himself as a good Christian. At Eleusis, he destroyed the ancient temple of Demeter, the Greek goddess of agriculture, along with everything else there. Eleusis had also been the site of the Eleusinian Mysteries, the best known of the secret ceremonies of the ancient Greek religions. Several imbecilic members of the Catholic priesthood, at various sites in the empire, went so far as to praise this and similar acts of desecration. It was "God's will" they claimed, and in such acts of destruction, the barbarians were actually "furthering the works of the Lord." One doubts, however, that these priests would have been so enthusiastic if the savagery was being carried on in closer proximity to their own precincts. In this assault, as with certain others, men and boys were massacred, and many women and girls were enslaved. The city was totally destroyed, and it has never been rebuilt by its survivors. Eleusis marked a watershed in Alaric's "progress" through Greece. Never had the troops under his command displayed such inhumanity as they did at that doomed city. But why such unparalleled brutality there as opposed to most other towns? The Battle of the Frigidus River has been distortedly portrayed as the ultimate contest between Christianity, supported by the Eastern Empire, and paganism, sustained by the West. The Visigoths had suffered ten thousand dead in that struggle (they claimed), and now, by a quirk of fate, they found themselves in the very heartland of where those ancient religions had evolved. The God of the Christians had won, and those of ancient Greece had been vanquished. Alaric saw his presence in Greece not only as an occasion to ensure that the expiration of the old gods remained permanent but also to wreck vengeance on the very nation that he saw as being most responsible for his people's most recent sufferings. Eleusis suffered most savagely for the very reason that it remained the most revered center of the ancient religions. In its tragic but by no means unique way, the devastation and slaughter there came to symbolize Alaric's entire march through Greece. This most ancient nation of Europe would eventually be left ravaged with shattered cities and half-starved populations where any populations were left at all. He left nothing of value, as his kind never does.

Soon afterward, the Visigoths crossed into the Department of Argolis and destroyed the city of Megara. It was ironic that Megara, along with the Anatolian city of Melitus, were the cofounders of the joint colony of Byzantium in 660 BC. Now, over a millennium later, that magnificent capital was totally impotent when it came to assisting its mother city in any way. But why destroy Megara so completely? Perhaps it was because of the simple fact that it *was* one of the mother cities of Constantinople. Alaric might have been sending a warning to both Milan and the eastern capital of what might be in store for them if they did not take him and the plight of his people more seriously. The butchery at Megara was as terrible as it had been at Eleusis.

The new year of 396 found the Visigoths pressing on to the Isthmus of Corinth and the city of the same name. As with the Pass of Thermopylae, the Corinthian isthmus could have been defended, but it was not. The city of Corinth was looted but not heavily damaged, and it has managed to recover fairly well since then. Plunging straight south, Argos was the next to fall, and then, after entering the Department of Laconia, came Sparta. Argos was looted, but no permanent disrepair was sustained. Sparta was another story. From its days of glory in centuries past, Sparta had, by the time of Alaric's arrival, shrunk to the size of a village of no great importance. But its current insignificance could not save it. Again, the question of why this village, long in a state of decline? The answer may lie in its history. Sparta, as we all know, was the most militant of the ancient Greek city-states. Alaric probably thought that its destruction would enhance his reputation as a conqueror and strike even greater fear into the minds of the ruling authorities throughout the empire. The Visigoths destroyed it utterly to the point where it is now completely abandoned. They then moved on to bring death and devastation to the cities of the western departments of Messenia and Elis, including the fabled city of Olympia. After having silenced the peninsula, the Visigoths suddenly fell silent themselves. They remained in the Peloponnese for the remainder of the year and appeared to be giving serious thought to settling there. If only they had.

The Peloponnese is a mountainous region, though less so than that part of Greece lying to the north of the Gulf of Corinth. Nonetheless, the elevations do reach seven thousand feet in places, and the higher reaches of the mountains are all well forested. There is a narrow coastal plain along the south shore of this gulf, but along the west coast of the peninsula, it broadens out to as much as twenty miles in places. On the south shore of the peninsula, the rivers that flow into the Gulf of Messenia and the Gulf of Laconia have extensive alluvial plains. The influence of prevailing westerly winds means that the west coast and the mountain ranges closest to it receive abundant rainfall. It is this part of the peninsula that is most suitable for agriculture and settlement. To the east, the rainfall continually diminishes. The eastern part of the peninsula is rugged and stony with thinner, poorer, and less well-watered soils. As a result, this area is given over more to the raising of sheep and goat herds than the growing of cereal crops. The Peloponnese would have made as good a homeland as any for the Visigoths, and from a Roman standpoint, it was probably ideal. Greece is over eight centuries removed from its golden age under Pericles. It has been a political backwater for ages, and with Rome's military focus on the Rhine and the Danube, its strategic consequence has declined accordingly. It's a warm and beautiful country, but the Visigoths had come only to savage, not settle it.

The year 396 may be broadly described as one of peaceful cooperation between Stilicho and Eutropius. Stilicho would be busy strengthening the defenses of the West while Eutropius was consolidating his own position in Constantinople. When Rufinus' family had been banished to Jerusalem, Emperor Arcadius had confiscated all his property for the state. Eutropius then appropriated most of Rufinus' wealth in land, money, and urban property for himself. But as the year progressed, one dismaying development gave all the warning required that there would be further conflict ahead for the two halves of the empire. The master of offices made his first major political move: he brought false charges of plotting to seize the throne against the great field marshal Timasius. Using a highly tainted witness and a rigged judicial panel, Timasius was found guilty and banished for life to the Great Oasis in Egypt. Stilicho could do nothing to rescue his old friend. Eutropius was on his way to becoming a second Rufinus, just as Gainas had feared.

There is no question that Stilicho's failure to defeat Alaric once and for all at the foot of Mount Olympus led directly to the catastrophe that befell Greece during the rest of the year. However compelling the justifications for lifting the siege at Mount Olympus, the subsequent savagery that Greece endured would always remain as almost the greatest misjudgment of Stilicho's career and the most deplorable stain on his reputation.

CHAPTER 10

Our Last Campaign in Albion (396–398)

PART 1: THE VIEW FROM HADRIAN'S WALL

STILICHO REALIZED THAT THEODOSIUS had been remiss in failing to visit the prefecture of the Gauls when resident in Milan. To make certain that no such feelings of neglect arose this time, a tour of the Rhineland by the twelve-year-old Honorius was arranged. Late in December 395, I had received a letter from Margareta in which she mentioned that her husband, Rufius, had taken ill again. I had not yet responded when my regiment was ordered to escort Honorius and Stilicho to Trier. At the end of February, the Splugen Pass was still snowbound. In order to traverse the Alps, we had to swing eastward through Verona and Trent and use the Brenner Pass. The journey of almost eight hundred miles took us until the end of April. Week by week, we were informed of the catastrophe that was befalling the land of the Hellenes. We were disgusted and demoralized by the blatant criminality of Alaric and his followers and not just because of the sufferings of the citizens of Greece. His behavior there proved beyond the slightest doubt that Theodosius's federate arrangement with the Visigoths had been a complete failure. We could never turn our backs on Alaric again with all that that might mean for the defense of the frontiers.

Our tour, like the identical one with Valentinian II in 389, contained many stopovers. Starting at Bregenz on Lake Constance and continuing at several other stops along the Rhine, Stilicho received envoys from Gaul and Britain. The frequency and length of these meetings raised suspicions that there might be more to this tour than we had been led to believe. Several regiments of cavalry had been sent ahead of us when we left Milan. We assumed that they were returning to their home bases in Gaul, but what Stilicho had in mind for some of them was something quite different.

Upon arriving in Trier, I dropped by Margareta's home in the city. One of the servants informed me that she had been living at her country villa since her husband died two months earlier. This did not surprise me. In her letter, Margareta said that Rufius' illness was the most serious since they had been married. His advanced age and frailty when I had last left Trier made me wonder if I would ever see him again. While his death had been in the normal course of events and certainly not unexpected, I was sorry to hear that he was gone. In the three years that we had lived next door to Rufius and Margareta, they had proven themselves to be the best of friends. I arrived at Rufius' country estate on the Moselle, but when I asked the servant who answered the door if Margareta was in, he informed me that she was living next door in, as he put it, "her own place." This was my first indication that something was amiss. I went next door to where I had enjoyed the happiest years of my life. It was difficult to believe that four years had passed. My knock on the door was answered by Margareta herself.

"Marcus!" she said, throwing her arms around me as we kissed and hugged one another. "I'm so glad you're here, and you're just in time for dinner. I've been cooking a roast this afternoon, and it's almost done. I could really use the company, especially yours."

Margareta's doing her own cooking was nothing unusual. She did it all the time when she and Rufius were married. No servants were present. I explained that I had learned of Rufius' death at her home in the city. We consoled one another on our bereavements but did not dwell on them inordinately.

"How come you're living here now instead of at your former domicile?"

"Stepmothers," she explained, "especially ones who are a generation younger than the father, are rarely popular with the children. I thought

I got along with them reasonably well when their father was alive. Unfortunately, that atmosphere of civility went into the tomb with my late husband. His will left most of his estate to his children, as it should have. He also left me with a comfortable legacy, though hardly enough to go live on one of the rivieras somewhere. But the kiddies begrudge me even that. The will is currently in probate and is being contested by the family. I don't know when or how it will end." After a brief silence, she changed the subject, sort of. "It's been almost four years since Makila died. Have you met anyone new?"

"No, not really," I replied. "Shortly after I moved into my new apartment in Milan, I met an Ostrogothic girl who lived in the same building with her three-year-old daughter. She's tall, blond and good-looking but also very distant and aloof, difficult to get to know. We went out together several times, dinner, the theatre, and so forth. I don't think anything would have developed. In any case, soon after we met, the problem with Alaric in Thessaly erupted. When I returned to Milan at year's end, she had moved without leaving word with anyone as to where they were going. End of story. I wish I had something more exciting to report, but, unfortunately, that's it."

After an excellent dinner, we spent a couple of hours talking of many things. Of failed loves, different roads that we might have taken in life, or changes that we would like to have seen in the roads that we did take. Finally, we reflected that we would not be sitting together having this conversation had it not been for the tragedies that had befallen us. We had known one another now for over a dozen years. That night we became lovers.

I spent the night at Margareta's villa and the following morning was quite proud of the fact that we really had not had much sleep at all. Apart from the squadron (providentially not mine) that had drawn escort duty for the emperor when we arrived in Trier, the rest of us were given the day off. The officers, however, were to be in attendance that evening at a banquet being held to honor the new emperor of the West. After breakfast, we returned to the bedroom. Candor dictates that I admit to having fantasized about this situation since the first day I saw Margareta in the city library when I was still a teenager. She was in her midforties by now but as beautiful as ever. While basking in the warmth of the afterglow, as they say, I informed her of our plans for the evening.

"Incidentally, gorgeous, I hope that your social calendar is free tonight."

"It's embarrassingly blank for far too much of the time these days," she replied. "What do you have in mind?"

I informed her that she was to be my guest at the banquet that night.

"You and me as a public twosome," she considered. "I like that. We should certainly raise more than just a few eyebrows in the process. By the way, I've been meaning to ask you, just what is our new emperor like?"

"Well, in the person of His Majesty Honorius, the citizenry of the West will instantly recognize the full cost of their dissatisfaction with the two previous legitimate holders of that office. Gratian was an excellent emperor. Ah, but he wasn't good enough for you, was he? 'Give us Magnus Maximus!' you all cried—and look what he accomplished for you. Valentinian II, if given a chance, I think, would have developed into a responsible monarch. But you would rather have Arbogast lead you all around by the nose. Now you are about to receive, how shall I put this, a less-than-precocious twelve-year-old boy for your chief of state. At the risk of belaboring the obvious, do you see a pattern emerging here? Hmmm?"

"Go ahead, rub it in," she replied. "In general, I guess we deserve such jibes but don't include me with the jerks that supported those revolts. The only rebel from the West who ever succeeded was Constantine, as you will insist on calling him, the Great. Every other one paid with his head impaled on a pole. But, in spite of the odds, too many of us never seem to learn."

"Do you sometimes wonder," I said, "whether anyone pays any attention at your government and history seminars? Events over the past dozen years or so tend to cast doubts on their effectiveness."

"At a superficial glance," she replied, "the more shallow minded among us might arrive at that conclusion. However, you must remember that neither Magnus Maximus nor Arbogast ever attended my lectures."

"Well said. By the way, what has been the public attitude to the appointments here in Gaul that Theodosius and Stilicho made since the defeat of Arbogast?"

"Same circus, different clowns." She shrugged. "No one seems to care very much."

We then returned to better things.

Her villa had an indoor bath, so after indulging ourselves there during the afternoon, we left for the banquet. On the ride into the city, I explained how, when I was living at her villa, Chlogius had informed me of the intra-family dispute between Arbogast and Arbitio's family that had ultimately led to Arbitio's switching sides at the Battle of the Frigidus. I mentioned that Stilicho might want to visit her place as a result.

The welcoming speeches were as fawning as ever, and one could notice a number of dozers among the guests before they were over. It was all too remindful of the reception held for young Valentinian in 389. Once again, the praetorian prefect of the Gauls and many of the leading officials of his several dioceses had traveled to Trier for the celebration to honor Honorius. Stilicho's speech was quite upbeat. Afterward, I introduced him to Margareta, and arrangements were made for him and Honorius to visit her villa the following day. After the banquet was over, we dropped by her home in the city to pick up a couple of servants to get the villa shipshape for the imperial visit.

Honorius was only twelve, very awkward in many respects, stunted in stature and mind. The danger signs were all there and had been duly observed by the notables at the banquet. Tragically, every male descendent of Theodosius I without exception would be immature and inadequate. They would all, however, have one thing going for them. During the fourth century, the concept of a hereditary monarchy had taken deep root. From the time that Constantine I established himself as sole emperor seven decades earlier, no usurper had succeeded in taking the throne. A dynasty might come to an end, as Constantine's did with Julian, but all attempts to overthrow the reigning imperial family would end in failure.

Margareta, childless herself, was very good with children, and when the imperial party arrived the next day, she treated our young emperor very well. Stilicho and I, and several other members of his party, sat down at the table where Chlogius had informed me about Arbitio, and we enjoyed the view of the Moselle and its wine. During the trip up from Milan, it became known that Stilicho was thinking of extending Honorius's tour to London. This possibility got me to thinking that perhaps I could work in a visit to my family. I asked Stilicho about it but received no direct answer.

"Our immediate purpose here," he replied, "is to secure the Rhine. It will involve inspecting every fortification from Strasbourg to the North Sea and recruiting as many Frankish volunteers from Germany as we can handle. That's all I can say at the present."

Shortly thereafter, our afternoon party came to an end. Just as they were leaving, Honorius ran back to Margareta and threw his arms around her. They hugged and kissed, and Margareta was beaming as the little emperor ran back to the imperial carriage. We stood in the road outside the gate and waved as they headed back to Trier. A short while later, I hitched up another wagon that Margareta had at her villa, and her two servants returned to the city also. We then sat at our by now historically famous table as the warm spring afternoon started to fade and enjoyed some more wine.

"It looks to me," I remarked, "that you've just made a friend in the highest of high places."

"Just when I thought all hope was lost," she laughed, "I find myself in the arms of our emperor himself. By golly, there's life in the old girl yet."

"I thought we had already proved that to our mutual satisfaction," I kidded her. "Should I start getting jealous of the little twerp?"

"He is kind of a woebegone little fellow, isn't he?" she observed. "He certainly must be lonely what with having lost his mother when he was three and then both his stepmother and father within eight months of one another. I'm sure that his sister, Serena, will do her best for him, but she has her own young family to think about. Besides, a sister can't extend the love to a young boy that a mother can."

"If you ever get tired of life here in Trier, then you might just have an opening available at the palace in Milan. You've really made a hit with young Honorius."

"Thanks but no thanks," Margareta replied. "I'll stay where I am. I couldn't get a word out of him when he first arrived, but by the end, we were getting along famously. At the same time, I couldn't help but remind myself that he was the successor to Constantine the Great, Julian the Apostate, and Valentinian I. Try as I may, I just cannot picture Honorius, sword in hand, galloping off to keep the barbarians at bay."

"Yes," I said, "it does appear that the weakest of all links has been added to the chain. Of course, he is just a child. But based on the way Arcadius has turned out, I wouldn't bet the villa here on any great leap forward in the intellectual development of his little brother."

"What do you think is going to happen with Alaric?" Margareta asked, abruptly changing the subject.

"Nothing good. The catastrophe in Greece shows plainly the bankruptcy of our trying to resolve the strategic danger that he poses to us on the cheap. We keep hoping that Alaric will transform into a responsible Roman, but that does not appear likely. In 391 and 395, the decision was made to give him one more chance. Well, we certainly know what he did with this last opportunity, don't we? There is also a psychological dimension to the conflict with Alaric. The longer that we delay confronting him, the stronger he grows in the public mind and his own. By letting him off the hook twice, we have enhanced his reputation to the point where he is now regarded by many as being the equal of any of our top generals. He's not. He has never 'won' anything on his own. He is no friend of Rome and neither are any of his followers. Since the East refuses to oppose him, that responsibility will probably wind up on Stilicho's doorstep once again. If it does then large numbers of western troops will have to be used to defeat him. Alaric poses a similar strategic danger to the empire that usurpers always have. Stilicho will never be able to guard the frontiers properly as long as he has to look over his shoulder to see what the Visigoths are doing in the Balkans."

"In other words, in spite of the fact that Gaul and Italy have the same population, roughly five million each, Italy's strategic requirements will always come before those of Gaul?"

"Exactly darlin'," I replied, "but you must remember that Italy is far richer than Gaul."

"The widely held view of Stilicho is that he is far more of a diplomat than he is a general," Margareta went on. "Even at the Frigidus, Stilicho was subordinate to Timasius, and the only campaign in which he was ever in complete command was that first engagement with Alaric back in, when was it, 392? In any case, Theodosius called it off for political reasons. There is a growing feeling here in Gaul that Stilicho may not really be up to the job and that the only reason he is generalissimo in the West is due to his connection with the imperial family. Many of the people here in Gaul who are usually in the know had rarely, if ever, heard of Stilicho prior to our defeat last September."

"Stilicho's political actions prior to the Frigidus," I reminded her, "that led to Arbitio's changing sides cost thousands of lives and swung the victory to Theodosius. Generally, I agree with your assessment of him. However, if Stilicho should 'accommodate' Alaric in any way in the future, then I think he will be letting his hopes outweigh his experience."

"Well," Margareta said, "you're certainly confirming my longstanding suspicions that the government's policy toward Alaric and his crowd is shear escapism that is designed to ward off confrontation at almost any cost."

"The cost I fear will be the West beyond the Alps," I answered, "should anything go wrong here. The frontier garrisons are probably as good as ever. But the Army of Gaul is now a de facto imperial field army, meaning that it will be treated by Stilicho like the two Theodosius created in the East."

"Wait a minute," she interrupted. "You're saying that our field army won't be returning? I thought that several regiments already had."

"Correct. But Italy counts for more than Gaul. Should Alaric pose any threat to Italy, then that is where the West's military focus will reside. We don't know where Alaric will go next. The regiments that you referred to might be the only ones from the original Gallic field army that do return here. But they will be incapable of dealing with any massive invasion on their own should one occur. That is why it is so important for the current stalemate between Milan and Constantinople to be resolved. Until the two capitals agree, we will never be able to construct a coherent policy to deal with the Visigoths. The only reality that Alaric understands is a sword pointed at his throat."

"And the moment it is taken away," Margareta added, "we are back at square one. What do you know about Eutropius?"

"Not much. The most bothersome thing is that the real political leader of the East is once again a man with no military background. Gainas is Stilicho's ally, and our best hope is that Eutropius will utilize him as his chief general. That would facilitate cooperation between the two capitals on military matters and presumably lead to a coordinated campaign against Alaric."

"So be it," Margareta said. "But if there is no agreement, then what?"

There was an awkward silence on my part.

"Then," I started slowly, "other barbarians will be emboldened to emulate Alaric. The message we have been sending into Germany since the day Theodosius started accommodating the Visigoths is that future aggressors may be able to accomplish the same end. They may no longer have to worry about paying an overly high price for attacking us. The longer we play chess with Alaric, the less of a deterrent to invasions our army will appear to be."

We savored an early dinner and then retired for the evening.

The next morning, our regiment embarked on a schedule that alternated between training exercises and border patrol activity. Two of the cavalry regiments that had preceded us had left for Britain shortly before we arrived. We were surprised to hear this but didn't think much of it at the time. We should have. During May and June, Stilicho and his staff spent a great deal of time successfully negotiating with German Franks to provide recruits for the army. As had often been the case in the past, these agreements permitted the settling of thousands more Franks on the Roman side of the Rhine. Our regiment was conducting border patrols when the announcement was made. Since we were geographically convenient, we were ordered to help in the supervision of the crossing. It came off without any major problems and the new immigrants were settled in northern Gaul with their distant relatives.

After ten days of such activity, we received new orders. Earlier in the year, intelligence had determined that an alliance had been formed between Saxons in northwest Germany and the Picts of Caledonia. There were rumors that some Scottish tribes in Ireland might be planning to act in concert with these two by attacking Britain along the northwest coast of Wales. It was then that we learned where the two regiments that had preceded us were situated. One was positioned in eastern Britain between Brancaster, on the south shore of the entrance of the Wash, and Colchester. It was along that portion of the coast that the Saxons had most recently struck but with little success. The second regiment was positioned in Chester to assist Legion XX Valeria Victrix in combating the Scots if and when they arrived. My regiment and the one that was accompanying us were heading for Hadrian's Wall. It was announced that Honorius would be returning to Milan and that Stilicho would soon be leaving for London for meetings with the vicar of the Diocese of Britain. Subsequently he would be establishing his headquarters in York to conduct the defense of the island.

We covered the three-hundred-mile distance from Trier to Boulogne in a little over three weeks. Then we sailed under escort of a fleet of powerful dromon warships from the British Fleet. After a brief stopover in Dover, we sailed for the port of Newcastle. It is on the Tyne River near the eastern end of the most famous defensive fortification the empire ever built. The distance from Dover to Newcastle is a little over three hundred miles by sea, and the only port that we put into during this time was Brancaster. Fortunately, the weather held, and we saw no sign of any

Saxon pirate fleets. Traveling up the east coast of Britain gives one an excellent idea of just how sparsely populated the island is relative to other dioceses. The region between the Thames estuary and the Wash, that bulges out into the North Sea, is a rich farming area containing many large estates. Their main crops are wheat and barley. Farther inland, where it is hillier, sheep ranches prevail. Proceeding northward along the coast, we could see several of these villas on the Black Water River estuary near Colchester. North of there, the population thins out. There are few major port facilities along the east coast because there is little need for them. We often traveled long distances without seeing any sign of human activity on land or sea. Near the end of August, we arrived at Newcastle.

Hadrian's Wall was constructed between 122 and 136, generally in an east to west manner. Its purpose is to act as a demarcation line between barbarism and civilization and to control traffic between the two. On too many occasions, it has had to act as a barrier. It was built by the three legions permanently stationed in Britain, although, once completed, they did not provide the troops to man it. It extends from Wallsend, at the beginning of the Tyne River estuary, westward just over seventy-three miles to Bowness on the south shore of Solway Firth. At first sight, the wall appeared somewhat smaller than I had always imagined it, and as a result, my immediate reaction was one of disappointment. Being familiar with the towering walls of Rome, Constantinople, and numerous other cities and fortresses, I had expected Hadrian's Wall to be of comparable size. Such is not the case. It stands twenty feet high and measures from six to ten feet in thickness. (The latter dimension includes the parapet along its north face.) When first constructed, small forts called mile castles were attached to the wall on its south side to control passage through it in both directions. Such fortifications typically measure sixty by fifty feet, have front and rear gates with double doors, and possess a tower over the northern gate. They can house as many as thirty-two men. Between the mile castles, two turrets were erected in the wall. They measure two stories in height and are spaced one-third of a mile apart from one another and their nearest mile castle. They are generally manned by six soldiers. While construction was underway, a major revision was made to the original plan: it was decided to incorporate fifteen major forts into the wall. The area north of the wall had proven to be more difficult to manage than had initially been envisaged. These forts are designed to house units of varying sizes and nature and have granaries attached that can hold up to one year's worth of food supplies. Soon after it had "opened for business," it was realized that the wall had, in some respects, been overdesigned. As a result, a number of the mile castles and turrets were closed. So too were some of the small forts that lined the Cumberland coast because the danger from that direction had been overestimated. While I served in northern Britain, the following types of units were assigned either to the wall forts or the advanced screening forts north of the wall and towers along the Cumberland coast to the south of the west end of the wall:

- three 512-man standard cavalry regiments
- one thousand-man augmented cavalry regiment
- two 480-man standard infantry regiments
- two thousand-man augmented infantry regiments
- seven five-hundred-man standard infantry/cavalry regiments
- two thousand-man augmented infantry/cavalry regiments

This gives a nominal force total of eleven thousand men under the command of the duke of Britain. By the time I arrived there, however, this number had been reduced considerably from what the "full-strength" numbers imply. The revolt of Magnus Maximus in 383, while he was count of Britain, had resulted in Theodosius's shipping several thousand British cavalry troops that had served in the usurper's army to the East once that war was over. These men were drawn from regiments stationed on the wall and in the island's mobile central reserve. Their numbers were never replaced. As a result, when it came to launching the current campaign against the Picts, Scots, and Saxons, Stilicho had been forced to transfer units from the continent to assist the reduced British garrisons. Many individual British regiments with which we campaigned were at less than half-strength. Instead of combining the most seriously reduced units into larger ones, the duke of Britain had decided to leave them as they were, with a view to building them back up to full strength over the long haul. He had been partly successful at this when the current danger arose.

The transfer of thousands of British soldiers and their families to Illyria and Thrace after 388 created special recruiting problems for Britain. Northern Britain and Caledonia are sparsely populated. British units recruit locally to a very high degree, and by "locally," I mean British and not barbarian. The recruiting pool in northern Britain has never been large to begin with. Some recruits from north of Hadrian's Wall would enroll in our regiments occasionally but not in great numbers. Very few Picts have ever joined the Roman Army. In any event, the population of the Caledonian highlands is so small that the Picts have generally posed more of a tactical problem than a strategic threat. Nonetheless, the strength of our shrunken units on the wall had been reduced to the point where assistance from the continent would be required when any major threat to it appeared. They could not be built back to full strength from the indigenous population.

The designations of the regiments that man the wall strike one who is new to the area as odd for units that are all recruited locally. Exotic names, such as the First Spanish Asturian Cavalry Regiment, the First Dacian Infantry Regiment, and the Second Thracian Infantry/Cavalry Regiment echo their far-distant origins. The soldiers currently enrolled in these regiments have never seen the lands where their units originated. But some of them are descended from the soldiers that first garrisoned the wall almost three hundred years ago.

The wall starts at Wallsend where the Tyne River estuary begins. It follows the Tyne Gap and the Eden Valley that separate the Pennine Mountains to the south from the Cheviot Hills to the north, throughout its length. It proceeds westward, north of the Tyne, across a region known as the Central Plain of Britain. This plain starts on the east coast and sweeps south down and around the Pennine Mountains in somewhat of a U shape, coming back up their west flank to the area at the west end of the wall. The Central Plains are a rich farming area, and there are numerous large estates in the Ouse River Valley that wends its way south toward York and the North Sea. Their main crops are wheat and oats. The part of the Central Plains lying to the west of the Pennines, however, is virtually undeveloped and no great estates have been established there. After crossing the eastern part of this plain, the wall climbs into the hill country formed by the Cheviot Hills and the Pennines. Apart from the towns that have grown up around certain major fortresses along the wall, the population density rapidly declines in this area. The soil is of a poorer quality than is found in the Central Plains, and agriculture is limited to small farms and the raising of sheep. Most of the wall resides in this hill country before descending back down to the Central Plains again at its western end.

Shortly after our arrival at Newcastle, we departed for a fortress that lies roughly ten miles north of Carlisle and its associated wall fort, Stanwix, toward the wall's western end. It is called Netherby and has to be one of the loneliest postings in the empire. Already stationed there was the First Spanish Aelian Infantry Regiment. It was originally an augmented regiment of a thousand men but was now drastically under strength. To get to our new base, we took the highway called the Military Way that runs close by the wall for almost its entire length. There are two highways leading north from Hadrian's Wall toward Caledonia. The eastern one runs from Halton north through our other advanced fort at High Rochester and on to the south shore of the Firth of Forth. The western highway runs from Carlisle through Stanwix and Netherby to the western end of the old Antonine Wall. The western highway has fallen into disrepair beyond Netherby, though many sections are still passable.

Hadrian's Wall was completed in 136. Two years later, Hadrian died. His successor, Antoninus Pius, extended the northern frontier to the northwest by one hundred miles to the narrowest part of the island: the line running from the Firth of Clyde on the west to the Firth of Forth on the east. Ideally, this is where Hadrian's Wall should have been built, but perhaps that emperor felt that constructing his wall there would have proven too confrontational to the Caledonian tribes to the north. In any event, Antoninus Pius ordered a new wall to be built along this line. Its construction began in 142. The same three legions that constructed Hadrian's Wall must have been rather disgruntled to find themselves employed in the construction of the wall of his successor just six years after the completion of the first. The Antonine Wall, made entirely of turf, is a decidedly down-market version of its predecessor. Given its building material and the fact that its length is only about thirty-seven miles long, it took only one year to construct it. While it is about fifteen feet wide, it is only ten feet in height. It originally contained nineteen forts, most of which were destroyed by our army when this line was finally abandoned for Hadrian's Wall in 186. However, several forts of the more northerly wall were maintained into the 200s as advance observation posts to guard against any hostile actions by the Picts who live to the north of it.

Our intelligence had been correct on the issue of the Picts, Saxons, and the Scots of Ireland planning an attack on Britain. Nonetheless, formulating and coordinating alliances between barbarians that speak three different languages and that reside on as many different land masses separated by large expanses of water are problematical to say the least. As a result, their attack on Britain was late in coming. There was another reason why it took longer than expected for the situation to develop. That was because of the highly original approach taken to secure the northern frontier three decades earlier. Once his armies had re-secured the island, Count Theodosius had a series of observation/signal towers constructed along the east coast south of the wall from the Tees River Estuary to Scarborough. They were built to serve a similar purpose to their small fort counterparts on the west coast in Cumberland. During their attacks in the late 360s, the Picts, tired after generations of banging their heads against the wall to no great success, had attacked us by way of a naval end run around it in the east. Thousands of their soldiers had caught us by surprise in that maneuver and had wrought great damage before they were checked and defeated.

The area between Hadrian's Wall and the long-abandoned Antonine Wall is the frontier between the Celtic peoples of Britain and the Picts of Caledonia. The Picts are not a Celtic nationality. They are the remnant of the aboriginal people that lived throughout Britain prior to the arrival of the Celts, centuries before the arrival of the Romans. North of the Antonine Wall is Caledonia proper, and since the late 200s, the Picts had become far more aggressive than they had been previously. The Celts living between the two walls have, in general, been favorably disposed toward Rome since our frontier in the north was finalized. But when the West went into revolt as it did in 286 and 350, the Picts attacked the wall and caused havoc in the northern part of the island. When insufficient Roman troops were available to protect them, the Celts, north of Hadrian's Wall, have more or less been forced to go along with the designs of the Picts. Count Theodosius tried to change this. He appointed four men to rule as prefects over the four main Celtic tribal groupings north of the wall. From Rome's standpoint, they were to act as our clients and on our behalf in their territories. To the people they ruled, they were kings in all but name. As required, their small tribal armies would be supplied by Rome and supported by Roman units from the wall when the Picts threatened. Now this new arrangement was to be put to the test for the first time.

I do not wish to exaggerate the size of the threat facing us. The whole enterprise turned out to be not a major campaign at all. Instead, it was a series of small, relatively minor engagements involving only a few hundred troops to a side, due in part to the difficulties of coordination between our enemies.

In early September, I led my cavalry squadron north from Netherby on a deep reconnaissance patrol. It was conducted in cooperation with soldiers from the Selgovian tribe that resides to the immediate north of the western section of the wall. I was able to converse with these tribesmen in my native Celtic, but it was not always easy, especially since the dialects are somewhat different. I had hardly spoken any Celtic in the fifteen years that I had been away from the island. It was awkward at first to start thinking in that language again. From Netherby, we traveled the old Roman highway that heads northwest before heading north into the Southern Caledonian Uplands. Not long out of Netherby, we crossed the Esk River that empties into Solway Firth. The valley of this river is low lying and quite swampy. Once again, I had to marvel at the ingenuity of the original army engineers who constructed the highway through this area three centuries earlier. Crossing points on the lower reaches of the river are limited. The route the builders followed lies along the only ridge in the vicinity that always remains above flood level. Almost twenty miles out of Netherby, we passed by the old Hadrianic fort of Birrens located on a small plateau. It had been abandoned back in 184 during the reign of Commodus. The road's quality was not of the highest order, but given that we had abandoned this region two centuries earlier, we couldn't really complain. This scouting expedition would be tinged with sadness throughout. Beyond Birrens, there is greater relief to the land, and while crossing over one of these hills, we saw a long-abandoned signal station platform. On several occasions, we passed by other Roman highways branching off our own either to the west or the northeast. These only served to remind us that in the past we had been greater than in our own lifetimes. It wasn't the same sort of shrinkage that I had witnessed on the continent that had been caused from pressure from without. Nonetheless, the unnerving sight of these abandoned forts, signal stations, and highways signified retreat nonetheless.

Once we reached the Annan River, the highway turned straight north, and we continued up the east side of the Annandale. We passed around several low mountain ranges and across their associated valleys that run in a southwest to northeast direction. We passed by two more abandoned Roman forts. The elevation increased, and we eventually reached the point where we were in a region of desolate moors that was several hundred feet higher than we had been back in Netherby. We saw very few people in this area of rough and hilly grasslands and occasional bogs. The ones we did see were mainly sheepherders. The numerous quarry pits that provided building materials for the road bed are still visible at various points along the highway in spite of the passage of time. Having made it into the true uplands, we started to transfer from the upper reaches of the Annandale west to the valley of the Clyde River. Upon reaching the north-flowing Clyde, we stayed overnight on the grounds of what had once been a large Roman Army camp. From this point, we would start our gradual descent to the Caledonian lowlands to the north. In this area, a lengthy stretch of the highway clings to the lower reaches of the steep hillsides that rise above the Clyde. We had to exercise caution because in places rockslides covered part of the highway and in a few spots the outer portions of the road had slid down toward the river. None of these obstacles proved insurmountable. We were constantly on the alert for an ambush, but nothing of that sort happened.

We were stricken by a sudden downpour along this section, but as luck would have it, we were within easy reach of the by now crumbling Crawford Castle. In spite of having been abandoned for two centuries, enough of it was sufficiently usable to afford shelter until the weather cleared. It had been our main fortress on the upper Clyde. At Crawford, we were surprised to discover another Roman highway paralleling our own on the opposite side of the river. It went off to the southwest, where it entered the Nith River Valley that parallels the Annandale about fifteen miles to the west. The two highways joined at Crawford. We had been blessed by the fact that most of the bridges along our route were still serviceable. After crossing the bridge to the other side of the river, I started down this other highway for a short distance. Staring down that road, I almost swore that I could see the ghosts of our Roman predecessors from centuries past.

Thus far, we had discovered no suspicious activity. None of the locals we spoke to had seen or heard anything about an impending attack against Hadrian's Wall. Or if they had, they weren't admitting it. Having no choice, we pressed northward. We had proceeded cautiously throughout the operation. After entering the uplands, I had forbidden the setting of fires at night so as not to give our position away. All the same, even more vigilance was called for now because the lowlands, which we were now approaching, have the highest population density of any region in Caledonia.

North of Crawford, the highway climbs over a large hill before returning to the riverside. We soon came to an intersection. According to my map, the highway we were on continued northeast all the way to the south shore of the Firth of Forth on the east side of the island. The highway branching off to our left crossed the Clyde by bridge and continued northwest to the western end of the Antonine Wall. We were halfway there. I decided to take this latter route. After traveling about ten miles through the hills, we settled down for the evening while it was still light. Not long after dark, we sighted a glow to the north of us. We carefully made our way toward it but it seemed to take forever to get there. Finally we spotted the campfires of the Picts and their Celtic allies. They were encamped by the old Roman fortress of Castle Dykes. There was no need to get too close since in the days ahead they would be coming to us. I decided to withdraw to a more secure location at a higher elevation. With the exception of when we stayed at former Roman forts in bad weather, we had always camped well off the road so as not to arouse the suspicions of the Picts if and when any of them came our way. We were always careful to remove all evidence of our ever having camped anywhere. The following day, from our high vantage point, we could see the Pict's army coming south. We estimated their number to be no more than about seven hundred men.

I sent one of my subdecurions and two others back to Carlisle with the enemy force estimate, along with their current axis of approach. Over the next couple of days, we withdrew southward through the uplands with the army of the Picts and Celts following us. We almost never let them out of our sight because of the possibility that they might suddenly turn left up one of the valleys to strike the wall in a more central location. My subdecurion and his team returned from Carlisle to tell me that plans were well underway to provide an appropriate reception. The enemy approach did not change. They stuck to the highway until they emerged from the southern edge of the uplands. At that point, they were about twenty-five miles from Netherby. By that time, we had withdrawn to join the other units with which our regiment was associated in a defensive position about ten miles to the west of our fort. These were the Mauritanian Regiment from Burgh-by-Sands, the Gallic Petriana Cavalry Regiment from Stanwix, the Second Tongrian Infantry/Cavalry Regiment from Castlesteads, and the First Spanish Aelian Infantry Regiment from Netherby. The Pict's army must have been stunned at what they saw awaiting them. We later learned that they had heard of the problems that the Visigoths had caused in Greece. The duke of Britain had "withdrawn" a number of regiments from the western end of the wall and spread the rumor to the north that these units were headed for Europe. Actually, they had only been transferred temporarily into the Pennines to the south. The Picts fell for the ruse. Prisoners taken admitted they had also concluded that the central government would be incapable of sending reinforcements to the island at any time in the near future. They paid a heavy price for their miscalculations.

The Picts were not well organized. Along our entire European frontier, they are among the least advanced of any of the enemies we face. Our biggest difficulty with Britain was that problems in Europe had always prevented us from completing the island's conquest and frequently delayed our responding to enemy attacks there. None such would concern us this time. Where the Picts had expected to find almost no one, they found an army far larger than their own. They certainly did not lack courage but they did lack cavalry. After a delay, as they sized us up, they led a charge complete with blood-curdling war cries into the center of our line in an attempt to divide us in two. In a standard, classic maneuver, the center of our line, composed entirely of infantry, yielded ground while our cavalry encompassed the enemy from both sides. The Picts were mainly infantry and our cavalry units successfully hemmed them in like the Visigoths had done to us at Hadrianople. The Picts and their allies, although seeing that their situation was hopeless, fought bravely. The battle started in the middle of the afternoon and lasted into the early evening. Finally, when small groups of the Picts started to surrender, one group broke and ran for the north. Had this battle taken place in southern Europe, they might have been able to get away in the dark. However, at the high latitude of northern Britain, the twilight lasts much longer during the summer. Our regiment was ordered after those fleeing the battleground and we cut them down without mercy. So far as we knew, no one escaped, but one can never be certain of such things. Orders had come down that no stragglers were to make it back to Caledonia. We wanted the Picts in the homeland to be totally mystified by what had happened to this army of theirs that had marched off into oblivion.

The battle over, we tended our wounded, cremated the enemy dead after killing off their most seriously wounded, carted our dead back to their respective bases, and marched enemy captives off in the direction of slavery in the southern part of the island. However soundly we had defeated the Picts in the west, their fellow nationals on the other side of the island had coordinated their attacks with the Saxons with great precision. The Picts attempted to outflank the eastern end of Hadrian's Wall by launching a naval attack south of it in the manner that they had three decades earlier. This time, however, military intelligence, with help from our Celtic allies north of the wall, enabled the Roman side to anticipate the timing and the nature of the onslaught. As a result, we were far better prepared to withstand it.

Stilicho had ordered a large number of ships over from the continent and stationed most of them at Brough-on-Humber. Only a small number were stationed at Newcastle because its harbor facilities are quite restricted. The ships had been drawn from the lower Saxon Shore forts and as far away as the Rhine Fleet. Constant patrols were initiated along the east coast from Bridlington Bay north to well beyond Hadrian's Wall. When the attack came, our victory was swift and complete. The Picts had originally intended to land further south along the coast, but our concentrated patrolling forced them to land in the region where Count Theodosius had constructed the lookout towers. The warning went out and our naval squadrons were quickly on the scene to destroy the Pict's fleet. Once again, only small numbers of men were involved.

When in London, Stilicho had had the count of Britain, who commanded the subfield army on the island, divide his forces, placing half of them north of York to fend off the Picts and the other half in the region between the Wash and the Thames to defend against the Saxons. There are not many large estates in the northern part of the province, so damage was minimal. Before the Picts had penetrated far inland, they were contained and defeated after suffering very heavy casualties. At the same time, a smaller fleet of Saxons ships than we expected attempted a landing on the east coast between the Wash and the Thames. They were intercepted by our British Fleet. An impressive number of enemy ships were sunk well off the coast; dozens of Saxon soldiers drowned as a result. Their bodies washed up along the coastline for weeks. Many of those who made it ashore did not fare much better. A few large estates not far from the sea were attacked and set afire. These fires served as beacons for our counterattacking forces. It took several weeks to track the Saxons down but hunted down they were and killed in large numbers. Our casualties, in comparison, were far fewer.

The Scots of Ireland did not attack with their supposed allies. However, late in 396, some of them landed along the west coast of Wales. They met with no resistance and were not expelled. The south coast of Wales has been settled in the traditional Roman manner and the north coast has been fortified for centuries. But central and western Wales have been almost completely untouched by Roman civilization. There is a highway running the length of the western part of the country from Caernarvon in the north to Carmarthen in the south. Only a handful of small forts were built along its length, all of which are abandoned now. While a few highways penetrate the interior, no Roman has ever settled there. In fact, large tracts of central and western Wales are uninhabited. Travel in this area is difficult because the heavy annual rainfall makes any dirt road frequently impassable. The west coast of Wales is quite rugged and is frequently shrouded in rain and mist. The few people that do inhabit this region live in a mountainous isolation from one another. In late 396, Rome had more pressing things to consider than small groups of Irish invaders on the west coast of Wales. Nonetheless, it was an omen.

During the remainder of the year, we patrolled north of the wall to ensure that the Picts had learned their recent lessons well. On such patrols, as with our deep reconnaissance during the summer, everyone in my squadron was touched by just how lonely and empty these lands really are. Looking across the hills and crags, mile after mile for as far as the eye could see, there would be very little sign of human activity in any direction. In our entire military careers, none of us had felt more isolated than we did on those patrols. One thing to be said in its favor, though, is that it certainly is excellent cavalry country. On several occasions, I led my troops back up into the uplands. We explored many trackless valleys in this region, but only on occasion did we come across anyone, and they were just peasant families. How anybody could live such solitary lives was beyond any of us, but the most important thing as far as we were concerned was that everything appeared quiet. When the weather was nasty, we trained indoors. Netherby has a large indoor cavalry hall that was constructed back in 222 to permit indoor training when the weather is inclement. It was typical of those located at other fortresses housing cavalry regiments throughout Europe. There was no further enemy military activity along the wall that year.

I do not wish to give a distorted presentation of our scouting activities along the wall. All mobile units there must conduct patrols to the south of the barrier as well as the north. These patrols are not against rebels but rather against Caledonians who have managed to get over the wall at night in some area where patrolling activity was light at the time. On several occasions, we had to track down bandit gangs who had penetrated our defenses in such a manner and committed crimes in the settlements to the south. Usually these men, once captured, were immediately shipped south and into slavery, as long as they had not murdered anyone.

While the weather was obviously more awkward then, I preferred to patrol in the winter rather than in the summer. As long as the snow cover was light it was much easier to trail intruders through their footprints. In the worst such instance with which I was involved, a group of five bandits climbed the wall at night and attacked a small farmstead several miles to the south. My troops and I discovered their footprints about a mile north of the wall early the following morning. We followed them to the point where they had climbed over it, and then we passed through the nearest mile castle and continued to follow the trail until we came to the farmstead. The scene was terrible: the farmer and his older son had been murdered and one girl had been raped when the gangster's lookout warned of our approach. We had not seen the men leave the farmhouse because they had kept low and dropped down into a small ravine close to the house that hid them from our view. Following their trail was easy. We caught up to them within a short time and quickly captured them. I had my men execute all five on the spot and then had a burial detail from the nearest fortress come out to dispose of the corpses.

411

The invasion by the Huns into eastern Anatolia in the previous year had struck fear into the hearts of everyone in the eastern Mediterranean. They had captured several thousand Roman citizens and attempted to drive them into slavery. The timely arrival of our Army of the East had resulted in the crushing of this assault. This victory was an enormous morale booster for the entire empire. Nonetheless, throughout 396 people in the East feared that another such invasion would materialize soon. The Hunnish attack on Iran in 395 had also met with a humiliating defeat. Hasty diplomacy between the two assured that Romans and Iranians would act in concert with one another in the event of any future activity by the Huns through the Caucasus. In 396, this sector remained quiet.

For someone brought in from the outside, like myself, and temporarily assigned along the wall, it could be a very lonely existence. I had anticipated this possibility and brought some books along with me for study and entertainment. Our fort was ten miles north of the wall and had only a few civilian buildings associated with it. However, we were blessed by the fact that Carlisle, the most northerly provincial capital in the empire, lay only ten miles to the south. A sizable civilian town, covering over thirty acres, has grown up around the original fortress, although it is not as large as any of the Rhineland or Danube towns where I had served.

On January 1, 397, I once again swore my oath of allegiance to Arcadius and Honorius. Shortly into the New Year, I met a young woman in Carlisle named Helena Teresa. She was a twenty-two-year-old widow. Her husband had been a soldier in the Gallic Petriana Cavalry Regiment and had been killed in action against the Picts in an earlier battle. She worked in her father's tailoring and leather goods store where I had gone on occasion to get my kit repaired. We fell in love almost instantly and were soon in the midst of a most passionate relationship. Things were obviously quite serious between us, and we talked of getting married, but after several months, she started to back away. Perhaps we had overreacted to one another and became involved too soon. She had already lost one husband in the army and was hesitant to run the risk of losing another. She also did not like the idea of having to leave her family so far behind if we did get married. We remained friends but gradually drifted apart. The last time I saw her, she mentioned that she had met someone new. I was genuinely glad to hear it and wished her the very best. I always had the highest regard for her and I still think of her often. She is always in my prayers.

By the spring, the campaigning season was once more upon us. The previous year, Stilicho had stationed a small flotilla of ships at Cardiff, Neath, and Carmarthen on the south shore of Wales. Its purpose was to defend against any incursion from Ireland against southern Britain via Bristol Channel. Such an attack did come but the Irish were defeated and forced to surrender shortly after they landed on the north coast. On the east coast, the main assault came from the Saxons. They were met at sea and heavily defeated once again. The Picts attacked in conjunction with the Saxons, but this time their attack was launched against the center and the eastern end of the wall. They refrained from launching any sea attacks and left the western end of the wall alone. Their land assaults failed as bloodily as their sea and land offensive had the previous year. Again, all these attacks involved relatively small numbers of men. By this time, Stilicho had already left Britain for Milan. He could no longer abide the disgusting manner in which Alaric was savaging southern Greece without the government in Constantinople lifting a finger to do anything about it. Admittedly, Eutropius and his fellow ministers had to consider the danger posed by the Huns against Syria and eastern Anatolia. Alaric's attack on Greece was not the only item on their plate. Diplomacy with the Iranians, however, appeared to have resolved the jeopardous situation on the Euphrates, at least for the time being. Still, Constantinople refused to do anything about Alaric.

As a result of the casualties suffered recently by the regiments defending the central part of the wall, we were transferred to a more easterly location in August. For the rest of the summer, we patrolled the region north of the wall in conjunction with the Second Spanish

Asturian Cavalry Regiment. There were no major incidents. Then in late September, our tribune, Lucius Verennius, ordered the regiment together for a special announcement. We were being transferred to the old legionary fortress of Chester, a goodly distance to the southwest, where Legion XX Valeria Victrix had been stationed for the past three hundred years. The strategic situation had changed. The high command had concluded that Ireland now represented more of a threat than Caledonia. Our sister regiment, which had been stationed at Chester when we first arrived on the island, had already been transferred down to Caerleon near the north shore of the Mouth of the Severn. It had participated in the recent actions against the Irish there.

Leaving Hadrian's Wall we traveled down the eastern side of the Pennines to York. To the north of the Tees River, we entered a rich agricultural area of large estates centered on comfortable villas. Their numbers increased the closer we got to York. Having heard so much about this city over the years, I was glad that we had taken the easterly route to get to our new location. The route down the west side of the Pennines is shorter. However, it would have been more difficult to supply the troops along the way because of the lack of intensive agricultural development in that area. Besides, after ninety miles on the road in warm weather, we were all due for a visit to the legionary baths at York that certainly lived up to their reputation. That city, like London, is a purely Roman creation, having been founded in the year 71 as the fortress for Legion IX Hispana that was later transferred to the Rhineland and then to Armenia. It lies at the confluence of the Ouse and Foss Rivers and has direct access to the North Sea in spite of being located approximately sixty miles inland. Its legionary baths are among the most sumptuous in Britain. The bath building measures three hundred feet square; it seemed all the more impressive for its being located near one of the most isolated frontiers in the empire. The entire city of York is striking with the stately homes of the well-to-do lining both banks of the Ouse River. The stone-walled fortress of Legion VI Victrix lies on the north side of the river while most civilian businesses and living quarters stand on the south.

Shortly after we arrived, our tribune announced that a banquet would be held that evening to which all officers in our regiment were invited. Hosting it would be the duke of Britain whose headquarters is also there. It was a pleasant way of thanking us for all the efforts that we had extended in defending Britain's northern frontier during the past year. Numerous other top commanders also attended. Introductions were made and we sat down to what was unquestionably our finest meal since we arrived on the island. The duke and his associates asked us about our patrolling duties that we had conducted in the southern uplands and the battle that we had fought near Netherby the previous year. In particular, they were interested in the details that we could provide about the Battle of the Frigidus three years earlier. None of them had been there. In return, we obtained details from them on the land and sea campaigns along the east coast for both the previous year and this. Finally, the conversation got around to the situation in Greece.

"Now that we've filled you in about our patrolling and campaigning activities," our tribune said, "perhaps you would be good enough to tell us about what has been going on in the East. With all the time that we've spent patrolling in the uplands, about the only solid information that we received was that Stilicho had taken his field army to Greece to confront Alaric and that there had been another invasion by the Huns."

"That's true," the duke replied. "Earlier this year, the Huns struck again out of the Caucasus invading our two Armenian provinces in the Diocese of Pontus. Once again, our eastern forces inflicted a defeat on them that appears to have been as severe as the one they suffered in 395. The most shocking aspect to this defeat is that no less a personage than Eutropius, the eastern master of offices, traveled to Roman Armenia to take control of the fighting himself."

"What?" I gasped, thinking that perhaps I had overshot my wine limit for the evening.

"Hard to believe, isn't it?" the duke said. "Seasoned soldiers everywhere, in their first reaction, were disgusted to hear it. But give him or it, whatever you want to call him, his due: if the battle had gone the other way, he would have suffered the same as everyone else. I'm certain that the part Eutropius played was minimal. No doubt the marshal of the East and his staff handled the military responsibilities, as they did in 395. In any event, our Asian forces appear to be handling themselves far better against the Huns than was anticipated in many quarters.

"The situation in Greece has improved also, as far as we can tell. Stilicho landed his mobile field army at Corinth to have it out with Alaric once and for all. The isthmus has been blockaded, and a number of small scale battles have been fought, with the Visigoths being bested in every one of them. But no showdown battle yet."

"In addition to his field army," the garrison commander added, "the generalissimo also took much of the Adriatic Fleet with him. This he used to resupply and refortify the ports around the Peloponnese: Aegium and Aegira on the south shore of the Gulf of Corinth, Patras and Dyme on the Gulf of Patras along with Pylus, Methone, Asopus, and almost every other port that you can name around the peninsula. Once fortified, these towns have been used as bases to strike at Alaric's forces almost anywhere we choose. As the duke mentioned, there have been a number of small engagements all around the Peloponnese, 1,500 men to a side at the most, nothing more, and Alaric's army has lost them all."

"It sounds," I said, "like more is being accomplished this time than when we spent four months parked at the foot of Mount Olympus."

"That was too soon after the last civil war," the duke of Britain replied. "Another factor that is impacting Alaric is that he left forces north of Corinth to continue plundering those departments for anything that was missed during their earlier raids. Now, not only can they not join him, but they in turn are under attack by our Army of Illyria from the north, small as its numbers may be to this point. Stilicho has sent some men up from Corinth to help them in this."

"So," the garrison commander continued, "we are hopeful that the Peloponnese will turn out to be Alaric's tomb and that he will have plenty of company in that regard."

The atmosphere was positive regarding Greece, and not before time. If Alaric and his army could be crushed once and for all, then we could concentrate our attention back to the frontiers. Once again, positive indicators would prove be mere prelude to disaster where Alaric was concerned. It had been an excellent feast with most informative conversations, but all too soon it was time to go. Back at our encampment, I requested the following day off from our tribune to attend to some personal business in the city. It was granted, and as things turned out, I would have a long day ahead of me.

The next morning, I headed for the city's basilica. It had been over half my lifetime since Ardovanda and her family had been transferred by my neighbor of so many years ago, Silanus, to his estate here at York. I spent the morning going through town records. Silanus had died in 390, and his estate had been inherited by his three daughters, who were quite a bit older than I. I double-checked to see if he had possessed more than one estate in this vicinity but he had not. His daughters in turn had sold the property. Determining where the place was, I rode out to it. Actually, I had ridden right past it the previous day as our regiment approached York. Coming to the villa, I informed the owner that I was looking for a friend of mine who had been moved to this estate from Cirencester in 381. He said that he wasn't aware of any Franks working as tenant farmers on his land but I was free to ask his tenants about her if I wanted to. I thanked him and spent the whole afternoon doing just that. I managed to track all his tenants down and asked them about Ardovanda and her family. None were Franks, and none had ever heard of any Franks working on this property. I had drawn a blank. I headed back to York and spent that night at the Imperial Post roadhouse.

The following day, I headed southwest from the city and soon rejoined my regiment on the highway that would take us through Manchester to Chester. This route crosses the Pennines at one of their narrowest points. Once again, we found ourselves passing by the large estates of wealthy landowners, but there were fewer of them. Soon there were none at all as we started to climb to the higher elevations. The distance to cross the moors was somewhat over ten miles, after which we started our descent back down to the plains. The distance from Hadrian's Wall to our new location was about 180 miles. Along the way, I started to notice something at the towns that I had also seen along the wall but thought quite proper on the northern frontier. On the wall, some gateways had been either completely bricked up due to overbuilding in the first place or narrowed for the exercise of greater control and protection. In every town that we came to, I noticed the same thing as far as the narrowing of their wall gates was concerned. Even in towns that had so far been beyond the reach of the Picts and the Saxons, the town councils were taking proper precautions. Another sign of the times.

By the middle of October, we were settled into our new quarters at Chester. Its legionary fortress had originally been constructed to house Legion XX Valeria Victrix back in the first century when a legion still contained 5,500 men. It now contained about 1,100, but this did not mean there was plenty of empty space for us. Over the decades, many older buildings had deteriorated and been torn down. Some civilian establishments had sprung up in their place. This had happened in a number of legionary fortress towns. When new independent cavalry regiments were established, they had to be housed either in leftover barracks that were still available or in private homes. About three-quarters of our complement could be housed within the fortress.

We no sooner arrived in Chester than we received some startling news courtesy of the legionary commander. Emperor Arcadius, at the behest of Eutropius, had suddenly declared Stilicho to be a public enemy and ordered him out of Greece. The earlier cooperation that Eutropius had exhibited with Stilicho had been designed to gain time for him to consolidate his own position. For the second time in two years, Arcadius had betrayed himself for the witless fool that he was; a puppet forever to be played by others. Eutropius had perhaps convinced himself that the triumph that the Eastern Empire had scored in Armenia earlier in the year had really been his and his alone. Over the course of the past two years, the eastern master of offices had removed several key army generals from their positions and sent them into exile. He had now been able to go Rufinus one better and all by himself. With "his" victory over the Huns in hand, Eutropius would countenance not the slightest hint of rivalry within his domain. And the proconsulate of Greece was part of the Eastern, not the Western Empire.

Eutropius had raised no objection to Stilicho's taking action against Alaric initially and did not for several months. Why would he? Eutropius was using Stilicho to do what he himself could not or would not do: seriously weaken Alaric and his people to the point where they would be willing to settle down on terms that would be more agreeable to Constantinople. Eutropius, like Rufinus before him, had come to see Stilicho as his foremost personal rival. That was a danger that Alaric would never be. But in recognizing that Alaric posed no personal threat, they failed to see the peril that he represented to the empire as a whole. Stilicho was caught in the same position that he had found himself in at the foot of Mount Olympus. His reaction would be the same.

We quickly settled into our new quarters and started patrolling the north coast of Wales with cavalry and mounted infantry from Legion XX Valeria Victrix. This shoreline runs from Chester, at the head of the Dee River estuary, westward approximately sixty miles to Caernarvon. From there, our naval base at Holyhead on the island of Anglesey conducted patrols southward along the west coast of Wales. I mentioned earlier that toward the end of 396, a small number of people from Ireland had migrated to the Lleyn Peninsula that lies thirty miles to the south of Holyhead. They appeared to pose no danger to us, and the flotilla at Holyhead was able to keep a close eye on them. What we were more concerned with was the danger of a large-scale invasion. The north coast of Wales is thinly populated, and along its entire length, there are only two fortresses and one civilian village. The small number of people who live there are pure Celtic stock. The rugged interior of the country provides excellent pasturage at its higher elevations, while grain crops are grown on the occasional tiny farm that one spots every now and again in the valleys. Mostly, however, it is just empty.

Our first patrol along the coast was uneventful. When we returned to Chester, our regiment and the legion were ordered into the arena for an address by the legionary commander.

"Gentlemen," the prefect began, "I have important information for you. It will no doubt impact us in some fashion but exactly how is impossible to foresee at the moment. To begin with, Gildo, count of Africa, has switched his allegiance from the Western to the Eastern Empire."

A loud series of groans and curses went up from the assembly. The first thing that crossed everyone's mind at that moment was that we might be recalled to the continent to put down the revolt. Gainas had been correct: the death of Rufinus had indeed produced another Rufinus in the form of Eutropius. Once he had solidified his position in the eastern capital, Eutropius started moving against the West or more accurately against Stilicho during the summer of 397. Count Gildo's daughter, Salvina, was married to a cousin of the two emperors on their mother's side. The couple lived in the imperial palace with Arcadius. Salvina had been sent to Constantinople as a hostage during the reign of Theodosius I to secure her father's allegiance. Eutropius used her and her husband, Nebridius, as emissaries to persuade the count of Africa to transfer his loyalty from the West to the East. After being paid a considerable sum of cash, Count Gildo joined Eutropius in his conflict with Stilicho, bringing the provinces contained within the Diocese of Africa with him. Thus, the two imperial brothers, whose control over their domains was entirely out of their hands, were now in conflict with one another. Stilicho had been caught by surprise but not for long.

The legion prefect continued, "Immediately after he had switched his allegiance, Count Gildo announced the termination of all grain shipments to Rome. To counteract this shortage, Lord Stilicho has organized barge trains to transport grain from Gaul down the Rhone River and along the coast to Italy. I will provide more information on this revolt as it becomes available to me."

The answer to the African dilemma lay within Gildo's own family. Extreme hostility had existed between Gildo and his younger brother, Mascazel, for many years. It reached its peak when Gildo switched his allegiance to the East. Mascazel was totally opposed to this and events would prove that he had far more foresight on the issue than did his brother. Feelings at this point became so strained that Mascazel fled Africa in fear for his life and went to Milan. In a most terrifying act of blind revenge, Gildo arrested and executed Mascazel's children. Mascazel had had a successful, though not overly lengthy, military career earlier in his life, so Stilicho outfitted him with sufficient ships and an army drawn from a number of legions in Gaul. It would take several months to put this invasion force together. No African dumb enough to go into rebellion had ever been capable of putting together sufficient forces to defend himself against the central government. Why did Gildo think his luck would be any different unless he had been promised military support by Eutropius? Unfortunately, the legion commander was only halfway through his address.

"There is also news from Illyria," he went on, "and if you thought that the revolt in Africa was disturbing, wait until you hear this. When the Visigoths left the Peloponnese, they headed northwest into Epirus in the western part of the Diocese of Macedonia. They started trashing it just as they had its eastern part in 395. At this point, the government in Constantinople negotiated a settlement with Alaric to stop him from destroying the entire prefecture. We all know by now that Alaric's ideas on 'negotiating' are no better than those of an untutored savage. That point notwithstanding, Constantinople has granted Alaric his wish for a high command in the Roman Army. And not just any command: Alaric is the new marshal of Illyria. He has signed a new federate treaty with Constantinople that we must all hope and pray has more substance and greater longevity to it than did our last pact with them. If we hear of any earthquakes in the vicinity of the eastern capital, it will probably be Emperor Theodosius turning over in his tomb."

At this, an enormous eruption of cursing went up among the assembly of soldiers. "Those stupid sons of bitches," someone yelled, and a great cheer went up from the throng. None of us could initially believe what we had just heard.

"One further item in connection with the foregoing," the legion prefect continued. "The Visigoths captured several thousand Roman citizens during their Illyrian rampage. The most revolting aspect of this new federate treaty is that Alaric and his horde have been allowed to keep their Roman slaves!"

We were all dumbfounded.

Eutropius had completed his predecessor's plan. That pathetic halfwit Arcadius had learned nothing whatever from his father about statecraft. Granting Alaric any command in the Roman Army, let alone such a vital one as this, was the very antithesis of what Theodosius wanted and what Stilicho would never have permitted. The government of the East had obviously descended into a theater-of-the-absurd-become-reality world in which no one could see our strategic dangers clearly. Their sense of reality had completely evaporated. The key word for Theodosius when it came to dealing with the Visigoths was "management," even though the leader of the "nation" that we were attempting to "manage" had tried to murder him. All hope for the success of this policy rested on complete cooperation between Milan and Constantinople. Without a common effort, with the two halves of the empire mutually assisting one another when required, the policy was doomed to failure. There was so much to be gained by cooperating, and yet the two capitals had come to see each as the other's greatest adversary. The empire was dividing into two distinct countries. As things turned out, the treaty did buy four years of peace in Illyria and the West. The East would suffer considerable turmoil from other quarters, but the West would not be directly affected; at least not immediately.

That night at supper in the officer's mess, all the talk concerned the two items that the legion's prefect had addressed.

"Any choice comments on what we heard in the arena this afternoon?" my tribune asked.

"I would expect," I replied, "that in due course we will be informed that the agreement with Alaric is a one-time-only, special dispensation for him alone that will not be repeated for any other barbarian cutthroat under any circumstances."

"Quite so, until the next time," my tribune responded.

"With Stilicho," one of the decurions said, "being declared a public enemy by the government of the East, do you think we are going to have to endure another civil war? We are all getting bloody-well fed up with the mindless self-destructiveness that those who govern us have exhibited over the last fourteen years. At least if things go wrong, this time historians will not be able to blame the West."

"If there was going to be a civil war," I suggested, "then Stilicho would have marched his army to Constantinople, not back to Milan. Stilicho is a strict constitutionalist. When given an order signed by an emperor, he will obey it even when he knows full well that the emperor in question is a complete idiot who probably doesn't even know that the order exists. Eutropius probably stuck a pile of papers in front of Arcadius, telling him that they contained nothing of import, just minor routine items that required the imperial signature. The dummy no doubt signed them all while reading none, and the rest, to coin a phrase is history. We should all bear in mind, however, that the end result of Rufinus' getting Arcadius to order Stilicho out of Macedonia in 395 was that Rufinus was butchered before the year was out. I would expect Stilicho to react to the treachery of Eutropius just as he did to that of Rufinus."

We were all stunned by the suddenness and quick pace with which events had unfolded during the few weeks since we had left Hadrian's Wall. Another decurion spoke up: "It's ironic, isn't it? After all the devastation and slaughter of innocents that he has caused in Macedonia and Greece, Alaric is now charged with defending them."

"Yes," Lucius Verennius agreed. "Clever fellow that Alaric. By trashing such wide swaths of the place, he has certainly made his new job easier, hasn't he? After all, there can't be very much left to defend by now."

We all laughed at this gallows humor but at the same time we realized there was nothing funny here at all.

"It just occurred to me," I said. "Now that Alaric is marshal of Illyria, the government in Constantinople will consider his army as just another Roman field army. It would be nice if the Visigoths felt the same way."

"What a hope!" a legionary centurion chimed in.

"Indeed," I replied, "but as marshal of Illyria, Alaric will have control over not only his federate army but also our Army of Illyria. It falls under his jurisdiction."

"Jesus Christ!" my tribune erupted. "I never thought of that, but you're right. Can anybody see the commander of the Army of Illyria taking orders from Alaric if he feels that they are not in Rome's best interests?"

"No," the legionary centurion replied, "but we will certainly have the makings of a most confusing civil war when he doesn't."

"Eutropius' granting of Alaric's demand," Lucius Verennius said, "is ridiculous. Alaric can be either a Roman or a Visigoth insofar as his military ambitions are concerned. He cannot be both. I cannot imagine how the Illyrians must feel, both soldiers and civilians. But it just occurred to me that there is an aspect to Alaric's wanting his high Roman military office beyond simply satisfying his ego. He has no ambitions as a 'Roman.' The title is just window dressing. But one thing that this crazy treaty will give Alaric and his army above all is access to Roman arsenals throughout Illyria."

"So now," a decurion suggested, "we are going to forge the weapons for the Visigoths to kill us in our next confrontation with them. How generous."

A dull silence fell over the group at that point. We had pretty well exhausted the topic by that time, so many of us started to retire for the evening.

In the weeks ahead, the treaty details were published and posted in public forums throughout the empire. One item was missing that had been present in the previous "agreement." Instead of being settled in a new "homeland" as they had been in Lower Moesia, the Visigoths were not going to settle necessarily anywhere in Macedonia. They would be billeted in private homes in cities there, just as most field armies and their families are when there are no local barracks to accommodate them.

Alaric's men would be paid as Roman soldiers. The entire Visigothic nation under Alaric was being considered as a mobile field army and its dependents, not as peasant settlers as all other barbarian immigrants have been from time immemorial. This treaty was causing even more hard feelings than its predecessor had. The general feeling was that Alaric would break it just as he did the last one: whenever it suited him.

The various tribes of Northern Ireland are collectively known as the Scots and they present the greatest danger of invasion to the northern part of Britain. It is never easy for any invader from Ireland to strike Britain. The distance between the two islands varies, but on average, it is about sixty miles. During inclement weather, especially in the winter, the Irish Sea can be difficult. We were, therefore, surprised when a scouting flotilla operating from our base at Holyhead, early in November, reported that a large fleet of ships had assembled at Dublin well after the end of the traditional campaigning season. Dublin is the only settlement in Ireland that comes close to approximating what civilized people would call a city. It is primarily the main trading center for the various island tribes and also serves as the gathering center for Irish fleets attacking northern Wales. (Wexford, in the extreme southeast corner of Ireland, is the focal point for their attacks along the Bristol Channel.) This is one reason why Rome built legionary fortresses at Chester on the Dee estuary and Caerleon on the estuary of the Severn River; these rivers are natural invasion routes for the Irish tribes.

We had scouting parties constantly on patrol and extra troops were stationed at Holyhead itself because of its exposed location. We patrolled night and day because the Irish were known to occasionally strike at night. That's what they did this time by outflanking our fleet at Holyhead and landing on the north coast of Wales midway between Caernarvon and Chester. Their strategy appears to have been to strike south into the mountains and then circle around to the south of Chester to strike at richer pickings further inland. The plan was sound but the weather did not cooperate. A snowstorm came up suddenly out of the west while the Irish were at sea and blew many of their ships off course. Instead of invading in a focused area, the enemy was spread out across many miles of coastline. Our patrols were spread out as well, checking for every eventuality. Unfortunately, every eventuality was what happened but in small concentrations.

The whole thing was a mess from both an Irish and Roman point of view. Many Irish did not know where they were nor could they make contact with their comrades. Roman scouting parties, finding invaders everywhere though in admittedly small numbers, sent out scouts to fetch reinforcements. The scouting parties kept running into one another all along the coast, telling themselves of invaders in their sectors. That first, terribly confused night, the scouting reports made it seem that all of Ireland had landed on top of us. My squadron was patrolling to the east of Caernarvon and everything remained quiet in our sector. When scouts from the east informed us of an invasion in their area, I sent couriers back to Caernarvon to inform them of the situation.

That in turn got the fleet moving from Holyhead that, in the days ahead, sought out and burned every ship they could find along the north shore. One way or another, the Irish were here to stay.

Riding to the east, we first came across a pitched battle between a century of our mounted infantry and about fifty invaders. This group of Irish was soon beaten. A few got away into the mountains to the south but we could do nothing about them at the time. In the blowing snow and not knowing the size of the invasion force, we slaughtered all enemy soldiers that we captured. Under the circumstances we had no time for prisoners. At sunup we pushed east again. Fighting continued all through the day and into the next night. By the end of our first full day, three of my men had been killed and four had been wounded. Medical units from the fort at Caernarvon did everything that they could for the wounded. After two full days, my troops were exhausted and were withdrawn from combat to eat and get a little sleep. On the third day, as we were rushing eastward down the highway to relieve a hard-pressed century from Legion XX Valeria Victrix, we were ambushed by an Irish tribe known as the Scots. These Scots reside primarily in Northern Ireland although in recent years some of them have been seen migrating to the northeast across what we call the North Channel into Caledonia. One onrushing Scot thrust his spear into my horse. As I quickly dismounted, I ruptured a muscle in my right leg. It was as painful as a sword thrust and at first I thought that an arrow may have pierced it. The Scots had launched their ambush prematurely. A second cavalry squadron came up immediately behind us and helped retrieve the situation. About twenty Scots had taken part in the attack. But after three days and nights in the snow and freezing cold with virtually no food, a lot of the fight had gone out of them. We killed most of them and took several prisoners. A few ran off south of the highway in an attempt to get into the mountains but most of them were hunted down and killed.

The overall situation appeared to be under control by this time, so we did not execute our prisoners. Instead we tied them up and marched them off to Chester for interrogation and subsequent shipment into slavery. By this time, I could no longer walk, the pain was so intense. I handed command of my squadron over to a subdecurion. A medic wrapped a bandage tightly around my damaged leg and dispatched me, along with a number of other wounded men, back to the hospital at Caernarvon so our injuries could be more completely attended to. The only thing I needed was rest, as there was nothing more the doctors could do for me. By that time, the invasion had been pretty well suppressed. Infantry from both the legion and independent regiments were busy hunting down those invaders that had escaped southward.

Caernarvon stands on a low hill near the narrow Menai Strait that separates the island of Anglesey from Britain proper. A large number of wounded from the western end of the combat zone had been transported there for medical treatment. The fort and its associated garrison are, however, not large, and their medical staff was vastly overtaxed. As a result, as soon as any of the ambulatory wounded were sufficiently recovered, they were sent back to Chester. I only stayed there for one night and was on my way the next morning with a number of others.

Once back in Chester, I was relegated to desk duty and spent much of the time helping the legionary adjutant process paperwork while my leg healed. I was made responsible for getting a complete casualty report prepared on the campaign that would eventually go to the count of Britain. He has responsibility for all military units on the island that are not under the jurisdiction of the duke of Britain in the north or the count of the Saxon Shore in the southeast. While doing this, I managed to confirm my worst fears about just how severe our regiment's losses had been. Ideally, a cavalry regiment has 512 officers and men divided into sixteen squadrons of thirty men each plus a small headquarters staff. Before arriving in Britain, our strength had been beefed up to about five hundred men. But our total complement had been reduced to three hundred in just the fifteen months that we had resided on the island. We had been permitted to recruit locally while in Britain. However, under the terms of their enlistment, such British reinforcements would remain on the island and be absorbed into local units when our regiment returned to the continent. It was the only reasonable thing to do given the degree to which Britain's overall garrison had been reduced in recent years. At the same time, it would present a serious recruiting problem for us once we returned to the continent, but that was for the future.

The year 397 was drawing to a close and enormous though unseen changes were looming ahead of us. I had no way of knowing it at the time, but I had fought my next to last campaign on the frontier. The ending of the epoch marked by the premature death of Theodosius had been further confirmed during the year by the death of Bishop Ambrose. Whether one admired or detested him, there was no denying that he had been perhaps the foremost intellect of his time. Tragically, his intolerant attitudes set the tone in virtually every aspect of our national life in the century that lay ahead.

January 1, 398, saw us once again taking our oaths to the emperors but with little or no enthusiasm. Arcadius' ordering Stilicho out of Illyria for the second time in two years had betrayed to us all just how totally unqualified he was for his office. The only good thing that could be said about Honorius at this time was that he was too young to indicate what an utter imbecile he would be as an adult. Later in the month, with my injured leg back to normal, I returned to my regiment but not as a squadron commander. My tribune placed me on his staff, and under the circumstances, I think it was for the best. The accumulated injuries over the years had reduced my capacity to serve in a direct combat roll. I would become the regimental quartermaster at the beginning of the New Year. In March, the Irish launched an invasion on the north coast of the Bristol Channel but they did this on their own. The Picts and Saxons would remain quiet all year, and this Irish attack was quickly defeated. We continued our patrols along the north shore of Wales until the beginning of April. At that time, all the regiments that had been sent to the island in 396 were ordered returned to the continent. I requested and was granted permission to visit my family in Cirencester, about 150 miles to the south of Chester.

Part 2: Homecoming

Crossing the bridge across the Dee River, I left Chester and headed south along the north-south highway whose original purpose had been to serve as the baseline for the conquest of western Britain. It connects the legionary fortress of Chester at the northeast corner of Wales to its sister fort at Caerleon in the southeast. Several miles out of Chester, I crossed the Dee again and continued through a region of small farms. It was not until I entered the vicinity of Wroxeter, almost forty miles south of Chester that large estates complete with country villas started to appear. From Wroxeter, the highway headed southwest into the hill country. As it climbed into the higher elevations, it provided good views of the land to the west. Having traveled over sixty miles, I had just arrived at the small town of Bravonium when the heavens opened up. Stilicho's universal pass had proven universally handy. Changing horses at every Imperial Post station, I had expected to make Gloucester at least by the end of the first day until the rain arrived. Bravonium was really a walled village. With none of the usual accoutrements of civilization to boast of, I had to simply settle for a good night's sleep. South of the village, the road rather gently snaked its way through the hills. Most farms were of the small peasant variety with only a few large estates. Crossing the Severn River at Gloucester that suddenly changed and there were villas everywhere. I headed down the highway southeast toward Cirencester and eventually came to my family's villa. Everything looked pretty much the same except that the trees that were young when I left were all quite tall now. My father had torn down an old barn and built a much larger one.

I knocked on the door several times, but there was no answer. The door was unlocked, so I entered. To our mutual surprise, a child of about three was standing in front of me.

"Well," I asked him, "whose little boy are you?"

He turned and ran off terrified to the back of the house. I called out, but when no one answered, I decided to follow him. As I was passing through the kitchen, my sister Maria Patricia suddenly appeared at the door leading out onto the rear courtyard. She stared at me incredulously.

"Remember me?" I asked, not quite knowing if she recognized me. "I just happened to be in the neighborhood and thought I'd drop by."

"Good God, Marcus, it is you, isn't it?" she asked after an awkward silence.

I gathered her up into my arms and we almost crushed one another. "Yes, it's me all right, although I can understand why the beard would throw you off."

"You are the last man that I ever thought would grow one of those things," she said in her disapproving tone that had not changed over the years.

"I never thought I would either," I replied. "I only grew it to cover a scar that resulted from a wound I received years ago in Illyria. I've never shaved it off since then. Perhaps I'm afraid at what I might find underneath."

She commiserated with me over the loss of my family and we discussed them for some time. The conversation then turned to other things.

"The last several months have not been kind to our family either," she said. "To begin with, our mother died about six months ago and Valeria died just three weeks ago tomorrow."

I was naturally shocked to hear this since her last letter had made no mention of our mother or sister suffering any illness. Our mother's death had been quite sudden and our sister had died from pneumonia.

"By the way, whose little boy is that?" I asked.

"He's our nephew," she replied. "Valeria's son. She also has an older son of six and a two-year-old daughter."

"And her husband is my old friend Donatius?" I asked.

"Yes, but he can't look after all these children on his own," she replied. "Donatius and Valeria purchased the old Statilius place up the road a piece with help from Donatius' father. Now Donatius drops the children off either at his parents' place or here when I'm around. Everything is kind of mixed up at the moment, but we'll eventually get things straightened out one way or another, eh?"

Maria Patricia had married a doctor in Cirencester and lived there with their daughter. But since our mother and sister had passed away, she had spent a lot of time at the family estate helping our father.

"How is Dad doing and where is he?" I asked.

"Not very well. An elderly couple can appear to be getting along fine. But you just don't realize how dependent one might have been on the other until the other dies. Dad's health has been declining for years but we didn't realize how totally reliant he was on Mom until she was gone. Valeria used to drop by every day after Mom died, but then she took sick, and now everything has devolved on me. As long as someone is here, he's fine, but I just don't trust him by himself, especially during the colder weather. He's already taken one bad fall. He hadn't been up in the hay loft in ages, but one day when he was all alone, he suddenly became curious as to what was up there. When he was coming down the ladder, he fell and knocked himself unconscious. He just lay on the floor for hours before coming out of it. I'm afraid he might accidently torch the place someday. As for Gratian, he's turned out to be just as worthless as you always said he would."

"I had a feeling you were saving the best for the last," I said. "You never mentioned him in your letters."

"What few there were of them," she apologized. "I would get these letters from you as thick as a book and take a whole week to read one.

431

They were the most interesting letters that I'll ever read but I felt so intimidated by them when it came to writing you back. After all, what would I have to say that you would find all that interesting?"

"When you live the sort of life I do," I replied, "all letters are appreciated. Don't ever stop writing to me. Besides, I wasn't that frequent a writer myself."

"Yes," she said, "but I could tell that you thought of me often by all the different dates that appeared in the different sections of your letters. I couldn't expect to receive anything from you when a civil war was on. Do you realize that in the seventeen years you have been away, the West has been in revolt for almost half that time?"

"I never thought of it that way, but you're right."

"I do promise to write more frequently in the future though." She smiled. "I'll give you the lowdown on Gratian later. Suffice it to say for the moment that he married your old heartthrob Veronica within a year after you left. Dad saw the wisdom of your suggestion only after you were gone. Old pop wanted to link our family to her daddy's transportation outfit regardless. A couple of years later, though, Veronica's father sold it to a larger company headquartered in London. Gratian spends most of his time between there and York these days. Look, why don't you go and see Dad now? He's sitting out in the courtyard reading as he likes to do every day."

We walked over to the back door, and I could see that the paved portion of the courtyard had been extended considerably from when I was a boy.

"That's our mother's tomb at the southeast corner," she added. "Valeria is buried in a similar one at her husband's villa. Good luck."

I walked toward my father, wondering what sort of a reception I would get. He never looked up until I was almost at the little table beside his chair.

"Do you remember me, Dad?" I asked.

He looked up with an uncomprehending expression on his face. It took a few moments for it to sink in, and then he stood up and threw his arms around me.

"You've come back!" he exclaimed, almost shouting. "If you hadn't called me 'Dad,' I wouldn't have recognized you with that beard. Your sister let me read the letters that you sent her. Don't let on to her that I told you."

"That's okay," I said. "I expected she would. After all, they were intended to inform everyone. By the way, I have something for you. It's the money that your friend Silvianus owed you. Seventeen years late but it's all there nonetheless."

"I remember Silvianus explaining to me what had happened once word got around that you had left home." My father smiled. "He offered to pay me again, but I took him at his word. We had been friends for many years. He's dead now; passed away about five years ago. But look, you also owe me an explanation of what happened after you left. So let's have it."

I spent the rest of the afternoon telling him of what my life had been like since I left home. He wanted to know about the daughter-in-law and three granddaughters that he would never see. He was especially fascinated by the fact that Makila had been an Axumite and was flabbergasted when I described my friendship with Valentinian II and my association with Theodosius and Stilicho. Our conversations continued through supper and long into the evening. He wanted to know all about Hadrian's Wall and was quite surprised when I told him about the reconnaissance patrol I had led to within thirty-five miles of the Antonine Wall. My sister joined us periodically as household chores permitted. My father eventually started to get tired, but before he retired for the evening, there was something he wanted to say that he had difficulty articulating. He had tried several times during the course of our discussions but had always stopped short and changed the subject. Finally he said, "God but I wish that you hadn't left us, son. Your mother and I drove you away, didn't we?"

He was too vulnerable, and while I hesitated to give him a direct answer, it could not be entirely avoided.

"When I look back," I began, "on my life in Britain, I cannot think of any time that I felt I belonged or fit in. I experienced very little sense of fellowship or purpose here. Nothing ever worked out in the way that I hoped, and I became convinced that nothing ever would. I was always a spectator and never a participant. And whenever I did attempt to participate, the results were disastrous or embarrassing, in any event a failure, regardless of the endeavor. It was as though a preclusive process was at work in almost everything I did, and I simply got fed up forever being on the outside looking in. The future was one that you had determined for me and it would have been a mirror image of a past that I despised. I don't blame all my problems on you. Perhaps the Fates simply had other things in store for me. Whatever the reason, my life here was like an endless jail sentence without my having any idea of what my crime was.

"Having traveled extensively in Europe, I can think of no finer place in which a couple can live and raise a family than in Britain. But that doesn't mean that I haven't cursed the life I had here prior to leaving. It was slow at first, but on the continent, avenues opened up for me that would never have existed here."

"So you wouldn't consider asking for a posting here?" he asked.

"No. I'm here strictly on assignment. I've never belonged here permanently."

He was quite tired by this time and he soon went to bed.

I then went outside and stood beside my mother's tomb. She and I had not been close, but standing where she lay, I was quite overcome emotionally. At first, I was surprised at this reaction because when I had left home in 381 I had absolutely detested her. But then I realized that, in many cases, when people die, what saddens us most is the realization that our relationship with them was so much less than it might have been; so many missed opportunities that would never return. It was certainly true in our case.

Cirencester had not changed much in my absence. There was little in the way of new construction since I left. I visited old friends in and around the town but quickly learned something I had not expected to. Not having seen or communicated with them for so many years, I thought we would have an enormous number of things to talk about. It didn't turn out that way. Too many years had passed and our lives had taken paths that were much too divergent. What we thought would be important for the other to know in too many instances turned out to be quite the opposite. So I decided to spend the rest of my time at home and simply discard the ancient friendships for the fading memories that they had become.

I stayed a total of five days with my family, and it turned out to be quite pleasant. My father had mellowed considerably over the years but no longer socialized to the extent that he used to. Of course, one reason for that was that he was starting to outlive some of his friends, and beyond a certain age, we no longer make new ones the way we did when we were younger. The loss of my mother hit him quite hard also and was perhaps the main reason that he chose to be more homebound than he might have been otherwise.

My brother Gratian had turned into an outright scoundrel. This I learned from a lengthy discussion with my sister. Gratian had made good on his boast as a teenager that he would never be faithful to any wife for long. I took a certain cynical satisfaction from that in the sense that I thought he and Veronica deserved one another. She had given birth to a baby girl within a year after their marriage but they had had no more children; at least not between them. He had sired two illegitimate children and, as could be expected, ignored responsibility for them. My father, at my mother's insistence, had seen that they and their mothers were well provided for. My father had also had to spend a considerable sum of money to keep Gratian out of prison for dealing in stolen goods several years later. He was just no damned good for anything except getting into trouble. After an appropriate amount of money had found its way to the local priest, the marriage between Gratian and Veronica had been annulled. Gratian had then remarried a rich widow in London and all communication between him and the rest of our family had ceased. It was probably just as well.

I approached my father on the question of Ardovanda and her family. I told him what I had discovered, or rather failed to discover, at York.

He was puzzled. So far as he knew, our neighbor had shipped them off to his estate there. But with Silanus dead now and so much time passed, I would never know her fate.

"There is no question in my heart and mind that Ardovanda was, is and always will be the love of my life," I told my father. "Our star-crossed love was doomed to fail from the start as far as the two of you were concerned. But from the moment I discovered that you had transferred her family to York, I determined that I would never live here or anywhere near this place. For me it had to be Ardovanda or no one. I will never forget what was said to me on the matter and I will never forgive what was done. Besides, there was no way in hell that I would ever consider spending the rest of my life with that witch Veronica."

Once again, I was learning that there are many problematical relationships in our lives that never have a satisfactory resolution to them. It would be nice if the sand could flow upward through the hourglass, just once in a while.

Finally, it was time for me to leave for the continent. In complete contrast to my leave-taking in 381, I genuinely hated to depart the place. These people were the only immediate family I had now. It was odd. When I lived there, it was the focus of all my problems. Now it was my port in the storm. The peace and prosperity that Britain enjoyed, in spite of the attacks on its periphery, were in such stark contrast to what I had witnessed in Thrace and other places. But the island's tranquility was deceiving. The victories that we had achieved in Britain and Syria would prove to be no more than momentary distractions. Their chief accomplishment was to take public attention briefly from the greatest danger we faced. This was not Alaric and his Visigoths. It was the growing alienation between Milan and Constantinople and the virulence of that disruption. With our manpower resources reduced drastically, as a result of our last civil war, our world was becoming ever more destabilized. We had no one to blame but ourselves. In one of history's cruelest tricks, the consequences of the Gothic Revolt would ultimately be felt most severely in the West, not the East. No one could have foreseen this in 398. Nonetheless, the groundwork was being laid. On the day of my departure, I bade a tearful farewell to my father and sister, nephews and nieces and headed south to Cirencester. I would never see them again.

Instead of heading southeast to Silchester, I headed southwest to Bath. I didn't know if I would ever get the chance to see one of the most mystifying ruins in the empire again, so I decided to take advantage of what might be my last opportunity. If the world was bound and determined to collapse in utter chaos, it would have to do it without me for at least a little while. One thing that impressed me, wherever I traveled in Britain, was that the highways all continued to be well maintained. The distance from Cirencester to Bath is thirty miles. For much of this stretch, the highway sits atop a high embankment that is anywhere from four to six feet in height. Where the embankment is lower, there is a usually a well-cleaned ditch on one or both sides. Even though there were several deep valleys to cross, I made good time. Eventually I started the steep descent down the north side of the Lower Avon River Valley to the city of Bath. The region near Bath is one of the most densely settled and richest on the island. The landscape is dotted with villas in every direction.

After changing horses there, I left the Fosse Way and branched off onto a more southeasterly highway. Shortly out of Bath, this road climbs steeply out of the valley but then levels out through a more forested and less populated area. Approximately twenty miles south of Bath, I turned east, near the headwaters the Wylye River, onto one of the oldest Roman highways in Britain. Its prime function is to connect to the iron mining region further west in the Mendip Hills. But its main purpose for me was that it would take me to the Salisbury Plain and that mystical place known as Stonehenge. My father had taken us there when we were children, and like most people who have seen it, I've been forever fascinated by it. Stonehenge is an ancient site. Its main feature is a circular array of tall, upright stones. The largest weighs almost fifty tons and measures thirty feet in length. This stone circle is about one hundred feet in diameter. It, in turn, is contained within a circular ditch and embankment that measures almost 350 feet across. The entire complex was constructed over a period of four centuries, starting about 1800 BC. The ditch was the earliest part of the site to be constructed, and the earth so excavated was used to build the embankment. Also put in place at this time was the thirty-five-ton block of sandstone known as the "Heel" stone. It lies about seventy-five feet outside the ditch on the northeast side in what is referred to as the "avenue" that leads out from a break in the embankment. Two centuries later, over seventy large pillars were transported onto the center of the site. Thirty of these stones were stood upright to form the circular array and topped by an unbroken series of stone lintels. Inside this circle is a U shaped series of five stand-alone pairs of upright stones, each pair also topped by a lintel. Later a smaller circle of stones was added between the outer circle and U-shaped structure.

The more chauvinistic Celts like to maintain the fiction that the structure was built by a race of Celtic giants, who have conveniently disappeared, and was connected to Druidism. There is no truth in any of this. Its construction long predated the Celtic arrival, and the first mention of the Druids occurs only in the third century BC. Besides, the Druids usually held their worship services in forests, not stone structures. Stonehenge remains a mystery since we do not know who built it or why. Walking among its stones, with a number of other tourists, I could not help but reflect that construction first started at this site a thousand years after the construction of the Great Pyramid of Cheops and a thousand years before the founding of Rome. Now, at a remove of four decades from my last trip home and with all the chaos and devastation with which we have been engulfed since then, I often think of that visit to Stonehenge. The pharaohs are gone, and the people who built Stonehenge have vanished. What is Rome's future to be?

To a degree, I believe that future has been written in the stones of Hadrian's Wall. In the two centuries following its completion, the wall was attacked on a number of occasions, and sometimes the damage was severe. But even during the worst times, the wall, its fortifications, and civilian settlements would be rebuilt once the region had been secured. The reason was that it was universally recognized that Hadrian's Wall and the other fortified areas of Britain were not just there to defend the island. They served as the northwest defensive network for Gaul and Spain as well. In 367, the worst attacks in Britain's history occurred simultaneously when the Irish, Caledonians, and Saxons struck in the west, north, and east respectively. Our most crushing defeat at this time came when the duke of Britain, who commanded the northern frontier, was defeated and slain, and Hadrian's Wall was overrun. The count of the Saxon Shore was also killed far to the south. The wall and its fortifications were all repaired, but the smallest of the associated civilian villages that were destroyed were not rebuilt. The civilians in these villages who survived the attacks were now housed within the wall fortifications. The failure to rebuild these settlements did not seem that important at the time. It was comparable, in a sense, to the constriction of the continental cities for defensive purposes that had occurred in the previous century. Coupled with this, however, was the fact that when I left Britain in 398, the total garrison on the island was the smallest since it was annexed by Rome. In combination, they were indications of things to come.

It had been an enjoyable day, but eventually it was time to go. If only I had sent my wife and children to live at the family homestead five years earlier. I permitted myself to daydream about what it would have been like if they had accompanied me to Stonehenge some time. But the Fates had determined otherwise. It was late, and I spent the night at Old Sarum, the next town up the road. The distance from Old Sarum to Silchester is only thirty-seven miles, but due to a driving rainstorm, that was as far as I got the following day. I stayed at its Imperial Post roadhouse that is quite large. It is a two-storied building that surrounds a courtyard and has attached baths and stables. I was the only soldier there, but there were several civil servants who were staying the night. They were traveling on official business for the diocese or their individual provinces. They were surprised to find that a fellow Briton had served in the Eastern Army in both civil wars and had spent so much time in Illyria and Thrace as well as the north of Britain. My main interest was the situation in Africa. While still stationed at Chester, we had been informed that Stilicho had outfitted Mascazel with a fleet stationed at the port of Pisa. In addition, a small force consisting of five thousand Gallic soldiers had been placed at Mascazel's service. That much I knew early in the year, but none of us had heard anything in the meantime. The civil servants informed me that they had just received information two days earlier that Mascazel's invasion had been a complete success. Scouts had pinpointed exactly where Gildo was staying, and the small force that he had at his disposal was not overly inclined to risk their lives on his behalf. Perhaps with the assistance of a judicious bribe, Gildo's small army had gone over to Mascazel. Gildo, knowing full well what sort of mercy to expect from his brother, hanged himself; a most fitting end. Eutropius, upon discovering Stilicho's plan, had ordered the praetorian prefect of the East, Caesarius, to rush to Count Gildo's aid. Caesarius, pointing out the far more immediate dangers to be faced on the eastern frontier, refused to do so and was dismissed as a result. Eutropius then elevated himself to that office. I was up at dawn the next morning and on my way to London.

The city looked pretty much as I remembered it. But what made me reflect above all over how much time had passed was the extent to which my cousins' children had grown. Also, my only uncle had died, as had one of my two aunts. I spent two days in London getting caught up on family matters. I also attempted to get in touch with my brother Gratian but was told that he and his wife were currently visiting one of their (meaning her) country estates. The city appeared prosperous and in good shape. Nonetheless, there had been very little major new construction that was readily apparent, either private or public, apart from churches. The reason for this economic stagnation was the shrinkage of the army that had taken place when British regiments were shipped to the continent, defeated in two civil wars, and distributed among mobile field armies 1,500 miles to the east.

My regiment arrived during my second day in the city. I was on my way back to Italy.

CHAPTER 11

Tragedy in the East (399–401)

THE INFANTRY AND CAVALRY regiments being withdrawn from Britain arrived in London on a staggered schedule. This was done so as not to overtax local resources. The men who were still recuperating from wounds could not travel at the same rate as those in good health. In addition, they frequently required longer rest periods. With a thousand miles still ahead of some of us once we landed on the continent, this presented a problem. The wounded were grouped together and allowed to proceed at their own pace. That way, they would not retard the progress of everyone else. With ulterior motives in mind, I generously volunteered to be one of the officers in charge of them. From London, we sailed down the Thames and shipped across the Gallic Strait to Boulogne.

When we arrived in Reims, we heard that Mascazel had died in Milan. Details were maddeningly scanty, but it appeared to have been an accident. From Reims, we traveled eastward to Metz and then went down the Moselle River Valley. I secured lodging for the men at the barracks in Trier for a three-day layover and then went to the baths. The rest would do them good and me better. I then headed back up the road we had just traveled. It was raining heavily when I arrived at Margareta's country villa. She answered the door herself and gave me a long, lingering kiss.

"Are we all alone?" I asked.

"Yes," she replied, "the servants are all in town."

Not having seen her for so long, I couldn't wait any longer. We made love in the middle of her living room floor.

"Good Lord," she laughed, "don't you have any willpower at all?"

"Of course I do," I replied. "I must have. I've never used any of it yet."

We retired to her bedroom. She was a most remarkable woman, ageing so gracefully that she did not appear to have aged at all across the years I had known her. After spending a couple of hours getting "reacquainted," she made us a late-night supper. That completed, we brought one another up to date on how we had spent our lives during the past two years and eventually got around to current events.

"What happened to Mascazel?" I asked. "In Reims, we heard that he died in a tragic accident in Milan, but we were given no details."

"What one chooses to believe," she replied, "depends on whether you are a supporter or a detractor of the great field marshal. The positive view says that what happened was an accident. After a banquet at Stilicho's headquarters, the two men went for a horseback ride through the city. It had been raining for several days, and even the small streams had been transformed into raging torrents. While crossing a bridge over a normally small creek, Mascazel's horse slipped on the wet pavement, causing its rider to fall over the railing and drown. The negative view is that Stilicho pushed him. According to both versions, Stilicho and Mascazel each had their bodyguards with them. In the negative version, Stilicho's men prevented Mascazel's from rescuing him. With the positive version, the whole thing happened so quickly that no one could do anything before the ill-fated African slipped beneath the turbulent waters below. You know the generalissimo better than I do. What do you think?" She was challenging me for an answer, and for a while, I was at a loss for words.

"When someone says, 'That is a good question,'" I finally responded, "It usually means that they do not have a good answer. Mascazel's two older brothers, Firmus and Gildo, both committed acts of treason. Honorius's grandfather Theodosius, who had been appointed count of Africa by Valentinian I, took three years to crush a difficult revolt by Firmus by 375. Firmus was captured but committed suicide in prison. An interesting aspect to Firmus' family is that of his two younger brothers: Gildo fought with Count Theodosius, while Mascazel fought with

Firmus. If your negative view is correct, then Stilicho must have felt that the disease runs in the family, so why not settle the account now instead of waiting for some future date when it may be far more difficult? On the other hand, you said that Mascazel's bodyguard was with him."

"That's what I've heard," she said.

"If the negative view is correct, then what happened to them?"

"Haven't heard," she replied. "Perhaps they were bribed to keep their mouths shut. The practice is hardly foreign to our body politic and armed forces, you know. Let me get you some more wine."

Just watching her walk across the room was worth the trip from London to Trier. She was the very personification of elegance in everything she did and was a godsend to me. I spent three full days with Margareta at her country estate. I loved this woman but would never really know how she felt about me. Perhaps it was because she was older. Perhaps it was because of our different social backgrounds that she always seemed to be holding back, not really giving of herself fully. But to my boundless gratification, after I had lost my family, she was always there when I needed her with chilled wine, a hot supper, and a warm bed. I could be content with that.

Well rested by now, our group of walking wounded took to the road. I wondered about recent developments. Over the past two years, we had engaged in military campaigns in Britain, Greece, eastern Anatolia, and Africa. My hope was that the recent frequency of warfare was an anomaly. My fear was that it was not. With the tens of thousands of men that the Roman Army had lost over the past two decades, we were ill suited to face such dangers on a prolonged basis. At Mainz, half the wounded men headed north to where their regiments were stationed at fortresses down the Rhine. The rest of us arrived in Milan at the beginning of August. Reattached to my regiment, I soon assumed my duties as the regimental quartermaster. One serious problem we faced was that of rebuilding ourselves to full strength. Over the past three years, the difficulty of recruiting volunteers had magnified considerably. While Theodosius resided in Milan from 388 to 391, a considerable number of Visigothic volunteers had joined regular Western Roman Army units stationed on the upper Danube and in northern Italy. However, the political difficulties between East and West after 395, the rise of Alaric, and the strengthening of Hunnish control north of the Danube staunched the flow of such volunteers to the West. Stilicho had retained a number of regiments from the Army of Gaul and attached them to his new Army of Italy. As a result, he was very reluctant to draw down any more units from there to respond to problems elsewhere. The units taken from Gaul to assist Mascazel had been returned to their home bases as soon as the crisis in Africa was over. The only region left from which we could obtain recruits for Italy consisted of our provinces of Rhaetia and Noricum and the area to their immediate north on the upper Danube. The numbers available were rather small.

I settled in a private apartment near the one I had previously. I was now thirty-three and past my sixteenth anniversary in the service. Even though I was living in the western capital, it was a lonely existence. Where women were concerned, I had always been somewhat like a camel in the desert, and as the years went by, the oases seemed to be getting farther and farther apart. Something had to be done; after all, it had been six years since I had lost Makila and the children. For the first few years after that, I simply didn't want to meet anyone new. Theodosius's second civil war and Stilicho's campaigns in Thessaly and Britain had kept me extremely busy. That was satisfaction enough at the time. However, it fell far short of what I ultimately needed. Since I was living off base, I frequented a laundry about three blocks from where I lived. I immediately became friendly with a girl who worked there named Aureliana. She and her mother and four sisters ran the establishment. Her father had died when she was in her teens. As had been happening for generations, her family had migrated up from Sicily about seventy years earlier. I asked her out the fourth time I went to the place, and to my delight, she accepted. We went out for dinner and attended a theatrical presentation. All in all, the evening was most pleasant, and we hit it off quite well. We have all had such first dates where everything is wonderful but is followed by subsequent get-togethers where the whole thing goes headfirst into the shitter. This time, however, I had a very comfortable feeling about Aureliana.

The next morning, a messenger approached me shortly after I arrived at the cavalry hall. I was to report to Stilicho's headquarters immediately. Upon arrival, a secretary told me to be seated in a small anteroom that led to his office. I had been there only a few minutes when Andreas and Julianus, my two associates from my last visit to Constantinople, arrived.

"Well," said Julianus, the younger of the two, in a low voice so as not to be overheard, "I guess your presence along with us determines what we're here for."

"Any idea whom the target is this time?" I asked.

"Eutropius is the most obvious choice," Andreas replied, "but if Stilicho sends anyone after him, it certainly won't be us."

"You're right," I replied. "But if not him, then who?" Neither one had an answer. "I haven't been in town long, but ever since I reached Trier, I've been hearing two stories about the death of Mascazel. Was his death an accident or was it arranged?"

They both shrugged.

Andreas replied, "You must keep in mind that Stilicho is a Christian and the son of a barbarian father. What else does the pagan aristocracy need to know about him to hate him? The rumor that Stilicho had personally pushed Mascazel off the bridge probably got started before the poor bugger even hit the water."

"And the water was quite high," Julianus tossed in. "It was a week in which a number of people drowned while crossing bridges in this region. The rains had been terrible for days. Whenever it stopped raining, people would come out of their houses to run their chores. But that didn't mean that the streams would stop rising. People would start to cross a bridge that was high and dry when suddenly a wall of water would come rushing down, and they would never be seen again. We heard that's what happened to Stilicho and Mascazel. A surge of water swept about a foot over the bridge and startled Mascazel's horse, hurling his rider to his doom. It almost knocked Stilicho and several of the bodyguards over as well."

I felt better about the incident, but historians will always hold it open for debate.

We sat in silence for a while before the door to Stilicho's office opened and he invited us in. We were informed that the three of us had once again been chosen to perform a "special service" on the state's behalf.

"I'm dispatching the three of you to Constantinople. However, don't be alarmed; it won't be like the last time. Since I have been declared a 'public enemy' by Eutropius, it has become extremely difficult for me to keep in communication with my contacts there. I'm sending the three of you with highly confidential documents for Gainas. The alienation that Constantinople has introduced into the relations between East and West cannot be permitted to continue indefinitely. I will be using the three of you as my personal couriers to communicate with Gainas and others in the eastern capital as required. Gainas sent me several passes with his imprimatur to allow western couriers to use the Imperial Post in the East. Needless to say, any attempts on your part to use the passes that I gave you in either of the two eastern prefectures would probably be frowned upon by the authorities there."

We all laughed but fully understood the danger. Stilicho referred to a large wall map of Constantinople and pointed out exactly where Gainas' headquarters was. We then left to inform our commanding officers of our new assignments and got our gear together for the trip. Once again, I passed through the Julian Alps and down the Sava River Valley. We noticed that the fortifications in the pass between Aquileia and Emona were unoccupied. Theodosius had stripped them of their defenders to support the Eastern Army as he pressed westward in 394. The heavy casualties suffered at the Frigidus prevented our re-manning these forts because the demand for troops on the frontier and in the field armies was so great. We would pay a heavy price for this. As had been previously arranged, we joined up with a wagon train prior to crossing the boundary between the Western and Eastern Empires at Belgrade. It was just a precaution. While the declaration of Stilicho as a "public enemy" by the government of the East in the previous year was tantamount to an act of war, that was as far as it went. The hostilities between East and West would remain at the personal and diplomatic level, not the military and commercial. There had, however, been instances of eastern soldiers on the boundary checking the credentials of individuals entering from the West on a random basis. In our case, we crossed over without incident.

The trip to the eastern capital was uneventful. To be on the safe side, we traveled on a lot of back roads that Andreas was quite familiar with. We met with Gainas and gave him Stilicho's documentation. He, in turn, gave us a collection of documents to take to Stilicho and engaged us in a rather lengthy conversation. When Gainas had arrived in Constantinople on November 20, 395, he held the rank of marshal of cavalry. As such, he was one of the highest-ranking officers in the empire and one of the most respected. Upon securing his position as the successor to Rufinus, Eutropius had appointed Gainas to be the head of Arcadius' bodyguard. Gainas held this post for a relatively short time before being promoted to the office of marshal of Thrace. This was the position that Stilicho had held prior to the Battle of the Frigidus. Unfortunately, by this time the office had more appearance than substance to it. The field armies of Thrace and Illyria had suffered enormous casualties during our most recent civil war. They were still markedly under strength. The two imperial field armies were only marginally stronger. With the exception of the Army of the East, which had contributed the fewest units to the recent civil war, the rebuilding of all our field armies was proving most difficult.

In his new capacity, Gainas' most important responsibility had been recruiting Visigoths from Thrace and the region north of the Danube into his field army. Eutropius, inheriting the disastrous plan that Rufinus had set in motion, decided to make the best of it by having Alaric's Visigothic Federate Army fill the role that had previously been the responsibility of our Army of Illyria. This latter army still existed but was taking too long to rebuild itself to full strength.

"It has been no easy undertaking," Gainas told us. "The lower Danube is as penetrable now as it has ever been. Its military resources were spent by our last civil war and the mass evacuation by Alaric's followers. Its manpower pool has shriveled drastically. It's more of a manpower puddle now. To the north of the Danube, there are even greater drawbacks to recruiting. Since the Huns consolidated their control there, it has become increasingly difficult to obtain recruits from that area other than on Hunnish terms. You know what that means: money. So until the barrels run dry from other sources, we will try and avoid that option."

"What effect," Andreas asked, "has the promotion of Alaric to marshal of Illyria had on our recruiting activities among the Visigoths?"

Gainas gave each of us a cold, hard stare and then looked out the window for a few moments, perhaps to compose himself. Andreas had definitely hit a raw nerve.

"What I'm getting at," Andreas continued, "is that that bastard Eutropius has ..."

At that point, Gainas raised his left hand and shook his head. It was obvious that he did not wish to discuss the eunuch any further. He did, however, leave us in no doubt that he was disgusted with Eutropius' decision to elevate Alaric to an office that was, in effect though not organizationally, superior to his own. In theory, Alaric and Gainas were both field marshals and therefore of equivalent stature. Alaric, however, had a real field army, one that by Roman standards was a full-strength field command. The Army of Thrace was still being rebuilt and was a long way from its prewar establishment. Gainas hated Alaric and Eutropius, as did we all, but in the politically charged atmosphere of the capital of the East, it is never wise to broadcast one's attitudes too freely.

"As was feared by everyone," Gainas replied, "except the civilian powers that be here, the 'legalization' of Alaric's status within the Roman framework has made his army appear more attractive to young Gothic recruits than it had been previously. Our Eastern Army is particularly dependent upon such volunteers. For the past three years, we have been competing with Alaric for their services, and thanks to the decision to which you just referred, those problems have been compounded severely. The training for Alaric's army is less severe than is our own, and now their pay is the same. The alleged advantage to Rome of Visigothic manpower that Theodosius did his best to secure in the Treaty of 382 has been completely eroded by the Treaty of 397. Visigothic volunteers are still joining our army, a small stream in the East, a trickle in the West, meaning Italy. We have managed to rebuild the Army of Thrace up to reasonable strength, but that of Illyria is woefully short. That was another vital factor leading to Alaric's promotion: we simply don't have enough Roman soldiers left in Illyria to defend it. I know why Eutropius did what he did. But like our late Emperor Valens, he looked only at the credit side of the ledger while ignoring the liabilities that such a policy would create. Our enlistment numbers are nowhere near where they should be."

At that point, several tribunes were announced to Gainas, and we were dismissed. While in Constantinople, we heard rumors that Eutropius was planning on holding the office of Eastern consul for the following year. The three of us thought it too bizarre to be worthy of consideration. It wasn't. We headed back to Milan. Andreas and Julianus were good company. They belonged to two different cavalry regiments in Stilicho's field army and had participated in his Peloponnesian campaign the previous year. Andreas was a Thracian, and Julianus had been born in Africa, though his family had migrated to Italy when he was quite young. We delivered Gainas' documents to Stilicho and then returned to our regular duties. Soon after, we heard that Eutropius was indeed planning to hold the office of Eastern consul for 399. It was now Stilicho's turn to wage a propaganda war against the grand chamberlain. Abundant details were leaked to the public about just how corrupt Eutropius' regime had become. During the year, Constantinople and several other cities in the East were damaged by earthquakes. The capital and Thrace were stricken by serious flooding as well. Many took these as omens boding ill for those in power.

When I first saw her after returning to Milan, Aureliana appeared concerned over not having seen me for several weeks. It was the first time anyone had expressed concern of that nature since that terrible day in Carnuntum. We started seeing one another regularly and realized that it had been a case of love at first sight for the both of us. I had been worried about our age difference from her standpoint; I was thirty-three when we met, while she was only twenty-one. However, she insisted that it was of no concern to her.

On January 1, 399, Eutropius became Eastern consul. It was the straw that broke the camel's back. The public had tolerated Eutropius to this point, even though it despised him. Now he had gone an office too far. The crowds in the Hippodrome wasted no time in letting him know what they thought of his assuming his new position, but he ignored their protests. Stilicho ensured that everyone was fully aware of Eutropius' corruption, courtesy of details provided by Gainas, some of which my two fellow decurions and I had delivered the previous year. It would come to mark the beginning of his downfall. The degree to which Eutropius had underestimated the public reaction and overreached was remarkable. At the peak of his power, his judgment was starting to slip. The mere idea of this eunuch occupying the honored office of consul only reignited people's hatred of him for the manner in which he had "rewarded" Alaric for devastating Greece. Stilicho refused to recognize Eutropius' consulship and declared all laws passed by the government of Arcadius void in the West. This included religious laws ordering the destruction of all pagan temples. Arcadius had signed such a law in July 398. Since the laws promulgated by each emperor were valid in the other's domains, some temples were destroyed by mobs of fanatical Christians in Africa, Gaul, and Spain. What Stilicho wanted above all on the domestic front was order. To this end, he issued an injunction for the protection of pagan temples throughout the Western Empire while continuing the prohibitions on pagan religious practices. He did, however, allow pagan festivals to be celebrated.

With his daughter Maria now married to Honorius, the generalissimo had much about which to be satisfied. In the four years since Theodosius died, the West had fared far better under Stilicho's leadership than had the East under the shortsighted and avaricious regimes of Rufinus and Eutropius. In the West, Africa had been secured with a minimum of bloodshed, Britain had been successfully defended against barbarian onslaughts, and the Rhine and Danube were quiet. In the East, while the Huns had been defeated twice in eastern Anatolia, Greece and Macedonia had been devastated by Alaric and his horde, and Thrace had suffered from both the Huns and the Visigoths. In addition, the eastern economy was severely strained, and political turmoil was about to reach the boiling point. On the personal front, Aureliana and I were married in late January. She became pregnant in February. Life had suddenly become good again.

Near the end of April 399, I was made a member of an officer task force. We were sent north into our transalpine provinces of Rhaetia and Noricum.[27] Our mission was distasteful to us, but we had no choice. More than four years had passed since the Battle of the Frigidus, but the manpower shortfall in the Army of Italy (derived mainly from the Army of Gaul) was still severe. The short-term solution was to make up the numbers from the frontier garrisons. We were to inspect mobile regiments on the upper Danube for the purpose of selecting the most capable for reassignment. It was always dangerous to weaken the frontier even for the shortest time. The dukes commanding these front-line provinces would have to make good their numerical losses by hiring more recruits from north of the Danube. Thus the Germanization of our army would be ratcheted up another notch. In generations past, the infusion of German recruits into a regiment would represent a minority of the total complement. The remainder would consist of Romans or Romanized Germans who would in turn Romanize the new recruits. Now in all too many frontier units, the German recruits were becoming the majority. The long shadow cast by the Frigidus River was bringing too many Germans into our army in too short a time span. "Romanization" was not taking effect, and standards of training were starting to suffer as a result. What the empire required above all was peace and prosperity that would grant the time and the money to build the army back to what it had been. Unfortunately, the dogs of war would not stay leashed long enough to permit this to happen. My friend Stephanus had recently been promoted to decurion. Since he was a native of Augsburg and knew the area well, I managed to convince our leadership that he should be a member of our party as well.

The southern parts of both Rhaetia and Noricum are quite mountainous. As a result, they are thinly populated. Noricum has always been the richer of the two because of its heavier concentration of mineral wealth. Their northern regions are where most agriculture is carried out but the farms tend to be small. During the first two centuries of the imperial period, a number of large villas were established in these provinces. A majority of those in Rhaetia have been long abandoned. Most of their proprietors had been Italian landowners who had tended to use them as summer homes to escape the heat of Italy. By the 350s, it was more important to escape the dangers posed by the Alemanns. As we traveled along the highways, we would sometimes see the ghostly ruins of a large country home whose once prosperous farmlands were in the process of being reclaimed by nature. It was an eerie feeling to know that you were passing through a world long departed.

Supply officers such as me find this situation particularly vexing all along our European frontier. While in recent decades we had had more soldiers manning frontier outposts than ever before, there were many vast estates and smaller farms along both the Rhine and the Danube lying abandoned. In generations past, many of their owners had been slaughtered in barbarian raids. Others had been forsaken due to chronic insecurity. If these farms had been able to remain in production, then it would have made the problem of supplying the army on the frontier much easier in terms of time and money. But as things stand, our frontier forces must, to a substantial degree, be supplied from sources well to the rear of the front lines. This is true all across Europe.

The commercial importance of Rhaetia has never been of any great consequence, but it does have one rather interesting idiosyncrasy: they age their wine in wooden barrels that are sealed with the resin from local conifers instead of ceramic jars, as is done elsewhere throughout the Roman world. However, as a communications link between Gaul and the East, it had been indispensable. One of the greatest political tragedies of my lifetime, among so many, was the lapsing of that connective as East and West drifted apart in a way that would have been unthinkable to previous generations. Wealthier Noricum is more heavily populated and the more Romanized. While it provided a fair harvest of soldiers in centuries past, it is no longer capable of doing so. Our task would not be easy. Its population has shrunk, and its cities, like those in other frontier areas, are heavily fortified. My previous passages through this region had been too brief for me to get a feel for what it was really like. Being native to the area, it was Stephanus who drew my attention to the changes that had occurred since his youth. A number of the small Roman towns now had Alemann villages attached to them. Some Alemanns worked as tenant farmers on the few large country estates that were still in operation. Others tended their own small farms whose excess produce went to feed the towns and garrisons. In some cases, they had established small hamlets on the grounds of abandoned estates and had managed to bring them at least partly back to life.

The compositions of the garrisons had changed since I first passed along the upper Danube in 383. During the 380s, when Valentinian II reigned over the prefecture of the Italies, Theodosius had reinforced its northern fortresses with Visigothic volunteers. The region was becoming increasingly German and less Roman in its cultural, commercial, and military aspects. Without realizing it at the time, or perhaps being unwilling to admit it, we were watching our civilization fading away before our eyes. The shrunken towns in Gaul, Illyria, Thrace, and the upper Danube, the increasing number of German settlements along our side of the frontier, the abandoned villas in so many provinces, and the fortification of so many that still remained were all indicative of a civilization that was failing to sustain itself in spite of its best efforts.

We were not on a conscription drive. Anyone on the Roman side of the Danube wanting to join the army was free to volunteer for a garrison legion or regiment. Fortress by fortress, we inspected units of both infantry and cavalry to ascertain their fitness for Stilicho's Army of Italy. Notices had gone out to all the garrison commanders on the frontier to be prepared. It was a slow process as we traveled along the

Danube from Neuburg, to the northeast of Augsburg, all the way to the border with Pannonia, which is only about ten miles west of Vienna. We left the smallest fortresses alone; after all, we were not there to "strip the frontiers," as some critics have charged. It was mainly from the larger garrisons that we would select a cavalry squadron or infantry century. Once they had all been gathered, escort troops were sent up from south of the Alps to take them to training bases in northern Italy. There they would either be reassigned to existing formations or, in some cases, be placed in entirely new "Honorian" infantry or cavalry regiments. It was a depressing exercise in that we all knew we should be moving troops from the interior to the frontiers, not in the opposite direction. From the time we left Milan to the time we returned took over four months. We used different passes in going through the Alps on the outgoing and return journeys. As with my earlier trip to the eastern capital, I noticed that the fortifications in the passes had all been abandoned. Occasional maintenance was done on them for when they would have to be reoccupied during an emergency. But no longer did they possess permanent garrisons. The troops that had previously manned them had been absorbed into either the frontier legions or our field army. Yet another extension of the shadow of 394.

It was good to get back to Aureliana, who, by early September, was seven months along. One of her sisters had been living with her at our apartment to keep her company while I was away. The first full day we were together, she sensed that something was wrong but didn't say anything. I invited Stephanus over for supper that night, and after we had finished, we started to loosen up after a couple of glasses of wine.

"What's the matter, hon?" Aureliana finally asked. "You haven't been very talkative since you got back. Did the trip go all right?"

"We did everything we were ordered to," I replied, "but we weren't overjoyed with the results. Look at it from our own provincial perspectives as veterans of almost seventeen years. If destiny smiles on us, then we will make tribune someday. Stephanus and I have come up through the ranks, as did every other officer in our recruiting party. Yet we are now seeing Germans who were leaders within their own tribes back in the Black or Bavarian Forests or wherever presenting themselves to Roman recruiters with a couple of hundred retainers, relatives, and so on. They are being made tribunes almost on the spot within the frontier legions and regiments."

"And to add insult to injury," Stephanus remarked, "Marcus and I will have to salute these yahoos should we happen to run into them at any time in the future."

"We've been doing this for centuries," I went on, "but in the past, its purpose was to attract foreigners with particular abilities, such as Iranians with special archery talents or Moroccan tribesmen who are great javelin throwers. But now it's being done wholesale. Even under Theodosius, when we took in thousands of Visigoths, they were accepted as though they were Roman-born volunteers and trained as Roman soldiers. We still regained control. Now a lot of that traditional influence seems to be fading away."

"But why?" my wife asked.

It occurred to me that when I killed my first enemy soldier, Aureliana had been only five years old.

"We've suffered too many men dead in too short a period of time," Stephanus replied. "We lost twenty thousand at Hadrianople in 378. Ten years later, we lost several thousand more in the civil war of 388. Six years later, we lost perhaps forty thousand at the Frigidus."

"We don't really know," I explained, "what the exact casualty figures were for either of the civil wars. The government has done an excellent job of hushing them up for fear of causing panic among the public and making the frontiers appear overly tempting to the Germans, Iranians, and Huns. The figures that Stephanus just mentioned are probably pretty close to the truth."

"In addition," Stephanus said, "consideration must be given to the men who were killed in the aftermath of Hadrianople when Theodosius was containing the Visigoths up to 382. There were no large battles, but there were a good many small ones. During the sixteen-year reign of Theodosius, we may have lost as many as eighty thousand men when you add in those forced to retire because of the seriousness of their wounds."

We sat in silence for a few moments, pondering what we had just said.

"And then," I continued, "with all those thousands of holes to plug in the dam, the state was inherited by a pair of cockeyed children."

"That is our biggest problem," Stephanus said. "Even if that bastard Alaric had never been born, we would still have the problem of our two infantile emperors. We all know that Arcadius is a fool and a coward; based on what I've heard since we returned from Britain, his little brother seems to be following in his footsteps. How could Theodosius have sired such a pair of utter dolts for sons?"

"How could Germanicus Caesar have sired Caligula?" I replied. "The biggest problem with an absence of leadership at the top is that it fosters division of authority all the way down the line. Too many men come to feel that they have the right to exercise authority in the emperor's name."

Another thing bothering everyone was the unsettling situation that had developed in the east several months earlier.

In the spring of 399, the contagion unleashed two years earlier when Eutropius made Alaric marshal of Illyria spread to Asia Minor. In 386, thousands of Ostrogoths who had been defeated in the Battle of the Danube were settled as tenant farmers in Phrygia in the Diocese of Asia in western Anatolia. There had been little trouble with them and several new cavalry regiments had been raised for the Roman Army from among their numbers. They were grouped into a special legion under the command of Count Tribigild, a distant cousin of Gainas, whom the latter had enticed to join the army about a dozen years earlier. In the most recent campaign against the Huns in Roman Armenia, this legion had served with distinction. However, when these Ostrogoths saw how well Alaric, in rebellion, had been treated by the government, they felt that as loyal "Romans," they were deserving of similar rewards. They too wanted federate status and Tribigild made demands for a higher command in the Roman Army. It is difficult to see what "federate status" was going to buy these Ostrogoths that they did not already have. They had been settled in Anatolia for over a decade and had done as well as anyone else there. As regards Tribigild, there was no mystery as to what motivated him and his military followers: unadulterated greed. The government in Constantinople, finally recognizing reality, refused these demands and as a result had a full-scale revolt on their hands.

They were not the only ones disenchanted with the government. Deserters from regular regiments, disgruntled townsmen fed up with the ever-increasing rates of taxation, escaped slaves and a number of other malcontents soon joined Tribigild. The lack of military training on the part of many of them made it more of a mob than an army. Constantinople, however, underestimated Tribigild and responded very slowly to him. As a result, a minor cut was allowed to expand into a hemorrhage. Bolting westward out of Phrygia, they struck through Lydia to the proconsulate of Asia on the west coast of Anatolia. There was a stampede of refugees in an attempt to escape to the offshore islands. Tribigild's army, however, quickly became bogged down with all the loot it had acquired in this prosperous area and headed back to Phrygia to gather up their families. The Ostrogoths and their newfound friends then rampaged through Phrygia, where they had been settled for over a decade. For a while, it looked as though western Anatolia would suffer the same fate as Greece.

An important factor here is that the Ostrogoths in Anatolia lacked the numbers that Alaric's horde did. Nonetheless, Tribigild's men were on a roll. They struck north toward the south shore of the Sea of Marmara. Eutropius reflected a poor understanding of the danger by the manner in which he deployed the two under strength imperial field armies. The Grand Chamberlain transferred Gainas from the command of the Army of Thrace to the Second Imperial Army. Command of the First Imperial Army was given to a general named Leo. Leo had been a garrison commander but was an empty uniform in so important an undertaking as this. He had remained in the army well beyond retirement age, in spite of his physical disabilities, and should have been put out to grass years earlier. He had never before commanded large forces in the field but he was deemed politically safe by Eutropius. That mattered above all.

Eutropius dispatched Leo and his army across the Hellespont to confront Tribigild. Gainas had been on another recruiting drive in Thrace when he was informed of his change of command and the fact that Eutropius had already ordered Leo south. Gainas was angered when he returned to the capital and discovered that the unqualified Leo had been placed on the same level as himself and that he had not been given overall command of the entire operation. After a lengthy argument with Eutropius and other civilian officials, Gainas was placed in charge of the expedition while Leo remained in command of his own rather small field army. Gainas and Leo advanced against Tribigild and forced the latter to retreat through Phrygia to Pamphylia on the southwest coast. Leo soon realized that his own army was considerably outnumbered by the Ostrogoths he was confronting. He requested reinforcements from Gainas who complied by sending newly recruited Visigothic volunteers to join him. With a good lead on Gainas' army group, the Ostrogoths found themselves in unfamiliar territory. Whether it was overconfidence or a lack of familiarity with the terrain, the Ostrogoths blundered into a severe defeat at the hands of a hastily put together Roman militia when they were trapped in a mountain pass near the town of Side.[28] Leo's army arrived on the scene as Count Tribigild, and his surviving forces were attempting to retreat in the direction from which they had come. Trapped between the two forces, Tribigild managed to bribe a corrupt Roman officer among the newly arrived regulars with some of the loot taken from his recent pillaging. As a result, the count and three hundred of his followers escaped destruction. To worsen the situation, several regiments of the newly arrived regulars deserted the Roman Army and went over to Tribigild. Tribigild immediately turned this force on the remains of Leo's depleted army and defeated it, killing Leo in the process. In the following weeks, large numbers of the more ill-trained among Tribigild's followers, who had deserted him in extremis near Side, rejoined his army once again.

To further confuse the picture in the East, the Iranian King Bahram IV died at this time and was succeeded by Yazdegerd. Rumors immediately spread that the new king was planning an invasion of Rome's easternmost provinces. Such proved not to be the case. However, the possibility alone was enough to send Arcadius into a state of complete panic. He sent a direct embassy to Stilicho requesting military assistance at both ends of Anatolia. The price Stilicho demanded in return was that Eutropius be discharged from office. When Arcadius heard this he was more confused than ever. The emperor felt an endless debt of gratitude to Eutropius for having brought him his wife, Eudoxia, and could not bring himself to dismiss his greedy and increasingly incompetent chief minister. It was at this juncture that Eutropius made the incomprehensible mistake of insulting and bullying the empress over some minor matter. He soon discovered how quickly one's luck can completely run out. The empress went to Arcadius who was finally forced to consider dumping the Grand Chamberlain. At this time, a convergence occurred between this domestic squabble, the demand by Stilicho, and the military fiasco that continued to worsen in western Anatolia.

Historians are in general agreement that at this point Gainas joined up with his cousin, Tribigild, and turned traitor. I disagree completely. From the beginning of his rebellion, Tribigild had been demanding the resignation of Eutropius. Even those with the greatest reason to hate Tribigild could agree with him on that issue. The incapability Eutropius had displayed in dealing with Tribigild only made things worse. Gainas, at all costs, wanted to avoid yet another needless round of shedding blood among soldiers who were technically all part of the Roman Army. At this point Gainas joined forces with his rebel cousin and marched on Constantinople. Historians make too much of the fact that Gainas and Tribigild were related. So were Theodosius and Magnus Maximus but that did not stop the former from having the latter's head impaled on a pike. Their blood relationship had nothing to do with Gainas' subsequent actions. Gainas was the supreme commander of this ad hoc army group that consisted of the two under strength imperial field armies along with the Ostrogoth auxiliaries. With Tribigild as his deputy Gainas marched north. He arranged a meeting with Emperor Arcadius at the end of July in Chalcedon across the Bosporus from the capital. Gainas was now at the peak of his power and influence and he did not hesitate to use it. Having suffered enough embarrassments at the hands of eastern officialdom, there were numerous old scores to settle. Gainas demanded that Arcadius remove everyone that he, Gainas, considered an enemy to himself and the army. The emperor complied at once: Eutropius was banished to Cyprus; Saturninus, the chief judge who banished Timasius, was sent into exile himself; the recently appointed praetorian prefect of the East, the civilian Count John, who was a favorite of the imperial couple, and several other civil servants with anti-army or anti-barbarian attitudes also found themselves among the unemployed; criminal charges against Tribigild were dropped. Tribigild and his followers were reintegrated into the regular army and arrangements made to transfer them to Thrace. Eutropius' chickens had come home to roost. Tribigild saw himself as an eastern version of Alaric, while Gainas had suddenly seen his fortunes rise to the same level as those of Stilicho. Gainas and Stilicho were friends and generally operated in concert with one another. But during the years that he had been in Constantinople and Thrace following the death of Theodosius, Gainas had become very much his own man.

The depredations of Tribigild and his army had disrupted seven provinces. Gainas requested Fravitta, marshal of the East, to assist him by sending army units into those provinces to quell disturbances and maintain order. Tribigild's units were folded into the Army of Thrace but shortly after this Tribigild fell ill and died. In August, Gainas proceeded to Constantinople to work with Arcadius in constructing a new government. Aurelian was selected as praetorian prefect of the East. He was the brother of Caesarius, Eutropius' predecessor in the same office, who had been fired for refusing to help Count Gildo in the previous year. Aurelian had compiled an excellent record over the years as an honest and dependable civil servant. Caesarius' integrity was also beyond reproach, but in one area the brothers had a profound difference of opinion. Caesarius was an ardent believer in Theodosius's policy of integrating barbarians and especially the Visigoths into Roman society. Aurelian, on the other hand, recognized that the policy of allowing a barbarian nation within a nation to exist within the empire had been a calamitous failure. To him, the recent disaster with Tribigild and his Ostrogoths was a murderous reminder of how bankrupt the whole idea of "federate treaties" with any barbarian people really was. The choice of Aurelian by Gainas struck many people as odd, but it must be remembered that Gainas thought of himself as far more Roman than Visigothic. Above all, Gainas appeared to be reaching out to the most capable people he could find to administer the Eastern Empire. A number of other appointees at this time were of a similarly high caliber.

As the last year of the fourth century of the Christian era approached, the two halves of the empire seemed to be in sync with one another to a greater degree than since the death of Theodosius. Stilicho had maintained open lines of communication with his eastern contacts during Tribigild's uprising. While I had been selecting new additions from the upper Danube for the Army of Italy, Andreas and Julianus had delivered Stilicho's reply to Emperor Arcadius' request for military support if necessary. In October, the three of us traveled once again to Constantinople. Following the accidental (or otherwise) death of Mascazel, Stilicho's officials in Africa uncovered incriminating correspondence from Eutropius to Count Gildo that led to Gildo's revolt against the West. We delivered this evidence to Aurelian who was preparing charges of treason and corruption against the former Grand Chamberlain. The evidence we delivered would prove vital on both counts. Eutropius was subsequently returned from Cyprus in November, tried for treason by Aurelian, and executed in Chalcedon.

Gildo had been granted the title of marshal of Africa in spite of the paucity of troops stationed there. It was purely for political reasons: Theodosius was determined to assure his loyalty during the revolt of Arbogast. From a military standpoint, it was unjustified. Stilicho made sure that loyalty in that diocese would not be a problem in the future when he appointed his brother-in-law, Bathanarius, as count of Africa in 401. There was no way of knowing that it would turn out to be a death sentence.

I arrived back in Milan just in time for the birth of our first son, Marcellus. My wife and I were developing a wonderful home life together and the world appeared to be calming down. There had been only minor military activity all year in the West. With the execution of Eutropius and the death of Tribigild, the East seemed scheduled for a quieter time ahead as well. Then a strange thing happened. Aurelian was announced as the eastern consul for the year 400. Stilicho, who was to be the western consul for the year, refused to acknowledge him as such. Many of us were surprised by Stilicho's reaction and thought it to be a needless aggravation to relations between the two halves of the empire. As the late Theodosius's right-hand man, Stilicho's attitude may have been based on Aurelian's anti-barbarian attitude, which was quite "anti-Theodosian," and about which he had been quite outspoken. Puzzled as many were by this turn of events, Stilicho's action would soon appear to have been quite prescient.

The latter half of 399 proved a good one for bringing the eastern field armies up to strength. Several thousand of Tribigild's followers were distributed to the Army of Thrace, the Army of Illyria, and the two imperial field armies. As a result of this, Gainas felt sufficiently confident at the beginning of 400 to settle one more point of personal aggravation: he fired Alaric as marshal of Illyria and announced that the eastern government would stop paying the Visigothic Federate Army as Roman soldiers. This enhanced Gainas' reputation throughout the East and led to his being announced as consul-designate for the year 401. For the West, however, Stilicho immediately recognized the dangers that a disgruntled Alaric might pose and almost felt betrayed by Gainas' actions. Relations between the two men were never the same again. Stilicho would have much preferred Alaric's status to remain as it had been since 397. After all, the Visigoths had been quiet since then and appeared content with their situation in Macedonia.

Alaric was in a quandary. Abandoned by the East and on terrible terms with Stilicho, the Visigothic chieftain did not know which way to turn. His first concern was that at long last, under Stilicho and Gainas, West and East would present a united front against him. He and his people could be facing oblivion. In response to this danger, he did something that no other Visigothic leader had ever done: he had himself proclaimed king. He knew this was a dangerous move that would win him no friends among the Roman hierarchy. The only monarchs that could reign on Roman soil would be Roman emperors. Alaric did not, however, proclaim himself "king of the Visigoths." That would have been too much of an affront to Roman dignity. It might also have turned his worst fear into a self-fulfilling prophecy. By taking the title of "king," period, Alaric would obtain the authority he needed to have his followers obey whatever decisions he may be forced to take in the future that were in their best interests as he saw them. He was not trying to rally all Visigoths throughout the empire to his cause. Rome would inconceivably go a long way toward accomplishing that end for him, but that lay in the future. Alaric and his followers simply stayed put while determining their next course of action. The stunning developments that occurred in neighboring Thrace during the last half of the year 400 did nothing to enhance their well-being or sense of security. Alaric would turn elsewhere to find a permanent residence for his people. It was not a question of if but when. His direction was determined for him.

After several months in office, Aurelian's old anti-barbarian sentiments came to the fore and he started acting upon them. From the start, he had problems putting his policies into effect. He made the colossal mistake of dismissing many high-ranking men who were barbarian born in both the army and the civil service before determining whether there were sufficient numbers of Roman-born officers and officials to replace them. Aurelian appeared quite inept when it was determined that there were not. Thus, many barbarians recently sacked had to be restored to their former positions. This happened, not surprisingly, while Gainas was conducting troop inspections in Thrace. When he returned to Constantinople in April 400, Aurelian was sent into immediate retirement. It was shortly after this that Gainas' fortunes started to decline.

Gainas' overthrow of Eutropius had proven quite popular and the change of government that he had created had proven successful in the eyes of the army and public alike. There was, however, one sore point between the public and Gainas and that involved the quartering of members of the two imperial field armies within the eastern capital. There was nothing new in this. But what aggravated the relationship between civilians and these particular soldiers more than usual was that so many of them were newly arrived Visigoths and Ostrogoths whose level of discipline was far inferior to that of other troops stationed in the city. There was almost continual friction between the civilian population and these new soldiers who in numerous instances arrogantly behaved as though they were members of an occupying army. Some felt this way because, having been recently recruited from Tribigild's mob, they may have gotten away with murder before and felt they could do so again. This coupled with the public's memory of Hadrianople and Thessalonica created a tinderbox that only needed a flash to set it off. In May and June, the frequency of such disturbances increased. While most were minor incidents, some were serious, and bloodshed resulted. Gainas decided, correctly, that his best course of action was to withdraw as many of his soldiers as possible from the city and reestablish them elsewhere.

On July 12, 400, the soldiers of the two imperial field armies that were stationed in the city and their families started their evacuation. Some ill-defined altercation occurred between the departing Goths and Roman civilians. Fighting broke out, and soon thousands of people were involved. Civilians in apartments lining the street along which the Goths were withdrawing started throwing anything that they could lay their hands on including pots, pans, vases and pieces of furniture. An all-consuming hatred of the Goths going back over a century boiled to the surface. As word spread, people started pouring into the area to kill any Goth in the evacuating force whom they could lay their hands on. People climbed atop numerous buildings and started hurling roof tiles down on the trapped Gothic soldiers and their families. The uprising was completely spontaneous. The city garrison soon closed all the gates in the wall and, instead of trying to defend their fellow soldiers, joined in the slaughter themselves, as did the Imperial Guard regiments. The order for these two sections of the army to join in the massacre came directly from Emperor Arcadius. This, in turn, only served to encourage more civilians to join in the killing and thus it went on. Many soldiers in both the garrison and the Imperial Guards were Visigoths but their loyalty to Rome was never in question. The killing continued for hours. "Remember Thessalonica" was the most commonly heard rallying cry for those attacking the retreating field troops. In the most pathetic outrage of all about seven hundred Visigoths barricaded themselves in a Catholic church that administered to the small minority of Visigoths who were Catholic. Arcadius himself ordered that the church be set on fire and that anyone trying to escape should be slain. And they were: men, women, and children. The blood frenzy reached such a terrifying state that by the time the slaughter was over, seven thousand Goths were dead. Thessalonica had indeed been remembered, right down to the body count.

Twice on that terrible day, Emperor Arcadius had reacted in a total panic to the developing situation: first by sending the garrison and the Imperial Guards against the retreating Visigoths and then by ordering the incineration of the Gothic Catholic church. But in a purely personal way, the ultimate enormity was yet to come. Gainas was just outside the city at the time, getting the new quarters for his evacuating troops ready. When he found out what was going on inside the city, he attempted to reenter but found all the gates barred to him. Perhaps this was what prompted the emperor's third overreaction. Arcadius called the Senate together and had it declare Gainas a public enemy.

What wretched feelings of rejection and isolation must have run through Gainas' mind on that terrible night when he learned that he had been declared an outlaw. This man had served the empire his entire adult life with total dedication. Now he found himself stripped of all titles and authority because of events that had spun out of control on a single day in which he himself had taken the lead in trying to rectify previous disturbances in a peaceful manner. When any man is declared a public enemy, his soldiers have the right, indeed the obligation, to desert him. That never happened with Stilicho in 397. Stilicho was an agent of the Western, not the Eastern, government and thus had a power base that was independent of the government that was trying to condemn him. That was not the case with Gainas. Many, but not all, of his soldiers did abandon him at this point. He had to run for his life and he struck north for Thrace.

He knew he was heading for a dry well, but where else could he go? During August and September of 400, Gainas and his dwindling army scoured Thrace in a desperate attempt to sustain themselves. The gates of all its cities remained closed to them. They even attempted to cross the Danube but found their way blocked by a combination of the Moesian Fleet of the Roman Navy and the Huns. Increasingly wracked by desertions, Gainas turned his army southward to re-cross the entire Diocese of Thrace. He attempted to cross into Anatolia where he might improve his fortunes among the remnants of Tribigild's followers who had remained there. That was not to be. Upon declaring Gainas a public enemy, Arcadius had ordered Fravitta, marshal of the East, to hunt Gainas and his remnant army down and destroy them. Fravitta was respected but not well known in the West, as most of his career had involved duty on the eastern frontier. What was known was that Gainas and Fravitta were on unfriendly terms. It was Fravitta who had ordered the fleet to prevent Gainas from crossing the Danube and now he would stop him from crossing into Asia. Fravitta rounded up all the ships that he could find along the coast of the Sea of Marmara and the Dardanelles. Gainas and his followers, who soon broke into the Thracian Chersonese near Gallipoli on the north shore of the Dardanelles, found no ships available. When they did manage to put together a slapdash flotilla of hastily constructed rafts, Gainas' followers were slaughtered and scattered by the navy on December 23, 400. Shortly after that, Gainas was captured and summarily executed by order of Fravitta. On January 3, 401, Gainas' severed skull appeared impaled on a pike in Constantinople. This final indignity happened because Fravitta insisted upon it.

Over the past four decades, it has been a standard practice among historians to denounce Gainas in the most disdainful terms. The historians, of course, are all Romans writing either in the grand old pagan tradition or in the relatively recent Christian manner. In all cases, Gainas is painted in the blackest possible fashion, by the pagans because he was a Goth and a Christian and by the Christians because he was an Arian and not a Catholic. As far as I am concerned, there was no treason on Gainas' part at all. It was he who was the victim of a panicky emperor and an over reactive Senate.

Gainas was a man of humble origins, born north of the Danube. He had a talent for languages and had mastered both Latin and Greek by the time he was twenty. Tall, powerfully built, and with long, flowing blond hair, his style and appearance were emulated by many young soldiers of the time, regardless of their national or provincial origins. Gainas was ultimately a tragedy but in his earlier days he had been a very appealing figure to soldiers on both sides of the Danube. He and Stilicho were about the same age. The two met shortly after joining the Roman Army and had been close friends ever since. Gainas built an enviable reputation during Theodosius's containment and pacification campaign against the Visigoths. During the 380s and 390s, he advanced rapidly through command positions. At the time of the civil war of 394, he was the highest-ranking Goth in the Roman Army. Gainas' most conspicuous hallmarks were his loyalty to Rome and his devotion to duty, and he never failed to inspire similar reactions in those who served under him. One of his favorite expressions was "a bargain made is a bargain kept." I saw Gainas in combat on three occasions: briefly at the Battle of the Danube in 386, at length during the Battle of the Frigidus in 394, and again during the standoff at the foot of Mount Olympus in 395. I had never seen this man appear anxious even during the most dangerous circumstances at the Frigidus, and in those few instances where he didn't have an answer to a problem, he never hesitated to take council with those who may. In every sense, he was a soldier's soldier. It was in Stilicho's employ that he led the assassination of Rufinus in 395, and it was on that mission that I had worked most closely with him. He was Stilicho's eyes and ears in the eastern capital, and he certainly kept his career-long friend informed on affairs there. It was his first lengthy posting to the great capital of the Eastern Empire and it may have had a disorienting influence on him. He saw the great general Timasius stripped of power by Eutropius and driven into exile. He witnessed the downfall of other fine officers on the basis of the slightest suspicion however ill founded. He saw the appalling corruption of Eutropius and his cronies who quickly confiscated the estates of the fallen and was sickened by it all. At the same time, he saw men promoted to fill military positions whose qualifications were considerably less than his own. It seemed that during much of his time in Constantinople, his own career had been placed in a state of suspension. He had approached Eutropius on several occasions requesting appointments to which he was fully entitled on the basis of experience and seniority. Each time, except the last, his requests were ignored. He had served the empire long and commendably. Gainas had been completely loyal his entire life and had always seen himself as a Roman first and foremost. He had risked his life many times for the empire, while Alaric had done so only once for a period of two days. Yet in 397, Alaric, who was responsible for killing and enslaving thousands of Roman citizens, was rewarded for his treason and criminality with one of the highest commands in the country. At the same time, Gainas saw himself remaining subordinate to a eunuch whose most conspicuous "service to the state" had been to find a wife for his dull-witted emperor.

In spite of a lifetime of loyal and dedicated service to the House of Theodosius, Gainas had been brought down by the confusing events of a single day. Those of us who knew and admired him were shattered by his tragedy and not just because of the purely personal aspect of it. There was a broader issue involved here that the gloating politicians, to their eventual regret, never considered. Gainas was the foremost example of how a Visigoth could enter Roman service and rise to the uppermost levels of imperial officialdom. That was what Theodosius's policy toward them was meant to achieve from the very beginning. If a Goth could be Romanized to the highest degree possible and still be brought down and slaughtered for no other reason than that he was a Goth, then what possible hope was there for integrating the Visigothic nation as a whole into the matrix of Roman society? This question arose in Alaric's mind as well at this time. Alaric might have pondered the fate of Tribigild as well, though it wouldn't have done him any good.

The tragedy of Gainas made me wonder if a pattern was not emerging. The six leaders of the Eastern Army who fought on the Frigidus in 394 should have had excellent futures ahead of them. Ultimately, the Fates would turn on them all. Bacurius was the only one of them killed in the battle itself. Theodosius died four months later, but his health had never been robust. Timasius had fallen afoul of Eutropius in 396 and been banished to a godforsaken oasis in Egypt, though he was subsequently rescued from it, in failing health, by his son. Now Gainas had suffered a terrible end. Only Saul and Stilicho were left. I no longer envied them.

During 400, most of my time was taken up by routine quartermaster duties. In addition, I also helped the adjutant in handling the record keeping for the new additions to our regiment that had been acquired the previous year. Consisting mainly of Visigoths and Alemanns, they turned out pretty well. During the year, we even received a small stream of Italian civilian recruits. The rest of the time was spent with my family. Our young son was developing rapidly, and in April, Aureliana informed me that she was pregnant again. I was overjoyed at the news, but at the same time, I worried about having forced her into motherhood too quickly. At age twenty-three, I think she might have liked the two of us to have had more time to ourselves before the children started to arrive. But at age thirty-five and having already lost one family, rightly or wrongly, I didn't want to wait.

During the spring, Stilicho sent me as a courier to Ravenna to convey his plans for augmenting the Adriatic Fleet. Nothing major, but Stilicho was good at sending members of his staff on secondary assignments to territory with which they had no familiarity simply to get them acquainted with it. I had never been to Ravenna, Rome's main naval base on the Adriatic. It is located about 180 miles southeast of Milan just north of the Via Aemilia and on the southern fringe of the broad plain of the Po. The city is surrounded by a strong wall and, more importantly, by broad swamps along its landward boundaries. About four centuries ago, Emperor Augustus constructed Classis, the port of Ravenna, about three miles to the south. Its harbor can hold well in excess of two hundred ships. The swampy approach to Ravenna/Classis makes this city/port almost impregnable because of the difficulty of drawing up a large army anywhere close to the walls. Neither archers nor artillery can be brought within range other than over the causeway leading to the landward approach road or the coastal highway that runs up from Rimini through Ravenna to Concordia, just to the west of Aquileia. After delivering the documentation, I toured the city and the port and arrived at rather mixed feeling about the place. Often plagued with fog, it is quite humid much of the year. No river flows through the place, but it does have an aqueduct to provide fresh water. In addition, Augustus built a canal from the most southerly mouth of the Po (roughly a dozen miles to the north) that brings a flow of water through the city. From this main canal, numerous smaller ones divide the city into a grid of small islands connected by numerous bridges. Transportation through much of Ravenna can be provided either by road or by boat. The harbor is kept clean by the water from the canals continually emptying into it, along with the constancy of the Adriatic tides.

I had had little opportunity to consider how best to invest my considerable financial reward from Theodosius after the Battle of the Frigidus. What with the campaigns in Thessaly in 395 and Britain during 396–398, the recent recruiting drive on the upper Danube, and other things, I had simply banked the money. In my spare time, I had looked into investing in properties in the Milan area. However, being the western capital, prices for everything seemed exorbitant. The devastation of Greece had struck fear into the hearts of people everywhere. Almost every city in the empire, including Rome, was either building walls if it had none or repairing them if it did. My biggest strategic concern was the Rhine. What would happen if we were off combating a breakthrough into Gaul when a similar deluge came across the upper Danube? In addition to myself, I once again had a family to consider. The more I looked Ravenna over, the more it seemed to develop a sudden attraction based on its strategic location alone. There were certainly prettier towns around, but sitting between the sea and the swamps, I could not think of a safer one. I checked with several real estate agents to get a feel for property values in the area. They were considerably less than in Milan.

Upon returning to Milan, I mentioned to Stilicho my thoughts about purchasing rental properties in Ravenna. He owned a number of estates and knew far more about property values and investments than a novice like myself. I was surprised by his response.

"We never know what the future holds for us," he replied. "I think that property investments in Ravenna at this time would be an excellent idea. I'm considering some there myself."

I got the names of several well-respected real estate lawyers, agents, and bankers from him. I was soon on my way to building my own small financial empire. Or more properly, a financial principality, I suppose. By the year's end, I had purchased two apartment blocks in the most fashionable part of Ravenna along with several large vacant lots in the same area. My intention was to hang onto the lots for perhaps five years and see if their land value appreciated. Knowing Stilicho's legal and financial contacts, I also hired a management firm to administer and maintain my properties for me, collect the rents, pay the taxes, and so on. By the beginning of 401, I had gained a considerable rental income.

In July 400, like everyone else in the empire, we had become long-distance spectators to the calamity unfolding in Thrace. As it dragged on through the summer, autumn, and into the winter, we all came to realize that the end was inevitable. When it finally came in January 401, my comrades and I felt a sickening sense of relief that it was finally over. The destruction caused by Alaric, the Hunnish invasions, the treason of Tribigild, and the confused conflict with Gainas had meant that the East, unlike the West, had known virtually no peace at all since Theodosius died. Its land, people, and treasure had suffered brutally in Europe and Asia. What we had no way of knowing at that time was that the beginning of the fifth century would also come to symbolize the end of its current time of troubles. Now it was to be the turn of the West.

CHAPTER 12

The Approaching Tide (401–406)

In late January 401, our second son, Aurelius, was born. We named him after his maternal grandfather. Marcellus, who was now fourteen months, had to learn that it would take a while before his little brother would actually be a playmate for him.

In spite of the convulsions that the East had gone through during the last half of 400, Stilicho and Fravitta saw eye to eye on most issues. East and West appeared to start the new century on a harmonious note. We all crossed our fingers that the situation would remain that way. In February, I was promoted to tribune and appointed to Stilicho's staff. When not commanding in the field, I had acquired considerable experience as a supply officer over the years. As a result, I was made deputy quartermaster for the Army of Italy. My main duties would involve supplying the field army both in peacetime and when on campaign. The four praetorian prefects have responsibility for acquiring all food and material supplies for the army and delivering them to the supply depots within their respective prefectures. The army quartermaster corps determines what those supplies should be. In addition, it is incumbent upon us to transport these supplies to the units in the field during wartime. In one vital regard, I did manage to over celebrate my promotion. A month later, Aureliana informed me that she was pregnant again.

During the spring, we received disquieting intelligence reports about tribal movements to the north of the upper Danube. In recent years, our relations had been good with the Alemanns living across this stretch of the river. But large numbers of Asding Vandals, with some Visigothic and Alan support, were starting to move into the area between it and the Main River. Should they turn hostile, this would place Rhaetia and Noricum at risk and, ultimately, Italy. The Asding Vandals, like the Ostrogoths, remaining Visigoths, and other Germanic peoples north of the lower Danube, were chafing under the frightful over-lordship of the Huns. According to friendly Alemanns and Roman spies, a segment of the Asding Vandals at least had broken free of Hunnish control and started moving westward into Bohemia. This in turn put pressure on the Alemanns north of the Danube. Soon the whole weary picture was starting to look all too familiar.

The quartermaster staff from the Army of Italy traveled north across the Alps to assess the situation. No major campaign had been conducted in this area in many years. We first determined the condition of the various storage depots that would have to be used if conditions heated up. Most of my summer was spent supervising work crews all across the transalpine region repairing storehouses and granaries as required. At the same time, the engineering corps was attending to bridge and highway repair. There was little doubt that a major invasion was about to take place into Rhaetia or Noricum or both. The biggest problem was trying to determine where it would occur across a three-hundred-mile section of the frontier.

In spite of his having been so unceremoniously dispossessed of his office at the beginning of the previous year, Alaric remained uncharacteristically quiet. Determining his next course of action was no easy affair. His council members were giving him contradictory advice, but the council he took with himself gave the wisest recommendation: sit tight and do nothing; at least for the time being. After the uprising in Constantinople in the previous July, Alaric and his followers, like the rest of us, watched in stunned amazement as the fortunes of Gainas collapsed. The destruction of Gainas, however, did nothing to enhance Alaric's position. In Fravitta, Alaric had an enemy that was just as hostile as Gainas. In fact, he was more dangerous since he had the full support of the army, the Senate, and the emperor behind him. Shortly after executing Gainas, Fravitta was named consul-designate for the year 401 in his place.

When word started getting around about the impending invasion by the Vandals and their allies, Alaric sent a letter to Stilicho offering to assist in defending the area. Stilicho politely refused the offer. From a purely military standpoint, Stilicho and Jacobus, his marshal of cavalry, felt they possessed enough resources to contain the invasion. More importantly, Stilicho did not want the Visigothic federates residing anywhere in the Western Empire given their deplorable inventory of atrocities in Greece. Alaric, however, was not the type to take no for an answer.

As the summer wore on into the early autumn, it appeared ever more likely that the attack was going to happen against Rhaetia. Even by straining its resources to the limit, its meager population and supply base could not sustain its local garrisons plus the Army of Italy for a prolonged period. For that reason, most army supplies had to be brought up from the Po River Valley. In addition to supervising construction projects across the Alps, I worked with civilian officials in northern Italy. Together we secured supplies and transported them north to the supply depots in the transalpine region. Every time more units were called in to augment the Army of Italy, our supply requirements changed accordingly. In October, while I was taking one of our last supply trains north out of Italy before the snows blocked the passes, the Asding Vandals and their allies invaded. They struck at several points across the frontier of Rhaetia and western Noricum. It was larger than originally anticipated and this led to a fateful decision.

At the beginning of 400 when Gainas had fired Alaric, Stilicho had reoccupied the fortifications in the Hrusica Pass in the Julian Alps. This was in case Alaric decided to make a thrust westward into Italy. At the time, he did not, but the pass remained garrisoned anyway. For the war against the Asding Vandals, Stilicho had also reoccupied the Alpine pass fortifications across northern Italy. This was to block barbarian penetrations from Rhaetia or Noricum that got past our frontier forces and the Army of Italy. When the actual invasion did come in October, its magnitude was of such a nature that every available soldier in Italy had to be pressed into service. This included moving the troops defending the Hrusica Pass to Rhaetia. We were just that strapped for manpower. Their removal did not go unnoticed by the Visigothic sovereign, who was never one to permit a golden opportunity to slip by.

While preparing the last wagon train of the year, I was sending couriers out to check on snow conditions in the various passes. The previous week, after bringing the Western Sacred Consistory up to date on the situation north of the Alps, Stilicho had taken the last elements of the Army of Italy north through the Splugen Pass. Its high elevation leads to its early closing almost every winter. We had just left Milan and were traveling northeast of the city when one of my couriers arrived to inform me that this pass had already been plugged with snow drifts by a sudden storm. As a result, I had to bring the train through the Julier and Rescia passes farther to the east that were still open. This took us into the upper reaches of the Inn River Valley. While this region is quite beautiful in the summer, studded as it is with magnificent Alpine peaks, it can be equally terrifying in the winter when the weather turns bad. This route lacks any sizable towns, and numerous wagon trains have perished on it over the years when caught in sudden snowstorms. Having commandeered as many wagons as I could find, I had them loaded to less than half their legal limits to enable us to travel at a faster rate. As a result, we exited the mountains on their northern side before they were hit by subsequent storms. These closed virtually all the passes to us, except the Brenner Pass, for the rest of the winter.

The fighting was quite heavy throughout October and November, and in a way, we were fortunate that winter set in early. The Asding Vandals had based their invasion plans on being able to break through or bypass our frontier defenses and get through the Alpine passes prior to the snowfall mounting up. They were met by a far larger army than they had anticipated, and that, joined with early heavy snows, prevented them from reaching any of the passes through the Alps. The Asding Vandals had spread their attack out in order to avoid any concentrated counterattacks by our forces. As a result, instead of any major battles, we were involved in a large number of small confrontations. The Asding Vandals could not break into any of the towns since they were all fortified, and for the same reason, they could not gain access to any of our supply depots. Like virtually all barbarians then they lacked siege equipment. Once the snows set in they were stuck but then so were we. We had to make do with the supplies we had but they were plentiful. However, once their supplies were exhausted, the Asding Vandals had to forage for whatever they could find. In Rhaetia, for reasons I have explained earlier, that wasn't very much. Attacking long-abandoned villas gained them nothing and as the snows accumulated their situation became desperate. A few thousand of them had been killed while the weather remained good. Once it turned bad and it was difficult for them to either advance or retreat, they started to surrender in large numbers. Our own casualties had been relatively small and we could count the campaign as a success. It took until late December before we completed our mopping-up operations. By that time, the snows in the more mountainous regions were too deep for conducting operations of any kind. Along the Danube the local garrisons, supplemented by units from the Army of Italy, captured or killed hundreds of Asding Vandals and others trying to get back into Germany. The following spring several hundred bodies of the invaders were found in the approaches to a number of the Alpine passes. Hundreds more must have frozen or starved to death in the forests.

About the middle of November, I ran into Stephanus near Salzburg in Noricum. He and his squadron were leading a line of prisoners back to a holding facility near that city. We had not seen one another since leaving Milan.

"I see that you've had a successful day," I remarked, nodding toward the captives. "Where is this lot from?"

"You'd be surprised," Stephanus replied. "I know I was when I discovered the background of some of them."

"How is that?"

"Well, we've got the standard run-of-the-raid barbarian for the most part; largely Vandals but with a small component of Alans and a few Visigoths." he replied.

"So what's the surprise?"

"There's a new element among the invaders that I have never seen before," he went on. "We have about eighty-five captives here, and six of them are Romans."

"*What?*" I asked, almost stupefied.

"That was our reaction too when we found out," Stephanus continued. "I first heard of such occurrences about three weeks back. The first ones to be captured were summarily executed for treason. But as we bagged more of them, the order came down to treat them as regular prisoners if they were originally civilians. Those who were deserters from our army, and there have been only a few, are still being executed."

"Where are they from?"

"The downstream dioceses mostly, Thrace and Dacia" he replied. "When you and I first started serving in Illyria, remember how we heard about how some civilians had joined the barbarians because they were fed up having the hell taxed out of them by the government while getting no protection in return? Well, these chaps have carried the process one step further. They've gone north of the Danube to join with various barbarian factions instead of waiting for the barbarians to come to them. Thrace has been so thoroughly trashed by all the military activity within it over the past twenty-five years that it is about as economically viable as the Sahara. We both know that."

"Yes," I replied wearily. "Shrunken cities and burned out villas everywhere you look."

"The eastern government's recognition of Alaric," Stephanus went on, "triggered a few of our native-born co-nationals there to offer their services to the barbarians. Not Alaric, mind you. I've interrogated some of these Roman renegades myself and they hate him as much as we do. The trouble is they hate the Roman government just as much. Their rationale is that if the government can enter into cooperative arrangements with our most dangerous enemies then they can too. In many cases they are the sons of landowners whose estates were destroyed in years past. Now they are being taxed to pay the salaries of the very men who drove them into near poverty in the first place. It's a hell of a situation."

"So these civilians," I said, "some of whom would rather chop their thumbs off than serve with our own army, are volunteering to serve our enemies."

"And then being conscripted into our own army, should they manage to escape execution upon capture," Stephanus continued. "You and I just finished putting our lives on the line for almost two years to secure Britain, only to return to the continent and find our fellow citizens ready to stab us in the back as a show of gratitude. Is the world going bloody-well crazy or what?"

"I wish I knew," I replied lamely, "but let's not make judgments that are too sweeping on the basis of the actions by these poor bastards."

That night, we got together in Salzburg to catch up on some long-overdue drinking and to toast once again our long-departed comrades.

About a month prior to winding down our northern campaign, the issue of Alaric suddenly occupied front and center stage once again. Stilicho was headquartered at Augsburg for this expedition, and toward the end of November, he called his staff together for a special meeting.

"Gentlemen," he began, "you are all to be congratulated for a job well done. This campaign is starting to wind down and what our soldiers in the field cannot accomplish, 'General Winter' should do for us. However, every silver lining has its cloud and I've brought you here to discuss an altogether different matter concerning Alaric and his army. Once he heard the conflict here in the transalpine provinces was in full swing, he took the offensive and invaded northeastern Italy from Pannonia through the Julian Alps on November 18."

"That goddam son of a bitch," Saul exploded. "The next time we should hang him from—"

"I know, I know," Stilicho cut him off.

"Where is he and what direction is he heading?" Saul went on, cooling down somewhat.

"That's what I'm monitoring," Stilicho continued. "Look, this has not come as a complete surprise to me. I've had agents tracking Alaric ever since we started moving men and supplies north for this campaign. Everything remained normal until about a month ago when he and his followers suddenly packed up and started moving north from their bases in Illyria and then west. Having waited until the harvest was in, the Visigoths are well supplied with food. They are also well provisioned militarily since they have been obtaining supplies from the various arsenals along the way. The managers of these weapons depots have been dealing with him as though his former title of marshal of Illyria was still in effect."

"So his presence in Italy comes as no surprise to Constantinople either," Saul considered.

"Apparently not," Stilicho replied, almost smiling. "Our good friends in the eastern capital appear intent on getting Alaric as far removed from their jurisdiction as possible. But two can play that game. I know we all have families in the Po River Valley, but they will be secure. The cities are all heavily walled and garrisoned, and the Visigoths have no siege equipment worthy of the name. The walled cities in Greece all survived unscathed."

"Where is he now?" Saul repeated.

"Between Emona and Aquileia," Stilicho replied. "It's too early yet to say what direction he will eventually head, but I'll keep you and our field commanders informed as soon as I'm informed myself. The big advantage for Alaric in moving now is that the Army of Italy will be involved on the frontier for most of the winter. We are not going to pack up and return to Italy until we've accomplished our objectives here; that means completely destroying all invaders in Rhaetia and Noricum."

At that point, we all expressed our agreement by continually slapping our hands on the conference table.

"The big disadvantage for Alaric," Stilicho went on, "is that the harvest has also been collected in Italy and is secure in the cities and towns. The Visigoths are going to have to make do with whatever food supplies they brought with them. When those stocks run down, they are in trouble. They won't be able to requisition military equipment in Italy either the way they have in the East for the past four years. As soon as military and meteorological conditions permit, I will be returning to

Italy with whatever forces this theater can spare. You will notice that several of your fellow tribunes are missing from this meeting. That's because I sent them off to Trier this morning to order several regiments from Gaul and Britain to join us for the upcoming campaign in Italy. We'll make up with garrison troops whatever shortfall we suffer to confront Alaric. Any questions?"

"Yes," I said. "Have we been able to determine who the leader or leaders are of the forces that we're battling here in Rhaetia and Noricum?"

"Yes, we have," Stilicho replied, "but he appears to have made it safely back north of the Danube. None of us had heard of him before. The odd thing is that, in spite of the enemy soldiers here being mostly Asding Vandals, they were led by an Ostrogoth named Radagaisus."

It would not be the last time we would encounter him.

We were all disheartened by what we had just heard. At the same time, Stilicho's address served to encourage us to redouble our efforts to crush the invading Asding Vandals and their allies. As was always the case at this time of year, our men guarding the Alpine passes were soon withdrawn for their own safety. We were immediately hit with a series of snowstorms that closed virtually all the passes for the winter, resulting in the ironic situation in which Alaric was snowed into Italy and Stilicho was snowed out. We had patrols out almost every day that weather permitted, tracking down the invaders. The transport troops that I had at my command were continually checking the conditions at our supply depots to ensure that our field troops would be fully supplied at all times with whatever they required. As 401 passed into 402, this was becoming more difficult, as our supplies started running low. However, by that time, reports of barbarian activity anywhere had dropped off drastically.

Stilicho kept us informed of Alaric's progress throughout this period. Initially, it was difficult to see exactly what the Visigothic objective was. Their rate of advance was not overly great, and there appeared to be a degree of aimlessness to it all. Alaric did not reach Aquileia until mid-December 401 when he laid a half-hearted siege on the city. There was no question of his taking it, so the siege was soon lifted. Instead he settled for sacking several small undefended towns in the vicinity whose inhabitants had already been evacuated to safety. At the end of January, he was near Verona. By this time, Stilicho felt that the transalpine region was sufficiently secure that he could take several legions from the regular army along with some federate cavalry regiments and advance south through the Brenner Pass to attack the Visigoths. Hundreds of Vandal prisoners volunteered to join two hastily formed federate cavalry regiments and also joined Stilicho's southward trek. The remaining legions and independent regiments comprising the Army of Italy were to follow as soon as military conditions allowed and the Alpine passes were usable. Most of his staff left with him at that time except for a few of us like me.

As a general comment, the federate regiments participating in this campaign constituted a prime example of how such units were supposed to be utilized. Some of these regiments were comprised of Alans and some of Visigoths who were not Alaric's followers. The point is they came from small groups of barbarian settlers, none of whom numbered more than five thousand people. Each group had signed its own private treaty with Rome and was defending the empire to our mutual advantage in agreement with the stipulations of its contract. It was with small groups like this that the federate concept worked best for both them and us. Somewhere between these smaller associations and the nation within a nation that Alaric's horde constituted, there appeared to be a critical mass beyond which control by the central government was impossible. This was especially true with a Roman leadership that was divided. Not once had Alaric and his followers ever acted to defend the empire from external aggression, and our distrust of them had now risen to the point where we felt it impossible to use them in that capacity. While our British campaign was going on, Alaric was rampaging through Greece. While we were fighting Radagaisus for the first time in the transalpine provinces, Alaric invaded Italy. The Fates, however, would continue to protect Alaric until the peculiar destiny they had designed for him had been fulfilled. Only then would they abandon him, as they eventually abandon us all.

My chief responsibility now was to transport all the food and supplies that were available to the supply depots leading to the Brenner Pass for the Army of Italy, the federate cavalry regiments, and the new regiments coming down from Gaul and Britain. This proved quite time-consuming since the winter of 401–402 had been more severe than is typical in much of Europe. The snows melted later than usual. As a result, Alaric and his horde had little trouble crossing any rivers during the early phase of their campaign. It was remarkable that, with almost all the mountain passes plugged with snow, so that neither man nor beast could traverse them, rumors had no problem making it through at all. We soon heard that Emperor Honorius and his government were planning on moving the capital of the Western Empire from Milan to Arles in southern Gaul. This was soon confirmed when Stilicho was informed of such by imperial courier while on his return march south. That piece of information certainly didn't come as a morale booster for those of us who had family members in Milan. After all, if the government did not have faith in the considerable defenses of the city against an army with no siege equipment, what hope should the rest of the population be expected to have? The generalissimo was furious at this blatantly cowardly proposal and quickly convinced the Western Sacred Consistory to reconsider.

The emperor of the West was now eighteen years of age and was turning out to be every bit as feckless as his brother. All of northern Italy had been thrown into a panic when Alaric's invasion was announced since the Army of Italy and certain garrison troops were north of the Alps. But once the initial shock subsided, the population calmed down and was determined to stand up to Alaric. It would have been nice if our cowardly emperor had shown a similar resolve.

It's odd, but after all these years, what I remember most about Honorius is just how uncouth he appeared both as a child and as an adult. Any description of Honorius's character (if indeed he may be said to have possessed such a thing) will inevitably appear superficial, a caricature, regardless of how articulate and sincere the writer. He would live his entire life as little more than a vegetable in human form, his eyes permanently focused on infinity, a man-boy with a blank past, a very shaky present and no meaningful future. No one paid much attention to Honorius during the early years of his reign. But as he aged, it became quite obvious that of the long line of emperors who had graced and disgraced the throne, Honorius was the most pitiful of the lot. A common wisecrack among us soldiers at the time was "Where is Caligula when we could really use him?" Honorius was born a lazy old man, totally lacking in intelligence. His physical appearance was most ungainly. He had a large head perched on top of a rather dwarfish body, and his arms dangled a little too close to his knees to avoid comparisons to an ape. His large eyes were always half-closed and made him appear to have just awakened, though not for long. His mouth was unusually small, but that didn't matter since he never had anything to say anyway. He was, without question, the most rattlebrained and unsophisticated lout who has ever reigned.

While his reign would prove to be the most disastrous of any emperor, Honorius could not help but be involuntarily comical on occasion. He was like a circus clown or one of those characters seen sometimes in comedy theatrical productions who, by their mere presence, automatically invite mockery or laughter or shame. To rise to the level of an arch-mediocrity would have been for Honorius a Herculean task. On those rare occasions when a question or statement of fact was placed before him, the emperor would reply initially with an uncomprehending stare. Then he would start looking desperately around him in the hope that one of his advisers would come up with a response before the silence became too embarrassing. There was not the slightest hint of constructive thought processes being carried out behind those large, drooping eyes. How such a meager individual could come to occupy the highest office in the world's greatest state will always remain my favorite example of how damnably capricious the Fates can be. Christianity can boast as much as it wants to about having abolished them. It's lying. The Fates are not only alive; they are thriving.

By March, Alaric was laying siege to Milan but to little effect. Commerce was disrupted, but the city had been well provisioned. The approach of Stilicho's army encouraged Alaric to continue his drive to the west. Captured Visigothic soldiers claimed that their objective was Gaul. That came as a surprise to everyone, as we thought they would strike south into central Italy with its insignificant military establishment but rich estates and cities. Perhaps the strategic blunder he had committed in Greece of isolating himself in the Peloponnese with no way out was a lesson well learned. Whatever the reason, he avoided the temptation and headed southwest from Milan toward the Via Julia Augusta. This coastal highway runs from Genoa through the Italian and Gallic Rivieras to Arles. Once there, he could strike west or north or perhaps into Spain. All was by no means unified on the king's council. His leading cavalry commander, to whom Alaric might have been distantly related, held serious misgivings about the king's long-range policy for his people, or lack thereof. This was Sarus. He had fought under Alaric's leadership from the very beginning and was a veteran of the Frigidus like so many of the rest of us. As he matured, however, Sarus had come to see the terrible shortcomings in both Alaric's character and his plans of action. To Sarus, as to all Romans, Alaric seemed to possess no positive vision for the future of his followers. They seemed to be just so many swords for hire. It wasn't Alaric's fault that he was fired in Illyria, but once again, his idea of long-range national ambition had reverted to determining which undefended city to attack next and little more. It just wasn't good enough.

At one council meeting after leaving the environs of Milan, Sarus suggested that they consider settling down permanently with the western government's permission. Sarus was very outspoken. He was on the council to advise and advise he did. He pointed out that they had been fortunate in not having to engage in major combat since leaving Illyria. They had been unable to gain access to a single fortified city to replenish their supplies after traveling 75 percent of the way across northern Italy. Sarus suggested that they negotiate a new treaty with Milan and settle somewhere in the West where they could furnish their own food supplies. Alaric expressed his usual contempt for such a sedentary existence, but Sarus had replied, "When we are allies of Rome, we eat, and when we are its enemies, we starve." Somewhat of an exaggeration but not by much. This conflict of opinion between the leader and the led was not limited to Alaric and Sarus, as subsequent developments would prove.

Alaric suddenly announced to his entourage that a vision had appeared to him imploring him to march on Rome. Everyone was stunned, especially when, within a week, he tried to capture the small northwestern town of Hasta and failed. This was hardly a promising inauguration to a march on the Eternal City. Moving southwestward to the even smaller town of Pollentia, the Visigoths pitched camp to rest up over the Easter holiday. Because of the ongoing religious observances, the Visigoths felt that they were under no immediate danger of attack. This was a major miscalculation. The reinforcements Stilicho had ordered from Gaul and Britain had not yet arrived. This meant that the Visigoths outnumbered the Romans but Stilicho was under severe political pressure to have a showdown with Alaric once and for all. This was understandable: if Rome could not defeat the Visigoths in the very heartland of the empire, then where could we defeat them? Stilicho launched an attack on Alaric's unsuspecting camp on Easter Sunday, April 6, 402. Stilicho's deputy commander for the assault was the Alan general Saul who launched the main cavalry attack. The camp was overrun; several members of the Gothic nobility along with almost their entire national treasury (that consisted of all the plunder they had stolen in Greece and elsewhere and included the scarlet robes of Emperor Valens that they had taken at Hadrianople) were captured. Part of Alaric's baggage train was taken and destroyed as well. The Visigoths suffered numerous casualties among their infantry but Alaric managed to launch a counterattack with his cavalry. In the ensuing charge, our Alan cavalry was driven back and Rome suffered a cardinal loss in the death of Saul. Now only one leading general from the Frigidus remained. The battle was in doubt for hours before Alaric's army managed to stage an orderly withdrawal to the south. Technically, some historians have claimed the battle resulted in a draw. But given that it was the Visigoths who retired from the field and especially when what followed subsequent to the battle is considered, I've always thought that it was more than just a marginal Roman victory.

Stunned at this attack and by the manpower and material damage he had suffered, Alaric was at a loss as to what to do. So deep in Italy, his losses could not be replaced by reinforcements. Rome, of course, did not have that problem. At least not yet since units called down from the north and west would continue to arrive in the weeks ahead. Alaric halted his forces after reaching the Mediterranean coast and traveling just a short distance to the east. Rome was out of the question. Instead Alaric agreed to negotiate a peace agreement with Stilicho. This time, however, the peace would be dictated, not negotiated: Alaric and his followers would leave Italy altogether and immediately; the Visigoths would return *all* Roman prisoners and slaves to Stilicho while Rome would release none of the Visigoths that it had captured; Alaric and his followers would be granted no provisions by the government, but they would be allowed to purchase supplies, under Roman supervision, with what little was left of their national treasury. By this time, it consisted only of the money they had accumulated while working in the employ of the eastern government. This was a humiliation for Alaric but he had no choice. The message was clear. If they wanted to avoid acute malnutrition on top of bankruptcy then the quicker they got out of Italy the better. Progress was slow. This time they took a more southerly route back to the vicinity of Verona.

While all this was going on, I had been working with the staff of the praetorian prefect of the Italies to get supplies positioned in the north of Italy and Rhaetia for the British and Gallic troops that were soon to arrive. While they were coming through the Alps, we received news of what had happened at Pollentia. I was disappointed to see that the British unit that was joining us was a regiment from Legion II Augusta stationed at Caerleon, the centuries-old legionary fortress nearest my home. With luck, I hoped it would be returning there soon. It never did.

Alaric was retreating eastward under close supervision, but for me, the most important thing at this time was getting home to see my family once again and to meet the latest addition. My mother- and sisters-in-law had no doubt taken good care of Aureliana, but again I felt guilty about not being there for her when she needed me most. I had missed almost a whole year out of the lives of my wife and children but circumstances would not permit much time for a family reunion yet. Business with the office of the praetorian prefect did, however, enable me to get to Milan for two days before returning to the field. Assistance from that office was essential: as long as Alaric was in Italy, the Army of Italy had to remain on a war footing just in case Alaric changed his mind regarding the recent agreements he had made. After all, if he did, it would not be the first time. And it wasn't.

Bursting through the door of the apartment, I scared the hell out of everyone in the place. My wife, her mother, two of her sisters, and our sons were there along with our new baby daughter, Margareta Ardovanda. She had been born the previous November and was now almost five months old. Marcellus, true to form, ran off to hide in one of the back rooms, and Aurelius, now fifteen months, took off after him. I was also rather stunned to see a tall, beautiful girl with deep reddish-brown hair named Claudia. She was my wife's cousin and had come up to Milan from Florence about a month after I had left for Rhaetia the previous year. Everyone excused themselves and left, knowing that Aureliana and I wanted to be alone. We had a lot to get caught up on. Now I had two sons who didn't know who I was and a daughter who would soon feel the same way if I didn't find another line of work.

"First of all," Aureliana said once everybody had left, "I want you to know that everyone is healthy and there were no problems with the delivery. Incidentally, I noticed the glow that came over you once you spied Claudia."

"Quite so," I replied with a big smile on my face. "She's a knockout."

"And knocked up too," my wife continued. "That's why she's here. She's not married, and to avoid a family embarrassment in Florence, she was shipped up here last October for the duration of the pregnancy and probably beyond. Her mother and my mother are sisters. I hadn't seen her since we were quite small."

"How old is she?"

"Twenty-three," my wife replied.

"And who's the lucky daddy?"

"An Alan cavalryman that she took up with," my wife replied stiffly. "Several thousand of them are settled across northern Tuscany and Umbria as you know. Her father almost killed her when he found out about it. After he gave her a severe beating her mother sent her up here to us. She's a wonderful girl, and it's really a shame this has happened. She's been living with me ever since she arrived and has been a big help."

"When is her baby due?" I asked.

"Early May some time."

"Well now we can return the favor," I said. "Claudia can stay on living here, and you can help her when her baby arrives because I'll be leaving the day after tomorrow."

"You just got here!"

"I know, but until Alaric and his bunch are out of Italy completely, all soldiers are on active duty. I'm just here checking up on supply requirements with the praetorian prefect's office."

"Is Alaric coming back this way?" she asked apprehensively.

"No. He's taking a more southerly route past Piacenza and Cremona. The army is following him closely to ensure that he does. Once Claudia's baby is born, what happens? Are she and her Alan boyfriend going to get married? If not, is she going to keep the baby or what?"

"You know what the law is regarding marriages between Romans and barbarians," she said.

"Sure, but dispensations are obtained all the time to get around it," I informed her, "and being on Stilicho's staff, I would have no difficulty in obtaining one for them—if that is, in fact, what they want."

"She didn't even know she was pregnant until after her Alan lover was called up," Aureliana said.

"If she never sees her boyfriend again for any reason," I said, "and she doesn't want to keep the baby, would you be interested in adopting it?"

"Are you serious?"

"Of course I am," I replied.

"That's wonderful!" she exclaimed. "You know I've been wondering about how to go about approaching you on the subject because I've been thinking the exact same thing."

Aureliana was a tall, raven-haired, and very pretty girl, and she possessed a very warm and understanding heart. She was always willing to do things for people, especially when they were suffering hardships of one kind or another. In any case, my having brilliantly set the mood without even trying, we had an early supper, put the children to bed, and had the rest of the evening to ourselves. Throughout my brief stay, the boys remained quite suspicious, giving every indication that they wanted nothing to do with me. Only time could change that. The following day after I was finished at the praetorian prefect's office, I dropped around my mother-in-law's place to see Claudia. I obtained the name of the man who was the father-to-be of her child and the name of the regiment that he was in. She did not know what she was going to do if she had to face life as an unwed mother, so I assured her that Aureliana and I would be willing to adopt her child if she, herself, agreed. After that, it was one more precious night at home before heading back into the field.

Once the Visigothic retreat was well underway, Stilicho visited Rome to apprise the Senate of the conditions set forth in the recent agreement. In addition, he managed, after lengthy discussions, to get them to provide more financial resources. They would not, however, go along with his request for conscription in Italy to meet the danger. The Senate put a greater value on the remuneration they would obtain through the efforts of their slaves and tenant farmers than they did in clearing Alaric out of northern Italy. The Senate attitude on this issue was most peculiar. Given the barbaric ruination of Greece, one would think that the Senate would be only too willing to offer up their tenants and slaves to defend the empire and especially Italy. Instead they were as parsimonious as they could possibly be. Their attitude might have arisen from their simply being too damned rich. Many of them own not just one but many estates and not just in Italy. They have land holdings in Africa, Spain, Gaul, Britain, and Anatolia as well. To begin with, what were the odds on any one of their estates being attacked? In other words, why suffer a definite loss against only a possible loss? Secondly, the richest were so rich that they would only suffer marginally even if any of their Italian estates were attacked. Patriotism was mostly a dead notion for this lot. The Fates, however, had some surprises in store for them that would manifest themselves quicker than any of us could have imagined.

I rejoined the Army of Italy shadowing Alaric's eastward retreat. I checked into the status of Claudia's lover and discovered that he had been killed at Pollentia during the Visigothic counterattack that had also taken the life of our Alan general Saul. He had been cremated along with the other battlefield dead. This made Claudia's situation all the more difficult. At the same time, I started thinking about a solution to it that was altogether different from what Aureliana and I had discussed. That would have to wait until I returned to Milan.

Throughout the Visigothic retreat, Stilicho had spies in Alaric's camp. Word soon arrived that Alaric, big surprise, was going to break his agreement to leave Italy via the Julian Alps. Instead, he was going to strike north from Verona and pass through Trent on his way to the Brenner Pass, Rhaetia, and Gaul. Word of this was brought to us in early July before Alaric reached Verona. As a result, Stilicho was able to position troops in the mountains north of that city sufficient to block any thrust in that direction. At the beginning of August, Alaric's horde was in the vicinity of Verona when he stopped. Stilicho wasted no time in launching an immediate attack that, once again, caught Alaric off guard. The Visigoths immediately tried to put their "northern strategy" into effect but, upon finding the highway to the north blocked, were forced to establish a fortified position on the nearest high ground they could find. This time, however, unlike Thessaly in 395 and the Peloponnese in 397, there would be no government order demanding that Stilicho withdraw. With their food supplies running low and the summer heat at its peak, the Visigoths were soon wracked with malnutrition and disease. His cavalry suffered defeat at the hands of our Alans and desertions in his ranks were soon rampant. Alaric's greatest loss at Verona was the desertion of his two leading cavalry commanders, Sarus and Ulfilas, who deserted with hundreds of their men to our side. Numerous attempts to break out of the trap were defeated with heavy casualties that only prompted more desertions. This was the worst defeat of Alaric's career. The siege went on for weeks and just when most of us felt that Alaric would soon be either surrendered to us or captured, a truce was called. As a result, a meeting was held between Stilicho and Alaric that went on for hours. When it was concluded, Stilicho called another meeting at which all members of his staff were ordered to be present.

It was the briefest such meeting I ever attended.

"A new agreement has been negotiated. Under its arrangements, Alaric and his Visigoths will be leaving Italy immediately for Pannonia. Their good conduct has been guaranteed by their surrender to us, as hostages, of several dozen members of their nobility. They have also surrendered a sizable portion of their baggage train that we will be destroying in full sight of them later this afternoon."

We all sat there staring at one another in total disbelief.

"My lord," I asked, "why are we not executing Alaric to be done with him once and for all? This is the chance that we have been all waiting for ever since—"

"Enough," Stilicho interrupted me in a voice much louder than usual. "We will have use for Alaric in the future."

At that point, we were dismissed.

Later that afternoon as the Goths departed past Verona, we set fire to a massive collection of several hundred of their wagons, most of which were in bad shape. We kept those in good repair for ourselves. We wanted to make life difficult for them, but at the same time, we did not want to impair the rate of their easterly progress to any marked degree. The sense of dejection that we all felt was beyond description. In 391, 395, 397, and now at the Battle of Verona in 402, a Roman army had maneuvered Alaric into a position to either destroy him militarily or at least starve him into surrender. And on every occasion, he was allowed to slip away. A cynic could well observe that we must have been totally triumphant in our dealings with Alaric at Verona. After all, we hardly ever had to engage in combat with him again. Of course, at the time of his next arrival, we had nothing left with which to confront him. For the time being, however, Alaric stuck to his word and led his people back to the Diocese of Pannonia. Disappointed as we may have been, the method behind Stilicho's "madness" soon became apparent.

During the past year, I had spent only two days (or rather two nights) at home. Our successes notwithstanding, we were all tired and badly in need of some rest and relaxation. An understanding wife is vitally important in these circumstances and I was fortunate to have been twice blessed in this regard. Aureliana had not expected me to be away for nearly as long as I was when I left for Rhaetia the previous year. Neither did I. But a soldier's wife must get used to this sort of thing just as the soldier must abide being absent from his wife and children. Claudia was heartbroken when I informed her that her Alan boyfriend had been killed at Pollentia. I assured her that Aureliana and I would see to it that she did not suffer from want of anything from a financial standpoint. Claudia's baby daughter had been born in May and the two of them had continued to live at our apartment as we had agreed. Now that I was home on a permanent basis, she and her baby had to move back in with my mother-in-law. She was in no state of mind then to determine whether she was going to keep the baby or not, and I assured her that there was no need to rush the decision. After returning home, I approached Aureliana on what had occurred to me since I left Milan to rejoin the army.

"What do you think about this idea? Claudia needs a husband and Stephanus really needs a wife. What say we introduce them and see what happens?"

"Stephanus?" she said surprised. "He is a good-looking hunk. He's about your age, isn't he?"

"Two months older. It's about time he settled down, whether he realizes it or not. What do you think?"

"I'll check with Claudia tomorrow," she answered, "and you check with Stephanus. If they are agreeable then let's do it."

The following day, I approached Stephanus, whose regiment was stationed in Milan, and discussed my proposal with him.

"You know," he said, "where women are concerned, my standards are of the highest order."

"She's alive," I replied with a straight face.

"Standards met." He laughed. "You're on."

I described Claudia in the most glowing terms and candidly told him that if I was not already married, I'd be making a play for her myself.

Several days later, Aureliana and I had the two of them over for supper, and they seemed to hit things off quite well. Later in the evening when we were sitting around talking, Aureliana asked Stephanus and me, "Do you think that we are finally free of Alaric?"

"No," I replied, "we will not be free of Alaric until the day he dies. By that time, we will have to contend with his successor, whomever that may be, and the whole monotonous stage play will simply continue as it has. Christ, I wish I wasn't so damned bitter about what happened at Verona! We *had* him! Regardless of the casualties, we should have captured him and had him summarily executed."

"I agree completely," Stephanus said. "Given all the desertions that had already depleted his ranks, I think we could have defeated him, absorbed and assimilated his people, and been done with this ridiculous notion of a kingdom of the Visigoths."

"I think," I continued, "I had a sort of epiphany on that last day near Verona. I was as angry as anyone to see Alaric leave the place alive. Then I remembered something that Stilicho said at his meeting near the end of last November when he informed us of Alaric's invasion. When Saul and Stilicho were discussing Constantinople's support of Alaric against us, Stilicho remarked, 'Two can play that game.' Somehow I think he plans to use Alaric to do unto them as they have done unto us. But each half of the empire cannot go on indefinitely using Alaric as a proxy to conduct a civil war with the other. If we do, then sooner or later something is going to break. The East has been doing that with us, off and on, for seven years now. I think we are now going to adopt the same policy with respect to them. I hoped Stilicho and Gainas would combine to destroy Alaric. When Gainas fell, some of us hoped that Fravitta would agree to accomplish the same end. Alaric's invasion here means that Fravitta does not have the influence at the court of Arcadius that we hoped he would. We are going to continue to look inward rather than outward."

"You're saying that Stilicho is going to have Alaric attack the East?" Aureliana asked.

"I don't know," I replied. "The first hint of how we are going to use Alaric will be reflected by where Stilicho settles him in Pannonia. That has not been publicly announced yet."

She then asked, "Did Stilicho say anything specifically at that last meeting that you had with him on what future operations you might be going on?"

"No. I'm on his staff but I'm not exactly part of his inner circle. My biggest concern remains what it has always been: the frontier. The most responsible way for Stilicho to have conducted the Battle of Verona would have been to destroy Alaric, forget the treachery of Constantinople, and concentrate on defending the Rhine and the upper Danube. It's been six years since Stilicho and Honorius visited the Rhine. I think it's time for another visit that should include Britain and Spain as well. Honorius is utterly useless as a national leader. So why not send him on a grand tour to let the provinces at least know that the central government is aware that they still exist? His handlers might even be able to manage the little shit to the point where he didn't even make too much of a fool of himself."

"Wouldn't that surprise us all?" Aureliana laughed. "When the Visigoths were besieging the city, we had old ladies, even my mother, claiming that they were ready to man, or woman, the walls to pour boiling oil or water down on Alaric's horde while our craven emperor ..."

"The elect of God," Stephanus chimed in.

"... was planning on hightailing it off to Arles," Aureliana continued.

"A most pleasant town at that time of the year," I remarked.

"Especially when you've got eighty thousand Visigoths after you," my wife continued. She usually wasn't this political and really felt herself on a roll.

"We were utterly disgusted with his cowardice," she said. "He's almost nineteen years old, and he has no more backbone now than when he was nineteen months. He is a pea-brained, gutless jackass who is a disgrace to his office. Is he never going to grow up?"

"The next time the Visigoths try to capture him," Stephanus suggested, "perhaps we should let them have him. God only know he is of no value to us. By the way, girls, your holy fathers must have been an enormous comfort to you while the city was encircled." Stephanus, always the cynical pagan, couldn't resist getting in a few jabs at the Catholic Church.

"Marginally more so than the emperor," Claudia replied after having been rather quiet for some time. "They were all quite certain that the Second Coming of Christ along with the Apocalypse was just around the corner and we had all better repent in a hurry or be forever damned. A special concern for me under my then-current circumstances."

By that time, the wine was starting to get to us, and we all had a good laugh.

"Sounds like what I've heard happened after Hadrianople a quarter century ago," Stephanus said. "At that time, even the venerable Bishop Ambrose was running about bewailing the approach of the forces of Gog and Magog, whatever the hell they are."

"Including the book of Revelation in the Bible," I suggested, "might be regarded eventually as one of the less responsible decisions that the church fathers ever made. There was considerable debate in the last century as to whether that book should be a part of the Bible at all. The church cannot even agree on who wrote it. Its inclusion to this point has been far more of an embarrassment than anything else. Every time something goes drastically wrong, some of the leading churchmen can be relied upon to panic and start proclaiming the end of the world."

"With considerable relish, of course," Stephanus added. "After all, it does help to keep the troops in line, at least for a week or two."

We had no idea at the time of how many opportunities the near future would offer these same churchmen to indulge their eschatological fantasies. It was just as well. Stephanus escorted Claudia home, and the two of them started seeing one another on a regular basis. Aureliana and I counted the evening as a success, and so did they. Three months later, they were married.

At the beginning of September, the government announced that the capital of the Western Empire was being moved from Milan to Ravenna. We had been hearing rumors of such a move for several weeks, but the city to which we would be transferred had not been certain. The official statement said that "On the advice of the Western Sacred Consistory, Emperor Honorius …" and so on. One could imagine how much "advice" Honorius would need to turn tail and flee in almost any direction that was away from a real or imagined enemy. It could not escape the public's notice that Ravenna is a seaport. The implication, of course, was that the next time push came to shove, Honorius could take flight over water as well as land. Everyone was shocked when the announcement was made, including those of us who had first heard the rumor. Milan had been the seat of government for the Western Empire for almost a century and a half. It had been chosen to provide the emperors with close proximity to the frontier so as to better control events. Moving the capital to Ravenna so quickly after the invasion of Italy sent a shudder throughout the West. One could sense public confidence, which had been quite resilient just a year earlier, starting to decline. The image of the emperor of the West feeling that he needed broad swamps in addition to stout walls to cower behind served to further stimulate defensive fortifications, both private and public, everywhere. Property values started to decline in Milan and soar in Ravenna. As a result, I would do quite well for myself and my growing family. The contempt for the sons of Theodosius was now universal. An emperor is born to face the enemy, not run from him at every approach. After the Battle of Verona, the Senate granted Honorius a triumph in Rome. Two years would pass before the lazy little bugger got around to celebrating it.

In October, we moved to the new capital. As our residence, we chose a large apartment in one of the blocks we owned. Now that Ravenna was the western capital, it underwent somewhat of a building boom. I sold a few of the vacant lots I had purchased earlier at a handsome profit and started the construction of two new apartment buildings, one in Ravenna proper and the other at Classis. With Aureliana pregnant by year's end with our fourth child, we decided it was time to construct a private home for ourselves. That project got underway during the following spring.

In the autumn of 402, I had celebrated my twentieth year in the army. By year's end, I was thirty-eight years of age and was starting to think about whether I wanted to continue with the military or retire and get into private business of some sort. Staying in for my full enlistment had definite benefits. As a veteran, both my wife and I would be exempt from the poll tax and all custom duties. In addition, I would be exempt from having to serve as a town councilor, an obligation that had proven ruinous for many a man even in the best of times. In addition, there would be a tax-free grant of a dozen acres of crown land (somewhere) that I would probably cash in. Not a bad future actually. My inclination, however, was to stay with the army at least for a while yet. It was really the only life that I knew and I still enjoyed it.

In October 402, after settling into our new headquarters, Stilicho called a special meeting of his staff. Its purpose was to inform us of what had really transpired at his conference with Alaric two months earlier.

"I know that many of you were disappointed with the fact that Alaric was permitted to leave Italy after the Battle of Verona. Last year in Rhaetia, when we were first informed of his invasion, my intention was to destroy him once and for all. So what changed my mind? First of all, Illyria. Since the Battle of the Frigidus, the prefecture of Illyria has increasingly become bandit country. Here we are, eight years after that battle, and the Army of Illyria is still under strength. Apart from a thin line of forces along the Danube, there are insufficient troop concentrations anywhere in the interior to police the place. Civil authority minus any means of law enforcement is no authority at all. You all know that I am as disgusted with Alaric's behavior in Greece as anyone. But in all fairness to him, once he was established as marshal of Illyria in 397, he and the civilian administration of the prefecture worked well together. His losing his office was not his idea. The four years in which he occupied the dioceses of Macedonia and Dacia were probably the most peaceful they have known since our last civil war. During the past year, since

Alaric left, civil disorder has increased again. The East is determined to do anything it can to hang on to the prefecture except reestablish control there. That situation cannot be allowed to go on indefinitely. Again, in fairness to Alaric, he did offer his services to us in the conduct of our recent campaign in the transalpine provinces. You all know why I rejected his overture and I stand by that decision. At the same time, we cannot afford any more surprises from the East. After all, what might they throw at us the next time; an army of Huns? I think Alaric learned something positive while he was marshal of Illyria: he has far more to gain by working with us than by fighting against us. Over the past two months, the praetorian prefect of the Italies has had a commission assessing the damage done by the invasion. Their work is ongoing and will not be complete for several months. However, it appears that the damage caused was far less than might have been expected considering the size of the incursion force. There was nothing to compare to Greece six years earlier.

"My second consideration is our campaign in Rhaetia and Noricum. Some of you at this table were part of the recruiting campaign that was conducted there early last year. The results were not overwhelming. Again, the number of federates that we signed up after our war there came to about 1,500. Such numbers speak for themselves. We cannot afford the luxury of facing enemies to the north and east of us simultaneously. As a result, a new agreement has been made with Alaric, but before I get into the details of that, a brief historical background might be in order. The prefecture of Illyria, as it was originally constituted, consisted of three dioceses, Pannonia, Dacia, and Macedonia, along with the proconsulate of Greece. That was its composition at the time of the Battle of Hadrianople when it was still part of the Western Empire. As a result of Hadrianople and the civil wars, the prefecture, or certain of its components, have bounced back and forth between East and West at various times. The Diocese of Pannonia was ceded back to the West in 395 as the quid pro quo for our returning the various elements of the eastern field armies to the jurisdiction of Constantinople. As of November 1, we are renaming that diocese to 'Western Illyria.' On that date, Alaric will assume the title of count of Illyria, and his field army will be in the employ of the western government. The prefecture of Illyria will be officially referred to as 'Eastern Illyria' by the western government. The Visigothic Federate Army is in the process of taking up positions in the lower Sava River Valley. This area is the breadbasket of our Diocese of Western Illyria, so the Visigoths cannot complain that they are not being well provided for. They are to be paid as Roman soldiers, just as they were when employed by Constantinople. Should they be attacked, we will assist them if required. Should we be attacked, we may call on them to assist us if the situation calls for it. Alaric is the supreme commander for the diocese. That means all Roman and Visigothic army units there report to him."

There was a brief question-and-answer period, but it covered minor items and cast no new light on what we had just been told. The particulars were illuminating, but they did not come as a surprise. After Verona, it was just a matter of time before the details of the agreement became public knowledge. In the following years, Alaric and his men conducted themselves as a normal Roman field army would. The East, though it felt threatened, did nothing to provoke a confrontation. In tribute to both Stilicho and Alaric, the agreement worked well. When it collapsed, it was the fault of neither man. After the meeting, several members of the quartermaster's staff of the Army of Italy and I were ordered to determine the supply requirements of Alaric's army. This assignment would not go into effect until the beginning of the New Year. It would take until then for Alaric and his people (it was no longer fashionable to refer to them as a "horde") to get settled in the cities and towns along the Sava River. The information that we gathered would be reported to the praetorian prefect of the Italies. He, in turn, would make the necessary arrangements to enable Alaric to withdraw these supplies from our storage depots and obtain weapons from our arsenals. Of significance on a different level in 402 was the death of the western senator Symmachus at the age of fifty-seven. In his prime, he had been considered the leader of the Roman Senate, but being a devout pagan, his influence declined as the imperial court came ever more under the domination of the Catholic Church.

Four years had passed since I had last seen Margareta. I mentioned her to Aureliana in terms of our academic association, our long friendship, and her being mine and Makila's landlady and neighbor while we lived in Trier. I gave Aureliana the general impression that Margareta was older than she was and, needless to say, I never mentioned just how intimate our relationship really was. After all, that would have served no purpose whatever, would it? Margareta and I did keep in touch with one another, as we had always done. When I told her that Aureliana and I had gotten married, she responded with a most generous wedding gift. When I returned to Milan after the Battle of Verona, I wrote a very lengthy letter to her explaining everything that had happened over the past year or so. I mailed it after we had taken up our new residence in Ravenna. Late in December, I received a letter from her thanking me for what I had sent her but explaining that she was no longer holding her seminars as she had in the past. She had been ill for several weeks and had been periodically confined to her bed at the country villa where she had decided to spend the winter. Although she tried to make it sound like nothing serious, it didn't take much to read between the lines. There appeared to be something seriously wrong, but with the winter settled in, communications would be difficult until the spring arrived. I saw Stilicho, explained the situation with Margareta, and requested that I be sent on any special courier assignment that he might have with Trier.

At the beginning of 403, our quartermaster task force left for the Sava River Valley. We did not meet with Alaric until we had completed our assessment. To that point, we had been dealing with members of his council. They provided the raw data we required for the praetorian prefect's office. Based on what we were told, the Visigothic Federate Army then numbered about ten thousand men, and this army, combined with its dependents, amounted to seventy-five thousand people. Stilicho had specialists make estimates for both as they left Verona the previous summer. Our numbers were a little lower than what they had arrived at but that was to be expected: Alaric had padded his figures in anticipation of some of his deserters returning to the fold once things had settled down. He also knew that Stilicho had other means of ascertaining these numbers and did not want to be caught inflating them too much. Alaric only appeared before us at a special dinner he gave on our behalf just prior to our leaving. He was a handsome man, shorter than I expected, and his Latin was quite good. He introduced himself to us before the dinner. In a brief speech afterward, he stated the hope and full expectation that relations would continue to go well between us now that all past "misunderstandings" had been cleared up. (An understatement if there ever was one.) The following day, we left for Italy, and we were back in Ravenna by the beginning of March.

Shortly after my return, I was called into Stilicho's office where I received a nasty shock. "Marcus, I'm sending you to Trier with special instructions that will be conveyed from there to the count of Britain. Intelligence reports from north of the Danube are indicating that a westward movement by various barbarian groups into Bohemia and Bavaria might be occurring in the near future. While nothing of the sort has started yet, the initial estimates for enemy troop strengths are considerably larger than they were two years ago. If these estimates are correct, then we will need all the troop support that we can muster. As a result, I'm going to be withdrawing Legion XX Valeria Victrix from Chester along with several independent regular and federate cavalry regiments currently stationed on the island."

"This will seriously undermine public confidence there," I said, "in spite of our having done so much to restore it."

"I'm not intending this as a permanent move," Stilicho replied, "but rather as a temporary relocation. You are as well acquainted as anyone with how difficult our manpower situation is."

"What about going back to the Senate again to request a troop call up here in Italy?" I suggested. "I know they turned you down the last time, but with this new information, perhaps they will relent."

"Such an approach will certainly be made," Stilicho said, "but in the meantime, we need trained professionals. I know that it's not easy for you, as a native Briton, to see these troops being withdrawn from your homeland. But Britain is quiet for now, and we cannot afford to have troops sitting idle there when Italy itself is endangered. Besides, bringing these troops down from Britain will make my job before the Senate a little easier. I will be able to claim that the frontier troop strengths have already been reduced to the minimum. I'm sending you on this mission because you are the only Briton on my staff, and I think it appropriate that you transmit the order. In addition, it will give you a chance to visit your friend Margareta, whom you mentioned was in ill health."

I appreciated this last, understanding gesture.

"There is an upside to this assignment," Stilicho continued. "Following the Battle of Verona, several cavalry regiments were returned to Gaul that had been brought down from there last year. In addition to their role in Gaul, they are also to be used as a reserve that can be drawn upon by the count of Britain should the need arise. This is similar to what we did back in 396. I hope this will serve to relieve any British fears that the recent and current withdrawal of their legionary forces signals any sort of downgrading in the magnitude of their importance to us."

"When do I leave, sir?"

"Go home now and spend the rest of the day with your family," the generalissimo replied. "I'm having the transfer orders drawn up now. You will report here first thing tomorrow morning to pick them up and leave immediately."

The Alpine passes were not clear of snow yet, so I traveled the most southerly route, taking the Via Aemilia from near Ravenna to Dertona, from where I headed south on the short Via Postiana to Genoa. There I connected with the Via Julia Augusta that would carry me along the lush, rich Riviera coastline all the way to Arles. As I turned north at Arles and raced through the valleys of the Rhone and Saone Rivers, I was once again on the familiar ground that I had traveled as a teamster over twenty years earlier. The weather remained good, and the rest of the trip was easy until I entered the Moselle River Valley, where I got drenched in a couple of heavy spring downpours. I passed Margareta's villa and continued into Trier to deliver Stilicho's orders to the praetorian prefect of the Gauls. After my business was finished there, I visited the baths and returned back up the Moselle, apprehensive of what I might find.

Turning into Margareta's villa, even the birds seemed uncommonly quiet. One of her servants answered the door and, taking my cloak, said, "Hurry, sir, there isn't much time." She led me to the bedroom door and then backed away. I entered and was stunned by what I saw.

Margareta was lying in her bed and looked as if she had aged at least ten years since I had last seen her. Her once-blond hair had partly turned white, and it was obvious that she was in considerable pain.

"Marcus," she said, struggling to sit up, "how did you know to come?"

"I've never known you to be sick a day in your life and your giving up your seminars told me that things must be more serious than you were letting on in your last letter."

"I've been writing another letter to you"—she waved to a nearby table—"whenever I've been able to get up, but it seems to have been taking forever. A historian's ultimate duty is to tell the truth but the most difficult truth of all is to face the fact of being fatally ill." She stopped suddenly and winced in pain. I then took her in my arms and kissed her and ran my fingers through her hair as I had done so often in the past. She then pushed away slightly and looked at me, smiling.

"Seeing you has long been my most enjoyable social highlight. I've always felt such a confusion of feelings about you. You're my lover, you're the son that I never had, and in the innermost recesses of my heart and mind, I've often thought of you as the husband that I wished I had had all my life."

I held her close. "I fell in love with you the first time I ever saw you. I will always remember that day in the library as one of the most beautiful in my life. I read somewhere that every man, at least once, falls in love with a woman from the generation that went before him. I know that it's been true in my case because for me that woman was you. I have wished so often that I had been born a generation earlier or that you were born one later so that we might have fallen in love as we have and lived our entire lives together. You're my woman of a thousand fantasies."

"Only some of which we ever fulfilled, I gather." She smiled.

"It's probably just as well," I said.

"I hate to change the subject," she interrupted, "but I must. I'm not going to recover, Marcus."

"Surely there must be—" I started, but she cut me off.

"No, there isn't," she said, tears welling up in her eyes. I laid her back on the large pillow behind her, as it was obvious that she was in considerable agony. "I don't have much time," she said finally, her voice weak and cracking. "My appetite is gone, and I've been passing blood for weeks but listen. My affairs are all in order. Two years ago, I sold my estate in Aquitaine. I had not been there in ages, and while I had thought of it as a possible retirement retreat for my golden years, I felt that by the time I got there, I wouldn't know anyone anymore. As it turned out, the gold turned to lead anyway. Having no children of my own has been my biggest disappointment in life, and I am so proud that you named your daughter Margareta Ardovanda after me. I have not heard the name Ardovanda before."

"It's a Frankish name," I said.

"Probably named after another old love, but my name came first, and that's what counts." She laughed, and so did I. "I own this estate and my home in Trier," she continued. "With the money I received from the sale of my estate in the south, I also purchased two small villas here just a few miles upriver. They provide good rental income. I also have a considerable sum of money on deposit in several banks in town. A copy of my will is on the table over there with your unfinished letter. Take them both with you. I have named you as my sole heir. The will is registered at the basilica, and the joint executors are you and my lawyer Demetrius Galerius. His office is just off the forum on the north side of the basilica. He's a decent and honest man. I taught his sons years ago. They are both civil servants now. I have always …"

At that point, she yelled out in a convulsion of pain and gripped her lower abdomen.

"There's nothing that you or anyone else can do." She struggled on. "A year after I sold my estate in Aquitaine, I had a small mausoleum built for myself in the pagan cemetery just outside the city. Everything is taken care of." The pain gradually subsided, and she started to breathe more easily.

"It's such a comfort to me having you here," she said. "At the same time, I wish that you didn't have to see me looking like this. I'm such a mess. I …"

I leaned over and kissed her. "That day when I first saw you, I was convinced that I was looking at as beautiful a woman as I had ever seen or could ever hope to see. You were beautiful then, and you still are now.

No amount of illness or the passing of time could ever diminish you in that regard. You have always been in my prayers from that very first day, you are now, and you always will be."

"I've always given a damn about you too." She smiled, and her eyelids started getting heavy. "Stay with me this night."

"Of course I will."

At that point, I took her in my arms again and held her for the longest time. It was as though I thought that simply by holding onto her, she could continue living. Even after I realized that she had fallen asleep, I continued holding her past midnight. Then I laid her gently back onto the large pillow, pulled the covers up on her, and called her servant. This woman had her own small bed in Margareta's bedroom in case she was needed during the night. I went down the hall to sleep in what had once been my children's bedroom. Just sitting there on the edge of the bed, I was overcome by all the memories that flooded back from over ten years earlier, and I cried as I had not done since that dreadful day in Carnuntum.

"Sir, come quickly," the female slave called to me from the doorway. I got up quickly and ran to the main bedroom. It was already light out.

"She's gone," the trembling slave barely whispered to me.

I checked Margareta's pulse in several places, but there was none. She had died quietly in her sleep during the night. Another female slave appeared at the door and started crying. I rode into town and met with her lawyer. The funeral was held the following day. I informed her stepson who now lived in the large villa next door. But none of Rufius's family came to the funeral that was, otherwise, well attended. It was also an occasion for me to get reacquainted with some old friends, such as Gaiso, whom I had not seen in years.

The lawyer entered her will into probate, and everything went without a hitch. I had him sell the three villas that she owned on the Moselle along with her home in the city. These things occurred over a period of about six months, and it was not until December that I received the cash from these transactions along with her bank investments. I had considered holding onto the villas as rental properties, but the distance from Trier to Ravenna is just too great for that. If you are a responsible landlord then you should live in close proximity to the properties that you own. Management companies are all very well and the most reputable among them do an admirable job. I have always used them to manage my properties but such companies can change over time or be purchased outright. Great distances only magnify the problems that arise when less scrupulous managers start handling one's affairs. When I finally received the cash from these transactions, I was more depressed than elated. I had spent some of the happiest and most important years of my life in that region, and I hated cutting my last connection with it in this way. I daydreamed occasionally of what it would be like in retirement relaxing in the beautiful garden of Margareta's villa overlooking the Moselle. But a daydream was all that it could ever be. My life in Gaul had come to an end years ago and I had to look to the future. It was just as well that I had not pressed my bemusement at Trier too far. The day would soon arrive when the daydream would be smashed forever.

From Trier, I raced northward through the Ardennes Forest to Bonn and visited the grave of my friend Gregorian. He who we were all certain had such a glorious future before him. Twenty years! How could so much of my life have passed so quickly? We were little more than boys when we had started out together. I then struck north to Xanten in the company of a cavalry squadron that just happened to be on patrol along the Rhine. I had sworn to share the financial award that Theodosius had granted me with Chlogius's widow. My plan was to take the money for her out of the cash that I would be receiving from Margareta's estate. The lawyer handling the probate had assured me that there were sufficient funds in Margareta's accounts to fulfill my obligation. I simply wanted to ensure exactly where Chlogius's widow lived so the lawyer would know where to transmit the funds. Eight years had already passed, and this was the first opportunity that I had had to go there. I discovered that she had died in 399. She and Chlogius had had no children. It was turning into a heartbreaking trip all around. I returned to Trier and visited Margareta's tomb before continuing back along the same route that I had taken. Going through Rhaetia and then south into Italy would have been quicker but I wanted to see the Riviera coast again with its crystal-clear air and golden sunshine, endless beaches, and splendid villas. What a way to live!

Construction on our new home in Ravenna was completed by the end of August. We moved in shortly after the birth of our second daughter, Licinia Juliana. Aureliana's mother's health had started to go into decline during the previous year, so in the autumn of 403, we had her moved down from Milan to live with us. With a live-in babysitter, Aureliana and I were afforded a little more time to attend the theater, dine out and attend government functions and so on. Generally, Ravenna was working out rather well for us even if, from the standpoint of surrounding scenery, it left something to be desired.

The remainder of the year 403 passed by uneventfully from a military and political standpoint. In Margareta, I had lost a fine friend and a wonderful love, but in passing, she had enriched me to a far greater extent than I had ever thought possible. The firm that I used to manage my properties in Ravenna had offices all over Italy. In addition to Ravenna, Milan, and Aquileia in the north, they had offices in Rome and the Bay of Naples area. It was recommended to me that I might wish to invest in properties in the bay area. That part of Campania has always been popular as a vacation area, as a playground for the rich, and as a retirement area for those who can afford it. It was also suggested that the recent invasion of northern Italy might get the upper classes in the Po Valley to think about more southerly climes. The latter point, however, was not borne out by any exodus of the wealthy. The subsequent agreement that Alaric made with our central government served to allay fears in this regard. When I had some spare time, I did manage a quick trip to the Bay of Naples and was simply overwhelmed by the beauty of the place. Naples struck me as a little too congested, but Sorrento on the south shore of the bay, near the isle of Capri, was just right. The whole Bay of Naples area was too pricey for my resources, but just south of there lays the Gulf of Salerno. Its north shore running from south of Sorrento through Amalfi toward the city of Salerno is a very attractive area, and it was there that I decided to start looking for real estate investments.

Aureliana originally felt that our new home was too large, but it was gradually getting filled. My wife was surprised when I commented that as the children got older they would want their own rooms. She had never had a bedroom of her own until we got married, and even then, it was only half hers.

A memorable death, from a national standpoint, during 403 was that of Princess Flaccilla, the eldest daughter of Arcadius and Eudoxia. Born on June 17, 397, she took suddenly ill and died in the midst of a personal confrontation between her mother and the patriarch of Constantinople, John Chrysostom. The patriarch had insulted the empress and her friends in public by denouncing their luxurious lifestyles. The empress interpreted the sudden death of her daughter as a direct punishment from God for her having dared to argue against His chief representative in the eastern capital. Emperor Arcadius, who had always lived a reclusive life, now withdrew more than ever from the public view. He was overwhelmed by his daughter's death and never really accepted it. From that day forward, he almost never ventured outside his palace walls. Whenever he did, the populace of Constantinople would flock to see him, certainly not out of admiration but simply out of curiosity.

The year 404 dawned peacefully. While the frontiers remained quiet, it was a year of significant passings both personal and national. At the beginning of the year, the same task force that I had worked on the previous year was reassembled and traveled to the Sava River Valley. We performed our annual reassessment of Alaric's requirements. The figures had risen very slightly. At the beginning of April, I received a letter from my sister informing me that our father had died in January. When the first parent dies, we have passed a significant milestone in our lives but much remains the same. The other parent is still living in the same home and much appears the way that it always has. But when the second parent dies, we know that we have passed a watershed. We have lost the last direct connection to those countless generations of ancestors that went before us and have ourselves become the older generation. At the national level, Empress Eudoxia died as the result of a miscarriage on October 6. Claudius Claudianus, the Egyptian-born finest poet of our age who had served the court of Honorius, also died, and the best of the eastern generals, Fravitta, was assassinated under very mysterious circumstances. I shall have more to say on this latter item further on.

I was informed that I had inherited half my father's estate but I notified his lawyer that I wanted my share to go to my sister. It was the least I could do as my way of compensating her for all that she did for him over the years. My brother Gratian had attended his funeral, the first time that he had been home in years. If it was money that he smelled then he was out of luck. By the time my father died, he was so fed up with his younger son that he had disinherited him completely.

It was in 404 that Emperor Honorius decided to accept the Senate's invitation to hold a triumph in Rome. A decade and a half had passed since Theodosius had held the last triumph there and the city fathers would go all out to make the celebration rank with the finest such exhibitions of the past. A special honor guard of grizzled veterans such as me was selected to accompany Honorius, Stilicho, and hundreds of other government functionaries as they traveled from Ravenna to Rome. Officials representing every diocese in the Western Empire would be attending. As for our group, we followed the coastal highway from Ravenna through Rimini, Ancona, and Potentia until we turned off at Firmo. From there we headed southwest, linking up with the Via Salaria for the second half of our journey. We entered through the Salarian Gate in the northeast corner of the city. Men such as me, who were now into their third decade of military service, were quite proud of our record to the state as we had every right to be. Our generation had sacrificed mightily on behalf of our emperors and we were as deserving of representation in Honorius's cortege as anyone. It was just as well that not a single one of us had the slightest notion of how contemptuously the Fates had already started to mock us and our lifetimes of endeavor. That realization lay in a quickly approaching future.

Much had changed since I first visited Rome in 388. After the walls had been restored on the orders of Stilicho in 401–402, they contained 381 towers. Hadrian's Tomb that lies just across the Tiber and beyond the northwest side of the city had also been fortified. Many of the gates had acquired new bastions. Those made of solid marble had in far too many instances had their materials obtained from the destruction of pagan temples. Even the Temple of Mars had been sacrificed in this manner despite its immense size. The destruction of so many ancient monuments to provide building materials for defensive purposes meant that the very heart of the empire was gradually being reduced by the same process that so many provincial towns had been forced to go through in generations past. The enhanced fortifications only served to remind everyone of the city's increasing danger instead of giving the populace a renewed sense of safety.

This triumph was to celebrate not only the recent victory over the Visigoths but also the defeats inflicted on the Picts, Scots, and Saxons in Britain, the victory over the barbarians in the transalpine provinces, and the defeat inflicted on Gildo in Africa. Saxon, Pict, and Scottish prisoners were hauled out of slavery and brought in all the way from Britain to march in the parade along with more recent prisoners from north of the Alps. In spite of the fact that the triumph was triggered by the Battle of Verona, the number of Visigothic prisoners appearing in the parade was not great. For political reasons, we did not want to rub too much salt into Alaric's wounds now that he was once again our loyal and devoted ally. As in the Triumph of Diocletian and Maximian, great mobile maps of the provinces where the battles had occurred preceded the prisoners and the war loot attributed to them. Since this was also the tenth year of the reign of Honorius and Arcadius, their decennalia was also celebrated at this time. Representatives of almost every western legion marched in the parade. I was strongly reminded of the first such occasion that I attended in Constantinople back in 386. The Senate spared no expense on this triumph held in the name of Honorius to celebrate the victories of Stilicho. However, in retrospect, an interesting question arises over the event's timing. In the light of subsequent developments, one could say that the Senate was, to say the least, premature in their desire to celebrate the defeat of the Visigoths. On the other hand, perhaps the city fathers were exhibiting a preternatural sense that time was running out. In 404, there was no hint of the impending catastrophe that was about to engulf us. After all we had accomplished over the past two decades, we had no reason to believe that we could not manage any future problem that confronted us. In terms of human destruction, the biggest disasters that we had come through had been the two civil wars. But they had merely laid the foundation for the greatest of all our calamities that still lay ahead of us. It too would be self-generated.

After the units had filed by Honorius and Stilicho and the other dignitaries on the reviewing stand, they were dismissed. They soon found their way to the numerous stadiums and arenas throughout the city, where every conceivable type of entertainment was being provided. Chariot races at the Circus Maximus, gladiatorial combat at the Coliseum, and comparable exhibitions at the various smaller arenas throughout the city. I naturally attended some of the chariot races at the Circus Maximus. However, given that I was going to reach the age of forty before the year was out, I spent more time attending theatrical presentations and simply lounging in some of the baths that I had missed on my earlier visits. As a member of the official military escort, there were certain functions that I had to attend. One of these was the first day of gladiatorial combat at the Coliseum. Various attempts had been made over the generations since Constantine I to abolish these games but to no avail. Pagans and most Christians alike loved these bloodbaths and simply could not shake themselves loose from these ancient traditions. On that first day, an aged monk named Telemachus jumped from the stands down onto the arena floor. He tried to interpose himself between two gladiators and wrestle their weapons from them.

For his efforts, the less-than-appreciative spectators in the lower rows promptly stoned him to death with a hail of debris. (The roots of Christianity in Rome were still a little shallow even sixteen years after I had first visited the place.) But the man's sacrifice had the desired effect. Honorius soon issued an edict abolishing gladiatorial fights forever and it stuck. It was ironic how this weakest of weak princes was able to bring this about while similar edicts of his far more powerful predecessors had been dead letters. The fact, of course, was that the martyrdom of Telemachus had given a life and substance to this ruling that its forerunners had lacked.

I guess it was because middle age was starting to appear just over the horizon but I had more interesting things to do than just sit around being entertained all day long. I obtained permission to break away for a few days and went down to Naples, where I worked with an agent to expand my burgeoning real estate holdings. By the end of the year, I had purchased a villa high up on the cliffs at Sorrento overlooking the Bay of Naples. I rented it out for many years. Then, after finally retiring, my family and I moved into it, and it was there that I eventually finished writing this book. I also acquired a hotel there to cater to the tourists who come to visit the nearby Isle of Capri. As a final investment at this time, I obtained several large plots of land on the north shore of the Gulf of Salerno near the village of Amalfi. We were going to do all right for ourselves, come what may. I took time to get a better appreciation of the area than I had in previous visits. The more I saw, the more I knew I was making the right decision in planning a future move to this area. That, however, would not be for some time.

The years 403 and 404 were peaceful ones for the empire as a whole, but relations between East and West cooled off after the earlier warming period. Civilian officials continued to encounter great difficulty enforcing the authority of Constantinople in Eastern Illyria. Disorder continued to grow in the prefecture as bandit gangs multiplied. In places, it was starting to fall into the same degree of decrepitude as the Diocese of Thrace. In addition, Visigothic soldiers stationed along the Sava River were not averse to launching raids of their own into eastern territory. Honorius wrote a letter to his brother expressing his regrets for the breakdown of law and order in the prefecture but took no responsibility for it. Stilicho, for his part, did not reprimand Alaric for this freebooting activity. It was actually quite trivial considering the manner in which the eastern capital had inflicted Alaric on the West in 401. It had been common knowledge since 402 that the chief advocates in Constantinople for supplying Alaric from Roman arsenals and food depots during his march on Italy were Empress Eudoxia and Count John. He was now the chief finance minister and was very close to the empress. In 401, when Arcadius' only son, the future Emperor Theodosius II, was born, it was widely rumored that the true father of the child was not Arcadius but the count. Fravitta, still the leading field marshal in the East and no friend of Alaric, had strongly opposed the entire plan of encouraging the Visigothic leader to strike westward. It was ironic that the Visigothic-born Fravitta was striving to maintain the unity of the empire while his Roman-born civilian masters seemed intent on generating as much discord as possible. They still saw Stilicho as their chief enemy. Count John and his supporters felt that if they could embroil Stilicho and Alaric in another war, it would distract Stilicho from his real or imagined designs on the East, whatever they may be. Their ongoing distrust of Stilicho was now in the process of transforming their fears into a bizarre self-fulfilling prophecy.

In circumstances as mysterious as the death of Promotus in 391, Fravitta was assassinated under conditions that have been impossible to determine with any accuracy. The whole empire, with the exception of certain top civilian officials in the eastern capital, was outraged at the murder of this most loyal, devoted, and capable general. Promotus, Timasius, Gainas, Fravitta, the eastern government seemed to possess a boundless and most perverse appetite for consuming its best generals regardless of their nationality. Its paranoid civilian leaders seemed neither to know nor care what the continual killing off of their finest officers would mean to the morale and capabilities of the army rank and file. Preserving their own positions of privilege and furthering their own political agendas, regardless of how ultimately ruinous and unrealistic, was all that mattered to them. The East, for the moment, seemed to be coming unstuck again, but the danger soon passed.

We in the West counted ourselves fortunate that, with the exception of Gildo's revolt in Africa, we had been spared the political instability that had stricken the East repeatedly since the death of Theodosius.

We could not know how quickly this eastern contagion would spread to the West or that its virulence would increase geometrically as it did so. The celebrations surrounding Honorius's triumph in Rome went on for six weeks, and the emperor remained in Rome for several months after that. Most of us who were members of Stilicho's staff were excused after a couple of weeks, and that suited me fine. I was glad to get back home to Aureliana and our four children.

The death of Fravitta meant that relations between East and West, already cool, got downright frigid. With Count John now the supreme civilian authority in Constantinople, it was obvious that Stilicho had a personal antagonist every bit as conniving as Rufinus and Eutropius. Stilicho was certain that Count John would approach Alaric with a view to using him as Eutropius had. There was no way in which the generalissimo was going to allow the eastern court the opportunity to bribe Alaric into another westward thrust. Stilicho launched a preemptive political strike by having a special meeting with Alaric late in the autumn of 404. They agreed to a joint invasion of the prefecture of Illyria at the first opportunity in the New Year. The objective would be to reattach it in its entirety to the Western Empire in the manner that it had been during the reigns of Valentinian I and Gratian. Once the re-annexation was complete, Alaric would be reappointed to his former office of marshal of Illyria. The only difference would be that this time his loyalty, to the extent that he had any, would be to Honorius and not Arcadius. The current prefecture of Illyria (known in the West now as Eastern Illyria) would be reunited with our Diocese of Western Illyria. Alaric would be the supreme commander of both federate and Roman troops within the new, expanded prefecture. The hope was that this would secure the eastern approaches to Italy and preserve for the West the native Roman population there as a recruiting pool for the Roman field armies in Italy as well as that of Illyria to the extent that that would be possible. In what would amount to a de facto declaration of war against the East, Honorius, at Stilicho's insistence, would appoint Jovius as praetorian prefect of Illyria as soon as the military campaign was ready to proceed. The problem was that others had military ambitions of their own.

Alaric might not be the best man to enforce Roman authority in Illyria. However, after nine years of buggering around on the subject and accomplishing very little, neither West nor East could come up with a better prospect. Thus, Stilicho ordered Alaric to move from the Sava River Valley southward to Epirus in the Diocese of Macedonia. This was an outright seizure of eastern territory, but Constantinople did nothing to stop it. Stilicho never thought they would. Thus, as the New Year was about to dawn, the West was getting ready to add the prefecture of Illyria to the realm of Honorius. It never happened.

During the past two decades, the government had permitted thousands of barbarian federates, apart from Alaric's Visigoths, to settle on Roman territory, usually in small groups. When they were called up for service, they were paid as Roman soldiers. From a financial standpoint, it was a good deal for the government; using federates instead of regular troops meant a lower annual military payroll and no pension benefits to be paid when they stopped serving. After a campaign, they might be admitted into the Roman Army as regulars. In numerous cases, entire federate units were so incorporated in regions where regular army units had suffered particularly severe casualties. One problem these federates posed was that they were responsible for their own training when not on active duty. As long as their numbers were small, this was not a problem. But as the years passed, they posed an ever-increasing percentage of the troops used on campaigns. In cases where entire regiments of them were admitted to the regular army, their lower standards of training would prove to be a major contributing factor to the deterioration of our own centuries-old training standards. This was especially true in the West. Those who wanted permanent employment as soldiers and could not get into the regular army started hiring themselves out to the private armies of aristocratic landlords. The richest aristocrats had had their own small private armies for generations. The increased influx of federates meant that it became a buyer's market for those noblemen wanting to expand the miniature armies they already had or create new ones. This in turn made enforcing any law in the countryside that had a negative impact on the aristocracy all the more difficult for the government to enforce. Especially in the West.

Writing this account almost a half century after the death of Theodosius I and as a veteran who joined the Roman Army when Gratian was emperor of the West, I can claim unequivocally that there is nothing positive to be said about any of these developments. The "privatization" of our national defense to an increasing degree has been a disaster for the West. When I was conscripted in 382, there was not the slightest doubt among any of us that we were joining the finest army in the history of the world. Now it's just our mob versus their mob, and may the best mob win. As my friend Stephanus put it, "This rent-a-soldier program just hasn't worked out."

At the beginning of 405, Aureliana informed me that she was pregnant again. In February, her mother died. It was going to be a difficult year all around. Early in the spring, information again started to filter down from north of the Alps that there were tribal movements going on beyond the Danube. A number of Stilicho's staff officers were sent north to analyze the situation, but it was difficult for any of us to pinpoint exactly what was going on. Because of my familiarity with the area, I was a member of the group sent to Rhaetia to work with the local commanders on the issue. Interviews with Alemanns on both sides of the river turned up nothing except that the name "Radagaisus" kept cropping up. When he had been defeated and driven northward in 402, he had apparently withdrawn back to the east from whence he had come. Since then, annual rumors circulated as far west as Bohemia and Bavaria that he was getting another invasion force together, but nothing happened. During the spring, Stilicho decided to postpone the re-annexation of Eastern Illyria, and Alaric was so notified. Conditions on the Danube were too uncertain. To invade Eastern Illyria at this time would be to risk a war on two fronts, and the West lacked the manpower for such a contingency.

After two weeks of frustration, I volunteered to lead a group of men northward across the Danube and up the ancient trade route that parallels the Naab River. The Naab is a left bank tributary that enters the Danube at Regensburg. It is short and has a roughly north-south alignment. The trade route that it parallels eventually reaches the Elbe River at a point not far from where it empties into the North Sea. Our purpose was to follow the Regensburg-Elbe trade route to a point about seventy miles north of the Danube unless we ran into anything dangerous beforehand. At the seventy-mile mark, we would intersect with an east-west trail that, at this point, parallels the easterly flowing Ohre River, a tributary to the Elbe. To the west, this route soon connects with the headwaters of the Main River and follows it all the way to where it empties into the Rhine at our fortress city of Mainz. What we did upon reaching the Ohre River would depend on what we had found out to that point, if anything.

I chose several Franks and Visigoths with whom I had been serving for years. In addition, I brought along a couple of Alemanns from Legion III Italica. These latter had been stationed at Regensburg for the past ten years and I required them as guides. We traveled in civilian dress, although we carried our weapons and armor with us. The Franks would be used for interrogating any West Germans whom we came across while the Visigoths would do the same for any East Germans. Many Romans think that the Germans have no difficulty understanding one another's languages, but that is not always the case. The Goths, Vandals, and Gepids, all being East Germans, can converse among themselves. This is somewhat the case for the Franks, Alemanns, and Saxons, who are West Germans. There are, however, linguistic differences among and between those East and West Germans that evolved at considerable distances from one another.

I was surprised at how rapidly the population thinned out once we got ten to fifteen miles north of the Danube. Beyond that, we could travel for an hour at a stretch and hardly see anyone. Each of us had two mounts. This way we could continually switch horses without overly tiring them and thus make better time. As we approached the east-west trail at the Ohre River on the third day, we ran into a group of Burgundians. This particular Germanic nation is not notably warlike, and when they have engaged in hostilities, they have usually come out on the losing side. They originated in Scandinavia as neighbors of the Goths, but their numbers are much smaller. By 350, the Burgundians had located themselves along the upper Main River to the north of the Alemanns and to the south of the Lombards, the latter of whom had beaten up on them in times past. This was my first encounter with Burgundians, and I was at first apprehensive. However, the men under my command assured me that there was nothing to be worried about. The Burgundians said that they had been under no pressure from the east and that as far as they knew there were no large-scale movements of any kind from there heading in our direction. They had, however, heard the same rumors as everyone else. Our reception being friendly, I decided to turn east and follow the easterly trade route along the Ohre River for a while. To the north of us were the southern slopes of the Ore Mountains that would now be forming part of Rome's northern frontier if the wars of Marcus Aurelius had been brought to a successful conclusion. We took a Burgundian guide with us and traveled east for two days into Bohemia, covering about sixty miles in the process. The guide would take us no further because we were approaching the lands of the Lombards, who are a subtribe of the Sueves (or Swabians). He made it quite clear that the Lombards were nobody's friends but their own and very difficult to get along with at the best of times. I could tell that my men were starting to get anxious, and frankly, so was I. We had traveled further into the wilderness than I had intended and had only taken supplies for ten days.

Not wanting to run short of those, we turned around and headed west. We had traveled about a mile back along the trail when we came across three Lombard men out hunting. I used the Burgundian as a translator. What they told us was not encouraging. They had heard that Radagaisus was once again putting together an invasion force that would be far larger than the one that he commanded four years earlier. They confirmed that Radagaisus was an Ostrogoth. Exactly where he was amassing this force they did not know, but they believed that it was off to the southeast somewhere. The Lombards had not been asked to join it. One important piece of information they gave us, if true, was that the invaders were waiting for the harvest to be collected before they struck. In 401, they had expected to be able to break into Roman cities and steal our grain supplies. When this plan failed, they had been quickly reduced to starvation and surrender. By using a much larger force, Radagaisus planned not to let that happen this time. We thanked the men and returned to Regensburg as soon as possible.

In Augsburg, I passed this information along to others at Stilicho's headquarters. Similar probes had been made into barbarian territory from Noricum and Western Illyria but to no avail. I had reconnoitered about 130 miles into barbarian territory. That had surprised the others who had generally limited their penetrations to no more than seventy-five to one hundred miles. I suggested that we all try to extend our reconnaissance patrols to 150 miles, but it was pointed out that this was more difficult to do from the more easterly provinces of the Western Empire. Our political relationships with German tribes in that area were more complex, and the Hunnish presence there had kept the region in constant turmoil for almost three decades. My men and I repeated our trip north again during the summer and early fall, but we came up empty as far as any new information was concerned. We finally concluded that whatever was coming would be starting farther east than in Bavaria or western Bohemia. We also started thinking that the attack, if and when it came, might be directed against the Eastern Empire rather than the West.

Our difficulties in obtaining valid information about the impending invasion were compounded by our bad relations with Constantinople. By seizing its two provinces of Epirus and establishing Alaric in them, it was impossible to ask the East to cooperate with us on our intelligence-gathering activities. In spite of the quiet spring and summer, the rumors kept coming. Once the harvest was in, we went on an advanced state of alert. The first "firm" estimate that we heard for the invasion force arrived in early autumn and came in at two hundred thousand. We were taken aback when we heard this and staggered even more so when the estimate shot up to four hundred thousand a couple of weeks later! It was obvious that if either of these estimates was even close to the truth, the standing forces of the Army of Italy would not be adequate for the challenge. Stilicho had already ordered Alan and Hun federates in to assist and it was beginning to appear that we would need every one of them. For this campaign, Stilicho selected Sarus to act as his chief of cavalry, thus assuming the same position that Saul the Alan had held at the Battle of Pollentia. Stilicho called in regiments from Gaul to assist once again, and by the time our total force was assembled, we had thirty legions and cavalry regiments at our disposal. In November, the onslaught came and from a place and direction that we did not expect.

During the autumn, southern Britain was subjected to serious raids. A man named Niall had been proclaimed "high king of Ireland" and led a confederation of tribes on these assaults along the south coast and the Bristol Channel. Considerable damage was done to certain estates in these areas, but with our mounting concerns on the Danube, we had no immediate means with which to retaliate.

Radagaisus had assembled his forces far to the east of us. His staging area was at least two hundred miles beyond the Danube in the region known as Transylvania. It is cradled on the northeast by the Carpathian Mountains and to the south by the Transylvanian Alps. He was planning on setting himself up as a rival to Alaric once he had defeated the Roman Army. He was intent on ruling both the Ostrogoths and the Visigoths and had learned several vital lessons from his previous misadventure.

This time he concealed his hand by establishing his staging ground far from Roman territory. Neither would his forces engage in a broad front attack. Moving rapidly westward out of the Carpathian foothills, they traveled across Transylvania and down the Mures River Valley. The Mures had formed part of the northern frontier of the empire prior to 270 when our Dacian territories had extended well to the north of the lower Danube. The last 150 miles of the Mures is navigable. Thus, the horde was able to use both the river and the old Roman highway that runs along its south bank to transport them to the point where the Mures empties into the Tizsa River. This is only ninety miles north of where the Tizsa empties into the Danube not far from Belgrade. From there it was about sixty-five miles due west to the north-south segment of the Danube coming down from Budapest. In early November, they crashed across the Danube on a section to the southeast of Lake Balaton that was only lightly held by a few regiments of our federate allies. These federates were quickly swept aside not because of any particular skill on the part of the barbarians but simply by their numbers. Cutting a swath of destruction through Western Illyria, they drove to the northwest and continued into Noricum and Rhaetia. These areas had still not fully recovered from the previous invasion four years earlier.

As soon as we heard where they had invaded, we moved the Army of Italy into Venetia, centered on Aquileia. Our first reaction was that Radagaisus might be heading for the cities of Poetovio and Emona en route to breaking through the Julian Alps and into Venetia. That was certainly the most direct way to get into Italy. It appeared that what we might be facing was another battle in the vicinity of the Frigidus River and the Hrusica Pass. Immediate consideration was given to reactivating the old palisade fortress that Arbogast had constructed eleven years earlier. This assumption, however, was wrong. Our scouting parties north of the Alps continued to report a westerly progress by the barbarians. In retrospect, the transfer of the Visigoths from the Sava River Valley to Epirus during the previous autumn was most unfortunate. Radagaisus had invaded just to the north of where Alaric and his people had been stationed. Positioned down in Epirus, however, Alaric would play no part in this conflict. Radagaisus had kept his people in reasonably good order to this point by maintaining their focus on the prime objective. He bypassed to the south all our frontier outposts on the upper Danube, heading westward for the highway between Linz and Salzburg. Then he struck south to the Brenner Pass. Its defenders fought well but were overwhelmed. As our (bad) luck would have it, the autumn of 405 had been mild, and the snows were late in arriving. Unlike four years earlier, Radagaisus led his people into Italy with a minimum of difficulty. As our scouts reported the enemy progress, the Army of Italy moved westward in parallel with them. Our army had other problems in addition to that of determining which pass or passes the enemy would select to break through. Once the news of the invasion on the Danube reached Italy, large numbers of people started fleeing south. The estimated figure of four hundred thousand barbarians understandably struck fear into everyone. Thousands of refugees soon clogged the highways. That only made our task of transporting troops and supplies all the more difficult once we knew where to move them. The congestion on numerous roads was terrible, and many supply trains were seriously delayed in getting to their destinations as a result.

Stilicho was soon being criticized for not stationing his large army north of the Alps to combat this horde the way that he had done in 401. But Radagaisus was not a fool. He had spies in northern Italy and the transalpine provinces to determine just what our troop dispositions were. Had Stilicho moved the Army of Italy north of the Alps immediately upon hearing of the invasion, Radagaisus would have probably gone through the Julian Alps instead. Stilicho has also been criticized for not having the frontier garrisons attack Radagaisus on his northern flank as he passed by to their south. The problem was we did not know if more attacks were going to be mounted from north of the Danube in spite of the evidence to the contrary. If there were then the frontier troops would be required to combat them. As Radagaisus tore across our provinces in Pannonia, Noricum, and Rhaetia, our scouts came up with a more reliable estimate of about seventy-five thousand for the total invasion force that included men, women, and children. It was only after several weeks had gone by and no further attacks came that we realized the initial panicky estimates of the enemy force size had no basis in fact.

Nonetheless, seventy-five thousand (if that figure was accurate) was still a considerable number to contend with, although no larger than Alaric's invasion force had been in 401.

What terrified the populace most about Radagaisus was the man's utter savagery. A devoted pagan, on more than one occasion early in his campaign he offered captured Roman civilians as human sacrifices to his gods. Whereas Alaric's forces, when in Italy, were reasonably well behaved (to the extent that that expression can be used to describe any invading force of barbarians) Radagaisus's ill-trained mob was anything but. The barbarians poured down the Via Claudia Augusta from the Brenner Pass and broke out into the valley of the Po. The fortified cities held out once again just as they had against Alaric. Small villages and towns where such fortifications could not be justified were laid waste, as were individual farms at every opportunity. The one thing that eventually worked in our favor was that the invaders were truly barbarians. Many of them had never been trained as soldiers, and once they had broken into northern Italy, their cohesion dissolved. They struck in every direction at once. The army came to feel like it was in a similar situation to the one that it faced in 401–402. The trouble was that now we were fighting on the wrong side of the Alps, and there were far more of the enemy.

In the autumn, our third daughter was stillborn. I did not find out about it for months. Before leaving for the north, I had arranged for Claudia to live with my wife in the period leading up to her delivery. Aureliana was heart-struck, and regardless of what anyone said or did, it was impossible to comfort her. Claudia was able to stay with her for several weeks afterward. Having another woman around, especially one her own age and to whom she was so close, was a big help. I had fathered seven healthy children before losing this one and could not help but take this tragedy as an omen.

Once it became clear that the invasion force was far smaller than originally estimated and that no further attacks appeared imminent, orders went north to the Danube. Certain frontier garrison troops and cavalry regiments were to head south immediately and join the Army of Italy and its federate allies. There was fighting going on everywhere throughout the winter but usually in small groups. As we entered 406, we appeared to have gained the upper hand, but it was going to take a long time to bring all the invaders under control. With a war of this intensity being brought into the political and commercial heartland of Italy, the Senate was finally forced to acquiesce with a request by the emperor and his advisers for conscription throughout the prefecture. In April, an order went out for army volunteers that applied to both free men and slaves. The terms of payment were different for the two, but the latter, by their act of volunteering, also gained their freedom. Through the spring and into the summer, battles raged across much of the Po Valley. Soon thousands of enemy dead could be found all across northern Italy. The civilian population, however, had suffered horribly in the initial stages.

By the middle of the summer, Radagaisus had lost control of the majority of his people. He had, however, managed to maintain his authority over a solid core of roughly fifteen thousand that suddenly plunged south out of the Po Valley, across the Apennines, and into Tuscany. They attacked the town of Fiesole. It lies a few miles northeast of Florence and just to the north of the Arno River and the Via Cassia, the highway running from Florence to Rome. After overrunning the town, Radagaisus and his army were trapped and surrounded by our forces. The only terms that Stilicho was willing to listen to were those of unconditional surrender. The battle raged on night and day. We practically emptied the arsenals in northern Italy. Catapults rained rocks on Radagaisus's army to the point where they must have felt they were the victims of a volcanic eruption. When they weren't dodging rocks, there were the hundreds of thousands of arrows to contend with. Several attempts to break through the Roman lines were met with utter ferocity by our federate allies, the Huns of King Uldin who took no prisoners. The Roman cavalry under Sarus and Ulfilas also performed quite well. Finally, after absorbing thousands of casualties in what were increasingly hopeless circumstances, Radagaisus led a peace party out under a flag of truce to negotiate with Stilicho. According to the surrender terms, Stilicho agreed to spare the life of the Ostrogothic leader. Once Radagaisus was in Roman custody, Stilicho ordered his execution. The date was August 23, 406.

"You promised that I would live!" Radagaisus yelled at Stilicho.

"I lied," was Stilicho's unemotional reply.

Radagaisus was immediately beheaded. Two years to the day, Stilicho would no doubt reflect on this moment.

From the enemy soldiers that surrendered, Stilicho selected twelve thousand of the best to add to the Roman Army directly or to enjoin as federates. The vast majority of these were Goths. The casualties the barbarians had suffered were enormous. Our own military casualties, in comparison, were far fewer. Time, however, was above all in increasingly short supply. We had taken thousands of captives all across northern Italy. Italian slave markets, stretched beyond their limits, had not seen such a glut in many generations; nor would they ever again.

This barbarian incursion had disrupted the economy of northern Italy as nothing had ever done. Property damage was considerable and much time would be required for the region to heal. With warfare being conducted everywhere, the planting of crops in the Po Valley had been drastically curtailed. To avert a famine, we had to arrange for food to be shipped in from Gaul, Africa, and southern Italy well before the military campaign had been brought to a close. However, that was not our greatest problem once Radagaisus and his army had been destroyed. As I mentioned earlier, the Fates had already started to mock us; we simply had not heard their laughter yet.

Several weeks later, Stilicho held a meeting back at his headquarters in Ravenna that involved his staff and top field generals. These commanders had been requested, subsequent to the execution of Radagaisus, to determine the status of all regular and federate units that had participated in the campaign. In addition to casualty reports, Stilicho ordered an assessment on how each legion and independent regiment (including federates) had performed. Most, but not all, frontier legions were ordered to return to their home bases. Likewise, a majority of the cavalry regiments. It was the responsibility of me and my staff to determine the food and material requirements en route for them. We would provide this data to the offices of the praetorian prefects of the Italies and the Gauls. We were also ordered to assess the status of our storage depots throughout the war zone. Many of those located in small villages and hamlets had been destroyed. It would take us into the following spring to get them rebuilt. This made resupplying the units returning home all the more difficult while they traveled through Italy. Certain cavalry regiments that had been brought down were retained along with a couple of frontier legions. We knew what that meant. Stilicho was in the process of resuming his plans to add Eastern Illyria to Honorius's realm. Originally scheduled for the latter half of 405, this undertaking was now rescheduled for sometime in 407. Everyone present was sworn to keep all matters pertaining to Illyria in strictest confidence. However, with Alaric having been parked in Epirus for the past two years, the West's intentions for that area were hardly the best-kept secret in the empire.

This long meeting was almost over when a messenger arrived with a communication from the praetorian prefect of the Gauls. Stilicho broke the seals and had not read very far into the document.

"Jesus Christ!" he erupted and then stomped down to the end of the long room where he stood staring out the windows for several minutes. The rest of us just sat there looking quizzically at one another, trying to guess at what had set him off like this. My first thought was that Alaric had broken loose again, but that was not the case. After he had composed himself, Stilicho returned to his chair at the head of the table.

"It appears," he began, "that our good friends in Britain have, as is their time-honored custom, gone into revolt."

Swearing could be heard coming from all around the table.

"Who's leading it?" I asked.

"A civilian named Marcus." Stilicho smiled. "A friend of yours, a relative perhaps?"

Everyone sat there grinning at my expense.

"Not bloody likely," I responded. "When did this revolt break out?"

"In April," Stilicho continued, "When I withdrew Legion XX Valeria Victrix and the one regiment from Legion II Augusta, I knew that the British would be understandably disturbed. I notified the vicar of Britain and his five provincial governors that several regiments that had been returned to Gaul were also available to the count of Britain as a reserve should the need arise. What the hell more could I have done?"

The generalissimo looked tired and drawn and seemed to have aged noticeably in recent months. Over the past dozen years, he had become Rome's personification of the Greek god Atlas, carrying all the Western Empire's burdens on his shoulders.

"What are we going to do about it?" I asked.

"For the moment, nothing," Stilicho replied. "As long as the revolt is confined to the island, it might just die out by itself. As experience tells us, however, these British contagions rarely remain confined to Albion alone. Our first priority is to get Alaric settled throughout Illyria on our behalf. Once that is decided, we will deal with the rebellion in Britain unless the situation worsens there in the near future."

"Lord Stilicho," Sarus submitted, "might not the very act of our becoming involved in Eastern Illyria serve to induce the British revolt to spread to the continent? We have already stripped the defenses of Britain and the Rhine to the minimum to help combat Alaric and Radagaisus. If we now send those same units to fight in Eastern Illyria, then they would find themselves in closer proximity to Constantinople than Rome, leave alone Gaul and Britain. Such knowledge could very well prove sufficient to shove the Gauls over the edge.

"In addition, it seems to me that your strategy with respect to our impending eastern campaign is based on the assumption that the East will not fight for Illyria. But what if it does? We could find ourselves involved in a full-scale civil war there. If Gaul joins Britain, then Spain will join them both, and we will have a simultaneous civil war in the West. Under those circumstances, how would we be able to defend the frontiers? For the past ten months, we have been fully focused on eliminating Radagaisus and his army. What has happened north of the upper Danube during that period? We simply do not know. Where exactly are the Asding Vandals that were driven back across the upper

Danube during the first campaign against Radagaisus? There were precious few Asding Vandals captured during the war just concluded. With all due respect, my lord, I believe that we should focus our current attention on crushing the rebellion in Britain. The presence of several additional regiments alone in Gaul might be enough to alleviate their strategic fears and bring Britain back into the fold. While we're doing that, we could also be upgrading our intelligence on the upper Danube and the Rhine."

We were deeply impressed by the manner in which Sarus had raised concerns that were common to a number of us. Sarus had the reputation of being somewhat of a hothead but the way in which he articulated our concerns over the focus of our strategic policy would haunt many of us there for the rest of our lives. Stilicho himself hailed from the Eastern Empire and had a number of other members on his staff who were native Illyrians. They firmly believed that only by enabling Alaric to resume his old post of marshal of Illyria could our eastern flank be secured in such a way that we could subsequently concentrate our attention on suppressing the British revolt and strengthening the Rhine frontier. The easterners downplayed the danger of Gaul's joining the revolt in Britain by using one of Sarus's arguments against him. Their reasoning was that the risk of denuding the frontier of even more troops in order to engage in civil war with Honorius's government would be enough to guaranty their loyalty.

Seeing his longtime friend outnumbered in this way prompted the usually reserved Ulfilas to counter the easterner's logic.

"That has never stopped them before," he shot back. "Magnentius, Magnus Maximus, Arbogast were all willing to risk the Rhine to achieve victory. Things will be the same this time if we permit the situation there to deteriorate through inadvertence. There is also a timing problem that is not being addressed here. It will be next spring at the earliest before we can invade Eastern Illyria and probably the autumn, if all goes well, before such a campaign could be brought to conclusion. What is being proposed here is that we allow the Rhine to be dangerously undermanned for an entire year at a minimum. No way will our enemies grant us that much of a hiatus. Neither will we be able to do anything about the rebellion in

Britain during that time; inattention to it will only cause it to fester and spread. As regards Alaric, his army is still in the process of recovering from its defeat at Verona four years ago. After Radagaisus's first defeat in 401–402, it took him almost four years to build up a sufficient force to reinvade and that was with a recruitment pool that was readily available. Down in Epirus with no available volunteers for two hundred miles, Alaric has to rebuild his strength from within. He's not going to do that anytime soon. As I understand it, we are provisioning Alaric, but because of the dislocations caused by our recent war, we have been unable to pay him. Keep on supplying him and start paying him, including his back pay, and he will remain quiet. Put Illyria on the back burner while we look after things in the northwest. That should be our first priority."

Sarus and Ulfilas had done their best, but in the end, their arguments availed us nothing. The "Illyria first" plan remained in place, and the northwest would be secured only after Alaric and Jovius were firmly ensconced in their new responsibilities.

As mentioned, the war in northern Italy had thoroughly disrupted the planting of crops in the spring of 406. But it is questionable how bountiful the crop yields would have been for that year. The winter of 405–406 had been quite mild, and as a result, the volume of snowmelt for the spring runoff was lower than normal. This was followed by a very dry spring and summer. The situation in our transalpine provinces and in Germany had been much the same. With so many other more immediate problems to deal with, we failed to give this situation north of the Alps much consideration at the time. We should have.

At the beginning of October, I was appointed chief quartermaster of the Army of Italy. I started to oversee the reconstruction of all damaged and destroyed military storage depots. Italy was our first priority. Then my staff and I crossed the Alps and inspected all such facilities in our provinces there. The Pannonian provinces in Western Illyria had suffered considerably. Construction on these facilities was carried out by the engineering corps or private contractors where available and proceeded until the winter settled in and brought such activity to a halt. I managed a side trip to Carnuntum that was close by. It was the first time since 392 that I had had a chance to visit the graves of my first wife and three eldest daughters. While we were in Noricum, we heard that the usurper Marcus had been slain in Britain but that, in his place, a new usurper, Gratian II, had been proclaimed. Like his predecessor, this Gratian was rumored to be a businessman with no military background. Such bizarre choices only served to confirm my longstanding conviction that the good people of Britain were quite unsuited to such underhanded carry-on.

The winter set in early and would prove to be severe in more ways than one. Much construction remained to be done in our devastated provinces, but it would have to wait until the following year. I returned to Ravenna and compiled a lengthy report on the status of our supply facilities. The fact that northern Italy had been required to import so much food in 406 coupled with the widespread destruction there meant that our supplies would probably be minimal come the spring of 407. This would probably lead to another delay in the start of the campaign to re-annex Eastern Illyria.

I was glad to have the holiday season upon us once again. I had missed the previous one completely because of the ongoing war. The loss of our daughter, which I didn't know about at the time, had badly marred it for my wife and family. But for this year, I was home, and we were at peace in spite of the ongoing rebellion in Britain. I just felt so damned tired. The position I held was quite prestigious and I certainly appreciated the confidence that my superiors, above all, Stilicho, had shown in me. But all the traveling was starting to wear me out. When I had my new home constructed in Ravenna, I had the architect design a courtyard for it like the one that I had enjoyed so much at Margareta's country villa near Trier. Of course, in Ravenna, surrounded by its city walls, I had nothing like the view that the villa at Trier afforded overlooking the Moselle. But I could make do. Unfortunately, the winter was proving so cold that I could not spend anytime outside enjoying it. Christmas came and went, and the New Year approached. And then it happened.

Collapse on the Rhine (407)

CHAPTER 13

WHILE WE WERE CONCENTRATING our efforts on defeating Radagaisus in Italy, we had suffered a dreadful intelligence failure in Germany. On December 31, 406, an alliance of over 250,000 barbarians broke across the frozen Rhine along a fifty-mile front between our fortress cities of Mainz and Koblenz. They consisted of the following:

- eighty thousand Asding Vandals
- fifty thousand Siling Vandals
- thirty thousand Alans
- twenty-five thousand Sueves
- twenty thousand Burgundians
- fifty thousand Alemanns

What propelled these people against our western frontier at this time was a combination of events. Initially for the Vandals and Alans, there was the desire to get out from under the brutal, overarching dominance of the Huns. After failing to break into Italy in 401, they had moved even further to the west. Crowding in with the Burgundians, Alemanns, and Sueves generated a demographic pressure previously unknown in the region. For the first few years, bountiful harvests sustained them all, but in 406, things changed. A very dry summer generated lower than average crop yields in central Europe. Shear desperation created by the prospect of widespread hunger left the Vandals, Alans, and their new

532

neighbors with a momentous decision to make. News of the disaster that had befallen Radagaisus and his followers soon penetrated the barbarian hinterlands. Three consecutive German invasions of Italy between 401 and 405 had all been defeated. With another invasion across the Alps offering no greater likelihood of success, by the tens of thousands these peoples started migrating westward well to the north of the Danube. Their line of march would change the course of history.

Like the Goths, the Vandals are (or at the time were) divided into two main groups: the Asdings and the Silings. Ethnically and linguistically, there might be a prehistoric link between the Vandals and the Goths because, up to a point, their histories parallel one another. Both evolved in southern Scandinavia before voyaging to northeast Germany. The Vandals migrated first and had firmly established themselves on the south shore of the Baltic by the time the Goths arrived. After several decades of living under their Vandal overlords, the Goths broke away, but there is an underlying attitude of distrust between the two that continues down to the present day. By the first century BC, the Siling Vandals had moved roughly two hundred miles south from the shore of the Baltic Sea to the region that straddles the upper Oder River. From them, this region, now known as Silesia, derives its name. It was there that they made their homes for the next four hundred years. The Asding Vandals remained near the mouth of the Vistula River for a couple of centuries before migrating to the area north of the lower Danube. In the late fourth and early fifth centuries, thousands of them settled within the empire and were granted federate status. However, the vast majority of them remained north of the Danube. It has been an utter cataclysm for civilized peoples everywhere that they did not stay there. Up to the beginning of the fifth century, Rome had had a hideous history of conflict with the Goths while having only sporadic flare-ups with the Vandals. This would now change. In 406, the Asding Vandals linked up once again with their distant cousins from Silesia. They continued moving westward down the valley of the Main River.

Migrating with the Asding Vandals were the Alans. Their alliance was a strange one in that the Alans, who are very primitive and socially unsophisticated, are a non-Germanic people. As mentioned earlier, they originated in the Caucasus Mountains and most were compelled to leave that region by the Hunnish onslaught. This occurred in the mid-360s around the time that I was born. Their lack of any kind of social structure hindered their organizing a defensive strategy against these Mongoloid invaders. As a result, some were quickly subjugated, while the remainder was driven westward along the north shore of the Black Sea until they came into contact with the Ostrogoths. In alliance with the Ostrogoths, the Alans attempted to defeat the Huns. When that failed, the Alans fragmented even more. Some fled south with Ostrogothic remnants to join their migration into the empire with the Visigoths in 376. These Alans, however, were a small percentage of the overall Alan "nation." Those remaining north of the lower Danube linked up with the Asding Vandals. Eventually they became part of the barbarian alliance moving west. The Alans practice no settled agriculture of any kind. Instead, they live entirely off their herds of animals or what they can hunt. They construct no permanent buildings and, like the Goths, live out of their wagons. All boys are trained to ride horses at an early age, which is essential in order to participate in their pastoral existence. That is one reason why, like the Huns, you never hear of Alan infantry, only Alan cavalry.

The Burgundians were another East Germanic peoples caught up in this great westerly migration, though perhaps they were involuntary participants. Like the Vandals and the Goths, the Burgundians originated in southern Scandinavia.[29] Tacitus first recorded the Burgundians as a subtribe of the Vandals. He located them as living between the Siling Vandals on the Oder River and the Goths to the northeast on the Vistula about the year 100. The tribal movements that the East German peoples underwent during the third century forced the Burgundians to relocate to the upper reaches of the Main River by the year 260. Once there, they started accompanying their westerly neighbors, the Alemanns, in attacks on Roman territory, but they were not overly successful. At least they had never managed to settle on Roman lands. By the time of Julian the Apostate, the Burgundians had moved (or been pushed) down to the mouth of the Main and had thus wedged themselves between the Franks to the north and the Alemanns to the south along the Rhine River.

The Sueves are a people who are difficult to define geographically. Most frequently, they are associated with the area named after them, Swabia, that is located to the northeast of the great bend in the Rhine River near Basel in the extreme southwest corner of Germany. However, small groupings of them are spread over much of the German interior. Up to the end of 406, they, like the Vandals, had been no more difficult to deal with than most other Germans. That too was about to change. After they occupied northwestern Spain, they would establish a reputation for almost unparalleled savagery as they forced a most appalling dark age upon those unfortunate peoples. That is for a later telling.

Another Germanic nation that played a major role in the invasion of December 31, 406, was that of the Alemanns. The Alemanns are actually a tribal confederation, some of whose components originated along the Elbe River to the northeast. When Roman control over Swabia collapsed about the year 260, the Alemanns and Sueves quickly moved into this triangular reentrant. As a result, the region has been known as Swabia or Alemannia ever since. Individual Alemann tribal elements have indeterminate backgrounds. Nonetheless, once they had confederated themselves, they were a power to be reckoned with. Throughout the latter fourth century, the Emperors Julian, Valentinian I, and Gratian had to conduct major campaigns against them. Small groups of them had been permitted to settle on Roman territory in both Gaul and Rhaetia but in much smaller numbers than the Franks on the lower Rhine. Certain of their officers had risen to the highest positions in the Roman Army. But the feeling of at least some degree of mutual trust and respect that had developed over several generations between Romans and Franks would never exist between Romans and Alemanns.

At the end of December 406, all was ready. These various nationalities had positioned themselves in the Burgundian lands fronting on the frozen Rhine. On the last day of the year, spearheaded by the Alans under their two kings, Goar and Respendial, they smashed across in the most devastating invasion that the West has ever seen. Its consequences have proven to be irreversible. I have often thought of how fortunate the passings of certain people were in the years leading up to that terrible watershed. Symmachus, Claudian, Margareta, my father and mother and others of their generation never had to witness, or worse yet be victims of, the terrifying ruination of our Western Roman Empire, the beginning of which can be dated to that awful day. Gaul would now suffer the murderous desolation that had been the fate of Thrace. It should have never turned out that way. There was a major difference in the targeting selection of these barbarians from what they had done in the past. They had usually avoided the fortresses because it was suicidal to attack them. Barbarian attacks generally went against the undefended towns and large estates in the interior. They would suffer during this invasion also, as badly as they ever had, but only after the frontline fortresses had been attacked. What prompted this change was the fact that the invaders were facing starvation, and it was the middle of winter. The fortress cities on the front line were well provisioned. Faced with the slow death of starvation, these invaders were all too willing to risk death in battle to achieve the food supplies of the garrison storehouses.

Early in January 407, I attended Stilicho's first staff meeting of the year. This was before news arrived of the Rhineland invasion. Stilicho's attitude was still to wait out developments in Britain instead of taking direct action against the island itself. Support for the first usurper had collapsed and perhaps it would for the second as well. Stilicho also announced that Honorius had appointed Jovius as praetorian prefect of Illyria. This surprised us. Originally this appointment was to occur after our invasion of Eastern Illyria was underway early in the spring. In preparation for this, provisioning for both the Visigothic Federate Army and the Army of Italy had been underway since shortly after the defeat of Radagaisus. Publicly announcing Jovius's appointment meant that the invasion date had been moved up but was known only to a few. The situation in Britain had prompted this. Strictly speaking, Jovius's authority extended only to Western Illyria, but this would be temporary. After Stilicho and Alaric had re-annexed Eastern Illyria, the reconstituted prefecture would be entirely under the administration of Jovius and Alaric. There already was a praetorian prefect of Illyria, meaning Eastern Illyria, named Clearchus, who had been appointed in 401 by Constantinople. He would shortly be unemployed. It all sounded very straightforward.

With members of my staff, I was to continue to monitor the reconstruction of military storage depots across northern Italy and the frontier provinces, weather permitting. Bad weather kept us in Ravenna for almost a week and gave me a few extra days with the family before heading back north. Late in the afternoon on the day before I was supposed to leave, I received the biggest political shock of my life to that point. A courier arrived and delivered me a letter from my sister. I had received a letter from her just two months earlier and she didn't usually write that frequently. My first thought was that there had been some sort of family tragedy. In a sense, there had been, or was about to be, but certainly not of the kind I would have predicted.

November 20, 406
My Dear Marcus:

I don't know how to tell you this. You are well aware of the revolt that broke out in Britain last spring under the nominal leadership of a rich merchant in London. I say "nominal" because I don't believe the poor man had much choice in the matter. A group of rebellious army officers, who are refusing to send any more British soldiers to the continent, had forced this man, named Marcus, to be proclaimed "emperor." They chose him primarily because he was rich and could finance their cause that they were certain would also find solid support in Gaul. The Gauls, though equally unwilling to send any more of their soldiers east, refused to join the revolt. Marcus, seeing his ambitions crumbling, tried to back out of his "imperium." Not willing to accept this, his top officers murdered him at the beginning of November and immediately started seeking out a replacement.

I still have difficulty believing that the man they chose is our brother Gratian! Neighbors and townspeople besieged our old homestead when the news was made public in Cirencester. I think I was the last person in Britain to find out. I haven't seen Gratian since Dad's funeral, and given what happened to his predecessor, I don't know if we ever will. Everything is still very confused. As of this writing, Gaul has still refused to join the British revolt. I hope and pray to God that none of this will pose a danger to you or perhaps even to ourselves.

I believe that the main reason Gratian was chosen by the army here is because of the considerable wealth of his second wife (whom I have never met) and his close business association with his predecessor. I'm afraid for him when her money runs out. If there is some way for you to arrange it, please write and let me know what the official view from Ravenna is on this.

Your loving sister,
Maria Patricia

I sat there stunned at what I had read. When I had been silent for a long time, Aureliana came in and asked me if anything was wrong. She sat down beside me and I read the letter to her. She asked me if my brother's action placed us in any danger and I assured her that it didn't. At the same time, it certainly put my position on Stilicho's staff in a different light. The following morning, I went to his office and showed him my sister's letter.

"Perhaps this creates an opportunity for us," he considered. "The first thing I want you to do is turn over your current responsibilities to your chief deputy. I'm going to call a meeting of the entire staff as soon as I can gather everyone together. I want their and your input as to what our future course of action should be. Your relationship to the new usurper may or may not cause me to alter my 'wait and see' policy on the British revolt."

The meeting dealt briefly with issues pertaining to the impending Illyrian campaign before concentrating on the developing situation in Britain. It continued late into the afternoon. The most important decision arrived at was to send me to London with an offer to my brother. Gratian was to be appointed vicar of Britain, no punitive actions were to be taken against any rebelling army units, and a promise was made to increase the strength of the small field army in Britain at the earliest opportunity once spring had arrived. Aureliana fully understood why I was uniquely qualified for this mission. She had grown used to the idea of having me around a little more once Radagaisus and his horde had been destroyed. Being away in Italy meant that I was still able to get home at the end of every month for a while. With a long-distance trip, it was impossible to tell when I would be back.

The following day at Stilicho's staff meeting, all the official documentation for my mission was reviewed. All was ready for me to leave when three couriers from northern Gaul arrived. It was then that we were informed of the invasion.

"Happy goddamned New Year!" Stilicho exploded.

The news that Mainz and Bingen had both fallen with heavy military and civilian casualties struck us all like a thunderbolt. The fortifications of Mainz were as strong as any site in the prefecture. The couriers, all tribunes, then provided us with the details available to them when they left Trier. The battle at Mainz had gone on for days, with the city garrison being besieged by several thousand barbarians, mainly Alemanns. The invaders had brought primitive siege equipment with them, but there were so many that it was good enough to get the job done. Legion XXII Primigenia, my first legion, was almost wiped out. The city underwent severe damage during the fighting and numerous fine buildings were destroyed. Many inhabitants were massacred, a goodly number of these in the city's largest church. Given that the Alemanns are all pagans and mostly savages, the idea of slaughtering defenseless civilians anywhere, leave alone in a church, would not be considered particularly reprehensible to them. After Mainz had been captured and trashed, this branch of the invading army moved south along the west bank of the Rhine.

The frontier running from Mainz to Augst is under the control of the count of the Strasbourg Tract, a position created by Stilicho in 396. His available forces were overwhelmed by the thousands whom they faced. It did not help that a number of the best cavalry regiments from this command were now in Italy awaiting the planned offensive against Eastern Illyria. The Alemanns were attacking city after city as they drove up the Rhine. The path they followed was somewhat typical of the sort of raiding activity conducted by West Germans as opposed to the East Germanic peoples. The West Germans rarely raid all that far away from their home territory. We all know about the far-ranging Frankish attacks through Gaul, Spain, and into North Africa in the third century. The Alemanns had also cut deeply into Gaul at that time. But invasions like that were the exceptions that proved the rule. It has always been the East Germans, primarily the Goths and Vandals, who have been the great wayfarers among the Germanic peoples. They above all have undermined the foundations of our Western Empire.

The Burgundians crossed the Rhine to the north of the Alemanns. In spite of their East German origins, a century and a half of living among the West Germans seems to have sapped these people of their wanderlust. Once they entered Roman territory, the Burgundians almost decided to call it quits. They moved downstream to a point between Koblenz and Cologne and simply settled there. Their participation in the great invasion was essentially over. In fact, if the invasion had been limited to the Alemanns and the Burgundians, it could have probably been contained with the reduced forces that we had on hand. The nation that made this invasion a catastrophe was that of the Vandals.

Driving across an undefended portion of the Rhine, the Vandals' spearhead was led by the Alans under their two kings. Immediately Rome got a break but simply lacked the forces to take full advantage of it. A dispute between the two Alan leaders caused Goar and his followers to desert to the Romans. An immediate counterattack by the Roman Army and Frankish federates against the Vandals resulted in their King Godegisel being slain along with thousands of his followers.

Though the number is open to question, estimates as high as twenty thousand have been given for the number of enemy killed in this initial battle. Ultimately it didn't matter. The Roman Army fought well in spite of being vastly outnumbered but was unable to defeat the second wave of the Vandal/Alan/Sueve onslaught led by King Respendial and was driven off. The Vandals proclaimed Godegisel's son, Gunderic, as king and their invasion continued into northern Gaul with Trier as their first objective.

All our planning was thrown into confusion and our trip was delayed until we considered these recent developments. Instead of going through the Rhineland or central Gaul to get to Boulogne, as we would have done normally, we would travel to Bordeaux in Aquitaine. Just to the north of that city, on the east bank of the Garonne River, is the port of Blavia (Blaye). In spite of its location, it comes under the jurisdiction of the duke of the Armorican Tract.[30] This command consists of the coastal fortifications lying between the mouth of the Seine and the mouth of the Garonne. Seven of its eight fortresses lie in Armorica. Blavia (Blaye) is the only one that does not. Andreas, Julianus, and I were to leave the next day.

I showed up early at Stilicho's headquarters the next morning, and as I did, three more couriers arrived from Gaul. After they spoke privately with Stilicho, another full staff meeting was called. Trier was now under attack by the Vandals, Alans, and Sueves. Speyer and Worms on the Rhine had also fallen to the Alemanns.

"Marcus," Stilicho said, "I want you, Andreas, and Julianus to leave immediately for Blavia. I've redrafted the introductory part of your letter so that it's now generic rather than being specifically addressed to your brother alone. Given the instability that exists there, we must be prepared to face the possibility that your brother may no longer be in charge by the time you arrive."

"That has occurred to me also," I replied.

Stilicho continued, "You are to make the offer that we originally addressed to your brother to whomever the usurper happens to be when you arrive on the island."

After seeing our families briefly, we were off for the northwest. Aureliana had told me recently that she was pregnant for the sixth time. I swore to her that I would do everything I could to be with her when her time came, but she knew that no promises could be made. In the meantime, her cousin Claudia could help her as she had done in the past. We raced up the Via Aemelia then cut south to the coast at Genoa. There would be no time for sightseeing as we rode through the Riviera on the Via Julia Augusta. The entire south coast of Gaul is a cultural, social, and commercial extension of Italy. Coming up from the coast, these Mediterranean plains sweep around the south and southwest edges of the Alps. Reaching about seventy miles up the Rhone, they then follow the southeastern and southern edges of the Cevennes Mountains before swinging around to the Pyrenees. Especially this early in the year, we could appreciate its warmth and dryness compared to the almost never-ending dampness of Ravenna. The bright sunshine and beautiful architecture of this area are enough to raise even the most depressed spirits. At every city and town we passed through, we inquired at the office of the urban prefect or provincial governor about the latest news from up north. To the point where we reached the Rhone, nothing major had occurred since we had left Ravenna so far as anyone knew. At Arles, that changed.

We were informed that Strasbourg had fallen with a considerable loss of life and destruction of property. Once we moved west of Arles, I was in territory that was new to me. Everything west of Italy was new to my comrades since they had never been in the prefecture of the Gauls before. We were in the plain of Languedoc between the Cevennes and that part of the Mediterranean Sea known as the Gulf of Lions. We continued on to Nimes and Narbonne. Past Nimes, the population tends to thin out somewhat. There was another route to Bordeaux through the Cevennes, but heavy rains had caused floods in the mountains that rendered taking that highway inadvisable. At Narbonne, we turned west and passed up the Aude River Valley through the Gate of Carcassonne. This is the gap between the Cevennes Mountains to the north and the Pyrenees that permit one to pass from the Mediterranean plains to those of Aquitaine. The eastern or upper plains of this region contain the finest soils in Gaul for growing grains, while the western or lower plains concentrate on wine production. We would pass by many large and wealthy estates, some with villas that would rival anything in Italy. This indeed was one of the richest and wealthiest regions in the empire and, to a degree, would continue to maintain itself as such in the increasingly difficult years ahead.

At Toulouse, we learned that the Garonne River was in flood further downstream where it takes in the runoff from the Cevennes and mountains further to the north. For that reason, we took the highway that runs straight west from Toulouse and that stays well to the south of the river. Our journey west of Narbonne took us parallel to the Pyrenees. These mountains, which run for 270 miles from the Mediterranean to the Atlantic, pose a much more formidable barrier between Gaul and Spain than do the Alps between Italy and its neighbors. This in spite of the fact that nowhere do the Pyrenees reach the elevation of the Alps. The difference lies in the fact that travel through the Alps is facilitated by a large number of easily accessible passes. There are far fewer of these corridors in the Pyrenees through which we have constructed only three major highways. From the plains of Aquitaine, these mountains rise quite sharply, and where the valleys on their northern and southern slopes join, they rarely do so in a pass that lies at a conveniently low elevation. The northwest face of this range receives the heaviest rainfall of any location in Gaul, but the Garonne is the only large river to flow from this chain. The rest of them are small. As I mentioned, the Pyrenees are a formidable barrier. But they would not prove formidable enough.

Pressing on to the northwest, we stayed overnight in Elusa (Eauze). We spent much of the evening in pleasant conversation with the inn keeper and several of his friends who dropped by to visit. Things might not have been so friendly if they had known we were the assassins of Rufinus, their town's most famous native son. Continuing on to Bordeaux, we were informed by the city prefect that Trier had fallen. This was a staggering loss. The former imperial capital had met the same fate as Mainz. It had been stormed, its garrison defeated, its citizenry slaughtered or driven off. While the main army of the Vandals, Alans, and Sueves was overrunning Trier, smaller bands of barbarians were savaging the rich estates along the Moselle. After Trier, the Vandals and their allies were reported heading southwest to Reims but were slowed by severe weather. The size of the breach in our Rhine defenses had doubled and then tripled since January 1. These fortifications could only be reclaimed with the greatest difficulty. As we left the urban prefect's office, Andreas spoke the thought that was on all our minds.

"I know this involves you most personally, Marcus, but should the military deterioration in the north worsen, I can't see a rebellious British army having much use for a civilian 'usurper.'"

No argument there. We continued on to the port of Blavia and reported to the office of the navarch (commander) of the flotilla stationed there. Stilicho had left it up to us to make a decision at Bordeaux as to whether we would travel to Boulogne by land or by sea. With the chaos deepening in the interior, we decided to travel on the next dromon warship leaving on patrol duty up the coast. Winter weather is always uncertain and we were held up for several days by heavy rainstorms. A further storm forced us into the port of Nantes after traveling about two hundred miles out of Blavia but we learned nothing more there about conditions in the interior. I had decided to meet with the duke of the Armorican Tract. We needed an update on military conditions in northern Gaul and the Rhineland as well as the political situation in Britain. His jurisdiction is mainly a coastal command. We learned that he was in the process of inspecting fortifications between Nantes and the estuary of the Seine and could be found at any of the sites in between. The storm over, we again set sail to the northwest.

Armorica is the least populated and least Romanized part of Gaul. In some areas, its ancient Celtic language is still spoken. Not only its location but its geography tends to isolate it. While its rugged coastline serves to facilitate its defense, its interior is heavily dissected by streams laden with runoff from its frequent storms. As a result, land communications are difficult. Its soils are rich, however, and with a greater population, it could be quite productive agriculturally. When I was a teamster, shellfish from this region rivaled the product that we transported up from the Mediterranean. If only it could have remained thus.

We found the duke at the small town of Brest on the westernmost promontory of Gaul. We were already early into the month of March. The garrison adjutant informed us that the duke had arrived about an hour before we had and a meeting had just started between him and the garrison commander. Showing him the documentation that I possessed bearing the seal of Emperor Honorius encouraged him to interrupt the meeting on our behalf. After introductions were made, I came quickly to the point.

"Sir," I said addressing the duke, "our mission is as follows: I've been instructed by His Majesty and Lord Stilicho to make an offer of reconciliation to the usurper who calls himself Gratian II. First of all, I would like you to inform us of what the current situation is regarding the rebellion in Britain."

The duke and the garrison commander quickly looked at one another; I knew instantly that something was wrong.

"You could have saved yourself a trip," the duke responded gruffly. "The would-be Gratian II is dead. He was assassinated ten days ago and replaced by a soldier who has proclaimed himself Constantine III. I was informed of this only three days ago."

"This new usurper is unknown to us," the garrison commander added.

"As were his two predecessors," the duke snorted. "He is neither the duke of Britain, the count of Britain, nor the count of the Saxon Shore. I know the top commanders there and he isn't one of them. I strongly suspect that he was chosen because of his name."

"The first Constantine got away with his rebellion in Britain," said the garrison commander. "Perhaps this guy figures he can keep the streak going."

The duke and the garrison commander both laughed. I just sat there stunned to realize that my brother was dead and that he had met his end in such a grim manner. I excused myself for a few moments and walked down to the end of the room to stare out the window. It was sunny with a pleasant breeze, and everything looked so peaceful. I returned to the table.

"Gentlemen, the reason I was chosen for this mission is that the late, aforementioned Gratian was my younger brother."

They both gasped at this revelation and offered apologies but I quickly assured them that none were necessary.

"My brother was an intelligent and highly articulate fool," I told them. "We were not close, and almost twenty-six years have passed since I last saw him. A sister of ours informed me of his 'power grab.' When I informed Stilicho of this, he appointed me for this mission on the hope that I would be able to talk sense into my brother and the army."

"If I am allowed to ask," the duke said, "what were the conditions that Lord Stilicho was offering?"

I told him.

"Sounds reasonable to me," the duke replied. "Offering the highest civilian posting to the leader of a rebellion who is himself a civilian would have gotten him off the hook nicely. But a civilian posting for a soldier will not be enough. I wish I knew more about this new usurper, but unfortunately none of us do."

"What's the situation here in Gaul?" Julianus asked, almost afraid to.

"The good news," the duke said, "is that all the fortresses from Cologne north along the Rhine have either held out against attacks or have not been attacked at all. Cavalry units from those forts have been launching continual assaults against the Vandals and their allies. But there is just so damned many of the enemy that it's been impossible to stop them. They are currently approaching Reims, and God only knows where they will go from there."

"The bad news," the garrison commander said, "is that we have no other forces left in northern Gaul to confront the Vandals. Also, the Alemanns are continuing to push south up the Rhine. Their next target of consequence will probably be Basel and then where will they go?"

"The most important question," the duke said, "that has been circulating among everyone in Gaul is, what is Stilicho going to do and why hasn't he started doing it already? Nothing angered the population here more than the emperor's proclamation announcing Jovius as the new praetorian prefect of Illyria. The timing was atrocious, arriving here as it did shortly after the Rhineland had started going up in flames. How can the generalissimo be planning on marching east when Gaul is undergoing the largest invasion in its history?"

"Neither the emperor nor Stilicho," I said, "was aware of the invasion when they decided to make Jovius's appointment public. I am certain that the Illyrian expedition will be suspended indefinitely. Regarding our response to the invasion here, remember that for nine months the Army of Italy and its associated forces were fighting Radagaisus. The enormity of our victory there notwithstanding, we did suffer considerable casualties that we are still trying to replace."

"And a lot of the casualties," said the garrison commander, "were Gallic and British troops. If they had not died defending Italy then they would be available now to defend Gaul. All we hear about here is 'Italy, Italy, Italy.' Damn it there is more to the Western Empire than Italy!"

"But there might not be," the duke warned, "if we do not stem this current invasion. In terms of numbers, it is the biggest single attack that Gaul has ever suffered. To make matters worse, we simply do not have adequate forces with which to defeat them. Now should be the time for the East to come to the aid of the West in the way we helped them after Hadrianople three decades ago. But the political atmosphere between the two capitals is such that no such help will be forthcoming. Whatever is done here will be accomplished with western units. Lord Stilicho had better make his mind up in a hurry as to how he is going to respond to this catastrophe."

From there we headed up the coast to Boulogne where the duke of Lesser Belgium was headquartered. We ran into some difficult weather but still managed to make the trip from Brest to Boulogne in five days with a good wind behind us. During the trip, my comrades and I discussed the sort of offer that might appeal to the new usurper. What we came up with was much broader than what Stilicho had offered. At the same time, the situation had changed so drastically since we had left Ravenna that we really had no choice.

The coastal command of the duke of Lesser Belgium extends from the Seine estuary to that of the Rhine and was a relatively new creation. It consists of those coastal fortifications that originally formed the continental portion of the command of the count of the Saxon Shore. In

395, Stilicho had set it up to prevent any future usurper in Britain from having automatic access to the continent. We met with him and received basically the same demand that we had heard earlier for Ravenna: act strongly in support of the beleaguered forces in Gaul. The status report that he provided was what we had heard at Brest but he added that the three major military commands in Britain were all actively supporting the would-be emperor. There had been little dissention from army elements over his proclamation while there had been with his two predecessors. From there we sailed to Dover.

Its garrison commander sent a courier to London to inform the usurper that we would be arriving shortly with recommendations for a peaceful resolution to the rebellion. Arriving in London, we reported to the vicar's palace where the usurper was holding court. Our reception was cool but not hostile. Constantine was in his late forties and had been a tribune in command of a cavalry regiment. I later looked up his personnel records back in the capital; he was hardly the nobody that many were trying to make him out to be. His record was modest but he was capable. The three of us met with Constantine and two of his top generals. We were thoroughly frisked by a fruity-looking bugger that obviously enjoyed his occupational responsibilities. Then we were ushered into a meeting room where Constantine and I sat on opposite sides of a long table. I handed the documents from Stilicho to the usurper. After he broke the seal and read them, Constantine looked up and said, "This is unacceptable."

"Let me explain a few things," I said. "This was drawn up on the assumption that we would be speaking to a civilian for whom Lord Stilicho was willing to make a legitimate political appointment. You are a soldier, so you will want something more. But as a soldier, you must surely realize that the one thing the empire cannot put itself through is yet another civil war. The breakthrough on the Rhine is a direct result of the last such war we had almost thirteen years ago, from which we have still not recovered."

"The only way to avoid that," Constantine stated, "is to have Honorius recognize me as his co-emperor."

"Let's set that aside for the moment," I suggested, "and consider—"

"No, let's not," Constantine interrupted. "Without Honorius and Stilicho being willing to accede to this one and only demand that I am placing on them, there is nothing else to discuss."

"The second document," I said, pretending to ignore what I had just heard, "requests you to determine whether any units from Britain can be sent to the defense of Gaul."

"Is Stilicho planning on sitting back and doing nothing to stem this barbarian tide himself?" Constantine asked rather testily.

"He will act at the earliest opportunity," I replied. "The Army of Italy is still in the process of being rebuilt as the result of our war with Radagaisus and being reoriented from the Illyrian theater to fight in Gaul."

"The way we heard it here," Constantine replied huffily, "is that your army slaughtered Radagaisus."

"Ultimately, we did," I said, "but a soldier of your experience knows full well that all armies, regardless of the extent of their victories, pay a heavy price for them. The Army of Italy is no different. We are trying to rebuild it as quickly as possible but these things take time. What Lord Stilicho wants from you is participation in our defeat of the barbarians in northern Gaul. You've read what he said. He wants you to cooperate with him. We had discussions in Ravenna, prior to the collapse on the Rhine, on creating a second field army in Gaul. After all there are six of them in the East if you include Alaric's Visigothic Federate Army. The current Army of Gaul will remain under the command of Chariobaudes. I will recommend to Stilicho that you be made the commander of the second field army, whatever it is eventually called, and that Ravenna make whatever payments to your soldiers that you might have promised them. That should keep them satisfied."

"You're just adlibbing now," Constantine said contemptuously, "without any idea of what your masters back in 'Swamp City' will say about your proposals."

"Of course I'm extemporizing," I said. "Under the circumstances, what else can I do? Nonetheless, my recommendations are realistic and I wouldn't be making them if I didn't think that Ravenna would find them acceptable."

"Why should I be satisfied with anything less than I have right now?" Constantine asked.

"At the moment," I replied, "there is no reason for anything to change as far as your proclamation is concerned. Help Honorius to the greatest extent that you can in northern Gaul and be rewarded for it. You know as well as I do that, apart from Julian the Apostate and his illustrious uncle whose name you bear, every man who attempted to seize the throne from northwest of the Alps has wound up with his head impaled on a stake prior to making a tour of the major cities. There is no need for a repetition of that dreary tradition yet again."

An awkward silence ensued. Awkward for Constantine, not me, because I had said just about all I could on the matter. It was up to the usurper now. He got up and started to pace about the room.

"I'll think about it," he said. "It would help if you would make arrangements for the duke of the Armorican Tract and his counterpart in Lesser Belgium to come over to my side when I do cross the strait, as I will have to. Reims could fall soon, and if the Vandals continue their march to the west, then I will have to cross sooner rather than later."

"You can appreciate that I cannot make that decision on my own," I replied. "We're talking treason here regardless of how noble the intent. What I will do is discuss the matter with Stilicho when I get back to Ravenna and recommend that he tell both dukes not to resist your crossing, to remain neutral."

"That's fair," Constantine replied rather too quickly.

We continued to discuss the deteriorating military situation in Gaul for a while, and then I astonished him by telling him that I was the older brother of his predecessor. He quickly assured me that he had had nothing to do with Gratian's assassination. I told him that I believed him and gave him assurance that I bore him no ill will. Secondly, I asked him to write a letter to my sister assuring her that no action would be taken against Gratian's extended family by his government—that to allay the fears that she had expressed to me in her letter. I then wrote her a quick letter myself. I explained the reasons for my visit to Britain along with why the military disaster unfolding in Gaul precluded my visiting her or even our relatives in London. A courier was then dispatched carrying both letters.

Our business in London completed, I then ordered the trierarch in command of our ship to set sail for Bordeaux. Once again, we had to put into Nantes for a couple of days due to a severe storm, but other than that, the trip went smoothly enough. In Bordeaux, we caught up on the military situation to the north. Rome's fortunes had declined even more. We left immediately for Ravenna, 750 miles to the east. Since the trip from Bordeaux to London was 950 miles, by the time we arrived back in the capital, our round-trip had covered 3,400 miles. By now it was the latter half of April. I reported to Stilicho and informed him of what had transpired between Constantine and us in London. The generalissimo first offered his condolences on the death of my brother and called an immediate staff meeting. He did not object to anything that I reported. My first hint that the local mind-set may not yet be properly oriented was when I went to see Stilicho's secretary to have my presentation added to the list of items to be covered. He added me at the bottom of the list, so I ordered him to put me at the top where I belonged. After all, half the Western Empire was starting to hang in the balance.

At the staff meeting, the first item of business was an update of the military situation in Gaul. After attacking Basel at the great bend of the Rhine, the Alemanns struck to the southwest and sacked the small town of Avenches just to the east of Lake Neuchatel. That was as far south as this particular army of invaders went. Earlier, Stilicho had dispatched several regiments in a "left hook" that eventually took them through Geneva. From there, they continued northeastward to Avenches, where they inflicted several minor defeats on the Alemanns. Our regiments were too outnumbered to inflict major damage on them. Nonetheless, our attacks had been sufficient to halt the momentum and change the direction of their progress. From Avenches the enemy retreated northeast and attacked Windisch, the onetime legionary base that lies twenty miles to the east of Basel. Returning back down the Rhine, many simply settled on the vacant lands along the Roman side of the frontier between the Rhine and the Vosges Mountains. Now that the spring thaw was well underway, Stilicho had sent units of the Army of Italy north to occupy all the fortifications in our northwestern and western Alpine passes in case the Alemanns changed their minds. Fortunately for Italy, they did not.

The situation regarding the northern wing of the barbarian invasion continued to deteriorate. The Vandals, Alans, and Sueves were in the process of cutting a swath of death and destruction across the entire length of northern Gaul. After Trier, they had attacked Reims, where they slaughtered a large number of civilians, including Bishop Nicasius in his own church. They then swung to the northwest along the highways that would take them to Soissons, Amiens, Cambrai, and Arras. This was really the proper point for me to speak, but instead I was astonished to learn that plans were still going forward for Stilicho and Alaric to launch their joint attack into Eastern Illyria. Several other minor issues were discussed, and finally it was my turn. The points my two comrades and I made were these: with the replacement of "Gratian II" by "Constantine III," the political situation had hardened in Britain; unless we sent a large army north and quickly, Gaul could very well go over to the usurper; we would pay the donation to Constantine's troops that he had promised them. We also recommended that the two coastal dukes in Gaul be advised to allow Constantine's forces to land on the continent without interference to combat the barbarians. There was an undercurrent of grumbling as soon as I was finished. Stilicho had a tendency to let discussions at these meetings be as freewheeling as possible to get every opinion out on the table. They were not long in coming.

"How the hell to you expect us to pay the sort of donation you have recommended to Constantine's troops?" growled one of the representatives from the finance ministries. "This is an open invitation for all troops to rebel to simply get a pay raise for themselves."

"If you have a better recommendation," I replied, "then I'd be glad to hear it. It is essential that we get whatever troops that Britain can afford involved in the war against the Vandals as soon as possible."

Silence.

"Our first order of business," Sarus said, "must be to cancel the operation against Eastern Illyria. We've already got two crises on our hands and yet we're deliberately planning a third!"

"I hear you," Stilicho said. "The early victory that we achieved over the Vandals was rendered academic by their second assault wave. Even if we accept the probably exaggerated figure of twenty thousand Vandal dead in their first assault, that would still leave well in excess of two hundred thousand barbarians of all varieties to contend with, assuming our original estimates are correct. Our total troop strength in Britain is twelve thousand men: 5,500 under the count of Britain, 1,200 on the Saxon Shore, and 5,300 manning Hadrian's Wall. At the most, I cannot see Constantine bringing over more than five thousand men. If he tries to strip the Saxon Shore forts or Hadrian's Wall of any more troops than they have already lost then he might very well face a revolt of his own. In British eyes, he will be no longer acting in their strategic interests."

At that point, a young tribune whom I had never seen before spoke up. While I had never met him, I had heard of him by reputation, which was excellent. His star was definitely in the ascendant.

"I don't think we have any choice," Constantius said. "If Constantine brought every soldier in Britain with him, it would not be enough to enable him to defeat the Vandals minus outside assistance. We must postpone the Illyrian operation one more time, bring Alaric back from Epirus, and send a joint Roman/Visigothic force into Gaul to destroy the barbarians. Gaul and Britain must come first. We can worry about Illyria later."

"It will not be easy," the gruff financial official reminded us, "to convince the population of northern Italy that Alaric will do them no harm this time around. There will be strong opposition from the Senate also for the same reason."

"A large number of those same senators own property in southern Gaul," Stilicho said. "If the Vandals turn south, then their properties there will be in grave danger."

No one was thinking in terms of Spain yet.

The meeting's end result was that my two comrades and I were ordered to retrace our steps to northern Gaul and Britain. This was quite difficult on our families. After being away for most of the year thus far, I could spend only two nights at home with Aureliana and the children. Most importantly, everyone understood the gravity of the developing situation. We headed off with the high purpose of avoiding another civil war. Conditions to the north, however, were starting to outrun our ability to respond.

When we arrived at Bordeaux, we discovered that the British revolt had taken a serious turn for the worse. The urban prefect informed us that the usurper had already crossed to the continent and the forces under the commands of the dukes of the Armorican Tract and Lesser Belgium had declared their loyalty to him. That meant that the port at Blavia, downstream from Bordeaux, was now in the usurper's hands. We continued on anyway. The garrison commander and the navarch in charge of its flotilla confirmed that their garrison and fleet had joined the rebels. This had happened shortly before our arrival. In addition, we learned that Constantine had appointed two field marshals to handle his troops. They were Justinianus and Nebiogastes, the two generals who had attended the usurper during our meeting with him in March. This was administrative overkill for just five thousand soldiers. Obviously, Constantine was counting on many troops in northern Gaul coming over to him. He would not be disappointed. Not yet.

We were in a quandary. The navarch offered to provide us passage to the north if we still desired to go. It was obvious that he and the garrison commander wanted to avoid civil war if at all possible. They were not alone in this desire, but the problem now was how this end could be accomplished. The garrison commander offered us a conference room to determine what course of action we wanted to pursue.

He then added as an afterthought, "Oh, by the way, there is something that we forgot to mention to you. Constantine has two sons. He announced before leaving Britain that he had renamed them Julian and Constans." He then smiled and closed the door behind him.

"Goddam son of a bitch," I exploded, once we were inside. "Why couldn't the bastard have waited another week or two?"

"Perhaps," Andreas suggested, "the situation up there has worsened to the point where he could not delay any longer."

"Do any of us see any point in continuing this trip?" Julianus asked.

"Unless either of you can provide a good reason for going forward," I replied, "I can't."

"At our London meeting in March," Julianus continued, "I'll bet the three of them probably fell off their chairs laughing at us before we had left the building."

"For a pair of men who claimed no knowledge of him," Andreas said, "the two coastal dukes appear to have gone over to the usurper rather quickly, don't you think?"

"It wouldn't be the first time that a cash exchange cemented an instant friendship," I replied. "Let's not forget Eutropius and Gildo. Look, the purpose of our mission has been completely undermined. We were to confirm our original suggestion to the dukes that they offer no resistance to Constantine. Instead, they have already gone over to him. We were to confirm our offer of the office of field marshal to the usurper once this invasion had been defeated. Instead, he has created two field marshals of his own before firing a single arrow at the enemy. I think we can safely conclude that Constantine was unimpressed with our peace offering and that we should return to Ravenna immediately." My two comrades agreed.

"By the time we get back," Julianus observed, "we will have covered almost five thousand miles between our two trips."

"And every foot was a waste of time," Andreas groaned.

We attended the baths and had dinner that evening with the navarch and garrison commander. The garrison was small. In fact, numerous cities and towns of southern Gaul, even substantial ones, have no garrisons at all. We thanked them for their hospitality and told them that we would not be continuing on our journey. Two days later, we arrived in Toulouse. It had been a long day, and the weather was already starting to get hot, so before having supper, we headed for the baths. Once again, our thoughts came back to our aborted mission and what its failure would mean for the future.

"Another civil war will be suicidal," said Andreas. "We've been through two of them already and know only too well the consequences."

"The most ominous thing that we heard in Bordeaux," said Julianus, "was that Constantine has two sons and has renamed them after two emperors who were held in high esteem by the Gauls. The usurper has ambitions that far exceed his sharing the throne of the West with that pipsqueak Honorius. Constantine's ultimate hope is probably to see Constans as emperor in Trier and Julian ruling in Ravenna. There is no way in which war can be avoided."

"Such a conflict," I said, "will be doubly suicidal for the West because it will involve only the two western prefectures. Constantinople can just sit back and watch. I wonder if the Fates have placed a special curse on us. With Gaul suffering the worst invasion in its history and with soldiers in shorter supply than ever, we are about to start slaughtering ourselves again; hardly the wisest preparation for going to war against our real enemies."

"It's beginning to appear," Julianus said, "that we *are* our real enemies!"

"About the only good thing to be said about it," Andreas reasoned, "is that the numbers involved should be relatively small. At the Frigidus, we had about a hundred thousand to a side. Since this next civil war will involve only the West, each side will do well to muster twenty thousand men, if that, for it."

"That will make Alaric more important to us than ever," Julianus said.

"Setting the civil war possibilities aside for the moment," Andreas said, "the situation we are facing here is far more complex than the one that confronted the East after Hadrianople. It took the united resources of East and West to stabilize the frontier of the lower Danube, in part with Visigothic recruits. Here in the West, we have to face our own version of the 'Danube crossing' entirely on our own. In addition to the Franks, whom we long ago entrusted with the defense of the lower Rhine, we are planning on increasing our German 'nationalities' problem by another order of magnitude by bringing in Alaric's Visigothic Federate Army to help us defeat the Vandals. Two decades after the Visigothic entry into Thrace and Illyria, conditions are still unsettled there. What sort of a nightmare are we ultimately going to wind up with here? The Vandal troop strength plus that of their allies is more than that of the Visigoths thirty years ago, but our resources to counter them are drastically less. And those will be reduced even further after we have completed warring with ourselves. The crisis in northern Gaul is starting to spin out of control and could easily spill over into the neighboring dioceses."

"And at this juncture in our long and illustrious history," I said, "we have the most pathetic pair of meatheads imaginable reigning over us."

"Might not Constantine," Julianus said, "be making the same mistake that Magnus Maximus made? That earlier usurper convinced himself that Theodosius was too far away and too involved with the Visigoths in the Balkans to reclaim the West for his junior colleague. What he failed to take into account was Theodosius's dynastic ambitions for his younger son. We all know that Theodosius planned to have Honorius inherit part—and after 392, all—of the Western Empire. Both civil wars that we served in were fought to secure the succession for Honorius as much as anything. Magnus Maximus and later Arbogast failed to appreciate the strength of the ambitions of the true power behind the western throne."

"Okay," I said, "I'll continue the analogy for you. Honorius is an imbecile held in universal contempt not just in Britain and Gaul but, given his less than ennobling performance during the recent invasions of the imperial heartland, Italy as well. If Honorius was on his own, then the Army of Italy would probably go over to the usurper in an instant. Such is not the case. Since Stilicho's son Eucherius is engaged to Galla Placidia, the emperor's half sister, he would make a logical successor should anything happen to Honorius, who, if there is truly a God in heaven, will never have any children of his own. Theodosius always referred to Eucherius as his grandson, which he is by virtue of his mother's adoption by Theodosius. Just as Theodosius would not let a usurper take over the prefecture of the Gauls, neither will Stilicho and for the same reason. I know nothing about Eucherius's capabilities. However, I am certain that he cannot possibly be less effective than his two distant cousins for whom our signal humiliation is to hail as 'Augustus.'"

"I've never heard you sound so pissed off over the, to be polite, lack of effective direction from the thrones East or West," Julianus said, "but I agree. Can you imagine the chaos that would reign if Honorius did not have Stilicho behind him?"

We could not imagine the affairs of the West being managed by anyone but Stilicho. But unknown to us at the time, there were others who could.

After Reims, Soissons fell. At that juncture, the Vandals divided their forces into two groups to continue their path of rape, slaughter, and destruction ever closer to the coast. There were no forces stationed in great numbers anywhere in the interior of Gaul, and with help so slow in arriving from the outside, the local civilian populations would have declared their loyalty to anyone showing up with a sword in his hand that was on their side. The barbarians continued their drive to the northwest, with their southern prong heading for Amiens while the northern force drove for Cambrai and Arras. Though more spread out than in the south, many large villas were still to be found in that area. Tragically, many of them went up in flames. At Arras, the two columns rejoined and continued their push to the northwest. With this oncoming tide advancing toward Boulogne, Constantine had very little choice but to land on the continent. By joining his forces with those of the two coastal dukes, a more coherent defense could be offered. The Vandals and their allies advanced to within twenty-five miles of Boulogne. Their objective might have been to attempt to seize ships and invade Britain. Regardless of what prompted them to travel that far west, the presence of Constantine's army on the coast caused them to halt at the town of Therouanne. Without making contact, they retreated eastward and sacked the city of Tournai before turning to the southwest. Whatever threat they had presented to Britain was over. The threat they posed to the empire as a whole, however, had just begun.

Arriving back in Ravenna, Stilicho agreed with my decision to abort our mission. To continue it would have served no purpose. He had been informed about Constantine's landing in Gaul just shortly before we arrived. Since we had left, an expeditionary force had been put together under the command of Sarus. It was felt that Alaric's army was too far away, down in Epirus, to provide an effective counter to the Vandals at this time. There was also strong political opposition to the idea of transporting Alaric's army across northern Italy. The locals remembered his last visitation quite vividly. Sarus's forces came primarily from the Army of Italy and the Alan federates stationed in the upper part of the peninsula. This force was still in the process of being gathered and provisioned when we arrived. At that point, I resumed my regular position as chief quartermaster for the Army of Italy.

The original mission for Sarus's army had been based on its attacking the Alemanns along the upper Rhine while Constantine attacked the Vandals and their allies in the northwest. Once it was determined that Constantine was going to remain in revolt, that mission was changed. The swiftness with which Constantine was able to secure his position in Gaul was testimony to just how unpopular the government of Honorius and Stilicho there had become. The Roman forces along the Rhine had quickly joined the usurper's cause. He ordered the reconstruction of Trier and established his headquarters there. However, his stay in the Rhineland was temporary. Honorius's government in Gaul had retreated southward and reestablished the capital of the prefecture in Arles. This was to be a temporary relocation; like much else transpiring in Gaul at the time, it would prove permanent. The reconstruction of other destroyed or damaged fortresses along the Rhine was also ordered once Constantine's army reoccupied them. He then launched a few minor attacks against the Vandals and their allies in the interior to bolster what was left of public morale in the region. One major victory was claimed, but none of these actions were sustained.

Gathering the forces at his disposal as quickly as he could, he proceeded to march up the Moselle and then down the Saone, pausing only after his army had reached Lyon. Constantine's main purpose, indeed at this time his only purpose, was to establish his authority, from a purely Roman standpoint, in Gaul. He avoided combat with the barbarians to the greatest degree possible in order to concentrate his resources on whatever forces Stilicho sent against him from Italy. At this point, the chief officials who remained loyal to Honorius fled to Italy. They could not have fared worse by going over to the usurper.

For several weeks, a series of directives in the name of Honorius had been delivered to Stilicho ordering him to attack Constantine's forces. The emperor's civilian advisers seemed to have no idea of the difficulties involved in putting a large expeditionary force in place. A number of historians have criticized Stilicho for his "fixation" on Eastern Illyria to the detriment of the West. These imputations are justified up to the spring of 407, but once the full scale of the barbarian onslaught became apparent, as had the treachery of Constantine, Stilicho gave it his full attention. One problem with assembling Sarus's expeditionary force was that certain key units of the Army of Italy were still involved in mopping up activity against remnants of Radagaisus's army in Noricum and Pannonia. These were small-scale operations but were nonetheless time-consuming. My men were now concentrating their efforts on upgrading and repairing our storage depots in the Italian northwest as well as determining the provisions required for Sarus's forces. Fortunately, this area had been the least impacted by the most recent invasion. At the same time, with the collapse of Honorius's civilian and military authority west of the Alps, we had to treat southern Gaul as an extension of Italy. Limenius, who was praetorian prefect of the Gauls under Honorius, was as helpful as he could be, but legitimate authority in Gaul was now restricted to most of Aquitaine and the Mediterranean plains. Food supplies were plentiful in this region, but for the most part, the expeditionary force had to obtain its provisions from Italy. Transporting these supplies from their collection points to the forces in the field occupied our command for much of the spring and summer.

Parked down in Epirus, Alaric's frustrations were growing daily. He felt that he had learned the proper lessons from his disgraceful adventure in Greece in 395–396 and had conducted himself in a proper

"Roman" manner ever since. From 397 to 401, he had reestablished and maintained order in the prefecture of Illyria on behalf of the government in Constantinople. His four years as marshal of Illyria had taught him and most of his followers that the best way for them to survive and advance themselves was to remain within the Roman military structure and to cooperate with Roman civilian authorities. His position with respect to Italy was that he had invaded it because he had nowhere else to go. Gainas had fired him, and Stilicho did not want him.

As a military count in Western Illyria in the employ of Rome, Alaric had done all that was asked of him. In 404, he had occupied Epirus for Honorius and had been ready to invade Eastern Illyria with Stilicho until unforeseen events had twice postponed the expedition. He came to feel that occupying Epirus had placed him too far out of Rome's watchful eye. Radagaisus had come and gone, and now the Vandals and "Constantine III" had both invaded Gaul, and still there was no call from Stilicho. Alaric was beginning to feel like the forgotten man of Roman politics. Well, there was certainly one way to fix that. He composed a lengthy letter to Stilicho.

Radagaisus's army had punched a large hole in our central Danubian defenses when it broke through. Stilicho recognized that he would have to plug it somehow, and we had discussed the problem on several occasions after Radagaisus had been executed. No decision had been reached, but in late 406, it was felt that it could be put off until the impending Illyrian campaign had been completed. The last day of the year changed all that. In the spring, Alaric's letter arrived, and Stilicho read it to us at one of his staff meetings. Though he had never been there, Alaric suggested that he and his army be moved to Noricum. There they could act to block any more invasions like the one that Radagaisus and his horde had just put the Western Empire through. He reminded Stilicho of the manner in which he had returned law and order to Illyria and assisted its civilian administration for four years, the last one for free after he had been fired by Gainas.

Finally, to the cash-strapped government at Ravenna, Alaric reminded them that by returning responsible government to Noricum, greater tax revenues could expect to flow into the coffers of the central government. Stilicho realized by this time that his Illyrian ambitions had been postponed again, if not cancelled outright.

"Gentlemen," he began, "this letter makes a lot of sense to me, and I'm inclined to take him at his word. I am going to issue orders to Alaric transferring his army and their dependents from Epirus to Noricum. We can await his arrival there and see how the situation develops in Gaul before we start drawing up plans to use his army against the Vandals, Sueves, and Alans. The distance between Noricum and Epirus is about six hundred miles. It will take several months to get Alaric's army and their families moved to their new locations. Once that is settled, Alaric's army can be transferred to Gaul to assist in suppressing Constantine's revolt and then the Vandals and their allies. As some of you probably cannot wait to remind me, this marks a complete about-face in my attitude toward Alaric from what it was just a short while ago. But when certain salient facts change, our conceptions have to change in response. A year or so ago, the Rhine was in no danger, and there was no hint of rebellion anywhere. All that has changed now and we have to respond accordingly."

"There is one aspect to this move," I suggested, "that Alaric did not mention. Sarus brought it up during one of our staff meetings last year. Stationed in Epirus for over two years, he has been almost totally dependent on internal growth to obtain new recruits. Gothic warriors coming down from the north to join him have been few and far between. As a result, the total number of men enrolled in his army and their dependents has, at best, remained stationary. Relocated in Noricum, he will have access to the frontier once again and be able to build his strength, perhaps at our expense, from that source as well."

"There is an element of danger," Stilicho answered, "in everything we do. But I don't see why Alaric's army should appear more attractive than our own to any potential new hires from across the Danube."

"Part of our previous agreement with Alaric," I said, "was that he would be reappointed marshal of Illyria, or Greater Illyria if you will, once the campaign there came to a successful conclusion. Once our operations against the Vandals and their allies are concluded, is he still going to have the rank of field marshal, and if so, where will he be serving?"

"The campaign in Gaul," Stilicho replied, "will be far more difficult than the one in Illyria would have been. By the time it is over, Alaric will have earned that rank. Several months back, we discussed a complete reorganization of our army in Gaul. Chariobaudes, our current marshal of Gaul, and Alaric will both play a major role in it, but the details must await the completion of the campaign."

The meeting adjourned, and I went back to repairing and rebuilding our storage depots. The work went well, and we completed the entire project by the late spring.

At this point, a bizarre thing happened. The rumor reached Rome and Ravenna that Alaric had died. Once again, our plans were thrown into uncertainty, and the expedition to Gaul was temporarily postponed while we determined exactly what the situation was down in Epirus. Within ten days, we had determined that Alaric was in fact alive, and our plans to combat the usurper went ahead.

On the diplomatic front, relations between East and West deteriorated further in 407. Patriarch John Chrysostom of Constantinople had been banished to Armenia by Emperor Arcadius several years earlier. His deposition had resulted from a combination of political infighting within the church between Constantinople and Alexandria and several personal confrontations between John and the late Empress Eudoxia. They were finally pitted against one another as a result of a sermon that he delivered that was quite condemning of women in general and the empress in particular, whom the patriarch compared to the biblical Jezebel. John appealed to Pope Innocent in Rome. He in turn went to Emperor Honorius to request intersession with his brother in the eastern capital to have John brought back from exile and reinstated. Honorius sent off a delegation of priests to Constantinople to affect this end, but they were arrested and immediately thrown into prison upon their arrival. Sending them was a naive act in the first place. From the reign of Constantine I onward, secular and ecclesiastical politics had been inextricably intertwined. This condition only worsened as time went on. Since Alaric had been occupying Epirus on Honorius's behalf for over two years by this time, one wonders just how the emperor of the West and his civilian advisers thought the eastern government would react. In retaliation for this insult, Stilicho ordered the closing down of all ports throughout the Western Empire to shipping from the eastern provinces. Trade is a two-way street, and when sanctions are imposed by one side on the other, both sides generally pay a price. This was thought to be a considerable overreaction in the opinion of many and one that started to undermine Stilicho's good relations with the mercantile element.

In late May, Sarus and his army were dispatched to combat Constantine. Many of us privately questioned the choice of Sarus as the commander for such a vital undertaking. He was a crack cavalry officer and had proved himself to be a first-class replacement for Saul the Alan as the chief cavalry commander for the Army of Italy. But he had never been in charge of a major expedition like this before. Most leading officers in Italy had assumed that Stilicho would be leading our forces in this campaign. His main reason for staying in Italy was the danger of an attack through the central Alps by some of Constantine's forces. The Alemanns had agreed to allow small numbers of the usurper's army to pass up the upper Rhine into Rhaetia and Noricum. They managed to suborn some of our regiments there with generous cash allocations.

Thus, there was the danger of Constantine's launching a two-pronged attack on Italy: one through the western and one through the northern Alps. In addition, there was still the lingering doubt as to whether we could really accept Alaric as one of our "fellow Romans," his protestations of loyalty notwithstanding. Stilicho wanted to be in Italy when Alaric arrived in Noricum just in case.

Sarus's forces headed west to the Rhone and then north. Constantine's army headed south from Lyon, and they met in the vicinity of Valence. Initially, things went well for our side. One of Constantine's field marshals, Justinianus, was killed early in the fighting. The other field marshal, Nebiogastes, entered into negotiations with Sarus under flags of truce but was promptly murdered by him. Sarus's diplomatic capacity was apparently limited. Constantine promptly appointed two generals, Gerontius and Edobichus, to replace his fallen chieftains, and they eventually defeated Sarus's forces. Leading a disorganized retreat through the Alps, Sarus lost much of his supply train to bandit gangs lurking in the regions he was forced to pass through.

Though Sarus had been defeated, it had been no easy victory for Constantine's army. Our forces had inflicted heavy casualties on the usurper in spite of being outnumbered and had slowed their rate of advance considerably. Once Sarus's army had withdrawn from Gaul, it should have been an easy matter for Constantine to reach the coast about 120 miles to the south. There were no central government forces left in Gaul. Instead, not until the following year did the usurper firmly establish his authority there. I was between Valence and Orange when I heard of Sarus's defeat. I ordered a retreat of my own. We moved quickly south to Arles and then east along the Riviera highway, the Via Julia Augusta. I gave my men orders to set fire to our wagons if Constantine's advance units started to catch up with us. They never appeared. After returning to Ravenna for a few days, I traveled north to Noricum. There I would inspect the construction work being done on our damaged storage depots in order to prepare for Alaric's arrival.

The year was turning into a total disaster. In January, we were planning to annex Eastern Illyria. The year looked promising. Before the summer was over, not only had our eastern ambitions been scuttled but Britain, Gaul, and part of the upper Danube had been lost to the central government. The Vandals and their allies continued to savage north-central Gaul with impunity. The only harmonious note was that the Alemanns that had attacked the upper Rhine seemed to have settled down somewhat. The defeat of Sarus's expedition meant that Stilicho and Alaric would have to lead a joint effort against Constantine during the New Year and attempt to do something against the Vandals. Our plate of crises was definitely overflowing.

On a personal basis, tragedy occurred also. Late in the autumn, Aureliana delivered a baby girl that was stillborn, as our previous child had been. We would have no more. I had fathered nine children across two marriages and now five of them were dead. The death of our fifth child in 405 had been a bad omen for events at the national level in 406. I could only wonder at what terrible tragedies the death of our last child might portend for the following year.

For Stilicho, this year had been the worst of his life both politically and militarily. During our wars of 401, 402, and 405–406, we had never doubted that we would be successful regardless of the difficulty in achieving those victories. But by the end of 407, the confidence of previous years had evaporated and a palpable sense of defeat was in the air. In spite of successfully concluding the recent war with Radagaisus in what was the greatest victory of his military career, Stilicho had been subjected to a great deal of criticism from the Senate and the public. They were angered by the manner in which the invaders had been able to penetrate the Alps and cause so much damage in northern Italy. While Stilicho had many critics and numerous outright enemies, we would learn too late that in the fullest sense he had no rivals. From being at the peak of his power, he suddenly found himself increasingly isolated. It began to appear that the strain of shouldering so many exacting burdens across more than a decade had become too much for him. There were too many problems demanding concurrent resolutions with scarce resources on the basis of inadequate information. His tragic misjudgment on Britain was the most profound indicator to date that he was losing his grip on affairs. No national leader can ever allow rebellion to go unchecked under any circumstances, regardless of how remote the province. And yet he did. The dominos were gradually being set in place.

By the end of August 406, the army was exhausted after nine months of warfare against the invaders. There was no way in which it could have been immediately marched off to Britain. Nonetheless, Stilicho had four months in which to take decisive action of some kind against the revolt, and yet he ignored it. His focus at this time was entirely on Eastern Illyria. His indecisiveness over Britain and his slowness in responding to the barbarian invasion puzzled and angered many. The public perception of Stilicho declined throughout 407 as the news from Gaul continued to worsen. If Sarus had been successful then public opinion would have changed. But Sarus's failure meant that we would have to undertake the whole process against Constantine all over again at the earliest opportunity. In the meantime, after an entire year, nothing had been accomplished against the Vandals and northern Gaul lay shattered.

On Christmas Day 407, a fateful decision was made by Emperor Honorius and his civilian advisers. As Honorius's authority in Britain and Gaul dissolved, the emperor decided to reemphasize his dominion throughout the West in a most bizarre manner: he ordered Stilicho to burn the Sibylline Books. Going along with this was a major political error on Stilicho's part: it needlessly poisoned his relations with the pagan section of the Senate that had been rather good up to that point. The Sibyl of Cumae (near Naples) had compiled nine books of prophecies, six of which she had burned as the result of a dispute with the last of the seven kings of early Rome. The remaining three books had been enshrined in the Temple of Jupiter on the Capitoline Hill in Rome and were to be consulted only in times of crisis. The news of the destruction of this most ancient connection with our historical foundations infuriated the pagan population of Rome. One more vital link to our ancient past had been reduced to ashes and to no purpose other than to secure the place of our mentally retarded emperor and his closest associates in the

Christian afterlife. In every respect, the descendants of Theodosius I have been far more suited to be residents of a monastery or convent than an imperial palace. They have possessed absolutely no political sense at all. Like a pair of monks, Honorius and Arcadius were in the world but not of it. They thought that prayer and pious living alone could make everything right with the universe. To gain greater favor from God, Honorius soon issued laws that allowed only Catholic Christians to hold the top administrative posts in his government. As the real world contracted around him, he sought to live in an ever-more repressively religious one. Like his father before him, Honorius was consumed with fear for his soul. Unlike his father up to the massacre in Thessalonica, he had no sense of having to balance his own intense religious convictions to any degree with political concessions to the real world that he had been born to administer. Forever in fear of having their souls consigned to the damning fires of hell, the ineptitude of the emperor and his advisers would guarantee that thousands of innocent souls in their domains would be consumed by conflagrations of a far more immediate nature.

By year-end, Constantine's forces had entered the Mediterranean plains of Gaul but would not complete their occupation until the spring. He would then move his military headquarters to Arles and continue to maintain the prefectural capital there. This latter act was understandable given the length of time that it would take to rebuild Trier and the continuing instability across northern Gaul. Nonetheless, it would have serious political repercussions in Britain.

We had firm control of all the Alpine passes, but serious questions had arisen as to how loyal our frontier forces would remain unless victory against the usurper was achieved in the New Year. Alaric's people were getting settled in Noricum on the northern frontier, and we had started making preliminary plans for an offensive against the usurper the following spring. To be engaging in what was turning out to be a prolonged civil war while Gaul was being savaged by a barbarian invasion was truly a political obscenity, but we had no choice. It was said that Constantine was in control of Gaul, but in fact that claim was a gross exaggeration. His zone of authority included all the Atlantic coast fortifications, the fortresses of the Rhineland still in Roman hands, and the valleys of the Moselle, the Saone, and the Rhone down to the Mediterranean. It somewhat resembled a huge question mark that was quite appropriate under the circumstances.

The approach of the year-end holiday season was marred when my good friend Stephanus was injured during a cavalry training exercise. He had reached the rank of tribune and had commanded one of the regiments in Honorius's bodyguard for the past three years. The regiment was going through some routine maneuvers when his horse toppled over on top of him and Stephanus broke his right leg in two places. It took longer than usual to set, and he was stricken with a severe limp as a result. Because of this, he retired from the army, took his pension, and soon obtained a job as a supervisor on the docks at nearby Classis. I regretted his forced retirement in that he was my last link to the various Imperial Guard regiments that we had served in over the years. He had always kept me abreast of their various goings-on, and now there was no one to whom I was close in any of them. There had been a complete turnover of officers during the past decade. Fewer and fewer men were left that either of us had known across the years.

My family and I shared a pleasant Christmas in spite of our recent bereavement. Aureliana started pressing me, ever so slightly, to think about retiring from the army and administering our investments full-time. They were returning a solid income. Their returns would never elevate me into the senatorial class (joke), but they would enable us to still live comfortably without my army pay. I was now forty-three years old and had completed over twenty-five years of service. If the empire was at peace, I would have given it more serious consideration. But given the terrible circumstances in which we found ourselves, the government had ordered the army to release no one from its ranks or officer corps until the current crisis was resolved. I did assure her that once that occurred, I would give more serious thought to her request. As we know, the crisis would prove incapable of resolution. In less than a year, our brilliant civilization that had been constructed during a period of over fifty generations would be plunging headlong into an unimaginable disaster. In less than a year, we would be teetering on the edge of an age of darkness.

CHAPTER 14

The Curse of the Vestal Virgin (408)

I am entering on the history of a period rich in disasters, frightful in its wars, torn by civil strife, and even in peace full of horrors ... There were three civil wars; there were more with foreign enemies; there were often wars that had both characters at once. There was success in the East, and disaster in the West ... Gaul wavered in its allegiance; Britain was ... abandoned. Now too Italy was prostrated by disasters either entirely novel, or that recurred only after a long succession of ages; cities in Campania's richest plains were swallowed up and overwhelmed; Rome was wasted by conflagrations, its oldest temples consumed; the sea was crowded with exiles.

—*Tacitus: The Histories, Book I*

OUR GREATEST HISTORIAN WAS referring to the year AD 69, known as the year of the four emperors. And yet now, at a point 339 years later, I can think of no more appropriate introduction to the final two chapters of my history. Tacitus was reflecting on just a single year, and regardless of how profound the events of that year, its outstanding issues were wrapped up in a short period of time. Our current fortunes, however, were about to take a turn for the worse by orders of magnitude that Tacitus could have never imagined. With the exception of Olympius, the master of offices, and his henchmen, there were none of the traditional Roman villains such as Caligula or Nero or Caracalla involved in the tragedies that were about to befall us. The fools who would soon emerge would be detested not only because they were monstrously evil but because they subjected the country to the tyranny of the most monumentally incompetent governance, if it may be called that, that we had ever been forced to suffer.

Immediately after the New Year began, we started planning for the upcoming campaign. Stilicho, newly returned to Ravenna from Rome, seemed reinvigorated by the brief Christmas holiday and we were all inspired by this. Working with emissaries from Alaric's camp and others, we determined the supplies required for both regular and federate troops. Alaric's army estimate held firm at ten thousand men. We stationed three thousand of them permanently in Noricum. They would assist regular and other federate forces already there defending against any enemies attacking Italy while the rest of us were off in Gaul. Alternatively, they could be used to strike westward at Constantine should his army decide to invade Italy through the northern Alps. Alaric's remaining seven thousand men would operate as allies with the Army of Italy and the Alan, Vandal, Hun, and non-Alaric Visigothic federates that were under our control. It was a very substantial body that the usurper would be hard-pressed to emulate. The supplying of this expeditionary force was quite involved because we were preparing for two campaigns in one. After defeating Constantine and reincorporating his forces into our regular army, we would continue on into central Gaul. There we would defeat the Vandals and their allies. Simultaneously, diplomatic efforts would be made to establish peace treaties with the Burgundians and Alemanns. The general feeling was that the Burgundians, whose numbers were the smallest of the invaders, could be dealt with reasonably. The Alemanns would be more difficult. If they were not amenable to diplomacy then they too would have to be defeated.

The Burgundians had effectively taken themselves out of the fight shortly after landing on our side of the Rhine. The Alemanns appeared to be doing the same thing but even if they remained hostile, they were at least isolated from the Vandals and their allies. Allowing for the Alans that had deserted to our side at the very beginning, we felt that of the remaining horde of Vandals, Alans, and Sueves we would be facing an army of about thirty-five thousand men. As the Visigoths had done in Thrace thirty years earlier, the Vandals and their allies had brought their families with them to settle permanently. It was indicative of the vastly changed circumstances north of the Danube wrought by the Huns, who were hated and feared by everyone. There would be no going back.

Most of our arms factories have facilities for manufacturing different types of armaments. Some specialize in certain types of weapons as opposed to others. There are, or at the time were, a total of twenty government arsenals in the Western Empire. Nine were located in Gaul to supply our soldiers on the Rhine and the Gallic forts along the Saxon Shore. Against the six factories in Italy, the usurper would normally have held an advantage over us in weapons manufacture. The barbarian invasion had changed all that. The arsenal at Trier was one of the two most important shield-manufacturing centers in Gaul. In addition, it had the largest crossbow production facilities in the West. It had all gone up in smoke. Nor was that the only arsenal that the barbarians had destroyed after looting it. Constantine had also lost his main sword factory at Reims when it was heavily damaged during the sack (and re-sack) of that town. Subsequently, the multipurpose arsenal at Amiens had been destroyed. One advantage that Constantine had over the central government was that Autun is the only factory that manufactures the special heavy body armor that the cavalry uses.

Italy had been fortunate during the war with Radagaisus in that none of its cities containing arsenals had fallen to the invaders. Our new shields would be provided mainly by Lorch and Carnuntum on the Danube, along with Cremona in Italy. The devastating fire of 392 had destroyed the civilian sector of Carnuntum but the arms factory there was still in operation in 408. The arsenal at Concordia, just west of Aquileia, provided the largest percentage of our arrows, while most of our breastplates came from Mantua, our bows from Pavia, and our swords from Lucca, just to the northeast of Pisa. The logistics were the most difficult of any campaign in which I had participated; almost from the beginning things went wrong.

Early in the New Year, Empress Maria died. Sad and unexpected as her death was, at a very young age, what made its aftermath sadder yet was that Stilicho had Honorius marry her younger sister, Thermantia, shortly afterward. When I arrived home on the day that the new betrothal was announced, my wife was incensed. Her cousin Claudia had heard about it earlier in the day while shopping in a local market and had come over to tell Aureliana right away.

"Marcus, what can Stilicho be thinking about?" my wife asked. "It is common knowledge that Honorius and Maria never consummated their marriage. For Stilicho to marry his second daughter to our imperial slug is incomprehensible. What miracle can Thermantia bring about that Maria was unable to generate across a decade? Everyone will see this as an act of just how desperate Stilicho and Serena are to establish legitimate descendants of their own on the throne."

I guided her over to our large couch in the living room where we snuggled up for a brief lesson in coldblooded politics of the gentler sort.

"Anyone having even a mere passing acquaintance with Honorius," I began, "knows that no genitalian fantasy of any kind has ever crossed whatever the emperor has that passes for a mind. The public will make the judgment that you just described and the public will be wrong. Marrying Maria and now Thermantia to Honorius has nothing to do with a desire to see descendants on the throne. It has everything to do with control. Stilicho has known for as long as anyone that Honorius is impotent and mentally retarded. The last thing that Stilicho or Serena want is grandchildren by Honorius because they would probably be as mentally damaged as he is. Think of Rufinus and Eutropius. They contested one another to provide a wife for Arcadius. Imperial descendants were certainly on Rufinus' agenda, though, for obvious reasons, not that of Eutropius. Their central contest was for control of Arcadius through the wife that only one could provide. The public is correct, however, to believe that Stilicho and Serena want a grandson to reign someday on the western throne. But that grandson, if he ever arrives, will be the son of Eucherius and Galla Placidia."

As it turned out, Stilicho would achieve neither, and marrying Honorius would be the least tragic aspect of Empress Thermantia's brief reign.

When our planning sessions started at the beginning of the year, we were astonished when Stilicho announced that Honorius had expressed an interest in being present at some of our meetings. The rest of us stared at one another in disbelief. We could only hope that our less-than-nimble-minded chief of state not embarrass us or himself too much. It was a requirement he seldom met. Honorius, on the few occasions that he did attend, would slouch in half-asleep, looking like he had dressed himself in the dark. He would sit at the head of the table, like a piece of furniture, watching the world pass him by. He never said anything and never made it through any of our sessions without dozing off. When the meeting was over, Stilicho would gently nudge him awake and lead him out of the room. We would all stand, salute him as he left with a "Hail, Augustus," and then burst out laughing the moment the door had closed. Once while snoring his way through one of my presentations, the little runt farted so loudly that he woke himself up. His bloodshot eyes spent several awkward moments looking up and down both sides of the table trying to determine what had happened.

Sarus quipped afterward, "Well, we certainly know what His Majesty thought of your presentation, don't we? Come to think of it, that is probably the only utterance that any of us will ever be able to quote verbatim from him."

Once it had been announced that Stilicho had selected Alaric as his deputy for the campaign, criticisms arose. From the Senate came the complaint that Stilicho was employing a proven barbarian enemy of Rome to go against a usurper who was at least a Roman and whose main reason for rebellion was Stilicho's own inattention to our northwest frontier. Stilicho countered that gripe by asking the Senate if its members would prefer that he left Alaric unattended on Italy's northeast frontier while he went off to combat Constantine on his own. Silence. More importantly, opposition to this arrangement also arose from within our own ranks: Sarus and Ulfilas as well as other Visigoths did not want to serve under Alaric in any capacity. These men had abandoned Alaric at Verona and proved their loyalty to the empire on numerous occasions, especially during the war of 405–406, while Alaric, in the fullest sense, never had. Another frequently heard senatorial comment, coming now even from men who had staunchly supported Stilicho ever since the death of Theodosius I, was that Constantine had at least done something, however half-heartedly, to combat the Vandals. The longer it took Stilicho to come to grips with the barbarians, the more the odious rumor was spread that the main reason for his failure to do so was that they were Vandals, he was half-Vandal and so on. This claim had circulated frequently across the years in spite of Stilicho's being unable even to speak their language. The notion that Stilicho was linked in some sort of preposterous conspiracy with these invaders to place his only son, Eucherius, on the throne was soon making the rounds. This particular slander had its source at the top of the civilian power structure in the form of Olympius, the master of the secretariat, who came originally from a province bordering the Black Sea.

Shortly before Honorius and Thermantia were married, Alaric placed a demand on Rome that sounded outrageous to the uninformed. It was not as unreasonable as many historians have made it out to be. However, the timing of the arrival of Alaric's ambassadors in Ravenna was politically unfortunate from Stilicho's standpoint because it added to the suspicions that were undeservedly pointing in his direction from mounting sources. Stilicho was unhappy with the demand payment but he determined that it would be in everyone's best interest if it was acceded to. Leaving the Visigothic emissaries in Ravenna, Stilicho took Alaric's "request" with him to present it to the Senate. What Alaric demanded was four thousand pounds of gold to pay his men for the three years of "service" that they had provided in Epirus waiting for orders to attack Eastern Illyria that never came. On top of that were their recent traveling expenses from Epirus to Noricum. The Senate went into convulsions when it heard the details. The extent to which certain of its more exercised members almost stroked over the issue was a reflection of how removed from reality their world was from that which was starting to close in on them from the frontiers. Individuals comprising the richest stratum of the Senate, with estates on two (and sometimes three) continents, could each make that much money in a single year. The late Symmachus spent two thousand pounds of gold on celebratory games in honor of the Senate's appointing his son to the office of praetor just a few years earlier. Alaric's demand was to support his following of seventy-two thousand that included an army of almost ten thousand men over a period of three years. For what the Visigoths were going to do on our behalf in Gaul, it would have been cheap at twice the price. After the imperial wedding, Stilicho had a difficult time persuading the senatorial tightwads to come up with the money. Negotiations dragged on for several days. Finally, after reminding them that the longer they debated the issue, the closer the Vandals were approaching their estates in Gaul (if they had not been already torched), the Senate gave in and agreed to pay up. While this was going on, we continued planning the campaign that had originally been scheduled to begin either in late June or early July.

Shortly after their wedding, the imperial couple prepared to leave Rome. They were going north to review the Army of Italy prior to its marching west to reclaim Gaul. At this time, the news arrived that the usurper had moved his headquarters from Trier to Arles. Spain was now cut off from Italy. With only a small military establishment of their own, the Spanish provinces would have little choice but to recognize Constantine. With his realm continuing to shrink and Italy and Africa obviously next on the usurper's list, Honorius was starting to panic. To make matters worse, news arrived in Rome shortly after the emperor left that his brother, Emperor Arcadius, had died suddenly on May 1 in Constantinople. He had been succeeded by his only son, Theodosius II, who was only seven years of age. Official confirmation of Arcadius' death was received in Ravenna and Rome on May 15. It was quickly conveyed to Honorius, who was accompanied on the journey by his master of the secretariat, Olympius. Stilicho had returned to Ravenna.

The character of Olympius can only be painted as monochromatically black. Originally a supporter of Stilicho, Olympius had sensed the strong shift in the mood of the Senate, the equestrian order, and the public toward the field marshal since the Vandal invasion. Senators possessing estates in Gaul had seen these properties either destroyed or at the very least placed in grave danger. The equestrians, involved in every aspect of commercial activity with the East, had seen their security shrink considerably. There was no relief in sight with respect to the trade embargo. Both social orders had been impressed with the manner in which the East had managed to keep the barbarians in its employ in check (or in some cases in the ground) in recent years.

Alaric's devastation of Greece in 395–396 and the turmoil generated by Gainas' troops during their residency in Constantinople had caused the government there to radically alter its policy of enrolling Germans into the Roman Army. As federates, they had proven themselves thoroughly treacherous (at least in the case of Alaric). In the regular army, the revolt of Tribigild and the unruliness of Gainas' troops had led to outright civil war. There was no massive discharge of Germans from the Eastern Army during and after 401, as some historians have claimed. There was, however, a major change in the recruiting policies of the eastern government from that point on. Constantinople determined to become less dependent on German recruits than it had been previously. It started an internal recruiting drive among the difficult people of Isauria in south-central Anatolia. The chief product this region has been famous for is its bandit gangs, and the people there have been barely governable at best from time immemorial. The government decided to put their lack of civility to good use in the army. To the extent that foreign mercenaries were still required, it started enrolling greater numbers of Armenians and Iranians. While some Germans did remain in top command positions, their numbers started to decline, as did their percentage in the ranks. Historians have pointed out that the Eastern Empire generally sought to solve its problems through diplomatic rather than military means. Reasonable as this sounds, it must be recognized that once Alaric's Visigoths left Illyria and headed west, the Eastern Empire was free of massive barbarian hordes trying to occupy its territory for several decades. However, from the same point of departure, the West would never enjoy that luxury again.

Seeing how Constantinople had started to reduce its dependence on Germans, certain cabinet ministers in the government of Honorius, in alliance with certain members of the Senate, started thinking along the same lines. They concluded, with catastrophic consequences, that what had been accomplished in the East could be duplicated in the West. The extent to which the daydreams of these men, led by Olympius, glibly ignored factors of paramount importance and became reality is reflected in the deplorable state of affairs that we see in the West today. The severity of the dangers we faced were poorly understood by the best intellectual minds in Italy; by Olympius and his associates, not at all. The term "Olympian self-confidence" soon took on a whole new meaning.

The East has certain advantages over the West that Olympius and his clique of overeducated ignoramuses never took into account:

+ From 401 on, the Western Empire had been at a serious strategic disadvantage with respect to the Germans. Italy had been under continual attack from across the Danube and Alaric and now Gaul was being inundated by the Vandals and others. The Eastern Empire was under no such threat after 401 because the Huns kept a very heavy-handed control over their subject Germanic peoples north of the lower Danube. The Persian Empire of Iran also kept the peace along the eastern frontier. During the terrible third century when the empire was last stricken with massive invasions, the East Germans struck the eastern half of the empire while the West Germans attacked our western provinces. Now large segments of both East and West German populations were savaging our western territories.

+ The East was subject to occasional attacks by the Huns, but, terrible as these could be, they were strictly raids. The Huns were not seeking to settle permanently within the empire at this time. Such was not the case in the West. First the Visigoths and now the Vandals and their allies were in the process of obtaining permanent domiciles of some sort on imperial territory be they stationary or mobile in character.

+ In Europe, the Western Empire has a frontier along the Danube and Rhine combined that is over twice as long as that of the Eastern Empire along the lower Danube. In addition, the Western Empire had to defend the lengthy coastline of the island of Britain that is as long as its Rhine and Danube frontiers combined. The military requirements of the West are much greater than those of the East and the notion of the Western Empire being able to get along without German army recruits was preposterous. Astoundingly, Olympius and his xenophobic cohorts gave no thought whatever to where replacements could be found, even if it were possible to expel the Germans from the Western Army.

+ Unlike the East, the West had no alternative source of foreign mercenaries except the Germans. Unlike the East, the West had long been tapping its largest source of domestic manpower for the army: the Gauls.

The list could go on, but the point is clear. The West could not defend itself without German volunteers as the East appeared to be slowly growing capable of doing. Olympius also never gave any thought to another vital question: if the Germans could be expelled from the Western Army, where would they go? He would certainly discover the answer to that one the hard way. Olympius considered himself as God's very own gift to the Roman people. He and his coconspirators were consumed by an almost pathological rage against all things German in the Roman military and political systems. He had a dream of "re-Romanizing" the Western Roman Army but no plan to accomplish it because by this time it was impossible. By midsummer of 408, the irrational expectations of Olympius and his supporters would hurl us into an apocalypse, though not the one that the book of Revelation has in mind.

During their journey north, it appears that Olympius started to poison the mind of the impressionable Honorius against his father-in-law whenever Thermantia was not present. Slowly at first and then with growing intensity over the weeks ahead, the master of the secretariat continually baited his conversations with the emperor with lies concerning Stilicho's ambitions for his son Eucherius. He virtually swore the emperor to secrecy on these matters by "confiding" to him that Stilicho's "conspiracy" was quite widespread and that the emperor's life would be in danger if he were to discuss these matters with the wrong man. Olympius would be Honorius's sole conduit on the "conspiracy." He concocted the story that Stilicho had been plotting to replace the emperor with Eucherius, who was a few years younger than Honorius. Olympius, the master manipulator, had already been confiding this slander to several top Roman officers in Honorius's bodyguard with an anti-German orientation like himself.

The emperor had arrived in Bologna when he received official confirmation of the death of his brother. He proposed to go to Constantinople with certain advisers to set up a regency for his nephew. This was a reflection of how isolated Honorius and certain of his civilian counselors were from the political realities of the eastern capital. The Eastern Empire had had its fill of western overlords during the reign of his father and was determined to rule itself after he died, come what may. Both Stilicho and Olympius, in separate audiences, argued against this but for different reasons. Stilicho argued quite correctly that Honorius's being present in the eastern capital might be just the invitation that the usurper would require to invade Italy, thus upsetting Stilicho's plans to strike first. The generalissimo also raised essentially the same arguments that he had presented seven years earlier when Honorius wanted to flee westward over the Alps to Arles to get away from Alaric. However unintentional, the emperor's trip to the eastern capital would appear like he was attempting to flee from yet another dangerous situation. Olympius, on the other hand, argued that if the emperor left for Constantinople, then Stilicho would proclaim his son Eucherius as emperor of the West. Stilicho's own arguments for the emperor to remain in Italy undermined the lies that Olympius was spewing, but Honorius, instead of seeing through his chief minister's treachery, was simply confused. These arguments went back and forth through the late spring and early summer of 408. I still find it incredible that Stilicho apparently had no idea of the machinations that Olympius was concocting against him.

The decision to pay Alaric his four thousand pounds of gold resulted in a delay to our plans to secure Gaul. As chief quartermaster of the Army of Italy, Stilicho commissioned me to transport the payment from Rome to Virunum, where Alaric had established his headquarters. This city is in the Julian Alps just north of the Loibl Pass. Stilicho also had other new responsibilities for me.

"In my direct correspondence with Alaric," he told me, "and through comments from his officers here in Ravenna, he has expressed complete confidence in you both as a quartermaster and as a liaison officer. You have done just about everything that you can from a supply standpoint, so I want you to hand over your duties in that area to your chief deputy. I am going to need you for all liaison activity that I conduct with Alaric from now on."

We moved as quickly as we could on the transfer, but given the lengthy distance to be covered and the large security force that had to be arranged for protection, our plans to attack Constantine were pushed out into the late summer. As our incredibly rich wagon train moved north from Rome, we were joined by Alaric's liaison officers who had left Ravenna once all planning was complete. As befit a payment of this magnitude (or "ransom," as detractors in the Senate called it), Alaric gave us a truly royal welcome when we arrived. When the transfer was completed, I dispatched my men and our large security detail back to Ravenna. I remained with Alaric for a further three days in order to review with him and his top officers the detailed plans that we had drawn up for the invasion of Gaul. Alaric was actually quite knowledgeable on the details, as his liaison officers in Ravenna had kept him informed of the progress made as time went along. A few minor questions arose that I could not answer but I promised to get a response back to him as soon as I returned to Ravenna. I was impressed with how eager Alaric and his staff were for the campaign to open at the earliest opportunity and I left his camp in high spirits.

While my men and I were transporting Alaric's gold, the political situation in Italy became more chaotic. The emperor had summoned Stilicho from Ravenna to Bologna just after our invasion plans had been finalized. Honorius restated that he wanted to go to Constantinople to establish a regency. As it turned out one was already in the process of being created under the nominal leadership of Princess Pulcheria, the oldest sister of Theodosius II. (The former was only nine years old but she was a precocious little brat.) Their dull-witted uncle in Ravenna, however, was obstinate and insisted that *he* do it. There were numerous arguments over the matter. Finally, in the worst decision of his career, Stilicho suggested that he, himself, go to Constantinople with certain of Honorius's key advisers and four legions to establish the regency for Theodosius II as Honorius wished. After all, the emperor of the West was now the senior emperor, to the extent that term still meant anything. Stilicho apparently saw an opportunity to reactivate his long-standing ambition to be the single regent for the two reigning emperors, East and West. This aspiration had been abandoned for all practical purposes by 402 due to military conditions in the West (especially in Britain and the Danube region) and the development of political conditions in the East during the past thirteen years that were far beyond his control. Stilicho, in a corollary decision that was just as dreadful as the first, appointed Alaric as the new supreme commander of the western expeditionary force. This truly shocked everyone. When Olympius heard this, he immediately changed his conspiracy theory: he now told Honorius that Stilicho was going to depose young Theodosius and place Eucherius on the eastern instead of the western throne. Honorius was more confused than ever. Small wonder.

By his subsequent actions, Honorius showed greater trust in Stilicho than Olympius. The warnings of the latter notwithstanding, Honorius signed the papers that Stilicho's secretaries drew up for him, giving Stilicho authority to establish a regency for Theodosius II in Honorius's name. Honorius also granted Alaric supreme command, until Stilicho's return, of the campaign against the usurper in Gaul. Alaric was given the permanent rank of field marshal. Stilicho emphasized that this rank was not of the temporary variety that would expire once the campaign had been completed. Having already spent an inordinate amount of time at Bologna, the emperor then left for Ravenna before continuing on to Pavia as he had originally intended. Stilicho, however, remained at Bologna awaiting the arrival of his four legions for his mission to the East. Honorius's final decision forced Olympius' hand.

When I returned to Ravenna, I was astounded to learn of the new developments. I rode immediately to Bologna and reported to Stilicho. He congratulated me on the completion of the mission, but when I questioned him on the recent command change, he grew quite defensive.

"I was staggered," I started off, "to learn in Ravenna that you are going to Constantinople while Alaric is taking over as supreme commander of our expeditionary force. You are vitally needed in Gaul for what is unquestionably the most important campaign in your life, not off in the East."

"The emperor has ordered me to go, and I must obey," was Stilicho's less than inspired response. "The only alternative was for him to go to Constantinople himself, and we all know what a bad example that would set."

"But back in 401–402, the Army of Italy was north of the Alps, and Alaric was the enemy," I countered. "The circumstances are quite different this time. We have a total of over thirty thousand soldiers about to march off and combat the usurper. I think the Senate and the public would be quite understanding about the emperor's absenting himself to go to the eastern capital under current conditions. Why not reconsider and let Honorius go east while you remain as supreme commander of the expedition?"

"I've had all these discussions with the emperor, his cabinet, legionary commanders, and others while you were away," Stilicho replied. "The decision is final."

"My lord, you must allow me to speak plainly. Appointing Alaric as the new captain-general will certainly not sit well with either the Roman officers such as Vincentius, our marshal of cavalry, or those Visigoths like Sarus and Ulfilas, who deserted Alaric to come over to our side in the first place, or for that matter—"

"I realize all that," he cut me off, "but the decision is final. Besides, Vincentius has been in questionable health lately and is in full agreement with Alaric's appointment."

"Twice you have taken an expeditionary force into Greece," I continued, "and twice you have returned to the West upon being ordered to do so by your adversaries in Constantinople via a document signed by the eastern emperor. What makes you think that things will be any different this time? You are not required there, while you are desperately needed here. If they order you to return for a third time then you will, after accomplishing nothing. We don't really know what Alaric's capabilities are as a 'Roman' commander. Sarus didn't fare too well last year on the first major command that he was given, and besides—"

"Sarus didn't have anywhere near the number of troops that Alaric will have," Stilicho said, cutting me off again, his voice rising. "Besides, as I said, the decision is *final!*"

He then handed me a document with the imperial seal on it.

"I want you to leave immediately for Virunum," he ordered, "to deliver this new commission to Alaric, designating him supreme commander and promoting him to field marshal. I want you to leave immediately."

Julianus and Andreas, who were to accompany me, were waiting in Ravenna. With all further argument of no value, I left. I never saw him again.

Ravenna lies almost due east of Bologna but is difficult to access from there since no major highway directly connects the two. I could only spend one night at home. At sunup the following morning, I had to bid Aureliana and the children goodbye once again for the trip back north. Before leaving, I looked at myself in our full-length mirror. The sun was just starting to break across the horizon, and its light gave a strange reddish-orange color that reflected off the mirror. It suddenly came back to me. I was looking at the bearded apparition whom I had seen in my strange dream twenty-seven years earlier during my first night alone on the road when I left home. I shuddered and felt suddenly cold at the realization but had no idea of how to interpret it. However, I knew that it was a terrifying omen.

We expected to be able to return to Ravenna briefly before having to report to Pavia, south of Milan, for the invasion of Gaul. It was at Pavia that the Army of Italy was headquartered. My comrades were as bitter as I was over the command change. Even if Stilicho was going east as the result of an imperial directive, it would certainly appear that his previous obsession with Eastern Illyria had reoccupied front and center stage once again. The timing could not have been worse. In Virunum, Alaric was astounded and elated to discover that Stilicho had appointed him as captain-general of the campaign and promoted him. We returned back through the Loibl Pass to Aquileia and stayed there overnight.

Earlier when we had passed through the city, there had been heavy military traffic to the west. Now there was none. That would soon change when Alaric's forces came marching down from the north. For the moment, however, it was almost eerily quiet like the lull that precedes the hell of battle. It would be hell all right but one the likes of which none of us could possibly have foreseen. We had just left Aquileia the following morning when two dispatch riders approached us from the west at top speed. Sensing something was wrong, we blocked the road three abreast to stop them but they tried to ride around us. As prearranged, I went after the one on the left while my two comrades went after the other one. My man's horse stumbled when his rider veered him sharply off to the south of the road. My two comrades had quickly knocked their man off his horse and tied him up. As my man hit the ground, he had tried to get up and draw his sword at the same time, but I had already dismounted and had my sword at his throat. I took his sword and marched him across the highway to where my friends were holding the other rider.

"My apologies for the inconvenience," I said, smiling, "but your haste made us suspicious. Where are you going?"

They looked at one another but said nothing.

"This can be easy or it can be difficult," Andreas suggested.

"We're from the Army of Italy heading west to join it," I said. "Seeing you coming at such a high rate of speed and recognizing you as couriers, we just wanted to ask you if anything was wrong."

"I think you could say that," the man that I had captured replied slowly.

Since Andreas, Julianus, and I still had our swords drawn, he went on to tell us of events that had taken place in Pavia three days earlier. We stood there listening to the details of an unfolding nightmare, barely able to believe our senses. After he was finished, I removed the documents they were carrying from their saddlebags. They were addressed to the provincial governor of Venetia and Istria and the garrison commander of Aquileia. The couriers were aghast when I broke the imperial seals on them. The penalty for doing so was death they reminded me. They didn't have to. Given what we had just heard, I might already be on someone's death list. The documents were almost identical. We then drove their horses off in opposite directions.

"My apology again, chaps," I said, "for the bother that we've caused you, but it couldn't be helped. You have your responsibilities while my comrades and I have ours. Start walking back toward Concordia."

Since I was the highest ranking of the three, I might be the only one that was in any real danger. Andreas and Julianus were not willing to take that chance. We raced back through Aquileia and then north toward Virunum. We ran into Alaric's forces as they were entering the Loibl Pass.

"I didn't expect to see you again until Pavia," Alaric said as we exchanged salutes. "Is anything wrong?"

"Everything is wrong," I replied. "We interrupted a pair of dispatch riders just to the west of Aquileia. They informed us, and these documents provide the details, that the entire top echelon of Stilicho's supporters among the government of Honorius was massacred on August 13. It happened while they were attending an address that Honorius was giving to the Army of Italy as it was about to leave for the frontier."

"What, uh, what about Stilicho and Honorius?" Alaric asked, obviously staggered by this revelation.

"Honorius is alive," I replied. "Stilicho and his supporters, not the emperor, appear to be the main targets of this revolt. We were told that as the emperor was in the middle of his speech, Olympius, master of the secretariat, gave a signal to a group of soldiers in Honorius's bodyguard to start the slaughter of all Stilichoians, civilian and military. The rampaging soldiers eventually so lost control that they started killing innocent civilians and stealing anything that they could carry off. As near as I can make out, only a small minority of the regular Roman Army units have been involved in the conspiracy."

"That's all it requires," Alaric replied.

I then read off the names of the victims from the documents I had seized from the couriers:

+ Chariobaudes, marshal of Gaul
+ Vincentius, marshal of Cavalry (second in command to Stilicho)
+ Limenius, praetorian prefect of the Gauls
+ Longinianus, praetorian prefect of the Italies
+ Salvius, count of domestics
+ Naemorius, master of offices
+ Patroinus, minister of finance
+ Ursicinus, minister for the imperial estates

I then handed the list to Alaric.

"As for Stilicho," I continued, "the couriers could tell us nothing except that he was not among those murdered at Pavia. When we left to come here, he was still in Bologna."

We sat there in silence for a few moments.

Shaking his head, Alaric asked, "What prompted such an act of madness?"

"According to the couriers, Olympius told certain anti-German Roman soldiers in Honorius's bodyguard that Stilicho was planning to overthrow young Theodosius in Constantinople and to place his own son Eucherius on the eastern throne. Given that, we can safely assume that Olympius and his fellow conspirators have already started moving against Stilicho in some manner. Only full-blooded Romans appear to have been involved in the massacre."

"This list is incredible," Alaric said. "Among the top government officials, who can Stilicho have left to support him?"

"The only ones I can think of are his brother-in-law, Bathanarius, the count of Africa," Andreas replied, "along with Jovius."

"Who has been named to succeed Stilicho?" Alaric asked.

"According to the couriers," Julianus replied, "no one, yet."

"You fellows are welcome to remain with us if you'd like," Alaric said.

We thanked Alaric and readily accepted his hospitality. Later we learned that a number of lower-echelon supporters of Stilicho had also perished at Pavia on that terrible day. Perplexed at what to do for the moment, Alaric turned his forces around and marched them back to Virunum to await events. My comrades and I decided to stay with the Visigoths until the political situation in Italy clarified. To be on the safe side, I had one of the Visigothic barbers give me a shave. When he was finished, I could hardly recognize myself. I had been wearing that beard for over twenty years to cover the facial scar that I had received in Illyria. The scar had almost completely vanished by now. If I could hardly recognize myself, then the odds were that no one else would either. Perfect.

Stilicho had some of his legionary commanders with him at Bologna when he received word of the catastrophe at Pavia. Their legions, however, had not yet arrived. Initially, all was confusion everywhere. Stilicho tried to determine whether Honorius was still alive or whether he had also been a victim of the plot. If Honorius had been slain, then the possibility existed that Constantine may have been behind the whole affair or that a second usurper may have been proclaimed. In that case, in which political direction had the Army of Italy gone or had it split? If Honorius had been slain, then loyal army elements might proclaim Eucherius emperor in his place since he was next in line to the throne. About the same time we had learned of the revolt in Pavia, Stilicho received word that Honorius was alive. He was puzzled as to what the emperor's attitude was toward him and moved his own headquarters back to Ravenna.

I suggested to Alaric that my comrades and I return to Aquileia in civilian dress and try to shed some light on just what was happening. Surprisingly, the seaport revealed nothing new. We rode on down the coast and then turned into Padua. It was obvious that something had happened, as a large crowd had gathered in the forum. I stopped a man and asked him what all the excitement was about.

"Stilicho is dead," he replied. "He was executed two days ago."

"Good God!" Julianus gasped. "Where?"

"Ravenna."

"We just arrived in town," I said. "What else has happened?"

"What do I know?" the man replied. "I'm just a shoemaker."

We pushed on to read the official proclamation for ourselves. It was brief and brutal. We then fanned out individually through the huge throng to try to discover what else there was to know. I spoke to several soldiers of the Padua garrison as well as numerous civilians and the news only grew worse. Padua is midway between Aquileia and Ravenna, and the temptation to return there to see our families was very strong. At the same time, we wouldn't be much use to them dead. After meeting up again, we left immediately for Virunum and reported to Alaric.

"No, no, *no!*" Alaric yelled when I told him that Stilicho had been executed. "Has the whole goddamned world gone insane?"

"The Italian portion of it certainly has," Andreas agreed.

"There is more," I said after an awkward silence.

"There always is," Alaric replied angrily.

"The emperor is now under the domination of this xenophobic megalomaniac, Olympius. This master of the secretariat has issued orders to all garrison commanders in Italy to carry out a mass slaughter of the families of all federate troops resident in their cities and towns."

"*What?*" Alaric and practically everyone else in his company gasped.

"Almost half the thirty thousand soldiers stationed in Italy are federates," I continued. "I should know since I've just spent the whole year to this point establishing provisions for them. Italy is facing a holocaust of innocent people, perhaps civil war within its own army, and an invasion by Constantine's army."

We all just sat around and started drinking. There was nothing else to do. After Stilicho had returned to Ravenna, a peculiar event occurred that is difficult to understand. The only units in his vicinity were several cavalry regiments, including one under the command of Sarus. Sarus and his men attacked and slaughtered members of Stilicho's Hunnish bodyguard but could not find the generalissimo himself. I firmly believe that it was prompted by blind revenge over Alaric's being given command of the upcoming operation against the usurper. As I've already said, both Sarus and Ulfilas had sworn never to serve with Alaric in any capacity.

Would Sarus have killed Stilicho if he had found him? He may have if he thought it would ingratiate him with Rome's new masters. That part of the assault is a mystery to which we will never know the answer.

On the night of August 22, the garrison commander of Ravenna received orders from Pavia signed by Honorius, but written by Olympius, ordering the arrest of Stilicho. Stilicho heard of this first and took refuge in a church. At dawn the following day, a century of troops under the command of Count Heraclian went to the church. Heraclian met with Stilicho and the bishop, showing him the document sent to the garrison commander, signed by Honorius, ordering his arrest. Heraclian pointed out the obvious, namely that nowhere in the document was there an order for the execution of the field marshal. Stilicho was simply to be taken into custody. As an additional show of good faith, Heraclian then marched his soldiers into the church and had them all swear an oath before the bishop that they were not there to take Stilicho's life. I am certain that Stilicho never believed this charade for a moment. But he would obey the order for one very simple reason: the emperor's signature was on the document, and Stilicho had never once disobeyed an imperial directive. Immediately after Stilicho exited the church, Count Heraclian halted his troops. He produced a second document also signed by Honorius but written, like the first, by Olympius. It ordered the summary execution of Stilicho. By this time, some of the members of Stilicho's bodyguard, who had not been with the group of men attacked by Sarus, had caught wind of what was happening. They immediately rushed to the church and offered to defend their leader, but he waved them off.

The public was puzzled why Stilicho acted the way he did at the end. Was he simply determined to spare the empire yet another civil war on top of the mounting crises that were already besetting it, even at the cost of his own life? Was it his sense of duty to the orders of the imperial family even when he was certain those orders were fabricated? He knew that Rufinus and Eutropius were behind the directives signed by Arcadius in 395 and 397, but he obeyed them. So too would he obey this final order. To do otherwise would have made a lie of his entire life.

Stilicho had never thought much of Heraclian. He came from a well-to-do family, was extremely good-looking, and had always been considered as a young man of great promise. He had been a reasonably good student and a rather capable practitioner but had spent most of his adult life ultimately falling short of expectations. He had acquired a wide variety of experience but had never developed what many thought his capacities to be either as an army officer or as a civilian administrator. Those early hopes were never really satisfied, though now, for a brief period in his life, he thought they might be. His glory would be of the basest and most transient variety. Heraclian always confused greed with fulfillment. He was an opportunist who was quite content to spend his life living for the compulsion of the moment. He was an also-ran who would achieve his highest office for the worst of reasons. If that involved bringing down better men than he was then so be it. Whichever way the current was carrying was the wave of the future as far as Heraclian was concerned. Like too many men in positions of great power in our history, Heraclian would settle for being cunning without ever acquiring wisdom. As long as his responsibilities had been much subordinated to his superiors, his inadequacies were not obvious. In the army, as a lower-echelon officer where his scope for initiative was limited, he was quite popular. But whenever he was given a position of any genuine authority, he foundered. He was never more tragically out of his element than on the morning of August 23, 408. Stilicho approached Heraclian and quoted the ancient epitaph, "As you are now, so once was I; as I am now, so shall you be." He then knelt before Heraclian and was beheaded. Eucherius, who had been living with his father, fled Ravenna shortly after Stilicho's arrest and made it to Rome, where his mother had recently been residing.

Stilicho had been as devoted to the empire as any statesman in our history. He had worked as prodigiously as anyone to preserve it: driving the Picts and Saxons from Britain, suppressing the revolt in Africa, securing the upper Danube, delivering Italy from Alaric and Radagaisus. He was the universal fireman. He worked against overwhelming odds, and the most invidious aspect to his demise was that he was crushed not by his formal enemies but by those who should have been his strongest supporters. In his last year, I saw him age prematurely as his self-doubt and recent failures closed in on him. At the end, the empire witnessed the most powerful man in the land strip himself of all armor and sacrifice his own life rather than plunge the state into yet another civil conflict. He was a man possessed of the most fascinating contradictions: a deeply religious man and yet one who never hesitated to kill an opponent when he thought it necessary. The most tragic aspect to his career was that, while he had devoted his entire life to the preservation and unity of the empire, he had witnessed its division and, in the West, the dawn of its shattering. He could be a statesman with few peers or an assassin without hesitation. At heart, he was an idealist who was never really driven by personal ambition. For the deeply determined Stilicho, the empire came before all. Often willing to compromise if it benefitted the common good, defeat was unacceptable under any circumstances. He respected his adversaries. Not because of any misdirected feelings of sympathy but because he admired in them the qualities that we so admired in him. Now he was gone. As subsequent events unfolded, I would sometimes wonder if Stilicho had really chosen death over the ultimate disappointment.

Stilicho's greatest failing, in the eyes of his enemies, was his greatest virtue: he was a conciliator. Bishop Ambrose had been Stilicho's strongest supporter among the church hierarchy, but by the time the end came, Ambrose had been dead for a decade. During that period, the church leadership came to dislike Stilicho for his pacific policies toward the pagans that it saw as betrayal of his own Christianity as well as the legal statutes suppressing paganism. At the same time, the pagans would always despise Stilicho because of the promulgation of those laws in the first place and the termination of the liberal policies of Eugenius at the Frigidus, not to mention his burning of the Sibylline books. The church obtained its revenge shortly after Stilicho's execution: all endowments to the pagan religions were cancelled; images of all pagan gods were ordered to be pulled down throughout the Western Empire; all pagan temples were ordered confiscated or destroyed; all pagan games and festivals were prohibited. In November 408, all pagan soldiers were ordered banished from the army. Neither government nor church cared that this supremely stupid act would deprive the Western Empire of some of its finest soldiers among the shrunken number that it still had under its command at the very moment when it had never had a greater need for them. The church enforced the above laws that many provincial governors had been wisely ignoring for years without any prompting from Stilicho. Nothing so impressed me about the depths of surrealism into which political thinking in Italy had descended as the fact that Stilicho's death was initially of no great interest to the populace at large. His execution should have shaken the peninsula as if some force of nature had vanished. But it didn't. Some actually cheered his passing. In short order, however, they would be rudely awakened from their illusions.

Olympius immediately promoted a general named Varanes to Stilicho's position of marshal of infantry, the top military office in the Western Empire. Varanes was of Iranian descent, and to receive that position so quickly, he was obviously one of the conspirators. He and Stilicho had known one another for a long time. They had worked well together in the past, but in recent years Varanes had become discontented with what he felt was the excessive favoritism that Stilicho had shown to barbarian generals such as Saul, Sarus, and now Alaric. He saw assignments that he thought should have come his way going to younger barbarian generals with less experience. His alliance with Olympius was a natural combination of the military with the political. Varanes' subsequent lack of effort completely substantiated Stilicho's lack of faith in him. The other top military positions went to Turpilio as marshal of cavalry and Vigilantius as count of domestics. These men were second or third raters at best and soon found themselves hopelessly out of their depth. They inspired no confidence whatever in the troops under their command but it soon didn't matter. Within several weeks, they had relatively few soldiers left to command.

It is difficult to know how many innocent members of the families of federate soldiers were slaughtered on the orders of Olympius. I believe the number of such murder victims stood in the dozens at the most. The more sensational writings on the subject have claimed a death toll in the thousands but they can be discounted for the following reasons. Many regular garrison soldiers, who were ordered to carry out the massacres, were federates themselves prior to joining the regular army. They were being asked to murder the families, in some cases, of friends and even relatives. It staggers belief that Olympius and his fellow butchers actually thought that such an order would ever be carried out on the vast scale that they intended. Many Italian families who had been forced to house these barbarian dependents, to their very great credit, refused to betray them to their would-be executioners. Many of the remaining garrison troops, who had joined the army directly, were either barbarians or of barbarian descent. Once the secret order to massacre the families of federate troops became public knowledge, barbarian troops in the regular army feared that they and their families might be next.

Within a week of the massacre in Pavia and Stilicho's execution, barbarian troops, first by the dozens, then in the hundreds and finally by the thousands began to desert the Roman Army in Italy. Many joined with federate deserters to filter north with their families to where Alaric was stationed. This included virtually all twelve thousand of the Gothic and other soldiers that Stilicho had recently acquired from Radagaisus's army. Others hired themselves out to the private armies of rich landowners. Many senators suddenly realized that they would have to form private security forces to protect their Italian estates, just as their families had been doing for generations in Gaul and Illyria on their other land holdings. Other deserters simply formed bandit gangs. The Army of Italy dissolved within a matter of a few weeks. Many towns lost the bulk of their garrisons almost literally overnight. In some cases, fighting broke out between loyal and deserting regulars in the process. It was an atrocious state of affairs that the amoral monstrosities now running the government had no idea how to correct. The simple fact was that there was no way in which these degenerates could stop the ongoing chaos that they had created. They *were* the problem; only their replacement could rectify matters to whatever extent they could be rectified. It would take several years for any sort of responsible government to reappear in Italy. By then, too much time would have passed and too much damage been done for any semblance of the status quo ante to be reestablished.

I pointed out to Alaric that he could not stay in the vicinity of Virunum indefinitely.

"My lord, there is a strong possibility that a number of deserting Romans and federates will soon ask to enter your service. Should that occur, this camp will soon draw down its food stocks. You are going to have to move to a region where your army and dependents can be more easily sustained. Pannonia perhaps."

"Yes, I know," Alaric agreed. "I've been thinking about that. Once the new government was installed, I was certain they would send emissaries to clarify their attitude toward us. But we have heard nothing. I've been discussing it with my council and the idea of a move back to Pannonia has come up. We were quite satisfied with the arrangements we had there back in 402. We could certainly maintain our greater numbers more easily there than we can here in Noricum."

"Has Constantine made any attempt to contact you?" I asked.

This question rather startled Alaric.

"No," he replied. "Why do you ask?"

"If I was Constantine, I know I would. He's the only Roman I can name at the moment who seems concerned over the strategic dangers facing the Western Empire. I would think that he would want to employ you on the same terms that Stilicho did."

"What puzzles me," Alaric said, "is why, given the death of Stilicho and the collapse of the Army of Italy, Constantine has not already attacked Italy through the western Alps. Perhaps he is just as much of a loser as the ones that Olympius has appointed to replace Stilicho and the men of his command. It's an interesting point that you raise though. I just hadn't given it any thought yet, but you're right. I should. Getting back to your original point, my council and I have agreed to send a delegation to Ravenna. Its purpose will be to get agreement on our responsibilities to the new government and to come to an understanding on our provision and remuneration. I'd like you to help us put the documentation for it together." I did.

Olympius set to work providing the appearance of leadership while lacking any sense of how his ends could be accomplished. Widespread torture of Stilicho's closest associates and their families was often followed by their executions. It was the only way in which Olympius felt he could convey the idea that the government was in firm control of a crisis that was entirely of his own making. By the nature of his own base character, Olympius could only think the worst of others. His was a most dwarfed and stunted spirit. Taking over as the new master of offices for the Western Empire, Olympius held the most powerful civilian office in the land. But the more authoritative the political office, the more addictive and self-delusional it can become. As the consequences of Olympius' revolt became manifest to all, the more the master spider became tangled in his own web. Everything he did to alleviate the mounting disaster was as effective as changing the bedding while the house is burning down. As conditions deteriorated, Olympius' paranoia mounted. He saw conspirators everywhere. At the most dangerous point in its history, the Western Empire needed leadership of the highest order. Instead, it found itself led not only by an utterly useless emperor but by a murderous and equally incapable malcontent of a chief minister as well. In the stupidest misjudgment of his life, the esteemed Bishop Augustine of Hippo Regius (Annaba) in Africa sent congratulations to Olympius on his "well-deserved promotion."

The biggest problem with Olympius and his supporters was that their entire perspective of what lay ahead for Rome was wrong. Olympius thought of himself as the foremost defender of the empire, but what he was "defending" was a version of the state that had not existed for over a century. He and his henchmen were blindly attempting to resurrect a past that was long beyond retrieval. In so doing, they generated the biggest catastrophe in Roman history. Stilicho had seen more clearly than anyone what future path Rome should take. He sensed the direction in which history was heading; his enemies could not. Stilicho had hoped to enroll the Visigoths along the lines that the Franks had been entrusted to be junior partners in the administration and defense of the empire.

Olympius could only look backward, but in murdering Stilicho, he sealed Rome's future.

It is one thing to assassinate a universally detested tyrant like Rufinus who will be mourned only by his immediate family. It is quite another to murder a man who is widely respected and broadly supported. Regardless of how sweeping Olympius' purge, many of Stilicho's supporters would slip through the net. Among those of us who did, there would breed an inextinguishable desire for vengeance. In addition to trying to conduct the affairs of state, Olympius would have to be on constant alert against men aiming at him. He would prove no more successful at the latter than at the former.

The initial enthusiasm of Olympius' inquisitors and torturers began to wane. Over the weeks subsequent to August 23, they discovered not the slightest trace of a conspiracy among any of their hapless victims. The man in charge of the guard of the imperial bedchamber and the tribune of notaries divulged nothing under torture. Olympius, who was present at their inquisition as he was at the others, decided to execute them in a novel manner: instead of decapitating them, he ordered them clubbed to death. He would eventually have cause to regret this innovation. They were among his last victims. Early in the following year, his chief investigators refused to carry the purge any further. It had all been a ferocious and bloodthirsty waste of time and talent that had sacrificed the future of the Western Empire and the well-being of its citizens in the process.

I do not believe that Honorius was directly involved in the slaughter of his own cabinet officers at Pavia on August 13. It was all reminiscent of what had happened to Rufinus back in 395. According to eyewitnesses, Honorius appeared terrified when the massacre began and had to be quickly reassured by Olympius that the revolt was not aimed at him. With respect to the execution of Stilicho, I do not know. Throughout the reigns of Honorius and Arcadius, officials would simply place stacks of government documents in front of the emperors. They would be arranged in such a way that only the line at the bottom of the page was showing where they had to apply their signatures. They hardly ever read anything that their officials placed before them. I suspect that Olympius stacked the orders to arrest and execute Stilicho somewhere in the middle of a pile. Honorius signed them as he always signed everything that was placed before him. Whenever the emperor discovered that he had signed some outrageous order resulting in the judicial murder of some innocent, Olympius would "remind" him that he, Olympius, had fully informed the emperor of what the specific order was about at the time he signed it. Honorius would almost always reply with, "Oh, yes, I remember now."

There is no question that Honorius knew what he was doing when Olympius had him sign an order of execution for his first cousin once-removed, Eucherius. Serena, fearful of this, had already obtained sanctuary for him in a church in Rome. Empress Thermantia, still a virgin, was now dethroned and sent to Rome to live with her mother. The ex-empress was accompanied on her journey by two palace eunuchs named Terentius and Arsacius. The eunuchs also carried the execution order for her brother with them. When they discovered that Eucherius had obtained church sanctuary, they decided not to pursue him there. They could wait.

In no time, Olympius was as desperate for money as he was for soldiers. Apart from the dioceses of Africa and Western Illyria, no external sources of tax revenue were coming into Italy at all. Britain and Gaul were under the nominal control of the usurper, and Spain was cut off. Even if Gaul had been still loyal, its economy was being so thoroughly trashed by the barbarians that it would have made no difference. To cover the crashing tax revenues, Olympius ordered the confiscation of all property belonging to civilians who had been appointed to their offices by Stilicho. Fortunately for the intended targets, the man whom Olympius appointed to the task was Heliocrates. He was a decent man who was as disgusted as most of us were with the tragedy that Olympius had caused. In numerous cases, he advised the intended victims well in advance so that they could ferret away their wealth in such a way that his official investigation would discover little or nothing to confiscate.

After several weeks had gone by, refugees started entering Alaric's camp in numbers that far exceeded our expectations. By this time, Alaric's delegation was ready to leave for Ravenna. As he had requested,

I helped the delegates draw up the list of demands that included the following:

- The treaty he had signed with Stilicho would be maintained and his army would continue to act in the service of Rome.
- Hostages would be exchanged.
- Permission was requested to transfer Alaric's (increasing) army from Noricum southeast to Pannonia.
- Remuneration was requested from Rome to cover his traveling expenses from Noricum to Pannonia. The traveling distance was small since the two areas border one another.

The list of suggested hostages was interesting. The Visigoths would send several sons of their own nobility to Rome, while Rome would send Aetius, the son of Gaudentius, and Jason, the son of Jovius. Gaudentius came from a rich family in the province of Scythia at the mouth of the Danube and had held important military and civilian positions. His son, Aetius, was quite young at the time but would have a brilliant future ahead of him. Jovius, the praetorian prefect of Western Illyria, was the only one of Stilicho's three praetorian prefects to survive the slaughter on August 13. We had feared that he would be one of Olympius' early victims, but on one of my visits to Aquileia, I discovered he was still alive. The only reason for that was that he was not present in Pavia on that terrible day. Jovius had been on Olympius' original death list. What enabled him to survive the subsequent purge was that the central government's administration had fallen apart so completely and quickly. It also did not hurt that Jovius was considered to be somewhat of a lightweight. He would prove himself to be a true chameleon who knew how to survive almost any reversal of fortune. It's always nice to know someone like that. My main hope for survival was to link up with him somehow, but so soon after Stilicho's overthrow, no one knew where Jovius was. Jovius and Alaric had become friends while working together in Epirus.

Honorius and Olympius not only rejected Alaric's proposition but also made it quite clear that the accord he had signed with Stilicho was terminated and his services were no longer required. This in spite of the usurpation of Constantine, Gaul's going up in flames, and the ongoing disintegration of the Army of Italy. The wretched stupidity of the new men in control of the government was completely unfathomable. In addition to all the other disasters, they were now goading Alaric to no purpose and giving no thought to how he would react. In truth, Olympius had no actual policy toward the Visigoths. The negotiations, if they may be dignified as such, that dragged on over the next two years were nothing more than a rutted path to further disaster. Varanes and Turpilio could do nothing to prevent the ongoing crumbling of the Roman military establishment in Italy while the anti-German attitude of the government prevented it from appointing Sarus or Ulfilas to command those few troops that Honorius had left.

The fact that the empire had survived so many disasters over the centuries led Olympius and his allies to conclude that time was inevitably on our side. By rejecting all proposals from Alaric, they deluded themselves that they were in control of events. Time had generally gone against Rome's enemies in the past, and they were confident that it would this time as well. Olympius could not comprehend that time is only of value if used in a positive way. The journey determines the destination. By doing nothing constructive, time was gradually shutting down our options. Events were controlling us. Instead of determining how best to achieve a lasting peace with the Visigoths, we would be forever left with trying to minimize defeat.

The rejection of Alaric's embassy left the king with little choice. He announced in late September that he was going to march on Rome and did so immediately after giving strict orders to his troops to be on their best behavior at all times. He also sent orders to his brother-in-law Athaulf to join him. Athaulf had long been posted on the central Danube in command of a mixed federate force of Visigoths and Huns in Rome's service. Once assured that there were no opposing Roman forces before him, Alaric started through the Loibl Pass as he had done a month earlier. Another example of how removed from reality the dream world of the Senate was occurred shortly before this on September 13. On that date, it passed a law that considerably reduced the land tax on senatorial estates in Italy. It had been Stilicho's policy to pay Alaric from revenues derived from this tax. They had no idea of what lay ahead of them.

My own role in Alaric's first march on Rome seems bizarre in retrospect, but under the circumstances, it was quite reasonable. I wanted to get word to my wife that I was alive. However, I dare not risk it until I could determine whether my name was on Olympius' lengthy (and growing) list of purge victims. I thought it prudent to contact Jovius first once I could determine where he was. In the meantime, I would act as Alaric's liaison with all the garrison commanders along the first stage of our route to Rome. I knew them all throughout the Diocese of Italy where most storage depots for the Army of Italy were located. But the diocese includes only the northern third of Italy along with Rhaetia on the upper Danube. The southern two-thirds of the Italian peninsula along with Sicily, Sardinia, and Corsica constitute the Diocese of the City of Rome, also known as Suburbicaria. I did not know the men running the garrisons there as well, but it was not a concern. As long as we could provision ourselves without too much difficulty in the northern diocese, we would have no trouble reaching Rome. I also requested that Alaric add Stilicho's son Eucherius to his list of desired hostages. Not knowing at that time what Honorius's attitude was toward his distant cousin, we knew that Eucherius would be far safer with us than in the church in Rome. After all, church sanctuary, through no fault of its own, had not accomplished anything for his father. Alaric agreed.

The cities we approached did not resist. Incredibly, Stilicho's orders for them to provision both the Roman and Visigothic armies on their way to the now-aborted campaign in Gaul were still in effect. Honorius and Olympius had not countermanded them. On that basis, even cities like Aquileia, which still maintained a large garrison and had suffered few desertions, allowed Alaric's army to obtain provisions and move on. In succession, Concordia, Altinum, Padua, Verona, Cremona, and Rimini opened their gates to us. It might seem odd that we would travel as far west as Cremona before turning southeast to the Adriatic. First and foremost, we wanted to ensure that we could provision ourselves to the greatest degree possible before entering the more southerly diocese where our reception might be hostile. At Rimini, we arrived at the Adriatic and picked up the Via Flaminia. It would transport us 170 miles southward and complete our journey to Rome. We had no way of knowing that our approach to the Eternal City would almost complete the destruction of Stilicho's family.

When news of our arrival at Rimini reached Rome, the population and government there went into a state of utter panic. Fearing that his church sanctuary would prove insufficient, Eucherius escaped the city and rode north to join Alaric, where he would certainly find greater security. At our end of the line, we had no knowledge of this. We all felt that the closer Alaric's army got to Rome, the stronger would be the probability of our finding some sort of military impediment in our path. There was nothing. At Fulginium, about eighty miles north of Rome, Andreas, Julianus, and I rode ahead and entered the town to scout it out. It had no garrison. As we approached the forum, we noticed a small crowd gathered around a bulletin board.

"I'm almost afraid to look at the damned thing," Julianus said. "Every time we've done this for the past two months, the news has only gotten worse."

We dismounted, tethered the horses, and walked over.

"Jesus Christ!" said Andreas after we had read the latest pronouncement. "The madness just won't stop, will it?"

We stood there in silent rage for a few moments.

"I would imagine that this has occurred to you two as well," Julianus said, "but over the past two months, as the Western Empire has marched ever closer to its self-imposed crucifixion, just whose side are we on now?"

"We're on our own side," I replied. "We are Romans, not Visigoths, but there is no way we can work for the current government, and besides, we might all be somewhere on Olympius' death list. I think we should continue as we have: consider ourselves as outlaws in the government's eyes until we receive definitive proof to the contrary."

"I agree," said Andreas. "Continue to work with Alaric and do whatever we can to get him employed by the government against the usurper and perhaps even the Vandals. The last two months have seemed like an eternity but I don't see how this government can last. It is universally detested and is incapable of having any of its orders carried out except for the slaughter of innocents that have fallen into its grasp."

After we arrived back at our camp, I went straight to Alaric.

"What did you find out?" he asked.

"First of all, you can remove Eucherius's name from your list of hostages."

"What happened?" he demanded.

"He escaped from Rome and rode north to join us. Unfortunately, he was captured en route, returned to Rome, and executed. He was only nineteen. One thing I would suggest is that when we arrive at the city, you demand that the authorities there turn over Serena to us. Eucherius's failed attempt to join us will only have placed his mother's life in greater jeopardy. The conspiratorialists, especially now that her son has been executed, will no doubt see Serena as more of a 'danger' to the city than they might have previously."

"Good idea," Alaric replied. "God, I'm sorry to hear about Eucherius. He was the only one of Theodosius's male blood relatives that held any promise. I can hardly believe that we'll be there in just a few days."

The rest of the world would find it impossible to believe as well. I subsequently learned that after he was captured by imperial troops, Eucherius had been taken back to Rome and executed under the approving eyes of the eunuchs Terentius and Arsacius. Fearful of falling into the hands of the Visigoths, the two eunuchs sailed to Genoa and then returned to Ravenna to report the death of the emperor's cousin. They were rewarded with offices previously held by two of Olympius' other victims.

We pressed on to the town of Narnia situated less than forty miles from Rome. It was there that we encountered our first opposition, although the town possessed no garrison. It simply refused to open its gates to us. Some of Alaric's generals wanted to lay siege to the place, but their king reminded them that their objective was Rome and not Narnia, a town that they had never heard of until they bumped into it. While we were encamped before the city, a terrible thunderstorm broke out and Alaric decided to switch our line of approach. Since we could not continue to Rome along the Via Flaminia without passing through

Narnia, we turned eastward along a connecting highway to the town of Reate where we continued south along the Via Salaria. We were well into the month of October when the walls of Rome slowly started to loom ahead of us. I could not help but reflect that just two months earlier I had carried Stilicho's orders to Alaric promoting him to field marshal. Those plans were nothing more than historical footnotes now and Alaric was about to lay siege to Rome itself. The closed city gates would keep us out, but by posting heavy guard units at each of them, Alaric would ensure that nothing got in. The first Visigothic siege of Rome had begun.

In addition to stopping all traffic in and out of the city, Alaric sent units down the Tiber River to the Mediterranean ports of Portus Augusti and Ostia to block them off on their landward sides. Many people throughout the empire still think of Ostia as the port of Rome. In fact, Ostia was superseded long ago by the newer Portus Augusti because of heavy silting in the harbor of the former. Ostia is still used but primarily for the overflow traffic that Portus Augusti cannot handle from time to time. Alaric then established his headquarters at a comfortable location just outside Rome and waited. Unless you count the fact that it closed its gates, Rome had made no preparations for the siege whatsoever. The wait was a short one.

Alaric was surprised at how easy it was to lay siege to Rome as compared to Constantinople. With direct access to the sea, it was easy to supply the eastern capital and Ravenna. Besieging either one of those places was a waste of time. In addition, they had been chosen as the national capitals of our universal empire because they were also difficult to assault by land. When Rome was established in 753 BC as a village with no guarantee of what its future might be, such considerations were impossible to take into account. Since neither food nor military assistance could be expected from the outside, it was not difficult to foresee what course events would take in the weeks that followed. The daily grain ration per person was reduced to one half and then one-third the standard quota. Famine set in and disease quickly followed. With the Visigoths blocking all the exits, the citizens of Rome could not bury their dead in the cemeteries outside the walls as prescribed by law for all cities throughout the empire. Corpses were starting to pile up, not just from the famine but from all causes. It was soon common knowledge that the poorest members of the population were starting to cannibalize the dead. It was at this time that the dowager Empress Laeta, widow of Emperor Gratian, living in Rome on a government pension, opened her home to numbers of hungry people and fed them from her own resources.

The Senate had originally believed that help would soon be sent from Ravenna. But this mistaken notion was simply one more indication of the imaginary world in which its members dwelt. Now for a senator, "starvation" might mean being served a slightly undercooked piece of roast lamb in a declining restaurant. For the masses, it was the real thing. When Ravenna sent no relieving army, reality slowly started to dawn. When the stench of the rotting corpses finally became unbearable, the Senate relented and decided to send a delegation to negotiate with Alaric. Things did not go well. The curious rumor had taken root in Rome that the leader of the barbarians currently besieging the city was not really Alaric but rather some unnamed protégé of Stilicho who wanted to take revenge on Rome. To satisfy themselves on this issue, the Senate sent as one of the delegates Johannes, who was chief of the imperial notaries and had met Alaric years earlier. I was glad to see him because I had also known Johannes for many years through our association with Stilicho and I knew I could trust him. The other delegate was a Spanish senator named Basilius who had also served as a proconsul. The two men were taken by guards to Alaric's tent. Alaric permitted me to attend the conference.

It got off to a dreadful start when Alaric said to the two, "The first thing that I want you to do is bring Stilicho's widow, Serena, to us. Given the appalling manner in which Rome has treated his family, we fear for her safety."

Johannes and Basilius looked uneasily at one another. Finally, Basilius said, "That will not be possible, my lord."

"Why not?" Alaric demanded.

The two ambassadors sat again in silence for a few moments.

"Immediately after your army laid siege to Rome," Basilius replied, "the Senate arrested Serena on suspicion of planning to betray the city to you."

"That is utterly ridiculous. I've never communicated with the woman. And then what?" Alaric asked angrily.

"She was executed, my lord," replied Johannes.

"*Executed!*" Alaric exploded.

The two ambassadors jumped at this, and then a deathly silence fell around the conference table.

"What was the method of execution?" I asked.

"She was strangled," Johannes replied.

"So the Senate even lacked the decency to offer her poison," I said.

Johannes and Basilius just sat there in silence.

"What other recent executions have been carried out concerning Stilicho's family and supporters?" I demanded.

"Eucherius was executed," Basilius said.

"We know about that. Who else?" I said.

"We received word," Basilius answered, "on the day before the siege began that, on orders from Ravenna, Bathanarius, count of Africa and Stilicho's brother-in-law, had been arrested and executed."

"Who was appointed in his place?" demanded Druma, one of Alaric's generals.

"Heraclian," replied Johannes, "as a reward for executing Stilicho. He has already been taken to Carthage on a dromon warship to assume his new office."

I had been deeply shaken once again by what I had just heard. As for Heraclian, what else could one have expected? Why work for promotion when one can achieve it with far less effort through judicial murder? But the most tragic aspect to what we had just been told concerned Serena and Galla Placidia. Without the slightest shred of evidence, the Roman Senate, having learned nothing from the bloody-minded turmoil of the past two months, had ordered the lovely Serena to be arrested and garroted in a dungeon. How could these men be so ferociously stupid as to think that their murdering this innocent woman in the most excruciating manner possible would secure the city? At the same time, what could be more fitting in this time of societal and military collapse than for the true character of Galla Placidia to emerge? By special invitation, the emperor's half sister had stormed into the Senate in full rant to address its members on the alleged danger that Serena posed to the city. Galla Placidia, who had always been jealous of Serena's position within the imperial family, saw this as the chance of a lifetime. In a thoroughly defamatory speech to the city fathers, she strongly recommended that her cousin Serena be executed. Galla Placidia, the only surviving child of Theodosius I and Galla, was only six years old when her father died. She had been raised from that day forward by Stilicho and Serena almost as one of their own daughters. This was their reward. She continued to live on in the former home of Stilicho, Serena, and Eucherius in Rome; at least for a while. It alone among Stilicho's vast property holdings was not confiscated. To those of us who would be forever proud to think of ourselves as "Stilicho's men," Galla Placidia from that day forward would be known as the "bitch queen."

The embassy, suddenly remembering what it had been sent out for, announced that Rome was prepared to negotiate, provided Alaric's terms were reasonable.

"Otherwise," said Basilius, "the citizens of Rome will rise as one man to fight to the death to defend its honor."

At this point, Alaric burst out laughing and coldly replied, "The more compact the grain, the more readily it falls to the scythe."

Basilius' boast was nothing but hot air, and both sides knew it. Alaric called their bluff immediately by dictating to the envoys a list of nonnegotiable demands. The Roman representatives were aghast at what they heard.

Alaric then added, "Oh, by the way, be sure to remind the Senate that all this could have all been avoided if only Stilicho were still alive. You can make as many empty threats against me as you like, but I can bring you to your knees without firing a single arrow. I learned much as Stilicho's adversary. That's why I became his and Rome's ally. Don't be the cause of any more corpses piling up in your streets."

Johannes asked, "If all these commodities were to be surrendered to you then what would the residents of the city have left to themselves?"

"Their lives," Alaric replied.

There was no laughing this time.

After the meeting, I asked Johannes to determine whether my name was on Olympius' list of purge victims. He assured me that it was not but promised to double-check to make sure. After explaining to him how my comrades and I happened to be with Alaric, he suggested that the Senate might have use for us given our intimacy with the Visigothic king. Johannes was a career civil servant and would briefly aspire to Rome's ultimate place in the sun. That, however, was a long way off. Johannes then surprised me by stating that Jovius was in Ravenna. Given his close association with Stilicho, that was the last place I expected him to be. Johannes explained that Honorius had insisted on bringing him back from Dalmatia because he was one of the only men the emperor now felt he could trust as a capable administrator. We were already into early December, and my two comrades and I wanted desperately to see our wives and children. Facilitating that would take some time. Johannes said that if we wanted to write letters to our wives, he would send them by imperial courier. We were grateful for the offer and got our letters off at our next meeting.

The envoys returned, shaken, to report to the city fathers. There was considerable debate as to whether to accede to Alaric's exactions. Pope Innocent even considered a request to allow pagan rituals to be performed to deliver the city, provided they were conducted in private. When informed that the rituals would have to be performed in public with the full participation of the Senate, the idea was dropped. Negotiations continued for some time and Alaric, to grant the Senate some measure of dignity, reduced some of his demands slightly. Ultimately the Senate had no choice but to capitulate and provided Alaric with the following: five thousand pounds of gold, thirty thousand pounds of silver, four thousand silk tunics, three thousand scarlet-dyed woolen cloaks, and three thousand pounds of pepper. Since the Senate had just paid Alaric four thousand pounds of gold a few months earlier, it was no easy matter to come up with this new volume of riches on such short notice. The senators are all quite wealthy, but they do not maintain that much of their wealth in Rome itself. In order to comply with Alaric's demands, all pagan statues in the city were stripped of their gold and silver jewelry. When that failed to measure up to the required amount, those statues that were themselves made of gold or silver were melted down into ingots. For both Christian and pagans alike, one of the most telling moments in Roman history arrived when the golden statue of Virtus, the ancient god of courage, was melted down.

To collect the required ransom, Alaric granted the city three days. He lifted the siege for that period on certain gates and permitted food stuffs to be shipped in from the countryside and the Mediterranean ports. Rome was also permitted to bury its dead. At this time, thousands of slaves escaped from the city and the barbarian slaves among them, many former soldiers of Radagaisus, joined Alaric. Rome would pay many times over for the crimes that it had committed against the family of Stilicho. During the three-day grace period, the Senate sent a fast embassy to Ravenna to persuade Honorius to agree to the payment. The senators did not want to be accused by Ravenna of doing anything illegal on their own after the ransom was paid. They also carried with them Alaric's demand for hostages and the conclusion of a treaty that would reappoint him and his army to Roman service. The emperor agreed to both the ransom and the demands. Once the monies and goods were paid, Alaric withdrew from the city north to Etruria to await the arrival of the promised hostages and the new treaty. His army had now bloated up to forty thousand with all the Roman Army deserters and slaves that had joined it since August. During the autumn, Scot, Pict, and Saxon raiders attacked Britain, causing considerable damage to coastal areas. Pleas for help from the island went unheeded by the usurper and were just so much background noise in Ravenna amidst all the other calamities befalling us by that time. Thus the hideous year 408 drew to a close, the most calamitous in living memory. Rome had passed its ultimate watershed. It just didn't know it yet.

In the late spring of 408, knowing full well that Stilicho and Alaric were soon going to march against him, Constantine betrayed his ineptitude. Having appointed his son Constans as vice-emperor,

Constantine sent him with a sizable army under the command of Gerontius to take over the Spanish provinces. Theoretically, this was reasonable from a strategic standpoint: Constantine feared that Stilicho may launch a two-pronged attack on him simultaneously from Italy and Spain. But he should have concentrated his attentions on Italy. His plan called for a lightning campaign in Spain that would bring his soldiers back in time for the impending onslaught by Stilicho. While extending one's authority into new territory always looks good on the map, it gains a conqueror nothing if he is unable to destroy his adversary's army in the process. All such activity does is consume resources to no purpose. Had there been substantial forces loyal to the central government resident in Spain, then Constantine's invasion would have made sense. He would have had to take Spain to secure his rear. The fact is that the Roman Army establishment in Spain is very small and has been for centuries. The most important thing for Constantine to do at the time was to prepare solid defensive positions in the Alps to prevent Stilicho and Alaric from penetrating Gaul. His invasion of Spain required him to send the bulk of his army there. As the campaign took longer than planned, Constantine was unable to take advantage of the upheaval that convulsed Italy when Stilicho's government was overthrown. We would soon realize that the real reason for Constantine's Spanish misadventure was his determination to wipe out those relatives of Honorius who were still living there.

The "army" they faced was a hastily put together collection of independent centuries, slaves, and tenant farmers led by four brothers. Didymus, Verenianus, Theodosiolus, and Logadius were cousins of Honorius who mounted a spirited but ultimately ineffective defense. After their defeat, Didymus and Verenianus were captured along with their wives and taken to Arles by Constans. The other two brothers escaped by sea with Theodosiolus going to Italy while Logadius went to Constantinople. Constantine immediately rewarded his son by proclaiming him co-emperor. In a move that would have serious consequences for Britain, the usurper ordered several more regiments from the island to the continent to support his expanded area of jurisdiction. My fellow Britons would just never learn.

Gerontius had been left in Spain in command of all Roman and federate troops. One of his first decisions was to replace Spanish troops guarding the highways and passes through and around the Pyrenees with Gallic soldiers because of their greater experience. This immediately caused hard feelings with Spanish units because they felt that maintaining the security of these passes and highways was their responsibility. Fighting broke out in some places between Gallic and Spanish regiments over this issue. Gerontius finally got things under control by giving these responsibilities to federate troops instead.

In the meantime, the Vandals, Alans, and Sueves continued their trail of devastation through Gaul, free of any interference. After striking Reims for the second time, they drove south and attacked Troyes in central Gaul. While Rome ignored the barbarians, King Gunderic of the Vandals kept a close eye on Roman troop movements. When Constantine marched south to combat Sarus in 407, King Gunderic realized that to continue his southern drive would place his army in too close a proximity to Roman forces. Tempting as the valley of the Rhone was, the barbarians drove west from Troyes and attacked Orleans. From there they gradually wheeled to the south and drove across the Loire River into Aquitania. They would spend almost two years from the autumn of 407 until the latter half of 409 plundering this beautiful region. It had, heretofore, been as peaceful and prosperous as any region in the empire. And Rome obliged by plunging Italy into cataclysm and dragging out the civil war with Constantine for four long years.

Tours and Poitiers fell in succession, but in Aquitania, the rate of the barbarian advance noticeably slowed. After all, with no opposition, why rush? Besides, Aquitania was so much richer than the lands they had been passing through since leaving the Rhine and the Moselle. There were rich estates to attack everywhere. Generally, those that were fortified managed to hold out while those that were not met with destruction. The Vandals felt that since there were so many of the latter, why struggle with the former? There were refugees, rich, poor, and middle class fleeing to anywhere they could find sanctuary. Barbarians seemed to be everywhere in a region that had not seen them in almost a century and a half. One commentator has remarked that this invasion turned all of Gaul into a flaming funeral pyre.

As the barbarians approached the Pyrenees, they sent out probes into the few mountain passes with highways going through them. These were reconnaissance patrols whose objective was to determine how well guarded the passes were or for that matter if they were guarded at all. Their objective was not to force a passage through the mountains at this point. They were all beaten off by the troops guarding them and did not return for another year.

The End of Eden

CHAPTER 15

Give me the wine and the dice now, and damn anyone
who cares about tomorrow. Death is twitching my ear:
"Get on and live," he says. "I'm coming, I'm coming."

—Vergil

DURING THE EARLY MONTHS of 409, things moved quickly but not to
the advantage of anyone except the Vandals. When after several weeks
Alaric had heard nothing more from Ravenna, he requested the Senate to
send another delegation to Honorius to determine the cause of the delay.
Several meetings were held between Alaric's staff and groups of senators.
On one of these occasions, I was invited into the city to talk with such a
group at the private home of one of them, Priscus Attalus. He had been
chosen by the Senate to head the delegation. Regarding me, they wanted
the opinion of a Roman, who was not in an adversarial position to Alaric,
on what the Visigothic king's real objectives were. In truth, I doubted
that I could add anything to what they had already been told. However,
I explained Alaric's position as clearly as I could:

"Gentlemen, Alaric wants nothing more than what he has been
spelling out to both Rome and Ravenna ever since Stilicho's overthrow.
He wants his appointment as a field marshal in the Roman Army to be
reconfirmed by His Majesty. He wants the Visigothic Federate Army
to be regarded as a regular Roman field army and to be paid as such by
the government of the Western Empire on an annual basis. In return, he

will serve wherever the interests of Rome demand. It's that simple. The government at Ravenna must put aside its prejudice against the Visigoths and accept Alaric and his army as allies. The longer that we refuse to do this, the longer Gaul will be consumed in flames and the longer the government will continue to be starved of tax revenues from the western dioceses. If another massive invasion of Italy were to occur, what army, other than that of Alaric, would be available to defend it? The Army of Italy has dissolved."

"What's in this for you?" Attalus asked.

This question annoyed me, but then Attalus himself annoyed me. Like most senators, he had an overblown sense of his own importance and always assumed that he was more knowledgeable than whomever he was speaking to, regardless of the subject.

"What's in it for me," I replied, "is what's in it for you and every other citizen in the Western Empire. When you meet with Ravenna, you must convince them that the only way to get Alaric out of Italy is to grant his demands that are entirely reasonable. Having done that, the emperor must commission someone, preferably the most competent *Roman* general there is, to command a joint Roman/Visigothic army, just as Stilicho had, to combat Constantine and the Vandals in that order. In addition, all antifederate and antipagan orders pertaining to the army that have been issued since the murder of Stilicho must be rescinded. If the government in Ravenna continues its boneheaded objections to the only responsible course of action that is possible then it has forfeited its right to govern."

Priscus Attalus was an Ionian Greek. Back in 398, when Stilicho had pressed to have conscription introduced in Italy, Attalus had headed up a delegation of senators to protest. This class of men, in times past, thought themselves the lords and masters of the world. They still considered themselves "born to command" even though they had long been shorn of their ability to control events. They, who had been so recently contemptuous and dismissive of events on the frontier, now found the frontier on their doorsteps. I hoped at this time they were all thoroughly enjoying the success of that remonstration. After the meeting, Johannes confided to me that Jovius had started to lead an increasingly open opposition to Olympius. He was able to get away with this because he had the Ravenna garrison's support. This was the same garrison that had been given orders to arrest Stilicho on the night of August 22, 408.

The Senate was soon solidly supporting Alaric in his demands. It recognized that if no agreement was reached between Honorius and the Visigoths, then Rome, not Ravenna, would be the object of Alaric's displeasure. Ravenna was invulnerable and provincial. Rome's incalculable wealth was legendary and the whole world was now aware of how assailable the Eternal City was. Nonetheless, Olympius arrogantly dismissed the embassy and cancelled the arrangements to which Honorius had previously agreed. As had happened back in the autumn, Ravenna was once again refusing to exchange hostages with Alaric and denying him and his army service on behalf of Rome. The full measure of the catastrophic nature of Rome's predicament could best be measured by the fact that Honorius was finally arousing himself, however slightly, from his lifetime of torpidity. In December 408, he had ordered five under strength legions to be sent from Dalmatia to Italy to garrison the city of Rome. The safest way to do this would have been to send this entire army by ship around Italy to the ports of Rome and avoid any contact with Alaric. By having the soldiers disembark at Classis and march across country, there was almost no way in which such contact could be avoided. This should have been the last thing that Ravenna wanted. Alaric discovered this and started planning to march north to intercept them. Alaric did not know these soldiers were being sent to garrison Rome. He feared they might be the first installment of a plan to corner him in Italy the way that he had been in Greece.

My two comrades and I wanted no part of a conflict between Romans fighting for Olympius and the Visigoths. The time had come for the three of us to take leave of Alaric. I thanked him for his hospitality and told him that one way or another I was determined to get back to Ravenna, provided I could do it without losing my head in the process. I told him how to get in touch with me there if I could be of any assistance in the future and he thanked me for the help that I had extended to him in the past.

"And by the way," he said, "the next time your wife suggests that you consider a change of occupation, be sure and give her advice more serious thought than you did the last time."

We both laughed.

Andreas, Julianus, and I then traveled south, past Rome to the Bay of Naples, Sorrento, and the Amalfi Coast and checked in on my properties. It was early February by now, and we had a pleasant stay while awaiting developments up north. News was not long in arriving. Alaric's army ambushed the oncoming Roman units, killing or capturing a sizable number of them. Shortly after this, one hundred or so Roman soldiers did make it to Rome, attending Attalus and the other members of the senatorial delegation on their return trip. While in Sorrento, I picked up part of the last six months' rent money from my managing agent. Because of the turmoil up north, he had been unable to transfer the monies to Ravenna on a monthly basis as we had arranged. I agreed to have him continue to bank the rents until the chaos settled down.

Once we heard about the Roman defeat, we headed back to Rome. I went to Attalus' home to get the details on the rejection. He was understandably depressed but said the Senate was about to send another embassy under the leadership of Pope Innocent to reiterate Alaric's (and their) recommendations. While I was there, Attalus called for Johannes to come over. Attalus had, of course, seen Jovius when he was in Ravenna and mentioned me to him. Given that he had not heard anything about me over the past six months, Jovius had feared that I might have been one of the unannounced victims of the purge. Jovius told Attalus that I was not on Olympius' hit list and that he wanted me back in Ravenna to help reconstruct the Army of Italy. Johannes arranged to have me added to Pope Innocent's delegation to get me inside the city. Otherwise, it would have been virtually impossible for me to enter. Honorius and Olympius were so paranoid that they had long ago halted all traffic into and out of the city without special passes. My diplomatic immunity would take care of that. I also arranged for my two comrades to accompany me under the same conditions. I was granted a special audience with the pope that was much like the one I had earlier with Attalus. The pope had considered allowing pagan rites to be performed in private to relieve the siege of Rome. That said he was a man who, in drastic circumstances, would place the well-being of the citizenry ahead of his own religious convictions. While a strong believer in Catholic supremacy, he was above all a conciliator when it came to settling most controversies with which he was confronted. I briefed Pope Innocent as I had the senators. I also went so far as to suggest that he threaten Honorius with excommunication unless he agreed to Alaric's demands; the Pope refused to consider it.

We left for Ravenna on the following day. Alaric provided bodyguards for the delegation to protect it from bandit gangs that had sprung up in various parts of northern Italy as the anarchy increased. I was not a member of the party that met with Olympius and Honorius and I didn't really want to be. Its chances for success were not great and it managed to live down to my expectations. Either in spite of or because of the defeat inflicted on his five legions, Honorius reiterated his earlier rejection of all Alaric's demands. The important thing for me was that I was home. Once inside Ravenna, the three of us reported immediately to Jovius. He gave us a hearty welcome and then apprised us of the political situation as he saw it. We returned the favor by explaining Alaric's situation to him. He was surprised to hear that Alaric's army had swelled to forty thousand, but that was to be expected. Never in our history had army intelligence sunk to such a low level. He gave us new passes to replace the ones that Stilicho had issued to enable us to use the imperial post service and to guarantee us passage into and out of Ravenna. I told Jovius that I had given some thought to retiring from the army, especially since there really wasn't much of an army left anymore in Italy.

"I sympathize entirely with your anger and frustration," he said, "because I've gone through and am still going through the same agonies as you. You three are Stilicho's men just as I am and that metaphorical turd in the punch bowl who is the author of all our misfortunes resides just a few buildings up the street. However, his star is definitely on the wane. This is strictly between the four of us but getting rid of him and his cohorts one way or another is my first order of priority. Can I rely on you to assist me in that as the need arises?"

We all agreed, and Jovius told us to take the next two weeks off with our families but to be available on short notice if he should need us. He then paid us the six months' back pay that we would have earned under normal circumstances. Nothing like half a year's salary to revive one's flagging interest. It was a warm, sunny pre-spring day. When I received no answer to my knock on the front door, I entered and proceeded through the house to the courtyard in the back.

"I just happened to be in the neighborhood," I said, "and thought I'd drop by."

The children looked at me in a state of shock, while Aureliana, who was reclining in a lounge chair looked like she had seen a ghost and burst out laughing. Then she started to cry. At first, they had not recognized me without my beard. It was good to be home.

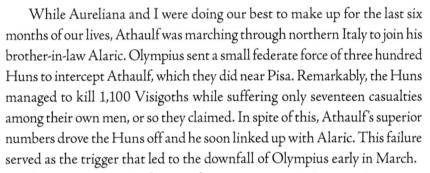

While Aureliana and I were doing our best to make up for the last six months of our lives, Athaulf was marching through northern Italy to join his brother-in-law Alaric. Olympius sent a small federate force of three hundred Huns to intercept Athaulf, which they did near Pisa. Remarkably, the Huns managed to kill 1,100 Visigoths while suffering only seventeen casualties among their own men, or so they claimed. In spite of this, Athaulf's superior numbers drove the Huns off and he soon linked up with Alaric. This failure served as the trigger that led to the downfall of Olympius early in March.

A messenger arrived at my home one morning requesting me to report to Jovius. I was surprised and pleased at what I heard when I arrived. Jovius, the Frankish general Allobichus, the Ravenna garrison, and certain eunuchs at the palace were about to deliver a demand that Olympius be removed from office. The message was duly communicated to the emperor but Olympius had already heard about the plot. Before Honorius could arrest him, the master of offices escaped across the Adriatic to Dalmatia. We would have to settle for the remaining smaller fish. Immediately, Jovius was made praetorian prefect of the Italies and started cleaning house. Allobichus arranged for the fleet at nearby Classis to stage a demonstration demanding that Turpilio, marshal of infantry, and Vigilantius, marshal of cavalry, be replaced. The presence of Allobichus in Ravenna to begin with showed that the new regime was not completely anti-German. If anything it was primarily anti-Gothic. I did not know Allobichus, though he had a good reputation gained through years of service in the Rhineland. I accompanied Jovius to the imperial palace where we were granted an immediate audience with the emperor. Appropriately enough, the little runt was sitting on a throne that looked five sizes too big for him. Jovius did all the talking, stating in no uncertain terms that unless the two leading military officers in the Western Empire were dismissed immediately, he would be unable to control the garrison. At the thought of a rebellion on his front steps, Honorius ordered Jovius to do whatever the garrison troops were demanding. Turpilio and Vigilantius were ordered sent into exile, as were those palace eunuchs that had been most closely associated with Olympius and who had carried out the execution of Eucherius. Terentius was banished to the east, while Arsacius was imprisoned in Milan. The exile of the two military leaders was where I came in.

We had brought two centuries of garrison troops with us. I ordered them into the offices of Turpilio and Vigilantius where the two field marshals were arrested at their desks. They were taken to the garrison jail. When I reported to Jovius's headquarters, I found Andreas and Julianus waiting. Jovius had drawn up orders for Honorius to sign, banishing Turpilio and Vigilantius. My two comrades and I were to escort them there. We spent the rest of the day reviewing the details and making the proper arrangements. Late that afternoon, both Turpilio and Vigilantius had their right hands branded with the letter S. They were puzzled by this, but we weren't.

The following morning, we set sail heading east across the Adriatic. Our two prisoners, bound in chains, had been told they were being exiled to an island off the coast of Dalmatia. Roughly ten miles off the Italian coast, the water starts to get deep. At that point, the prisoners were brought to the center of the deck.

"Gentlemen," I addressed them, "we have reached your place of exile."

"You bastards," Turpilio spat at us just before Julianus struck him across the face with a blow that I can still hear. I ran him through with my sword in an area where I knew he would not be killed instantly.

"That was for Serena," I said as he dropped to his knees.

Julianus then ran him through again and said, "That was for Eucherius."

Andreas then slit his throat and added, "That was for Stilicho."

We stood there watching the traitorous wretch writhe on the deck, literally drowning in his own blood. I then yanked him up into a kneeling position and rammed his head down onto the execution block that had been brought over to where he was lying. Andreas was a powerfully built man. It took but one blow to decapitate the former marshal of infantry. It was then the turn of Vigilantius, who rained curses down upon us throughout. As a final act, their right hands were amputated. Their heads and bodies were then wrapped in sailcloth, weighted with stones and chains, and committed to the deep. Their right hands were brought back to Jovius as proof that the task had been completed.

What disappointed us in this exercise was that it was impossible for us to apprehend Varanes, the chief military conspirator who had immediately replaced Stilicho. As the summer of 408 had dragged into the autumn, Varanes realized the hopelessness of the situation he had done so much to create. He resigned at the beginning of 409 and went to Constantinople where he served as eastern consul for the year 410. It was a reward for his "good works" on the East's behalf. He was succeeded by Turpilio. The Roman general Valens and the Frankish general Allobichus replaced Turpilio and Vigilantius respectively. They, too, were Stilicho loyalists, but our troubles were not over yet as far as the top command was concerned.

Shortly after this, Honorius appointed another very capable barbarian general, a supporter of Stilicho with long service in the Roman Army, to the post of count of Western Illyria. Generidus was an honorable man and at first refused his promotion because of the law issued the previous November forbidding pagans such as him from holding positions in the army. Generidus persuaded Honorius to rescind this law before he would assume his new office.

Bringing Spain over to his side and getting its defenses in order to ward off an invasion by the Vandals, Alans, and Sueves was more time-consuming that Constantine had envisioned. The usurper decided that his first priority regarding Italy was to come to an understanding with Ravenna that would get him recognized as co-emperor of the West. Jovius persuaded Honorius to accept such an alliance to offset the possibility of Constantine's invading Italy once sufficient numbers of his forces had returned to Gaul from Spain. In addition to the strategic dilemma he faced, Honorius had the problem of doing whatever he could to save the lives of his two cousins who were under arrest in Arles. As a result, the emperor extended recognition to Constantine and sent him an imperial robe as proof of this.

Jovius invited Alaric and his brother-in-law Athaulf to a conference in Rimini, about thirty miles southeast of Ravenna on the coast, to work out a new federate treaty. I went with him and found nothing unreasonable about Alaric's requests that consisted of the following: permission to garrison the provinces of Venetia and Istria (in northeast Italy proper), Noricum, and Dalmatia; a fixed annual payment for his army and its dependents; a fixed annual grain supply; reappointment to the rank of field marshal in the Roman Army; recognition of the Visigothic Federate Army as a regular Roman field army. Jovius discussed with Alaric and Athaulf the recent extension of recognition that Honorius had granted to Constantine. He also mentioned the need for Alaric and Constantine to cooperate as allies to defeat the Vandals and the others before the latter could invade Spain. Alaric was surprised by the former but favorably disposed to this latter suggestion. From Rome's standpoint, what better way to get Alaric and his army out of Italy and accomplish something positive for a change? The Visigothic demands were written down and reviewed. Jovius then went to his temporary office in Rimini to send the letter by dispatch riders to Ravenna for review by Honorius and his military commanders. After Jovius had gone to his office, we retired to the hotel that had been set aside for Alaric, Athaulf, and their bodyguard for some socializing. Tall, dark featured, and very quiet, Athaulf was an Ostrogoth. It was difficult to draw any conclusions as to his character on the basis of that first meeting. I told them their demands were reasonable but from a negotiating standpoint they should be prepared to give up the idea of garrisoning Venetia and Istria. Just use it as a bargaining point. Their presence there would irritate Italian patriotic pride too much. I also told them to stick to all the other demands and not make any changes to them without hearing sound alternatives from Honorius first. Any early shifting in their position would be interpreted by Ravenna as a sign of weakness, regardless of who was in charge.

What we had no way of knowing was that Jovius wrote a private letter to Honorius, in addition to the one containing Alaric's demands. In it he requested that Alaric be made joint commander of Roman and barbarian forces in the peninsula, in other words, "marshal of Italy." Jovius hoped that by elevating Alaric to this new high office, his territorial requests could be reduced. Several historians have criticized Jovius for this action, but I don't agree with them. It was a responsible suggestion for a cabinet minister to make to his sovereign, simply as a point for discussion. Late the following day, Honorius's return letter arrived. Given Honorius's record of obstruction for the sake of obstruction, Jovius should have first read the letter privately and, if need be, summarized it for presentation to Alaric. When he called the meeting, I assumed that he had and was surprised to see him break the imperial seal in front of us. The emperor rejected all Alaric's demands once again and, in the most contemptuous language, vowed never to consider making any Goth a field marshal in the Roman Army. Alaric erupted when he heard this insult, ordered his army to march on Rome, and stormed out of the meeting. We were all shocked at the severity of this rejection, but who had really authored it? Jovius and I returned to Ravenna along with the rest of his staff.

That fateful letter of rejection had also been critical of Jovius. It denounced him for suggesting that Alaric be appointed field marshal since that alone was for the emperor to determine. I have often wondered if Allobichus was the real force behind this particular rejection of Alaric's demands. Allobichus had been slowly trying to reconstruct the Army of

Italy, many of whose former members had deserted to Alaric. Allobichus would have wanted them back, and there was a question of whether Alaric would return them if they did not wish to return voluntarily. Allobichus' own star was in the ascendant for the moment and here was Jovius suggesting that Alaric be made his superior. It would be understandable for the Frank to be opposed. Valens, Allobichus' nominal superior, had been promoted beyond his capabilities and did not appear to be doing much of anything at this time.

Honorius ordered all Roman forces that he could find along with a large contingent of Huns to counter Alaric. Another embassy arrived from Constantine at this time. In return for being granted recognition, he promised British, Gallic, and Spanish soldiers to aid Honorius in his conflict with Alaric. Incredibly, it was announced that the two cousins of Honorius held captive in Arles were dead. Constantine had his ambassadors claim, pathetically, that the two brothers had been executed by mistake and not on his orders. Even a moron like Honorius wouldn't buy that one. But the situation in Italy was beyond desperate. Honorius had no choice, for the moment, but to accept what he was told. It would be learned later that Didymus and Verenianus had, in fact, been executed prior to the arrival of the first embassy earlier in the year. Once a traitor, always a traitor. Only further treachery could be expected from the usurper.

The day after the second embassy from Constantine left for Arles, I was summoned to Jovius's office. I would now learn that Jovius, like virtually all civil servants, would rather hang onto his job than risk losing it by taking a stand on principle. He would appear in such sharp contrast to the recent fine example that Generidus had set. The meeting started off with the odd comment that with the dissolution of the Army of Italy, Honorius had been forced to admit that Constantine now possessed the only Roman army that was capable of combating the Visigoths. Help would be arriving from that quarter in the weeks ahead. He explained decisions that had been made with respect to bringing in the Huns and what few Roman units were available in Italy to counter Alaric. He immediately asked me to help him and Allobichus start bringing in supplies from Dalmatia in the form of livestock and grain to supply them. All I could do initially was sit there staring at him in total disgust and disbelief.

"For me personally, this is the straw that finally broke the camel's back. For years now, you have supported the policy of Theodosius and Stilicho of accommodating the Visigoths within the Roman system. After being Alaric's friend all these years, you are now going to reverse yourself by 180 degrees and completely reject the whole program? And all because you were called to task by a mentally retarded emperor for giving him perfectly sound advice?"

"I have not reversed myself at all," Jovius angrily denied. "I have been opposed to Alaric's demands from the very beginning."

"The beginning of what? The beginning of yesterday? You are now sitting there telling me that all the years that you spent in Pannonia and Dalmatia and Epirus working with Alaric on behalf of Stilicho were just a sham? Not only is the Western Empire politically and intellectually bankrupt, but it will soon be financially destitute as well. We have no tax revenues arriving from Britain, Gaul, or Spain and just a trickle from Illyria. There is no guaranteed revenue source for the central government apart from Italy and Africa, and at the rate Italy is collapsing in chaos, we will not be able to count on it much longer either. Law and order has almost disappeared, bandit gangs are running around all over the place, the Visigoths have already trashed numerous large estates to sustain themselves as their supplies run low, and all you can deliver to the populace is more of the same? There's imagination for you. I can't take this crap anymore. I'm resigning here and now."

"Not so fast," Jovius said, obviously stunned. "There is something else that I want you to know. When I originally returned to Ravenna, I discovered that your name was on Olympius' list of Stilicho's officers and officials that were to be purged. I saw to it that your name was removed. When I didn't hear anything about you, I thought that perhaps you had already been purged and that Olympius had lied to me. Fortunately, that turned out not to be the case. I think you owe me one."

He certainly sounded sincere but I couldn't help but feel that it was just a con job. At the same time, I didn't want to burn all my bridges to him.

"If that's the case," I said, "then you are right, I do owe you one. But this isn't it. I'll not be a party to the precipitation of a war on Italian soil that is entirely avoidable. You do, however, have my everlasting gratitude. If there is ever an especially sensitive mission that you think I would be qualified to perform on Rome's behalf then feel free to call on me."

With that, I got up and left his office. My army career was over. Or so I thought. It was still in the forenoon when I arrived home.

"What happened that you're home so early, hon?" Aureliana asked.

"Your husband now ranks among the unemployed," I replied. "Somewhat belatedly, I've decided to take your advice of last year and resign from the army."

I then explained the blowup that I had just had with Jovius.

"When I returned to my office, I wrote up my letter of resignation. I was surprised, but my hand was visibly shaking as I wrote it. I guess it was due to the shock of realizing that I was ending a career that had spanned almost twenty-seven years. I honestly hoped that Jovius would keep fighting for what he and I honestly believed to be the only responsible policy that Rome can now have with respect to Alaric. This morning, I was forced to the conclusion that I had misjudged him. The only cause he will ever be loyal to is himself. In any case, I submitted my letter of resignation to the Central Records Office."

I then explained what Jovius had said about removing my name from Olympius' death list and also stated my reservations on the veracity of that claim.

"It seems like what you're telling me," Aureliana said, "is that Alaric is now one of the good guys. And yet not all that long ago, you wanted to hang him from the nearest tree."

"Alas, my sweet," I replied, "as one matures, the term 'good guys' appears to become ever more relative. I am unaware of any government official in Rome or Ravenna to which that term could be applied, so I guess you are correct."

"What are you going to do now?" she asked apprehensively.

"Sit on my ass and do nothing, at least for the time being. Even with the disruption of money flows coming in from our southern properties, we've still got enough income from our local rents to live on. And if times get tougher, we can always sell some property."

"Well," she said, "we always knew that this day would arrive sooner or later. Now you can cut out our local property manager and handle that activity for yourself."

She was right, of course. I could now be a direct, instead of an indirect, landlord. But there was no need to rush these things. I decided to take a few weeks' rest. During this period, I started getting my memoirs in order. Reading those words that went back over twenty years brought back a rush of emotions that I had almost succeeded in putting out of my mind, though not out of my heart. I then wrote up the events as they had transpired since August 408. Once that was done, I took my diary notes from the British campaign and wrote up that adventure as a complete chapter. It was gradually dawning on me that I actually liked writing. So I decided to put off the landlord routine for a while and write a complete memoir. During this time, word arrived that Toulouse had fallen to the Sueves. Shortly after this, reality of a more local nature raised its ugly head once again.

The initial Hun force estimate of ten thousand had been greatly exaggerated, but Alaric, when it came to his attention, must have believed it. He halted his march on Rome and quickly sent off another embassy to Ravenna. This one was composed of bishops from various cities in northern Italy. In what can only be described as an overreaction, Alaric drastically reduced his demands, just as I had warned him not to. He now asked only for permission to garrison Noricum; a fixed annual grain supply to be determined by the government; permission to serve as a Roman army commander at a level to be determined by the government. As he had done before, he pointed out the need to secure tax revenues for the central government from Noricum. The demand for an annual gold payment was dropped. It was a surprise to hear that he was willing to serve the emperor in a reduced military capacity, but this might have reflected problems that Alaric was starting to have within his own ranks. His army had been on and off the march for over seven months by this time and was running into supply problems. These had been severely aggravated by the manner in which his ranks had swollen in 408. Regardless of the motivation, Alaric was being reasonable once again, as he had been throughout this ordeal. In addition, he included a letter to Honorius that almost pleaded for understanding. It reflected that Alaric, in addition to suffering supply problems, was also under political pressure from his generals who despaired of ever reaching an accommodation with Rome. He asked the government not to risk the safety of Rome by rejecting his demands any longer. He said he did not wish to see this great city, this world capital with over a thousand years of history behind it, damaged in any way. Nothing that he stated in his official request and his personal letter was unjust or excessive. But the change in government in March had brought no change in attitude. To add to his troubles, Alaric had betrayed himself as a weak negotiator in Ravenna's eyes by altering his position before he really had to. Ravenna would see this as a form of victory. He also had another problem: the chameleon had changed his colors. All Alaric's demands were rejected.

I have often wondered how serious Alaric was in expressing the desire to settle in Noricum or earlier in Pannonia. Strategically, this would make sense from Rome's standpoint, in that Alaric's army would be protecting Italy's northeast frontier. Supposedly. But at the same time, there would be the possibility that they would face similar dangers to the ones they faced a generation earlier on the lower Danube, and we all know how well that turned out.

The following morning, there was a loud knock at my door by a courier from Jovius's office. I was asked to come at once.

"Marcus," Jovius said as I entered his office, "I have a special ambassadorial mission for you. It's our official response to Alaric's latest demands."

"Let me guess. Total rejection, right?"

"That's right."

"Why did you pick me for the job? You could have sent any diplomatic courier."

"I know that," he replied, "but you know Alaric and he respects you. I didn't want this to be delivered by a total stranger."

There was no point in pursuing this part of the conversation any further.

"Tell me," I asked, "is the common rumor that we have all heard in the marketplace true?" I then told him what my wife's cousin Claudia had heard while shopping in the city's main market.

Jovius looked down at the floor and simply said, "You can go now."

I headed south to where Alaric was, ashamed of playing any further part in this dreary and endless charade. But as Jovius had said weeks earlier, I did owe him one. Arriving in Alaric's camp, I was escorted to his command tent, where Athaulf was also present.

"Marcus!" Alaric exclaimed. "Good to see you. What's the occasion?"

"I'm here as a personal favor to our erstwhile friend Jovius," I replied.

"Why do you say 'erstwhile'?" Athaulf asked.

Athaulf's Latin was difficult to understand at times. He had spent all his time in Roman service on the frontier. Alaric's Latin, on the other hand, had almost no trace of a German accent after all the time that he had spent just about everywhere but the empire's frontiers. I handed Alaric the document from Jovius.

"What I've just given you is the latest rejection of your demands by Honorius. Jovius can now be considered completely on the emperor's side in refusing to deal with you. After our last meeting in Rimini, when the emperor upbraided him in addition to insulting you, Jovius decided he would do whatever it took to hang onto his job. He swore an oath on the emperor's head and then had all Honorius's cabinet ministers do likewise. The oath they swore was that they would never make peace with you and that they would forever consider you to be an enemy of the Roman Empire. People have been talking about this all over Ravenna."

"You said that this oath was sworn on the emperor's head?" Alaric said quizzically. "I don't understand."

"It appears," I began, "that Jovius felt that if the oath was merely sworn on a Bible that the men present might at some point try and squirm out of it. His fear was that when anyone breaking such an oath eventually appeared before the Almighty in the great beyond, he would be able to sweet-talk his way through the pearly gates with our all-forgiving Lord. In other words, such an oath would not be taken all that seriously. On the other hand, by swearing on the emperor's head, punishment for breaking such an oath would be far more immediate and severe. There would be no forgiveness."

Alaric and Athaulf sat there in silence for a while and then spoke briefly to one another in Gothic.

"What's the situation with respect to the ten thousand Huns?" Athaulf asked.

"Shortly after the fiasco at Rimini," I replied, "Jovius asked me to help him set up the supplies required for them. That was his way of telling me that he had reversed his position on reconciling Ravenna's differences with you. I got pissed off and resigned. Since then I haven't heard a word about them. From the beginning, I think it was just so much Ravenna swamp gas. Another thing that happened at that time was that Constantine, once Honorius granted him recognition, promised to send troops to Italy to help Honorius combat you. That might have played more of a role in persuading Jovius to reverse himself than anything else. However, like the Huns, neither have the Gauls, the Spaniards, nor the Britons shown up yet. Since retiring in Ravenna, I've managed to renew several contacts from the old days to keep me abreast on what's going on. Everything seems quiet regarding external troop support for Honorius. Apart from Gaul, about the only place Honorius could obtain any troops now would be from Dalmatia or the upper Danube, and I've heard nothing about that."

"Am I dealing with the biggest collection of bloody idiots on the surface of the globe?" Alaric asked.

"You most certainly are," I replied.

"It's remarkable," Alaric went on, "how just a year ago we expected to have defeated Constantine by this time and to be already engaged in combat with the Vandals. Did Stilicho ever say what he was planning on doing with them once they had been defeated?"

"We discussed it several times," I replied. "His general thinking was that we might settle them in Armorica since it is the most sparsely settled part of Gaul. And as they were already in the neighborhood ..."

"Have there been any personnel changes of note in Ravenna?" Athaulf asked, suddenly changing the subject.

"Not that I'm aware of," I replied, "but one thing that I've heard is that an Eastern Illyrian, one of the youngest generals in the army, is being called to Ravenna, though in what capacity I don't know. I've met him only once. He's very sharp and was a protégé of Stilicho. His name is Constantius and the rumor is that he is going to take over one of the two top command positions."

"Constantius?" Alaric and Athaulf almost said in unison.

"I got to know him fairly well," Alaric said, "while I was count of Western Illyria. Athaulf met him also on the occasion of his making tours of inspection of frontier fortifications over the years. He's very capable, younger than I am. His arrival is a good sign. I think we could work well together."

Alaric, Athaulf, and I spoke for a while on many things, including our families. We had a sumptuous dinner and good wine, and the next morning I was up early to leave for Ravenna. When I asked Alaric if he was going to return to Rome, he replied, "What choice do I have?"

I thanked them for their hospitality and headed north. I never saw Alaric again.

In September, I was pleasantly surprised when my old friend Gaiso was appointed minister of finance. He had withdrawn from Gaul with the rest of Honorius's government and had been working in Milan until called down to Ravenna. If the Western Empire had been united and at peace then it would have been a most prestigious posting. With the land wracked by invasion, dissention, and civil war, his job would be most difficult.

On Tuesday, September 28, 409, the Vandals, Alans, and Sueves suddenly burst through the Pyrenees along the main road from Bordeaux to Pamplona. Their passage through the mountains lasted fifteen days. The federates posted in the pass proved incapable of defending it. The number of federates employed for this purpose was relatively small, and yet they had to defend all the passes. To break through, the Vandals had to choose but one. Certain of these federate regiments then joined the invaders. The Vandals had learned in Gaul what the Visigoths had learned thirty years earlier in Thrace: thoroughly destroying the agricultural economy of an area one year prevents it from sustaining you the next. The Vandals had so disrupted Gaul that they had little choice but to seek fresh fields of slaughter to the south. They had been in Gaul for over two years. They would remain in Spain for twenty.

Having largely ignored the ruination of Gaul, Constantine realized he could not sit idly by and watch Spain consumed in the same fashion. The usurper quickly sent Constans back to Spain with another general named Justus to replace Gerontius. When Gerontius heard that he was about to be fired, he was incensed, went into revolt against "Constantine III" and "Constans II," and proclaimed a subordinate, a capable young officer named Maximus, as emperor in Tarragona. With the bulk of their army now in revolt, Constantine and his son found themselves in a very difficult position. The usurper now had to focus his attention on Spain because of a danger that would have never existed if he had not gone there in the first place. Gerontius, to ensure victory, took on some of the Vandal invaders as federates to go against Constans and Justus. The situation was getting crazier all the time. In the ensuing battle, Maximus and Gerontius were victorious, and Constans retreated back to Arles. Thus, the very thing that Constantine had invaded Spain to avoid had come about anyway in a fashion that he could never have imagined.

With this latest rejection of his proposals for a treaty of alliance, Alaric marched on Rome for a second time. He went straight for the jugular by seizing Rome's Mediterranean ports. He didn't bother laying siege to the city. Holding the ports gave him all the leverage he needed, as the painful memories of the previous year's famine were only too fresh in the public mind. After threatening to parcel out the food stocks in Portus Augusti to his army and then to set fire to the rest, the Senate was only too willing to listen to his demands. Alaric ordered the Senate to proclaim Attalus, the urban prefect of Rome, as emperor. Once this was done, Attalus made Alaric marshal of infantry, and Athaulf count of domestics.

When news of this reached Ravenna, Honorius sent orders to Heraclian, count of Africa, to stop shipping grain to Rome. Once again, Honorius, well provisioned and secure in Ravenna, appeared willing to fight to the last inhabitant of the Eternal City to get his own way. Alaric recommended to Attalus that a sizable Visigothic force under his general Druma be sent to Africa to overthrow Count Heraclian and resume the grain supply to the city. But Attalus, who was unwilling to merely play the role of a puppet, ignored this advice. He was reluctant to send Visigothic troops to fight Roman soldiers, especially in Africa where no Visigoth had ever set foot. Instead he chose to send a Roman force under the command of a recently promoted Roman general named Constans. Once Africa was brought over to the side of Attalus, Honorius would have to see the light. This was a perfectly sound decision, but Attalus had no military background.

The force he assembled was much too small for the task. When Alaric complained about this, Attalus ignored him again. As Stilicho usually exercised power silently, Attalus would employ no power loudly. When this force had sailed off, Attalus marched against Honorius in Ravenna with a small force, but before leaving, he made another important decision. He arrested Galla Placidia to use as a bargaining chip in the diplomatic battles with Honorius that lay ahead. As things turned out, Attalus and Alaric placed greater value on the "bitch queen" than did her half brother. But then, retarded though he was, he knew her better.

Aureliana, along with a lot of other people in Ravenna, were quite frightened by the thought of the city being placed under siege and attacked. We were only too familiar with the horror stories from the recent siege of Rome. Aureliana wanted to leave the city and go to live at our properties at Sorrento or along the Amalfi Coast that she had never seen. Probably the easiest way for us to get there would have been to take the coastal highway along the Adriatic down to Vasto or Siponto and then to turn west to get to the Bay of Naples area. But with chaos reigning in the countryside, I felt that traveling almost any route to the south could prove more dangerous than simply staying put. With the emperor in residence, Ravenna was the best provisioned city in Italy. Our food supplies at this time were coming mainly from Dalmatia. Besides, it was common knowledge that Honorius had ordered the assembly of a fleet at the suburban port of Classis. It was to take him off to safety in Constantinople with his young nephew Theodosius II if he failed to hang on in Ravenna. That would have been the best possible outcome for Rome. I finally managed to convince my wife that Attalus had no intention of sacking Ravenna if and when Honorius did flee the place. Like so much else, it would turn out to be so much wishful thinking. It was coming to dawn on almost everyone that Rome's time of being mistress of the Mediterranean died the same day that Stilicho did. Only an act of divine intervention could halt the avalanche of self-destruction into which we had plunged ourselves.

The terrified Honorius sent a delegation of his ministers, headed by Jovius, to meet Attalus with an offer to reign jointly with him, as he was already reigning jointly, sort of, with Constantine. Attalus, with an invasion fleet on its way to Africa and no army apart from the small garrison of Ravenna to oppose him, felt quite confident about his chances of success. He would only offer Honorius the opportunity to abdicate and live the rest of his life as a private citizen in exile. Jovius, as usual the eager opportunist, saw fit to switch sides once again, as it was "obvious" that Attalus would win. Jovius was acting like a rat swimming back and forth between two sinking ships. Jovius, on his own and without telling Attalus, let it be known that Honorius would be mutilated before being sent into exile. This was to panic the terrified Honorius into taking ship to Constantinople as quickly as possible. All hope appeared to be lost for Honorius when a large fleet arrived from Constantinople in December.

It carried four thousand troops and had been sent out by Anthemius, praetorian prefect of the East, on the advice of Varanes. Anthemius and his fellow "mandarins" were quite satisfied running their own fiefdoms on behalf of the eight-year-old Theodosius II. They did not want his blundering, pigheaded dunce of an uncle anywhere near the eastern capital. This unexpected arrival bolstered Honorius's determination and he decided to stay with his new garrison. Lucky us. The only good thing that could be said about the year 409 was that it was over.

The new year of 410 started with a situation that was eerily reminiscent of conditions a century earlier. Like then, we now had six claimants to the two imperial thrones. In the East, the eight-year-old Theodosius II had his throne all to himself with not a usurper in sight. In the West, five grown men, all of whom were acting like eight-year-olds, claimed to be emperor of the West. The great irony of the western situation was that the more claimants appeared the less of a realm there was to claim. The Vandals had caused the total disruption of government across much of northern and all of western Gaul. The destruction in Gaul had isolated Britain. Northern Spain and southern Gaul were undergoing a civil war of their own, and Italy was in chaos. With the exception of Africa, the economy of the entire Western Empire was in collapse. Bandit gangs were showing up everywhere. The downward slide of our fortunes that had started in August 408 continued without letup. It was almost as though our society had suddenly become prepossessed to see all the brilliant achievements of the past swept away. Government had deteriorated into nothing more than crisis management, and management of the most incompetent order it was. When Honorius was a boy, someone always had to clean up after him. His toys and clothes were always strewn about. Now, as an adult, it was his nation that lay about him in pieces.

Early in the New Year, Attalus' young general, Constans, and his inadequate invasion force were defeated in Africa by the forces of Count

Heraclian. Constans himself was killed in the attack. The year would continue to be awkward for young men with that name. The failure of Attalus' African campaign caused Alaric to recommend once again that a Visigothic force under Druma be sent there.

One morning, at the beginning of February, an imperial courier arrived at my home. Honorius was requesting me to attend a special audience that same afternoon. Its purpose was not disclosed. Arriving at the palace, I was ushered into the imperial presence and was surprised to see I was the only one there apart from the emperor, one of his secretaries, and a man I had never seen before. The secretary did all the talking. After I saluted Honorius, I was told that my old friend Gaiso was being considered for the vacant position of master of offices. I was very pleased to hear this. He had obviously impressed the right people in the short period that he had been at court. I was puzzled as to why I had apparently been brought into the selection process since I was not concerned with imperial finances in any way. The secretary told me that it was due to a combination of my excellent service record combined with the fact that I had known Gaiso longer than any man in Italy. I was asked numerous questions about him and I replied as elegantly and positively as I could. I was thanked for my input and was dismissed. As I was leaving, the new man in the meeting decided to leave as well. I struck up a conversation with him and he introduced himself as Theodosiolus, the emperor's cousin. A very amicable fellow, we would become good friends in the years ahead. On February 12, 410, it was announced that Gaiso had been promoted to this most important office. He had only been finance minister for five months, but his star had risen very quickly. Several days later, Aureliana and I were invited to a party at Gaiso's home to celebrate his promotion.

During the party, he and I talked about what should be done about the army high command since under the current leadership it was obviously foundering. I suggested that both current leaders, Valens and

Allobichus, be replaced. Both men were well intentioned but their efforts to reconstruct the Army of Italy had not accomplished much. Valens was little more than a figurehead and as events would soon show, Allobichus was more interested in politics than the Army of Italy per se. As midlevel officers, in August 408 they had been promoted to positions that were beyond their capabilities. The only field marshals in the West under Stilicho were Chariobaudes and Vincentius, both of whom were slain at Pavia. I suggested that, for political reasons, a native-born Roman would have to fill the position of master of infantry and it should be someone who had worked well with the Goths in the past. Constantius, who was still in Western Illyria, was my recommendation for that post, in spite of his being one of the junior generals in the army at the time. He had been born in Naissus, the hometown of Constantine the Great, came from a military family, and was known to Alaric and Athaulf. Fortunately, he was low enough down in the army hierarchy back in 408 to have escaped the purge. For master of cavalry, I suggested Ulfilas or Generidus but made known my own preference for Ulfilas. His devotion to duty had been exemplary and the fact that he was a Visigoth would act as a beacon to attract Visigothic deserters from 408 back to the colors. Generidus was getting on in years, and I felt that all the campaigning that would lie ahead of us to rectify matters to whatever extent that was still possible could prove too much for him. Sarus I ruled out. Because of his murderously eccentric behavior just before Stilicho's execution, he could simply no longer be trusted.

Within a few weeks, Attalus, who had been so confident of success at the beginning of December, saw his support crumbling rapidly. The defeat of his expeditionary force meant that Rome would remain shorn of its African grain supplies. Famine had already broken out in central Italy but this time Alaric could not be blamed. The arrival of eastern troops in Ravenna meant that Honorius could withstand any siege by Alaric's troops indefinitely. Jovius sensed the change in wind direction and, once again, switched sides, rejoining Honorius in Ravenna. The man lacked all credibility. Anyone else would have been handed his head for such carryon, but the luck of Jovius held. He tried to bring Alaric over with him, but Alaric remained loyal to the "chief of state" that he had created; at least for the moment. Lifting his siege of Ravenna that had caused those of us on the inside little discomfort, Alaric then sent his army on campaign through some of the northern provinces of Italy to enforce the authority of Attalus. Only Bologna held out for Honorius. As a result, Alaric, lacking the wherewithal to lay siege to a city that was well provisioned and defended, let it go. By this time, the Senate had swung around to Alaric's view that his general, Druma, should attack Count Heraclian in Africa. Imperial pride be damned, Rome was starving. Attalus, for the same political reasons that he had used the previous year, again refused to send federate troops across the Mediterranean. That was the last straw for Alaric. The alliance between himself and Attalus dissolved, the latter having exhausted whatever usefulness he may have had.

Alaric came to another conclusion as well. Attalus' opposition to his suggestion of a Visigothic invasion of Africa led Alaric to see in Attalus a similarly obstinate attitude as had been displayed by Honorius throughout. No Roman emperor would ever accept the Visigoths as partners in managing the empire. Roman pride would never permit it. Alaric feared that even if Honorius were driven from his throne, Count Heraclian may, as Gildo had before him, take Africa into the Eastern Empire instead. There seemed to be no end to it. Alaric decided to admit that his scheme to elevate Attalus had been a failure. Accordingly, in May, at Rimini, Alaric dethroned his creation but not before being assured by Honorius that no harm would befall Attalus or any of his supporters. As added insurance, Attalus and his family remained members of Alaric's entourage. As a token of his renewed allegiance, Alaric shipped the purple robe and crown of Attalus to Honorius. Galla Placidia, however, remained a hostage with Alaric.

Late in the spring, once the snows had melted in the Alpine passes, Constantine finally sent some units into northern Italy. Almost a year late, he was finally fulfilling his promise to Honorius to send troops to combat Alaric, but they were taking forever to arrive. Soon after this development, a rumor started that the young general Constantius, who was currently up in Pannonia on the Danube, would soon be posted to Ravenna. No one seemed to know exactly what his responsibilities would be and for a while nothing came of it. My longtime friend Stephanus and I, along with our wives, would get together every Friday evening to get caught up on the week's events while our children would play together in the courtyard. We only lived a couple of blocks away from one another. For Stephanus and me, it was a continuation of an ancient drinking tradition from our army days, whether we had any new news for one another or not. Early in the summer, we would have a most unusual Friday.

"Well, have you heard the latest?" Stephanus asked before he was halfway through the door.

"No," I replied. "I guess I haven't and I'm almost afraid to ask."

"Allobichus has been assassinated."

"What? By whom?"

"You've got to pull your head out of your memoirs, old buddy," he chided me. "The world is passing you by. It's a big mystery, but it happened this afternoon in the emperor's presence. The main theory is that Constantine has been using Alaric simply as a pretext to get his troops into northern Italy without opposition. He had made an alliance with Allobichus to overthrow Honorius. Allobichus' reward in this was to be his promotion to marshal of infantry for the Western Empire. His, meaning Allobichus', opposition to Alaric all these months has been a stalling tactic until Constantine could get to within striking distance of Ravenna."

"This would have happened last year," I said, "if Constantine had not gone belly-up in Spain."

"Of course," Stephanus went on. "Rumor has it that once Honorius had either been driven out of Ravenna or killed, Constantine was planning on making the alliance with Alaric that Alaric has been demanding all along."

What made the whole story plausible was that Constantine immediately started withdrawing his regiments, whose numbers were not great to begin with, back into Gaul as soon as he was informed of the assassination. The usurper had no time to spare in Italy anyway, as his ambitions were all collapsing in on him. He had felt that his son, Constans, with federates brought down from the Rhine, would be able to handle Gerontius while he himself attended to affairs in Italy that could no longer be postponed. Stilicho and Sarus had recognized years earlier that the Western Empire could not afford simultaneous wars on two fronts. It should have been doubly obvious to Constantine that his ravaged *half* of the Western Empire could not afford that luxury either. He chose to ignore the danger.

While Constantine was involved in Italy, Gerontius carried his campaign into Gaul where he defeated "Constans II" at Vienne. Constantine returned through the Alps as quickly as he could. When he reached the Rhone Valley, he discovered that his son had already been executed by his former chief general. Constans had been a monk when his father went into revolt and persuaded his elder son to join him; a most tragic choice. Constantine retreated south, with his younger son, Julian, to his capital at Arles. A year earlier things had never looked better for him. Now he had lost Spain, his hopes in Italy had been dashed and his elder son was dead. Gerontius laid siege to Arles and Constantine remained bottled up there for the rest of the year.

Negotiations began for a face-to-face meeting between Alaric and Honorius. Most of us were surprised that Honorius would even consider such a thing. Talks dragged on through June and ended in July when they agreed to meet outside Ravenna. The conference never took place. Alaric left the bulk of his army at Rimini and continued north up the coastal highway with a few hundred troops. Along the way, he was suddenly attacked by Sarus. Nothing had been heard of Sarus since the execution of Stilicho, and his materialization at this time appeared more than just a little suspicious. Alaric's forces, after a tough fight, managed to drive Sarus and his men off. Not unreasonably, Alaric concluded that Honorius and his advisers were behind the attempted assassination.

Alaric returned to his army at Rimini and ordered it to march on Rome for the third and final time. He realized that his ambitions to work within the Roman system would never come to fruition. They too had died with Stilicho. By now, the Visigoths could launch the siege with their eyes shut. Rome was surrounded, the gates sealed, all traffic in and out halted, and the Mediterranean ports blockaded because there was still a small amount of grain coming in from Sicily. The third siege was similar to the first. A terrible famine grew steadily worse, and once again the dead started to pile up in the streets. Late at night on August 24, two years plus a day from the execution of Stilicho, the Salarian Gate in the northeast corner of the city was mysteriously opened. Who opened it has never been established although one rumor claimed that it was Anicia Faltonia Proba, a member of the most powerful family in the city. It struck me as total nonsense why anyone of the ruling class would do such a thing, given the dreadful fate that had befallen Serena on the basis of no evidence whatever. The story was that she did it to alleviate the suffering in the current siege and not repeat the appalling casualties of the first one. My own theory is that Alaric had infiltrated some of his own men into the city shortly after arriving there with orders as to which gate to open and when. After all, an entire new generation of Visigoths had grown up within the empire and those who had served in the Roman Army were quite conversant with Latin. Quite a number of them were serving with Alaric now.

The word spread like wildfire. Thousands of Visigoths camped outside the walls started pouring through the Salarian Gate and into all quarters of the city. Specific orders were given by Alaric that the churches of St. Paul and St. Peter were to be spared and so they were. Numerous other churches were sacked and so were many residential quarters. Entering the city where they did, the Visigoths came almost immediately to the Palace of Sallust just north of the Baths of Diocletian.

It was the first luxurious target to be pillaged and set on fire. The palace and its beautifully landscaped grounds and gardens had been constructed by the historian Sallust 450 years earlier. It had become crown property during the reign of Tiberius Caesar and many subsequent emperors had resided there and enriched the place with expensive art works. One of its water reservoirs is over six hundred feet long. The entire property was largely trashed. The area to the east of the Gardens of Sallust, in the triangular area bounded by the Via Salaria, the Via Nomentana and the Aurelian Wall, was the original focus of wealth in the city. It was immediately sacked and burned. But more enticing properties lay ahead. In centuries past, as the Senate expanded its numbers eventually into the high hundreds, additional residential quarters had to be acquired. These were found first on the Palatine and then the Aventine Hill as the various imperial palaces took over the Palatine. The next target for the barbarians was the Baths of Diocletian where the damage was quite severe.

With most of the northeastern part of the city being pillaged and much of it set on fire by the initial invaders, the subsequent barbarian thousands who flooded through the Salarian Gate had to look for fresh targets. In the Roman Forum and the forums of Trajan and Augustus, all in close proximity to one another, Visigothic horsemen pulled over many ancient statues that had stood in place for centuries. With the exception of the two churches that Alaric had declared off limits, most of the churches were looted of whatever treasures they possessed. Some of those treasures were considerable. Constantine I alone had poured enormous amounts of silver plate and candelabras, many of them encrusted with emeralds and rubies, gold and silver chalices, along with at least one solid silver altar, along with countless other riches into numerous churches around the city. His successors continued this practice, though in a more subdued manner. Gold leaf was now torn from the walls and ceilings of many of the churches; massive silver statues of Christ and the apostles and countless angels all standing about five feet in height were carried off; golden candles; gold and silver rings. All these riches that Constantine I and his successors had poured into the churches to get their souls into heaven were now being stolen and carried off by forty thousand barbarian gangsters. The Christian and Jewish catacombs outside the city were also plundered. After they were through stealing everything they could carry off, the Visigoths wantonly set fire to many of the buildings they looted, regardless of whether they were private homes or churches; destruction for the sake of destruction. Several convents were invaded, with many nuns being raped and some being murdered. It was reported that many nuns committed suicide rather than be raped by the barbarians. It must be remembered that many in Alaric's hoard were still pagans and held no aspect of the Christian religion in reverence. Thousands of citizens were tortured in their homes to divulge where their money was. In the richest areas of the city, many slaves that had previously run away during previous sieges and joined Alaric had led the Visigoths back to their former places of enslavement to wreck whatever vengeance they could on their former masters. While all this wanton carnage and desecration was going on, a great number of Romans escaped the city. Many fled into the countryside, while thousands of others took ship with little more than the clothing they were wearing. They distributed themselves to some of the islands off the west coast of Italy as well as Africa, Libya, Egypt, the Levant, and Anatolia. Their destitution was the living proof of just how far Rome had fallen.

Though the point of entry was at the northeast corner of the city, the invaders knew well that its richest quarter was on the Aventine Hill on the extreme south side to the west of the Baths of Caracalla and to the south of the Circus Maximus. It was here that most senators had their residences. In the days that followed, none of them escaped looting and many of them were set on fire. On the Caelian Hill, to the east of the Aventine, the Valerian Palace was heavily damaged by fire, as were numerous other buildings in this sector. The raping, killing, stealing, and burning went on for three days. In just that short period of time, the Goths managed to strip Rome of almost every ounce of gold and silver that could be found in any form. Rich clothing, portable art, and everything else that they could lift they loaded onto an estimated five hundred to six hundred wagons and carts and headed out of the city on August 27. Their complete baggage train and all their newly acquired captives took another three days to leave the city. Alaric still had Galla

Placidia as a captive but she was treated well. In fact, far better than she deserved. I have never seen an estimate of how many people were killed during the sacking of the foremost city in the world. At least several thousand were slain and many thousands more were enslaved. Rome had finally paid the price for the disaster that had commenced at Pavia and Ravenna in August 408.

As the shockwaves rippled out from Rome, all inhabitants in the empire felt the ground shake beneath their feet. With Rome now joining the list of ravaged cities in Greece and Gaul, how could anyone anywhere feel secure? Everyone knew, from the most educated to the least articulate, that the world had passed through a catastrophic historical boundary in time from which we might never recover. We had been taught as children that regardless of how uncertain our individual futures might be, that of the empire was guaranteed. Now the empire was being proven to be mortal also. When I was a little boy, mothers, in warning their children to be home before dark, would tell them that if they were not, then "Hannibal will get you." Every child growing up in Roman society had been hearing that expression for over six hundred years. It's fallen out of fashion now. Today, Hannibal is everywhere.

When Constantine the Great was on his deathbed, seventy-three years earlier, he predicted that the number thirteen would prove fatal for the Roman Empire. Many people tried to make sense of this prophecy in view of the recent disaster but no one could. Perhaps no one ever will.[31]

The couriers from Rome arrived with the news that the city had fallen. They were ushered into the imperial presence by two palace eunuchs.

"What is it?" Honorius demanded.

"Your Majesty," one courier began, "Rome has been taken."

"That cannot be," Honorius howled almost in physical pain. "I was feeding him just a little while ago …"

"No, no, Your Majesty," one of the eunuchs interrupted. "Not your pet chicken. The *city* has been taken by Alaric and his Visigoths."

There was an agonizing silence.

"All right," the emperor finally replied. He looked around the room with those large uncomprehending eyes of his, rose from his throne, and left. That was all there was to it.

Alaric now had a startling new plan that had been thought out well beforehand. If he could not serve Rome then he would damned well control it in perpetuity. The past two years had shown how easily the Eternal City could be dominated from Carthage. After stocking up their food supplies, he determined to march the entire length of Italy. It has puzzled many why Alaric and his army only spent three days in Rome. The reason was that he could not stay there any longer if he was to get to the toe of Italy before the winter storms set in. The Goths marched through Capua and Nola, tried and failed to take Naples and kept on going. When their food supplies started to run out, they had to live off the land and many estates and towns without walls suffered accordingly. The plan was that once they had arrived at the southern tip of the peninsula, they would take ship to both Sicily and Africa and seize those grain-rich regions. His Visigoths would settle Africa but only garrison Sicily. The idea of being a mercenary just wasn't working out. Food supply had always been a problem for the Visigoths. In Africa, the problem would be what to do with it all. The Visigothic hierarchy started dreaming of getting rich and staying that way at Rome's expense. Not without reason.

The distance from Rome to Reggio in the toe of Italy is over 350 miles. The Visigoths arrived there three months after leaving Rome. By this time, tens of thousands of their family members had joined them. Two years had passed since the Army of Italy had disintegrated and Ravenna's attempts to rebuild it had produced little. What is often overlooked, however, is that the Roman Navy remained in good shape throughout this period. In 397, when Alaric was trapped in the Peloponnese, Stilicho made certain that every ship in every harbor in the peninsula was his own. Alaric and his people could not lay their hands on anything that floated. In 410, the world was in the process of being completely transformed.

Once Alaric had started south, the government had three months to come up with a plan to prevent him from achieving his new objectives. The masterminds running what was left of the Roman armed forces in Italy did absolutely nothing. The idea of doing anything probably never occurred to them. As a result, the story spread that Alaric was able to accumulate a fleet of ships, but no one knew how large it was. They had been loaded with supplies and had already set sail across the narrow Strait of Messina for Sicily when a terrible storm arose. The ships that had already left the harbor were either sunk or driven ashore and those at dockside were so heavily damaged as to be unusable. Catholic priests in Carthage claimed that their nonstop praying was what had saved them from the ruination that Western Europe was enduring. It was difficult to gainsay them. We all knew that it wasn't because of anything Ravenna did. Details were maddeningly scarce. Alaric then turned his army northward with a view to seizing ships at more northerly ports, but this plan, too, would fail. The last surviving general from the Battle of the Frigidus River in 394 didn't realize it, but by now the Fates had also abandoned him.

Shortly after Stilicho was executed, Olympius had ordered all public inscriptions bearing his name to be erased. Oddly enough, while visiting the home of Attalus in Rome in 409, I came across one that escaped this desecration right across from the Senate house. It's not surprising that it survived. It had been so poorly rendered as a work of public art that perhaps those commissioned to carry out Olympius' order concluded that it had already suffered sufficient dishonor. It praises the gallantry and devotion of the army and the courage and determination of Stilicho. It had been placed in the Roman Forum to commemorate the defeat of Radagaisus in 406. Given that Rome itself would suffer the ultimate desecration at the hands of the Visigoths within four years, it was appropriate that this most recent "monument" would rank as the shabbiest memorial in the city. By itself, the victory was indeed great and deserving of the most considerate commemoration. But the quality of craftsmanship had fallen to such a low level and the state had become so strapped for funds that this vulgar exercise was all the aesthetically destitute Senate could come up with. It consists of two blocks, the base composed of travertine, while the upper block of marble had been rudely removed from another statue and its original lettering effaced. It was truly an utterly deficient monument and yet perversely in harmony with the times.

Our victory in 406 would be almost the last great triumph that a Roman army would achieve over barbarian invaders in the West during my lifetime. Two years later, events would plunge us into the early evening of history's greatest epoch.

In the previous year, what is certain to be the last triumphal arch was raised in Rome to commemorate the defeats, one marginal, one substantial, inflicted on Alaric and his Visigoths in 402. It was insolent to the point of boasting that Rome had obliterated the Gothic nation from the face of the earth. It has been said that dying institutions erect their own mausoleums. If that is true then that silly arch certainly qualifies for that "honor" in the most literal sense. Without even realizing it, many thousands of Visigoths must have passed under it as they sacked the city just five years later.

What cynics like myself found most amusing in all of this was the contorted logic to which Catholic Church leaders resorted. They came up with the most ludicrous explanations as to why God had permitted the sacking of Rome and the widespread devastation of Gaul and now Spain in spite of the empire's being officially Christian. Some told us that we were being punished for being insufficiently attentive to living as God wanted us to. There was certainly nothing like the gang rape, mass slaughter, enslavement, and universal impoverishment of tens of thousands of innocent men, women, and children to get that point across. That prize fool, Paul Orosius, found himself in the biggest quandary. He styles himself a historian but he is simply a religious propagandist of the most amateurish variety. The original basis for his history was to show how all evils that had afflicted the world had occurred prior to Christ's birth and that since then, everything had been just wonderful. As his native Spain started to go up in flames, even he must have had second thoughts, though he could never admit to them.

This nonsense reminded me of the position that pagan leaders had taken when Emperor Gratian had been assassinated in 383. That emperor, as a pious Catholic, had ordered the removal of the Altar of Victory from the Senate. From the reign of Augustus, senatorial sessions had commenced with sacrifices being performed at this altar. When Gratian was slain, pagan priests claimed that it was the revenge the gods took for his having removed the altar and his refusing to assume the title of pontifex maximus of the ancient religions as all his predecessors had done.

As for myself, while I am religious in a private sense, I have almost nothing but contempt for the involvement of the Catholic Church in political matters. There are many who subscribe to the belief that all human affairs are presided over by Providence. But unless the Supreme Being is a supreme idiot, I have witnessed too much innocence butchered in the world to see the hand of God overly manifest in the destiny of any of us. My religious convictions were strongest when I was a teenager, but the older I get, the more my faith contracts. The only part of the Bible in which I have complete belief is the first page or so of the book of Genesis. All any of us has to do is look out the window to see creation. Beyond that, it's all myth and speculation.

We had first witnessed the act of Roman provincials actually joining up with barbarian invaders to a small degree after the Battle of Hadrianople in 378. By the summer of 410, it had happened again in Gaul and was now starting to occur in Italy and Spain. Roman society was disintegrating in all three regions. Ever more private citizens gravitated to the large, fortified private estates that had started multiplying immediately after Alaric had invaded Italy in 401. Most of them were able to withstand the invaders. Those provincials in endangered areas who were unable to find protection with a landowner or join the barbarians in some cases formed bandit gangs of their own. Chaos was spreading like a plague all over Western Europe. Trade and commerce were grinding to a halt. Highways were falling into disrepair throughout the West, causing what few goods that could be transported overland to move more slowly and cost more. Intraprovincial trade was becoming more important as commercial interdependence between the provinces collapsed. The widespread lawlessness only added to our woes.

In short order, we had become a very inward-looking society. At the beginning of the decade, the famous senator Symmachus had obtained horses from a friend of his in Spain. After wintering in Gaul, they continued on to Italy, where they were used by Symmachus' son in the celebratory games that he put on upon becoming praetor. It was a tradition that had gone on for centuries. By the end of the decade, all that was impossible. Instances of cannibalism had been recorded in northern Spain and Italy. Some poverty-stricken citizens of Rome coming ashore in Africa were arrested on orders of the venal Count Heraclian and sold into slavery. The corporate extent of our individual sense of loyalty had been suddenly compressed from the universal empire to the province to the estate and village. The process of unifying Europe and Africa, politically, culturally, socially, and economically, that Rome had carried on for over six centuries had become undone in just a few years. Like great birds of prey pecking out the eyes of their own kind, we have squandered the richest inheritance any people have ever had, far beyond the point of redemption. We are a people who have outlived our age.

By the latter part of 410, the people in Britain felt they had been completely betrayed by Constantine. They had tried to elevate him to the throne in 407 to defend Britain and the western continent against barbarian invasion. Instead, he had ignored the barbarians in Gaul; failed to defend the island when it came under attack in 408; added insult to this last injury by depleting the military strength of Britain further in 409 to support his European adventures; and fumbled away Spain by blundering into a second civil war with his top general, Gerontius, who was also British-born. In 402, the British people had seen their national capital removed from Milan to Ravenna, 180 miles further away. Now they had seen their prefectural capital moved from near the Rhine to the Mediterranean, over four hundred miles further distant from Britain. The Roman Army had defended them well when it had sufficient troops on the island to get the job done. But recent history had shown that Britain could not rely on that army to be on the island in sufficient numbers when the need arose. They had had enough and rose in revolt against those administrators that Constantine had appointed prior to leaving for the continent. It was, however, a peculiar revolt.

It was shortly after Constantine's officials had been dismissed from office (though by whom and in what fashion remains a mystery) and no one named to replace them that a rescript miraculously arrived from Ravenna in response to a request for aid from the former vicar of Britain. It advised the cities of the diocese to look out for their own defense. Civil government had been deliberately dissolved in Britain and it now consists of a collection of de facto city-states and fiefdoms. There were no imperial officials there still on the job when the rescript arrived. They had either left for the continent or retired to their estates in the British countryside. There was no intention of our cutting Britain adrift. The hope was that the Roman Army would return to the island as soon as conditions on the continent had returned to normal. They never did. We never could.

As I arrive at the end of this volume (writing in the autumn of 439), it is difficult for me to know for certain just what state Britain is in today. Most of the information that I have obtained has been received from Catholic priests who have managed to visit the island since I was there last. I do know that, while conditions are nowhere nearly as pleasant as when I lived or served there, neither are they as bad (yet) as what the Sueves have inflicted on northwestern Spain or what the Vandals and their allies brought to Gaul and the rest of Spain. Not having a mint of its own, Britain was dependent on bronze, silver, and gold coins being supplied from the mints on the continent. From the beginning of 407 onward, it was impossible for the continent to supply any coinage to the island. As a result, its economy has deteriorated back to the point where it is once again based on barter rather than money. Much of the island's financial well-being was based on its formerly large military establishment. With most of that removed and with no more money arriving to pay the remaining frontier regiments manning the Saxon Shore forts and those along Hadrian's Wall, the economy has shrunk drastically. The remaining soldiers are little more than a collection of local militias without an overall command structure to guide them. Empty are the offices of the vicar of Britain, the duke of Britain, the count of Britain, and the count of the Saxon Shore. The five provincial governments have vanished as well. They were all dissolved when the island revolted against Constantine and were never replaced with an administrative and command structure that was island-wide in scope. The militia soldiers sustain themselves by farming near the forts while manning the forts only in times of danger.

Trade within the island has declined severely, further running down the standard of living. I have heard that any new buildings put up there nowadays are constructed of timber that can be supplied locally. Masonry construction has been pretty well dispensed with throughout the island because of the difficulties involved in transporting the materials over long distances. The highways have fallen into a rather dilapidated state in many places and are, in any case, unsafe due to increased activity by bandit gangs. Rome's authority in northern Gaul, to the extent that it would eventually be reestablished, would be of a very tenuous nature and we would never be strong enough to consider a full-scale military invasion of the island to re-secure it. There would be too many problems to consider elsewhere in Gaul and Spain.

For their part, the Britons, though they still call themselves "Romans," have never made a serious attempt on their own to reunite with the continent. The manner in which Honorius's government eventually purged Constantine's supporters in Gaul was doubtless enough to give the Britons pause on the matter. The number of rural villas still in operation has gone into sharp decline since 410. The more isolated ones were the first to be abandoned, as the landowners opted in many cases to live within the protective walls of the nearest towns. I am unaware of any fortified villas on the island like those on the continent. At least I never saw any while I lived or served there. Even in the more densely populated areas, the quality of villa life has degraded due to the absence of both trade and the military establishment. As their fortunes have declined, many great landowners have found it difficult to maintain their large estates. The Britons might have tired of the unreliability of the Roman Army, but the economy started to suffer immediately once the Roman style of government had been discarded.

Pottery manufacture has almost ceased entirely in Britain, from what I hear. Its military market has largely vanished and its civilian market in the towns has become impoverished to the point where its products can no longer be afforded. On top of that, insecurity and lack of maintenance on the highways has made the provision of raw materials extremely difficult. All trades and businesses that are generally dependent on a money economy have almost disappeared. The multiplier effect, so prominent in a money-based economy, is totally absent in a barter system. Britain's divorce from the empire has proven to be little more than economic suicide.

In early November, a young centurion arrived at our home. He handed me a letter that invited me to a meeting that afternoon in Stilicho's old office. It was signed "Constantius, Marshal of Infantry." I immediately went to the forum, and sure enough, there was a posting from earlier in the morning announcing the promotion of Constantius and also that of Ulfilas to the corresponding cavalry position. For the first time in twenty-seven dreadful months, I had finally seen a posting in a forum that was positive. At the appointed time, I was ushered into Constantius' office.

"Welcome, Marcus," he said. "I'm glad you could come. I know that you've retired, but I also hope that you might be starting to find private life rather heavy on your hands. I remember you from that meeting that we attended with Stilicho several years back. Stilicho always spoke quite highly of you, and since the catastrophe of two years ago, the need for good officers has never been greater. I'm going to be leading a campaign next year, and I want you to be my chief supply officer. It's not going to be like the good old days. With the frontier moving into Italy, we are as disrupted as Gaul, Thrace, and Greece. But we will have to make do with what we've got. I've reviewed your official military record here, and I'm certain that you will be able to handle the job as well as anyone. Are you interested?"

"Absolutely," I replied, without giving it a second thought. The great memoir would just have to wait. Constantius then swore me to secrecy on everything that we discussed during the meeting.

"What will be the nature of the campaign?" I asked.

"I can't reveal any details yet. First of all, there is another matter that I want to discuss with you. It involves a last item of housekeeping that Jovius implied would be certain to interest you."

Leaving Constantius' office, I suddenly felt good and took a long walk around Ravenna in spite of the bitter cold. Was it really possible to retrieve the situation? I was convinced that the answer to that question would be no unless some sort of arrangement was worked out with the Visigoths in spite of their savagery in Rome and unless the Vandals were crushed in Spain. The sack of Rome had naturally raised the level of hostility between the empire and the Visigoths to a new level. Rome, however, had brought its disgrace entirely upon itself. Alaric had been entirely reasonable in his demands while Ravenna had acted throughout like the pack of fools they were. The central government had too many enemies to deal with at once. For the past two years, it had been attempting to do it with virtually no military establishment. Aureliana was stunned when I informed her that I had rejoined the army.

"I'm back on the payroll as of today," I said.

"Well there's no doubt that we could use the money," she said, "but what are they going to pay you with?"

"With Rome sacked, the government busted, and minimal tax revenues coming in, there is a real problem there. Fortunately, that's not my job. I don't know exactly when or where I'll be starting, but I came away with a good feeling from my meeting with Constantius. Sometimes I almost felt like I was talking to Stilicho."

Constantius had a brilliant future ahead of him, and in some respects, his career would resemble that of Constantius I: both men had brief reigns as emperors; both were farsighted and diplomats as well as soldiers; both made their major contributions to the empire prior to being hailed as Augustus. That evening, I looked at my ceremonial leopard skin for the first time in ages and was suddenly struck by the irony of its choice as our leading dress uniform. Everyone fears the leopard as the great man-eater it can be and rightly so. But it has a rather small heart for so large a body, and because of this, it tires easily. It's a brilliant sprinter but an inevitable loser over a long distance. We had come a very long way.

Ten days later, a dromon warship arrived in Ravenna from Dalmatia. By special order from Emperor Honorius, Olympius had been ordered back to the capital to resume his old duties as master of offices. Or that is what he thought. When he disembarked, I was waiting for him with a century of troops from the Ravenna garrison. His small personal bodyguard was ordered to step aside as I arrested him. He was placed in chains with his hands cuffed at the waist. We took him immediately to where Constantius was waiting in the main conference room at the palace. In addition to Constantius, Julianus and Andreas, each carrying a large club, were awaiting him. That must have given him some intimation of his fate. Constantius had been reading the list of formal charges against him and never looked up when Olympius was hauled into his presence. When he was finished reviewing the document, the generalissimo looked off to one side at nothing in particular, and then his face lightened up with a broad smile. He tossed the document to one side, having decided to dispense with a formal reading of the charges. Then, addressing Julianus and Andreas, Constantius said, "Gentlemen, in the immortal words that Emperor Caligula used on occasions such as this, 'Make him know that he is dying.'"

Julianus struck Olympius across the ankles to knock him to the floor. Then they pulverized him. Starting with the extremities, they smashed up his feet, ankles, and lower leg bones until they were a bloodied, mangled, almost unrecognizable mess. They took a particular delight in crushing his kneecaps before moving to higher latitudes. They passed rather lightly, relatively speaking, over his thighs, feeling that in a comparative sense, there was little satisfaction to be derived there. Besides, it would have been anticlimactic after the excruciating cries of agony that Olympius had shrieked while his kneecaps were being destroyed. His screams could be heard all over the palace. The executioners then paused for a moment to admire their craftsmanship as Olympius writhed on the floor in convulsions, uttering howls from an agony that knew no description. We all knew what was coming next.

This task was left to Andreas. After all, in such close quarters, they didn't want to start accidently whacking one another. Olympius' ankles were unchained, and Julianus kicked his mutilated legs apart as far as he could. A massive blow was then delivered to Olympius' genitals, the first of many. Before the first blow was driven to his crotch, his hands strained with surprising strength, given the depth of his torment, to protect himself but in vain. After the fifth blow fell upon his groin, he went unconscious. Eventually, Olympius was rolled over onto his stomach and the destruction of his spinal column from the bottom to the top took place. He was then rolled over on his back, the world's foremost quadriplegic. But his heart was still beating in spite of the unimaginable dismantlement his body had suffered. This was not mere revenge by "Stilicho's men." It was justice on behalf of every innocent victim of Olympius' appalling criminality.

I doubt if any man has ever looked like Olympius did when my associates were finished with him. By the time they had completed bashing his skull into an indescribable pulp, his eyes, brains, and teeth were scattered all over the floor. None of us had ever done or seen anything like it. When the one-man massacre was over, the janitors were called in.

Constantius quipped, "Needless to say, our late master of offices will not be receiving a state funeral. When you are finished mopping him up, chaps, burn him with the garbage."

He then dismissed Andreas and Julianus after thanking them for a job well done and asked me to come with him to his office.

"I timed this little exhibition," Constantius said, "to lift the nation's sagging spirits and our own. After all, the Christmas season is almost upon us, and God only knows we've had little enough for which to be grateful over the past two years. I'm setting up a meeting for shortly after the New Year. I'll notify you by courier as to when it will take place. It will be in the conference room that we just used."

"If the janitors have finished cleaning it up by then," I said, and we both had a good laugh.

"By the way," Constantius said, "how did you feel about the manner by which Olympius' execution was carried out?"

"I thought it was tastefully done in every respect," I replied, and we had another good laugh.

"I'm curious," I continued. "What is the status of the Army of Italy? I heard that Valens and Allobichus were starting to rebuild it but I never did hear or see anything in the way of concrete progress."

"They really didn't accomplish very much," Constantius said. "Valens was in over his head, and as we know, the late Allobichus had other things on his mind. They managed to rebuild several cavalry regiments. They are composed mainly of Visigothic soldiers from the Roman Army who deserted to Alaric after Stilicho's execution. They started to drift back to us when Olympius was overthrown and they realized the danger to them and their families was over. Along with that was the fact that their backbones and navels were starting to rub together because Alaric simply could not provide for them all. Nothing like an empty stomach to let one know where one's interests lay. Regardless of their motivation, they do provide a core on which we can build."

"What is the situation with Alaric now?" I asked.

"I have sent scouts down to southern Italy to monitor the situation. As we all know, his invasion plans for Sicily and Africa were dashed by storms and he's still heading north, probably looking for more ships for another attempt. There is no way in hell that he is going to succeed in that. I've already ordered the Adriatic Fleet to our southern coast to block any such attempt. I've also ordered them to do exactly what Stilicho did in Greece a decade ago by tracking them up the coast to round up every ship in every port if necessary to foil whatever the Goths' plans may be for any future seafaring adventures at our expense. It's staggering to think that such things never occurred to our predecessors."

Our conversation continued for the better part of an hour as we got to know one another better.

"Tell me," Constantius asked, "why do you think we are in the predicament we are in today?"

"The simple answer to that is Arcadius died," I replied. "Oversimplified to be sure, but if the late Arcadius was still with us, then I'm certain our campaign against the Vandals in Gaul would have started earlier in 408 instead of the late summer. That would have given the conspirators far less time to put their act together. But one could also say it was Stilicho's failure to defeat Alaric once and for all in 395 or 397."

"Speaking of the siege at Mount Olympus," Constantius asked, "what exactly happened there? I was fairly new to the army at that time and was stationed in a garrison in northern Illyria. We were all astonished when the abandonment of the siege was announced."

I filled him in on the details as I saw them and as I have recorded in an earlier chapter.

"I have heard that you participated in the siege at Mount Pholoe in the Peloponnese two years later," I said, "while I was off defending Britain from the Saxons, Picts, and Scots. Now it's your turn to tell me what happened there."

"It was my first major campaign," Constantius answered, "and it was as much of a disappointment to me as your Mt. Olympus exercise was to you. We had had several minor engagements with the Visigoths and bested them in every contest before bottling them up around Mt. Pholoe. As at Mt. Olympus, we had serious disciplinary problems—not so much with the Roman units but with a number of the Germanic federate regiments.

"For the campaign of 397, Stilicho used far more newly recruited barbarian federate troops than had been the case in the campaign two years earlier. Quite a number of them proved to be as much of a problem as allies as the Visigoths were as enemies. The Visigoths had of course by this time ransacked Greece and were quite rich with all the gold and silver they had collected during their Hellenic rampage; gold that they did not have at hand at Mt. Olympus. They had no trouble bribing several federate regiments to simply abandon the fight, thus creating a large gap in the cordon we had set up that could only be filled by thinning our lines considerably. At the same time, as you mentioned in the campaign of 395, regular western troops from Gaul started protesting their posting to Greece when their real concern was for their homeland over a thousand miles to the northwest. If Stilicho's plan had been to bring the Visigoths to a decisive battle, then there would probably have been no problem with the Gauls. But when they realized they were there for a long-term siege in order to minimize casualties, the remonstrations began. Then on the heels of the desertion by certain of the federates came the order declaring Stilicho a public enemy and ordering him and his army back to Italy. Eutropius had come to believe, as many did and still do from two years earlier that the long siege at Mt. Pholoe was little more than a cover for Stilicho to arrange an alliance with Alaric. Those of us who participated in either or both campaigns know that there was no truth in any of these suspicions, but the rumors continued to grow and in no small way helped to pave the way for his terrible downfall. It also prompted Eutropius to start negotiating with Count Gildo to transfer his loyalty from Honorius to Arcadius. Stilicho's 397 campaign in Greece was a total waste of time, and it ultimately proved to be the final blow, self-inflicted as it was, to his daydream of establishing a regency over Arcadius."

After the execution of Olympius and my meeting with Constantius, I went for another long walk around Ravenna. One thing that I had proven to myself over the years was that I knew how to be a survivor. Our rental properties were bringing in good returns, and if things didn't work out with the army, then we could live comfortably with the rental income alone. I was also determined to purchase a country estate of my own and fortify it as soon as finances permitted. My primary concern was that we might not be able to retrieve the situation and that the chaos could become even more severe in the future. When I was a boy, I had the dream of owning a large villa of my own some day on the coast of Africa with a spectacular view of the Mediterranean or the ocean. For some reason, the notion of living in the small coastal town of Tangier had a great fascination for me. In an empire at peace, that could have been possible. But the fact that the Visigoths were now situated at the toe of Italy and aiming at Africa while the Vandals had entered Spain, which is even closer to Africa, dashed that dream for good. Southern Italy, relatively poor though it may be, was becoming increasingly attractive to me. I was certain that the Visigoths would not stay there, and neither would any other barbarian nation. But for the time being, that would have to wait.

The end of the year 410 seems like a good place to finish this first volume of my memoirs. The next job will be to get it published and that won't be easy. It never is the first time out. I had originally planned on writing everything up in one volume, but as the project progressed, I realized that if I did, it would wind up being a thousand pages long. If I cannot get what I have already written published, then there is no point in writing the rest of it. I have found it to be a profoundly worthwhile undertaking, painful and wrenching as it was. At the end of his great history, which concluded shortly after the Battle of Hadrianople, Ammianus Marcellinus admonished those who would chronicle and analyze that which came after to do so "in the grand style." How grand my style is must be left to others to judge. I know that some will take exception to the title of this last chapter. They will claim that it is foolishly overdone, for what I have described in the period leading up to 408 sounds like anything but Eden as recorded in the Bible. That is true. But compared to what followed, not immediately but eventually, it was Eden all right.

ENDNOTES

1   The Saxon Shore acquired its name from the large-scale raids it had suffered a century earlier at the hands of Saxon pirates. It is the only place in the empire that took its name from the constant attacks thrust upon it by a single foreign invader. In Britain, it runs from the Wash, on the east coast, around to the Isle of Wight in the center of the south coast. In Gaul, it runs from the mouth of the Rhine to the mouth of the Seine.

2   Now known as the Strait of Dover.

3   The Isle of Thanet was joined to Britain during subsequent centuries as a result of the silting up of the channel that originally separated the two.

4   This is the ancient name for the Pregel River that flows through Kaliningrad, Russia.

5   Ancient Thrace corresponds approximately to modern Bulgaria.

6   Many Alans that were conquered by the Huns remained settled in their homelands in the Caucasus Mountains.

7   The ancient Roman city of Durostorum is the modern-day city of Silistra in northeastern Bulgaria.

8   The Roman city of Marcianopolis is the modern-day town of Reka Devnia in eastern Bulgaria.

9   In antiquity, the North Sea was known as the German Ocean, and the English Channel as the British Ocean.

10 A regular infantry cohort in the Roman Army contained about five hundred men, while special super-cohorts were twice as large. I have referred to such units as regiments throughout while recognizing that in terms of numbers the Roman cohort more closely approximated a battalion in a modern NATO army.

11 Passau, the Roman town of Castra Batava, lies on the south bank of the Danube on the border between Bavaria and Upper Austria.

12 Lorch, a suburb of the Austrian city of Enns, derives its name from the Roman town of Lauriacum.

13 The Roman city of Naissus is now the Serbian city of Nis.

14 The ancient town known to the Romans as Calisia is the modern Polish city of Kalisz. Roman ruins have been found there.

15 The Axumite/Ethiopian port of Adulis corresponds to the modern Eritrean port of Massawa (or Mitsiwa).

16 The Roman riverine naval fortress of Noviodunum is now the Romanian town of Isaccea.

17 Ratiaria is the modern-day Bulgarian town of Archar.

18 Novae is the modern-day Bulgarian town of Svishtov.

19 The Roman Diocese of Thrace contained all of modern-day Bulgaria (except its westernmost section), the Dobruja area of Romania, Turkey-in-Europe, and that part of modern Greece that is still known as Thrace.

20 The Roman town of Poetovio is the Slovenian town of Ptuj.

21 The Roman town of Marsonia is now the Croatian city of Slavonska Brod.

22 The Graeco-Roman town of Nicephorium (Greek)/Callinicum (Roman) is now the Syrian city of Raqqa at the confluence of the Euphrates River and its tributary, the Balikh.

23 The Roman towns of Curia and Magia correspond to the Swiss towns of Chur and Maienfeld, while Clunia is the Austrian town of Feldkirch.

24 The city of Grenoble derives its name from Gratianopolis.

25 The Roman town of Emona is now Ljubljana, the capital of Slovenia.

26 These winds have been measured at speeds of over sixty miles per hour.

27 Rhaetia consisted of the easternmost cantons of Switzerland, the western Austrian provinces of Vorarlberg and Tirol, and that part of Bavaria to the south of the Danube. Noricum consisted of that part of central Austria lying south of the Danube, along with northern Slovenia.

28 Side is the modern Turkish town of Selimiye on the Mediterranean coast.

29 Bornholm, the easternmost island of Denmark, was known as Borgundarholm as late as the thirteenth century.

30 Armorica is the ancient name for that part of northwestern France that lies to the south of the Seine, to the north of the Loire, and fronts on the sea.

31 In the year 1453, what was left of the Eastern Roman Empire fell to the Turks when they captured Constantinople. $1 + 4 + 5 + 3 = 13$.

Made in the USA
San Bernardino, CA
10 September 2019